Grammar *in use*
Intermediate

劍橋活用英語文法 中級

專為台灣學生
設計的自學
文法參考書
與練習本

附習題解答

Raymond Murphy
with William R. Smalzer

總審　**周中天教授**
前國立台灣師範大學翻譯研究所所長
現國立台灣師範大學國語文中心主任

譯者　**游毓玲**
國立彰化師範大學英語系暨研究所教授

CAMBRIDGE
UNIVERSITY PRESS

CAMBRIDGE UNIVERSITY PRESS
Cambridge, New York, Melbourne, Madrid, Cape Town, Singapore,
São Paulo, Delhi, Dubai, Tokyo, Mexico City

Cambridge University Press
79 Anson Road, #06-04/06, Singapore 079906

www.cambridge.org

This Taiwan bilingual edition is based on
Grammar in Use Intermediate Student's Book with Answers, Third edition
ISBN 978-0-521-73477-6 first published by Cambridge University Press in 2009.

© Cambridge University Press 2009, 2011

First published 2009
Taiwan bilingual edition 2011

Printed in Singapore by KHL Printing Co. Pte Ltd

Cambridge University Press has no responsibility for the persistence or
accuracy of URLs for external or third-party Internet Web sites referred to in
this publication, and does not guarantee that any content on such Web sites is,
or will remain, accurate or appropriate.

ISBN 978-0-521-14787-3 paperback Taiwan bilingual edition

Book design and layout: Adventure House, NYC

目錄

如果您不確定應該研讀哪些單元，請利用 **319** 頁的學習指引。

如果您不確定應該研讀哪些單元，請利用 319 頁的學習指引。

如果您不確定應該研讀哪些單元,請利用 **319** 頁的學習指引。

關於 *Grammar in Use Intermediate* 中譯版

由 Raymond Murphy 所編寫的 *Grammar in Use (Intermediate)*，是作者根據其多年的教學經驗所編寫而成的文法書，暢銷數十年，並已譯成多國語言。其特色為解釋清楚、少有艱深的文法術語，而最重要的是提供實用情境的例句，使學習者能將所學的文法應用於實際的語言使用情境。此譯本詳實的翻譯了原書中的文法解釋，但保留住原書少用文法專用術語的精神，並且針對意思與用法不易了解的句型提供例句中文翻譯，以協助讀者掌握各句型的意思。前一版的中文譯本發行後，廣受高中英文老師與大學教授的歡迎與推薦；此次新版針對部分內容進行調整，並且新增了八個單元說明片語動詞及一個單元講解 *wish* 的用法。這樣一本著重說明實用文法句型之用法的文法書，對於國內準備大學及研究所升學考試、全民英檢 (GEPT)、托福 (TOEFL)、多益(TOEIC)、雅思(IELTS) 等英文檢定考試的英語學習者，實在是一本倍增英文能力必備的利器。

感謝我的老師，前台灣師範大學翻譯所所長周中天教授、以及台灣師範大學英語系李櫻教授，擔任本書的審稿者，對於中文用字遣詞、文法內容多有指正；並感謝我的研究助理，呂佩蒞、林筱茜、陳冠霖幫我繕打中文稿件。最後感謝劍橋大學出版社新加坡亞洲總部的 Richard Walker、Katherine Wong、以及其他所有參與此書編輯工作的所有工作人員。

游毓玲 謹誌於
彰化師範大學英語系

關於譯者

譯者畢業於國立台灣師範大學英語系，美國伊利諾大學香檳校區 (University of Illinois at Urbana-Champaign) 語言學博士，現任國立彰化師範大學英語系暨研究所教授。長年從事英文閱讀與寫作的研究與教學，對於台灣學生學習英文所面臨的困難，特別在英文寫作方面，有深入的瞭解與研究。

給學生的話

本書是專為學習美語文法的學生所寫的，不需老師指導也可自行研讀。

如果您無法確切回答以下的問題，那麼這本書正是您所需要的文法書：

- *I did* 與 *I have done* 的用法有何不同？
- 何時使用 *will* 表未來式？
- 接在 *I wish* 之後的句型結構為何？
- *used to do* 與 *used to doing* 的意思與用法有何不同？
- 何時使用定冠詞 *the*？
- *like* 和 *as* 的用法有何不同？

本書針對許多諸如上述的英文文法要點皆有清楚的解說，每個文法重點之後並附有練習題。

程度

本書適合中級程度的學生(即已學習過基礎英文文法的學生)。全書著重在解說中級學生在使用英文時常遇到困難的文法結構；有文法問題的高級程度學生也可以使用本書，但本書不適合初學者。

本書架構

本書共有 142 個單元，每一單元解說一項文法重點。部份文法重點(例如，現在完成式或定冠詞the的用法)因內容較多，故涵蓋數個單元。各單元之表列請見目錄。

本書每個單元皆包括左右兩頁，左頁是文法重點的解釋和例句，而右頁則是練習題。書後並附有解答，供學生自行核對(第 328 頁)。

本書並附有七個附錄(第 286–295 頁)，內容包括有不規則動詞、動詞形式、拼字以及美式英文與英式英文之比較。

最後，本書並附有詳盡的索引(第 363–371 頁)。

本書使用方法

各單元並非根據難度依序排列，所以不需從頭研讀。每位學生的文法問題各不相同，因此您可以依據自己的問題與需要查閱各項文法重點。

建議您依下列的方法使用本書：

- 先利用目錄或索引找出您有興趣的文法重點所屬的單元。
- 如果您不確定需要研讀哪些單元，可以使用第 319 頁的學習指南。
- 研讀您所選擇之單元中，左頁的解釋以及例句。
- 練習右頁的習題。
- 利用書後所附的解答核對您的答案。
- 如果您的答案不正確，再研讀該單元左頁的解說以了解自己的問題所在。

當然，您也可以把本書當作參考書使用，不需做練習題。

補充練習

本書最後另有補充練習(第 296–318 頁)，針對不同單元裡的文法重點提供綜合練習。例如，練習 16 綜合 Unit 25 至 Unit 34 的文法要點。您在各單元之文法重點研讀與練習完畢後，還可以利用這些習題做額外練習。

給老師的話

Grammar in Use Intermediate 是以學生自習為目的所編寫的文法書,但是老師若需要在課堂上加強文法,本書也正是您所需要的補充教材。

本書對於中級和中上程度的學生最有助益(書中幾乎所有內容都與其學習相關),可作為修正其文法觀念的基準或練習新文法結構的工具。此外,本書對於有文法問題、需要一本文法書作為參考和練習的高級程度學生也有助益,但不適用於初學者。

本書的單元編排架構是以文法類別(現在式和過去式,冠詞和名詞,介係詞等)做區分;各單元並非依據其困難程度依序排列,因此不需從頭開始研讀。老師可以根據自己的教學大綱和學生的問題選擇相關單元彈性使用本書。

本書可用來進行文法重點的立即加強或稍後的修正、補救,可以全班一起使用,也可以由需要特別加強的學生個別使用。各單位的左頁(包含文法重點解說和例句)是依學生自習的目的編寫;然而老師也可以將相關重點和資料用作上課內容的基礎,學生則可以於課後利用左頁作為復習與參考之依據。各單元右頁的習題可以作為課堂練習或家庭作業。此外,若部分學生有個別的問題,老師可以指導他們自行研讀本書的某些單元。書後並有附加練習(詳見給學生的話)。

Grammar in Use 書中所採用的文法形式,為北美口說英文中最常使用並普遍廣為接受的用法。或許有部份以美語為母語的人會認為某些用法是不正確的,例如,*who* 作為受詞代名詞,或是以 *they* 指稱 he or she;但本書將這些用法皆視為標準用法。

Grammar in Use Intermediate 新版

新版 *Grammar in Use Intermediate* 與前一版不同之處如下:

- 本版新增八個單元講解片語動詞 (Unit 134 至 Unit 142),並新增一個單元講解 *Wish* (Unit 39)。Unit 40 至 Unit 79 及 Unit 81 至 Unit 134 則與第二版的單元編號不同。
- 部分單元內容經過改寫或重新組織;大部分單元內容中的例句、解釋與練習有些微的修改。
- 本版並擴充補充練習,新增的練習為 14–16、25、30–31 與 37–41。

Grammar *in use* Intermediate

劍橋活用英語文法 中級

現在進行式 (I am doing)

請看下面的範例：

Sarah is in her car. She is on her way to work.

She **is driving** to work.

上面的句子意思是，在說話者描述該情境的時刻，Sarah 正在開車；開車的動作正在進行、尚未結束。

am/is/are + **-ing** 為現在進行式的動詞形式：

I	**am**	(= I**'m**)	driv**ing**
he/she/it	**is**	(= he**'s**, etc.)	work**ing**
we/you/they	**are**	(= we**'re**, etc.)	do**ing**, etc.

I am doing something 意思是我正在做某件事；表示我已經開始做該件事，而且還沒有做完。

- Please don't make so much noise. **I'm trying** to work. (並非 I try)
- "Where's Mark?" "**He's taking** a shower." (並非 He takes a shower)
- Let's go out now. It **isn't raining** any more. (並非 It doesn't rain)
- (在宴會上) Hello, Jane. **Are** you **enjoying** the party? (並非 Do you enjoy)
- What's all that noise? What**'s going** on? (= What's happening?)

然而，動作即使並非發生在說話的當時，也可以使用現在進行式。例如：

Steve 正透過電話和朋友說話，他說：

> I**'m reading** a really good book at the moment. It's about a man who . . . .

在這個情境中，Steve 並非在說話的當時正在讀一本有趣的書；他的意思是他已經開始讀那本書，但是還沒有讀完，也就是說他還正在閱讀中。

其他例子如下：

- Kate wants to work in Italy, so she**'s studying** Italian. (雖然說話者在說這句話的時刻，Kate或許並非正在研讀義大利文。)
- Some friends of mine **are building** their own house. They hope to finish it next summer.

現在進行式可以與 **today** / **this week** / **this year** 等表時間的字和片語一起使用。 (這些時間都是接近現在的時間)：

- *A:* You**'re working** hard **today**. (並非 You work hard today)
  B: Yes, I have a lot to do.
- The company I work for **isn't doing** so well **this year**.

現在進行式也用來指最近正在發生的改變，特別適用於下列動詞以現在進行式表達時：

get	change	become	increase	rise
fall	grow	improve	begin	start

- **Is** your English **getting** better? (並非 Does your English get better)
- The population of the world **is increasing** very fast. (並非 increases)
- At first I didn't like my job, but **I'm beginning** to enjoy it now. (並非 I begin)

現在進行式與現在簡單式之比較 **Unit 3** 與 **Unit 4**　現在式表未來的意思 **Unit 18**

Exercises

1.1 依各句題意，從下列動詞中選出一個適當的字，並將正確的動詞時式填入空格。

> get   happen   look   lose   make   start   stay   try   ~~work~~

1. "You _re working_____ hard today." "Yes, I have a lot to do."
2. I _____ for Christine. Do you know where she is?
3. It _____ dark. Should I turn on the light?
4. They don't have anywhere to live at the moment. They _____ with friends until they find a place.
5. Things are not so good at work. The company _____ money.
6. Do you have an umbrella? It _____ to rain.
7. You _____ a lot of noise. Can you be quieter? I _____ to concentrate.
8. Why are all these people here? What _____ ?

1.2 將正確的動詞時式填入空格；若語意有需要，請使用否定詞 (例如，*I'm not doing*)。

1. Please don't make so much noise. I _m trying_____ (try) to work.
2. Let's go out now. It _isn't raining__ (rain) any more.
3. You can turn off the radio. I _____ (listen) to it.
4. Kate called me last night. She's on vacation in Quebec. She _____ (have) a great time and doesn't want to come home.
5. I want to lose weight, so this week I _____ (eat) lunch.
6. Andrew has just started evening classes. He _____ (study) German.
7. Paul and Sally had an argument. They _____ (speak) to each other.
8. I _____ (get) tired. I need a break.
9. Tim _____ (work) this week. He has a week off.

1.3 依照對話內容，將正確的動詞時式填入空格。

1. *A:* I saw Brian a few days ago.
   B: Oh, did you? _What's he doing____ these days? (what / he / do)
   A: He's in college now.
   B: _____ ? (what / he / study)
   A: Psychology.
   B: _____ it? (he / enjoy)
   A: Yes, he says _____ a lot. (he / learn)

2. *A:* Hi, Liz. How _____ ? (your new job / go)
   B: Not bad. It wasn't so good at first, but _____ better now. (it / get)
   A: What about Jonathan? Is he OK?
   B: Yes, but _____ his work at the moment. (he / not / enjoy) He's been in the same job for a long time, and _____ to get bored with it. (he / begin)

1.4 依各句題意，從下列動詞中選出一個適當的字，並將正確的動詞時式填入空格。

> begin   change   get   ~~increase~~   rise

1. The population of the world _is increasing___ very fast.
2. The world _____ . Things never stay the same.
3. The situation is already bad and it _____ worse.
4. The cost of living _____ . Every year things are more expensive.
5. The weather _____ to improve. The rain has stopped, and the wind isn't as strong.

現在簡單式 (I do)

A 請看下面的範例：

Alex 是公車司機，但是他現在正在床上睡覺。
所以我們說：

He is not driving a bus. (他正在睡覺。)

但是 He **drives** a bus. (他是公車駕駛員。)

drive(s)/work(s)/do(es) 等，為現在簡單式的動詞
形式：

I/we/you/they	**drive/work/do**, etc.
he/she/it	**drives/works/does**, etc.

B 現在簡單式用於一般性的陳述或說明，主要用於陳述一件經常性或重複發生的事，也用於
陳述事實或真理。

- Nurses **take** care of patients in hospitals.
- I usually **leave** for work at 8 a.m.
- The earth **goes** around the sun.
- The coffee shop **opens** at 7:30 in the morning.

要記得：

I **work** ...   但是   He **works** ...   They **teach** ...   但是   My sister **teaches** ...

有些動詞字尾應加-s或是加-es，參見附錄 6。

C 現在簡單式的疑問句與否定句，須在句子中加入 **do** 或 **does**。

do **does**	I/we/you/they he/she/it	**work?** **drive?** **do?**

I/we/you/they he/she/it	**don't** **doesn't**	**work** **drive** **do**

- I come from Japan. Where **do** you **come** from?
- I **don't go** to church very often.
- What **does** this word **mean**? (並非 What means this word?)
- Rice **doesn't grow** in cold climates.

以下兩個例句中 **do** 也是主要動詞 (do you **do** / doesn't **do**等)：

- "What **do** you **do**?"   "I work in a department store."
- He's always so lazy. He **doesn't do** anything to help.

D 現在簡單式可以用來表達我們做某一件事的頻率：

- I **get** up at 8:00 **every morning**.
- **How often** do you **go** to the dentist?
- Julie **doesn't drink** tea **very often**.
- Robert usually **plays** tennis **two or three times a week** in the summer.

E **I promise / I apologize** 等之用法

有時候我們可以藉由說一句話而完成該件事。例如，當我們答應做某事，我們說 I promise ...。
當我們建議某事，我們說 I suggest ...。

- **I promise** I won't be late. (並非 I'm promising)
- "What do you **suggest** I do?"   "**I suggest** that you spend less money."

同樣地，我們可以說：**I advise** ... / **I insist** ... / **I refuse** ... / **I suppose** ... 等，來表示勸
告、堅持、拒絕、認定某事。

現在簡單式與現在進行式之比較 Unit 3 與 Unit 4   現在式表未來的意思 Unit 18

Exercises

2.1 依各句題意，從下列動詞中選出一個適當的字，並將正確的動詞時式填入空格。

  cause(s)   connect(s)   drink(s)   live(s)   open(s)   ~~speak(s)~~   take(s)

1. Tanya __*speaks*__ German very well.
2. I don't _____ much coffee.
3. The swimming pool _____ at 7:30 every morning.
4. Bad driving _____ many accidents.
5. My parents _____ in a very small apartment.
6. The Olympic Games _____ place every four years.
7. The Panama Canal _____ the Atlantic and Pacific Oceans.

2.2 將正確的動詞時式填入空格。

1. Julie __*doesn't drink*__ (not / drink) tea very often.
2. What time _____ (the banks / close) here?
3. I have a TV, but I _____ (not / watch) it much.
4. "Where _____ (Hiroshi / come) from?"   "He's Japanese."
5. "What _____ (you / do)?"   "I'm an electrician."
6. It _____ (take) me an hour to get to work. How long _____ (it / take) you?
7. Look at this sentence. What _____ (this word / mean)?
8. David isn't in very good shape. He _____ (not / exercise).

2.3 依各句題意，從下列動詞中選出一個適當的字；若語意有需要，請使用否定詞。

  believe   eat   flow   ~~go~~   ~~grow~~   make   rise   tell   translate

1. The earth __*goes*__ around the sun.
2. Rice __*doesn't grow*__ in Canada.
3. The sun _____ in the east.
4. Bees _____ honey.
5. Vegetarians _____ meat.
6. An atheist _____ in God.
7. An interpreter _____ from one language into another.
8. Liars are people who _____ the truth.
9. The Amazon River _____ into the Atlantic Ocean.

2.4 根據提示，詢問 Liz 有關她自己和她家人的問題。

1. You know that Liz plays tennis. You want to know how often. Ask her.
   How often __*do you play tennis*__ ?
2. Perhaps Liz's sister plays tennis, too. You want to know. Ask Liz.
   _____ your sister _____ ?
3. You know that Liz reads a newspaper every day. You want to know which one. Ask her.
   _____ ?
4. You know that Liz's brother works. You want to know what he does. Ask Liz.
   _____ ?
5. You know that Liz goes to the movies a lot. You want to know how often. Ask her.
   _____ ?
6. You don't know where Liz's grandparents live. You want to know. Ask Liz.
   _____ ?

2.5 依各句題意，從下列詞語中選出適當者填入空格。

  I apologize   I insist   I promise   I recommend   ~~I suggest~~

1. It's a nice day. __*I suggest*__ we go for a walk.
2. I won't tell anybody what you said. _____ .
3. I won't let you pay for the meal. _____ that you let me pay.
4. _____ for what I did. It won't happen again.
5. The new restaurant downtown is very good. _____ it highly.

UNIT 3

現在進行式與現在簡單式 1 (I am doing 與 I do)

A

比較現在進行式與現在簡單式：

現在進行式 (I am doing)

現在進行式表示，在說話的當時或接近該時刻，某個動作正在進行，尚未結束。

I am doing
past   *now*   *future*

- The water **is boiling**. Can you turn it off?
- Listen to those people. What language **are** they **speaking**?
- Let's go out. It **isn't raining** now.
- "I'm busy." "What **are you doing**?"
- **I'm getting** hungry. Let's eat.
- Kate wants to work in Italy, so she**'s learning** Italian.
- The population of the world **is increasing** very fast.

表示暫時的狀況用現在進行式。

- **I'm living** with some friends until I find a place of my own.
- *A:* You**'re working** hard today.
  B: Yes, I have a lot to do.

現在進行式之用法，參見 Unit 1。

現在簡單式 (I do)

現在簡單式表示一般的事實，以及重複發生的事情。

←   I do   →
past   *now*   *future*

- Water **boils** at 100 degrees Celsius.
- Excuse me, **do** you **speak** English?
- It **doesn't rain** very much in summer.
- What **do** you usually **do** after work?
- I always **get** hungry in the afternoon.
- Most people **learn** to swim when they are children.
- Every day the population of the world **increases** by about 200,000 people.

表示永久的狀況用現在簡單式。

- My parents **live** in Vancouver. They have lived there all their lives.
- John isn't lazy. He **works** hard most of the time.

現在簡單式之用法，參見 Unit 2。

B

I always do 與 I'm always doing

I always do something 通常表示我每次都做某件事。

- **I always drive** to work. (並非 I'm always driving)

而 **I'm always doing** something 意思並不相同。例如：

I've lost my key again. **I'm always losing** things.
我又把鑰匙弄丟了。我總是掉東西。

I'm always losing things 意思是我經常掉東西，頻率已經高過正常狀況。

其他例子如下：

- You**'re always watching** television. You should do something more active.
  (= You watch too much television)
- Tim is never satisfied. He**'s always complaining**. (= He complains too much)

Exercises

3.1 判斷劃線部份的動詞時式是否正確；若不正確，請改為適當的時式。

1. Water <u>boils</u> at 212 degrees Fahrenheit.   _OK_
2. The water <u>boils</u>. Can you turn it off?   _is boiling_
3. Look! That man <u>tries</u> to open the door of your car. _____
4. Can you hear those people? What <u>do</u> they <u>talk</u> about? _____
5. The moon <u>goes</u> around the earth in about 27 days. _____
6. I have to go now. It <u>gets</u> late. _____
7. I usually <u>drive</u> to work. _____
8. "Hurry up! It's time to leave." "OK, I <u>come</u>." _____
9. I hear you've got a new job. How <u>does</u> it go? _____
10. Paul is never late. He<u>'s</u> always <u>getting</u> to work on time. _____
11. They don't get along well. They<u>'re</u> always <u>arguing</u>. _____

3.2 將正確的動詞時式填入空格。請使用現在進行式或現在簡單式。

1. Let's go out. It _isn't raining_ (not / rain) now.
2. Julia is very good at languages. She _speaks_ (speak) four languages very well.
3. Hurry up! Everybody _____ (wait) for you.
4. "_____ (you / listen) to the radio?" "No, you can turn it off."
5. "_____ (you / listen) to the radio every day?" "No, just occasionally."
6. The River Nile _____ (flow) into the Mediterranean.
7. The river _____ (flow) very fast today – much faster than usual.
8. We usually _____ (grow) vegetables in our garden, but this year we _____ (not / grow) any.
9. *A:* How's your English?
   B: Not bad. I think it _____ (improve) slowly.
10. Rachel is in New York right now. She _____ (stay) at the Park Hotel. She always _____ (stay) there when she's in New York.
11. Can we stop walking soon? I _____ (start) to feel tired.
12. *A:* Can you drive?
    B: I _____ (learn). My father _____ (teach) me.
13. Normally I _____ (finish) work at five, but this week I _____ (work) until six to earn a little more money.
14. My parents _____ (live) in Taipei. They were born there and have never lived anywhere else. Where _____ (your parents / live)?
15. Sonia _____ (look) for a place to live. She _____ (stay) with her sister until she finds a place.
16. *A:* What _____ (your brother / do)?
    B: He's an architect, but he _____ (not / work) right now.
17. *(at a party)* I usually _____ (enjoy) parties, but I _____ (not / enjoy) this one very much.

3.3 依各句題意，以 *always -ing* 之用法，完成 B 句。

1. *A:* I've lost my keys again.
   B: Not again! _You're always losing your keys_ .
2. *A:* The car has broken down again.
   B: That car is useless. It _____ .
3. *A:* Look! You made the same mistake again.
   B: Oh no, not again! I _____ .
4. *A:* Oh, I forgot my glasses again.
   B: That's typical! _____ .

現在進行式與現在簡單式 2
(I am doing 與 I do)

A

進行式用以表示動作或事件已經開始但是尚未完成 (例如，they **are eating** / it **is raining** 等)。有些動詞 (例如 know 以及 like) 並非表達動作的動詞，所以不能使用 I am knowing 或 they are liking。正確的用法應為 I **know**、they **like**。

以下動詞通常不可以使用進行式。

like	love	hate	want	need	prefer
know	realize	suppose	mean	understand	believe	remember
belong	fit	contain	consist	seem	

- I'm hungry. I **want** something to eat. (並非 I'm wanting)
- **Do** you **understand** what I **mean**?
- Ann **doesn't seem** very happy.

B

think

think 意思是 believe (相信)或「有某種意見」的時候，不可以使用進行式：

- I **think** Mary is Canadian, but I'm not sure. (並非 I'm thinking)
- What **do** you **think** about my plan? (= What is your opinion?)

但是，**think** 意思是「考慮」的時候，就可以使用進行式：

- I'm **thinking** about what happened. I often **think** about it.
- Nicky **is thinking** of quitting her job. (= she is considering it)

C

He is selfish 與 He is being selfish

He's being 意思與 He's behaving / He's acting 相同。比較下面例句：

- I can't understand why he**'s being** so selfish. He isn't usually like that.
  (**being** selfish 是指在當時表現得很自私。)
- He never thinks about other people. He **is** very selfish. (並非 He is being)
  (一般來說，他是個自私的人，不只是在說話的時候表現得很自私。)

am/is/are **being** 表示某人目前的表現，並不適用於表達一般性狀態的句子中：

- It**'s** hot today. (並非 It's being hot)
- Sarah **is** very tired. (並非 is being tired)

D

see   hear   smell   taste

通常 see、hear、smell、taste 等動詞只能使用現在簡單式，不可以使用進行式：

- **Do** you **see** that man over there? (並非 Are you seeing)
- This room **smells**. Let's open a window.

我們通常用 **can + see / hear / smell / taste**：

- I **can hear** a strange noise. **Can** you **hear** it?

E

look   feel

現代簡單式或進行式可用以表達某人看起來如何、感覺如何：

- You **look** good today.　或　You**'re looking** good today.
- How **do** you **feel** now?　或　How **are** you **feeling** now?

但是

- I usually **feel** tired in the morning. (並非 I'm usually feeling)

現在進行式與現在簡單式之比較 1 Unit 3　**have** Unit 16　現在式表未來的意思 Unit 18

Exercises

4.1 判斷劃線部份的動詞時式是否正確；若不正確，請改為適當的時式。

1. Nicky <u>is thinking</u> of giving up her job.   *OK*
2. <u>Are</u> you <u>believing</u> in God?   _____
3. <u>I'm feeling</u> hungry. Is there anything to eat?   _____
4. This sauce is great. It<u>'s tasting</u> really good.   _____
5. <u>I'm thinking</u> this is your key. Is it?   _____

4.2 請依各圖片的情境，用括號內的字完成句子 (做此練習以前，需先研讀 Unit 3)。

1. (you / not / seem / very happy today)
You don't seem very happy today.

2. (what / you / do?)
_____
_____
Be quiet! (I / think)
_____

3. (who / this umbrella / belong to?)
_____
_____
I have no idea.

4. (dinner / smell / good)
_____
_____

5. Excuse me. (anybody / sit / there?)
_____
_____
No, go ahead.

6. Ladies Gloves
(these gloves / not / fit / me)
_____
_____
They're too small.

4.3 將正確的動詞時式填入空格。請使用現在進行式或現在簡單式。

1. Are you hungry? __*Do you want*__ (you / want) something to eat?
2. Don't put the dictionary away. I _____ (use) it.
3. Don't put the dictionary away. I _____ (need) it.
4. Who is that man? What _____ (he / want)?
5. Who is that man? Why _____ (he / look) at us?
6. Alan says he's 80 years old, but nobody _____ (believe) him.
7. She told me her name, but I _____ (not / remember) it now.
8. I _____ (think) of selling my car. Are you interested in buying it?
9. I _____ (think) you should sell your car. You _____ (not / use) it very often.
10. Air _____ (consist) mainly of nitrogen and oxygen.

4.4 將動詞 *be* 的正確時式填入空格。請使用現在簡單式 (*am*/*is*/*are*) 或現在進行式 (*am*/*is*/*are being*)。

1. I can't understand why __*he's being*__ so selfish. He isn't usually like that.
2. Sarah _____ very nice to me these days. I wonder why.
3. You'll like Debbie when you meet her. She _____ very nice.
4. You're usually very patient, so why _____ unreasonable about waiting 10 more minutes?
5. Why isn't Steve at work today? _____ sick?

過去簡單式 (I did)

A 請看下面的範例：

Wolfgang Amadeus Mozart was an Austrian musician and composer. He **lived** from 1756 to 1791. He **started** composing at the age of five and **wrote** more than 600 pieces of music. He **was** only 35 years old when he **died**.

Wolfgang A. Mozart
1756-1791

莫札特是奧地利的音樂家與作曲家，生於 1756 年，卒於 1791 年。他 5 歲即開始作曲，一生作品超過 600 首音樂，他去世時年僅 35 歲。

lived / started / wrote / was / died 皆為過去簡單式動詞。

B 規則動詞的過去式是在動詞字尾加上 **-ed**：

- I work in a travel agency now. I **worked** in a department store before.
- We **invited** them to our party, but they **decided** not to come.
- The police **stopped** me on my way home last night.
- Laura **passed** her exam because she **studied** very hard.

有關 stop**ped**、stud**ied** 等動詞的過去式拼法，參見附錄 6。

但有許多動詞為不規則動詞，其過去式變化則不是以 **-ed** 為結尾。例如：

write	→	**wrote**
see	→	**saw**
go	→	**went**
shut	→	**shut**

- Mozart **wrote** more than 600 pieces of music.
- We **saw** Rose at the mall a few days ago.
- I **went** to the movies three times last week.
- It was cold, so I **shut** the window.

不規則動詞表，參見附錄 1。

C 過去簡單式的疑問句及否定句，必須使用助動詞 **did/didn't** ＋動詞原型 (例如，**enjoy / see / go** 等)：

I	enjoy**ed**
she	**saw**
they	**went**

	you	**enjoy?**
did	she	**see?**
	they	**go?**

I		**enjoy**
she	**didn't**	**see**
they		**go**

- *A:* **Did** you **go** out last night?
  B: Yes, I **went** to the movies, but I **didn't enjoy** the film much.
- "When **did** Mr. Thomas **die?**" "About 10 years ago."
- They **didn't invite** her to the party, so she **didn't go**.
- "**Did** you **have** time to write the letter?" "No, I **didn't**."

在下列例句中，**do** 的意思是「做」，為該句的主要動詞，故仍必須使用助動詞 **did**。

- What **did** you **do** on the weekend? (並非 What did you on the weekend?)
- I **didn't do** anything. (並非 I didn't anything)

D be 動詞 (**am/is/are**) 的過去式形態為 **was/were**：

I/he/she/it	**was/wasn't**
we/you/they	**were/weren't**

was	I/he/she/it?
were	we/you/they?

句中的動詞為 **be** 動詞時，不可使用助動詞 **did** 來形成疑問句及否定句。

- I **was** angry because they **were** late.
- **Was** the weather good when you **were** on vacation?
- They **weren't** able to come because they **were** so busy.
- Did you go out last night, or **were** you too tired?

Exercises

5.1 以下為 Debbie 對於她平常工作日所做的事情的描述：

> I usually get up at 7:00 and have a big breakfast. I walk to work, which takes me about half an hour. I start work at 8:45. I never have lunch. I finish work at 5:00. I'm always tired when I get home. I usually cook dinner a little later. I don't usually go out. I go to bed around 11:00, and I always sleep well.

Debbie

昨天是 Debbie 的工作日，請描述她所做的或沒有做的事。

1. _She got up at 7:00._
2. She _____ a big breakfast.
3. She _____ .
4. It _____ to get to work.
5. _____ at 8:45.
6. _____ lunch.
7. _____ at 5:00.
8. _____ tired when _____ home.
9. _____ dinner a little later.
10. _____ out last night.
11. _____ at 11:00.
12. _____ well last night.

5.2 依各句題意，從下列動詞中選出一個適當的字，並將正確的動詞時式填入空格。

buy   catch   cost   fall   hurt   sell   spend   teach   throw   ~~write~~

1. Mozart _wrote_ more than 600 pieces of music.
2. "How did you learn to drive?"   "My father _____ me."
3. We couldn't afford to keep our car, so we _____ it.
4. Dave _____ down the stairs this morning and _____ his leg.
5. Jim _____ the ball to Sue, who _____ it.
6. Ann _____ a lot of money yesterday. She _____ a dress that _____ $200.

5.3 James 剛度完假回來；請以問句詢問 James 度假的情形。

Hi. How are things?

Fine, thanks. I've just had a great vacation.

1. Where _did you go_ ?

   We went on a trip from San Francisco to Denver.
2. How _____ ? By car?

   Yes, we rented a car in San Francisco.
3. It's a long way to drive. How long _____ ?

   Two weeks.
4. Where _____ ? In hotels?

   Yes, small hotels or motels.
5. _____ ?

   It was very hot – sometimes too hot.
6. _____ the Grand Canyon?

   Of course. It was wonderful.

5.4 將正確的動詞時式填入空格；並依語意需要，使用肯定或否定形式。

1. It was warm, so I _took_ off my coat. (take)
2. The movie wasn't very good. I _didn't enjoy_ it very much. (enjoy)
3. I knew Sarah was very busy, so I _____ her. (disturb)
4. I was very tired, so I _____ the party early. (leave)
5. The bed was very uncomfortable. I _____ very well. (sleep)
6. The window was open and a bird _____ into the room. (fly)
7. The hotel wasn't very expensive. It _____ very much. (cost)
8. I was in a hurry, so I _____ time to call you. (have)
9. It was hard carrying the bags. They _____ very heavy. (be)

過去進行式 (I was doing)

A

請看下面的範例：

Yesterday Karen and Jim played tennis. They began at 10:00 and finished at 11:30.
So, at 10:30 they **were playing** tennis.
Karen 和 Jim 昨天打網球。他們 10 點開始打，11 點半結束。
所以 10 點半時，他們正在打網球。

They **were playing** 意思是他們正在打，還沒有結束。

was/were -ing 為過去進行式的動詞形式。

I/he/she/it	**was**	play**ing**
we/you/they	**were**	do**ing**
		work**ing**, etc.

B

I **was doing** something 表示在過去的某一段時間內，我正在做某一件事；這個動作在過去的某個時間點以前就已經開始，並且在該時間點之前還正在進行，尚未結束。

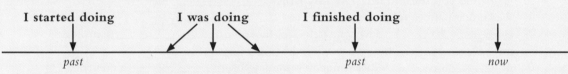

I started doing　　　**I was doing**　　　**I finished doing**

past　　　　　　　　　　　　　　　*past*　　　　　*now*

- This time last year I **was living** in Brazil.
- What **were** you **doing** at 10:00 last night?
- I waved to Helen, but she **wasn't looking**.

C

比較過去進行式 (**I was doing**) 與過去簡單式 (**I did**)：

過去進行式表示動作正在進行	過去簡單式表示動作已經完成
■ I **was walking** home when I met Dave. ■ Kate **was watching** television when we arrived.	■ I **walked** home after the party last night. ■ Kate **watched** television a lot when she was sick last year.

D

過去簡單式與過去進行式常同時使用，以表示某件事發生時，另一件事正在進行。
- Matt **burned** his hand while he **was cooking** dinner.
- It **was raining** when I **got** up.
- I **saw** you in the park yesterday. You **were sitting** on the grass and **reading** a book.
- I **hurt** my back while I **was working** in the garden.

某件事發生後，另一件事接著發生，則都必須使用過去簡單式。
- I **was walking** downtown when I **saw** Dave. So I **stopped**, and we **talked** for a while.

比較下面例子：

■ When Karen arrived, we **were having** dinner. (Karen 到達的時候，我們已經開始吃晚餐；當時我們正在吃。)	■ When Karen arrived, we **had** dinner. (Karen 到達後，我們才一起吃晚餐。)

E

有些動詞(例如 **know** 和 **want** 等) 通常不能使用進行式 (參見 Unit 4A)：
- We were good friends. We **knew** each other well. (並非 We were knowing)
- I was having a good time at the party, but Chris **wanted** to go home. (並非 was wanting)

Exercises

6.1 以過去進行式或過去簡單式，寫出你在以下各個時間的活動 (過去進行式不一定要選用)。

1. (at 8:00 last night) _I was having dinner._
2. (at 5:00 last Monday) _I was on a bus on my way home._
3. (at 10:15 yesterday morning) _____
4. (at 4:30 this morning) _____
5. (at 7:45 last night) _____
6. (half an hour ago) _____

6.2 依你自己的意思，以過去進行式完成下列各句。

1. Matt burned his hand while he _was cooking dinner_ .
2. The doorbell rang while I _____ .
3. We saw an accident while we _____ .
4. Lauren fell asleep while she _____ .
5. The television was on, but nobody _____ .

6.3 將正確的動詞形式填入空格；請使用過去進行式或過去簡單式。

1.

I _saw_ (see) Sue in town yesterday, but she _____ (not / see) me. She _____ (look) the other way.

2.

I _____ (meet) Tom and Jane at the airport a few weeks ago. They _____ (go) to Boston and I _____ (go) to Montreal. We _____ (talk) while we _____ (wait) for our flights.

3.

I _____ (ride) my bicycle yesterday when a man _____ (step) out into the street in front of me. I _____ (go) pretty fast, but luckily I _____ (manage) to stop in time and _____ (not / hit) him.

6.4 將正確的動詞形式填入空格；請使用過去進行式或過去簡單式。

1. Jane _was waiting_ (wait) for me when I _arrived_ (arrive).
2. "What _____ (you / do) at this time yesterday?" "I was asleep."
3. "_____ (you / go) out last night?" "No, I was too tired."
4. How fast _____ (you / drive) when the accident _____ (happen)?
5. Sam _____ (take) a picture of me while I _____ (not / look).
6. We were in a very difficult position. We _____ (not / know) what to do.
7. I haven't seen David for ages. The last time I _____ (see) him, he _____ (try) to find a job in Miami.
8. I _____ (walk) along the street when suddenly I _____ (hear) footsteps behind me. Somebody _____ (follow) me. I was scared and I _____ (start) to run.
9. When I was young, I _____ (want) to be a pilot.
10. Last night I _____ (drop) a plate while I _____ (do) the dishes. Fortunately it _____ (not / break).

現在完成式 (I have done)

A 請看下面的對話：

Dave: **Have** you **traveled** a lot, Jane?
Jane: Yes, **I've been** to lots of places.
Dave: Really? **Have** you ever **been** to China?
Jane: Yes, **I've been** to China twice.
Dave: What about India?
Jane: No, **I haven't been** to India.

Dave: 你到過很多地方旅行嗎？
Jane: 是啊！我去過很多地方。
Dave: 真的嗎？你去過中國嗎？
Jane: 是的，我去過兩次。
Dave: 那麼印度呢？
Jane: 沒有，我沒去過印度。

Jane's life
(a period until now)

past   now

have/has + **traveled/been/done** 等(過去分詞)為現在完成式。

I/we/they/you **have** (= **I've**, etc.)	**traveled**
he/she/it **has** (= **he's**, etc.)	**been**
	done, etc.

規則動詞的過去分詞為動詞原型字尾加上 **-ed**；但是許多重要的動詞都屬於不規則動詞 (例如 **done/been/written**等)。不規則動詞表，參見附錄 1。

B 現在完成式表達從過去到現在的一段時間，這段期間內完成的動作。在 **A** 部分的對話中，Dave 和 Jane 談論的是，直到說話的當時 Jane 一生曾經去過的地方。其他例子如下：

- **Have** you ever **eaten** caviar? (in your life)
- We've never **had** a car.
- "**Have** you **read** *Hamlet*?" "No, **I haven't read** any of Shakespeare's plays."
- Susan really loves that movie. She**'s seen** it eight times!
- What a boring movie! It's the most boring movie I**'ve** ever **seen**.

C 在下列例句中，說話者所談論的，也都是指從過去延續到說話當時的一段時間(**recently / in the last few days / so far / since breakfast**等)。

- **Have** you **heard** from Brian **recently**?
- I**'ve met** a lot of people **in the last few days**.
- Everything is going well. We **haven't had** any problems **so far**.
- I'm hungry. I **haven't eaten** anything **since breakfast**.
- It's nice to see you again. We **haven't seen** each other **for a long time**.

recently
in the last few days
since breakfast

past   now

D 當 **today / this morning / this evening** 等單字或片語所指的時間，在說話的當時尚未結束時，常使用現在完成式。

- I**'ve drunk** four cups of coffee **today**.
- **Have** you **had** a vacation **this year** (yet)?
- I **haven't seen** Tom **this morning**. **Have** you?
- Rob **hasn't studied** very hard **this semester**.

today

past   now

E It's the (first) time something **has happened** 使用現在完成式，表達這是某人生平第一次(或某某次)做某事。例如：

- Don is taking a driving lesson. It's his first one.
  It's the first time he **has driven** a car. (並非 drives)
  或 He **has never driven** a car **before**.
- Sarah has lost her passport again. This is the second time this **has happened**. (並非 happens)
- Bill is calling his girlfriend again. That's the third time he**'s called** her **tonight**.

This is the first time I**'ve driven** a car.

STUDENT DRIVER

Exercises

7.1 用括號內的語詞，配合 *ever* 寫出問句，詢問他人曾經做過的事。

1. (ride / horse?) _Have you ever ridden a horse?_____
2. (be / Mexico?) Have _____
3. (run / marathon?) _____
4. (speak / famous person?) _____
5. (most beautiful place / visit?) What's _____

7.2 依各句題意，從下列動詞中選出一個適當的字完成 B 句；並依語意需要，使用肯定或否定形式。

be	be	eat	happen	have	~~meet~~	play	read	see	see	try

A   **B**

1. What's Mark's sister like? — I have no idea. _I've never met_ her.
2. How is Diane these days? — I don't know. I _____ her recently.
3. Are you hungry? — Yes. I _____ much today.
4. Can you play chess? — Yes, but _____ in ages.
5. Are you enjoying your vacation? — Yes, it's the best vacation _____ for a long time.
6. What's that book like? — I don't know. _____ it.
7. Is Sydney an interesting place? — I have no idea. _____ there.
8. Mike was late for work again today. — Again? He _____ late every day this week.
9. Do you like caviar? — I don't know. _____ it.
10. I hear your car broke down again yesterday. — Yes, it's the second time _____ this week.
11. Who's that woman by the door? — I don't know. _____ her before.

7.3 依各句題意，以 *today* / *this year* / *this semester* 完成句子。

1. I saw Tom yesterday, but _I haven't seen him today_____ .
2. I read a newspaper yesterday, but I _____ today.
3. Last year the company made a profit, but this year _____ .
4. Tracy worked hard at school last semester, but _____ .
5. It snowed a lot last winter, but _____ .
6. Our football team won a lot of games last season, but we _____ .

7.4 參考範例，依各句題意完成下列各個對話。

1. Jack is driving a car, but he's very nervous and not sure what to do.
   You ask: _Have you driven a car before?_____
   He says: _No, this is the first time I've driven a car._____
2. Ben is playing tennis. He's not good at it, and he doesn't know the rules.
   You ask: Have _____
   He says: No, this is the first _____
3. Sue is riding a horse. She doesn't look very confident or comfortable.
   You ask: _____
   She says: _____
4. Maria is in Los Angeles. She has just arrived, and it's very new for her.
   You ask: _____
   She says: _____

現在完成式與過去簡單式 1
(I have done 與 I did)

A

現在完成式 (**I have done**) 可用以表達最近剛發生的事。

- **I've lost** my keys. **Have** you **seen** them?
- "Is Sally here?" "No, she**'s gone** out."
- The police **have arrested** two people in connection with the robbery.

但是在上述情形也可以使用過去簡單式 (**I lost**、**she went** 等)

- **I lost** my keys. **Did** you **see** them?
- "Is Sally here?" "No, she **went** out."
- The police **arrested** two people in connection with the robbery.

B

something **has happened** 表示該件事是剛發生的新訊息。

- Have you heard? Bill and Sarah **have won** the lottery!
  (或 Bill and Sarah **won** . . .)
- The road is closed. There**'s been** (there **has been**) an accident.
  (或 There **was** an accident)

表達舊的、不是最近發生的訊息，只能使用過去簡單式。

- Mozart **was** a composer. He **wrote** more than 600 pieces of music.
  (並非 has been . . . has written)
- My mother **grew** up in Chile. (並非 has grown)

比較下面例子：

- Shakespeare **wrote** many plays.
- My brother is a writer. He **has written** many books. (he still writes books)

C

使用現在完成式表示與說話此刻相關。

- I'm sorry, but I**'ve forgotten** your name. (= I can't remember it *now*)
- Sally isn't here. She**'s gone** out. (= she is out *now*)
- I can't find my bag. **Have** you **seen** it? (= do you know where it is *now*?)

但是在上述使用現在完成式的情形中，也可以使用過去簡單式(I lost、she went 等)

當說話此刻的情況已經不同時，只能用過去簡單式。

比較下面例子：

- It **has stopped** raining, so you don't need the umbrella.
  It **stopped** raining for a while, but now it's raining again.

D

過去簡單式和現在完成式都可與 **just**、**already**、**yet** 一起使用。

just 意指「不久之前」

- *A:* Are you hungry?
  B: No, I **just had** lunch   或   I**'ve just had** lunch.
- *A:* Why are you so happy?
  B: I **just heard** some good news.   或   I**'ve just heard** some good news.

already 用於表示某件事較預期的時間提前發生：

- *A:* Don't forget to mail the letter.
  B: I **already mailed** it.   或   I**'ve already mailed** it.
- *A:* What time is Mark leaving?
  B: He **already left**.   或   He**'s already left**.

yet 意指「到目前為止」；只用於疑問句與否定句，表示說話者期待某事發生：

- **Did** it **stop** raining **yet**?   或   **Has** it **stopped** raining **yet**?
- I wrote the letter, but I **didn't mail** it **yet**.   或   . . .I **haven't mailed** it **yet**.

Exercises

8.1 依各句題意，用括號內的語詞完成句子；請使用現在完成式或過去簡單式。

1. It _has stopped_ (stop) raining, so you don't need your umbrella.

2. *before* / *now*
   The town is very different now. It _____ (change) a lot.

3. I meant to call you last night, but I _____ . (forget)

4. Mary
   Mary _____ (go) to Peru for a vacation, but she's back home in Austin now.

5. Are you OK?
   Yes. I _____ (have) a headache, but I feel fine now.

6. You look great! You _____ (lost) weight.

8.2 判斷以下各題中，**(a)** 句或 **(b)** 句正確，亦或兩者皆可。

1.	a) My mother has grown up in Taitung.	b) My mother grew up in Taitung.	_b_
2.	a) Did you see my purse?	b) Have you seen my purse?	_both_
3.	a) I already paid the gas bill.	b) I've already paid the gas bill.	_____
4.	a) The Chinese invented paper.	b) The Chinese have invented paper.	_____
5.	a) Where have you been born?	b) Where were you born?	_____
6.	a) Ow! I cut my finger.	b) Ow! I've cut my finger.	_____
7.	a) I forgot Jerry's address.	b) I've forgotten Jerry's address.	_____
8.	a) Did you go to the store yet?	b) Have you gone to the store yet?	_____
9.	a) Albert Einstein has been the scientist who has developed the theory of relativity.	b) Albert Einstein was the scientist who developed the theory of relativity.	_____
10.	a) My father was raised by his aunt.	b) My father has been raised by his aunt.	_____

8.3 依各句題意，配合 *just*、*already* 或 *yet* 完成句子；請使用現在完成式或過去簡單式。

1. After lunch you go to see a friend at her house. She says, "Would you like something to eat?"
   You say: No, thank you. _I've just had lunch_ 或 _I just had lunch_ . (have lunch)

2. Joe goes out. Five minutes later, the phone rings and the caller says, "Can I speak to Joe?"
   You say: I'm sorry, _____ . (go out)

3. You are eating in a restaurant. The waiter thinks you have finished and starts to clear the table.
   You say: Wait a minute! _____ . (not / finish)

4. You are going to a restaurant tonight. You call to reserve a table. Later your friend says,
   "Should I call to reserve a table?" You say: No, _____ . (do it)

5. You know that a friend of yours is looking for a place to live. Perhaps she has been successful.
   Ask her. You say: _____ ? (find)

6. You are still thinking about where to go on vacation. A friend asks, "Where are you going
   on vacation?" You say: _____ . (not / decide)

7. Linda went to the bank, but a few minutes ago she returned. Somebody asks, "Is Linda still
   at the bank?" You say: No, _____ . (come back)

8. Yesterday Carol invited you to a party on Saturday. Now another friend is inviting you to the
   same party. You say: Thanks, but Carol _____ . (invite)

現在完成式與過去簡單式 2
(I have done 與 I did)

現在完成式不可用以談論發生在過去，且已經結束的時間(例如 **yesterday** / **10 minutes ago** / **in 1999** / **when I was a child**)，必須使用過去簡單式。

- It **was** very cold **yesterday**. (並非 has been)
- Paul and Lucy **went** out **10 minutes ago**. (並非 have gone)
- **Did** you **eat** a lot of candy **when you were a child**? (並非 have you eaten)
- I **got** home late **last night**. I **was** very tired and **went** straight to bed.

When ...? 或 **What time ...?** 的問句，必須使用過去簡單式。

- **When did** your friends **get** here? (並非 have ... gotten)
- **What time did** you **finish** work?

比較下面各例：

使用現在完成式或過去簡單式	只能用過去簡單式
■ Tom **has lost** his key. He can't get into the house. (或 Tom **lost** ...)	■ Tom **lost** his key **yesterday**. He couldn't get into the house.
■ Is Carla here or **has** she **left**? (或 **Did** she **leave**?)	■ **When did** Carla **leave**?

比較下面各例：

現在完成式 (**have done**)	過去簡單式 (**did**)
■ I**'ve done** a lot of work **today**.	■ I **did** a lot of work **yesterday**.
表達持續至此刻的一段時間，使用現在完成式，例如 **today** / **this week** / **since 1999**。	過去簡單式用以表達發生在過去，已經結束的時間，例如 **yesterday** / **last week** / **from 1999 to 2005**。

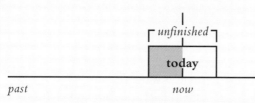 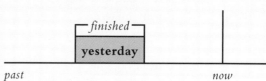

■ It **hasn't rained this week**.	■ It **didn't rain last week**.
■ **Have** you **seen** Lisa **this morning**? (It is still morning)	■ **Did** you **see** Lisa **this morning**? (It is now afternoon or evening)
■ **Have** you **seen** Tim **recently**?	■ **Did** you **see** Tim **on Sunday**?
■ I don't know where Lisa is. I **haven't seen** her. (= I haven't seen her recently)	■ *A:* **Was** Lisa at the party **on Sunday**? *B:* I don't think so. I **didn't see** her.
■ We**'ve been waiting** for an hour. (We are still waiting now)	■ We **waited** (*or* **were waiting**) **for an hour**. (We are no longer waiting)
■ John lives in Los Angeles. He **has lived** there **for seven years**.	■ John **lived** in New York **for 10 years**. Now he lives in Los Angeles.
■ I **have never played** golf. (in my life)	■ I **didn't play** golf **last summer**.
■ 今天是假期的最後一天，因此，你說：It's been a really good vacation. I**'ve** really **enjoyed** it.	■ 你的假期已經結束，因此，你說：It **was** a really good vacation. I really **enjoyed** it.

過去簡單式 **Unit 5**　現在完成式 **Unit 7**　現在完成式與過去簡單式 (1) **Unit 8**　現在完成進行式 **Unit 10** 與 **Unit 11**

Exercises

9.1 判斷下列各題畫線部份是否正確，並更正錯誤。

1. I've lost my key. I can't find it anywhere. _____ *OK* _____
2. Have you eaten a lot of candy when you were a child? _____ *Did you eat* _____
3. I've bought a new car. You have to come and see it. _____
4. I've bought a new car last week. _____
5. Where have you been last night? _____
6. Maria has graduated from high school in 2004. _____
7. I'm looking for Mike. Have you seen him? _____
8. "Have you been to Paris?" "Yes, many times." _____
9. I'm very hungry. I haven't eaten much today. _____
10. When has this book been published? _____

9.2 用括號內的語詞完成句子；請使用現在完成式或過去簡單式。

1. (it / not / rain / this week) *It hasn't rained this week.* _____
2. (the weather / be / cold / recently) The weather _____
3. (it / cold / last week) It _____
4. (I / not / read / a newspaper yesterday) I _____
5. (I / not / read / a newspaper today) _____
6. (Kate / make / a lot of money / this year) _____
7. (she / not / make / so much / last year) _____
8. (you / take / a vacation recently?) _____

9.3 依各句題意，將正確的動詞形式填入空格；請使用現在完成式或過去簡單式。

1. I don't know where Lisa is. *Have you seen* (you / see) her?
2. When I _____ (get) home last night, I _____ (be) very tired, so I _____ (go) straight to bed.
3. *A:* _____ (you / eat) at the new sushi place on Joe's birthday?
   B: No, but _____ (we / be) there twice this month.
4. There was a bus drivers' strike last week. There _____ (not / be) any buses.
5. Mr. Lee _____ (work) in a bank for 15 years. Then he quit.
6. Kelly lives in Toronto. She _____ (live) there all her life.
7. *A:* _____ (you / go) to the movies last night?
   B: Yes, but it _____ (be) a mistake. The movie _____ (be) awful.
8. My grandfather _____ (die) before I was born. I _____
   _____ (never / meet) him.
9. I don't know Karen's husband. I _____ (never / meet) him.
10. It's nearly lunchtime, and I _____ (not / see) Martin all morning.
    I wonder where he is.
11. *A:* Where do you live?
    B: In Rio de Janeiro.
    A: How long _____ (you / live) there?
    B: Five years.
    A: Where _____ (you / live) before that?
    B: In Buenos Aires.
    A: And how long _____ (you / live) there?
    B: Two years.

9.4 請參照例句，用括號內的提示，完成有關於你自己的描述。

1. (something you haven't done today) *I haven't eaten any fruit today.*
2. (something you haven't done today) _____
3. (something you didn't do yesterday) _____
4. (something you did last night) _____
5. (something you haven't done recently) _____
6. (something you've done a lot recently) _____

A

It has been raining.
請看下面的範例：

Is it raining?
No, but the ground is wet.
It has been raining.

正在下雨嗎？
沒有，但是地是濕的。
之前一直在下雨。

have/has been –ing 為現在完成進行式的動詞形式：

I/we/they/you	**have**	(= I**'ve**, etc.)	**been**	do**ing**
he/she/it	**has**	(= he**'s**, etc.)		wait**ing**
				play**ing**, etc.

現在完成進行式表達某一個動作持續到此刻才停止或剛剛才停止，與現在時間有關聯。

- You're out of breath. **Have** you **been running**? (= you're out of breath *now*)
- Jason is very tired. He**'s been working** very hard. (= he's tired *now*)
- Why are your clothes so dirty? What **have** you **been doing**?
- (在電話中) I'm glad you called. I**'ve been thinking** about calling you . . .
- Where have you been? I**'ve been looking** everywhere for you.

B

It has been raining for two hours.
請看下面範例：

It began raining two hours ago, and it is still raining.
How long **has** it **been raining**?
It **has been raining** for two hours.

天正在下雨。兩個小時前就開始下了。
下雨下了多久了？
已經下了兩個小時了。

現在完成進行式常與 how long、for 以及 since 一起使用，
表示某個動作目前仍持續進行中(例如在上班中)，或剛剛停止。

- **How long have** you **been studying** English? (= you're still studying English)
- Tim is still watching television. He**'s been watching** television **all day**.
- Where have you been? I**'ve been looking** for you **for the last half hour**.
- Christopher **hasn't been feeling** well **recently**.

現在完成進行式也可以表示一段時間以來不斷反覆的動作。

- Debbie is a very good tennis player. She**'s been playing since she was eight**.
- Every morning they meet in the same café. They**'ve been going** there **for years**.

C

比較現在進行式 **I am doing** (參見 Unit 1)與現在完成進行式 **I have been doing**：

I am doing *present continuous*	**I have been doing** *present perfect continuous*
now	*now*
- Don't bother me now. I**'m working**.	- I**'ve been working** hard. Now I'm going to take a break.
- We need an umbrella. It**'s raining**.	- The ground is wet. It**'s been raining**.
- Hurry up! We**'re waiting**.	- We**'ve been waiting** for an hour.

現在完成簡單式與現在完成進行式之比較 Unit 11 與 Unit 12　現在完成式與 *for / since* Unit 12 與 Unit 13

Exercises

10.1 請依圖片的情境，以現在完成進行式完成各句。

1. *earlier* / *now*
   They *'ve been shopping.*

2. *earlier* / *now*
   She _____

3. *earlier* / *now*
   They _____

4. *earlier* / *now*
   He _____

10.2 依各句題意，寫出問句。

1. You meet Paul as he is leaving the swimming pool.
   You ask: (you / swim?) *Have you been swimming?*
2. You have just arrived to meet a friend who is waiting for you.
   You ask: (you / wait / long?) _____
3. You meet a friend at the store. His face and hands are very dirty.
   You ask: (what / you / do?) _____
4. A friend of yours is now working at a gym. You want to know how long.
   You ask: (how long / you / work / there?) _____
5. A friend tells you about his job – he sells computers. You want to know how long.
   You ask: (how long / you / sell / computers?) _____

10.3 依各句題意，完成句子。

1. It's raining. The rain started two hours ago.
   It *'s been raining* for two hours.
2. We are waiting for the bus. We got to the bus stop 20 minutes ago.
   We _____ for 20 minutes.
3. I'm studying Spanish. I started classes in December.
   I _____ since December.
4. Jessica is working in Tokyo. She started working there on January 18.
   _____ since January 18.
5. Our friends always spend their summers in the mountains. They started going there years ago. _____ for years.

10.4 請以現在進行式 (*I am -ing*) 或現在完成進行式 (*I have been -ing*)，依各句題意完成句子。

1. *Maria has been studying* (Maria / study) English for two years.
2. Hello, Tom. _____ (I / look) for you all morning. Where have you been?
3. Why _____ (you / look) at me like that? Stop it!
4. Linda is a teacher. _____ (she / teach) for 10 years.
5. _____ (I / think) about what you said, and I've decided to take your advice.
6. "Is Kim on vacation this week?" "No, _____ (she / work)."
7. Sarah is very tired. _____ (she / work) very hard recently.

A

請看下面的範例：

Ling's clothes are covered with paint.
She **has been painting** the ceiling.

Ling 的衣服沾滿了油漆。
她一直在油漆天花板。

has been painting 是現在完成進行式。

這裡描述的重點是「油漆」這個動作本身；至於動作是否已經完成並不重要。在這個例子中，油漆天花板的動作還在進行中，尚未完成。

The ceiling was white. Now it is red.
She **has painted** the ceiling.

天花板過去是白色的，現在是紅色的。
Ling 已經將天花板漆好了。

has painted 是現在完成簡單式。

這裡描述的重點是某件事已經完成；**has painted** 表示已經完成的動作。意即，描述的重點是動作完成後的結果(油漆天花板的工作已經完成了)，而非動作本身。

比較下面各例：

- My hands are very dirty. **I've been fixing** the car.
- Joe **has been eating** too much recently. He should eat less.
- It's nice to see you again. What **have** you **been doing** since the last time we saw you?
- Where have you been? **Have** you **been playing** tennis?

- The car is OK again now. **I've fixed** it.
- Somebody **has eaten** all my candy. The box is empty.
- Where's the book I gave you? What **have** you **done** with it?
- **Have** you ever **played** tennis?

B

現在完成進行式用於描述或詢問某個動作已經進行了有多久 (how long)；該動作仍在進行中。

- How long **have** you **been reading** that book?
- Lisa is still writing her report. She**'s been writing** it **all day**.
- They**'ve been playing** tennis **since 2:00**.

- I'm studying Spanish, but I **haven't been studying** it very long.

現在完成簡單式用於描述或詢問某個動作已經進行了多少次 (how much、how many 或 how many times)；該動作已經完成了。

- How much of that book **have** you **read**?

- Lisa **has written** 10 pages today.

- They**'ve played** tennis three times this week.
- I'm studying Spanish, but I **haven't learned** very much yet.

C

有些動詞 (例如 **know/like/believe**) 通常不可以使用進行式。

- **I've known** about it for a long time. (並非 I've been knowing)

這類動詞參見 Unit 4A 中的表。但是必須注意，**want** 與 **mean** 可以使用現在完成進行式：

- **I've been meaning** to phone Pat, but I keep forgetting.

Exercises

11.1 依各句題意，用括號內的語詞造問句。

1. Luis started reading a book two hours ago. He is still reading it, and now he is on page 53.
   (read / for two hours) _He has been reading for two hours._
   (read / 53 pages so far) _He has read 53 pages so far._

2. Min is from Korea. She is traveling around Asia right now. She began her trip three months ago.
   (travel / for three months) She _____
   (visit / six countries so far) _____

3. Jimmy is a tennis player. He began playing tennis when he was 10 years old. This year he is national champion again – for the fourth time.
   (win / the national championships / four times) _____
   (play / tennis since he was 10) _____

4. When they graduated from college, Lisa and Amy started making movies together. They still make movies.
   (make / five movies since they finished college) They _____
   _____
   (make / movies since they finished college) _____
   _____

11.2 依各句題意，用括號內的語詞造問句。

1. You have a friend who is studying Arabic. You ask:
   (how long / study / Arabic?) _How long have you been studying Arabic?_

2. You have just arrived to meet a friend. She is waiting for you. You ask:
   (wait / long?) Have _____

3. You see somebody fishing by the river. You ask:
   (catch / any fish?) _____

4. Some friends of yours are having a party next week. You ask:
   (how many people / invite?) _____

5. A friend of yours is a teacher. You ask:
   (how long / teach?) _____

6. You meet somebody who is a writer. You ask:
   (how many books / write?) _____
   (how long / write / books?) _____

7. A friend of yours is saving money to take a trip. You ask:
   (how long / save?) _____
   (how much money / save?) _____

11.3 依各題題意，選用適當的動詞填入空格。請使用現在完成簡單式或現在完成進行式。

1. Where have you been? _Have you been playing___ (you / play) tennis?
2. Look! _____ (somebody / break) that window.
3. You look tired. _____ (you / work) hard?
4. "_____ (you / ever / work) in a factory?" "No, never."
5. "Hi, is Sam there?" "No, he _____ (go) for a run."
6. My brother is an actor. _____ (he / appear) in several films.
7. "Sorry I'm late." "That's all right _____ (I / not / wait) long."
8. "Is it still raining?" "No, _____ (it / stop)."
9. _____ (I / lose) my cell phone. _____ (you / see) it anywhere?
10. _____ (I / read) the book you lent me, but _____ (I / not / finish) it yet. It's very interesting.
11. _____ (I / read) the book you lent me, so you can have it back now.

How long have you (been) . . . ?

請看下面的範例：

Bob and Alice are married. They got married exactly 20 years ago, so today is their 20th wedding anniversary. They **have been** married for **20 years**.

Bob 和 Alice 是夫妻。他們 20 年前結婚的，因此，今天是他們結婚 20 週年紀念日，他們已經結婚 20 年了。

我們說 They are married. 現在簡單式表示他們是夫妻的事實。

但是 **How long have** they **been** married? 現在完成式，表示他們已經結婚多久了？
(並非 How long are they married?)

They **have been** married for **20 years**. 現在完成式，表示到目前為止他們已經結婚 20 年了。
(並非 They are married for 20 years)

現在完成式常與 how long、for 以及 since 一起使用，表示某個動作開始於過去，而且到目前仍持續進行。現在式與現在完成式之比較如下：

■ Bill is in the hospital.
但是 He **has been** in the hospital **since Monday**.
(並非 Bill is in the hospital since Monday)

past ——— *present*

■ **Do** you **know** each other well?
但是 **Have** you **known** each other **for a long time**?
(並非 Do you know)

present perfect

■ She's **waiting** for somebody.
但是 She's **been waiting all morning**.

now

■ **Do** they **have** a car?
但是 **How long have** they **had** their car?

I have known/had/lived 等是現在完成簡單式。

I have been learning / been waiting / been doing 等是現在完成進行式。

談論或詢問「有多久的時間」，較常使用現在完成進行式(參見 Unit 10)：
■ **I've been studying** English **for six months**.
■ **It's been raining since lunchtime**.
■ Richard **has been doing** the same job **for 20 years**.
■ "**How long have** you **been driving**?" "**Since I was 17.**"

有些動詞 (例如 **know/like/believe**) 通常不可以使用進行式：
■ How long **have** you **known** Emily? (並非 have you been knowing)
■ **I've had** a stomachache all day. (並非 I've been having)

這類動詞的用法參見 Unit 4A 與 Unit 10C。動詞 have 的用法，參見 Unit 16A。

動詞 **live** 和 **work** 可以使用現在完成簡單式，也可使用現在完成進行式。
■ John **has been living / has lived** in Montreal for a long time.
■ How long **have** you **been working / have** you **worked** here?

但與 **always** 一起使用時，必須使用現在完成式 (**I've done / I've lived** 等)。
■ **Have** you **always lived** in the country? (並非 always been living)

表達 I **haven't done** something **since/for** . . . 時，通常使用現在完成簡單式。
■ I **haven't seen** Tom **since** Monday. (= 我最後一次看到 Tom 是在星期一。)
■ Sue **hasn't called for** ages. (= Jane 最後一次打電話給我是很久以前。)

I haven't . . . since / for Unit 7C 現在完成進行式 Unit 10 與 Unit 11 *for* 和 *since* Unit 13

Exercises

12.1 判斷劃線部分的動詞時式是否正確；若不正確，請改為適當的時式。

1. Bob is a friend of mine. <u>I know him</u> very well. _____OK_____
2. Bob is a friend of mine. <u>I know him</u> for a long time. _____I've known him_____
3. Sue and Scott <u>are married</u> since July. _____
4. The weather is awful. <u>It's raining</u> again. _____
5. The weather is awful. <u>It's raining</u> all day. _____
6. I like your house. How long <u>are you living</u> there? _____
7. Gary <u>is working</u> in a store for the last few months. _____
8. <u>I don't know</u> Tim well. We've only met a few times. _____
9. I quit drinking coffee. I <u>don't drink</u> it for a year. _____
10. That's a very old bike. How long <u>do you have</u> it? _____

12.2 依各句題意，用括號內的語詞寫出問句。

1. John tells you that his mother is in the hospital. You ask him:
   (how long / be / in the hospital?) _How long has your mother been in the hospital?_
2. You meet a woman who tells you that she teaches English. You ask her:
   (how long / teach / English?) _____
3. You know that Erica is a good friend of Carol's. You ask Erica:
   (how long / know / Carol?) _____
4. Your friend's brother moved to Costa Rica a while ago. You ask your friend:
   (how long / be / in Costa Rica?) _____
5. Chris drives a very old car. You ask him:
   (how long / have / that car?) _____
6. You are talking to a friend about Scott. Scott now works at the airport. You ask your friend:
   (how long / work / at the airport?) _____
7. A friend of yours is taking guitar lessons. You ask him:
   (how long / take / guitar lessons?) _____
8. You meet somebody on a plane. She says that she lives in Chicago. You ask her:
   (always / live / in Chicago?) _____

12.3 依對話內容，完成 B 的回答。

	A	B
1.	Amy is in the hospital, isn't she?	Yes, she _has been_ in the hospital since Monday.
2.	Do you see Ann very often?	No, I _haven't seen_ her for three months.
3.	Is Margaret married?	Yes, she _____ married for 10 years.
4.	Are you waiting for me?	Yes, I _____ for the last half hour.
5.	You know Linda, don't you?	Yes, we _____ each other a long time.
6.	Do you still play tennis?	No, I _____ tennis for years.
7.	Is Jim watching TV?	Yes, he _____ TV all night.
8.	Do you watch TV a lot?	No, I _____ TV for ages.
9.	Do you have a headache?	Yes, I _____ a headache all morning.
10.	George is never sick, is he?	No, he _____ sick since I met him.
11.	Are you feeling sick?	Yes, I _____ sick all day.
12.	Sue lives in Miami, doesn't she?	Yes, she _____ in Miami for the last few years.
13.	Do you go to the movies a lot?	No, I _____ to the movies for ages.
14.	Would you like to go to Taiwan one day?	Yes, I _____ to go to Taiwan. (用 **always / want**)

for 與 since
When . . . ? 與 How long . . . ?

A

for 和 since 表達事情已經發生了有多久的時間。

for 後面接的是一段時間
(例如 2 小時、6 星期等)：

- I've been waiting **for two hours**.

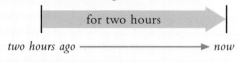

two hours ago ⟶ *now*

for		
two hours	a long time	a week
20 minutes	six months	ages
five days	50 years	years

- Kelly has been working here **for six months**. (並非 since six months)
- I haven't seen Tom **for three days**.

since 後面接的是一段時間的起點(例如 8 點鐘、星期一、1999 年等)：

- I've been waiting since **8:00**.

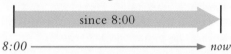

8:00 ⟶ *now*

since		
8:00	April	lunchtime
Monday	1985	we arrived
May 12	Christmas	yesterday

- Kelly has been working here **since April**. (= from April until now)
- I haven't seen Tom **since Monday**.

肯定句中，可以省略 **for**；否定句中則通常不省略。
- They've been married (for) **10 years**. (可省略 **for**)
- They **haven't had** a vacation for 10 years. (必須使用 **for**)

表一段時間的片語有 **all** 時(如 **all day**、**all my life** 等)，**for** 必須省略。
- I've lived here **all my life**. (並非 for all my life)

否定句中除了 **for**，也可以使用 **in**：
- They **haven't had** a vacation in 10 years.

B

比較 **When . . . ?** (使用過去簡單式)與 **How long . . . ?** (使用現在完成式)

A: **When** did it start raining?
B: It started raining **an hour ago** / **at 1:00**.

A: **How long** has it been raining?
B: It's been raining **for an hour** / **since 1:00**.

A: **When** did Joe and Carol first meet?
B: They first met { a long time **ago**.
{ **when** they were in high school.

A: **How long** have they **known** each other?
B: They**'ve known** each other { **for** a long time.
{ **since** they were in high school.

C

It's (= It has) **been a long time** / **two years** 等表示，自從(since)某事發生後已經過了很久/兩年(等)。
- **It's been two years since** I saw Joe. (= I **haven't seen** Joe for two years)
- **It's been ages since** we went to the movies. (= We **haven't gone** to the movies for ages)

其對應的問句句型為 **How long has it been since . . . ?**
- **How long has it been since** you saw Joe? (= When did you last see Joe?)
- **How long has it been since** Mrs. Hill died? (= When did Mrs. Hill die?)

Exercises

13.1 填入 *for* 或 *since*。

1. It's been raining _____since_____ lunchtime.
2. Sarah has lived in Chicago _____ 1995.
3. Joe has lived in Dallas _____ 10 years.
4. I'm tired of waiting. We've been sitting here _____ an hour.
5. Kevin has been looking for a job _____ he graduated.
6. I haven't been to a party _____ ages.
7. I wonder how Joe is. I haven't seen him _____ last week.
8. Jane is away at college. She's been away _____ last August.
9. The weather is dry. It hasn't rained _____ a few weeks.

13.2 以 *how long* 與 *when* 造問句。

1. It's raining.
   (how long?) _How long has it been raining?_
   (when?) _When did it start raining?_
2. Kate is studying Japanese.
   (how long / study?) _____
   (when / start?) _____
3. I know Jeff.
   (how long / you / know?) _____
   (when / you / meet?) _____
4. Rebecca and David are married.
   (how long?) _____
   (when / get?) _____

13.3 依各句題意，完成句子。

1. It's raining. It's been raining since lunchtime.   It _____started raining_____ at lunchtime.
2. Ann and Sue are friends. They met years ago.   _They've been friends for_____ years.
3. Mark is sick. He got sick on Sunday.   He has _____ Sunday.
4. Mark is sick. He got sick a few days ago.   He has _____ a few days.
5. Sarah is married. She's been married for a year.   She got _____ .
6. You have a headache. It started when you woke up.
   I've _____ I woke up.
7. Megan has been in France for the last three weeks.
   She went _____ .
8. You're working in a hotel. You started six months ago.
   I've _____ .

13.4 依各句題意，用括號內的字完成 B 句。

1. *A:* Do you take vacations often?
   B: (no / five years) _No, I haven't taken a vacation for five years._
2. *A:* Do you see Laura often?
   B: (no / about a month) _____
3. *A:* Do you go to the movies often?
   B: (no / a long time) _____
4. *A:* Do you eat out often?
   B: (no / ages) _____

請用 *It's been . . . since* 的句型重新回答上述的問題。

5. (1) _No, it's been five years since I took a vacation._
6. (2) No, it's _____
7. (3) No, _____
8. (4) _____

過去完成式 (I had done)

A

請看下面的範例：

At 10:30
Bye!

At 11:00
Hi!

Eric   Sarah

Sarah went to a party last week. Eric went to the party, too, but they didn't see each other. Eric left the party at 10:30 and Sarah got there at 11:00. So: When Sarah got to the party, Eric wasn't there.

He **had gone** home.

Sarah 上星期去參加一個宴會，Eric 也去了，但是他們沒見到面。Eric 10:30 離開，Sarah 11:00才到。當 Sarah 抵達宴會的時候，Eric 不在那兒。

他已經回家了。

had gone 為過去完成簡單式：

I/we/they/you he/she/it	**had**	(= I'**d**, etc.) (= he'**d**, etc.)	**gone seen finished**, etc.

過去完成簡單式為 **had** + 過去分詞 (**gone/seen/finished** 等)。

描述過去發生的事用過去式：

■ Sarah **got** to the party.

這是故事發生時間的起點；因此，要描述在這個時間點之前發生的事，就必須使用過去完成式 (**had** . . .)。

■ When Sarah arrived at the party, Eric **had** already **gone** home. (當 Sarah 抵達宴會時，Eric 已經回家了。)

其他例子如下：

■ When we got home last night, we found that somebody **had broken** into our house.
■ Karen didn't want to go to the movies with us because she'**d** already **seen** the film.
■ At first I thought I'**d done** the right thing, but I soon realized that I'**d made** a big mistake.
■ The man sitting next to me on the plane was very nervous. He **hadn't flown** before.
  或　. . .He **had** never **flown** before.

B

比較現在完成式 (**have seen** 等) 與過去完成式 (**had seen**) 之用法：

現在完成式

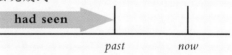

have seen

past　　　　　　　*now*

■ Who is that woman? I'**ve** never **seen** her before.
■ We aren't hungry. We'**ve** just **had** lunch.
■ The house is dirty. They **haven't cleaned** it for weeks.

過去完成式

had seen

past　　　*now*

■ I didn't know who she was. I'**d** never **seen** her before. (= before that time)
■ We weren't hungry. We'**d** just **had** lunch.
■ The house was dirty. They **hadn't cleaned** it for weeks.

C

比較過去簡單式 (**left**, **was** 等) 與過去完成式 (**had left**, **had been**等) 之用法：

■ *A:* Was Tom there when you arrived?
　B: Yes, but he **left** a little later.

■ Amy **wasn't** at home when I called. She **was** at her mother's house.

■ *A:* Was Tom there when you arrived?
　B: No, he **had** already **left**.

■ Amy **had** just **gotten** home when I called. She **had been** at her mother's house.

Exercises

14.1 依各句題意，用括號內的語詞完成句子。

1. You went to Jill's house, but she wasn't there.
   (she / go / out) _She had gone out._
2. You went back to your hometown after many years. It wasn't the same as before.
   (it / change / a lot) _____
3. I invited Rachel to the party, but she couldn't come.
   (she / make / plans to do something else) _____
4. You went to the movies last night. You got there late.
   (the movie / already / begin) _____
5. It was nice to see Daniel again after such a long time.
   (I / not / see / him in five years) _____
6. I offered Sue something to eat, but she wasn't hungry.
   (she / just / have / breakfast) _____

14.2 依各句題意，配合 **never . . . before**，用括號內的語詞完成句子。

1. The man sitting next to you on the plane was very nervous. It was his first flight.
   (fly) _He had never flown before._
2. A woman walked into the room. She was a complete stranger to me.
   (see) I _____ before.
3. Sam played tennis yesterday. He wasn't very good at it because it was his first game.
   (play) He _____
4. Last year we went to Mexico. It was our first time there.
   (be there) We _____

14.3 依各句題意，完成右邊的段落。各題左邊的 (1) 至 (3) 或 (1) 至 (4) 句組是依時間順序排列，因此，在完成右邊的段落時，有可能必須使用過去完成式。

1. (1) Somebody broke into the office during the night.
   (2) <u>We arrived at work in the morning.</u>
   (3) We called the police.

   We arrived at work in the morning and found that somebody _had broken_ into the office during the night. So we _____.

2. (1) Laura went out this morning.
   (2) <u>I tried to call her.</u>
   (3) There was no answer.

   I tried to call Laura this morning, but _____ no answer. She _____ out.

3. (1) Jim came back from vacation a few days ago.
   (2) <u>I met him the same day.</u>
   (3) He looked relaxed.

   I met Jim a few days ago. _____ just _____ vacation. _____ relaxed.

4. (1) Kevin sent Sally lots of e-mails.
   (2) She never answered them.
   (3) <u>Yesterday he got a phone call from her.</u>
   (4) He was very surprised.

   Yesterday Kevin _____ from Sally. He _____ very surprised. He _____ lots of e-mails, but she _____ .

14.4 請選用過去完成式 (**I had done**) 或過去簡單式 (**I did**)，並將正確的動詞時式填入空格。

1. "Was Ben at the party when you got there?" "No, he _had gone_ (go) home."
2. I felt very tired when I got home, so I _____ (go) straight to bed.
3. The house was very quiet when I got home. Everybody _____ (go) to bed.
4. Sorry I'm late. My car _____ (break) down on the way here.
5. We were driving on the highway when we _____ (see) a car that _____ (break) down, so we _____ (stop) to help.

過去完成進行式 (I had been doing)

A 請看下面的範例：

Yesterday morning

Yesterday morning I got up and looked out of the window. The sun was shining, but the ground was very wet.

It **had been raining**.

昨天早上我起床後往窗外看，太陽出來了，但是地上很濕。

之前一直在下雨。

It was *not* raining when I looked out of the window; the sun was shining. But it **had been** raining before.

昨天早上當我往窗外看，太陽出來了，沒有下雨；但是之前一直在下雨。

had been -ing 為過去完成進行式的動詞形式。

I/we/you/they he/she/it	**had**	(= I'**d**, etc.) (= he'**d**, etc.)	**been**	do**ing** work**ing** play**ing**, etc.

其他例子如下：

- When the boys came into the house, their clothes were dirty, their hair was messy, and one of them had a black eye. They'**d been fighting**.
- I was very tired when I got home. I'**d been working** hard all day.
- When I went to Tokyo a few years ago, I stayed with a friend of mine. She'**d been living** there only a short time but knew the city very well.

B 過去完成進行式表達在過去某事件發生以前，另一個事件已經持續發生了一段時間。

- We'**d been playing** tennis for about half an hour when it started to rain hard.
- Jim went to the doctor last Friday. He **hadn't been feeling** well for some time.

C 比較現在完成進行式 (**have been -ing**) 與過去完成進行式 (**had been -ing**) 之用法：

現在完成進行式	過去完成進行式
I have been -ing ➡	**I had been -ing** ➡
past *now*	*past* *now*
■ I hope the bus comes soon. I'**ve been waiting** for 20 minutes. *(before now)*	■ The bus finally came. I'**d been waiting** for 20 minutes. *(before the bus came)*
■ James is out of breath. He **has been running**.	■ James was out of breath. He **had been running**.

D 比較過去完成進行式 (**had been doing**) 與過去進行式 (**was doing**) 之用法：

- It **wasn't raining** when we went out. The sun **was shining**. But it **had been raining**, so the ground was wet.
- Stephanie **was sitting** in an armchair resting. She was tired because she'**d been working** very hard.

E 有些動詞 (例如 **know** 和 **want**) 通常不使用進行式：

- We were good friends. We **had known** each other for years. (並非 had been knowing)

這類動詞，參見 Unit 4A。

Exercises

15.1 依各句題意，用括號內的語詞完成句子。

1. I was very tired when I got home.
   (I / work / hard all day) *I'd been working hard all day.*
2. The two boys came into the house. They had a soccer ball, and they were both very tired.
   (they / play / soccer) _____
3. I was disappointed when I had to cancel my vacation.
   (I / look / forward to it) _____
4. Ann woke up in the middle of the night. She was scared and didn't know where she was.
   (she / dream) _____
5. When I got home, Mike was sitting in front of the TV. He had just turned it off.
   (he / watch / a DVD) _____

15.2 依各句題意，完成句子。

1. We played tennis yesterday. Half an hour after we began playing, it started to rain.
   We *had been playing for half an hour* when *it started to rain* .
2. I had arranged to meet Robert in a restaurant. I arrived and waited for him. After 20 minutes I suddenly realized that I was in the wrong restaurant.
   I _____ for 20 minutes when I _____
   _____ the wrong restaurant.
3. Sarah got a job in a factory. Five years later the factory closed down.
   When the factory _____ , Sarah _____
   _____ there for five years.
4. I went to a concert last week. The orchestra began playing. After about 10 minutes a man in the audience suddenly started shouting.
   The orchestra _____
   when _____

請依您自己的情況完成句子。

5. I began driving home from work. I _____
   when _____

15.3 請依題意選用過去進行式 (*I was doing*)、過去完成式 (*I had done*) 或過去完成進行式 (*I had been doing*)，並將正確的動詞時式填入空格。

1. It was very noisy next door. Our neighbors *were having* (have) a party.
2. We were good friends. We *had known* (know) each other for years.
3. John and I went for a walk. I had trouble keeping up with him because he _____ (walk) so fast.
4. Sue was sitting on the ground. She was out of breath. She _____ (run).
5. When I arrived, everybody was sitting around the table with their mouths full. They _____ (eat).
6. When I arrived, everybody was sitting around the table and talking. Their mouths were empty, but their stomachs were full. They _____ (eat).
7. Jim was on his hands and knees on the floor. He _____ (look) for his contact lens.
8. When I arrived, Kate _____ (wait) for me. She was upset with me because I was late and she _____ (wait) for a long time.
9. I was sad when I sold my car. I _____ (have) it for a long time.
10. We were exhausted at the end of our trip. We _____ (travel) for more than 24 hours.

have 與 have got

A

have 與 have got 表示「擁有」、「關係」、「疾病」、「病痛」等意思。

使用 have got 或 have，意思大致相同：

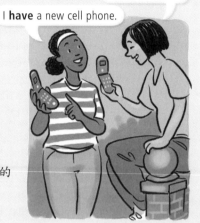

I **have** a new cell phone.

I**'ve got** a new cell phone, too.

- They **have** a new car. 或 They**'ve got** a new car.
- Nancy **has** two sisters. 或 Nancy **has got** two sisters.
- I **have** a headache. 或 I**'ve got** a headache.
- He **has** a few problems. 或 He**'s got** a few problems.
- Our house **has** a big yard. 或 Our house **has got** a big yard.

當 have 意思是「擁有」時，不可以使用進行式。

- We're enjoying our vacation. We **have** / **have got** a nice room in the hotel. (並非 We're having)

注意，使用 have 或 have got 意思雖然相同，但是疑問句與否定句的句型卻不相同：

Do you **have** any questions?	**Have** you **got** any questions?
I **don't have** any questions.	I **haven't got** any questions.
Does she **have** a car?	**Has** she **got** a car?
She **doesn't have** a car.	She **hasn't got** a car.

B

過去式為 had (不是 had got)。

- Ann **had** long hair when she was a child.

had 為主要動詞時，疑問句與否定句必須使用助動詞 **did/didn't**：

- **Did** they **have** a car when they were living in Miami?
- I **didn't have** a watch, so I didn't know what time it was.
- Ann **had** long hair, **didn't** she?

C

have breakfast / have trouble / have a good time 等

had 用於下列動詞片語中，表示動作或經驗，例如：

have	**breakfast / dinner / a cup of coffee / something to eat**
	a party / a safe trip / a good flight
	an accident / an experience / a dream
	a look (at something)
	a conversation / a discussion / a talk (with somebody)
	trouble / difficulty / fun / a good time, etc.
	a baby (= give birth to a baby) / **an operation**

在上述的表達方式中必須用 **have**，不可以用 **have got**。比較下面例子：

- Sometimes I **have** (= eat) a sandwich for lunch. (並非 I've got)

但是 I**'ve got** / I **have** some sandwiches. Would you like one?

此外，上述的 **have** 和其他表動作的動詞一樣，可依語意需要使用進行式(**am having**)：

- We're enjoying our vacation. We**'re having** a great time. (並非 We have)
- Mike **is having** trouble with his car. He often has trouble with his car.

在使用上述的動詞片語時，其疑問句與否定句必須使用助動詞 **do/does/did**：

- I **don't** usually **have** a big breakfast. (並非 I usually haven't)
- What time **does** Ann **have** lunch? (並非 has Ann lunch)
- **Did** you **have** any trouble finding a place to live?

Exercises

16.1 依各句題意以及括號內的提示，以現在式或過去式寫出 *have* 的否定句。

1. I can't get into the house. (a key) _I don't have a key._
2. I couldn't read the letter. (my glasses) _I didn't have my glasses._
3. I can't climb up on the roof. (a ladder) _____
4. We couldn't visit the museum. (enough time) We _____
5. He couldn't find our house. (a map) _____
6. She can't pay her bills. (any money) _____
7. I can't fix the car tonight. (enough energy) _____
8. They couldn't take any pictures. (a camera) _____

16.2 以 *have* 為主要動詞，使用現在式或過去式完成下列的問句。

1. Excuse me, _do you have_ a pen I could borrow?
2. Why are you holding your face like that? _____ a toothache?
3. _____ a lot of toys when you were a child?
4. *A:* _____ the time, please?
   B: Yes, it's ten after seven.
5. I need a stamp for this letter. _____ one?
6. When you took the test, _____ time to answer all the questions?
7. *A:* It started to rain very hard while I was taking a walk.
   B: Did it? _____ an umbrella?

16.3 描述你自己的情形。你現在擁有以下的物品嗎？十年前呢？

Now	*10 years ago (or 5 if you're young)*
1. (a car) _I have a car._ 或 _I've got a car._	_I didn't have a car._
2. (a bike) I _____	I _____
3. (a cell phone) _____	_____
4. (a dog) _____	_____
5. (a guitar) _____	_____
6. (long hair) _____	_____
7. (a driver's license) _____	_____

16.4 依各句題意，從下列動詞中選出適當者，並將正確的動詞時式填入空格。

have a baby	have a dream	have a talk	have trouble	have a good flight
have a look	~~have lunch~~	have a party	have a nice time	have dinner

1. I don't eat much during the day. I never _have lunch_ .
2. If you're angry with your friend, it might be a good idea to sit down and _____ with her.
3. We _____ last week. It was great – we invited lots of people.
4. Excuse me, can I _____ at your newspaper, please?
5. Jim is on vacation in Hawaii. I hope he _____ .
6. I didn't sleep well last night. I _____ about my exam.
7. *A:* _____ finding the book you wanted?
   B: No, I found it OK.
8. Crystal _____ a few weeks ago. It's her second child.
9. *A:* Why didn't you answer the phone?
   B: We _____ with friends.
10. *You meet your friend Sally at the airport. She has just arrived. You say:*
    Hi, Sally. How are you? _____ ?

used to (do)

A

請看下面範例：

幾年前

現在

David quit jogging two years ago. He doesn't jog any more. But he **used to jog**.

David 兩年前停止了慢跑，他現在不再慢跑了。
但是他過去經常慢跑。

He **used to jog** three miles a day.
He **used to jog** = he jogged regularly in the past, but he doesn't jog now.

他過去一天跑 3 英哩。

He **used to jog** 意思是在過去他曾經常常慢跑，但是現在他不再慢跑了。

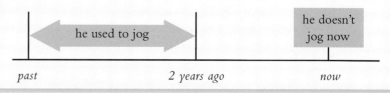

past   2 years ago   now

B

something **used to** happen 意思是過去某件事經常發生，但是現在已經不再發生了。
- I **used to play** tennis a lot, but I don't play very often now.
- David **used to spend** a lot of money on clothes. These days he can't afford it.
- "Do you go to the movies much?" "Not any more, but I **used to**." (= I used to go)

used to 也可以表示過去的一件事實，但目前這件事已經不再是事實。
- This building is now a furniture store. It **used to be** a movie theater.
- I **used to think** Mark was unfriendly, but now I realize he's a very nice person.
- I've started drinking coffee recently. I never **used to like** it before.
- Nicole **used to have** very long hair when she was a child.

C

used to do something 必定是過去式，沒有對應的現在式，所以不可以用 I use to do。
表示現在事實，必須使用現在簡單式 (I do)。比較下面例句：

| *Past* | he **used to play** | we **used to live** | there **used to be** |
| *Present* | he **plays** | we **live** | there **is** |

- We **used to live** in a small town, but now we **live** in Chicago.
- There **used to be** four movie theaters in town. Now there is only one.

D

used to do 的疑問句為 **did** (you) **use to . . .**?
- **Did** you **use to eat** a lot of candy when you were a child?

used to do 的否定句為 **didn't use to**：
- I **didn't use to like** him.

E

比較 **I used to do** 與 **I was doing** 之用法：
- I **used to watch** TV a lot when I was little. (我過去經常看電視，但是現在不再是如此了。)
- I **was watching** TV when Mike called. (Mike 打電話來的時候，我正在看電視。)

F

注意 **I used to do** 與 **I am used to doing** (參見 Unit 59) 的意思不同，結構與用法也不相同。
- I **used to live** alone. (我以前一個人住，但是我現在不是一個人住了。)
- I **am used to living** alone. (我一個人住；我不覺得一個人住奇怪或困難。)

Exercises

17.1 依各句題意，以 *used to* 和適當的動詞完成句子。

1. David quit jogging two years ago. He ___used to jog___ three miles a day.
2. Liz _____ a motorcycle, but last year she sold it and bought a car.
3. We moved to Spain a few years ago. We _____ in Paris.
4. I seldom eat ice cream now, but I _____ it when I was a child.
5. Tracy _____ my best friend, but we aren't friends anymore.
6. It only takes me about 40 minutes to get to work now that the new highway is open. It _____ more than an hour.
7. There _____ a hotel near the airport, but it closed a long time ago.
8. When you lived in New York, _____ to the theater very often?

17.2 Matt 改變了他的生活方式；他停止了做某些事，開始做另一些事：

He stopped { ~~studying hard~~ / going to bed early / running three miles every morning }   He started { ~~sleeping late~~ / going out every night / spending a lot of money }

請以 *used to* 與 *didn't use to* 完成有關 Matt 的描述。

1. ___He used to study hard.___
2. ___He didn't use to sleep late.___
3. _____
4. _____
5. _____
6. _____

17.3 比較 Karen 五年前所説的話與目前她所説的話：

請寫出句子描述 Karen 的改變。句子的第一部份請以 *used to / didn't use to / never used to* 表達。

1. ___She used to travel a lot___ , but ___she doesn't take many trips these days.___
2. She _____ , but _____
3. She _____ , but _____
4. She _____ , but _____
5. She _____ , but _____
6. She _____ , but _____
7. She _____ , but _____
8. She _____ , but _____
9. She _____ , but _____
10. She _____ , but _____

表示未來意思之現在式
(I am doing / I do)

現在進行式 (**I am doing**) 表未來意思之用法

這是 Ben 下週的行程表。

He **is playing** tennis on Monday afternoon.
He **is going** to the dentist on Tuesday morning.
He **is having** dinner with Ann on Friday.

星期一下午他將打網球。
星期二早上他將去看牙醫。
星期五他將和 Ann 吃晚餐。

在這些例子中，Ben 已經決定並安排好下星期一、二、
五要做這些事。

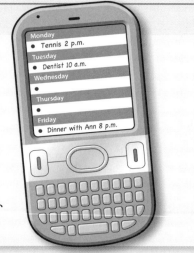

現在進行式可以表示未來已經安排好將進行的事。這種情況不可以使用現在簡單式(I do)。
  - A: What **are** you **doing** Saturday night? (並非 What do you do)
    B: **I'm going** to the theater. (並非 I go)
  - A: What time **is** Cathy **arriving** tomorrow?
    B: At 10:30. **I'm meeting** her at the airport.
  - **I'm not working** tomorrow, so we can go out somewhere.
  - Sam **isn't playing** football next Saturday. He hurt his leg.

表示未來已經安排好將進行的事也可以用 **I'm going to** (do)：
  - What **are** you **going to do** Saturday night?

但表示未來已經安排好、預定進行的事，使用現在進行式較為自然(參見 Unit 19B)。

will 並不用於表示未來已經安排好將做的事。
  - What **are** you **doing** tonight? (並非 What will you do)
  - Eric **is getting** married next month. (並非 will get)

表示即將要開始進行的動作，也可以使用現在進行式，特別是表示動作的動詞(**go/come/leave** 等)：
  - I'm tired. **I'm going** to bed now. Goodnight. (並非 I go to bed now)
  - "Tina, are you ready yet?" "Yes, **I'm coming**." (並非 I come)

現在簡單式 (**I do**) 表示未來意思之用法

現在簡單式用於時刻表、一般性行程等 (例如，大眾運輸工具時刻表、電影院放映時間等。)
  - My flight **leaves** at 11:30, so I need to get to the airport by 10:00.
  - What time **does** the movie **begin**?
  - It's Wednesday tomorrow. / Tomorrow **is** Wednesday.

現在簡單式可以用來描述某人既定且不會變更的計劃，例如固定的行程：
  - I **start** my new job on Monday.
  - What time **do** you **finish** work tomorrow?

但是在描述個人的安排時，較常使用現在進行式。
  - What time **are** you **meeting** Ann tomorrow? (並非 do you meet)

比較下面的例子：

現在進行式	現在簡單式
■ What time **are** you arriving?	■ What time **does** the plane **arrive**?
■ **I'm going** to the movies tonight.	■ The movie **starts** at 8:15 (tonight).

Exercises

18.1 你的朋友將要去渡假，請以括號內的提示寫出問句，詢問她的計畫。

1. (where / go?) _Where are you going?_ _____
2. (how long / stay?) _____
3. (when / leave?) _____
4. (go / alone?) _____
5. (travel / by car?) _____
6. (where / stay?) _____

Quebec.
Ten days.
Next Friday.
No, with a friend.
No, by plane.
In a hotel.

18.2 Ben 希望你去拜訪他，可是你太忙了無法成行。請根據以下所列你接下來幾天的行程，向他解釋你無法拜訪他的原因。

Monday
● Volleyball 7:30 p.m.
Tuesday
● Work late until 9 p.m.
Wednesday
● Theater
Thursday
● Meet Julia 8 p.m.
Friday
●

Ben: Can you come over on Monday night?
You: Sorry, but _I'm playing volleyball_ . (1)
Ben: What about Tuesday night then?
You: No, not Tuesday. I _____ . (2)
Ben: And Wednesday night?
You: _____ . (3)
Ben: Well, are you free on Thursday?
You: I'm afraid not. _____ . (4)

18.3 根據各題提示的時間，寫出你未來的行程。

1. (tonight) _I'm going out tonight._ 或 _I'm not doing anything tonight._ _____
2. (tomorrow morning) I _____
3. (tomorrow night) _____
4. (next Sunday) _____
5. (*choose another day or time*) _____

18.4 請選用現在進行式或現在簡單式，並將正確的動詞時式填入空格。

1. I _'m going_ (go) to the movies tonight.
2. _Does the movie begin_ (the movie / begin) at 3:30 or 4:30?
3. We _____ (have) a party next Saturday. Would you like to come?
4. The art exhibit _____ (open) on May 3.
5. I _____ (not / go) out tonight. I _____ (stay) at home.
6. "_____ (you / do) anything tomorrow morning?" "No, I'm free. Why?"
7. We _____ (go) to a concert tonight. It _____ (start) at 7:30.
8. I _____ (leave) now. I came to say good-bye.
9. *A:* Have you seen Liz recently?
   B: No, but we _____ (meet) for lunch next week.
10. *You are on the train to Boston and you ask another passenger:*
    Excuse me. What time _____ (this train / get) to Boston?
11. *You are talking to Julie:*
    Julie, I _____ (go) to the store now. _____ (you / come) with me?
12. *You and a friend are watching television. You say:*
    I'm bored with this show. What time _____ (it / end)?
13. I _____ (not / use) the car tonight, so you can have it.
14. Sue _____ (come) to see us tomorrow. She _____ (fly) from Seattle, and her plane _____ (arrive) at 10:15 a.m.

(I'm) going to (do)

A

I am going to do something 意思是「我已經決定要做某事」、「我打算要做某事」：

- *A:* **Are** you **going to watch** the football game on TV tonight?
- *B:* No, **I'm going to go** to bed early. I'm tired from my trip.
- *A:* I heard Lisa won some money. What **is** she **going to do** with it?
- *B:* She**'s going to buy** a new car.
- **I'm going to make** a quick phone call. Can you wait for me?
- This cheese smells awful. **I'm not going to eat** it.

B

I am doing 與 **I am going to do** 之比較

I am doing 表示我已經安排好將做某事；例如，已經安排好將要見某人、已經安排好將去某處：

- What time **are** you **meeting** Amanda tonight?
- **I'm leaving** tomorrow. I already have my plane ticket.

I am going to do something 表示我已經決定做某件事，但可能並非預先安排好要做的：

- "The windows are dirty." "Yes, I know. **I'm going to wash** them later."
  (= 我已經決定要洗窗戶，可是還沒安排何時洗。)
- I've decided not to stay here any longer. Tomorrow **I'm going to look** for another place to live.

上述兩種表達方式的意思差別通常十分細微，說話時兩種形式都有可能使用。

C

something **is going to happen** 表示未來有某事即將發生。請看下面的範例：

The man can't see the wall in front of him.
He **is going to walk** into the wall.

那個人看不見他前面的牆。

他將會撞到牆壁。

使用 something **is going to happen** 時，是指當時的情境令說話者相信某事即將發生。在這個例子中，拿著大箱子的男人正一步一步走向前面的牆，所以可以說 he **is going to walk** into it，他將會撞到牆壁。

going to

現在的狀況　　　　　　　　未來即將發生

其他例子如下：

- Look at those dark clouds! It**'s going to rain**. (the clouds are there now)
- I feel awful. I think **I'm going to be sick**. (I feel awful now)
- The economic situation is bad now, and things **are going to get** worse.

D

I was going to do something 意思是過去某個時候我本來想做某件事，但是沒有做。

- We **were going to fly** to New York, but then we decided to drive instead.
- Peter **was going to take** the exam, but he changed his mind.
- I **was** just **going to cross** the street when somebody shouted, "Stop!"

Something **was going to happen** 表示過去某事本來即將發生，但是沒有發生。

- I thought it **was going to rain**, but it didn't.

Exercises

19.1 依各句題意，用括號內的語詞，以 *going to* 完成各問句。

1. Your friend has won some money. You ask:
   (what / do with it?) _What are you going to do with it?_
2. Your friend is going to a party tonight.
   You ask: (what / wear?) _____
3. Your friend has just bought a new table.
   You ask: (where / put it?) _____
4. Your friend has decided to have a party.
   You ask: (who / invite?) _____

19.2 依各題題意，以 *going to* 完成對話。

1. You have decided to clean your room this morning.
   Friend: Are you going out this morning?
   You: No, _I'm going to clean my room._
2. You bought a sweater, but it doesn't fit you very well. You have decided to return it.
   Friend: That sweater is too big for you.
   You: I know. _____
3. You have been offered a job, but you have decided not to take it.
   Friend: I hear you've been offered a job.
   You: That's right, but _____
4. You have to call Sarah. It's morning now, and you intend to call her tonight.
   Friend: Have you called Sarah yet?
   You: No, _____
5. You are in a restaurant. The food is awful and you've decided to complain.
   Friend: This food is awful, isn't it?
   You: Yes, it's disgusting. _____

19.3 依各題題意，用括號內的提示完成句子。

1. There are a lot of dark clouds in the sky.
   (rain) _It's going to rain._
2. It is 8:30. Tom is leaving his house. He should be at work at 8:45, but it takes him 30 minutes
   to get there. (late) He _____
3. There is a hole in the bottom of the boat. A lot of water is coming in through the hole.
   (sink) The boat _____
4. Erica and Chris are driving in the country. There is very little gas left in the tank. The nearest gas
   station is miles away.
   (run out) They _____

19.4 依各句題意，從下列動詞中選出一個適當的字，並以 *was / were going to* 完成句子。

   buy   call   ~~fly~~   have   play   quit

1. We _were going to fly_ to New York, but then we decided to drive instead.
2. I _____ some new clothes yesterday, but I was very busy and
   didn't have time to go shopping.
3. Joshua and I _____ tennis last week, but he hurt his ankle.
4. I _____ Jane, but I decided to e-mail her instead.
5. *A:* The last time I saw Bob, he _____ his job.
   B: That's right, but in the end he decided not to.
6. We _____ a party last week, but some of our friends couldn't
   come, so we changed our minds.

will 1

A

I'll (= I will) 表示說話者於說話的當時，決定即將做某事：

- Oh, I left the door open. **I'll go** and shut it.
- "What would you like to drink?"　"**I'll have** some orange juice, please."
- "Did you call Julie?"　"Oh no, I forgot. **I'll call** her now."

上述的情形不可以使用現在簡單式 (**I do / I go** 等)表示：

- **I'll go** and shut the door. (並非 I go and shut)

I think I'll . . .、**I don't think I'll . . .** 意思是我認為我將做/不做某事：

- I am a little hungry. **I think I'll have** something to eat.
- **I don't think I'll go** out tonight. I'm too tired. (並非 I think I won't go out . . .)

口語中，**will** 的否定形式通常為 **won't** (= will not)：

- I can see you're busy, so **I won't stay** long.

B

will 不可以用來表示未來已經決定要做或已經安排好要做的事 (參見 Unit 18 與 Unit 19)：

- **I'm going** on vacation next Saturday. (並非 I'll go)
- **Are** you **working** tomorrow? (並非 Will you work)

C

will 經常使用於下列的情形：

主動表示將做某事

- That bag looks heavy. **I'll help** you with it. (並非 I help)

同意將做某事

- *A:* Can you give Tim this book?
- *B:* Sure, **I'll give** it to him when I see him this afternoon.

承諾將做某事

- Thanks for lending me the money. **I'll pay** you back on Friday.
- I **won't tell** anyone what happened. I promise.

請求某人做某事 (**Will you . . . ?**)

- **Will you** please **be** quiet? I'm trying to concentrate.
- **Will you shut** the door, please?

won't 可以用來表示某人拒絕做某件事。

- I've tried to give her advice, but she **won't listen**.
- The car **won't start**. (= the car "refuses" to start)

D

Shall I . . . ?　Shall we . . . ?

shall 用於問句 **Shall I . . . ?** / **Shall we . . . ?** 中，用來徵詢他人之意見
(特別是表示提供幫助或建議)：

- **Shall I open** the window? (= Do you want me to open the window?)
- "Where **shall we have** lunch?"　"Let's go to Marino's."

同樣的情形也可以用 **should**：

- **Should I open** the window? (= Do you want me to open it?)
- Where **should we have** lunch?

Exercises

20.1 依各句題意，以 *I'll* 與適當的動詞完成下列各句。

1. I'm too tired to walk home. I think ___I'll take___ a taxi.
2. "It's a little cold in this room." "You're right. _____ on the heat."
3. "We don't have any milk." "We don't? _____ and get some now."
4. "Can I wash the dishes for you?" "No, that's all right. _____ it later."
5. "I don't know how to use this computer." "Don't worry, _____ you."
6. "Would you like tea or coffee?" "_____ coffee, please."
7. "Goodbye! Have a nice trip." "Thanks. _____ you a postcard."
8. Thanks for letting me borrow your camera. _____ it back to you on Monday, OK?
9. "Are you coming with us?" "No, I think _____ here."

20.2 依各句題意，以 *I think I'll* 或 *I don't think I'll* 完成下列各句。

1. It's a little cold. The window is open, and you decide to close it. You say:
   ___I think I'll close the window.___
2. You're tired, and it's getting late. You decide to go to bed. You say:
   I think _____
3. A friend of yours offers you a ride in his car, but you decide to walk. You say:
   Thank you, but I think _____
4. You arranged to play tennis today. Now you decide that you don't want to play. You say:
   I don't think _____
5. You were going to go swimming. Now you decide that you don't want to go. You say:
   _____

20.3 判斷下列各句中劃線部份的動詞時式何者正確（參見 Unit 18 與 Unit 19）。

1. "Did you call Julie?" "Oh no, I forgot. ~~I call~~ / I'll call her now." (*I'll call* 為正確的動詞時式)
2. I can't meet you tomorrow. I'm playing / ~~I'll play~~ tennis. (*I'm playing* 為正確的動詞時式)
3. "I meet / I'll meet you outside the hotel in half an hour, OK?" "Yes, that's fine."
4. "I need some money." "OK, I'm lending / I'll lend you some. How much do you need?"
5. I'm having / I'll have a party next Saturday. I hope you can come.
6. "Remember to get a newspaper when you go out." "OK. I don't forget / I won't forget."
7. What time does your plane leave / will your plane leave tomorrow?
8. I asked Sue what happened, but she doesn't tell / won't tell me.
9. "Are you doing / Will you do anything tomorrow night?" "No, I'm free. Why?"
10. I don't want to go out alone. Do you come / Will you come with me?

20.4 依各句題意，以 *I'll / I won't / shall I / shall we . . . ?* 與適當的動詞，完成下列各句。

1. A: Where ___shall we have___ lunch?
   B: Let's go to that new restaurant on North Street.
2. A: It's Mark's birthday soon, and I want to get him a present.
   What _____ him?
   B: I don't know. I never know what to give people.
3. A: Do you want me to put these groceries away?
   B: No that's OK. _____ it later.
4. A: Let's go out tonight.
   B: OK, where _____ ?
5. A: What I've told you is a secret. I don't want anybody else to know.
   B: Don't worry. _____ anybody.
6. A: I know you're busy, but can you finish this report this afternoon?
   B: Well, _____ , but I can't promise.

A

will 不可以用來表示某人已經決定或安排好即將做某件事：

- Ann **is working** next week. (並非 Ann will work)
- **Are** you **going to watch** television tonight? (並非 Will you watch)

is working . . . ? 與 **Are** you **going to . . . ?** 之用法，參見 Unit 18 與 Unit 19。

但是在描述未來的事件時，我們不一定都是談論某人已經決定做某事。請看下面的範例：

Joe 和朋友正在電影院前排隊。

This is a very long line!

Don't worry. We**'ll get in**.

Joe

在這個例子中，**we'll get in** 意思並不是「我們已經決定要進去」。Joe 說這句話是表示他知道或他認為他們會進得去；所以，Joe 並非在描述已經決定或已經安排好要去做的事，而是預測未來將會發生的事。

will/won't 用來表示對未來的事件或情況之預測。

其他例子如下：

- Jill has lived abroad for a long time. When she comes back, she**'ll find** a lot of changes here.
- "Where **will** you **be** this time next year?" "I**'ll be** in Japan."
- That plate is hot. If you touch it, you**'ll burn** yourself.
- Tom **won't pass** the exam. He hasn't studied hard enough.
- When **will** you **find out** how you did on the exam?

B

will (**'ll**) 經常與下列的表達方式一起使用：

probably	■ I**'ll probably** be home late tonight.
I expect	■ **I expect** the test **will** take two hours.
I'm sure	■ Don't worry about the exam. **I'm sure** you**'ll** pass.
I think	■ **Do you think** Sarah **will** like the present we bought her?
I don't think	■ **I don't think** the exam **will** be very difficult.
I guess	■ *A:* What are you doing after dinner? *B:* I don't know. **I guess** I**'ll** read the paper.
I suppose	■ When **do you suppose** Jan and Mark **will** get married?
I doubt	■ **I doubt** you**'ll** need a heavy coat in Las Vegas. It's usually warm there.
I wonder	■ I worry about those people who lost their jobs. **I wonder** what **will** happen to them.

I hope 後的句子通常使用現在式：

- **I hope** Kate **passes** the exam.
- **I hope** it **doesn't rain** tomorrow.

will 1 Unit 20   *I will* 與 *I'm going to* 用法之比較 Unit 22   *will be doing* 與 *will have done* 用法之比較 Unit 23
未來式 附錄 3 英式英文 附錄 7

Exercises

21.1 判斷劃線部份的動詞時式何者正確。

1. Diane isn't free on Saturday. ~~She'll work~~ / She's working. (*She's working* 為正確的動詞時式)
2. I'll go / I'm going to a party tomorrow night. Would you like to come, too?
3. I think Amy will get / is getting the job. She has a lot of experience.
4. I can't meet you tonight. A friend of mine will come / is coming over.
5. *A:* Have you decided where to go on vacation?
   B: Yes, we'll go / we are going to Italy.
6. Don't be afraid of the dog. It won't hurt / It isn't hurting you.

21.2 依各句題意，從下列動詞中選出一個適當的字，以 *will ('ll)* 完成句子。

come	get	like	live	look	~~pass~~	see	take

1. Don't worry about the exam. I'm sure you *'ll pass* .
2. Why don't you try on this jacket? It _____ nice on you.
3. I want you to meet Brandon sometime. I think you _____ him.
4. It's raining. Don't go out. You _____ wet.
5. Do you think people _____ longer in the future?
6. Goodbye. I'm sure we _____ each other again soon.
7. I invited Sue to the party, but I don't think she _____ .
8. When the new road is finished, I expect that my trip to work _____ less time.

21.3 填入 *will ('ll)* 或 *won't*。

1. Can you wait for me? I _*won't*_ be very long.
2. You don't need to take an umbrella along. It _____ rain.
3. If you don't eat anything now, you _____ be hungry later.
4. I'm sorry about what happened yesterday. It _____ happen again.
5. I've got some incredible news! You _____ never believe what happened.
6. There's no more bread. I guess we _____ have to go shopping before we eat.
7. Don't ask Amanda for advice. She _____ know what to do.
8. Jack doesn't like crowds. I don't think he _____ come to our party.

21.4 在下列各題提示的時間你想你會在哪裡呢？請根據各題的時間提示，從下列用法中選出適當的形式，寫出你未來的行程。

I'll be . . .   **I'll probably be . . .**   **I don't know where I'll be . . .**   **I guess I'll be . . .**

1. (next Monday night at 7:45)
   *I'll be at home.* 或 *I guess I'll be at home.* 或 *I don't know where I'll be.*
2. (at 5:00 tomorrow morning)
   _____
3. (at 10:30 tomorrow morning)
   _____
4. (next Saturday afternoon at 4:15)
   _____
5. (this time next year)
   _____

21.5 依各句題意，從下列動詞中選出一個適當的字，並以 *do you think . . . will . . . ?* 完成問句。

be back	cost	end	get married	happen	~~like~~	rain

1. I bought Rosa a present. _*Do you think she'll like it*_ ?
2. The sky is dark and cloudy. Do you _____ ?
3. The meeting is still going on. When do you _____ ?
4. My car needs to be fixed. How much _____ ?
5. Sally and David are in love. Do _____ ?
6. "I'm going out now." "OK. What time _____ ?"
7. The future is uncertain. What _____ ?

I will 與 I'm going to

A 表未來的動作

比較 **will** 與 **(be) going to** 的用法與意思之不同：

Sue 正在和 Erica 談話：

Let's have a party.

That's a great idea. We**'ll invite** lots of people.

Sue

Erica

will ('ll): will 用於說話者於說話的當時，決定將做某件事。例子中，舉辦聚會是一個新的主意，是 Erica 和 Sue 談話時才決定的。

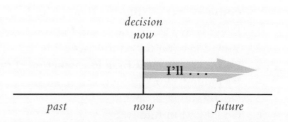

decision now

I'll . . .

past　　*now*　　*future*

當天稍晚，Erica 遇見 Dave：

Sue and I have decided to have a party. We**'re going to invite** lots of people.

Erica

Dave

going to: (be) going to 用於表示過去已經決定好了，將要做某件事。例子中，Erica 在和 Dave 談話之前，就已經決定要辦聚會、邀請同事參加。

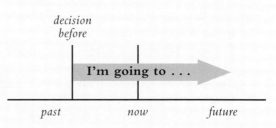

decision before

I'm going to . . .

past　　*now*　　*future*

比較下面的例子：

■ "Daniel called while you were out." "OK. I**'ll call** him back."
　"Daniel called while you were out." "Yes, I know. I**'m going to call** him back."
■ "Anna is in the hospital." "Oh really? I didn't know. I**'ll go** and visit her."
　"Anna is in the hospital." "Yes, I know. I**'m going to visit** her tonight."

B 表未來的情形或未來會發生的事 (預測未來)

用於預測未來的情形或將發生的事時，**will** 與 **going to** 的意思差別並不大。例如：

■ I think the weather **will** be nice later.
■ I think the weather **is going to** be nice later.

Something **is going to** happen，表示說話者是根據目前的情形判斷事情將會發生 (參見 Unit 19C)：

■ Look at those black clouds. It**'s going to rain**. (並非 It will rain)
　(We can see that it **is going to** rain from the clouds that are in the sky *now*.)
■ I feel terrible. I think I**'m going to be** sick. (並非 I think I'll be sick)
　(I think I**'m going to be** sick because I feel terrible *now*.)

will 通常不用於上述的情形。

其他的情況則使用 **will**：

■ Tom **will** probably **get** here at about 8:00.
■ I think Jessica **will like** the present we bought for her.
■ These shoes are very well made. They**'ll last** a long time.

22.1 依各句題意，以 *will ('ll)* 或 *going to* 完成句子。

1. *A:* Why are you turning on the television?
   B: ___I'm going to watch___ the news. (I / watch)
2. *A:* Oh, I just realized. I don't have any money.
   B: You don't? Well, don't worry. _____ you some. (I / lend)
3. *A:* I have a headache.
   B: You do? Wait a second and _____ an aspirin for you. (I / get)
4. *A:* Why are you filling that bucket with water?
   B: _____ the car. (I / wash)
5. *A:* I've decided to paint this room.
   B: Oh, really? What color _____ it? (you / paint)
6. *A:* Where are you going? Are you going shopping?
   B: Yes, _____ some things for dinner. (I / buy)
7. *A:* I don't know how to use this camera.
   B: It's easy. _____ you. (I / show)
8. *A:* Did you mail that letter for me?
   B: Oh, I'm sorry. I completely forgot. _____ it now. (I / do)
9. *A:* The ceiling in this room doesn't look very safe, does it?
   B: No, it looks as if _____ down. (it / fall)
10. *A:* Has Dan decided what to do when he finishes high school?
    B: Yes. Everything is planned. _____ a few months
    off. (he / take) Then _____ classes at the community
    college. (he / start)

22.2 依各題對話內容，以 *will ('ll)* 或 *going to* 完成句子。

1. The phone rings and you answer. Somebody wants to speak to Jim.
   Caller: Hello. Can I speak to Jim, please?
   You: Just a minute. ___I'll get___ him. (I / get)
2. It's a nice day, so you have decided to take a walk. Just before you go, you tell your friend.
   You: The weather's too nice to stay indoors. _____ a
   walk. (I / take)
   Friend: Good idea. I think _____ you. (I / join)
3. Your friend is worried because she has lost an important letter.
   You: Don't worry about the letter. I'm sure _____ it.
   (you / find)
4. There was a job advertised in the newspaper recently. At first you were interested, but then you
   decided not to apply.
   Friend: Have you decided what to do about that job you were interested in?
   You: Yes, _____ for it. (I / not / apply)
5. You and a friend come home very late. Other people in the house are asleep. Your friend
   is noisy.
   You: Shh! Don't make so much noise. _____ everybody up.
   (you / wake)
6. John has to go to the airport to catch a plane tomorrow morning.
   John: Ann, I need a ride to the airport tomorrow morning.
   Ann: That's no problem. _____ you. (I / take)
           What time is your flight?
   John: 10:50.
   Ann: OK, _____ at about 8:00. (we / leave)
   Later that day, Joe offers John a ride to the airport.
   Joe: John, do you want me to take you to the airport?
   John: No thanks, Joe. _____ me. (Ann / take)

will be doing 與 will have done

A

請看下面的範例：

These people are standing in line to get into the stadium.
這些人在球場前排隊，等候進場。

now

An hour from now, the stadium will be full.
Everyone **will be watching** the game.
1 小時後，球場將客滿。
每個人將正在觀看球賽。

an hour from now

Three hours from now, the stadium will be empty.
The game **will have ended**.
Everyone **will have gone** home.
3 小時後，球場將空無一人。
比賽將已經結束。
每個人將已經回家。

three hours from now

B

I will be doing something (未來進行式) 表示我將正在進行某件事。

■ I'm leaving on vacation this Saturday. This time next week, I**'ll be lying** on the beach or **swimming** in the ocean.
■ You have no chance of getting the job. You**'ll be wasting** your time if you apply for it.

比較 **will be doing** 與 **will do** 之不同：

■ Don't call me between 7 and 8. We**'ll be having** dinner.
■ Let's wait for Maria to arrive, and then we**'ll have** dinner.

比較 **will be doing** (未來進行式) 與現在進行式、過去進行式：

■ At 10:00 yesterday, Kelly **was** at the office. She **was working**. (過去)
It's 10:00 now. She **is** at the office. She **is working**. (現在)
At 10:00 tomorrow, she **will be** at the office. She **will be working**. (未來)

C

will be doing 也可以用來表示未來某個動作即將進行或發生，
例子如下：

■ The government **will be making** a statement about the crisis later today.
■ **Will** you **be going** away this summer?
■ Later in the program, I**'ll be talking** to the Minister of Education . . .
■ Our best player is injured and **won't be playing** in the game on Saturday.

在這些例子中，**will be doing** 的意思與用法，與現在進行式
表未來意思的用法類似。

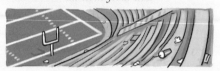
Later in the program,
I**'ll be talking** to . . .

D

will have done 為未來完成式，意思是在未來的某個時間以前，某事將已完成。
例子如下：

■ Sally always leaves for work at 8:30 in the morning. She won't be at home at 9:00 – she**'ll have gone** to work.
■ We're late. The movie **will** already **have started** by the time we get to the theater.

比較 **will have done** (未來完成式) 與現在完成式、過去完成式：

■ Ted and Amy **have been** married for 24 years. (現在完成式)
Next year they **will have been** married for 25 years. (未來完成式)
When their first child was born, they **had been** married for three years. (過去完成式)

will Unit 20 與 Unit 21　*by the time / by then* Unit 117C　未來式 附錄 3

Exercises

23.1 請先閱讀下面有關 Josh 的描述，並根據敘述，在以下各組句子中勾選出最適當的答案(可能複選)。

Josh goes to work every day. After breakfast, he leaves home at 8:00 and arrives at work at about 8:45. He starts work immediately and continues until 12:30, when he has lunch (which takes about half an hour). He starts work again at 1:15 and goes home at exactly 4:30. Every day he follows the same routine, and tomorrow will be no exception.

1. **At 7:45**
   a) he'll be leaving the house
   b) he'll have left the house
   c) he'll be at home ✓
   d) he'll be having breakfast ✓

4.  **At 12:45**
   a) he'll have lunch
   b) he'll be having lunch
   c) he'll have finished his lunch
   d) he'll have started his lunch

2.  **At 8:15**
   a) hc'll be leaving the house
   b) he'll have left the house
   c) he'll have arrived at work
   d) he'll be arriving at work

5.  **At 4:00**
   a) he'll have finished work
   b) he'll finish work
   c) he'll be working
   d) he won't have finished work

3.  **At 9:15**
   a) he'll be working
   b) he'll start work
   c) he'll have started work
   d) he'll be arriving at work

6.  **At 4:45**
   a) he'll leave work
   b) he'll be leaving work
   c) he'll have left work
   d) he'll have arrived home

23.2 請依照例句將正確的動詞時式填入空格；使用 **will be (do)ing** 或 **will have (done)**。

1. Don't call me between 7 and 8. ___*We'll be having*___ (we / have) dinner then.
2. Call me after 8:00. _____ (we / finish) dinner by then.
3. Tomorrow afternoon we're going to play tennis from 3:00 until 4:30. So at 4:00,
   _____ (we / play) tennis.
4. *A:* Can we meet tomorrow afternoon?
   B: I'm sorry I can't. _____ (I / work).
5. *B has to go to a meeting that begins at 10:00. It will last about an hour.*
   A: Will you be free at 11:30?
   B: Yes, _____ (the meeting / end) by then.
6. Ben is on vacation, and he is spending his money very quickly. If he continues like this,
   _____ (he / spend) all his money before the end of his vacation.
7. Do you think _____ (you / still / do) the same job
   10 years from now?
8. Lisa is from New Zealand. She is traveling around South America right now. So far she has
   traveled about 1,000 miles. By the end of the trip, _____
   (she / travel) more than 3,000 miles.
9. If you need to contact me, _____ (I / stay) at the Bellmore
   Hotel until Friday.
10. *A:* _____ (you / see) Laura tomorrow?
    B: Yes, probably. Why?
    A: I borrowed this CD from her. Can you give it back to her?

When I do / When I've done
when 與 if

請看下面範例：

Will you call me tomorrow?

Yes, I'll call you **when I get** home from work.

I'll call you when I get home from work 這個句子可分為兩部分：

主要子句部分　　　　　：I'll call you

以及 **when** 時間副詞子句部分：**when I get** home from work

該句話雖然是表示未來式 (tomorrow)，但是在 **when** 時間副詞子句中動詞時態必須是現在式 (**get**)。

when 時間副詞子句中，必須以現在式動詞表未來意思，不可以用 **will**。

其他例子如下：

- We'll go out **when** it **stops** raining. (並非 when it will stop)
- **When** you **are** in Los Angeles again, give us a call. (並非 When you will be)
- (對小孩說話) What do you want to be **when** you **grow** up? (並非 will grow)

在 **while / before / after / as soon as / until** 或 **till** 的時間副詞子句中，也是以現在式動詞表未來意思。

- I'm going to read a lot of books **while I'm** on vacation. (並非 while I will be)
- I'm going back home on Sunday. **Before I go**, I'd like to visit a museum.
- Wait here **until** (或 **till**) I **come** back.

B **when / after / until / as soon as** 的時間副詞子句中，也可以使用現在完成式 (**have done**)：

- Can I borrow that book **when** you**'ve finished** it?
- Don't say anything while Ben is here. Wait **until** he **has gone**.

現在完成式用以表示某一件事於另一件事之前完成，不可用以表示兩件事不是同時發生：

- **When I've called** Kate, we can have dinner.
  (我先打電話給 Kate，然後我們吃晚餐)

兩件事將同時發生，不可以使用現在完成式：

- **When I call** Kate, I'll ask her about the party. (並非 When I've called)

但是現在簡單式與現在完成式經常可以互換使用：

- I'll come **as soon as** I **finish**.　或　I'll come **as soon as** I**'ve finished**.
- You'll feel better **after** you 　或　You'll feel better **after** you**'ve**
  have something to eat.　　　　　　**had** something to eat.

C **if** 子句中，通常使用現在簡單式 (if I do / if I see 等) 表未來意思：

- It's raining hard. We'll get wet **if** we **go** out. (並非 if we will go)
- I'll be angry **if** it **happens** again. (並非 if it will happen)
- Hurry up! **If** we **don't hurry**, we'll be late.

D 比較 **when** 與 **if** 用法：

when 表示事情確定會發生：

- I'm going shopping later. (for sure) **When** I go shopping, I'll get some cheese.

if 表示事情可能會發生：

- I might go shopping later. (it's possible) **If** I go shopping, I'll get some cheese.
- **If** it is raining tonight, I won't go out. (並非 When it is raining)
- Don't worry **if** I'm late tonight. (並非 when I'm late)
- **If** they don't come soon, I'm not going to wait. (並非 When they don't come)

if Unit 36 至 Unit 38　*even if / even when* Unit 109D　*unless* Unit 112A

Exercises

24.1 依各句題意，用括號內的動詞完成句子。所有句子均表示未來將發生的事，動詞請用 **will / won't** 或現在簡單式 (如 **I see / he plays / it is** 等)。

1. I _ll call_ (call) you when I _get_ (get) home from work.
2. I want to see Jennifer before she _____ (go) out.
3. We're going on a trip tomorrow. I _____ (tell) you all about it when we _____ (come) back.
4. Brian looks very different now. When you _____ (see) him again, you _____ (not / recognize) him.
5. _____ (you / miss) me while I _____ (be) gone?
6. We should do something soon before it _____ (be) too late.
7. I don't want to go without you. I _____ (wait) until you _____ (be) ready.
8. Sue has applied for the job, but she isn't very well qualified for it. I _____ (be) surprised if she _____ (get) it.
9. I'd like to play tennis tomorrow if the weather _____ (be) nice.
10. I'm going out now. If anybody _____ (call) while I _____ (be) out, can you take a message?

24.2 請將下列各題中的兩個句子合併為一個句子。

1. You'll be in Los Angeles again. Give us a call.
   Give us a call when _you are in Los Angeles again_ .
2. I'll find a place to live. Then I'll give you my address.
   I _____ when _____ .
3. I'll go shopping. Then I'll come straight home.
   _____ after _____ .
4. It's going to get dark. Let's go home before that.
   _____ before _____ .
5. She must apologize to me first. I won't speak to her until then.
   _____ until _____ .

24.3 請依各句題意，完成句子。

1. A friend of yours is going on vacation. You want to know what she is going to do. You ask:
   What are you going to do when _you go on vacation_ ?
2. A friend of yours is visiting you. She has to go soon, but you'd like to show her some pictures. You ask:
   Do you have time to look at some pictures before _____ ?
3. You want to sell your car. Jim is interested in buying it, but he hasn't decided yet. You ask:
   Can you let me know as soon as _____ ?
4. A friend of yours is going to visit Hong Kong. You want to know where she is going to stay. You ask:
   Where are you going to stay when _____ ?
5. The traffic is very bad in your town, but they are going to build a new road. You say:
   I think things will be better when they _____ .

24.4 請依各題題意填入 **when** 或 **if**。

1. Don't worry _if_ I'm late tonight.
2. Chris might call while I'm out tonight. _____ he does, can you take a message?
3. I'm going to Tokyo next week. _____ I'm there, I hope to visit a friend of mine.
4. I think Beth will get the job. I'll be very surprised _____ she doesn't get it.
5. I'm going shopping. _____ you want anything, I can get it for you.
6. I'm going away for a few days. I'll call you _____ I get back.
7. I want you to come to the party, but _____ you don't want to come, that's all right.
8. We can eat at home or, _____ you prefer, we can go to a restaurant.

can、could 與 (be) able to

A

can 表示某事是可能的或經允許的，或某人有能力做某事。can 的用法為 can＋動詞原型(can do / can see 等)
- We **can see** the ocean from our hotel window.
- "I don't have a pen." "You **can use** mine."
- **Can** you **speak** any foreign languages?
- I **can come** and help you tomorrow if you want.
- The word "dream" **can be** a noun or a verb.

can 的否定形式為 **can't** (= cannot)：
- I'm afraid I **can't come** to your party on Friday.

B

(be) able to 可以代替 can，但是 can 較常用：
- We **are able to see** the ocean from our hotel window.

由於 can 只有 can (現在) 以及 could (過去) 兩種形式，因此，有些情況必須用 (be) able to 表達。比較下面的例子：

■ I **can't** sleep.	■ I **haven't been able to** sleep recently.
■ Tom **can** come tomorrow.	■ Tom **might be able to** come tomorrow.
■ Maria **can** speak French, Spanish, and English.	■ Applicants for the job **must be able to** speak two foreign languages.

C

could

could 有時用作 can 的過去式形式。could 特別常與下列動詞一起使用：

see   hear   smell   taste   feel   remember   understand

- We had a nice room in the hotel. We **could see** the ocean.
- As soon as I walked into the room, I **could smell** gas.
- She spoke in a very soft voice, so I **couldn't understand** what she said.

could 也用於表示某人有能力做某事，或獲得允許做某事：
- My grandfather **could speak** five languages.
- We were totally free. We **could do** what we wanted. (= we were allowed to do)

D

could 和 was able to 之比較

could 通常是表示一般的能力；但是描述某一特殊情況下所發生的事情時，則必須使用 **was / were able to** 或 **managed to**，而非 could。
- The fire spread through the building very quickly, but fortunately everybody **was able to escape** / **managed to escape**. (並非 could escape)
- We didn't know where David was, but we **managed to find** / **were able to find** him in the end. (並非 could find)

比較下面各例：
- Jack was an excellent tennis player when he was younger. He **could beat** anybody. (Jack 有能力擊敗任何人)

但是 Jack and Ted played tennis yesterday. Ted played very well, but Jack **managed to** / **was able to beat** him. (Jack 這次設法打敗了 Ted)

could 的否定形式 **couldn't** (= could not)則可以用於上述各種情形：
- My grandfather **couldn't swim**.
- We looked for David everywhere, but we **couldn't find** him.
- Ted played well, but he **couldn't beat** Jack.

Exercises

25.1 依各句題意，以 *can* 或 *(be) able to* 完成句子。

1. Eric has traveled a lot. He ___*can*___ speak four languages.
2. I haven't ___*been able to*___ sleep very well recently.
3. Nicole _____ drive, but she doesn't have a car.
4. I used to _____ stand on my head, but I can't do it any more.
5. I can't understand Michael. I've never _____ understand him.
6. I can't see you on Friday, but I _____ meet you on Saturday morning.
7. Ask Catherine about your problem. She might _____ help you.

25.2 用括號內的提示，完成有關於你自己的描述。

1. (something you used to be able to do)
   ___*I used to be able to sing well.*___
2. (something you used to be able to do)
   I used _____
3. (something you would like to be able to do)
   I'd _____
4. (something you have never been able to do)
   I've _____

25.3 依各句題意，從下列動詞中選出一個適當的字，並與 *can / can't / could / couldn't* 連用完成句子。

~~come~~   **eat**   **hear**   **run**   **sleep**   **wait**

1. I'm sorry I ___*can't come*___ to your party next week.
2. When Bob was 16, he _____ 100 meters in 11 seconds.
3. "Are you in a hurry?"   "No, I've got plenty of time. I _____ ."
4. I felt sick yesterday. I _____ anything.
5. Can you speak a little louder? I _____ you very well.
6. "You look tired."   "Yes, I _____ last night."

25.4 依各句題意，以 *was/were able to* 完成各個問題的答句。

1. *A:* Did everybody escape from the fire?
   B: Yes. Although the fire spread quickly, everybody ___*was able to escape*___ .
2. *A:* Did you finish your homework this afternoon?
   B: Yes, nobody was around to disturb me, so I _____ .
3. *A:* Did you have any trouble finding Amy's house?
   B: Not really. She'd given us good directions, so we _____ .
4. *A:* Did the thief get away?
   B: Yes. No one realized what was happening, and the thief _____ .

25.5 依各句題意，以 *could, couldn't* 或 *managed to* 完成句子。

1. My grandfather traveled a lot. He ___*could*___ speak five languages.
2. I looked everywhere for the book, but I ___*couldn't*___ find it.
3. They didn't want to come with us at first, but we ___*managed to*___ persuade them.
4. Laura had hurt her leg and _____ walk very well.
5. Sue wasn't at home when I called, but I _____ contact her at her office.
6. I looked very carefully, and I _____ see someone in the distance.
7. I wanted to buy some tomatoes. The first store I went to didn't have any good ones,
   but I _____ get some at the next place.
8. My grandmother loved music. She _____ play the piano very well.
9. A girl fell into the river, but fortunately we _____ rescue her.
10. I had forgotten to bring my camera, so I _____ take any photos.

could (do) 與 could have (done)

A

could 可以表示不同的意思。用法之一是作為 can 的過去式(參見 Unit 25C)：
- ■ Listen. I **can hear** something. (現在)
- ■ I listened. I **could hear** something. (過去)

could 還可以表示現在或未來可能的
動作(特別是提供建議的時候)。例如：

- ■ *A:* What would you like to do tonight?
  B: We **could go** to the movies.
- ■ *A:* When you go to New York next
  month, you **could stay** with Candice.
  B: Yes, I guess I **could**.

What would you like to do tonight?

We **could go** to the movies.

can 也可以表示現在或未來可能的動作(We **can go** to the movies 等)。但使用 **could** 所表示的可能性比使用 **can** 較低。

B

could 可以表示不是真實的動作，但 can 不可以。例如：
- ■ I'm so tired, I **could sleep** for a week. (並非 I can sleep for a week)

比較 can 和 could 的用法:
- ■ I **can stay** with Candice when I go to New York. (真實的)
- ■ Maybe I **could stay** with Candice when I go to New York. (可能的，不十分確定)
- ■ This is a wonderful place. I **could stay** here forever. (不真實的)

C

could 也可以表示，某件事於現在或未來有可能發生，但是can不可以。could 的意思與 **might** 或 **may** 的意思類似(參見 Unit 28 與 Unit 29)。
- ■ The story **could be** true, but I don't think it is. (並非 can be true)
- ■ I don't know what time Liz is coming. She **could get** here at any time.

D

談論過去發生的事，可以用 **could have** (done)。比較下面例子:
- ■ I'm so tired, I **could sleep** for a week. (現在)
  I was so tired, I **could have slept** for a week. (過去)
- ■ The situation is bad, but it **could be** worse. (現在)
  The situation was bad, but it **could have been** worse. (過去)

could have (done)表示過去某件事可能發生，但並未發生。
- ■ Why did you stay at a hotel when you were in New York? You **could have stayed** with Candice. (你有機會和 Candice 一起住，可是你沒有。)
- ■ I didn't know that you wanted to go to the concert. I **could have gotten** you a free ticket. (我沒有幫你取得入場券)
- ■ Dave was lucky. He **could have hurt** himself when he fell, but he's OK.

E

couldn't 表示某事現在不可能：
- ■ I **couldn't live** in a big city. I'd hate it. (= it wouldn't be possible for me)
- ■ Everything is fine right now. Things **couldn't be** better.

表示某事過去不可能用 **couldn't have** (done):
- ■ We had a really good vacation. It **couldn't have been** better.
- ■ The trip was canceled last week. Paul **couldn't have gone** anyway because he was sick. (他當時不可能去。)

Exercises

26.1 請參照例句，依各題對話內容，以 **could** 與括號內的字完成句子。

1. Where would you like to go on vacation? | (to San Diego) _We could go to San Diego._
2. What should we have for dinner tonight? | (fish) We _____
3. When should I call Angela? | (now) You _____
4. What should I give Ana for her birthday? | (a book) _____
5. When should we go and see Tom? | (on Friday) _____

26.2 判斷下列各句何者必須使用 **could** (而非 **can**)，並將句子改正。

1. The story can be true but I don't think it is. | _could be true_
2. It's a nice day. We can go for a walk. | _OK (也可以用 could go)_
3. I'm so angry I can scream. | _____
4. If you're hungry, we can have dinner now. | _____
5. It's so nice here. I can stay here all day,
   but unfortunately I have to go. | _____
6. A: Where's my bag. Have you seen it?
   B: No, but it can be in the car. | _____
7. Peter is a good musician. He plays the flute,
   and he can also play the piano. | _____
8. A: I need to borrow a camera.
   B: You can borrow mine. | _____
9. The weather is nice now, but it can change later. | _____

26.3 依各題對話內容，以 **could** 或 **could have** 與適當的動詞，完成句子。

1. A: What should we do tonight?
   B: We _could go_ to the movies.
2. A: I spent a very boring evening at home yesterday.
   B: Why did you stay at home? You _____ out with us.
3. A: There's a job advertised in the paper that I think you are really qualified for.
   B: I guess I _____ for it, but I like my present job.
4. A: How was your test? Was it hard?
   B: It wasn't so bad. It _____ worse.
5. A: I got very wet walking home in the rain last night.
   B: Why did you walk? You _____ a taxi.
6. A: Where should we meet tomorrow?
   B: Well, I _____ to your house if you want.

26.4 依各句題意，從下列動詞中選出一個適當的字，並與 **couldn't** 或 **couldn't have** 完成句子

~~be~~   be   come   find   get   ~~live~~   wear

1. I _couldn't live_ in a big city. I'd hate it.
2. We had a really good vacation. It _couldn't have been_ better.
3. I _____ that hat. I'd look silly, and people would laugh at me.
4. We managed to find the restaurant you recommended, but we _____ it
   without the map that you drew for us.
5. Paul has to get up at 4:00 every morning. I don't know how he does it. I
   _____ up at that time every day.
6. The staff at the hotel was really nice when we stayed there last summer. They
   _____ more helpful.
7. A: I tried to call you last week. We had a party, and I wanted to invite you.
   B: That's nice of you, but I _____ anyway. I was away all
   last week.

must (You must be tired 等)

must (not)

My house is next to the freeway. 我的房子就在高速公路旁。

It **must be** very noisy. 那一定很吵。

must 表示說話者確信某事必定是真的：

■ You've been traveling all day. You **must be** tired.
(旅行是很累人的。你已經旅行了一整天，所以你一定很累了。)
■ "Jim is a hard worker." "Jim? You **must be** joking. He's very lazy."
■ I'm sure Sally gave me her phone number. I **must have** it somewhere.

must not 表示說話者確信某事不是真的：

■ Their car isn't outside their house. They **must not be** home. (他們必定出門了。)
■ Brian said he would be here by 9:30. It's 10:00 now, and he's never late. He **must not be coming**.
■ They haven't lived here very long. They **must not know** many people.

請看下面句型：

I/you/he (etc.)	**must (not)**	**be** (tired/hungry/home, etc.) **be** (**doing/coming/joking**, etc.) **do/get/know/have**, etc.

must (not) have done

表過去式時，必須使用 **must (not) have done**：

■ "We used to live close to the freeway." "Did you? It **must have been** noisy."
■ There's nobody at home. They **must have gone** out.
■ I've lost one of my gloves. I **must have dropped** it somewhere.
■ She walked past me without speaking. She **must not have seen** me.
■ Tom walked into a wall. He **must not have been looking** where he was going.

請看下面句型：

I/you/he (etc.)	**must (not)**	**have**	**been** (tired/hungry/noisy, etc.) **been** (**doing/coming/looking**, etc.) **gone/dropped/seen**, etc.

比較 can't 與 must not

It **can't be** true 意思是我相信這是不可能的。

■ How can you say such a thing? You **can't be** serious!

比較 **can't** 與 **must not** 意思之不同：

■ A: Joe wants something to eat.
■ B: But he just had lunch. He **can't be** hungry already. (Joe 才剛吃過午餐，所以他不可能餓了。)
■ A: I offered Bill something to eat, but he didn't want anything.
■ B: He **Must not be** hungry. (我確信 Bill 不餓，否則他就會吃些東西了。)

Exercises

27.1 填入 *must* 或 *must not*。

1. You've been traveling all day. You __*must*__ be tired.
2. That restaurant _____ be very good. It's always full of people.
3. That restaurant _____ be very good. It's always empty.
4. You _____ be looking forward to going on vacation next week.
5. It rained every day during their vacation, so they _____ have had a very nice time.
6. You got here very quickly. You _____ have walked very fast.

27.2 請參照例句，依各句題意，以正確的動詞時式完成句子。

1. I've lost one of my gloves. I must __*have dropped*__ it somewhere.
2. They haven't lived here very long. They must not __*know*__ many people.
3. Ted isn't at work today. He must _____ sick.
4. Ted wasn't at work last week. He must _____ sick.
5. Sarah knows a lot about movies. She must _____ to the movies a lot.
6. Look. James is putting on his hat and coat. He must _____ out.
7. I left my bike outside last night and now it is gone. Somebody must _____ it.
8. Sue was in a difficult situation when she lost her job. It must not _____ easy for her.
9. There is a man walking behind us. He has been walking behind us for the last 20 minutes. He must _____ us.

27.3 請參照例句，依各句題意，用括號內的語詞加上 *must have* 或 *must not have* 完成句子。

1. The phone rang, but I didn't hear it. (I / asleep) __*I must have been asleep.*__
2. Julie walked past me without speaking. (she / see / me) __*She must not have seen me.*__
3. The jacket you bought is very good quality. (it / very expensive)
   _____
4. I can't find my umbrella. (I / leave / it in the restaurant last night)
   _____
5. Dave passed the exam without studying for it. (the exam / very difficult)
   _____
6. She knew everything about our plans. (she / listen / to our conversation)
   _____
7. Rachel did the opposite of what I asked her to do. (she / understand / what I said)
   _____
8. When I woke up this morning, the light was on. (I / forget / to turn it off)
   _____
9. I was awakened in the night by loud music next door. (the neighbors / have / a party)
   _____

27.4 依各句題意，以 *must not* 或 *can't* 完成句子。

1. How can you say such a thing? You __*can't*__ be serious!
2. Their car isn't outside their house. They __*must not*__ be home.
3. I just bought a box of cereal yesterday. It _____ be empty already.
4. The Smiths always go on vacation this time of year, but they are still home.
   They _____ be taking a vacation this year.
5. You just started filling out your tax forms 10 minutes ago.
   You _____ be finished with them already!
6. Eric is a good friend of Ann's, but he hasn't visited her in the hospital.
   He _____ know she's in the hospital.

may 與 might 1

請看下面的範例：

你正在找 Bob，沒有人確知他在那裡，但是你得到一些提示。

Where's Bob?

He **may be** in his office. (他可能在他的辦公室。)

He **might be having** lunch. (他可能正在吃午餐。)

Ask Ann. She **might know**. (她可能知道。)

may 與 **might** 都可用以表示某件事有可能發生：

- It **may** be true. 或 It **might** be true. (可能是真的)
- She **might** know. 或 She **may** know.

may 與 **might** 的否定形式為 **may not** 與 **might not**：

- It **may not** be true. (可能不是真的)
- She **might not** work here any more. (她可能不在這兒工作。)

請看下面句型：

I/you/he (etc.)	**may** **might**	(**not**)	**be** (true/in his office, etc.) **be** (**doing/working/having**, etc.) **do / know / work / want**, etc.

表過去的可能性，使用 **may have done** 或 **might have done**：

- *A:* I wonder why Kate didn't answer the phone.
  B: She **may have been** asleep. (她可能在睡覺。)
- *A:* I can't find my bag anywhere.
  B: You **might have left** it in the store. (你可能把它留在店裡了。)
- *A:* I was surprised that Sarah wasn't at the meeting yesterday.
  B: She **might not have known** about it. (她可能不知道。)
- *A:* I wonder why David was in such a bad mood yesterday.
  B: He **may not have been feeling** well. (他可能身體不舒服。)

請看下面句型：

I/you/he (etc.)	**may** **might**	(**not**) **have**	**been** (asleep/at home, etc.) **been** (**doing/working/feeling**, etc.) **known / had / wanted / left**, etc.

有時候 **could** 的意思與 **may** 和 **might** 類似：

- It's a strange story, but it **could be** true. (可能是真的)
- You **could have left** your bag in the store. (你可能把它留在店裡了。)

但是 **couldn't** 的意思與 **may not** 和 **might not** 不同。比較下面例子：

- Sarah **couldn't have gotten** my message. Otherwise she would have called me.
  (她不可能收到我的留言。)
- I wonder why Sarah hasn't called me. I suppose she **might not have gotten** my message. (她可能沒有收到我的留言，也可能收到了。)

---

could Unit 26 *may* 與 *might* 2 Unit 29 *May I . . . ?* Unit 35 *might* 與 *if* Unit 29B、 Unit 36C 與 Unit 38D
助動詞 (*can / could / will / would* 等) 附錄 4

Exercises

28.1 請參照例句，依各句題意，以 *may* 或 *might* 改寫句子。

1. Perhaps Elizabeth is in her office. _She might be in her office._ 或 _She may be . . ._
2. Perhaps Elizabeth is busy. _____
3. Perhaps she is working. _____
4. Perhaps she wants to be alone. _____
5. Perhaps she was sick yesterday. _____
6. Perhaps she went home early. _____
7. Perhaps she had to go home early. _____
8. Perhaps she was working yesterday. _____

第 9–11 題，請以 *may not* 或 *might not* 改寫句子。

9. Perhaps she doesn't want to see me. _____
10. Perhaps she isn't working today. _____
11. Perhaps she wasn't feeling well yesterday. _____

28.2 請參照例句，依各句題意，以正確的動詞時式完成句子。

1. "Where's Sam?" "I'm not sure. He might _be having_ lunch."
2. "Who is that man with Anna?" "I'm not sure. It might _____ her brother."
3. "Who was the man we saw with Anna yesterday?" "I'm not sure. It may _____ her brother."
4. "What are those people doing by the side of the road?" "I don't know. They might _____ for a bus."
5. "Do you have a stamp?" "No, but ask Sam. He may _____ one."

28.3 請參照例句，依各句題意，用括號內的字與 *may* 或 *might* 完成句子。

1. I can't find Jeff anywhere. I wonder where he is.
   a) (he / go / shopping) _He may have gone shopping._
   b) (he / play / tennis) _He might be playing tennis._
2. I'm looking for Tiffany. Do you know where she is?
   a) (she / watch / TV / in her room) _____
   b) (she / go / out) _____
3. I can't find my umbrella. Have you seen it?
   a) (it / be / in the car) _____
   b) (you / leave / in the restaurant last night) _____
4. Why didn't Dave answer the doorbell? I'm sure he was at home at the time.
   a) (he / not / hear / the doorbell) _____
   b) (he / be / in the shower) _____

28.4 請參照例句，依各句題意，以 *might not have* 或 *couldn't have* 完成句子。

1. A: Do you think Sarah got the message we left her?
   B: No, she would have contacted us. _She couldn't have gotten it._
2. A: I was surprised Kate wasn't at the meeting. Perhaps she didn't know about it.
   B: That's possible. _She might not have known about it._
3. A: I wonder why they never replied to our letter. Do you think they received it?
   B: Maybe not. They _____ .
4. A: I wonder how the fire started. Was it an accident?
   B: No, the police say it _____ .
5. A: Mike says he needs to see you. He tried to find you yesterday.
   B: Well, he _____ very hard. I was in my office all day.
6. A: The man you spoke to – are you sure he was Chinese?
   B: No, I'm not sure. He _____ .

may 與 might 2

A

may 與 might 都表示未來可能的動作、或可能發生的事：

- I haven't decided yet where to go on vacation. I **may go** to Hawaii.
  (我可能將會去夏威夷。)
- Take an umbrella with you. It **might rain** later. (可能會下雨。)
- The bus isn't always on time. We **might have** to wait a few minutes.
  (我們可能必須等。)

may 與 might 的否定形式為 **may not** 與 **might not**：

- Ann **may not go** out tonight. She isn't feeling well. (她可能不會出去。)
- There **might not be** enough time to discuss everything at the meeting.

比較 **will** 和 **may/might** 之用法：

- **I'll be** late this evening. (確定)
- I **may/might** be late this evening. (可能)

B

通常 may 與 might 的意思類似，可以互換使用，例如：

- I **may go** to Hawaii.　或　I **might go** to Hawaii.
- Lisa **might be** able to help you.　或　Lisa **may be** able to help you.

但是描述的狀況若不是真實情況時，只能使用 **might**：

- If I were in Tom's position, I think I **might** look for another job.

本例中描述的情況不是真的；因為我不是 Tom，所以我必須再找另一份工作。本句話不可使用 **may**。

C

may 與 might 也可以和進行式一起使用：**may/might be -ing**。比較 **may/might be -ing** 與 **will be -ing**：

- Don't call me at 8:30. **I'll be watching** the baseball game on TV.
- Don't call me at 8:30. I **might be watching** (或 I **may be watching**) the baseball game on TV. (我可能將正在看球賽。)

may/might be -ing 也可以表示未來可能的計畫。比較下面例子：

- **I'm going** to Hawaii in July. (確定)
- I **may be going** (或 I **might be going**) to Hawaii in July. (可能)

上句也可以用 I **may go** (或 I **might go**) to Hawaii 來表示，意思僅有些微的差別。

D

might as well / may as well

Rosa 和 Maria 剛剛錯過了公車；公車一小時才一班。

> What should we do? Should we walk?

> We **might as well**. It's a nice day, and I don't want to wait here for an hour.

We **might as well** do something 意思是我們應該做某件事，因為沒有更好的選擇，況且也沒有理由不做。也可以用 **may as well** 表示一樣的意思。

- *A:* You'll have to wait two hours to see the doctor.
  B: I **might as well go** home and come back.
- Rents are so high these days, you **may as well buy** a house.
  (買房子也一樣可行，不會比較貴。)

Exercises

29.1 依各句題意，以 **may** 或 **might** 完成句子。

1. Where are you going on vacation? (to Hawaii??)
   I haven't decided yet. *I might go to Hawaii.*
2. What kind of car are you going to buy? (a Toyota??)
   I'm not sure yet. I _____
3. What are you doing this weekend? (go to the movies??)
   I haven't made up my mind yet. _____
4. When is Jim coming to see us? (on Saturday??)
   I don't know for sure. _____
5. Where are you going to hang that picture? (in the dining room??)
   I haven't made up my mind yet. _____
6. What is Julia going to do when she graduates from high school? (go to college??)
   She's still thinking about it. _____

29.2 依各句題意，從下列動詞中選出一個適當的字，與 **might** 完成句子。

> **bite   break   need   ~~rain~~   slip   wake up**

1. Take an umbrella with you when you go out. It *might rain* later.
2. Don't make too much noise. You _____ the baby.
3. Watch out for that dog. It _____ you.
4. I don't think we should throw that letter away. We _____ it later.
5. Be careful. The sidewalk is very icy. You _____ .
6. I don't want the children to play in this room. They _____ something.

29.3 依各句題意，以 **might be able to** 或 **might have to** 及適當的動詞，完成句子。

1. I can't help you, but why don't you ask Jane? She *might be able to help* you.
2. I can't meet you tonight, but I _____ you tomorrow.
3. I'm not working on Saturday, but I _____ on Sunday.
4. I can come to the meeting, but I _____ before the end.

29.4 依各句題意，以 **might not** 完成句子。

1. I'm not sure that Ann will come to the party.
   Ann might not come to the party.
2. I'm not sure that I'll go out tonight.
   I _____
3. You don't know if Sam will like the present you bought for him.
   Sam _____
4. We don't know if Sue will be able to get together with us tonight.
   _____

29.5 依各題的情境，以 **might as well** 完成下列各句。

1. You and a friend have just missed the bus. The buses run every hour.
   You say: We'll have to wait an hour for the next bus. *We might as well walk.*
2. You have a free ticket for a concert. You're not very excited about the concert, but you decide to go.
   You say: I _____ _____ to the concert. It's a shame to waste a free ticket.
3. You've just painted your kitchen. You still have a lot of paint, so why not paint the bathroom, too?
   You say: We _____ . There's plenty of paint left.
4. You and a friend are at home. You're bored. There's a movie on TV starting in a few minutes.
   You say: _____ . There's nothing else to do.

have to 與 must

I **have to do** 表示必須做某事，我有義務要做某事：

- You can't turn right here. You **have to turn** left.
- I **have to get up** early tomorrow. My flight leaves at 7:30.
- Jason can't meet us tonight. He **has to work** late.
- Last week Nicole broke her arm and **had to go** to the hospital.
- Have you ever **had to go** to the hospital?

使用 **have to** 時，現在簡單與過去簡單式的疑問句中，必須使用 **do/does/did**：

- What **do** I **have to do** to get a driver's license?
  (並非 What have I to do?)
- **Does** Kimberly **have to work** tomorrow?
- Why **did** you **have to leave** early?

否定句必須使用 **don't/doesn't/didn't**：

- I **don't have to get up** early tomorrow.
  (並非 I haven't to)
- Kimberly **doesn't have to work** on Saturdays.
- We **didn't have to pay** to park the car.

You **have to turn** left here.

可以使用下列句型：

I'll have to / I won't have to ...
I'm going to have to ...
I might/may have to ... (我可能必須)

- They can't fix my computer, so **I'll have to buy** a new one.　或
  . . . so **I'm going to have to buy** a new one.
- I **might have to leave** the meeting early.　或　I **may have to leave** . . .

must 的意思與 **have to** 類似：

- The economic situation is bad. The government **must do** something about it.　或
  The government **has to do** . . .
- If you go to New York, you really **must visit** the Empire State Building.
  (或 . . . you really **have to** visit . . .)

但是 **have to** 較 **must** 常用

must 通常用於書面的規定與說明中：

- Answer all the questions. You **must write** your answers in ink.
- Applications for the job **must be received** by May 18.

You **must not** do something 意思是你必須不可以做某事，亦即你不可以做某事：

- Students **must not use** cell phones in class. (不允許)

比較 **must not** 和 **don't have to**：

- You **must keep** this a secret. You **must not tell** anybody.
  (不要告訴任何人)
- You **don't have to tell** Tim about what happened. I can tell him myself.
  (你不需要告訴 Tim，但是你若告訴他也無妨。)

have to 也可以用 **have got to** 來表示，意思相同。例如：

- **I've got to work** tomorrow.　或　I **have to work** tomorrow.
- **He's got to visit** his aunt tonight.　或　He **has to visit** his aunt tonight.

Exercises

30.1 依各句題意，以 *have to* / *has to* / *had to* 完成下列各句。

1. Jason can't join us tonight. He ___*has to*___ work late.
2. Beth left before the end of the meeting. She _____ go home early.
3. I don't have much time. I _____ go soon.
4. Kathy may _____ go out of town on business next week.
5. Eric is usually free on weekends, but sometimes he _____ work.
6. There was nobody to help me. I _____ do everything by myself.
7. Julie has _____ wear glasses since she was a small child.
8. Jeff can't pay his bills. He's going to _____ sell his car.

30.2 依各句題意，以 *have to* 與括號內的字完成下列問句。

1. "I broke my arm last week." "___*Did you have to go*___ (you / go) to the hospital?"
2. "I'm sorry I can't stay very long." "What time _____ (you / go)?"
3. _____ (you / wait) long for the bus last night?
4. How old _____ (you / be) to drive in your country?
5. How does Chris like his new job? _____ (he / travel) a lot?

30.3 依各句題意，從下列動詞中選出一個適當的字，並與 *have to* 完成句子。肯定句用 I *have to*，否定句用 I *don't have to*。

> ask   do   ~~get up~~   go   make   make   shave   ~~show~~

1. I'm not working tomorrow, so I ___*don't have to get up*___ early.
2. Steve didn't know how to use the computer, so I ___*had to show*___ him.
3. Excuse me for a minute – I _____ a phone call.
4. I couldn't find the street I wanted. I _____ somebody for directions.
5. Jack has a beard, so he _____ .
6. A man was injured in the accident, but he _____ to the hospital because it wasn't serious.
7. Sue is the vice president of the company. She _____ important decisions.
8. I'm not so busy. I have a few things to do, but I _____ them now.

30.4 依各句題意，以 *might have to*、*will have to* 或 *won't have to* 完成下列各句。

1. They can't fix my computer, so I ___*ll have to*___ buy a new one.
2. I ___*might have to*___ leave the party early. My son is going to call me if he needs a ride home.
3. We _____ take the train downtown instead of driving. It depends on the traffic.
4. Sam _____ go to jail if he doesn't pay all his old parking tickets.
5. Unfortunately, my father _____ stay in the hospital another week. The doctor is going to decide tomorrow.
6. If it snows all night, we _____ go to class tomorrow. It'll be canceled.

30.5 依各句題意，以 *must not* 或 *don't* / *doesn't have to* 完成下列各句。

1. I don't want anyone to know about this. You ___*must not*___ tell anyone.
2. He ___*doesn't have to*___ wear a suit to work, but he usually does.
3. I can sleep late tomorrow morning because I _____ go to work.
4. Whatever you do, you _____ touch that switch. It's very dangerous.
5. There's an elevator in the building, so we _____ climb the stairs.
6. You _____ forget what I told you. It's very important.
7. Lauren _____ get up early, but she usually does.
8. You _____ eat or drink on buses. It's not allowed.
9. You _____ be a good player to enjoy a game of tennis.

should

You **should do** something 意思是你必須、應該做某事，因為這是一件好事或對的事。

should 通常用於提供建議、忠告或意見：
- You look tired. You **should go** to bed.
- The government **should do** more to reduce crime.
- "**Should** we **invite** Susan to the party?" "Yes, I think we **should**."

should 經常與 **I think / I don't think / Do you think . . . ?** 一起使用：
- **I think** the government **should do** more to reduce crime.
- **I don't think** you **should work** so hard.
- "**Do you think** I **should apply** for this job?" "Yes, **I think** you **should**."

You **shouldn't do** something 意思是你不應該做某事，因為它不是一件好事：
- You **shouldn't believe** everything you read in the newspapers.

should 表達「必須」的意思沒有 **must** 或 **have to** 強：
- You **should** apologize. (道歉會是件好事。)
- You **must** apologize. / You **have to** apologize. (你應該道歉，別無選擇。)

should 也可以表示某事不對，或不符合說話者的期待：
- I wonder where Liz is. She **should be** here by now.
  (她還沒來，這並不尋常。)
- The price on this package is wrong. It **should be** $1.29, not $1.59.
- That man on the motorcycle **should be wearing** a helmet.

should 表示說話者期待某事將發生：
- She's been studying hard for the exam, so she **should pass**.
  (我預期她會通過考試。)
- There are plenty of hotels in this city. It **shouldn't be** hard to find a place to stay. (我不認為找個地方住會很難。)

You **should have done** something 意思是你過去應該做某事，可是你當時並沒有做：
- You missed a great party last night. You **should have come**.
  Why didn't you?
  (你沒來參加聚會，你應該來的。)
- I wonder why they're so late. They **should have been** here an hour ago.

You **shouldn't have done** something 意思是你當時做了某件事，可是你不應該做的：
- I feel sick. I **shouldn't have eaten** so much. (我吃太多了。)
- She **shouldn't have been listening** to our conversation. It was private.

比較 **should** (do) 與 **should have** (done)：
- You look tired. You **should go** to bed now.
- You went to bed very late last night. You **should have gone** to bed earlier.

ought to

ought to 可以用來代替 **should**，兩者意思相同：
- Do you think I **ought to apply** for this job?
  (= Do you think I **should apply**?)
- That's a terrible thing to say. You **ought to be** ashamed of yourself!
- She's been studying hard for the exam, so she **ought to pass**.

should 與 *had better* Unit 33B

Exercises

31.1 依各句題意，從下列動詞片語中選出適當者，並與 *should* 或 *shouldn't* 完成句子。·

go away for a few days	go to bed so late	look for another job
put some pictures on the walls	take a photo	use her car so much

1. Liz needs a change. _She should go away for a few days._
2. Your salary is too low. You _____
3. Eric always has trouble getting up. He _____
4. What a beautiful view! You _____
5. Sue drives everywhere. She never walks. She _____
6. Bill's room isn't very interesting. He _____

31.2 依各句題意，以 *I think* / *I don't think . . . should . . .* 完成句子。

1. Chris and Amy are planning to get married. You think it's a bad idea.
   I don't think they should get married.
2. I have a bad cold but plan to go out tonight. You don't think this is a good idea.
   You say to me: _____
3. Peter needs a job. He's just seen an ad for a job which you think would be
   ideal for him, but he's not sure whether to apply or not. You say to him: I think
   _____
4. The government wants to raise taxes, but you don't think this is a good idea.
   _____

31.3 依各句題意，用括號內的動詞，與 *should* 或 *should have* 完成句子。

1. Tracy _should pass_ the exam. She's been studying very hard. (pass)
2. You missed a great party last night. _You should have come._ (come)
3. We don't see you enough. You _____ and see us more often. (come)
4. I'm in a difficult position. What do you think I _____ ? (do)
5. I'm sorry that I didn't follow your advice. I _____ what you
   said. (do)
6. We lost the game, but we _____ . Our team is better than theirs. (win)
7. "Is John here yet?" "Not yet, but he _____ here soon." (be)
8. I mailed the letter three days ago, so it _____ by now. (arrive)

31.4 依各句題意，以 *should* / *shouldn't* 完成句子；有些句子為現在式，有些則為過去式。

1. I'm feeling sick. I ate too much. _I shouldn't have eaten so much._
2. That man on the motorcycle isn't wearing a helmet. That's dangerous.
   He _should be wearing a helmet._
3. When we got to the restaurant, there were no free tables. We hadn't reserved one.
   We _____
4. The sign says that the store opens every day at 8:30. It is 9:00 now, but the store isn't
   open yet.
   _____
5. The speed limit is 30 miles an hour, but Kate is driving 50.
   She _____
6. Mai gave me her e-mail address, but I didn't write it down. Now I can't remember it.
   I _____
7. I was driving right behind another car. Suddenly, the driver in front of me stopped,
   and I drove into the back of his car. It was my fault.
   _____
8. I walked into a wall. I wasn't looking where I was going.
   _____

假設語氣 (I suggest you do)

請看下面的範例：

Why don't you buy some nice clothes?

Lisa said to Mary, "Why don't you buy some nice clothes?"
Lisa suggested that Mary **buy** some nice clothes.

Lisa 對 Mary 說：「你為何不買些好看的衣服？」
Lisa 建議 Mary 買些好看的衣服。

在上例中，**buy** 是假設語氣用法，使用假設語氣時，主詞不論是第一人稱，還是第二、第三人稱，也不論是單數還是複數，一律使用動詞原型(例如：I **buy**, he **buy**, she **buy** 等。)

I/he/she/it we/you/they	**do/buy/be**, etc.

在下列動詞所接的名詞子句中，動詞皆為假設語氣動詞，因此必須為動詞原型：

demand	insist	propose	recommend	suggest

- I **insisted** he **have** dinner with us.
- The doctor **recommended** that I **rest** for a few days.
- John **demanded** that Lisa **apologize** to him.
- What do you **suggest** I **do**?

其他句型包括 It's **essential** / **imperative** / **important** / **necessary** / **vital** (that) something **happen**：

- It's **essential** that everyone **be** at work by 9:00 tomorrow morning. No exceptions.
- It's **imperative** that the government **do** something about health care.

上列的句型也可以用以下方式表達：

- It's **essential for** everyone **to** be at work by 9:00 tomorrow morning.
- It's **imperative for** the government **to** do something about health care.

假設語氣的否定動詞形式為 not + 動詞原型(例如 I **not be**、you **not leave**、she **not go** 等)：

- The doctor strongly **recommended** that I **not go** to work for two days.
- It's very **important** that you **not miss** this appointment with your eye doctor.

假設語氣動詞不論現在式、過去式、或未來式，皆為動詞原型：

- I insist you **come** with us.
- They insisted I **go** with them.

be 動詞之動詞原型為be，因此假設語氣動詞為 **be** (通常使用被動語氣)：

- I **insisted** that something **be done** about the problem.
- It's **essential** that this medicine not **be taken** on an empty stomach.
- The airline **recommended** we **be** at the airport two hours before our flight.

在 insist 和 suggest 之後，除名詞子句以外，也可以使用下面的句型：

- They **insisted on paying** for dinner. (參見 Unit 60A)
- It is a beautiful evening, so I **suggest going** for a walk. (參見 Unit 51)

在 suggest 之後不可以使用不定詞 (to + 動詞原型)：

- She **suggested that he buy** some new clothes. (並非 suggested him to buy)
- He **insists on going** with us. (並非 he insists to go)

Exercises

32.1 請參照例句，將下列各題中第一個句子改寫為第二個句子。

1. "Why don't you buy some new clothes?" said Lisa to Mary.
   Lisa suggested that _Mary buy some new clothes._

2. "I don't think you should go to work for two days," the doctor said to me.
   The doctor recommended that _I not go to work for two days._

3. "You really must stay a little longer," she said to me.
   She insisted that _____

4. "Why don't you visit the museum after lunch?" I said to her.
   I suggested that _____

5. "I think it would be a good idea to see a specialist," the doctor said to me.
   The doctor recommended that _____

6. "I think it would be a good idea for you not to lift anything heavy," the specialist
   said to me.
   The specialist recommended that _____

7. "You have to pay the rent by Friday at the latest," the landlord said to us.
   The landlord demanded that _____

8. "Why don't you go away for a few days?" Josh said to me.
   Josh suggested that _____

9. "I don't think you should give your children snacks right before mealtime,"
   the doctor told me.
   The doctor suggested that _____

10. "Let's have dinner early," Sarah said to us.
    Sarah proposed that _____

32.2 依各句題意，填入適當的動詞以完成句子。

1. It's imperative that the government _do_ something about health care.
2. I insisted that something _be_ done about the problem.
3. Our friends recommended that we _____ our vacation in the mountains.
4. Since Dave hurt Tracy's feelings, I stongly recommended that he _____ to her.
5. The workers at the factory are demanding that their wages _____ raised.
6. Lisa wanted to walk home alone, but we insisted that she _____ for us.
7. The city council has proposed that a new convention center _____ built.
8. What do you suggest I _____ to the party? Something casual?
9. It is essential that every child _____ the opportunity to get a good education.
10. Brad forgot his wife's birthday last year, so it's really important he _____ it
    this year.
11. It is vital that every runner _____ water during the marathon.

32.3 Tom 希望身體健康，他的朋友給了他一些建議：

Why don't you try jogging? — Linda

How about walking to work in the morning? — Sandra

Eat more fruit and vegetables. — Bill

Why don't you take vitamins? — Anna

請依上述 Tom 的朋友給他的建議，完成下列的句子。

1. Linda suggested that he _try jogging._
2. Sandra suggested that he _____
3. Bill suggested _____
4. Anna _____

had better　It's time . . .

A

had better (I'd better / you'd better 等)

I'd better do something 意思是我最好做某事；如果不做，就會有問題或危險。

- I have to meet Amy in 10 minutes. **I'd better go** now or I'll be late.
- "Do you think I should take an umbrella?"　"Yes, **you'd better**. It might rain."
- **We'd better stop** for gas soon. The tank is almost empty.

I'd better 的否定形式為 **I'd better not** (= I had better not)：

- "Are you going out tonight?"　"**I'd better not**. I've got a lot of work to do."
- You don't look very well. **You'd better not go** to work today.

注意：

> 此用法為 **had** better (在口語中通常縮寫為 **I'd** better / **you'd** better 等)：
> - **I'd better** go now = I **had** better go now.
>
> **had** 雖然是過去式形式，但是 **had better** 的意思是現在或未來，不是過去：
> - **I'd better go** to the bank now / tomorrow.
>
> **had better** 後接動詞原型，例如 **I'd better do** (而非 **I'd better to do**)：
> - It might rain. We**'d better take** an umbrella. (並非 We**'d better to take**)

B

had better 與 should

had better 與 **should** 的意思相近，但不完全一樣。**had better** 只用於表示特定的情況，而非普通的一般情況；**should** 則可以用於任何情況，以提供建議或意見。

- It's cold. **You'd better wear** a coat when you go out. (特定情況)
- You're always at home. You **should go** out more often. (一般情況，不可以用 had better go。)

此外，**had better** 與 **should** 不同之處在於，**had better** 通常表示如果不做某事，就會有問題或危險。**should** 則表示某件事應該做、去做比較好。比較下列各例：

- It's a great movie. You **should** go and see it. (但是你可以不去看)
- The movie starts at 8:30. You**'d better** go now, or you'll be late.

C

It's time . . .

此句型通常為 **It's time** (for somebody) **to do** something：

- It's time **to go** home. / It's time for us **to go** home.

也可以用下面的句型來表示：

- It's late. It's time we **went** home.

上面例句中的動詞雖然是過去式 (**went**)，但意思是指現在而非過去：

- It's 10:00 and he's still in bed. **It's time** he **got** up. (並非 It's time he gets up)

It's time you did something 意思是你早就該做某事，或開始做某事；這個句型通常用於批評或埋怨：

- **It's time** you **changed** the oil in the car. It hasn't been changed in a long time.
- The windows are very dirty. I think **it's time** they **were washed**.

也可以用 **It's about time . . .** ，此用法更加重批評的語氣。

- Jack is a great talker. But **it's about time** he **did** something instead of just talking.

Exercises

33.1 依各句題意，用括號內的語詞，與 *had better* 完成句子。

1. You're going out for a walk with Tom. It looks as if it might rain. You say to Tom:
   (an umbrella) _We'd better take an umbrella._

2. Alex has just cut himself. It's a bad cut. You say to him:
   (a bandage) _____

3. You and Kate plan to go to a restaurant tonight. It's a popular restaurant. You say to Kate:
   (make a reservation) We _____

4. Jill doesn't look very well – not well enough to go to work. You say to her:
   (work) _____

5. You received your phone bill four weeks ago, but you haven't paid it yet. If you don't
   pay soon, you could be in trouble. You say to yourself:
   (pay) _____

6. You want to go out, but you're expecting an important phone call. You say to your friend:
   (go out) I _____

7. You and Jeff are going to the theater. You've missed the bus, and you don't want to be late.
   You say to Jeff: (a taxi) _____

33.2 請判斷下列各句題意，若適用 *had better* 者請填入 *had better*；若不適用者請填入 *should*。

1. I have an appointment in 10 minutes. I _'d better_ go now or I'll be late.
2. It's a great movie. You _should_ go and see it. You'll really like it.
3. You _____ set your alarm. You'll never wake up on time if you don't.
4. When people are driving, they _____ keep their eyes on the road.
5. I'm glad you came to see us. You _____ come more often.
6. She'll be hurt if we don't invite her to the wedding, so we _____ invite her.
7. These cookies are delicious. You _____ try one.
8. I think everybody _____ learn a foreign language.

33.3 依各句題意，完成句子；注意需填入一個字或兩個字。

1. a) I need some money. I'd better _go_ to the bank.
   b) John is expecting you to call him. You _____ better call him now.
   c) "Should I leave the window open?" "No, you'd better _____ it."

2. a) It's time the government _____ something about the problem.
   b) It's time something _____ about the problem.
   c) I think it's about time you _____ about other people instead of only thinking
      about yourself.

33.4 依各句題意，以 *It's time . . .* 完成句子。

1. You think the children should be in bed. It's already 11 o'clock.
   It's time the children were in bed.

2. You haven't taken a vacation in ages. You need one now.
   It's time I _____

3. You're sitting on a train waiting for it to leave. It should have left five minutes ago.
   _____

4. You enjoy having parties. You haven't had one for a long time.
   _____

5. The company you work for is badly managed. You think some changes should be made.
   _____

6. Andrew has been doing the same job for the last 10 years. He should try something else.
   _____

would

would ('d) / wouldn't 用於表示想像的狀況或動作,
亦即該狀況或動作並非真實的:

- It **would be** nice to buy a new car, but we can't afford it.
- I**'d love** to live by the ocean.
- *A:* Should I tell Chris what happened?
  B: No, I **wouldn't say** anything.
  (站在你的立場,我什麼也不會說。)

would have (done) 用於表示想像中過去的狀況或
動作 (該狀況或動作在過去根本未發生):

- They helped us a lot. I don't know what we **would have done** without their help.
- I didn't tell Sam what happened. He **wouldn't have been** pleased.

比較 **would (do)** 與 **would have (done)**:

- I **would call** Sue, but I don't have her number. (現在)
  I **would have called** Sue, but I didn't have her number. (過去)
- I'm not going to invite them to the party. They **wouldn't come** anyway.
  I didn't invite them to the party. They **wouldn't have come** anyway.

would 經常與 **if** 的子句一起使用 (參見 Unit 36 至 Unit 38):

- I **would call** Sue **if** I had her number.
- I **would have called** Sue **if** I'd had her number.

比較 **will ('ll)** 與 **would ('d)** 之用法:

- I**'ll stay** a little longer. I've got plenty of time.
  I**'d stay** a little longer, but I really have to go now. (所以我不能再待下去。)
- I**'ll call** Sue. I've got her number.
  I**'d call** Sue, but I don't have her number. (所以我沒有打電話給她。)

有時候 **would/wouldn't** 為 **will/won't** 之過去式。
比較下面例子:

現在	過去
■ *Tom:* I**'ll call** you on Sunday. →	Tom said he**'d call** me on Sunday.
■ *Ann:* I promise I **won't be** late. →	Ann promised that she **wouldn't be** late.
■ *Liz:* Darn! The car **won't start**. →	Liz was annoyed because her car **wouldn't start**.

somebody **wouldn't do** something 意思是某人拒絕做某事:

- I tried to warn him, but he **wouldn't listen** to me. (他拒絕聽我的話。)
- The car **wouldn't start**. (車子發不動。)

would 也可以用於表示在過去會定期固定發生的事:

- When we were children, we lived by the ocean. In summer, if the weather was nice, we **would** all get up early and go for a swim. (我們定期、固定這麼做。)
- Whenever Richard was angry, he **would** walk out of the room.

would 用於上述用法時,意思與 **used to** 相似(參見 Unit 17):

- Whenever Richard was angry, he **used to walk** out of the room.

will Unit 20 與 Unit 21   *Would you . . . ?* Unit 35A   *would . . . if* Unit 36 至 Unit 38
wish . . . would Unit 39   *would like* Unit 35E 與 Unit 56   *would prefer / would rather* Unit 57

34.1 請參照例句，用括號內的提示，完成有關於你自己的描述。

1. (a place you'd love to live) _I'd love to live by the ocean._
2. (a job you wouldn't like to do) _____
3. (something you would love to do) _____
4. (something that would be nice to have) _____
5. (a place you'd like to go to) _____

34.2 依各句題意，從下列動詞中選出一個適當的字，並與 *would* 完成句子。

be   be   ~~do~~   do   enjoy   enjoy   have   pass   stop

1. They helped us a lot. I don't know what we _would have done_ without their help.
2. You should go and see the movie. You _____ it.
3. It's too bad you couldn't come to the concert yesterday. You _____ it.
4. Do you think I should apply for the job? What _____ you
   _____ in my position?
5. I was in a hurry when I saw you. Otherwise, I _____ to talk.
6. We took a taxi home last night but got stuck in the traffic. It _____ quicker
   to walk.
7. Why don't you go and see Claire? She _____ very pleased to see you.
8. Why didn't you take the exam? I'm sure you _____ it.
9. In an ideal world, everybody _____ enough to eat.

34.3 請參照例句，依句意將下列左方與右方的句子完成適當的配對。

1. ~~I'd like to go to Australia one day.~~	a) It wouldn't have been very pleasant. _c_
2. I wouldn't like to live on a busy street.	b) It would have been fun. _____
3. I'm sorry the trip was canceled.	c) ~~It would be nice.~~ _____
4. I'm looking forward to going out tonight.	d) It won't be much fun. _____
5. I'm glad we didn't go out in the rain.	e) It wouldn't be very pleasant. _____
6. I'm not looking forward to the trip.	f) It will be fun. _____

34.4 依各句題意，以 *promised* + *would / wouldn't* 完成句子。

1. I wonder why Laura is late. _She promised she wouldn't be late._
2. I wonder why Steve hasn't called. He promised _____
3. Why did you tell Jane what I said? You _____
4. I'm surprised they didn't wait for us. They _____

34.5 依各句題意，以 *wouldn't* 與適當的動詞完成句子。

1. I tried to warn him, but he _wouldn't listen_ to me.
2. I asked Amanda what had happened, but she _____ me.
3. Paul was very angry about what I'd said and _____ to me for two weeks.
4. Martina insisted on carrying all her luggage. She _____ me help her.

34.6 下列各句描述的都是在過去發生過很多次的事。依各句題意，從下列動詞中選出一個適當的字，並與 *would* 完成句子。

forget   help   shake   share   ~~walk~~

1. Whenever Richard was angry, he _would walk_ out of the room.
2. We used to live next to railroad tracks. Every time a train went by, the
   house _____ .
3. George was a very kind man. He _____ always _____
   you if you had a problem.
4. Brenda was always very generous. She didn't have much, but she _____
   what she had with everyone else.
5. You could never rely on Joe. It didn't matter how many times you reminded him to do something,
   he _____ always _____ .

Can / Could / Would you . . . ? 等
(表請求、提供協助、許可、與邀請)

A 請求他人做某事：

can 或 could 通常用於請求他人做某事：

- **Can you** wait a minute, please?

或　**Could you** wait a minute, please?

- Liz, **can you** do me a favor?
- Excuse me, **could you** tell me how to get to the airport?
- I wonder if **you could** help me.

但是在 **Do you think you could . . . ?** 的句型中，
通常不用 can 而是用 could：

- **Do you think you could** lend me some money until next week?

will 和 would 也可以用於請求他人做某事，
但是 can 和 could 較常使用：

- Liz, **will you** do me a favor?
- **Would you** please be quiet? I'm trying to concentrate.

Could you open
the door, please?

B 要求某事或某物：

Can I have . . . ?、**Could I have . . . ?** 或 **Can I get . . . ?** 可用於要求某物品：

- (在禮品店) **Can I have** these postcards, please? (或 **Can I get . . . ?**)
- (用餐中) **Could I have** the salt, please?

要求某物品也可以用 **May I have . . . ?**

- **May I have** these postcards, please?

C 請求許可：

can、could 或 may 都可以用於請求允許做某件事：

- (在電話中) Hello, **can I** speak to Tom, please?
- "**Could I** use your phone?" "Yes, of course."
- **Do you think I could** borrow your bike?
- "**May I** come in?" "Yes, please do."

may 較 can 和 could 正式，但較少使用。

請求允許做某件事也可以用以下句型：**Do you mind if I . . . ?**
Is it all right / Is it OK if I . . . ?:

- "**Do you mind if I** use your phone?" "No. Not at all."
- "**Is it all right if I** come in?" "Yes, of course."

D 提供協助：

Can I . . . ? 或 **May I . . . ?** 用於表示提供協助做某件事：

- "**Can I** get you a cup of coffee?" "Yes, that would be very nice."
- (在商店裡) "**May I** help you?" "No, thanks. I'm being helped."

may 較 can 正式。

E 提供與邀請：

Would you like . . . ? (而非 Do you like) 用於表示邀請或提供某種事物：

- "**Would you like** a cup of coffee?" "Yes, please."
- "**Would you like** to go to the movies with us tonight?" "Yes, I'd love to."

I'd like 為表示「我想要某事」的客氣用法：

- (在旅客服務中心) **I'd like** some information about hotels, please.
- (在商店裡) **I'd like** to try on this jacket, please.

Exercises

35.1 請參照例句，依各句題意，以 *Can you . . .* 或 *Could you . . .* 寫出問句。

1. You're carrying a lot of things. You can't open the door yourself. There's a man standing near the door. You say to him:
   Can you open the door, please? 或 *Could you open the door, please?*

2. You phone Ann, but somebody else answers. Ann isn't there. You want to leave a message for her. You say: _____

3. You're a tourist. You want to go to the post office, but you don't know how to get there. You ask at your hotel: _____

4. You are in a department store. You see some pants you like, and you want to try them on. You say to the salesperson: _____

5. You need a ride home from a party. John drove to the party and lives near you. You say to him:
   _____

35.2 請參照例句，依各句題意，用括號內的語詞寫出問句。

1. You want to borrow your friend's camera. What do you say to him?
   (think) *Do you think I could borrow your camera?*

2. You are at a friend's house and you want to use her phone. What do you say?
   (all right) *Is it all right if I use your phone?*

3. You've written a letter in English. Before you send it, you want a friend to check it for you. What do you ask?
   (think) _____

4. You want to leave work early. What do you ask your boss?
   (mind) _____

5. The woman in the next room is playing music. It's very loud. You want her to turn it down. What do you say to her?
   (think) _____

6. You are calling the owner of an apartment that was advertised in the newspaper. You are interested in the apartment and want to see it today. What do you say to the owner?
   (OK) _____

7. You're on a train. The woman next to you has finished reading her newspaper, and you'd like to have a look at it. You ask her.
   (think) _____

35.3 請參照例句，依各題對話的情境和內容，寫出問句。

1. Paul has come to see you. You offer him something to eat.
   You: _Would you like something to eat_ ?
   Paul: No, thank you. I've just eaten.

2. You need help replacing the memory card in your camera. You ask Kate.
   You: I don't know how to replace the memory card. _____ ?
   Kate: Sure. It's easy. All you have to do is this.

3. You're on a bus. You have a seat, but an elderly man is standing. You offer him your seat.
   You: _____ ?
   Man: Oh, that's very nice of you. Thank you very much.

4. You're the passenger in a car. Your friend is driving very fast. You ask her to slow down.
   You: You're making me very nervous. _____ ?
   Driver: Oh, I'm sorry. I didn't realize I was going so fast.

5. You've finished your meal in a restaurant and now you want the check. You ask the waiter:
   You: _____ ?
   Waiter: Sure. I'll get it for you now.

6. A friend of yours is interested in one of your books. You invite him to borrow it.
   Friend: This book looks very interesting.
   You: Yes, it's very good. _____ ?

If I do ... 與 If I did ... 之比較

A

比較下面兩個例子：

1) Sue 弄丟了她的手錶。她認為手錶可能在 Ann 家裡。她告訴 Ann：

Sue: I think I left my watch at your house. Have you seen it?
我想我把我的錶留在你家裡了。你有看到我的手錶嗎？

Ann: No, but I'll look when I get home. **If I find** it, I'll tell you.
沒有，但是我回家後會看看。如果找到了，我會告訴你。

在此例中，由於 Ann 覺得她有可能找到 Sue 的手錶，因此她使用的句型為

If I find ..., **I'll** ....

2) Carol 說：

If I found a wallet in the street, I'd take it to the police station.
如果我在街上找到皮夾，我會將它送給警方。

此例的情形與例 1 不同。在此例中，Carol 並不期待在街上找到皮夾。她只是想像一個不可能發生的情況。因此，Carol 用的句型為

If I found ..., **I'd** (= I would) .... （並非 if I find ..., I'll ...）

表示想像而非真實情況時，用 if + 過去式（例如，**if** I **found** / **if** there **was** / **if** we **didn't** 等）。

但意思並非指過去式：

- What would you do **if** you **won** a million dollars?
  （我們並不認為你真的會贏得一百萬。）
- I don't really want to go to their party, but I probably will go. They'd be hurt **if** I **didn't go**.
- **If** there **was** （或 **were**） an election tomorrow, who would you vote for?

if ... **was/were** 之用法，參見 Unit 37C。

If I **won** a million dollars . . . .
假如我贏了一百萬…

B

在 **if** 子句中，通常不可以用 **would**：

- I'd be very frightened **if** somebody **pointed** a gun at me.（並非 if somebody would point）
- **If** I **didn't** go to their party, they'd be hurt.（並非 If I wouldn't go）

C

在主要子句部分，可以使用 **would** ('d) / **wouldn't**：

- If you got more exercise, you**'d feel** better.
- I'm not tired. If I went to bed now, I **wouldn't sleep**.
- **Would** you **mind** if I used your phone?

除了 **would** 以外，也可以用 **could** 或 **might**：

- If you got more exercise, you **might feel** better.（你可能會覺得比較好。）
- If it stopped raining, we **could go** out.（我們可能可以出去。）

D

when 不可以用於上述表示「假如…」的句型中：

- They'd be hurt **if** I didn't go to their party.（並非 when I didn't go）
- What would you do **if** you were bitten by a snake?（並非 when you were bitten）

Exercises

36.1 請參照例句，依各句題意，填入適當的動詞形式。

1. They would be hurt if _I didn't go_ to their party. (not / go)
2. If you got more exercise, you _would feel_ better. (feel)
3. If they offered me the job, I think I _____ it. (take)
4. A lot of people would be out of work if the car factory _____ . (close down)
5. If I sold my car, I _____ much money for it. (not / get)
6. *(in an elevator)* What would happen if somebody _____ that red button? (press)
7. I'm sure Amy will lend you the money. I'd be very surprised if she _____ . (refuse)
8. Liz gave me this ring. She _____ very upset if I lost it. (be)
9. Dave and Kate are expecting us. They would be very disappointed if we _____ . (not / come)
10. Would Bob mind if I _____ his bike without asking him? (borrow)
11. What would you do if somebody _____ in here with a gun? (walk)
12. I'm sure Sue _____ if you explained the situation to her. (understand)

36.2 以 *What would you do if . . . ?* 的句型，詢問你的朋友下面問題。

1. (imagine – you win a lot of money)
   What would you do if you won a lot of money?
2. (imagine – you lose your passport)
   What _____
3. (imagine – there's a fire in the building)
   _____
4. (imagine – you're in an elevator and it stops between floors)
   _____

36.3 請參照範例，依各題的對話內容，完成句子。

1. *A:* Should we catch the 10:30 train?
   B: No. (arrive too early) _If we caught the 10:30 train, we'd arrive too early._
2. *A:* Is Ken going to take the driver's test?
   B: No. (fail) If he _____
3. *A:* Why don't we stay at a hotel?
   B: No. (cost too much) If _____
4. *A:* Is Sally going to apply for the job?
   B: No. (not / get it) If _____
5. *A:* Let's tell them the truth.
   B: No. (not / believe us) If _____
6. *A:* Why don't we invite Bill to the party?
   B: No. (have to invite his friends, too) _____

36.4 請依你自己的想法，完成下列各句。

1. If you got more exercise, _you'd feel better._
2. I'd feel very angry if _____
3. If I didn't go to work tomorrow, _____
4. Would you go to the party if _____
5. If you bought a car, _____
6. Would you mind if _____

If I knew . . .   I wish I knew . . .

A

請看下面的範例：

Sue 想要打電話給 Paul，可是因為她不知道 Paul 的電話號碼，所以她不能打。她說：

If I knew his number, I **would call** him.
假如我知道他的電話號碼，我就可以打電話給他了。

在例子中 Sue 說 **If I knew** his number，表示 Sue 事實上她並不知道 Paul 的電話號碼。她只是想像她如果知道的話會怎麼做。

If I **knew** his number . . . .

If + 過去式 (if I knew / if you were / if we didn't 等)表示描述的狀況僅為說話者的想像；動詞雖然是過去式，但是所表達的意思是現在式：

■ Tom would read more **if** he **had** more time. (but he doesn't have much time)
■ **If** I **didn't** want to go to the party, I wouldn't go. (but I want to go)
■ We wouldn't have any money **if** we **didn't** work. (but we work)
■ **If** you **were** in my position, what would you do?
■ It's a shame you can't drive. It would be helpful **if** you **could**.

B

動詞 wish 後接子句，也可用來描述說話者想像的狀況，其中動詞用法必須使用過去式(例如，**I wish I knew / I wish you were** 等)。wish 常表示說話者後悔或遺憾某件事並不是如他所希望的一樣：

I **wish** I **had** an umbrella.
我希望我有把傘。

■ I wish I knew Paul's phone number.
(我不知道 Paul 的電話號碼，覺得很遺憾。)
■ Do you ever **wish** you **could** fly? (you can't fly)
■ It rains a lot here. I **wish** it **didn't** rain so often.
■ It's very crowded here. I **wish** there **weren't** so many people.
■ I **wish** I **didn't** have to work tomorrow, but unfortunately, I do.

C

If I **was** / If I **were**

在 if 和 wish 的子句中，通常使用 I / he / she / it **were**；**was** 也可以使用，但較不正式。
例子如下：

■ **If I was** you, I wouldn't buy that coat.　或　**If I were** you, . . .
■ I'd go out **if it wasn't** so cold.　或　. . . **if it weren't** so cold.
■ **I wish Carol was** here.　或　**I wish Carol were** here.

D

在 if 和 wish 後接的子句中，通常不用 **would**：

■ **If I were** rich, I **would** have a yacht. (並非 If I would be rich)
■ **I wish I had** something to read. (並非 I wish I would have)

但有時候可以使用wish . . . would 的句型，例如，**I wish you would listen.** (參見 Unit 39D)。

E

注意 **could** 的用法，有時候意思是 would be able to，有時是 was / were able to：

■ You **could** get a better job　(you **could** get = you would be able to get)
if you **could** use a computer.　(you **could** use = you were able to use)

could Unit 25 與 Unit 26　*If I do* 與 *If I did* Unit 36　*If I had known / I wish I had known* Unit 38　*wish* Unit 39

Exercises

37.1 依各句題意，填入適當的動詞時形式。

1. If I ___knew___ (know) his phone number, I would call him.
2. I ___wouldn't buy___ (not / buy) that coat if I were you.
3. I _____ (help) you if I could, but I'm afraid I can't.
4. We would need a car if we _____ (live) in the country.
5. If we had the choice, we _____ (live) in the country.
6. This soup isn't very good. It _____ (taste) better if it weren't so salty.
7. I wouldn't mind living in Maine if the weather _____ (be) better.
8. If I were you, I _____ (not / wait). I _____ (go) now.
9. You're always tired. If you _____ (not / go) to bed so late every night, you wouldn't be tired all the time.
10. I think there are too many cars. If there _____ (not / be) so many cars, there _____ (not / be) so much pollution.

37.2 依各句題意，以 *if* . . . 完成句子。

1. We don't see you very often because you live so far away.
   If you didn't live so far away, we'd see you more often.
2. This book is expensive, so I'm not going to buy it.
   I'd _____ if _____
3. We don't go out to eat because we can't afford it.
   We _____
4. I can't meet you tomorrow. I have to work late.
   If _____
5. It's raining, so we can't have lunch on the patio.
   We _____
6. I don't want his advice, and that's why I'm not going to ask for it.
   If _____

37.3 依各句題意，以 *I wish* 完成句子。

1. I don't know many people (and I'm lonely). _I wish I knew more people._
2. I don't have a cell phone (and I need one). I wish _____
3. Amanda isn't here (and I need to see her). _____
4. It's cold (and I hate cold weather). _____
5. I live in a big city (and I don't like it). _____
6. I can't go to the party (and I'd like to). _____
7. I have to work tomorrow (but I'd like to stay in bed).
   _____
8. I don't know anything about cars (and my car has just broken down).
   _____
9. I'm not feeling well (and that's not pleasant).
   _____

37.4 請依你自己的想法，以 *I wish* 完成句子。

1. (somewhere you'd like to be now – on the beach, in Hawaii, in bed, etc.)
   I wish I _were at home in bed now._ _____
2. (something you'd like to have – a computer, a good job, more friends, etc.)
   _____
3. (something you'd like to be able to do – sing, speak a language, fly, etc.)
   _____
4. (something you'd like to be – beautiful, strong, rich, etc.)
   _____

If I had known . . .   I wish I had known . . .

A

請看下面的範例：

上個月 Brian 住院好幾天。Liz 並不知道這件事，所以她沒有去探望 Brian。前幾天他們見面了，Liz 說：

If I had known you were in the hospital, **I would have gone** to see you.
如果當時我知道你住院，我就會去探望你。

在例子中，Liz 說 **If I had known** you were in the hospital . . . ，表示她當時並不知道 Brian 住院。

表過去的情況時，必須使用 **if + had ('d)** . . . (例如，**if I had known/been/done** 等)：
- I didn't see you when you passed me in the street. **If I'd seen you**, of course I would have said hello. (but I didn't see you)
- I didn't go out last night. I would have gone out **if I hadn't been** so tired. (but I was tired)
- **If** he **had been looking** where he was going, he wouldn't have walked into the wall. (but he wasn't looking)
- The view was wonderful. **If I'd had** a camera, I would have taken some pictures. (but I didn't have a camera)

比較下面的例子：
- I'm not hungry. **If** I **was** hungry, I would eat something. (現在)
- I wasn't hungry. **If** I **had been** hungry, I would have eaten something. (過去)

B

If 子句中不可以使用 **would**；**would** 必須用於主要子句中：
- If I **had seen** you, I **would have said** hello. (並非 If I would have seen you)

注意縮寫 **'d** 可以是 **would** 或 **had** 的縮寫：
- **If I'd seen** you,   (I'd seen = I **had** seen)
  I'd have said hello.   (I'd have said = I **would** have said)

C

wish 子句中，動詞的用法與上述if子句中動詞的用法相同。I **wish** something **had happened** 意思是我很遺憾當時某事並沒有發生：
- I **wish I'd known** that Brian was sick. I would have gone to see him. (but I didn't know)
- I feel sick. I **wish** I **hadn't eaten** so much cake. (I ate too much cake)
- Do you **wish** you **had studied** science instead of languages? (you didn't study science)

wish 子句中，不可以使用 **would have**：
- The weather was cold on our vacation. I wish it **had been** warmer. (並非 I wish it would have been)

D

比較 **would do** 與 **would have (done)**：
- If I had gone to the party last night, I **would be** tired now. (我現在不累—與現在狀況不符。)
- If I had gone to the party last night, I **would have met** lots of people. (我昨晚並沒有見到許多人—與過去狀況不符。)

比較 **would have**、**could have** 和 **might have**：

- If the weather hadn't been so bad,
  - we **would have gone** out.
  - we **could have gone** out.
    - (= we would have been able to go out)
  - we **might have gone** out.
    - (= maybe we would have gone out)

had done Unit 14   *If I do* 與 *if I did* Unit 36   *If I knew / I wish I knew* Unit 37   *wish* Unit 39

38.1 依各句題意，填入適當的動詞形式。

1. I didn't know you were in the hospital. If ___*I'd known*___ (I / know), ___*I would have gone*___ (I / go) to see you.
2. John got to the station in time to catch the train. If _____ (he / miss) the train, _____ (he / be) late for his interview.
3. I'm glad that you reminded me about Rachel's birthday. _____ (I / forget) if _____ (you / not / remind) me.
4. Unfortunately, I didn't have my address book with me when I was on vacation. If _____ (I / have) your address, _____ (I / send) you a postcard.
5. *A:* How was your trip? Did you have a nice time?
   B: It was OK, but _____ (we / enjoy) it more if _____ (the weather / be) nicer.
6. I took a taxi to the hotel, but the traffic was bad. _____ (it / be) quicker if _____ (I / walk).
7. I'm not tired. If _____ (I / be) tired, I'd go home now.
8. I wasn't tired last night. If _____ (I / be) tired, I would have gone home earlier.

38.2 依各句題意，以 *If* . . . 完成句子。

1. I wasn't hungry, so I didn't eat anything.
   ___*If I'd been hungry, I would have eaten something.*___
2. The accident happened because the road was icy.
   If the road _____
3. I didn't know that Matt had to get up early, so I didn't wake him up.
   If I _____
4. I was able to buy the car only because Jim lent me the money.
   _____
5. Michelle wasn't injured in the crash because she was wearing a seat belt.
   _____
6. You didn't have any breakfast – that's why you're hungry now.
   _____
7. I didn't take a taxi because I didn't have any money.
   _____

38.3 想像你自己身處下面各題的情境之中，並以 *I wish* 完成句子。

1. You've eaten too much and now you feel sick. You say:
   ___*I wish I hadn't eaten so much.*___
2. There was a job advertised in the newspaper. You decided not to apply for it. Now you think that your decision was wrong. You say:
   I wish I _____
3. When you were younger, you didn't learn to play a musical instrument. Now you regret this. You say:
   _____
4. You've painted the door red. Now you think that red was the wrong color. You say:
   _____
5. You are walking in the country. You'd like to take some pictures, but you didn't bring your camera. You say:
   _____
6. You have some unexpected guests. They didn't call to say they were coming. You are very busy and you are not prepared for them. You say (to yourself):
   _____

wish

A

wish 可用於表示祝福，例如，**I wish you luck / all the best / success / a happy birthday** 等。

- **I wish you all the best** in the future.
- I saw Tim before the exam, and **he wished me luck**.

wish 表示祝福必須使用 wish somebody *something* 的句型 (例如，**luck / a happy birthday** 等) 但不能用於 wish that something *happens* 的句型；此種情形必須用 **hope** 表達。例如：

- I **hope** you **get** this letter before you leave town. (並非 I wish you get)

比較 **I wish** 與 **I hope** 之用法：

- **I wish** you **a pleasant stay** here.
- **I hope** you **have** a pleasant stay here. (並非 I wish you have)

B

wish 也用於表示，很遺憾某件事發生並非如我們所預期。其中動詞用法必須使用過去式 (**knew/lived** 等)，但是所表達的意思是現在。例子如下：

- **I wish** I **knew** what to do about the problem. (I don't know and I regret this)
- **I wish** you **didn't** have to go so soon. (you have to go)
- Do you **wish** you **lived** near the ocean? (you don't live near the ocean)
- Jack's going on a trip to Mexico soon. I **wish** I **was** going too. (I'm not going)

對過去發生的事表示遺憾，使用 **wish + had . . .**(**had known / had said** 等)：

- **I wish** I'**d known** about the party. I would have gone if I'd known. (I didn't know)
- It was a stupid thing to say. **I wish** I **hadn't said** it. (I said it)

其他例子參見 Unit 37 與 Unit 38。

C

I wish I could (**do** something) 意思是我很遺憾我不能做某件事：

- I'm sorry I have to go. **I wish** I **could stay** longer. (but I can't)
- I've met that man before. **I wish** I **could remember** his name. (but I can't)

I wish I could have (**done** something) 意思是我很遺憾我當時不能做某件事：

- I hear the party was great. **I wish** I **could have gone**. (but I couldn't go)

D

I wish (somebody) **would** (do something) 之用法。請看下面例句：

I wish it **would stop** raining.

下了一整天的雨了，Jill 不喜歡整天下雨。她說：
I wish it **would stop** raining.
但願不要下雨了。

Jill would like the rain to stop, but this will probably not happen.

意思是，Jill 但願不要下雨了，但是雨可能不會停。

I wish . . . would . . . 表示我希望某事發生或改變，但是我認為我希望的事不會發生。

I wish . . . would 常用於埋怨某個情況：

- The phone has been ringing for five minutes. **I wish** somebody **would answer** it.
- **I wish** you **would do** something instead of just sitting and doing nothing.

I wish . . . wouldn't 可用於埋怨某人重複做某件事：

- **I wish** you **wouldn't keep interrupting** me.

I wish . . . would 是表示希望某個動作或某個改變發生，而不是某個狀態。比較下面的例子：

- **I wish** Sarah **would** come. (= I want her to come)

但是 **I wish** Sarah **was** (或 **were**) here now. (並非 I wish Sarah would be)

- **I wish** somebody **would buy** me a car.

但是 **I wish** I **had** a car. (並非 I wish I would have)

I wish I knew Unit 37   *I wish I was / I wish I were* Unit 37   *I wish I had known* Unit 38

39.1 依各句題意，填入 *wish(ed)* 或 *hope(d)*。

1. I ___wish___ you a pleasant stay here.
2. Enjoy your vacation. I _____ you have a great time.
3. Goodbye. I _____ you all the best.
4. We said goodbye to each other and _____ each other luck.
5. We're going on a picnic tomorrow, so I _____ the weather is nice.
6. I _____ you luck in your new job. I _____ it works out well for you.

39.2 在下列情境中你會說什麼？以 *I wish . . . would . . .* 完成下列各句。

1. It's raining. You want to go out, but not in the rain.
   You say: ___I wish it would stop raining.___
2. You're waiting for Jane. She's late and you're getting impatient.
   You say to yourself: I wish _____
3. You're looking for a job – so far without success. Nobody will give you a job.
   You say: I wish somebody _____
4. You can hear a baby crying. It's been crying for a long time and you're trying to study.
   You say: _____

請依下列情境以 *I wish . . . wouldn't . . .* 完成句子。

5. Your friend drives very fast. You don't like this.
   You say to your friend: I wish you _____
6. Joe leaves the door open all the time. This annoys you.
   You say to Joe: _____
7. A lot of people drop litter in the street. You don't like this.
   You say: I wish people _____

39.3 判斷下面各題是否為正確的句子，並將不正確的句子改正。

1. I wish Sarah would be here now.   ___I wish Sarah were here now.___
2. I wish you would listen to me.   _____
3. I wish I would have more free time.   _____
4. I wish our house would be a little bigger. _____
5. I wish the weather would change.   _____
6. I wish you wouldn't complain all the time. _____
7. I wish everything wouldn't be so expensive. _____

39.4 依各句題意，用括弧內的字，請以適當的動詞形式完成各句。

1. It was a stupid thing to say. I wish ___I hadn't said___ it. (I / not / say)
2. I'm fed up with this rain. I wish ___it would stop___ . (it / stop)
3. It's a difficult question. I wish _____ the answer. (I / know)
4. I should have listened to you. I wish _____ your advice. (I / take)
5. You're lucky to be going to Peru. I wish _____ with you.
   (I / can / come)
6. I have absolutely no energy. I wish _____ so tired. (I / not / be)
7. Aren't they ready yet? I wish _____ up. (they / hurry)
8. It would be nice to stay here longer. I wish _____ to go now.
   (we / not / have)
9. When we were in Cairo last year, we didn't have time to see all the things we wanted to see.
   I wish _____ longer. (we / can / stay)
10. It's freezing today. I wish _____ so cold. I hate cold weather.
    (it / not / be)
11. Joe still doesn't know what he wants to do. I wish _____ .
    (he / decide)
12. I really didn't enjoy the party. I wish _____ . (we / not / go)

被動句型 1 (is done / was done)

A

請看下面的範例：

This house **was built** in 1935.

這棟房子建於 1935 年。

was built 為被動句。

比較主動與被動句型：

Somebody **built** this house in 1935. (主動)
受詞

This house **was built** in 1935. (被動)
主詞

主動句的動詞表示主詞所做的動作：

- My grandfather was a builder. **He built** this house in 1935.
- It's a big company. **It employs** two hundred people.

被動句的動詞則表示發生於主詞的事情：

- This house is pretty old. **It was built** in 1935.
- Two hundred people **are employed** by the company.

B

被動句通常用於施作動作的人或物不清楚或不重要的情況：

- A lot of money **was stolen** in the robbery.
  (某人偷了那筆錢，但不知道是誰偷的。)
- **Is** this room **cleaned** every day? (does somebody clean it? – it's not important who)

若需要指明是何人或何物做了該動作，則使用 **by**：

- This house was built **by my grandfather**.
- Two hundred people are employed **by the company**.

C

被動句型是 be (is/was等) + 過去分詞 (done/cleaned/seen 等)：

(be) done　　**(be) cleaned**　　**(be) damaged**　　**(be) built**　　**(be) seen**, etc.

不規則動詞的過去分詞(例如 **done/known/seen** 等)，參見附錄 1。

請看現在簡單式與過去簡單式的主動句型與被動句型：

現在簡單式

主動：**clean(s) / see(s)** 等

被動：**am/is/are** + **cleaned/seen** 等

Somebody **cleans** this room every day.

This room **is cleaned** every day.

- Many accidents **are caused** by careless driving.
- **I'm not** often **invited** to parties.
- How **is** this word **pronounced**?

過去簡單式

主動：**cleaned/saw** 等

被動：**was/were** + **cleaned/seen** 等

Somebody **cleaned** this room yesterday.

This room **was cleaned** yesterday.

- We **were woken** up by a loud noise during the night.
- "Did you go to the party?"　"No, I **wasn't invited**."
- How much money **was stolen** in the robbery?

Exercises

40.1 依各句題意，從下列動詞中選出一個適當的字，並以適當的時式(現在式或過去式)完成句子。

~~cause~~	damage	hold	invite	make
pass	show	surround	translate	write

1. Many accidents _are caused_ by dangerous driving.
2. Cheese _____ from milk.
3. The roof of the building _____ in a storm a few days ago.
4. You _____ to the wedding. Why didn't you go?
5. A movie theater is a place where films _____ .
6. In the United States, elections for president _____ every four years.
7. Originally the book _____ in Spanish, and a few years ago it _____ into English.
8. Although we were driving pretty fast, we _____ by a lot of other cars.
9. You can't see the house from the road. It _____ by trees.

40.2 以被動句型與適當的時式 (現在式或過去式)，完成下列問句。

1. Ask about glass. (how / make?) _How is glass made?_
2. Ask about television. (when / invent?) _____
3. Ask about mountains. (how / form?) _____
4. Ask about the planet Neptune. (when / discover?) _____
5. Ask about silver. (what / use for?) _____

40.3 依各句題意，填入適當的動詞時式 (現在簡單式或過去簡單式)，以及主動與被動句形式。

1. It's a big factory. Five hundred people _are employed_ (employ) there.
2. _Did somebody clean_ (somebody / clean) this room yesterday?
3. Water _____ (cover) most of the Earth's surface.
4. How much of the Earth's surface _____ (cover) by water?
5. The park gates _____ (lock) at 6:30 p.m. every evening.
6. The letter _____ (mail) a week ago, and it _____ (arrive) yesterday.
7. The boat hit a rock and _____ (sink) quickly. Fortunately everybody _____ (rescue).
8. Ron's parents _____ (die) when he was very young. He and his sister _____ (bring up) by their grandparents.
9. I was born in Chicago, but I _____ (grow up) in Houston.
10. While I was on vacation, my camera _____ (steal) from my hotel room.
11. While I was on vacation, my camera _____ (disappear) from my hotel room.
12. Why _____ (Sue / quit) her job? Didn't she like it?
13. Why _____ (Bill / fire) from his job? What did he do wrong?
14. The company is not independent. It _____ (own) by a much larger company.
15. I saw an accident last night. Somebody _____ (call) an ambulance, but nobody _____ (injure), so the ambulance _____ (not / need).
16. Where _____ (these pictures / take)? In Hong Kong? _____ (you / take) them?

40.4 依各句題意，以被動句型改寫下面各句。

1. Somebody cleans the room every day.   _The room is cleaned every day._
2. They canceled all flights because of fog.   All _____
3. People don't use this road much.   _____
4. Somebody accused me of stealing money.   I _____
5. How do people learn languages?   How _____
6. People warned us not to go out alone.   _____

被動句型 2 (be done / been done / being done)

A

請看下列主動與被動句型之用法：

與 **will** / **can** / **must** / **going to** / **want to** 等一起使用的被動句型之用法：

主動： **do/clean/see**, etc.	Somebody **will clean** this room later,
被動： **be + done/cleaned/seen**, etc.	This room **will be cleaned** later.

- The situation is serious. Something must **be done** before it's too late.
- A mystery is something that can't **be explained**.
- The music was very loud and could **be heard** from far away.
- A new supermarket is going to **be built** next year.
- Please go away. I want to **be left** alone.

B

與 **should have** / **might have** / **would have** / **seem to have** 等一起使用的被動句型之用法：

主動： **done/cleaned/seen**, etc.	Somebody **should have cleaned** this room .
被動： **been + done/cleaned/seen**, etc.	This room **should have been cleaned**.

- I haven't received the letter yet. It might **have been sent** to the wrong address.
- If you had locked the car, it wouldn't **have been stolen**.
- There were some problems at first, but they seem to **have been solved**.

C

現在完成式之被動句型：

主動： **have/has + (done)**, etc.	The room looks nice. Somebody **has cleaned** it .
被動： **have/has been + (done)**, etc.	The room looks nice. It **has been cleaned**.

- Have you heard? The concert **has been canceled**.
- **Have** you ever **been bitten** by a dog?
- "Are you going to the party?" "No, I **haven't been invited**."

過去完成式之被動句型：

主動： **had + (done)**, etc.	The room looked nice. Somebody **had cleaned** it .
被動： **had been + (done)**, etc.	The room looks nice. It **had been cleaned**.

- The vegetables didn't taste very good. They **had been cooked** too long.
- The car was three years old but **hadn't been used** very much.

D

現在進行式之被動句型：

主動： **am/is/are + (do)ing**	Somebody **is cleaning** this room right now.
被動： **am/is/are + being (done)**	This room **is being cleaned** right now.

- There's somebody walking behind us. I think we **are being followed**.
- (在商店裡) "Can I help you?" "No, thank you. I**'m being helped**."

過去進行式之被動句型：

主動： **was/were + (do)ing**	Somebody **was cleaning** this room when I arrived.
被動： **was/were + being (done)**	This room **was being cleaned** when I arrived.

- There was somebody walking behind us. We **were being followed**.

被動句型 **1, 3** Unit 40 與 Unit 42

Exercises

41.1 以 *it can* 或 *it can't* 解釋下面各單字的意思；必要時請查閱字典。

If something is

1. washable, *it can be washed.* .
2. unbreakable, it _____ .
3. edible, _____ .
4. unusable, _____ .
5. invisible, _____ .
6. portable, _____ .

41.2 依各句題意，從下列動詞中選出一個適當的字，以完成句子。

arrest   carry   cause   ~~do~~   make   repair   ~~send~~   spend   wake up

注意，有些句子需要用到 *might have*、*should have* 等。

1. The situation is serious. Something must _*be done*_ before it's too late.
2. I haven't received the letter. It might _*have been sent*_ to the wrong address.
3. A decision will not _____ until the next meeting.
4. Do you think that more money should _____ on education?
5. This road is in very bad condition. It should _____ a long time ago.
6. The injured man couldn't walk and had to _____ .
7. I told the hotel desk clerk I wanted to _____ at 6:30 the next morning.
8. If you hadn't pushed the policeman, you wouldn't _____ .
9. It's not certain how the fire started, but it might _____ by an electrical short circuit.

41.3 依各句題意，以被動句型改寫下面各句。

1. Somebody has cleaned the room. _*The room has been cleaned.*_
2. Somebody is using the computer right now.
   The computer _____
3. I didn't realize that somebody was recording our conversation.
   I didn't realize that _____
4. When we got to the stadium, we found that they had canceled the game.
   When we got to the stadium, we found that _____
5. They are building a new highway around the city.
   _____
6. They have built a new hospital near the airport.
   _____

41.4 依各句題意，用括號內的字，以主動或被動句型完成句子。

1. There's somebody behind us. (I think / we / follow) _*I think we're being followed.*_
2. This room looks different. (you / paint / the walls?) _*Have you painted the walls?*_
3. My car has disappeared. (it / steal!)
   It _____
4. My umbrella has disappeared. (somebody / take)
   Somebody _____
5. When I went into the room, I saw that the table and chairs were not in the same place.
   (the furniture / move) The _____
6. The man next door disappeared six months ago. (he / not / see / since then)
   He _____
7. I wonder how Jane is these days. (I / not / see / for ages)
   I _____
8. I wanted to use a computer at the library last night, but I wasn't able to.
   (the computers / use) All _____
9. Ann can't use her office this week. (it / redecorate)
   It _____
10. The photocopier broke down yesterday, but now it's OK. (it / work / again; it / repair)
    It _____ . It _____
11. A friend of mine was mugged on his way home a few nights ago. (you / ever / mug?)
    _____

被動句型 3

A

I was offered . . . / we were given . . . 等

有些動詞必須有兩個受詞，例如 **give**：

- Someone gave **the police** **the information**. (= Someone gave the information to the police)

  受詞 1　　　　受詞 2

因此，這類動詞可以有兩種被動的句型：

- **The police** were given the information. 或

  The information was given to the police.

屬於此類的動詞還包括有：

ask　　offer　　pay　　show　　teach　　tell

上述動詞使用被動句型時，較常使用人作為主詞：

- **I was offered** the job, but I refused it. (= they offered me the job)
- **You will be given** plenty of time to decide. (= we will give you plenty of time)
- **Have you been shown** the new machine? (= has anybody shown you?)
- **The men were paid** $200 to do the work. (= somebody paid the men $200)

B

I don't like being . . .

doing/seeing 等之被動句型為 **being done / being seen** 等。比較下面例句：

主動： I don't like **people telling me** what to do.

被動： I don't like **being told** what to do.

- I remember **being taken** to the zoo when I was a child.
  (= I remember somebody taking me to the zoo)
- Steve hates **being kept** waiting. (= he hates people keeping him waiting)
- We managed to climb over the wall without **being seen**. (= without anybody seeing us)

C

I was born . . .

I was born 意思是「我出生於 …」，必須使用過去式(而非 I am born)：

- I **was born** in Chicago.　　　　　　　　　　　　　　　　過去
- Where **were** you **born**? (並非 Where are you born?)　簡單式

但是

- How many babies **are born** every day?　　　　　　　　現在簡單式

D

get

被動句型中的 **be** 有時候也可以用 **get** 取代：

- There was a fight at the game, but nobody **got hurt**. (= nobody **was** hurt)
- I don't often **get invited** to parties. (= I'm not often invited)
- I'm surprised Ann **didn't get offered** the job. (= Ann **wasn't offered** the job)

get 只能用於描述事情發生或事情改變。例如，**get** 不可以用於下面的例句中：

- Jill **is liked** by everybody. (並非 gets liked – 因為這不是描述一件事情的發生。)
- He was a mystery man. Very little **was known** about him. (並非 got known)

get 通常用於非正式的口語中；**be** 則可以用於各種情形表示被動語氣。

get 也用於下列表達(但並不表示被動語氣)：

get married, get divorced (結婚；離婚)　　**get lost** (迷路)

get dressed (穿上衣服)　　　　　　　　　　**get changed** (換衣服)

Exercises

42.1 請參照範例，依各句題意，以被動句型改寫下面各句。

1. They didn't give me the information I needed.
   I _wasn't given the information I needed._
2. They asked me some difficult questions at the interview.
   I _____
3. Jessica's colleagues gave her a present when she retired.
   Jessica _____
4. Nobody told me about the meeting.
   I wasn't _____
5. How much will they pay you for your work?
   How much will you _____
6. I think they should have offered John the job.
   I think John _____
7. Has anybody shown you what to do?
   Have you _____

42.2 依各句題意，從下列動詞中選出一個適當的字，並以 *being* 形成被動句型完成句子。

> **give**   **hit**   **invite**   ~~**keep**~~   **pay**   **treat**

1. Steve hates _being kept_ waiting.
2. We went to the party without _____ .
3. I like giving presents, and I also like _____ them.
4. It's a busy road and I don't like crossing it. I'm afraid of _____ .
5. I'm an adult. I don't like _____ like a child.
6. Few people are prepared to work without _____ .

42.3 請自下面人名中選出五位，以正確的句型寫出他們出生於何年。

Beethoven	**Galileo**	**Elvis Presley**	1452	1869
John Lennon	**Mahatma Gandhi**	**Leonardo da Vinci**	1564	~~1901~~
~~**Walt Disney**~~	**Martin Luther King Jr.**	**William Shakespeare**	1770	1940
			1929	1935

1. _Walt Disney was born in 1901._
2. _____
3. _____
4. _____
5. _____
6. _____
7. And you? I _____

42.4 依各句題意，從下列動詞中選出一個適當的字，以 *get/got* 形成被動句型完成句子。

> **ask**   **damage**   ~~**hurt**~~   **pay**   **steal**   **sting**   **stop**   **use**

1. There was a fight at the game, but nobody _got hurt_ .
2. Ted _____ by a bee while he was sitting in the yard.
3. These tennis courts don't _____ very often. Not many people want to play.
4. I used to have a bicycle, but it _____ a few months ago.
5. Rachel works hard but doesn't _____ very much.
6. Last night I _____ by the police as I was driving home. One of the lights on my car wasn't working.
7. Please pack these things very carefully. I don't want them to _____ .
8. People often want to know what my job is. I often _____ that question.

It is said that . . .   He is said to . . .
He is supposed to . . .

A

請看下面的範例：

Henry 很老了，沒有人知道他確實的年齡，但是：

It is said that he is 108 years old.

或　　He **is said to be** 108 years old.

以上兩個句子的意思都是「大家說他 108 歲」。

其他動詞也可以使用上述兩種句型，特別是下列的動詞：

alleged   believed   considered   expected   known   reported   thought   understood

比較下列兩種句型：

- Cathy works very hard.
  It is said that she works 16 hours a day.　或　She **is said to work** 16 hours a day.
- The police are looking for a missing boy.
  It is believed that the boy is wearing a　或　The boy **is believed to be wearing** a white sweater and blue jeans.　　　　　a white sweater and blue jeans.
- The strike started three weeks ago.
  It is expected that it will end soon.　或　The strike **is expected to end** soon.
- A friend of mine has been arrested.
  It is alleged that he hit a police officer.　或　He **is alleged to have hit** a police officer.
- The two houses belong to the same family.
  It is said that there is a secret tunnel　或　There **is said to be** a secret tunnel between them.　　　　　　　　　　　　between them.

這兩種被動的句型經常用於新聞報導中，例如，報導意外事件：

- **It is reported that** two people were injured　或　Two people **are reported to have** in the explosion.　　　　　　　　　　　**been injured** in the explosion.

B

(be) supposed to

it is supposed to 之意思有時與 it is said to 相同：

- Let's go and see that movie. It**'s supposed to be** good.　(= it is said to be good)
- Mark **is supposed to have hit** a police officer, but I don't believe it.

be supposed to 還有其他的意思。**supposed to** 用於表達某事是預先計畫、安排好的，或是預期中應該會發生的；通常用來表示與真正發生的狀況不同：

- The plan **is supposed to be** a secret, but everybody seems to know about it.
  (= the plan is intended to be a secret)
- What are you doing at work? You**'re supposed to be** on vacation.
  (= you arranged to be on vacation)
- Jane **was supposed to call** me last night, but she didn't.
- Our guests **were supposed to come** at 7:30, but they were late.
- I'd better hurry. I**'m supposed to meet** Chris in 10 minutes.

you're **not supposed to** do something 意思是「你未獲允許做某事」或「不建議你去做某事」：

- You**'re not supposed to park** your car here. It's private parking only.
- Mr. Bruno is much better after his operation, but he**'s still not supposed to do** any heavy work.

Exercises

43.1 請參照範例，依各句題意，用畫底線的字以被動句型改寫各句。

1. It is <u>expected</u> that the strike will end soon. The strike _is expected to end soon._
2. It is <u>thought</u> that the prisoner escaped by climbing over a wall.
   The prisoner _is thought to have escaped by climbing over a wall._
3. It is <u>reported</u> that many people are homeless after the floods.
   Many people _____
4. It is <u>alleged</u> that the man robbed the store of $3,000.
   The man _____
5. It is <u>reported</u> that the building was badly damaged by the fire.
   The building _____
6. a) It is <u>said</u> that the company is losing a lot of money.
   The company _____
   b) It is <u>believed</u> that the company lost a lot of money last year.
   The company _____
   c) It is <u>expected</u> that the company will lose money this year.
   The company _____

43.2 下列為關於 Stan 的許多傳説，例如：

1. Stan speaks 10 languages.
2. He knows a lot of famous people.
3. He is very rich.
4. He has 12 children.
5. He was an actor when he was younger.

Stan

沒有人確知這些傳説是真是假；請以 ***supposed to*** 改寫以上的傳説。

1. _Stan is supposed to speak 10 languages._
2. He _____
3. _____
4. _____
5. _____

43.3 依各句題意，從下列詞語中選出適當者，配合 ***supposed to be*** 完成各句。

on a diet   a flower   my friend   a joke   ~~on vacation~~   working

1. What are you doing at work? You _are supposed to be on vacation._
2. You shouldn't criticize me all the time. You _____
3. I really shouldn't be eating this cake. I _____
4. I'm sorry about what I said. I was trying to be funny. It _____
5. What's this drawing? Is it a tree? Or maybe it _____
6. You shouldn't be reading the paper now. You _____

43.4 依各句題意，從下列動詞中選出一個適當的字，以 ***supposed to*** 完成句子。

arrive   block   call   ~~park~~   start

注意有些句子為否定意思，必須用 ***not supposed to***，例如第一題。

1. You _'re not supposed to park_ here. It's private parking only.
2. We _____ work at 8:15, but we rarely do anything before 8:30.
3. Oh, I _____ Helen, but I completely forgot.
4. This door is a fire exit. You _____ it.
5. My train _____ at 11:30, but it was an hour late.

have / get something done

請看下面的範例：

Lisa

Lisa 房子的屋頂在暴風雨中壞了，昨天有一位工人來修理屋頂。

Lisa **had** the roof **repaired** yesterday.
Lisa 昨天請人修了屋頂。

這句話的意思是 Lisa 安排了某人修屋頂，不是她自己修的。

have something done 表示我們安排某人為我們做某事。比較下面例子：
- Lisa **repaired** the roof. (Lisa 自己修的。)
  Lisa **had** the roof **repaired**. (Lisa 安排別人修的。)
- "Did you **paint** your apartment yourself?"　"Yes, I like doing things like that."
  "Did you **have** your apartment **painted**?"　"No, I painted it myself."

注意此句型中，受詞與過去分詞(**repaired/cut** 等)的位置與順序：

have	受詞	過去分詞
Lisa **had**	the roof	**repaired** yesterday.
Where did you **have**	your hair	**cut**?
Our neighbor has just **had**	air conditioning	**installed** in her house.
We are **having**	the house	**painted** this week.
How often do you **have**	your car	**serviced**?
Why don't you **have**	that coat	**cleaned**?
I don't like **having**	my picture	**taken**.

get something done

have something done 也可以用 **get** something done 來表示。**get** something done 通常用於非正式的口語中：
- When are you going to **get the roof repaired**? (= have the roof repaired)
- I think you should **get your hair cut** really short.

have something done 還有不同的意思，例如：
- Eric **had his license taken away** for driving too fast again and again.
  或　Eric **got his license taken away** for driving ...

上面例句的意思當然不是 Eric 安排某人把他的駕照拿走，而是他的駕照被警察拿走了。

have something done 在這種用法中表示，某人或他擁有的物品發生了不好的事：
- James **got** his passport **stolen**. (= his passport was stolen)
- Have you ever **had** your flight **canceled**? (= has your flight ever been canceled?)

Exercises

44.1 請依各圖片中的情境，在 a 與 b 句中，選出符合該圖片的句子。

1.	2.	3.	4.

Sarah	Bill	John	Sue

1.
a) Sarah is cutting her hair.
b) Sarah is having her hair cut.

2.
a) Bill is cutting his hair.
b) Bill is having his hair cut.

3.
a) John is shining his shoes.
b) John is having his shoes shined.

4.
a) Sue is taking a picture.
b) Sue is having her picture taken.

44.2 依各句題意，從下列動詞中選出適當者，以 ***To have something done*** 的句型完成句子。

~~my car~~   my eyes   my jacket   my watch   clean   repair   ~~service~~   test

1. Why did you go to the garage? _*To have my car serviced.*_
2. Why did you go to the cleaner's? To _____
3. Why did you go to the jeweler's? _____
4. Why did you go to the optician's? _____

44.3 請參照範例，依各句題意改寫句子。

1. Lisa didn't repair the roof herself. _*She had it repaired.*_
2. I didn't cut my hair myself. I _____
3. They didn't paint the house themselves. They _____
4. John didn't build that wall himself. _____
5. I didn't deliver the flowers myself. _____

44.4 依各句題意，用括號中的字，以 ***have something done*** 的句型完成句子。

1. We _*are having the house painted*_ (the house / paint) this week.
2. I lost my key. I'll have to _____ (another key / make).
3. When was the last time you _____ (your hair / cut)?
4. _____ (you / a newspaper / deliver) to your house every day, or do you go out and buy one?
5. *A:* What are those workers doing at your house?
   B: Oh, we _____ (garage / build).
6. You can't see that sign from here? You should _____ (your eyes / check).

以下各句請以 ***get something done*** 的句型完成句子。

7. How often _*do you get your car serviced*_ (your car / service)?
8. This coat is dirty. I should _____ (it / clean).
9. If you want to wear earrings, why don't you _____ (your ears / pierce)?
10. *A:* I heard your computer wasn't working.
    B: That's right, but it's OK now. I _____ (it / repair).

以下各句請以 ***have something done*** 的第二義 (參見D小節) 完成句子。

11. Did you hear about Pete? _*He had his license taken away*_ (license / take away).
12. Did I tell you about Jane? She _____ (her purse / steal) last week.
13. Gary was in a fight last night. _____ (his nose / break).

間接敘述 1 (He said that . . .)

請看下面的範例：

I'm feeling sick.

Tom

要把 Tom 話轉述給某人聽時，有以下兩種方式：

一是重述 Tom 的話(直接敘述)：
Tom said, **"I'm feeling sick."**

另一種則是間接敘述：
Tom said **that he was feeling sick.**

比較直接敘述與間接敘述之不同：

| 直接敘述： | Tom said, " I am feeling sick." |

| 間接敘述： | Tom said that **he was** feeling sick. |

在書寫形式中，引號
用於表示直接敘述。

使用間接敘述時，主要子句的動詞通常是過去式動詞 (例如 Tom **said** that . . . / I **told** her that . . .
等)，間接敘述的部分也是過去式：

- Tom **said** that he **was feeling** sick.
- I **told** her that I **didn't have** any money.

間接敘述子句前的 that 可以省略：

- Tom **said that** he was feeling sick. 或 Tom **said** he was feeling sick.

直接敘述中的現在式，在間接敘述中通常必須改為過去式：

am/is → **was**	do/does → **did**	will → **would**
are → **were**	have/has → **had**	can → **could**
want/know/go, etc. → **wanted/knew/went**, etc.		

比較下面直接敘述與間接敘述的用法：

你遇到 Jenny。下面是以直接敘述的方式
表示她所說的話：

Jenny

"My parents **are** fine."

"I**'m** going to learn to drive."

"I **want** to buy a car."

"John **has quit** his job."

"I **can't** come to the
party on Friday."

"I **don't** have much free time."

"I**'m** going away for a few days.
I**'ll** call you when I **get** back."

稍後，你以間接敘述的方式，告訴別人 Jenny 說
了什麼：

- Jenny said that her parents **were** fine.
- She said that she **was** going to learn to drive.
- She said that she **wanted** to buy a car.
- She said that John **had quit** his job.
- She said that she **couldn't** come to the
  party on Friday.
- She said she **didn't** have much free time.
- She said that she **was** going away for a few
  days and **would** call me when she **got** back.

直接敘述中的過去式(**did/saw/knew** 等)在間接敘述中仍然可以是過去式，或者也可以改為
過去完成式(例如 **had done** / **had seen** / **had known** 等)：

- 直接敘述: Tom said, "I **woke** up feeling sick, so I **didn't go** to work."
  間接敘述: Tom said (that) he **woke** up feeling sick, so he **didn't go** to work. 或
  Tom said (that) he **had woken** up feeling sick, so he **hadn't gone** to work.

Exercises

45.1 昨天你遇到好久不見的朋友 Rob.，以下是他對你所説的話：

1. I'm living in my own apartment now.

2. My father isn't very well.

3. Amanda and Paul are getting married next month.

4. My sister has had a baby.

5. I don't know what Eric is doing.

6. I saw Nicole at a party in June, and she seemed fine.

7. I haven't seen Diane recently.

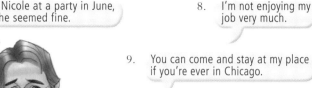

Rob

8. I'm not enjoying my job very much.

9. You can come and stay at my place if you're ever in Chicago.

10. My car was stolen a few days ago.

11. I want to take a trip, but I can't afford it.

12. I'll tell Amy I saw you.

請以間接敍述的方式，把 **Rob** 所説的話告訴你的另一個朋友。

1. _Rob said that he was living in his own apartment now._
2. He said that _____
3. He _____
4. _____
5. _____
6. _____
7. _____
8. _____
9. _____
10. _____
11. _____
12. _____

45.2 在下面各題的對話中，**A** 句是你的朋友對你所説的話，但是內容與他們之前對你所説的不同。請依各句題意完成 **B** 的答句。

1. *A:* That restaurant is expensive.
   B: It is? _I thought you said it was cheap_ .
2. *A:* Sue is coming to the party tonight.
   B: She is? I thought you said she _____ .
3. *A:* Ann likes Paul.
   B: She does? Last week you said _____ .
4. *A:* I know lots of people.
   B: You do? I thought you said _____ .
5. *A:* Pat will be here next week.
   B: She will? But didn't you say _____ ?
6. *A:* I'm going out tonight.
   B: You are? But you said _____ .
7. *A:* I can speak a little French.
   B: You can? But earlier you said _____ .
8. *A:* I haven't been to the movies in ages.
   B: You haven't? I thought you said _____ .

間接敘述 2

A

將直接敘述改為間接敘述時，動詞時式不一定需要改變。假如所轉述的話之內容還是真的，
並未改變，那麼就不需要改變動詞的時式：

- 直接敘述：Tom said, "My new job **is** very interesting."
  間接敘述：Tom said that his new job **is** very interesting.
  　　　　　(Tom 的工作很有趣，這個情形並未改變。)

- 直接敘述：Ann said, "**I want** to go to South America next year."
  間接敘述：Ann told me that **she wants** to go to South America next year.
  　　　　　(Ann 明年仍然想去南美洲。)

上述例句中，也可以將動詞時式改為過去式：

- Tom said that his new job **was** very interesting.
- Ann told me that she **wanted** to go to South America next year.

但是，當敘述的事件或狀態已經結束，則必須使用過去式。

- Paul left the room suddenly. He said **he had** to go. (並非 has to go)

B

然而當轉述的內容與事實不符時，則必須將時式改為過去式。請看下面的範例：

你幾天前遇見 Sonia，她說："**Joe is in the hospital**" (Joe 生病了。) (直接敘述)

當天稍晚你在街上見到 Joe。你說：
"I didn't expect to see you, Joe. Sonia said you **were** in the hospital." (並非 Sonia said you are in the hospital，因為很顯然的 Joe 並不在醫院裡。)

Joe is in the hospital.

Sonia said you **were** in the hospital.

Sonia　　Joe

C

say 與 **tell**

tell 用於有聽話者的情形，表示對某人說話：

- Sonia **told me** that you were in the hospital. (並非 Sonia said me)
- What did you **tell the police**? (並非 say the police)

TELL <u>SOMEBODY</u>

say 則用於其他的情況：

- Sonia **said** that you were in the hospital. (並非 Sonia told that . . .)
- What did you **say**?

SAY ~~SOMEBODY~~

say 也可以用於有聽話者的情形，句型為 **say** something **to** somebody：

- Ann **said** goodbye **to** me and left. (並非 Ann said me good-bye)
- What did you **say to** the police?

D

tell/ask somebody **to** do something

間接敘述中也可以使用不定詞 (**to do** / **to stay** 等)，特別是當 **tell** 和 **ask** 的意思是命令或
要求時：

- 直接敘述："**Stay** in bed for a few days," the doctor said to me.
  間接敘述：The doctor **told me to** stay in bed for a few days.
- 直接敘述："**Don't shout**," I said to Jim.
  間接敘述：I **told** Jim **not to** shout.
- 直接敘述："Please **don't tell** anybody what happened," Jackie said to me.
  間接敘述：Jackie **asked me not to tell** anybody what (had) happened.

也可以使用 Somebody **said** (not) **to** do something 之句型：

- Jackie **said** not **to tell** anyone. (並非 Jackie said me)

Exercises

46.1 以下是 Ann 對你所說的話：

I've never been to South America.

I don't have any brothers or sisters.

I can't drive.

I don't like fish.

Rosa has a very well-paid job.

I'm working tomorrow night.

Rosa is a friend of mine.

~~Dave is lazy.~~

Ann

但是稍後 Ann 對你所說的話與之前所說的不同。請參照範例，依各句題意完成你和 Ann 的對話。

	Ann	**You**
1.	Dave works very hard.	_But you said he was lazy._
2.	Let's have fish for dinner.	But _____
3.	I'm going to buy a car.	_____
4.	Rosa is always short of money.	_____
5.	My sister lives in Tokyo.	_____
6.	I think Peru is a great place.	_____
7.	Let's go out tomorrow night.	_____
8.	I've never spoken to Rosa.	_____

46.2 依各句題意，將 *say* 或 *tell* 以適當的時式填入。每題限填一個字。

1. Ann _said_ goodbye to me and left.
2. _____ us about your vacation. Did you have a good time?
3. Don't just stand there! _____ something!
4. I wonder where Sue is. She _____ she would be here at 8:00.
5. Jack _____ me that he was fed up with his job.
6. The doctor _____ that I should rest for at least a week.
7. Don't _____ anybody what I _____ . It's a secret just between us.
8. "Did she _____ you what happened?" "No, she didn't _____ anything to me."
9. Jason couldn't help me. He _____ me to ask Kate.
10. Gary couldn't help me. He _____ to ask Caroline.

46.3 下列各句是以直接敘述陳述的句子：

Don't wait for me if I'm late.

Mind your own business.

Don't worry, Sue.

Can you open your bag, please?

~~Hurry up!~~

Please slow down!

Will you marry me?

Do you think you could give me a hand, Tom?

依各句題意，從上述的直接敘述中選出適當者，並以間接敘述的方式，完成句子。

1. Bill was taking a long time to get ready, so I told _him to hurry up_ .
2. Sarah was driving too fast, so I asked _____ .
3. Sue was nervous about the situation. I told _____ .
4. I couldn't move the piano alone, so I _____ .
5. The customs officer looked at me suspiciously and _____ .
6. The man started asking me personal questions, so I _____ .
7. John was in love with Maria, so he _____ .
8. I didn't want to delay Helen, so I _____ .

問句 1

A

在問句中，助動詞必須置於主詞之前：

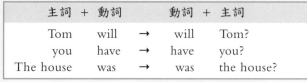

主詞 + 動詞			動詞 + 主詞	
Tom	will	→	will	Tom?
you	have	→	have	you?
The house	was	→	was	the house?

- **Will Tom** be here tomorrow?
- **Have you** been working hard?
- When **was the house** built?

記得，主詞必須置於助動詞或 be 動詞之後：
- **Is Catherine** working today? (並非 Is working Catherine)

B

do/does 用於現在簡單式的問句：

you	live	→	**do**	you live?
the film	begins	→	**does**	the film begin?

- **Do** you **live** near here?
- What time **does** the film **begin**?

did 用於過去簡單式的問句：

you	sold	→	**did**	you sell?
the train	stopped	→	**did**	the train stop?

- **Did** you **sell** your car?
- Why **did** the train **stop**?

若 **who/what** 為問句的主詞，則不用助動詞 **do/does/did**。比較下面例句：

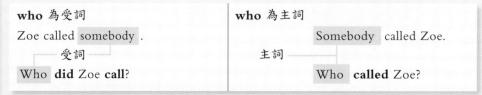

who 為受詞	**who** 為主詞
Zoe called somebody .	Somebody called Zoe.
受詞	主詞
Who **did** Zoe **call**?	Who **called** Zoe?

下面例句中，**who/what** 等為問句的主詞：
- **Who wants** something to eat? (並非 Who does want)
- **What happened** to you last night? (並非 What did happen)
- **How many people came** to the meeting? (並非 did come)
- **Which bus goes** downtown? (並非 does go)

C

注意下面以 **Who / What / Which / Where** 為首的問句中，介係詞出現的位置：
- **Who** do you want to speak **to**?
- **What** was the weather **like** yesterday?
- **Which** job has Ann applied **for**?
- **Where** are you **from**?

在較正式的用法中，可以使用介係詞 + **whom** 的句型：
- **To whom** do you wish to speak?

D

Isn't it . . . ? / **Didn't you . . . ?** 等 (否定問句)

否定問句常用於表示驚訝：
- **Didn't you** hear the doorbell? I rang it three times.

否定問句也用於表示期待聽話者同意我們的意見：
- "**Haven't we** met somewhere before?" "Yes, I think we have."

注意否定問句的回答中，**yes** 與 **no** 所代表的意義：
- **Don't you** want to go to the party?
  - **Yes.** (= Yes, I want to go)
  - **No.** (= No, I don't want to go)

注意以 **Why . . .** 為句首的問句中，否定助動詞出現的位置：
- **Why don't we** go out for a meal tonight? (並非 Why we don't go)
- **Why wasn't Mary** at work yesterday? (並非 Why Mary wasn't)

問句 2 Unit 48　附加問句 (. . . , do you? . . . , isn't it? 等) Unit 50

Exercises

47.1 請參照範例，根據 Joe 的回答，寫出問句。

1. (where / live?) _Where do you live?_ In Vancouver.
2. (born there?) _____ No, I was born in Toronto.
3. (married?) _____ Yes.
4. (how long / married?) _____ 17 years.
   _____
5. (children?) _____ Yes, two boys.
   _____
6. (how old / they?) _____ 12 and 15.
7. (what / do?) _____ I'm a journalist.
8. (what / wife / do?)_____ She's a doctor.

Joe

47.2 請參照範例，依各句題意，以 **who** 或 **what** 寫出問句。

1. Somebody hit me. _Who hit you?_
2. I hit somebody. _Who did you hit?_
3. Somebody paid the bill. Who _____
4. Something happened. What _____
5. Diane said something. _____
6. This book belongs to somebody. _____
7. Somebody lives in that house. _____
8. I fell over something. _____
9. Something fell on the floor. _____
10. This word means something. _____
11. I borrowed the money from somebody. _____
12. I'm worried about something. _____

47.3 請參照範例，用各題括號中的語詞，完成問句。

1. (when / was / built / this house) _When was this house built?_
2. (how / cheese / is / made) _____
3. (when / invented / the computer / was) _____
4. (why / Sue / working / isn't / today) _____
5. (what time / coming / your friends / are) _____
6. (why / was / canceled / the concert) _____
7. (where / your mother / was / born) _____
8. (why / you / to the party / didn't / come) _____
9. (how / the accident / did / happen) _____
10. (why / this machine / doesn't / work) _____

47.4 請依各題的對話內容，用括號中的語詞，完成表示驚訝的否定問句。

1. *A:* We won't see Ann tonight.
   B: Why not? (she / not / come / to the party?) _Isn't she coming to the party?_
2. *A:* I hope we don't see Brian tonight.
   B: Why? (you / not / like / him?) _____
3. *A:* Don't go and see that movie.
   B: Why not? (it / not / good?) _____
4. *A:* I'll have to borrow some money.
   B: Why? (you / not / have / any?) _____

問句 2 (Do you know where . . . ? / He asked me where . . .)

A

Do you know where . . . ? / I don't know why . . . / Could you tell me what . . . ?, etc.

我們說：　　　　　Where **has Tom** gone?

但是　　**Do you know** where **Tom has** gone? (並非 Do you know where has Tom gone?)

當問句(例如 **Where has Tom gone?**)為另一個句子的一部分時(例如 **Do you know . . . ? / I don't know . . . / Can you tell me . . . ?** 等)，主詞與動詞的順序必須改變。比較下面例句：

- What time **is it**?
- Who **are those people**?
- Where **can I** find Linda?
- How much **will it** cost?

但是 **Do you know** what time **it is**?
I don't know who **those people are**.
Can you tell me where **I can** find Linda?
Do you have any idea how much **it will** cost?

注意問句中有 **do/does/did** (現在簡單式與過去簡單式)等助動詞時，必須依下面的方式改變原問句：

- What **time does the movie begin**?

- What **do you mean**?
- Why **did she leave** early?

但是 **Do you know** what time **the movie begins**?
(並非 does the movie begin)
Please explain what **you mean**.
I wonder why **she left** early.

沒有疑問詞(**what**、**why** 等)的問句成為另一個句子的一部分時，前面需加上 **if** 或 **whether**：

- Did anybody see you?

但是 Do you know **if** anybody saw you?
或 . . . **whether** anybody saw you?

B

He asked me where . . . (轉述問句)

上述改變問句的方法，於轉述問句時也同樣適用。比較下面例句：

- 直接敘述：The police officer said to us, "Where **are you going** ?"

  間接敘述：The police officer asked us where **we were going** .

- 直接敘述：Claire asked, "What time **do the banks close** ?"

  間接敘述：Claire wanted to know what time **the banks closed** .

在轉述問句時，問句中的動詞通常會改為過去式(**were**, **closed** 等)。參見 Unit 45。

請看下面例子。你去參加工作面談，以下是訪談者對你所提的一些問題：

What **do you** do in your spare time?

Can you speak another language?

Are you willing to travel?

Why **did you** apply for the job?

How long **have you** been working at your present job?

Do you have a driver's license?

稍後你以間接敘述的方式，將以上的問題轉述給你的朋友聽：

- She asked if (或 whether) **I was** willing to travel.
- She wanted to know what **I did** in my spare time.
- She asked how long **I had** been working at my present job.
- She asked why **I had** applied for the job. (或 . . . why **I applied**)
- She wanted to know if (或 whether) **I could** speak another language.
- She asked if (或 whether) **I had** a driver's license.

間接敘述 Unit 45 與 Unit 46

Exercises

48.1 請參照範例，改寫下列各題括號中的問句。

1. (Where has Tom gone?) Do you know _____where Tom has gone?_____
2. (Where is the post office?) Could you tell me _____
3. (What time is it?) I wonder _____
4. (What does this word mean?) I want to know _____
5. (Has the plane left yet?) Do you know _____
6. (Is Sue going out tonight?) I don't know _____
7. (Where does Carol live?) Do you have any idea _____
8. (Where did I park the car?) I can't remember _____
9. (Is there a bank near here?) Can you tell me _____
10. (What do you want?) Tell me _____
11. (Why didn't Kelly come to the party?) I don't know _____
12. (How much does it cost to park here?) Do you know _____
13. (Who is that woman?) I have no idea _____
14. (Did Ann get my letter?) Do you know _____
15. (How far is it to the airport?) Can you tell me _____

48.2 你打電話給 Amy，可是她不在家；請以問句詢問以下三件事情：(1) Amy 在哪裡？(2) 她什麼時候回來？(3) 她是單獨外出嗎？

(1) Where is Amy? (2) When will she be back? and **(3) Did she go out alone?**

完成下面的對話。

A: Do you know where _____ ? (1)
B: Sorry, I have no idea.
A: That's all right. I don't suppose you know _____ . (2)
B: No, I'm afraid I don't.
A: One more thing. Do you happen to know _____ ? (3)
B: I'm sorry. I didn't see her go out. But I'll tell her you called.

48.3 你離開家有一段時間了，才剛回到家中。你遇見了你的朋友 Tony，他問了你以下的問題。

1. How are you?
2. Where have you been?
3. How long have you been back?
4. What are you doing now?
5. Why did you come back?
6. Where are you living?
7. Are you glad to be back?
8. Do you plan to stay for a while?
9. Can you lend me some money?

Tony

請以間接敘述的方式，將 Tony 問你的問題轉述給另一個朋友聽。

1. _____He asked me how I was._____
2. He asked me _____
3. He _____
4. _____
5. _____
6. _____
7. _____
8. _____
9. _____

助動詞 (have / do / can 等)
I think so / I hope so 等

下面例句中的動詞都是由助動詞與主要動詞兩個部份所組成：

I	**have**	**lost**	my keys.
She	**can't**	**come**	to the party.
The hotel	**was**	**built**	ten years ago.
Where	**do** you	**live**?	

這些例句中，動詞的第一個部份 **have** / **can't** / **was** / **do** 為助動詞。

要避免重複時可省略動詞，只用助動詞表示：

- "Have you locked the door?" "Yes, I **have**." (= I have *locked the door*)
- George wasn't working, but Janet **was**. (= Janet was *working*)
- She could lend me the money, but she **won't**. (= she won't *lend me the money*)

現在簡單式的助動詞為 **do/does**；過去簡單式的助動詞為 **did**：

- "Do you like onions?" "Yes, I **do**." (= I *like onions*)
- "Does Mark play soccer?" "He **did**, but he **doesn't** any more."

助動詞可以用於反駁他人所說的話：

- "You're sitting in my place." "No, I**'m not**." (= I'm not *sitting in your place*)
- "You didn't lock the door before you left." "Yes, I **did**." (= I *locked the door*)

You have? / **She isn't?** / **They do?** 等，可用於禮貌性表示對他人所說的話感興趣：

- "I've just seen David." "**You have**? How is he?"
- "Liz isn't feeling very well today." "**She isn't**? What's wrong with her?"
- "It rained every day during our vacation." "**It did**? What a shame!"
- "Jim and Karen are getting married." "**They are**? Really?"

助動詞與 **so** 和 **neither** 可以一起使用：

- "I'm tired." "**So am I**." (= I'm tired, too)
- "I never read newspapers." "**Neither do I**." (= I never read newspapers either)
- Sue doesn't have a car, and **neither does Mark**.

注意在 **so** 和 **neither** 後，助動詞須出現於主詞之前：

- I passed the exam, and **so did Paul**. （並非 so Paul did）

也可以使用 **not . . . either**，意思與 **neither** 相同：

- "I don't have any money." "**Neither do I**." 或 "I **don't either**."

I think so / **I hope so** 等

有些動詞後可以使用 **so**，以省略不需重覆的部份：

- "Are those people Australian?" "**I think so**." (= I think they are Australian)
- "Will you be home tomorrow morning?" "**I guess so**." (= I guess I'll be home . . .)
- "Do you think Kate has been invited to the party?" "**I suppose so**."

除上述例子外，還可以用 **I hope so** 和 **I'm afraid so**。

上述句型的否定形式如下：

I think so	→	**I don't think so**
I hope so / I'm afraid so / I guess so	→	**I hope not / I'm afraid not / I guess not**
I suppose so	→	**I suppose not**

- "Is that woman French?" "**I think so. / I don't think so.**"
- "Do you think it will rain?" "**I hope so. / I hope not.**" （並非 I don't hope so）

Exercises

49.1 依各句題意，以助動詞 (**do / was / could / should** 等) 完成句子。注意，因語意需求，有些句子需使用否定形式 (**don't/wasn't** 等)。

1. I wasn't tired, but my friends ___were___ .
2. I like hot weather, but Ann _____ .
3. "Is Eric here?" "He _____ five minutes ago, but I think he's gone."
4. Liz said she might call later on tonight, but I don't think she _____ .
5. "Are you and Chris coming to the party?" "I _____ , but Chris _____ ."
6. I don't know whether to apply for the job or not. Do you think I _____ ?
7. "Please don't tell anybody what I said." "Don't worry. I _____ ."
8. "You never listen to me." "Yes, I _____ !"
9. "Can you play a musical instrument?" "No, but I wish I _____ ."
10. "Please help me." "I'm sorry. I _____ if I _____ , but I _____ ."

49.2 請依第 1、2 題的回答方式，表達你不同意 Alex 所說的話。

1. I'm hungry.
2. I'm not tired.
3. I like baseball.
4. I didn't like the movie.
5. I've never been to South America.
6. I thought the exam was easy.

Alex

You are? I'm not.
You aren't? I am.
_____
_____
_____
_____

You

49.3 請依第 1 題的回答方式，以 **So . . .** 或 **Neither . . .** 表達你和 Lisa 的情形相同；或依第 2 題的回答方式，表達你的情形不同於 Lisa。

1. I feel really tired.
2. I'm working hard.
3. I watched TV last night.
4. I won't be at home tomorrow.
5. I like to read. I read a lot.
6. I'd like to live somewhere else.
7. I can't go out tonight.

Lisa

_So do I._
You are? What are you doing?
_____
_____
_____
_____

You

49.4 請參照各題的對話內容，根據括號中提示的字，以 **I think so**、**I hope so** 等完成對話。

1. (You don't like rain.)
   A: Is it going to rain?   B: (hope) ___I hope not._____
2. (You're not sure Sarah will get the job she applied for, but her chances look pretty good.)
   A: Do you think Sarah will get the job?   B: (guess) _____
3. (You're not sure whether Amy is married – probably not.)
   A: Is Amy married?   B: (think) _____
4. (You need more money quickly.)
   A: Do you think you'll get a raise soon?   B: (hope) _____
5. (You're a hotel desk clerk. The hotel is full.)
   A: Do you have a room for tonight?   B: (afraid) _____
6. (You're at a party. You have to leave early.)
   A: Do you have to leave already?   B: (afraid) _____
7. (You are going to a party. You can't stand John.)
   A: Do you think John will be at the party?   B: (hope) _____
8. (You're not sure what time the concert is – probably 7:30.)
   A: Is the concert at 7:30?   B: (think) _____
9. (Ann normally works every day, Monday to Friday. Tomorrow is Wednesday.)
   A: Is Ann working tomorrow?   B: (suppose) _____

附加問句 (do you? / isn't it? 等)

A

請看下面的範例：

You haven't seen Maria today, **have you**?
你今天還沒見到 Maria，是嗎？

No, I haven't.
沒有，我還沒。

It was a good movie, **wasn't it**?
這部電影很棒，不是嗎？

Yes, I loved it.
是啊！我很喜歡。

上述例句中的 **have you?** 與 **wasn't it?** 為附加問句。附加問句為迷你問句，經常於口語當中使用於句尾。附加問句中必須使用助動詞(**have/was/will** 等)。

現在簡單式使用助動詞 **do/does**；過去簡單式則使用助動詞 **did**(參見 Unit 49)：

■ "Lauren plays the piano, **doesn't she**?" "Well, yes, but not very well."
■ "You didn't lock the door, **did you**?" "No, I forgot."

B

通常肯定句後使用否定的附加問句：

肯定句＋否定附加問句
Maria **will** be here soon, **won't she**?
There **was** a lot of traffic, **wasn't there**?
Jim **should** take his medicine, **shouldn't he**?

否定句後使用肯定的附加問句：

否定句＋肯定附加問句
Kate **won't** be late, **will she**?
They **don't** like us, **do they**?
You **haven't** paid the gas bill, **have you**?

注意否定問句的回答中，**yes** 與 **no** 所表示的意思：

■ You're **not** going out today, **are you**?
  Yes. (= Yes, I am going out)
  No. (= No, I am not going out)

C

附加問句的意思是由語調來決定。當語調下降時，並非真正的問句，目的是求得聽話者的同意：

■ "It's a nice day, **isn't it**?" "Yes, beautiful."
■ "Eric doesn't look too good today, **does he**?" "No, he looks very tired."
■ She's very funny. She has a wonderful sense of humor, **doesn't she**?

如果語調上揚，則為真正的問句：

■ "You haven't seen Lisa today, **have you**?" "No, I haven't."
  (= Have you seen Lisa today by any chance?)

否定句＋肯定附加問句，通常用於要求某物、詢問訊息、或者請求某人做某事；此時附加問句的語調需上揚：

■ "You wouldn't have a pen, **would you**?" "Yes, here you are."
■ "You couldn't lend me some money, **could you**?" "It depends how much."
■ "You don't know where Lauren is, **do you**?" "Sorry, I have no idea."

D

Let's . . . ? 句型的附加問句為 **shall we?**：

■ **Let's** go for a walk, **shall we**? (語調上揚)

祈使句(**Do. . . / Listen. . . / Give. . .** 等)的附加問句為 **will you?**

■ **Listen** to me, **will you**? (語調上揚)

注意主詞為 I 時，否定附加問句為 **aren't I?**：

■ "**I'm** right, **aren't I**?" "Yes, you are."

Exercises

50.1 依各句題意，在下列各句中填入適當的附加問句。

1.	Tom won't be late, _will he_?	No, he's never late.
2.	You're tired, _aren't you_?	Yes, a little.
3.	You've lived here a long time, _____?	Yes, 20 years.
4.	You weren't listening, _____?	Yes, I was!
5.	Sue doesn't know Ann, _____?	No, they've never met.
6.	Jack's on vacation, _____?	Yes, he's in Peru.
7.	Mike hasn't called today, _____?	No, I don't think so.
8.	You can speak Spanish, _____?	Yes, but not fluently.
9.	He won't mind if I use his phone, _____?	No, of course he won't.
10.	There are a lot of people here, _____?	Yes, more than I expected.
11.	Let's go out tonight, _____?	Yes, that would be great.
12.	This isn't very interesting, _____?	No, not at all.
13.	I'm too impatient, _____?	Yes, you are sometimes.
14.	You wouldn't tell anyone, _____?	No, of course not.
15.	Listen to me, _____?	OK, I'm listening.
16.	I shouldn't have lost my temper, _____?	No, but that's all right.
17.	He'd never met her before, _____?	No, that was the first time.

50.2 請參照範例，依下列各句題意，寫出包含附加問句的句子，以請求聽話者同意你的意見。

1. You look out of the window. The sky is blue and the sun is shining. What do you say to your friend? (beautiful day) _It's a beautiful day, isn't it?_

2. You're with a friend outside a restaurant. You're looking at the prices, which are very high. What do you say? (expensive) It _____

3. You and a colleague have just finished a training course. You really enjoyed it. What do you say to your colleague? (great) The course _____

4. Your friend's hair is much shorter than when you last met. What do you say to her/him? (have / your hair / cut) You _____

5. You and a friend are listening to a woman singing. You like her voice very much. What do you say to your friend? (a good voice) She _____

6. You are trying on a jacket in a store. You look in the mirror, and you don't like what you see. What do you say to your friend? (not / look / very good) It _____

7. You and a friend are walking over a small wooden bridge. The bridge is very old and some parts are broken. What do you say? (not / very safe) This bridge _____

50.3 請參照範例，依下列各句題意，寫出包含附加問句的句子，以詢問訊息或者請求聽話者做某事。

1. You need a pen. Maybe Kelly has one. Ask her.
   Kelly, you don't have a pen, do you?

2. The cashier is putting your groceries in a plastic bag, but maybe he could give you a paper bag. Ask him.
   Excuse me, you _____

3. You're looking for Ann. Maybe Kate knows where she is. Ask her.
   Kate, you _____

4. You need a bicycle pump. Maybe Nicole has one. Ask her.
   Nicole, _____

5. You're looking for your keys. Maybe Robert has seen them. Ask him.
   Robert, _____

6. Ann has a car and you need a ride to the station. Maybe she'll take you. Ask her.
   Ann, _____

動詞 + -ing (enjoy doing / stop doing 等)

A

請看下面的例句：

- I **enjoy** read**ing**. (並非 I enjoy to read)
- Would you **mind** clos**ing** the door?
  (並非 mind to close)
- Sam **suggested** go**ing** to the movies.
  (並非 suggested to go)

Would you **mind** clos**ing** the door?

上述三個例句中的動詞 **enjoy**、**mind** 和 **suggest**，後面必須接 **-ing** (而非 to . . .)。

其他相同用法的動詞還包括：

stop	postpone	consider	admit
finish	avoid	imagine	deny
quit	risk	miss	recommend

- Suddenly everybody **stopped** talk**ing**. There was silence.
- I'll do the shopping when I've **finished** clean**ing** the apartment.
- He tried to **avoid** answer**ing** my question.
- Have you ever **considered** go**ing** to live in another country?

上述用法的否定形式為 **not -ing**：

- When I'm on vacation, I **enjoy not** hav**ing** to get up early.

B

下列動詞片語後也是接 **-ing**：

give up (= stop)
put off (= postpone)
go on (= continue)
keep 或 **keep on** (= do something continuously or repeatedly)

- Paula has **given up** try**ing** to lose weight.
- Jenny doesn't want to retire. She wants to **go on** work**ing**.
- You **keep** interrupt**ing** when I'm talking! 或 You **keep on** interrupt**ing** . . .

C

有些動詞可以使用 動詞 + 某人 + **-ing** 的句型：

- I can't **imagine George** rid**ing** a motorcycle.
- "Sorry to **keep you** wait**ing** so long." "That's all right."

注意此類句型的被動形式為 being **done/seen/kept** 等：

- I don't **mind being kept** waiting. (= I don't mind **people** keep**ing** me waiting.)

D

表示動作已經完成，可以用 **having done/stolen/said** 等來表示：

- They admitted **having stolen** the money.

但表達動作已經完成並不一定要用 **having done**，也可以只用 **-ing**：

- They admitted **stealing** the money.
- I now regret **saying** (或 **having said**) what I said.

regret 的用法，參見 Unit 54B。

E

本單元所列舉的動詞中，部分動詞(特別是 **admit/deny/suggest**)後面可以接 **that**：

- She **denied that** she had stolen the money. (或 She **denied** stealing . . .)
- Sam **suggested that** we go to the movies. (或 Sam **suggested** going . . .)

suggest Unit 32　*being done* (被動句型) Unit 41B　動詞 + *to* . . . Unit 52
動詞 + *to* . . . 或 *-ing* Unit 53C 與 Unit 54 至 Unit 56　*regret / go on* Unit 54B　*go on / keep on* Unit 138A

51.1 依各句題意，從下列動詞中選出一個適當的字，並將正確的動詞形式填入空格。

~~answer~~	apply	be	forget	listen	pay
lose	make	read	try	use	write

1. He tried to avoid _answering_ my question.
2. Could you please stop _____ so much noise?
3. I enjoy _____ to music.
4. I considered _____ for the job, but in the end I decided against it.
5. Have you finished _____ the newspaper yet?
6. Let's buy a house. I don't want to go on _____ rent every month.
7. I don't mind you _____ the phone as long as you pay for all your calls.
8. My memory is getting worse. I keep _____ things.
9. I've put off _____ the letter so many times. I really have to do it today.
10. What a mean thing to do! Can you imagine anybody _____ so mean?
11. Sarah gave up _____ to find a job in this country and decided to go abroad.
12. If you invest your money in the stock market, you risk _____ it.

51.2 依各題的對話內容，以 *-ing* 的形式完成句子。

1. What should we do? — We could go to the movies.
   She suggested _going to the movies_ .

2. You were driving too fast. — You're right. Sorry!
   She admitted _____ .

3. Let's go swimming. — Good idea!
   She suggested _____ .

4. You broke my DVD player. — No, I didn't!
   He denied _____ .

5. Can you wait a few minutes? — Sure, no problem.
   They didn't mind _____ .

51.3 依各句題意，以 *-ing* 的形式改寫句子。

1. She doesn't really want to retire.
   She wants to go on _working_ .
2. It's not a good idea to travel during rush hour.
   It's better to avoid _____ .
3. Should we leave tomorrow instead of today?
   Should we postpone _____ until _____ ?
4. Could you turn the radio down, please ?
   Would you mind _____ ?
5. Please don't interrupt me all the time.
   Would you mind _____ ?

51.4 依你自己的意思，以 *-ing* 的形式完成句子。

1. She's a very interesting person. I always enjoy _talking to her_ .
2. I'm afraid there aren't any chairs. I hope you don't mind _____ .
3. It was a beautiful day, so I suggested _____ .
4. It was very funny. I couldn't stop _____ .
5. My car isn't very reliable. It keeps _____ .

動詞 + to . . . (decide to . . . / forget to . . . 等)

A

offer	decide	hope	deserve	promise
agree	plan	manage	afford	threaten
refuse	arrange	fail	forget	learn

上述動詞後若接另一動詞，通常使用動詞 + **to** . . . 之不定詞形式：
- It was late, so we **decided to take** a taxi home.
- David was in a difficult situation, so I **agreed to help** him.
- How old were you when you **learned to drive**? (或 learned **how** to drive)
- Karen **failed to make** a good impression at the job interview.

此種用法之否定形式為 **not to** . . . :
- We **decided not to go** out because of the weather.
- I **promised not to be** late.

但是許多動詞後通常不可以使用不定詞 **to** . . . ; 例如 **enjoy/think/suggest** 等：
- I **enjoy** read**ing**. (或 enjoy to read)
- Sam **suggested** go**ing** to the movies. (或 suggested to go)
- Are you **thinking of** buy**ing** a car? (或 thinking to buy)

動詞 + **-ing** 之用法，參見 Unit 51；動詞 + 介係詞 + **-ing** 之用法，參見 Unit 60。

B

下列動詞後也必須使用 **to** . . .(不定詞)：

seem	appear	tend	pretend	claim

請看下面的例句：
- They **seem to have** plenty of money.
- I like Dan, but I think he **tends to talk** too much.
- Ann **pretended not to see** me when she passed me on the street.

不定詞也有進行式不定詞(**to be** doing)與完成式不定詞(**to have** done)：
- I **pretended to be** read**ing** the newspaper. (= I pretended that I **was** read**ing**)
- You **seem to have lost** weight. (= it seems that you **have lost** weight)
- Joe **seems to be** enjoy**ing** his new job. (= it seems that he **is** enjoy**ing** it)

C

dare 後所接的動詞可以使用動詞原型或不定詞 **to** . . . :
- I wouldn't **dare to tell** him. 或 I wouldn't **dare tell** him.

D

下面動詞後可以接疑問詞 (**what/whether/how** 等) + **to** . . . :

ask	decide	know	remember	forget
learn	understand	wonder	explain	

We **asked**	how	to get	to the station.
Have you **decided**	where	to go	for your vacation?
I don't **know**	whether	to apply	for the job or not.
Do you **understand**	what	to do?	

show / **tell** / **ask** / **advise** / **teach** 可以使用動詞 + 某人 + **what/how/where** + to do 某事
之句型：
- Can somebody **show me how to change** the film in this camera?
- Ask Jack. He'll **tell you what to do**.

動詞 + -ing Unit 51　動詞 + 受詞 + to . . . (want 等) Unit 53　動詞 + to . . . 或 -ing Unit 54 至 Unit 56

Exercises

52.1 請參照範例，依各題的對話內容，以 **to . . .** 的形式完成句子。

1. Should we get married? — Yes. | They decided _to get married_ .

2. Please help me. — OK. | She agreed _____ .

3. Can I carry your bags for you? — No, thanks. I can manage. | He offered _____ .

4. Let's meet at 8:00. — OK, fine. | They arranged _____ .

5. What's your name? — I'm not going to tell you. | She refused _____ .

6. Please don't tell anyone. — I won't. I promise. | She promised _____ .

52.2 依各句題意，以 **to . . .** 或 **-ing** 的形式完成句子 (動詞 + **ing** 之用法，參見 Unit 51)。

1. When I'm tired, I enjoy _watching_ television. It's relaxing. (watch)
2. It was a nice day, so we decided _____ for a walk. (go)
3. There was a lot of traffic, but we managed _____ to the airport on time. (get)
4. I'm not in a hurry. I don't mind _____ . (wait)
5. They don't have much money. They can't afford _____ out very often. (eat)
6. We've got new computer software in our office. I haven't learned _____ it yet. (use)
7. I wish that dog would stop _____ . It's driving me crazy. (bark)
8. Our neighbor threatened _____ the police if we didn't stop the noise. (call)
9. We were hungry, so I suggested _____ dinner early. (have)
10. We were all afraid to speak. Nobody dared _____ anything. (say)
11. Hurry up! I don't want to risk _____ the train. (miss)
12. I'm still looking for a job, but I hope _____ something soon. (find)

52.3 依各句題意，用括號中的字完成句子。

1. You've lost weight. (seem) _You seem to have lost weight._
2. Tom is worried about something. (appear) Tom appears _____
3. You know a lot of people. (seem) You _____
4. My English is getting better. (seem) _____
5. That car has broken down. (appear) _____
6. David forgets things. (tend) _____
7. They have solved the problem. (claim) _____

52.4 依各句題意，從下列動詞中選出一個適當的字，並以 **what/how/whether + to . . .** 的形式完成句子。

do ~~get~~ **go** **ride** **say** **use**

1. Do you know _how to get_ to John's house?
2. Can you show me _____ this washing machine?
3. Would you know _____ if there was a fire in the building?
4. You'll never forget _____ a bicycle once you've learned.
5. I was really astonished. I didn't know _____ .
6. I was invited to the party, but I haven't decided _____ or not.

動詞 +（受詞）+ to . . .
(I want you to . . . 等)

A

want	ask	help	expect
beg	would like	would prefer	mean (= intend)

上述動詞後必須接不定詞 **to** . . .。句型有下列兩種：

動詞 + **to** . . .　　　　　　　　　或　　　動詞 + 受詞 + **to** . . .

- We **expected to be** late.
- **Would** you **like to go** now?
- He doesn't **want to know**.

- We expected **Dan to be** late.
- Would you like **me to go** now?
- He doesn't want **anybody to know**.

注意，want 後面不可以接 that 子句：

- Do you **want me to come** with you? (並非 Do you want that I come)

help 後面可以接動詞原型或不定詞 **to** . . .：

- Can you help me **to move** this table? 或 Can you help me **move** this table?

B

tell	remind	force	encourage	teach	enable
order	warn	invite	persuade	get (= persuade, arrange for)	

上述動詞使用的句型為動詞 + 受詞 + **to** . . .：

- Can you **remind me to call** Ann tomorrow?
- Who **taught you to drive**?
- I didn't move the piano by myself. I **got somebody to help** me.
- Jim said the switch was dangerous and **warned me not to touch** it.

下面例句中的動詞為被動句型(**I was warned / we were told** 等)：

- **I was warned not to touch** the switch.

suggest 不可以使用動詞 + 受詞 + **to** . . . 之句型：

- Jane **suggested that I ask** you for advice. (並非 Jane suggested me to ask)

C　　**advise** 與 **allow** 可以使用下面兩種句型：

動詞 + **-ing** (沒有受詞)

- I wouldn't **advise** stay**ing** in that hotel.

- They don't **allow** park**ing** in front of the building.

請比較上面例句之被動句型：

- Park**ing** isn't **allowed** in front of the building.

動詞+受詞 + **to** . . .

- I wouldn't **advise anybody to stay** in that hotel.
- They don't **allow people to park** in front of the building.

- You **aren't allowed to park** in front of the building.

D　　**make** 與 **let**

make 與 **let** 使用的句型為動詞+受詞+動詞原型(**do/open/feel** 等)：

- I **made him promise** that he wouldn't tell anybody what happened. (並非 to promise)
- Hot weather **makes me feel** tired. (= causes me to feel tired)
- Her parents wouldn't **let her go** out alone. (= wouldn't allow her to go out)
- **Let me carry** your bag for you.

上述 **make somebody do** . . . 句型的被動句型為 (**be) made to** do . . .：

- We **were made to wait** for two hours. (= They **made us wait** . . .)

---

suggest Unit 32 與 Unit 51　*tell/ask somebody to* . . . Unit 46D　動詞 + *-ing* Unit 51　動詞 + *to* . . . Unit 52
動詞 + *to* . . . 或動詞 + *ing* Unit 54 至 Unit 56　*help* Unit 55C

Exercises

53.1 依各句題意，從下列動詞中選出一個適當的字，以 ***do you want me to . . . ?*** 或 ***would you like me to . . . ?*** 的句型完成句子。

~~come~~   lend   repeat   show   shut   wait

1. Do you want to go alone, or _do you want me to come with you_____ ?
2. Do you have enough money, or do you want _____ ?
3. Should I leave the window open, or would you _____ ?
4. Do you know how to use the machine, or would _____ ?
5. Did you hear what I said, or do _____ ?
6. Can I go now, or do _____ ?

53.2 請參照範例，依各題的對話內容，完成句子。

1. Lock the door. | OK.   She told _him to lock the door_____ .

2. Why don't you stay with us for a few days? | That would be nice.   They invited her _____ _____ .

3. Can I use your phone? | No!   She wouldn't let _____ _____ .

4. Be careful. | Don't worry. I will.   She warned _____ _____ .

5. Can you give me a hand? | Sure.   He asked _____ _____ .

53.3 請參照範例，依各句題意，將第一句話改寫成語意相近的句子。

1. My father said I could use his car.   My father allowed _me to use his car._
2. I was surprised that it rained.   I didn't expect _____
3. Don't stop him from doing what he wants. Let _____
4. He looks older when he wears glasses.   Glasses make _____
5. I think you should know the truth.   I want _____
6. Don't let me forget to call my sister.   Remind _____
7. At first I didn't want to apply for the job, but Sarah convinced me. Sarah persuaded _____ _____
8. My lawyer said I shouldn't say anything to the police. My lawyer advised _____ _____
9. I was told that I shouldn't believe everything he says. I was warned _____ _____
10. If you have a car, you are able to get around more easily. Having a car enables _____ _____

53.4 依各句題意，填入動詞的正確形式：***-ing***、不定詞 (***to do / to read*** 等)、或動詞原型 (***do/read*** 等)。

1. They don't allow people _to park_ in front of the building (park)
2. I've never been to Hong Kong, but I'd like _____ there. (go)
3. I'm in a difficult position. What do you advise me _____ ? (do)
4. The movie was very sad. It made me _____ . (cry)
5. Lauren's parents always encouraged her _____ hard at school. (study)
6. I wouldn't advise _____ at that restaurant. The food is terrible. (eat)
7. She said the letter was personal and wouldn't let me _____ it. (read)
8. We are not allowed _____ personal phone calls at work. (make)
9. "I don't think Alex likes me." "What makes you _____ that?" (think)

動詞 + -ing 或 to . . . 1
(remember / regret 等)

A

有些動詞後使用 -ing，有些則使用 to . . .。

動詞後使用 -ing：		
admit	finish	postpone
avoid	imagine	risk
consider	keep (on)	stop
deny	mind	suggest
enjoy		

其他例句參見 Unit 51。

動詞後使用 to . . .：		
afford	fail	offer
agree	forget	plan
arrange	hope	promise
decide	learn	refuse
deserve	manage	threaten

其他例句參見 Unit 52。

B

有些動詞後面可以接 -ing 或 to . . .，但意思不同：

remember

I **remember doing** something 意思是我做了某事，並且我記得我做了。
因此 **remember doing** something 意思是做了那件事以後記得做過了。

■ I know I locked the door. I clearly **remember locking** it.
(= I locked it, and now I remember this)
■ He could **remember driving** along the road just before the accident, but he couldn't remember the accident itself.

I **remembered to do** something 意思是我當時記得我必須做某事，所以我做了。
因此 **remember to do** 意思是做某事之前就已經記得必須做該件事。

■ I **remembered to lock** the door, but I forgot to shut the windows.
(= I remembered that I had to lock it, and so I locked it)
■ Please **remember to mail** the letter.
(= don't forget to mail it)

regret

I **regret doing** something 意思是我做了某事，現在我後悔做了那件事：

■ I now **regret saying** what I said. I shouldn't have said it.
■ It began to get cold and he **regretted not wearing** his coat.

I **regret to say** / **to tell** you / **to inform** you 意思是很遺憾我必須告訴你某事：

■ (正式信件) We **regret to inform** you that we cannot offer you the job.

go on

go on doing something 意思是繼續做某件已經在做的事：

■ The president **went on talking** for hours.
■ We need to change. We can't **go on living** like this.

go on to do something 意思是繼續去做另一件事：

■ After discussing the economy, the president then **went on to talk** about foreign policy.

C

下列動詞可以用 -ing 或 to . . .：
begin   start   continue   bother

請看下面例句：
■ It has **started raining**.　或　It has **started to rain**.
■ Don't **bother locking** the door.　或　Don't **bother to lock** . . .

但 -ing 之後不再接 -ing：
■ It's start**ing to rain**. (並非 It's starting raining)

Exercises

54.1 填入動詞的正確形式： **-ing** 或 **to . . .** ；注意有些句子中兩者都適用。

1. They denied _stealing_ the money. (steal)
2. I don't enjoy _____ very much. (drive)
3. I don't want _____ out tonight. I'm too tired. (go)
4. I can't afford _____ out tonight. I don't have enough money. (go)
5. Has it stopped _____ yet? (rain)
6. Our team was really unlucky yesterday. We deserved _____ the game. (win)
7. Why do you keep _____ me questions? Can't you leave me alone? (ask)
8. Please stop _____ me questions! (ask)
9. I refuse _____ any more questions. (answer)
10. One of the boys admitted _____ the window. (break)
11. The boy's father promised _____ for the window to be repaired. (pay)
12. If the company continues _____ money, the factory may be closed. (lose)
13. "Does Sarah know about the meeting?" "No, I forgot _____ her." (tell)
14. The baby began _____ in the middle of the night. (cry)
15. Julie has been sick, but now she's beginning _____ better. (get)
16. I enjoyed _____ you. I hope _____ you again soon. (meet, see)

54.2 以下是有關於 Tom 小時候的描述：

1. He was in the hospital when he was four.
2. He cried on his first day of school.
3. He said he wanted to be a doctor
4. He went to Miami when he was eight.
5. Once he fell into a river.
6. Once he was bitten by a dog.

他還記得第 **1**、**2** 和 **4** 項，但已經忘了第 **3**、**5** 和 **6** 項。請以 **He can remember . . .** 或 **He can't remember** 的句型敍述 Tom 記得和忘記的事。

1. _He can remember being in the hospital when he was four._
2. _____
3. _____
4. _____
5. _____
6. _____

54.3 依各句題意，選擇適當的動詞並填入動詞的正確形式： **-ing** 或 **to . . .**。

1. a) Please remember _to lock_ the door when you go out.
   b) *A:* You lent me some money a few months ago.
      B: I did? Are you sure? I don't remember _____ you any money.
   c) *A:* Did you remember _____ your sister?
      B: Oh no, I completely forgot. I'll call her tomorrow.
   d) When you see Amanda, remember _____ hello for me, OK?
   e) Someone must have taken my bag. I clearly remember _____ it by the window, and now it's gone.
2. a) I believe that what I said was fair. I don't regret _____ it.
   b) I knew they were in trouble, but I regret _____ I did nothing to help them.
3. a) Ben joined the company nine years ago. He became assistant manager after two years, and a few years later he went on _____ manager of the company.
   b) I can't go on _____ here any more. I want a different job.
   c) When I came into the room, Liz was reading a newspaper. She looked up and said hello and then went on _____ her newspaper.

動詞 + -ing 或 to . . . 2
(try / need / help)

try to . . . 與 try –ing

try to do 意思是「嘗試去做、努力去做」：
- I was very tired. I **tried to keep** my eyes open, but I couldn't.
- Please **try to be** quiet when you come home. Everyone will be asleep.

try 也有「試試看某件事，就當作是實驗或測試」的意思，例如：
- These cookies are delicious. You should **try** one. (= you should have one to see if you like it)
- We couldn't find anywhere to stay. We **tried** every hotel in the town, but they were all full. (= we went to every hotel to see if they had a room)

try 作為「試試看某件事」時，後面接 **–ing**：
- *A:* The photocopier doesn't seem to be working.
- *B:* **Try pressing** the green button. (= press the green button – maybe this will help to solve the problem)

比較下面例句：
- I **tried to move** the table, but it was too heavy. (so I couldn't move it)
- I didn't like the way the furniture was arranged, so I **tried moving** the table to the other side of the room. But it still didn't look right, so I moved it back again.

need to do、need to be done 與 need doing

I **need to do** something 意思是我必須做某事：
- I **need to get** more exercise.
- He **needs to work** harder if he wants to make progress.
- I don't **need to come** to the meeting, do I?

Something **needs to be done** 意思是有人應該把某事做好：
- My cell phone **needs to be charged**.
- Do you think my pants **need to be washed**?

need to be done 有時候會以 **need doing** 來表示：
- My cell phone **needs charging**.
- Do you think my pants **need washing**?

This room needs to be cleaned up.
這個房間應該要打掃。

help 與 can't help

help to do 或 **help do** 意思相同：
- Everybody **helped to clean up** after the party.　或
  Everybody **helped clean up** . . .
- Can you **help** me **to move** this table?　或
  Can you **help** me move . . .

I **can't help doing** something 意思是我無法阻止我自己做某事：
- I don't like him, but he has a lot of problems. I **can't help feeling** sorry for him.
- She tried to be serious, but she **couldn't help laughing**. (= she couldn't stop herself from laughing)
- I'm sorry I'm so nervous. I **can't help it**.
  (= I **can't help being** nervous)

55.1 請參照範例，依各句題意，從下列動詞片語中選出適當者，以「*try* + 提議」的句型完成句子。

call his office　~~change the batteries~~　**turn it the other way**　**take an aspirin**

1.	The radio isn't working. I wonder what's wrong with it.	Have you _tried changing the batteries?_
2.	I can't open the door. The key won't turn.	Try _____
3.	I have a terrible headache. I wish I could get rid of it.	Have you _____
4.	I can't reach Fred. He's not at home. What should I do?	Why don't you _____

55.2 請依圖片的情境，從下列動 詞中選出一個適當的字，以 *need* + 動詞的用法完成句子。

~~clean~~　cut　empty　paint　tighten

1. These pants are dirty. _They need to be cleaned._ 或 _They need cleaning._
2. The room doesn't look very nice. _____
3. The grass is very long. It _____
4. The screws are loose. _____
5. The garbage can is full. _____

55.3 填入動詞的正確形式。

1. a) I was very tired. I tried ___to keep___ (keep) my eyes open, but I couldn't.
   b) I rang the doorbell, but there was no answer. Then I tried _____ (knock) on the door, but there was still no answer.
   c) We tried _____ (put) out the fire, but we were unsuccessful. We had to call the fire department.
   d) Sue needed to borrow some money. She tried _____ (ask) Jerry, but he was short of money, too.
   e) I tried _____ (reach) the shelf, but I wasn't tall enough.
   f) Please don't bother me. I'm trying _____ (concentrate).

2. a) I need a change. I need _____ (go) away for a while.
   b) My grandmother isn't able to look after herself any more. She needs _____ (look) after.
   c) The windows are dirty. They need _____ (wash)
   d) Your hair is getting very long. It needs _____ (cut).
   e) You don't need _____ (iron) that shirt. It doesn't need _____ (iron).

3. a) They were talking very loudly. I couldn't help _____ (overhear) them.
   b) Can you help me _____ (get) dinner ready?
   c) He looks so funny. Whenever I see him, I can't help _____ (smile).
   d) The beautiful weather helped _____ (make) it a wonderful vacation.

動詞 + -ing 或 to ... 3
(like / would like 等)

A

like/love/hate

描述重複的動作時，下列動詞後可以使用 **-ing** 或 **to** ...。
請看下面例句：

- Do you **like** gett**ing** up early? 或 Do you **like to get** up early?
- Stephanie **hates** fly**ing**. 或 Stephanie **hates to fly**.
- I **love** meet**ing** people. 或 I **love to meet** people.
- I don't **like** be**ing** kept waiting. 或 ... **like to be** kept waiting.
- I don't **like** friends call**ing** me at work. 或 ... friends **to call** me at work.

但是

表示已經存在的情況通常用 **-ing** (而不用 **to** ...)。

例如：

- Paul lives in Vancouver now. He **likes** liv**ing** there. (He **likes** liv**ing** in Vancouver = He lives there and he likes it)
- Do you **like** be**ing** a student? (You are a student – do you like it?)
- The office I worked at was horrible. I **hated** work**ing** there. (I worked there and I hated it)

I like to do 與 **I like doing** 有時候表達的意思不同。

I like do**ing** something 意思是我做某事而且我喜歡做這件事：
- I **like** clean**ing** the kitchen. (我喜歡清理廚房)

I like to do something 意思是我認為做某件事是好的，但我不一定喜歡做這件事：
- It's not my favorite job, but I **like to clean** the kitchen as often as possible.

enjoy 和 **mind** 後面接 **-ing** (而不是接 **to** ...)：
- I **enjoy** clean**ing** the kitchen. (並非 I enjoy to clean)
- I **don't mind** clean**ing** the kitchen. (並非 I don't mind to clean)

B

would like / would love / would hate / would prefer

would like / would love / would hate / would prefer 後面通常接 **to** ...(不定詞)：
- I'**d like** (= **would** like) to go away for a few days.
- **Would** you **like to come** to dinner on Friday?
- I **wouldn't like to go** on vacation alone.
- I'**d love to meet** your family.
- **Would** you **prefer to have** dinner now or later?

比較 **I like** 與 **I would like** (**I'd** like) 之用法：
- I **like playing** tennis. / I **like to play** tennis. (一般而言，我喜歡這種運動。)
- I'**d like to play** tennis today. (我今天想打網球。)

would mind 後面必須接 **-ing** (而不是接 **to** ...)：
- **Would** you **mind closing** the door, please?

C

I would like **to have done** something 意思是我現在後悔我當時沒有做或不能做某事：
- It's too bad we didn't see Johnny when we were in Nashville. I **would like to have seen** him again.
- We'**d like to have gone** on vacation, but we didn't have enough money.

would love / would hate / would prefer 也可以使用上述的句型與用法：
- Poor Tom! I **would hate to have been** in his position.
- I'**d love to have gone** to the party, but it was impossible.

Exercises

56.1 你喜歡從事以下各題中提示的行業嗎？請參照範例，從下列動詞中選用適當的動詞與句型，表達你對從事各個行業的感覺。

like / don't like   love   hate   enjoy   don't mind

1. (fly) _I don't like flying. 或 I don't like to fly._
2. (play cards) _____
3. (be alone) _____
4. (go to museums) _____
5. (cook) _____

56.2 依各句題意，用括號內的動詞，以 *-ing* 或 *to . . .* 完成句子；注意有些句子中兩者皆可適用。

1. Paul lives in Vancouver now. It's nice. He likes it.
   (he / like / live / there) _He likes living there._
2. Jane is a biology teacher. She likes her job.
   (she / like / teach / biology) She _____
3. Joe always carries his camera with him and takes a lot of photographs.
   (he / like / take / photographs) _____
4. I used to work in a supermarket. I didn't like it much.
   (I / not / like / work / there) _____
5. Rachel is studying medicine. She likes it.
   (she / like / study / medicine) _____
6. Dan is famous, but he doesn't like it.
   (he / not / like / be / famous) _____
7. Jennifer is a very cautious person. She doesn't take many risks.
   (she / not / like / take / risks) _____
8. I don't like surprises.
   (I / like / know / things / ahead of time) _____

56.3 填入動詞的正確形式：*-ing* 或 *to . . .* ；注意有些句子中兩者皆可適用。

1. It's good to visit other places – I enjoy _traveling_ .
2. "Would you like _____ down?"   "No, thanks, I'll stand."
3. I'm not quite ready yet. Would you mind _____ a little longer?
4. When I was a child, I hated _____ to bed early.
5. When I have to catch a plane, I'm always worried that I'll miss it. So I like
   _____ to the airport ahead of time.
6. I enjoy _____ busy. I don't like it when there's nothing to do.
7. I would love _____ to your wedding, but unfortunately I can't.
8. I don't like _____ in this part of town. I want to move somewhere else.
9. Do you have a minute? I'd like _____ to you about something.
10. When there's bad news and good news, I like _____ the bad news first.

56.4 依各句題意，用括號內的動詞，以 *would . . . to have* (*done*) 的句型完成句子。

1. It's too bad I couldn't go to the wedding. (like) _I would like to have gone to the wedding._
2. It's a shame I didn't see the program. (like) _____
3. I'm glad I didn't lose my watch. (hate) _____
4. It's too bad I didn't meet your parents. (love) _____
5. I'm glad I wasn't alone. (not / like) _____
6. It's a shame I couldn't travel by train. (prefer) _____

prefer 與 would rather

A

prefer to do 與 prefer doing

prefer to (do) 與 **prefer –ing** 皆表示說話者普遍說來較喜歡某事：

- I don't like cities. I **prefer to live** in the country.　或　I **prefer living** in the country.

請比較 **prefer** 的三種句型之不同：

I prefer	something	**to** something else.
I prefer	**doing** something	**to doing** something else.
但是 I prefer	**to do** something	**rather than (do)** something else.

- I **prefer** this coat **to** the coat you were wearing yesterday.
- I **prefer driving to traveling** by train.

但是

- I **prefer to drive rather than travel** by train.
- Ann **prefers to live** in the country **rather than** in a city.　或　. . . **rather than live** in a city.

B

would prefer (I'd prefer . . .)

would prefer 表示在某一個情境下某人偏好什麼，並非指一般狀況：

- "**Would** you **prefer** tea or coffee?" "Coffee, please."

would prefer 後面必須接 **to do** (而非 doing)：

- "Should we take the train?" "No, I'**d prefer to drive**." (並非 I'd prefer driving)
- I'**d prefer to stay** at home tonight **rather than go** to the movies.

C

would rather (I'd rather . . .)

would rather (do) 與 **would prefer** (to do) 意思相同。**would rather** 後面必須接動詞原型(**do / have / stay** 等)。

比較下列例句：

- "Should we take the train?" { "I'**d prefer to drive**."
  "I'**d rather drive**." (並非 to drive) }
- "**Would** you **rather have** tea or coffee?" "Coffee, please."

否定形式為 I'**d rather not** (do something)：

- I'm tired. I'**d rather not go** out tonight, if you don't mind.
- "Do you want to go out tonight?" "I'**d rather not**."

此外還有 **would rather do** something **than do** something else 之句型：

- I'**d rather stay** at home tonight **than go** to the movies.

D

I'd rather you did something

I'**d rather** you **did** something 的句型中使用過去式，例句如下：

- "I'll fix your car tomorrow, OK?" "I'**d rather** you **did** it today." (= I'd prefer this)
- "Is it OK if Ben stays here?" "I'**d rather** he **came** with us." (並非 he comes)
- Shall I tell them, or **would** you **rather** they **didn't** know? (並非 don't know)

此句型必須使用過去式動詞，但是意思並非過去式。

比較下面例句：

- I'd rather **make** dinner now.

但是　I'd rather you **made** dinner now. (並非 I'd rather you make)

I'**d rather you didn't** (do something) 意思是我寧願你不做某事：

- I'**d rather you didn't tell** anyone what I said.
- "Should I tell Stephanie?" "I'**d rather you didn't**."

would prefer Unit 56B　*prefer* (one thing) *to* (another) Unit 133D

Exercises

57.1 你偏好什麼呢？請從括號內的動詞中選出你的偏好，並以 *I prefer* (something) *to* (something else) 的句型完成下列各句。

1. (drive / fly)
   I prefer driving to flying.
2. (tennis / soccer)
   I prefer _____
3. (call people / send e-mails)
   I _____ to _____
4. (go to the movies / watch videos at home)
   _____
   _____

請參照範例，以 *I prefer to* (do something) *rather than* (something else) 的句型，改寫第 **3、4** 句。

5. (1) *I prefer to drive rather than fly.*
6. (3) I prefer to _____
7. (4) _____

57.2 請依各句題意選出適當的動詞片語，並以 *I'd prefer . . .* 或 *I'd rather* 的句型完成下列各句。

eat at home	~~take a taxi~~	go alone
wait a few minutes	listen to some music	stand
go for a swim	~~wait till later~~	think about it for a while

1. Should we walk home? — (prefer) *I'd prefer to take a taxi.*
2. Do you want to eat now? — (rather) *I'd rather wait till later.*
3. Would you like to watch TV? — (rather) _____
4. Do you want to go to a restaurant? — (prefer) _____
5. Let's leave now. — (rather) _____
6. What about a game of tennis? — (rather) _____
7. I think we should decide now. — (prefer) _____
8. Would you like to sit down? — (rather) _____
9. Do you want me to come with you? — (prefer) _____

請以 *than* 或 *rather than* 的句型完成下列各句。

10. I'd prefer to take a taxi *rather than walk home.*
11. I'd prefer to go for a swim _____
12. I'd rather eat at home _____
13. I'd prefer to think about it for a while _____
14. I'd rather listen to some music _____

57.3 請以 *would you rather I . . . ?* 的句型完成下列各句。

1. Are you going to make dinner or *would you rather I made it* ?
2. Are you going to tell Ann what happened or would you rather _____ ?
3. Are you going to go shopping or _____ ?
4. Are you going to call Diane or _____ ?

57.4 請依各句題意以及你自己的意思，完成下列各句。

1. "Should I tell Ann the news?" "No, I'd rather she _didn't_ know."
2. Do you want me to go now, or would you rather I _____ here?
3. Do you want to go out tonight or would you rather _____ at home?
4. This is a private letter addressed to me. I'd rather you _____ read it.
5. I don't really like these shoes. I'd rather they _____ a different color.
6. *A:* Do you mind if I turn on the radio?
   B: I'd rather you _____ . I'm trying to study.

介係詞 (in / for / about 等) + -ing

A

介係詞 (**in/for/about** 等)後所接的動詞必須為 **-ing** 之形式。例句如下：

	介係詞	動詞 (**-ing**)	
Are you interested	**in**	work**ing**	for us?
I'm not very good	**at**	learn**ing**	languages.
Sue must be fed up	**with**	study**ing**.	
What are the advantages	**of**	hav**ing**	a car?
Thanks very much	**for**	invit**ing**	me to your party.
How	**about**	meet**ing**	for lunch tomorrow?
Why don't you go out	**instead of**	sitt**ing**	at home all the time?
Carol went to work	**in spite of**	feel**ing**	sick.

instead of somebody doing something 與 fed up with **people** doing something 等句型中，動詞必須為 –ing 之形式。

■ I'm fed up with **people** telling me what to do.

B

注意下列介係詞 + **-ing** 之用法：

before -ing 與 **after -ing**：
■ **Before going** out, I called Sarah. (並非 Before to go out)
■ What did you do **after finishing** school?

上面的例句也可以用 **Before I went** out 與 …**after you finished** school. 來表示。

by -ing 表示某事是如何發生的：
■ The burglars got into the house **by** break**ing** a window and climb**ing** in.
■ You can improve your English **by** read**ing** more.
■ She made herself sick **by** not eat**ing** properly.
■ Many accidents are caused **by** people driv**ing** too fast.

without -ing：
■ We ran 10 miles **without** stopp**ing**.
■ It was a stupid thing to say. I said it **without** think**ing**.
■ She needs to work **without** people disturb**ing** her. (或 … **without** be**ing** disturbed.)
■ I have enough problems of my own **without** hav**ing** to worry about yours.

C

to -ing (look forward **to** do**ing** something 等)

to 通常為不定詞(**to** + 動詞原型)的一部份，例如 **to** do / **to** see 等：
■ We decided **to go** out.
■ Would you like **to meet** for lunch tomorrow?

但是 **to** 也是介係詞(如同其他介係詞 **in** / **for** / **about** / **from** 等)。例句如下：
■ We drove from Houston **to Chicago**.
■ I prefer tea **to coffee**.
■ Are you looking forward **to the weekend**?

介係詞後面所接的動詞必須為 **-ing** 之形式(參見 A 中的說明)。

in do**ing**	**about** meet**ing**	**without** stopp**ing** (etc.)

因此，當 **to** 作為介係詞時，後面的動詞必須是 **-ing**的形式：
■ I prefer driving **to** travel**ing** by train. (並非 to travel)
■ Are you looking forward **to** go**ing** on vacation? (並非 looking forward to go)

be / get used to -ing Unit 59   動詞 + 介係詞 + **-ing** Unit 60   ***while / when -ing*** Unit 66B   ***in spite of*** Unit 110
介係詞 Unit 118 至 Unit 133

Exercises

58.1 請參照範例，改寫下列各句，使兩句話的意思相同。

1. Why is it useful to have a car?
   What are the advantages of _havinq a car_ ?
2. I don't intend to apply for the job.
   I have no intention of _____ .
3. Karen has a good memory for names.
   Karen is good at _____ .
4. Mark won't pass the exam. He has no chance.
   Mark has no chance of _____ .
5. Did you get into trouble because you were late?
   Did you get into trouble for _____ ?
6. We didn't eat at home. We went to a restaurant instead.
   Instead of _____ .
7. We got into the exhibition. We didn't have to wait in line.
   We got into the exhibition without _____ .
8. Our team played well, but we lost the game.
   Our team lost the game in spite of _____ .

58.2 依各句題意選出適當的動詞片語，並以 **by -ing** 的用法完成下列各句。

> borrow too much money   ~~break a window~~   drive too fast
> put some pictures on the walls   stand on a chair   turn a key

1. The burglars got into the house _by breaking a window_ .
2. I was able to reach the top shelf _____ .
3. You start the engine of a car _____ .
4. Kevin got himself into financial trouble _____ .
5. You can put people's lives in danger _____ .
6. We made the room look nicer _____ .

58.3 依各句題意，填入適當的動詞 (限填一個字)。

1. We ran 10 miles without _stopping_ .
2. He left the hotel without _____ his bill.
3. It's a nice morning. How about _____ for a walk?
4. We were able to translate the letter into English without _____ a dictionary.
5. Before _____ to bed, I like to have a hot drink.
6. It was a long trip. I was very tired after _____ on a train for 36 hours.
7. I was annoyed because the decision was made without anybody _____ me.
8. After _____ the same job for 10 years, I felt I needed a change.
9. We got lost because we went straight instead of _____ left.
10. I like these pictures you took. You're good at _____ pictures.

58.4 依各句題意，以 **I'm (not) looking forward to** 的句型完成下列各句。

1. You are going on vacation next week. How do you feel?
   I'm looking forward to going on vacation.
2. Diane is a good friend of yours and she is coming to visit you soon. So you will see her again soon. How do you feel? I'm _____
3. You are going to the dentist tomorrow. You don't enjoy going to the dentist. How do you feel?
   I'm not _____
4. Carol hates school, but she is graduating next summer. How does she feel?
   _____
5. You've arranged to play tennis tomorrow. You like tennis a lot. How do you feel?
   _____

be / get used to something (I'm used to . . .)

A

請看下面範例：

Lisa

Lisa 是美國人，現在住在東京。她剛開始在日本開車時，覺得非常困難，因為她必須靠左邊開而不是靠右邊開。靠左邊開對她而言很奇怪而且很困難，因為：

She **wasn't used to it**.
She **wasn't used to driving** on the left.
她那時不習慣。
她那時不習慣靠左邊開車。

但是經過多次練習以後，靠左邊開比較不奇怪了。所以：

She **got used to driving** on the left.
她習慣了靠左邊開車。

現在對她而言不是問題了：
She **is used to driving** on the left.
她現在習慣靠左邊開車。

B

I'm used to something 意思是某事對我而言並不陌生，或我已經習慣於某事：

- Frank lives alone. He doesn't mind this because he has lived alone for 15 years. It is not strange for him. He **is used to it**. He **is used to living** alone.
- I bought some new shoes. They felt strange at first because I **wasn't used to them**.
- Our new apartment is on a very busy street. I expect we'll **get used to the noise**, but for now it's very annoying.
- Diane has a new job. She has to get up much earlier now than before – at 6:30. She finds this difficult, because she **isn't used to getting up** so early.
- Barbara's husband is often away. She doesn't mind. She **is used to him** being away.

C

be/get used 後面不可以接不定詞：

- She is used **to driving** on the left. (並非 She is used to drive)

I **am used to** something 句型中的 **to** 為介係詞，而非不定詞的一部分；因此 **be used to** 後面必須接 **-ing**：

- Frank is used **to living** alone. (並非 Frank is used to live)
- Lisa had to get used **to driving** on the left. (並非 get used to drive)

D

注意 **I am used to doing** 與 **I used to do** 之語意與用法的不同：

I am used to (doing) something 意思是某事對我而言並不陌生或我已經習慣於某事：

- I **am used to the weather** in this country.
- I **am used to driving** on the left because I've lived in Japan a long time.

I used to do something 意思是我過去經常做某事，但是現在不做了。此用法只能用於過去式，不得用於現在式：

此句型為 I **used** to do (而非 I **am** used to do)：

- I **used to drive** to work every day, but these days I usually ride my bike.
- We **used to live** in a small town, but now we live in Los Angeles.

Exercises

59.1 參照本單元 A 小節的情況，考量以下兩個情境，並以 ***used to*** 及適當動詞完成下列各句。

1. Juan is Spanish and went to live in Canada. In Spain he usually had dinner late in the evening, but in Canada dinner was at 6:00. This was very early for him, and he found it very strange at first.

    When Juan first went to Canada, he ___*wasn't used to having*___ dinner so early, but after a while he _____ it. Now he finds it normal.
    He _____ at 6:00.

2. Julia is a nurse. A year ago she started working nights. At first she found it hard and didn't like it.

    She _____ nights, and it took her a few months to _____ it. Now, after a year, she's pretty happy. She _____ nights.

59.2 依各題的對話內容，以 ***I'm (not) used to*** 的句型完成句子。

1. You live alone. You don't mind this. You have always lived alone.
    Friend: Do you get a little lonely sometimes?
    You: No, ___*I'm used to living alone.*___

2. You sleep on the floor. You don't mind this. You have always slept on the floor.
    Friend: Wouldn't you prefer to sleep in a bed?
    You: No, I _____

3. You have to work long hours in your job. This is not a problem for you. You have always worked long hours.
    Friend: You have to work very long hours in your job, don't you?
    You: Yes, but I don't mind that. I _____

4. You usually go to bed early. Last night you went to bed very late (for you) and as a result, you are very tired this morning.
    Friend: You look tired this morning.
    You: Yes, _____

59.3 依各題情境，以 ***get/got used to*** 的句型完成句子。

1. Some friends of yours have just moved into an apartment on a busy street. It's very noisy.
    They'll have to ___*get used to the noise.*___

2. Sue moved from a big house to a much smaller one. She found it strange at first.
    She had to _____ in a much smaller house.

3. The children at school got a new teacher. She was different from the teacher before her, but this wasn't a problem for the children. They soon _____

4. Some people you know from the United States are going to live in your country. What will they have to get used to?
    They'll have to _____

59.4 依各句題意，填入適當的動詞 (限填一個字) (參見 C 小節)。

1. Lisa had to get used to ___*driving*___ on the left.
2. We used to ___*live*___ in a small town, but now we live in Los Angeles.
3. Tom used to _____ a lot of coffee. Now he prefers tea.
4. I feel very full after that meal. I'm not used to _____ so much.
5. I wouldn't like to share an office. I'm used to _____ my own office.
6. I used to _____ a car, but I sold it a few months ago.
7. When we were children, we used to _____ swimming every day.
8. There used to _____ a movie theater here, but it was torn down a few years ago.
9. I'm the boss here! I'm not used to _____ told what to do.

動詞 + 介係詞 + -ing (succeed in -ing / accuse somebody of -ing 等)

許多動詞使用「動詞 + 介係詞(in/for/about 等) + 受詞」之句型。

例如：

動詞 +	介係詞	+ 受詞
We **talked**	**about**	the problem.
You should **apologize**	**for**	what you said.

如果上述句型中的受詞為動詞，則必須為 **-ing** 的形式：

動詞 +	介係詞	+ -ing (受詞)
We **talked**	**about**	go**ing** to South America.
You should **apologize**	**for**	not tell**ing** the truth.

以下動詞也使用「動詞 + 介係詞 + 受詞」之句型：

succeed (in)	Have you **succeeded**	**in**	find**ing** a job yet?
insist (on)	They **insisted**	**on**	pay**ing** for dinner.
think (of)	I'm **thinking**	**of**	buy**ing** a house.
dream (of)	I wouldn't **dream**	**of**	ask**ing** them for money.
approve (of)	He doesn't **approve**	**of**	swear**ing**.
decide (against)	We have **decided**	**against**	mov**ing** to Chicago.
feel (like)	Do you **feel**	**like**	go**ing** out tonight?
look forward (to)	I'm **looking forward**	**to**	meet**ing** her.

上述動詞中，有些動詞還可以使用「動詞 + 介係詞 + 某人 + -ing」之句型 (approve of **somebody** doing something、look forward to **somebody** doing something)：

- I don't approve **of people** kill**ing** animals for fun.
- We are all looking forward **to Bob** com**ing** home.

下列動詞使用「動詞 + 受詞 + 介係詞 + -ing」之句型：

	動詞 + 受詞 +		介係詞	+ -ing (受詞)
congratulate (on)	I **congratulated**	Ann	**on**	gett**ing** a new job.
accuse (of)	They **accused**	us	**of**	tell**ing** lies.
suspect (of)	Nobody **suspected**	the general	**of**	be**ing** a spy.
prevent (from)	What **prevented**	you	**from**	com**ing** to see us?
keep (from)	The noise **keeps**	me	**from**	fall**ing** asleep.
stop (from)	The rain didn't **stop**	us	**from**	enjoy**ing** our vacation.
thank (for)	I forgot to **thank**	them	**for**	help**ing** me.
excuse (for)	**Please excuse**	me	**for**	not return**ing** your call.

上述動詞中，有些動詞常使用被動句型。例如：

- We **were accused of** tell**ing** lies.
- The general **was suspected of** be**ing** a spy.

動詞 apologize 也可以用「apologize to 某人 for」的句型：

- I apologized **to them** for keeping them waiting. (並非 I apologized them)

decide to . . . Unit 52A　介係詞 + *-ing* Unit 58　動詞 + 介係詞 Unit 129 至 Unit 133

Exercises

60.1 依各句題意，填入適當的動詞 (限填一個字)。

1. Our neighbors apologized for ___making___ so much noise.
2. I feel lazy. I don't feel like _____ any work.
3. I wanted to go out alone, but Joe insisted on _____ with me.
4. I'm fed up with my job. I'm thinking of _____ something else.
5. We have decided against _____ a new car because we can't really afford it.
6. I hope you get in touch with me soon. I'm looking forward to _____ from you.
7. The weather was extremely bad and this kept us from _____ out.
8. The man who was arrested is suspected of _____ a false passport.
9. I think you should apologize to Sue for _____ so rude to her.
10. Some parents don't approve of their children _____ a lot of television.
11. I'm sorry I can't come to your party, but thank you very much for _____ me.

60.2 依各句題意選出適當的動詞，配合介係詞完成下列各句。

carry	cause	escape	~~go~~	interrupt
live	see	solve	spend	walk

1. Do you feel ___like going___ out tonight?
2. It took us a long time, but we finally succeeded _____ the problem.
3. I've always dreamed _____ in a small house by the sea.
4. The driver of the other car accused me _____ the accident.
5. There's a fence around the lawn to stop people _____ on the grass.
6. Excuse me _____ you, but may I ask you something?
7. Where are you thinking _____ your vacation this year?
8. The guards weren't able to prevent the prisoner _____ .
9. My bag wasn't very heavy, but Dave insisted _____ it for me.
10. It's too bad Paul can't come to the party. I was really looking forward _____ him.

60.3 依各題的對話內容，填入適當的動詞型式，以完成下列各句。

1. You / Kevin — It was nice of you to help me. Thanks a lot.
   Kevin thanked ___me for helping him___ .

2. Ann / Tom — I'll take you to the station. I insist.
   Tom insisted _____ _____ .

3. You / Dan — I hear you got married. Congratulations!
   Dan congratulated me _____ _____ .

4. Sue / Jenny — It was nice of you to come to see me. Thank you.
   Jenny thanked _____ _____ .

5. You / Kate — I'm sorry I didn't call earlier.
   Kate apologized _____ _____ .

6. You / Jane — You're selfish.
   Jane accused _____ _____ .

片語、句型 + -ing

下列片語和句型中，必須使用動詞 **-ing** 的形式：

There's no point in . . . :
- **There's no point in** hav**ing** a car if you never use it.
- **There was no point in** wait**ing** any longer, so we left.

the point **of** do**ing** something 片語中也是使用動詞 **-ing** 的形式：
- **What's the point of** hav**ing** a car if you never use it?

There's no use / It's no use . . . :
- There's nothing you can do about the situation, so **there's no use** worry**ing** about it.
- 或 . . . **it's no use** worry**ing** about it.

It's (not) worth . . . :
- I live only a short walk from here, so **it's not worth** tak**ing** a taxi.
- Our flight was very early in the morning, so **it wasn't worth** go**ing** to bed.

此外也可以使用 a movie is **worth seeing**、a book is **worth reading** 的句型：
- What was the movie like? Was it **worth seeing**?
- Thieves broke into the house but didn't take anything. There was nothing **worth stealing**.

have trouble -ing, have difficulty -ing, have a problem -ing

have trouble do**ing** something 中的第二個動詞，必須是 **-ing** 的形式：
- I **had** no **trouble** find**ing** a place to live. (並非 trouble to find)
- Did you **have** any **trouble** gett**ing** a visa?
- People often **have** a lot of **trouble** read**ing** my writing.

have **difficulty** / **a problem** doing something 的用法與上述句型相同，也是使用動詞 **-ing** 的形式：
- I had **difficulty** find**ing** a place to live. 或
  I had **a problem** find**ing** a place to live.

下列語詞後所接的動詞必須是 **-ing** 的形式：

spend / waste (time)
- He **spent** hours try**ing** to repair the clock.
- I **waste** a lot of time daydream**ing**.

(be) **busy**
- She said she couldn't go with us. She was too **busy** do**ing** other things.

go swimming / go fishing 等

有許多一般性的活動，特別是體育活動，都可以用 **go -ing** 表示。例如：

go swimm**ing**　　**go** sail**ing**　　**go** fish**ing**　　**go** hik**ing**　　**go** ski**ing**　　**go** jogg**ing**

其他類似的表達方式的還有 **go** shopp**ing**、**go** sightsee**ing**。
- How often do you **go** swimm**ing**?
- I'd like to **go** ski**ing**.
- When was the last time you **went** shopp**ing**?
- I've never **gone** sail**ing**.

Exercises

61.1 依各句題意，以 ***There's no point . . .*** 的句型完成下列各句。

1. Why have a car if you never use it?
   There's no point in having a car if you never use it.
2. Why work if you don't need money?
   _____
3. Don't try to study if you feel tired.
   _____
4. Why hurry if you've got plenty of time?
   _____

61.2 依各題的對話內容，填入適當的動詞形式，以完成右邊的句子。

1. Should we take a taxi home?
2. If you need help, why don't you ask Dave?
3. I don't really want to go out tonight.
4. Should I call Ann now?
5. Are you going to complain about what happened?
6. Do you ever read newspapers?
7. Do you want to keep these old clothes?

No, it isn't far. It's not worth ___*taking a taxi*___ .
There's no use _____ .
He won't be able to do anything.
Well, stay at home! There's no point _____
_____ if you don't want to.
No, don't waste your time _____
now. She won't be home.
No, it's not worth _____ .
Nobody will do anything about it.
No, I'm usually too busy _____ care of the kids.
No, let's throw them away. They're not worth
_____ .

61.3 請參照範例，依各句題意完成下列各句。

1. I managed to get a visa, but it was difficult.
   I had trouble ___*getting a visa*_____
2. I find it hard to remember people's names.
   I have a problem _____
3. Sarah managed to get a job without any trouble.
   She had no difficulty _____
4. It won't be difficult to get a ticket for the game.
   You won't have any trouble _____ .
5. Do you think it's difficult to understand him?
   Do you have a problem _____ ?

61.4 依各句題意，填入適當的動詞 (限填一個字)，以完成下列各句。

1. I waste a lot of time ___*daydreaming*___ .
2. Every morning I spend about an hour _____ the newspaper.
3. "What's Karen doing?"   "She's going away tomorrow, so she's busy _____ ."
4. I think you waste too much time _____ television.
5. There's a beautiful view from that hill. It's worth _____ to the top.
6. There's no use _____ for the job. I know I wouldn't get it.
7. Just stay calm. There's no point in _____ angry.

61.5 依各句題意選出適當的動詞，並以適當的動詞形式，完成下列各句。

go riding   ~~go sailing~~   **go shopping**   **go skiing**   **go swimming**

1. Robbie lives by the ocean and he's got a boat, so he often ___*goes sailing*___ .
2. It was a very hot day, so we _____ at the pool.
3. There's plenty of snow in the mountains, so we'll be able to _____ .
4. Michelle has two horses. She _____ regularly.
5. "Where's Dan?"   "He _____ . There were a few things he needed to buy."

表目的之 to、for 與 so that

A

to ... 表示某人為何做某事(也就是表示動作的目的)：
- "Why are you going out?" "**To mail** a letter."
- A friend of mine called **to invite** me to a party.
- We shouted **to warn** everybody of the danger.

to ... 也可以表示某事/某物為何存在 (某事/某物存在的目的)：
- This fence is **to keep** people out of the yard.
- The president has a team of bodyguards **to protect** him.

B

to ... 還可以表示需要或必須做某事/物以達到某個目的：
- It's hard to find **a place to park** downtown. (一個可以停車的地方)
- Would you like **something to eat**?
- Do you have **much work to do**? (你必須做的事)
- I get lonely if there's **nobody to talk to**.
- I need **something to open** this bottle **with**.

類似的用法還有 **money** / **time** / **chance** / **opportunity** / **energy** / **courage** 等後加 to (do something) 等句型：
- They gave us **some money to buy** some food.
- Do you have **much opportunity to practice** your English?
- I need **a few days to think** about your proposal.

C

for ... 與 **to** ...

比較 **for** ... 與 **to** ... 用法：

for 後面接名詞	**to** 後面接動詞
■ I'm going to Spain **for a vacation**.	■ I'm going to Spain **to learn** Spanish. (並非 for learn, 並非 for learning)
■ What would you like **for dinner**?	■ What would you like **to eat**?
■ Let's go to the pool **for a swim**.	■ Let's go to the pool **to have** a swim.

for somebody to do something 意思是「為/給某人做某事」：
- There weren't any chairs **for us to sit on**, so we had to sit on the floor.

for -ing 或 **to** ... 表示某件事物的一般目的，或某件事一般的用途。
- Do you use this brush **for** wash**ing** the dishes? (或 ... **to wash** the dishes?)

What ... **for**? 可以用來詢問目的：
- **What** is this switch **for**?
- **What** did you do that **for**?

D

so that

有時候 **so that** 也可以表示目的：

特別是下列情形中通常使用 **so that** (而非 **to** ...)：

目的為否定之意時，用 **so that** ... **won't** / **wouldn't**：
- I hurried **so that** I **wouldn't** be late. (= because I didn't want to be late)
- Leave early **so that** you **won't** (或 **don't**) miss the bus.

與 **can/could** 一起使用時，句型為 **so that** ... **can** / **could**：
- She's learning English **so that** she **can** study in Canada.
- We moved to the city **so that** we **could** see our children more often.

Exercises

62.1 請參照例 1 的方式，自 A 框與 B 框中各選出一個句子後，組成一個新的句子。

A	B
1. ~~I shouted~~	I want to keep warm
2. I had to go to the bank	I wanted to report that my car had been stolen
3. I'm saving money	I want to go to Canada
4. I went into the hospital	I had to have an operation
5. I'm wearing two sweaters	I needed to get some money
6. I called the police	~~I wanted to warn people of the danger~~

1. _I shouted to warn people of the danger._
2. I had to go to the bank _____
3. I _____
4. _____
5. _____
6. _____

62.2 依各句題意，填入適當的動詞，以完成下列各句。

1. The president has a team of bodyguards _to protect_ him.
2. I didn't have enough time _____ the newspaper today.
3. I took a taxi home. I didn't have the energy _____ .
4. "Would you like something _____ ?" "Yes. A cup of coffee, please."
5. We need a bag _____ these things in.
6. There will be a meeting next week _____ the problem.
7. I wish we had enough money _____ another car.
8. I saw Kelly at the party, but we didn't have a chance _____ to each other.
9. I need some new clothes. I don't have anything nice _____ .
10. They've just passed their exams. They're having a party _____ .
11. I can't do all this work alone. I need somebody _____ me.

62.3 請依各句題意，填入 *to* 或 *for*。

1. I'm going to Spain _for_ a vacation.
2. You need a lot of experience _____ this job.
3. You need a lot of experience _____ do this job.
4. We'll need more time _____ make a decision.
5. I went to the dentist _____ a check-up.
6. I had to put on my glasses _____ read the letter.
7. Do you have to wear glasses _____ reading?
8. I wish we had a yard _____ the children _____ play in.

62.4 請依各句題意，以 *so that* 的句型完成句子。

1. I hurried. I didn't want to be late.
   I hurried so that I wouldn't be late.
2. I wore warm clothes. I didn't want to be cold.
   I wore _____
3. I left Dave my phone number. I wanted him to be able to contact me.
   I _____
4. We whispered. We didn't want anybody else to hear our conversation.
   _____ nobody _____
5. Please arrive early. We want to be able to start the meeting on time.
   Please _____
6. Jennifer locked the door. She didn't want to be disturbed.
   _____
7. I slowed down. I wanted the car behind me to be able to pass.
   _____

形容詞 + to . . .

A

hard to understand 等

比較下面例句中 (a) 與 (b) 之句型：

- Jim doesn't speak very clearly.

(a) It is **hard to understand** him .

(b) He is **hard to understand**.

(a) 句與 (b) 句的意思相同，但請注意 (b) 句的句型：

- He is hard **to understand**. (並非 He is hard to understand him.)

以下的形容詞也可以使用上述的句型：

| easy | difficult | impossible | dangerous | safe | expensive |
| cheap | nice | good | interesting | safe | exciting |

- Do you think it is **safe** (for us) **to drink this water**?
  Do you think this water is **safe** (for us) **to drink**? (並非 to drink it)
- The questions on the exam were very difficult. It was **impossible to answer them**.
  The questions on the exam were very difficult. They were **impossible to answer**.
  (並非 to answer them)
- Jill has lots of interesting ideas. It's **interesting to talk** to her.
  Jill **is interesting to talk to**. (並非 to talk to her.)

此句型也適用於形容詞+名詞：

- This is a **difficult question** (for me) **to answer**. (並非 to answer it)

B

(It's) nice of (you) to . . .

此句型表示說話者對聽話者所做的事情之感覺或評價：

- It was **nice of you to take** me to the airport. Thank you very much.

下列形容詞也可以用於此種句型。例如：

| careless | kind | mean | considerate | foolish | stupid | generous | unfair |

- It's **foolish of Mary to quit** her job when she needs the money.
- I think it was very **unfair of him to criticize** me.

C

I'm sorry to . . . / I was surprised to . . . 等

形容詞 + to . . . 表示某人對於某事的反應：

- I was **sorry to hear** that your father is ill.

下列形容詞也可以用於此句型。例如：

| happy | disappointed | glad | surprised | pleased | amazed | sad | relieved |

- Was Julia **surprised to see** you?
- It was a long and tiring trip. We were **glad to get** home.

D

the first (person) **to know** / **the next** (train) **to arrive**

the first/second/third 等與 **the last, the next, the only** 後使用不定詞(to . . .)：

- If I have any more news, you will be **the first** (person) **to know**.
- **The next** plane **to arrive** at gate 4 will be Flight 268 from Bogotá.
- Everybody was late except me. I was **the only** one **to arrive** on time.

E

something is **sure / certain / likely / bound to . . .** 的句型使用不定詞(to . . .):

- Carla is a very good student. She's **bound to pass** the exam. (= she is sure to pass)
- I'm **likely to get** home late tonight. (= I will probably get home late)

afraid / interested / sorry Unit 64 *It . . .* Unit 82C *enough* 與 *too* + 形容詞 Unit 101

Exercises

63.1 請參照範例，依各句題意改寫句子 (參見本單元 **A** 小節)。

1. It's hard to understand him.   He _is hard to understand._
2. It's easy to use this machine.   This machine is _____
3. It was very difficult to open the window.   The window _____
4. It's impossible to translate some words.   Some words _____
5. It's expensive to maintain a car.   A _____
6. It's not safe to stand on that chair.   That _____

63.2 請參照範例，用括號內的形容詞，以形容詞 + 名詞 + **to** . . . 的句型完成下列各句 (參見本單元 **A** 小節)。

1. I couldn't answer the question. (difficult)   It was a _difficult question to answer._
2. Everybody makes that mistake. (easy)   It's an _____
3. I like living in this place. (nice)   It's a _____
4. We enjoyed watching the game. (good)   It was a _____

63.3 請參照範例，依各句題意選出適當的形容詞，並以 **It** . . . 的句型完成句子 (參見本單元 **B** 小節)。

     careless   inconsiderate   ~~kind~~   nice

1. Sue has offered to help me. _It's kind of Sue to offer to help me._
2. You make the same mistake again and again.
   It _____
3. Dan and Jenny invited me to stay with them.
   _____
4. The neighbors make so much noise at night.
   _____

63.4 請參照範例，依各句題意，從下列字組中選出適當的語詞，以完成句子 (參見本單元 **C** 小節)。

     sorry / hear   glad / hear   ~~pleased / get~~   surprised / see

1. We _were pleased to get_ your letter last week.
2. I got your message. I _____ that you're doing well.
3. We _____ Paula at the party. We didn't expect her to come.
4. I _____ that your mother isn't well. I hope she gets better soon.

63.5 依各句題意，用括號內的字加上 **+ to** . . . 的句型完成句子 (參見本單元 **D** 小節)。

1. Nobody left before me. (the first) I was _the first person to leave._
2. Everybody else arrived before Paul.
   (the last) Paul was the _____
3. Jenny passed the exam. All the other students failed.
   (the only) Jenny was _____
4. I complained to the restaurant manager about the service. Another customer had already complained.
   (the second) I was _____
5. Neil Armstrong walked on the moon in 1969. Nobody had done this before him.
   (the first) Neil Armstrong was _____

63.6 依據各題題意，用括號內的字配合適當的動詞，完成下列各句 (參見本單元 **E** 小節)。

1. Diane is a very good student. She _is bound to pass_ the exam. (bound)
2. I'm not surprised you're tired. After such a long trip, you _____ tired. (bound)
3. Toshi has a very bad memory. He _____ what you tell him. (sure)
4. I don't think you need an umbrella. It _____ . (not likely)
5. The holiday begins this Friday. There _____ a lot of traffic on the roads. (likely)

to . . . (afraid to do) 與
介係詞 + -ing (afraid of -ing)

A　afraid to (do) 與 afraid of (do)ing

I am **afraid to do** something 意思是我不想做某事，因為這件事有危險性或不好的結果。
afraid to do 通常用於表示出自說話者意願的事情；亦即說話者可以選擇做或不做這件事：

- This part of town is dangerous. People are **afraid to walk** here at night.
  (因為怕危險，他們不想出去，所以他們不出去。)
- James was **afraid to tell** his parents what happened.
  (他不想告訴父母，因為他知道他們會生氣或擔心。)

I am **afraid of** something **happening** 意思是不好的事有可能會發生(例如意外)。
afraid of -ing 不可以用於表示出自說話者意願的事情：

- The sidewalk was icy, so we walked very carefully. We were **afraid of falling**.
  (我們可能會滑倒 – 並非 we were afraid to fall)
- I don't like dogs. I'm always **afraid of being bitten**. (並非 afraid to be bitten)

因此，You are **afraid to do** something because you are **afraid of something happening** 意思是你不願意/害怕做某事，因為你害怕有事情會因此而發生：

- I was **afraid to go** near the dog because I was **afraid of being** bitten.

B　interested in (do)ing and interested to (do)

I'm **interested in doing** something 意思是我想做某事，我喜歡做某事：

- Let me know if you're **interested in joining** the club. (並非 to join)
- I tried to sell my car, but nobody was **interested in buying** it. (並非 to buy)

interested to 一般常與 hear / see / read / learn / know / find 等動詞一起使用。I was
interested to hear it 意思是我聽到了某事，而我對這件事很感興趣：

- I was **interested to hear** that Tanya quit her job.
- Ask Mike for his opinion. I would be **interested to know** what he thinks.
  (= it would be interesting for me to know it)

此句型與 surprised to / delighted to 的用法相同(參見 Unit 63C)：

- I was **surprised to hear** that Tanya quit her job.

C　sorry to (do) 與 sorry for / about (do)ing

sorry to . . . 表示我們對於某事的發生，感到遺憾(參見 Unit 63C)：

- I was **sorry to hear** that Nicky lost her job. (= I was sorry when I heard that . . .)
- I've enjoyed my stay here. I'll be **sorry to leave**.

sorry to . . . 表示我們在做某事時，覺得很抱歉：

- I'm **sorry to call** you so late, but I need to ask you something.

sorry for (doing something)則表示對於我們做過的事感到抱歉：

- I'm **sorry for** (**about**) **shouting** at you yesterday. (sorry to shout)

上個例句也可以用下面的句型表達：

- I'm **sorry I shouted** at you yesterday.

D　注意下面各動詞之用法：

I **want to** (do) / **I'd like to** (do)	並非	I'm **thinking of** (doing) / I **dream of** (doing)
I **failed to** (do)	並非	I **succeeded in** (doing)
I **allowed** them **to** (do)	並非	I **stopped**/**prevented** them **from** (doing)

上面各動詞用法，參見 Unit 52、 Unit 53 以及 Unit 60。

動詞 + 介係詞 + -ing Unit 60　形容詞 + 介係詞 Unit 127 與 Unit 128　*sorry about / for* Unit 127

Exercises

64.1 依各句題意，用括號內的語詞，以 *afraid to . . .* 或 *afraid of -ing* 的句型完成句子。

1. The streets are unsafe at night.
   (a lot of people / afraid / go / out) _A lot of people are afraid to go out._
2. We walked very carefully along the icy path.
   (we / afraid / fall) _We were afraid of falling._
3. I don't usually carry my passport with me.
   (I / afraid / lose / it) _____
4. I thought she would be angry if I told her what had happened.
   (I / afraid / tell / her) _____
5. We rushed to the station.
   (we / afraid / miss / our train) _____
6. In the middle of the film there was an especially horrifying scene.
   (we / afraid / look) _____
7. The vase was very valuable, so I held it carefully.
   (I / afraid / drop / it) _____
8. I thought the food on my plate didn't look fresh.
   a) (I / afraid / eat / it) _____
   b) (I / afraid / get / sick) _____

64.2 依各句題意選出適當的動詞，並以正確的動詞形式填入空格中。

~~buy~~	get	know	look	read	start

1. I'm trying to sell my car, but nobody is interested _in buying_ it.
2. Julia is interested _____ her own business.
3. I was interested _____ your letter in the newspaper last week.
4. Ben wants to stay single. He's not interested _____ married.
5. I met Mark a few days ago. You'll be interested _____ that he's just gotten a job in Buenos Aires.
6. I don't enjoy sightseeing. I'm not interested _____ at old buildings.

64.3 依各句題意，用括號內的字，以 *sorry for / about* 或 *sorry to . . .* 的句型完成下列各句。

1. I'm _sorry to call_ you so late, but I need to ask you something. (call)
2. I was _____ that you didn't get the job you applied for. (hear)
3. I'm _____ all those bad things about you. I didn't mean them. (say)
4. I'm _____ you, but do you have a pen I could borrow? (bother)
5. I'm _____ the book you lent me. I'll buy you another one. (lose)

64.4 依各句題意，用括號內的字，以適當的動詞形式填入空格中。

1. a) We wanted _to leave_ the building. (leave)
   b) We weren't allowed _____ the building. (leave)
   c) We were prevented _____ the building. (leave)

2. a) Peter failed _____ the problem. (solve)
   b) Chris succeeded _____ the problem. (solve)

3. a) I'm thinking _____ away next week. (go)
   b) I'm hoping _____ away next week. (go)
   c) I'd like _____ away next week. (go)
   d) I'm looking forward _____ away next week. (go)

4. a) Lisa wanted _____ me lunch. (buy)
   b) Lisa promised _____ me lunch. (buy)
   c) Lisa insisted _____ me lunch. (buy)
   d) Lisa wouldn't dream _____ me lunch. (buy)

see somebody do 與 see somebody doing

請看下面的範例：

Tom 進入車內，把車開走。你看到上述的情形，
你可以說：

■ I saw Tom **get** into his car and **drive** away.
(我看到 Tom 進入車內，把車開走。)

此句型 see 後面的動詞為動詞原型 (**get/drive/do**
等)，而非 to . . .(不定詞)：

Somebody **did** something + I **saw** this

I **saw** somebody **do** something

Tom

請看下面的範例：

昨天你看到 Kate。Kate 當時正在等公車。你可以說：
■ I saw Kate **waiting** for a bus.
(我看到 Kate 正在等公車。)

此句型 see 後面用 **-ing** (**waiting/doing** 等)：

Somebody **was doing** something + I **saw** this

I **saw** somebody **doing** something

Kate

比較這兩種句型在意思上的差別：

I saw him **do** something 意思是某人做了某事(過去簡單式)，我看到他做該件事從頭到尾的整個
過程。
■ He **fell** off the wall. I saw this. → I saw him **fall** off the wall.
■ The accident **happened**. Did you see it? → Did you see the accident **happen**?

I saw him doing something 意思是我看到他正在做某件事(過去進行式)，並非他做整件事的過程。

■ He **was walking** along the street.
I saw this when I drove past in my car. } I saw him **walking** along the street.

描述事情時，有時候上述語意的差別並不重要，則兩種句型皆可使用：
■ I've never seen her **dance**.   或   I've never seen her **dancing**.

除了 **see** 和 **hear** 以外，其他有些動詞也可以使用這兩種句型：

■ I didn't **hear** you **come** in. (you came in – I didn't hear this)
■ Liz suddenly **felt** somebody **touch** her on the shoulder.
■ Did you **notice** anyone **go** out?

■ I could **hear** it **raining**. (it was raining – I could hear it)
■ The missing children were last **seen playing** near the river.
■ **Listen to** the birds **singing**!
■ Can you **smell** something **burning**?
■ I **found** Sue in my room **reading** my letters.

65.1 依各題的對話內容，完成對話中的答句。

1.	Did anybody go out?	I don't think so. I didn't see ___anybody go out___ .
2.	Has Sarah arrived yet?	Yes, I think I heard her _____ .
3.	How do you know I took the money?	I know because I saw you _____ .
4.	Did the doorbell ring?	I don't think so. I didn't hear _____ .
5.	Can Tom play the piano?	I've never heard _____ .
6.	Did I lock the door when I went out?	Yes, I saw _____ .
7.	How did the woman fall?	I don't know. I didn't see _____ .

65.2 請參照範例，依各圖片的情境，描述你和你的朋友看到、聽到、或聞到的事物。

1. ___We saw Kate waiting for a bus.___
2. We saw Dave and Helen _____
3. We saw _____ in a restaurant.
4. We heard _____
5. We could _____
6. _____

65.3 依各句題意選出適當的動詞，並以正確的動詞形式填入空格中。

climb	~~come~~	crawl	cry	explode	ride
run	say	~~sing~~	slam	sleep	tell

1. Listen to the birds ___singing___ !
2. I didn't hear you ___come___ in.
3. We listened to the old man _____ his story from beginning to end.
4. Listen! Can you hear a baby _____ ?
5. I looked out of the window and saw Dan _____ his bike along the road.
6. I thought I heard somebody _____ "Hi," so I turned around.
7. We watched two men _____ across the yard and _____ through an open window into the house.
8. Everybody heard the bomb _____ . It made a tremendous noise.
9. Oh! I can feel something _____ up my leg! It must be an insect.
10. I heard somebody _____ the door in the middle of the night. It woke me up.
11. When we got home, we found a cat _____ under the kitchen table.

-ing 片語 (Feeling tired, I went to bed early.)

A

請看下面的例子：

> Joe 當時正在打網球，他傷了他的膝蓋。
> 你可以說：
> - Joe hurt his knee **playing football**. (Joe 在打網球時傷了他的膝蓋。)
>
> 你覺得很累，所以你很早就上床睡覺。
> 你可以說：
> - **Feeling tired**, I went to bed early. ((因為)覺得很累，(所以)我很早就上床睡覺。)
>
> 上述例句中的 playing tennis 與 feeling tired 都是 -ing 片語。
> 如果 -ing 片語置於句首(如上面第二例所示)，後面通常有逗號(,)。

B

當兩件事同時發生時，其中一件事可以用 -ing 的句型來表達：
- Kate is in the kitchen **making coffee**.
  (= she is in the kitchen *and* she is making coffee)
- A man ran out of the house **shouting**.
  (= he ran out of the house *and* he was shouting)
- Do something! Don't just stand there **doing nothing**!

-ing 的動詞出現在主要子句之後，用於表示當主句的動作發生時，-ing 片語的動作正在進行；主句的動作通常較短，而 -ing 片語的動作較長、正在持續進行：
- Joe hurt his knee **playing football**. (= while he was playing)
- Did you cut yourself **shaving**? (= while you were shaving)

-ing 片語也可以用於 **while** 或 **when** 之後：
- Jim hurt his knee **while playing** football.
- Be careful **when crossing** the street. (= when you are crossing)

C

表示兩個動作一前一後發生的情況，可以用 **having done** 來描述第一個動作：
- **Having found** a hotel, we looked for someplace to have dinner.
- **Having finished** her work, she went home.

上述的例句也可以用 **After -ing** 來表達：
- **After finishing** her work, she went home.

若是兩個動作都很短暫，則可用 -ing(也就是 **doing** 而非 **having done**)來表示第一個動作：
- **Taking** a key out of his pocket, he opened the door.

上述句型較常用於書面文章中，較少用於口語表達。

D

-ing 片語也可以用於解釋某事，或說明某人為何做某事的原因；此時 -ing 片語通常置於句首：
- **Feeling** tired, I went to bed early. (= because I felt tired)
- **Being** unemployed, he doesn't have much money. (= because he is unemployed)
- **Not having** a car, she has trouble getting around. (= because she doesn't have a car)
- **Having** already **seen** the movie twice, I didn't want to go again with my friends.
  (= because I had already seen it twice)

此種用法較常用於書面文章中，較少用於口語表達。

Exercises

66.1 請參照範例，自 A 框與 B 框各中各選出一個句子，並以 *-ing* 片語之句型組成一個新的句子。

A
1. Kate was in the kitchen.
2. Diane was sitting in an armchair.
3. Sue opened the door carefully.
4. Sarah went out.
5. Linda was in London for two years.
6. Mary walked around the town.

B
She was trying not to make any noise.
She looked at the sights and took pictures.
She said she would be back in an hour.
She was reading a book.
She was making coffee.
She worked as a teacher.

1. _Kate was in the kitchen making coffee._
2. Diane was sitting _____
3. Sue _____
4. _____
5. _____
6. _____

66.2 請參照範例，將各題中的兩個句子合併，以 *-ing* 片語之句型組成一個新的句子。

1. Joe was playing football. He hurt his knee. _Joe hurt his knee playing football._
2. I was watching television. I fell asleep.
   I _____
3. The man slipped and fell. He was getting off a bus.
   The man _____
4. I was walking home in the rain. I got very wet.
   I _____
5. Laura was driving to work yesterday. She had an accident.
   _____
6. Two kids got lost. They were hiking in the woods.
   _____

66.3 請參照範例，將各題中的兩個句子合併，組成一個以 *Having* 開始的新句子。

1. She finished her work. Then she went home.
   Having finished her work, she went home.
2. We bought our tickets. Then we went into the theater.
   _____
3. They had dinner, and then they continued their trip.
   _____
4. After I'd done the shopping, I stopped for a cup of coffee.
   _____

66.4 請參照範例，將各題中的兩個句子合併，組成一個以 *-ing*、 *Not -ing* (參見本單元 **D** 小節) 或 *Having* (*done something*) 開始的新句子。

1. I felt tired. So I went to bed early.
   Feeling tired, I went to bed early.
2. I thought they might be hungry. So I offered them something to eat.
   _____
3. Sally is a vegetarian. So she doesn't eat any kind of meat.
   _____
4. I didn't know his e-mail address. So I wasn't able to contact him.
   _____
5. Sarah has traveled a lot. So she knows a lot about other countries.
   _____
6. I wasn't able to speak the local language. So I had trouble communicating.
   _____
7. We had spent nearly all our money. So we couldn't afford to stay in a hotel.

UNIT 67

可數名詞與不可數名詞 1

A

名詞可以分為可數名詞與不可數名詞：

可數名詞	不可數名詞

可數名詞
- I eat a **banana** every day.
- I like **bananas**.

banana 為可數名詞。

可數名詞有單數形(**banana**)與複數形
(**bananas**)。

可數名詞是指可以計算的東西，例如 one
banana (一根香蕉)、two bananas (兩根香蕉)。

可數名詞的例子如下：
- Kate was singing **a song**.
- There's **a nice beach** near here.
- Do you have **a $10 bill**?
- It wasn't your fault. It was **an accident**.
- There are no **batteries** in the radio.
- We don't have enough **cups**.

不可數名詞
- I eat **rice** every day.
- I like **rice**.

rice 為不可數名詞。

不可數名詞只有一種形式，即單數形(**rice**)。

不可數名詞是指不可以計算的東西，例如，
我們不可以說 one rice (一粒米)、two rices
(兩粒米)。

不可數名詞的例子如下：
- Kate was listening to (some) **music**.
- There's **sand** in my shoes.
- Do you have any **money**?
- It wasn't your fault. It was bad **luck**.
- There is no **electricity** in this house.
- We don't have enough **water**.

B

可數名詞單數通常要加 **a/an**：

    a beach   **a student**   **an umbrella**

單數可數名詞不可以單獨使用，其前一定要
加 **a/the/my** 等：
- I want **a banana**. (並非 I want banana)
- There's been **an accident**.
  (並非 There's been accident)

複數可數名詞則可以單獨使用：
- I like **bananas**. (通指香蕉這種水果)
- **Accidents** can be prevented.

不可數名詞通常不可以加 **a/an**，例如，不可
以說 a sand 或 a music。
不可數名詞通常使用 **a ... of** 的量詞，
例如：

    a bowl of / a pound of / a grain of rice

不可數名詞可以單獨使用 (不需加 **the / my /
some** 等)：
- I eat **rice** every day.
- There's **blood** on your shirt.
- Can you hear **music**?

C

some 和 **any** 可以和複數可數名詞一起使用：
- We sang **some songs**.
- Did you buy **any apples**?

many 和 **few** 通常和複數可數名詞一起使用：
- We didn't take **many pictures**.
- I have **a few things** to do.

some 和 **any** 也可以和不可數名詞一起使用：
- We listened to **some music**.
- Did you buy **any** apple **juice**?

much 和 **little** 和不可數名詞一起使用：
- We didn't do **much shopping**.
- I have **a little work** to do.

可數名詞與不可數名詞2 Unit 68　*children / the children* Unit 73　*some* 與 *any* Unit 83
many / much / few / little Unit 85

Exercises

67.1 下列各句中的名詞，有些須要加 *a/an*，有些不須要；請判斷各題 *a/an* 的使用是否正確，若有錯誤請加以改正。

1. Joe goes everywhere by bike. (He doesn't have car.)   _a car._
2. Helen was listening to music when I arrived.   _OK_
3. We went to very nice restaurant last weekend.   _____
4. I brush my teeth with toothpaste.   _____
5. I use toothbrush to brush my teeth.   _____
6. Can you tell me if there's bank near here?   _____
7. My brother works for insurance company in Detroit.   _____
8. I don't like violence.   _____
9. Can you smell paint?   _____
10. When we were in Rome, we stayed in big hotel.   _____
11. We need gas. I hope we come to gas station soon.   _____
12. I wonder if you can help me. I have problem.   _____
13. I like your suggestion. It's very interesting idea.   _____
14. John has interview for job tomorrow.   _____
15. I like volleyball. It's good game.   _____
16. Liz doesn't usually wear jewelry.   _____
17. Jane was wearing beautiful necklace.   _____

67.2 依各句題意，從下列名詞中選出一個字以完成句子，並依據各名詞的需要加入 *a/an*。

~~accident~~	blood	coat	cookie	decision	electricity
interview	key	minute	~~music~~	question	sugar

1. It wasn't your fault. It was _an accident_ .
2. Listen! Can you hear _music_ ?
3. I couldn't get into the house because I didn't have _____ .
4. It's very warm today. Why are you wearing _____ ?
5. Do you take _____ in your coffee?
6. Are you hungry? Would you like _____ with your coffee?
7. Our lives would be very difficult without _____ .
8. "I had _____ for a job yesterday." "You did? How did it go?"
9. The heart pumps _____ through the body.
10. Excuse me, but can I ask you _____ ?
11. I'm not ready yet. Can you wait _____ , please?
12. We can't delay much longer. We have to make _____ soon.

67.3 依各句題意，從下列名詞中選出一個字以完成句子，並判斷各名詞是否須要 *a/an*，或必須使用複數形。

air	day	friend	language	letter	line
meat	patience	people	~~picture~~	space	umbrella

1. I had my camera, but I didn't take any _pictures_ .
2. There are seven _____ in a week.
3. A vegetarian is a person who doesn't eat _____ .
4. Outside the movie theater, there was _____ of people waiting to see the movie.
5. I'm not very good at writing _____ .
6. Last night I went out with some _____ of mine.
7. There were very few _____ in town today. The streets were almost empty.
8. I'm going out for a walk. I need some fresh _____ .
9. Gary always wants things quickly. He doesn't have much _____ .
10. I think it's going to rain. Do you have _____ I could borrow?
11. Do you speak any foreign _____ ?
12. Our apartment is very small. We don't have much _____ .

可數名詞與不可數名詞 2

A 很多名詞可以作為可數名詞或不可數名詞，但通常意思不同。比較下面各例句：

可數名詞
- Did you hear **a noise** just now?
  (專指某一個的噪音)
- I bought **a paper** to read.
  (一份報紙)
- There's **a hair** in my soup!
  (一根頭髮)
- You can stay with us. There is **a** spare **room**. (屋子裡的一個房間)
- I had some interesting **experiences** while I was traveling. (曾經發生在我身上的一些事情)
- Enjoy your trip. Have a good **time**!

不可數名詞
- I can't work here. There's too much **noise**. (並非 too many noises)
- I need some **paper** to write on.
  (用來寫字的東西)
- You've got very long **hair**. (並非 hairs)
  (頭上所有的頭髮)
- You can't sit here. There isn't any **room**.
  (空間)
- They offered me the job because I had a lot of **experience**. (並非 experiences)
- I can't wait. I don't have **time**.

coffee / **tea** / **juice** / **beer** 等飲料通常為不可數名詞：
- I don't like **coffee** very much.

但 **a coffee** 是 a cup of coffee，**two coffees** 意思是 two cups of coffee：
- **Two** coffees and **an orange juice**, please.

B 下列的名詞通常是不可數名詞：

advice	baggage	behavior	bread	chaos	damage
furniture	information	luck	luggage	news	permission
progress	scenery	traffic	weather	work	

這些名詞不可以與 **a/an** 一起使用：
- I'm going to buy **some bread**. 或 ...**a loaf of bread**. (並非 a bread)
- Enjoy your vacation! I hope you have good **weather**. (並非 a good weather)

這些名詞通常不可以使用複數形 (通常不說 breads、furnitures 等)：
- Where are you going to put all your **furniture**? (並非 furnitures)
- Let me know if you need more **information**. (並非 informations)

news 為不可數名詞，並不是複數形：
- The **news was** very depressing. (並非 The news were)

travel 的意思泛指旅遊，為不可數名詞，因此不可用 a travel 來表示一趟旅行，而是用 **a trip**：
- They spend a lot of money on **travel**.
- We had **a** very good **trip**. (並非 a good travel)

比較下面的可數名詞與不可數名詞：

可數名詞
- I'm looking for **a job**.
- What **a** beautiful **view**!
- It's **a** nice **day** today.
- We had a lot of **bags** and **suitcases**.
- **These chairs** are mine.
- That's **a** good **suggestion**.

不可數名詞
- I'm looking for **work**. (並非 a work)
- What beautiful **scenery**!
- It's nice **weather** today.
- We had a lot of **baggage/luggage**.
- **This furniture** is mine.
- That's good **advice**.

Exercises

68.1 判斷下列各題劃線部份的名詞何者正確。

1. "Did you hear ~~noise~~ / a noise just now?"   "No, I didn't hear anything." (*a noise* 為正確答案)
2. a) If you want to know the news, you can read paper / a paper.
   b) I want to print some documents, but the printer is out of paper / papers.
3. a) I thought there was somebody in the house because there was light / a light on inside.
   b) Light / A light comes from the sun.
4. a) I was in a hurry this morning. I didn't have time / a time for breakfast.
   b) "Did you have a good vacation?"   "Yes, we had wonderful time / a wonderful time."
5. This is nice room / a nice room. Did you decorate it yourself?
6. Sue was very helpful. She gave us some very useful advice / advices.
7. Did you have nice weather / a nice weather when you were away?
8. We were very unfortunate. We had bad luck / a bad luck.
9. Is it difficult to find a work / job at this time?
10. Our travel / trip from Paris to Istanbul by train was very tiring.
11. When the fire alarm rang, there was total chaos / a total chaos.
12. I had to buy a / some bread because I wanted to make some sandwiches.
13. Bad news don't / doesn't make people happy.
14. Your hair is / Your hairs are too long. You should have it / them cut.
15. The damage / The damages caused by the storm will cost a lot to repair.

68.2 依各句題意，從下列名詞中選出適當的字以完成句子。注意：有些名詞必須用複數形式。

advice	chair	experience	experience	furniture	hair
information	job	~~luggage~~	permission	progress	work

1. I didn't have much *luggage* – just two small bags.
2. They'll tell you all you want to know. They'll give you plenty of _____ .
3. There is room for everybody to sit down. There are plenty of _____ .
4. We have no _____ , not even a bed or a table.
5. "What does Alan look like?"   "He's got a long beard and very short _____ ."
6. Carla's English is better than it was. She's made _____ .
7. Mike is unemployed. He can't find a _____ .
8. Mike is unemployed. He can't find _____ .
9. If you want to leave early, you have to ask for _____ .
10. I didn't know what to do. So I asked Chris for _____ .
11. I don't think Ann will get the job. She doesn't have enough _____ .
12. Rita has done many interesting things. She could write a book about her _____ .

68.3 請參見本單元 Unit 68B 名詞表中的名詞，並依各題情境，自表中選出適當的字以完成下列各句。

1. Your friends have just arrived at the station. You can't see any suitcases or bags.
   You ask them: Do _you have any luggage_ _____ ?
2. You go into the tourist office. You want to know about places to see in the city.
   You say: I'd like _____ .
3. You are a student. You want your teacher to advise you about which courses to take.
   You say: Can you give me _____ ?
4. You want to watch the news on TV, but you don't know when it is on.
   You ask your friend: What time _____ ?
5. You are at the top of a mountain. You can see a very long way. It's beautiful.
   You say: It _____ , isn't it?
6. You look out the window. The weather is horrible: cold, wet, and windy.
   You say: What _____ !

可數名詞與 a / an 和 some

A 可數名詞分為單數形與複數形，請看下面各例：

a **dog**	a **child**	the **evening**	this **party**	an **umbrella**
dogs	some **children**	the **evenings**	these **parties**	two **umbrellas**

a/an 可以用於單數可數名詞前：

- Goodbye! Have **a** nice **evening**.
- Do you need **an umbrella**?

單數可數名詞不可以單獨使用 (必須與 a/the/my 等一起使用)：

- She never wears **a** hat. (並非 She never wears hat)
- Be careful of **the** dog. (並非 Be careful of dog)
- What **a** beautiful day!
- I've got **a** headache.

B **a/an** 用來表示，某事物/某人是一個什麼樣的東西或人：

- That's **a nice table**.

複數可數名詞可以單獨使用：

- Those are **nice chairs**. (並非 some nice chairs)

比較下列單數名詞與複數名詞之用法：

■ A dog is **an animal**.	■ Dogs **are animals**.
■ I'm **an optimist**.	■ We're **optimists**.
■ Tim's father is **a doctor**.	■ Most of my friends are **students**.
■ Are you **a good driver**?	■ Are they **good students**?
■ Jill is **a really nice person**.	■ Jill's parents are **really nice people**.
■ What **a pretty dress**!	■ What **awful shoes**!

我們可以說某人有 **a long nose** / **a nice face** / **blue eyes** / **small hands** 等：

■ Jack has **a long nose**.	■ Jack has **blue eyes**.
(並非 the long nose)	(並非 the blue eyes)

描述某人的職業時必須用 **a/an**：

- Sandra is **a nurse**. (並非 Sandra is nurse)
- Would you like to be **an English teacher**?

C **some** 可以與複數可數名詞一起使用。**some** 的用法分為兩種。

意思與 a number of / a few of / a pair of 相同：

- I've seen **some** good **movies** recently. (並非 I've seen good movies)
- **Some friends** of mine are coming to stay this weekend.
- I need **some** new **sunglasses**. (= a new pair of sunglasses)

名詞意思為泛指某樣東西時，不可以與 **some** 一起使用 (參見 Unit 73)：

- I love **bananas**. (並非 some bananas)
- My aunt is a writer. She writes **books**. (並非 some books)

有時候名詞前使用 **some** 或沒有 **some**，意思並無差別：

- There are (**some**) eggs in the refrigerator if you're hungry.

意思是一些、部分，而非全部：

- **Some children** learn very quickly. (but not all children)
- Tomorrow there will be rain in **some places**, but most of the country will be dry.

Exercises

69.1 這些是什麼東西？請參照範例，完成下列各句。

1. an ant? *It's an insect.*
2. ants and bees? *They're insects.*
3. a cauliflower? _____
4. chess? _____
5. a violin, a trumpet, and a flute _____
_____
6. a skyscraper? _____

這些人是誰？請參照範例，完成下列各句。

11. Beethoven? *He was a composer.*
12. Shakespeare? _____
_____
13. Albert Einstein? _____
_____
14. George Washington, Abraham Lincoln, and John F. Kennedy?
_____

7. Earth, Mars, Venus, and Jupiter? _____
_____
8. a tulip? _____
9. the Nile, the Rhine, and the Mississippi?
_____
10. a pigeon, an eagle, and a crow? _____
_____

15. Marilyn Monroe? _____
_____
16. Elvis Presley and John Lennon? _____
17. Van Gogh, Renoir, and Picasso? _____
_____

69.2 依據各題的描述，自下列的名詞中選出各題中所描述的職業。

chef	interpreter	journalist	~~nurse~~
plumber	surgeon	travel agent	waiter

1. Sarah takes care of patients in the hospital. *She's a nurse.*
2. Gary works in a restaurant. He brings the food to the tables. He _____
3. Mary arranges people's trips for them. She _____
4. Kevin works in a hospital. He operates on people. _____
5. Jonathan cooks in a restaurant. _____
6. Jane writes articles for a newspaper. _____
7. Dave installs and repairs water pipes. _____
8. Linda translates what people are saying from one language into another so that they can understand each other. _____

69.3 依各句題意，於空格中填入 *a/an* 或 *some*，或空白。

1. I've seen *some* good films recently.
2. What's wrong with you? Do you have __*a*__ headache?
3. I know a lot of people. Most of them are __—__ students.
4. When I was _____ child, I used to be very shy.
5. Would you like to be _____ actor?
6. Do you collect _____ stamps?
7. What _____ beautiful garden!
8. _____ birds, for example, the penguin, cannot fly.
9. Do you enjoy going to _____ concerts?
10. I've been walking for three hours. I've got _____ sore feet.
11. I don't feel very well this morning. I've got _____ sore throat.
12. Maria speaks _____ English, but not very much.
13. It's too bad we don't have _____ camera. I'd like to take _____ picture of that house.
14. Those are _____ nice shoes. Where did you get them?
15. I'm going shopping. I want to buy _____ new shoes.
16. You need _____ visa to visit _____ countries, but not all of them.
17. Jane is _____ teacher. Her parents were _____ teachers, too.
18. I don't believe him. He's _____ liar. He's always telling _____ lies.

a / an 與 the

請看下面的例子：

I had **a** sandwich and **an** apple for lunch.
我午餐吃了一個三明治和一個蘋果。
The sandwich wasn't very good, but **the** apple was delicious.
三明治不怎麼好吃，但蘋果很可口。

John

Karen

在第一個例句中，John 說 **a** sandwich 以及 **an** apple 因為這是他第一次提及這兩樣東西。

在第二個例句中，John 再次提到三明治和蘋果時，他說 **the** sandwich 以及 **the** apple，因為 Karen 知道 John 所指的就是他中餐所吃的那個三明治和蘋果。

比較下列例句中 **a** 與 **the** 之用法：

■ **A** man and **a** woman were sitting across from me. **The** man was American, but I think **the** woman was British.

■ When we were on vacation, we stayed at **a** hotel. Sometimes we ate at **the** hotel, and sometimes we went to **a** restaurant.

the 用來指特定的某樣東西。比較 **a/an** 與 **the** 之用法：

■ Tim sat down on **a** chair. (房間中有許多椅子，Tim 坐在其中的一張椅子上。)
Tim sat down on **the** chair **nearest the door**. (特定的一張椅子，靠門的那一張。)

■ Paula is looking for **a** job. (並非特定的某一份工作。)
Did Paula get **the** job **she applied for**? (特定的一份工作，Paula 所申請的那一份。)

■ Do you have **a** car? (並非特定的某一部車。)
I washed **the** car yesterday. (我的車)

在某些情況下，說話者所指的某特定人、事、物很明確時，必須使用 **the**。例如，當我們在房間裡談論裡面的東西，就用 **the** light / **the** floor / **the** ceiling / **the** door / **the** carpet 等：

■ Can you turn off **the** light, please? (房間裡的燈)

■ I took a taxi to **the** station. (這個鎮上的車站)

■ (在商店裡) I'd like to speak to **the** manager, please. (這個店的經理)

同樣地，我們通常用 (go to) **the** bank / **the** post office：

■ I have to go to **the** bank and then I'm going to **the** post office.
(說話者通常指的是某一個特定的銀行或郵局。)

還有，我們通常用 go to **the** doctor / **the** dentist / **the** hospital：

■ Carol isn't very well. She went to **the** doctor. (她平常看的醫生)

■ Two people were taken to **the** hospital after the accident.

比較 **the** 與 **a** 的用法：

■ I have to go **the** bank today.
Is there **a** bank near here?

■ I don't like going to **the** dentist.
My sister is **a** dentist.

我們常用 once **a** week / three times **a** day / $1.59 **a** pound 等表達方式：

■ "How often do you go to the movies?" "About once **a** month."

■ "How much are those potatoes?" "A dollar **a** pound."

■ Helen works eight hours **a** day, six days **a** week.

Exercises

70.1 依各句題意，填入 **a/an** 或 **the**。

1. This morning I bought __a__ newspaper and _____ magazine. _____ newspaper is in my briefcase, but I can't remember where I put _____ magazine.
2. I saw _____ accident this morning. _____ car crashed into _____ tree. _____ driver of _____ car wasn't hurt, but _____ car was badly damaged.
3. There are two cars parked outside: _____ blue one and _____ gray one. _____ blue one belongs to my neighbors; I don't know who _____ owner of _____ gray one is.
4. My friends live in _____ old house in _____ small town. There is _____ beautiful garden behind _____ house. I would like to have _____ garden like that.

70.2 依各句題意，填入 **a/an** 或 **the**。

1. a) This house is very nice. Does it have __a__ yard?
   b) It's a beautiful day. Let's sit in _____ yard.
   c) I like living in this house, but it's too bad that _____ yard is so small.
2. a) Can you recommend _____ good restaurant?
   b) We had dinner in _____ very nice restaurant.
   c) We had dinner in _____ most expensive restaurant in town.
3. a) She has _____ French name, but in fact she's English, not French.
   b) What's _____ name of that man we met yesterday?
   c) We stayed at a very nice hotel – I can't remember _____ name now.
4. a) There isn't _____ airport near where I live. _____ nearest airport is 70 miles away.
   b) Our flight was delayed. We had to wait at _____ airport for three hours.
   c) Excuse me, please. Can you tell me how to get to _____ airport?
5. a) "Are you going away next week?" "No, _____ week after next."
   b) I'm going away for _____ week in September.
   c) Gary has a part-time job. He works three mornings _____ week.

70.3 請參照範例，依各句題意，判斷各題的名詞是否需要 **a/an** 或 **the**。

1. Would you like (apple)? _____an apple_____
2. How often do you go to dentist? _____
3. Could you close door, please? _____
4. I'm sorry. I didn't mean to do that. It was mistake. _____
5. Excuse me, where is bus station, please? _____
6. I have problem. Can you help me? _____
7. I'm just going to post office. I won't be long. _____
8. There were no chairs, so we sat on floor. _____
9. Are you finished with book I lent you? _____
10. My sister has just gotten job at bank in Atlanta. _____
11. We live in small apartment near hospital. _____
12. There's supermarket on corner near my house. _____

70.4 依你自己的情形，以 D 小節的片語 (**once a week / three times a day** 等) 回答下面各問題。

1. How often do you go to the dentist? _Three or four times a year._
2. How much does it cost to rent a car in your country? _About $40 a day._
3. How often do you go to the movies? _____
4. How often do you take a vacation? _____
5. What's the normal speed limit on highways in your country? _____
6. How much sleep do you need? _____
7. How often do you go out at night? _____
8. How much television do you watch (on average) _____

the 1

A

表示「唯一」或「只有一個」時必須用 **the**：
- What is **the** longest river in **the** world? (世界上只有一條最長的河。)
- **The** earth goes around **the** sun, and **the** moon goes around **the** earth.
- Have you ever crossed **the** equator?
- I'm going away at **the** end of this month.

下面例句中，一定要使用 **the**：
- Paris is **the** capital of France. (並非 Paris is capital of . . .)

描述某事物是一個什麼樣的東西時，則必須用 **a/an** (參見 Unit 68C)。比較下面例句中 **the** 與 **a** 之用法：
- **The** sun is **a** star. (很多星星中的一個。)
- **The** hotel we stayed at was **a** very nice hotel.

B

下列名詞片語中必須使用 **the**：**the sky** / **the sea** / **the ocean** / **the ground** / **the country** / **the environment**：
- We looked up at all the stars in **the sky**. (並非 in sky)
- Would you like to live in **the country**? (= not in a town or city)
- We must do more to protect **the environment**. (我們週遭的自然環境。)

space 意思是「太空」或「宇宙」時不加 **the**。比較下面例句：
- There are millions of stars **in space**. (並非 in the space)
- I tried to park my car, but **the space** was too small.

C

same 前面必須加 **the** (**the same**)：
- Your sweater is **the same** color as mine. (並非 is same color)
- "Are these keys **the same**?" "No, they're different."

D

我們說 (go to) **the movies** / **the theater**，「看電影」的片語中必須使用 **the**：
- I go to **the movies** a lot, but I haven't been to **the theater** in ages.

上面例句中的 **the movies** 和 **the theater** 並不是指特定的電影或戲院。

radio 前通常加 **the**，但是 **television** 前不加 **the**：
- I listen to **the radio** a lot.　　並非　I watch **television** a lot.
- We heard the news on **the radio**.　　並非　We watched the news on **TV**.

the television 意思與 the television set 相同，意思是電視機。
- Can you turn off **the television**, please?

E

breakfast　　lunch　　dinner

三餐的名稱前通常不加 **the**：
- What did you have for **breakfast**?
- We had **lunch** in a very nice restaurant.
- What time is **dinner**?

三餐的名稱前若有形容詞，則必須加 **a**：
- We had **a** very **nice lunch**. (並非 We had very nice lunch)

F

Gate 10　　Room 126 等

在名詞+數字的名詞片語中，不需加 **the**。例如：
- Our plane leaves from **Gate 10**. (並非 the Gate 10)
- (在商店裡) Do you have these shoes in **size 9**? (並非 the size 9)

同樣地，飯店裡 126 號房為 **Room 126**，書的第 29 頁為 **page 29**，測驗中的第 3 題為 **question 3**，火車站的第 6 月台為 **Platform 6** 等。

71.1 依各句題意，填入 *the* 或 *a*/*an*，或空白。

1. *A:* Where did you have ___–__ lunch?
   B: We went to __*a*__ restaurant.
2. *A:* Did you have _____ nice vacation?
   B: Yes, it was _____ best vacation I've ever had.
3. *A:* Where's _____ nearest drugstore?
   B: There's one on _____ next block.
4. *A:* Do you often listen to _____ radio?
   B: No. In fact, I don't have _____ radio.
5. *A:* Would you like to travel in _____ outer space?
   B: Yes, I'd love to go to _____ moon.
6. *A:* Do you go to _____ movies very often?
   B: No, not very often. But I watch a lot of movies on _____ television.
7. *A:* It was _____ nice day yesterday, wasn't it?
   B: Yes, it was beautiful. We went for a walk by _____ ocean.
8. *A:* What did you have for _____ breakfast this morning?
   B: Nothing. I never eat _____ breakfast.
9. *A:* Excuse me, where is _____ Room 225, please?
   B: It's on _____ second floor.
10. *A:* We spent all our money because we stayed at _____ most expensive hotel in town.
    B: Why didn't you stay at _____ cheaper hotel?

71.2 依各句題意，填入 *the* 或 *a*/*an*，或空白。

1. I haven't been to __*the*__ movies in ages.
2. I lay down on _____ ground and looked up at _____ sky.
3. Sarah spends most of her free time watching _____ television.
4. _____ television was on, but nobody was watching it.
5. Lisa and I arrived at _____ same time.
6. Have you had _____ dinner yet?
7. You'll find _____ information you need at _____ top of _____ page 15.
8. What's _____ capital city of Canada?

71.3 依各句題意，在名詞前加 *the* 或 *a*/*an* 或不加冠詞，以改寫下列各句 (參見 Unit 70)。

1. (Sun) is (star) __*The sun is a star.*_____
2. Paul lives in small town in country. _____
3. Moon goes around earth every 27 days. _____
4. I'm fed up with doing same thing every day. _____
5. It was very hot day. It was hottest day of year. _____
6. I don't usually have lunch, but I always eat good breakfast. _____
7. If you live in foreign country, you should try to learn language. _____
8. We missed our train because we were waiting on wrong platform. _____
9. Next train to San Diego leaves from Platform 3. _____

71.4 依各句題意，自下列名詞中選出一個適當的字，以完成句子。若題意有需要，請填入 *the*。

breakfast   ~~**dinner**~~   **gate**   **Gate 21**   **movies**   **question 8**   **ocean**

1. "Are you going out tonight?" "Yes, after __*dinner*__ ."
2. There was no wind, so _____ was very calm.
3. The test wasn't too difficult, but I couldn't answer _____ .
4. "I'm going to _____ tonight." "Really? What are you going to see?"
5. I didn't have time for _____ this morning because I was in a hurry.
6. Oh, _____ is open. I must have forgotten to close it.
7. *(airport announcement)* Flight AB123 to Tokyo is now boarding at _____ .

the 2 (school / the school 等)

比較 school 與 the school 之用法：

Claudia

Claudia is 10 years old. Every day she goes to **school**. She's at **school** now. **School** begins at 8:30 and ends at 3:00. (Claudia 今年 10 歲。她每天去上學。她目前正在學校裡上課。學校早上 8 點半上課，下午 3 點下課。)

表達學生去上學或在學校上課時，我們說 go to **school** 或 be in **school**；此種用法中，並未指某一所特定的學校，此時學校指的是一般性的概念。

Today Claudia's mother wants to speak to her daughter's teacher. So she has gone to **the school** to see her. She's at **the school** now. (今天 Claudia 的母親要和她的老師談話。所以她到學校裡見 Claudia 的老師。她人目前在學校裡面。)

例子中，Claudia 的媽媽不是學生，所以不能說 she is in school 或 she goes to school。她到特定的學校，也就是 Claudia 的學校，去見 Claudia 的老師，所以說 she goes to **the school**。

prison/jail、college、class 與 church 的用法類似。將這些場所當作一個概念，指的是他們的用途時，不可以加 **the**。比較下面例句：

- Ken's brother is in **prison** for robbery. (Ken 的弟弟是犯人，他在監獄裡服刑；此處 prison 並不是指某個特定的監獄。)

- When I finish **high school**, I want to go to **college**.

- Mrs. Kelly goes to **church** every Sunday. (去教堂作禮拜)

- I was **in class** for five hours today. (在高中或大學裡上課)

- Ken went to **the prison** to visit his brother. (Ken 是訪客，不是犯人。)

- Dan is a student at **the college** where I used to work. (某一所特定的學校，我以前在那裡工作的那一所。)

- Some workmen went to **the church** to repair the roof. (並不是去作禮拜)

- Who is the youngest student in **the class**? (一群特定的學生)

其他大部分的場所都必須加 **the**；例如，**the hospital** / **the bank** / **the station**。(參見 Unit 70C 與 Unit 71D)。

bed   work   home

我們通常說 **go to bed** (去睡覺)/ **be in bed** (在床上) 等，而非 the bed:
- It's time to go to **bed** now.
- Do you ever have breakfast **in bed**?

但是 - I sat down on **the bed**. (指某一件特定的家具，也就是某一張床)

我們通常說 **go to work** / **be at work** / **start work** / **finish work** 等，而非 the work:
- Ann didn't go to **work** yesterday.
- What time do you usually finish **work**?

我們通常說 **go home** / **come home** / **arrive home** / **get home** / **be (at) home**
- It's late. Let's go **home**.
- Will you be (at) **home** tomorrow afternoon?

the Unit 70 與 Unit 71，Unit 73 至 Unit 76   介係詞 (*in* bed / *at* school 等) Unit 120 至 Unit 122   home Unit 123D

Exercises

72.1 依各句題意，自下列名詞中選出一個適當的字，以介係詞 (*to/at/in* 等) + 名詞的方式完成各句。下列名詞可重複使用。

> **bed** ~~college~~ **home** **prison** **school** **high school** **work**

1. When Julie finishes high school, she wants to study economics _in college_____ .
2. In Taiwan, children from the age of seven have to go _____ .
3. Mark didn't go out last night. He stayed _____ .
4. There is a lot of traffic in the morning when everybody is going _____ .
5. Jeff hasn't graduated yet. He is still _____ .
6. Bill never gets up before 9:00. It's 8:30 now, so he is still _____ .
7. If you commit a serious crime, you could be sent _____ .

72.2 依各句題意，判斷 *school / college / church / prison* 等字是否需要加 *the*，並完成各句。

1. (**school**)
   a) Every semester parents are invited to __*the school*__ to meet the teachers.
   b) Why aren't your children in __*school*__ today? Are they sick?
   c) When he was younger, Ted hated _____ .
   d) What time does _____ usually start in your country?
   e) *A:* How do your children get home from _____ ? By bus?
      B: No, they walk. _____ isn't very far away.
   f) What sort of job does Jenny want to do when she finishes _____ ?
   g) There were some people waiting outside _____ to meet their children.

2. (**college**)
   a) In your country, do many people go to _____ ?
   b) The Smiths have four children in _____ at the same time.
   c) This is only a small town, but _____ is one of the best in the country.

3. (**church**)
   a) John's mother is a regular churchgoer. She goes to _____ every Sunday.
   b) John himself doesn't go to _____ .
   c) John went to _____ to take some pictures of the building.

4. (**class**)
   a) The professor isn't in his office at this time. He's in _____ .
   b) The teacher asked _____ to turn off their cell phones.
   c) I'll get a newspaper on my way to _____ this afternoon.
   d) Not even the best student in _____ could answer the question.

5. (**prison**)
   a) In some places people are in _____ because of their political beliefs.
   b) A few days ago, the fire department was called to _____ to put out a fire.
   c) The judge decided to fine the man $500 instead of sending him to _____ .

6. (**home/work/bed**)
   a) I like to read in _____ before I go to sleep.
   b) It's nice to travel around, but there's no place like _____ !
   c) Should we meet after _____ tomorrow?
   d) If I'm feeling tired, I go to _____ early.
   e) What time do you usually start _____ in the morning?
   f) The economic situation was very bad. Many people were out of _____ .

the 3 (children / the children)

A

泛指某一類的事物或人時，不可以使用 **the**：

- I'm afraid of **dogs**. (並非 the dogs)
  (**dogs** 泛指狗這種動物，而不是某一群特定的狗)
- **Doctors** are paid more than **teachers**.
- Do you collect **stamps**?
- **Crime** is a problem in most big cities. (並非 The crime)
- **Life** has changed a lot in the last 30 years. (並非 The life)
- Do you like **classical music** / **Chinese food** / **fast cars**?
- My favorite sport is **football/skiing/hockey**.
- My favorite subject at school was **history/physics/English**.

使用 **most** 時，例如 **most** people / **most** books / **most** cars 等，不可以加 the。

- **Most hotels** accept credit cards. (並非 The most hotels)

B

指特定的人或事物時要用 **the**。
比較下面的例句：

一般性的 (不加 the)	特定的人或事物 (加 the)
■ **Children** learn from playing. (一般孩童)	■ We took **the children** to the zoo. (一群特定的小孩，也許是說話者自己的小孩)
■ I couldn't live without **music**.	■ The movie wasn't very good, but I liked **the music**. (該部電影中的音樂)
■ All **cars** have wheels.	■ All **the cars** in this parking lot belong to people who work here.
■ **Sugar** isn't very good for you.	■ Can you pass **the sugar**, please? (桌上的糖)
■ Do **Americans** drink much tea? (一般美國人)	■ Do **the Americans you know** drink tea? (你所認識的美國人，而不是一般美國民眾)

C

有時「一般性的事物」與「特定的事物」之間，意思的差別並不很清楚。
比較下面的例句：

一般性的 (不加 the)	特定的人或事物 (加 the)
■ I like working with **people**. (一般人，民眾)	
■ I like working with **people who are lively**. (並非所有人，然而「充滿活力的人」仍是泛指某一群人)	■ I like **the people I work with**. (特定的一群人，和我一起工作的那群人。)
■ Do you like **coffee**? (泛指咖啡)	
■ Do you like **strong black coffee**? (並非所有的咖啡，但是「濃的黑咖啡」仍是泛指某一類咖啡。)	■ Did you like **the coffee we had after dinner last night**? (特定的咖啡，我們昨晚晚餐後喝的那一杯/那一種)

73.1 自下列名詞中選出四個，並依你個人的經驗，造句說明你喜歡或不喜歡該事物或人。

boxing	cats	fast food restaurants	football	~~hot weather~~
math	opera	small children	rock music	zoos

請以下列句型造句。

I like . . . / I don't like . . .   I don't mind . . .

I love . . . / I hate . . .   I'm interested in . . . / I'm not interested in . . .

1. _I don't like hot weather very much._
2. _____
3. _____
4. _____
5. _____

73.2 依各句題意，自下列名詞中選出適當者，並判斷是否需要加 **the**，以完成各句。

~~(the) basketball~~	(the) **grass**	(the) **patience**	(the) **people**
(the) **questions**	(the) **meat**	~~(the) information~~	(the) **hotels**
(the) **history**	(the) **water**	(the) **spiders**	(the) **lies**

1. My favorite sport is _basketball_ .
2. _The information_ we were given wasn't correct.
3. Some people are afraid of _____ .
4. A vegetarian is somebody who doesn't eat _____ .
5. The test wasn't very difficult. I answered _____ without any trouble.
6. Do you know _____ who live next door?
7. _____ is the study of the past.
8. George always tells the truth. He never tells _____ .
9. We couldn't find anywhere to stay downtown. All _____ were full.
10. _____ in the pool didn't look very clean, so we didn't go swimming.
11. Don't sit on _____ . It's wet from the rain.
12. You need _____ to teach young children.

73.3 依各句題意，判斷是否需要加 **the**，以選擇正確形式。

1. I'm afraid of dogs / ~~the dogs~~. (*dogs* 是正確答案)
2. Can you pass ~~salt~~ / the salt, please? (*the salt* 是正確答案)
3. Apples / The apples are good for you.
4. Look at apples / the apples on that tree! They're very big.
5. Women / The women live longer than men / the men.
6. I don't drink tea / the tea. I don't like it.
7. We had a very good meal. Vegetables / The vegetables were especially good.
8. Life / The life is strange sometimes. Some very strange things happen.
9. I like skiing / the skiing, but I'm not very good at it.
10. Who are people / the people in this photograph?
11. What makes people / the people violent? What causes aggression / the aggression?
12. All books / All the books on the top shelf belong to me.
13. Don't stay in that hotel. It's very noisy and beds / the beds are very uncomfortable.
14. A pacifist is somebody who is against war / the war.
15. First World War / The First World War lasted from 1914 until 1918.
16. I'd like to go to Egypt and see Pyramids / the Pyramids.
17. Someone gave me a book about history / the history of modern art / the modern art.
18. Ron and Brenda got married, but marriage / the marriage didn't last very long.
19. Most people / The most people believe that marriage / the marriage and family life / the family life are the basis of society / the society.

A

請看下面的例句：

- **The giraffe** is the tallest of all animals.
- **The bicycle** is an excellent means of transportation.
- When was **the telephone** invented?
- **The dollar** is the currency (= the money) of the United States.

在上述的例句中，**the** + 名詞並非用來指某一特定的事物。**The giraffe** 意思是「長頸鹿這種動物」，而非某一隻特定的長頸鹿。**The**+單數可數名詞可用來表示某一類的動物、機器等。

相同的，樂器名稱前加 **the** 也用來表示某一類的樂器：

- Can you play **the** guitar?
- **The** piano is my favorite instrument.

使用 **a** 時，意思不同；比較下面的例句：

- I'd like to have **a piano**.　　但是　I can't play **the piano**.
- We saw **a giraffe** at the zoo.　　但是　**The giraffe** is my favorite animal.

注意我們使用 **man**(而非 the man)表示人類：

- What do you know about the origins of **man**? (並非 the man)

B

the + 形容詞之用法：

the + 形容詞用來表示某一群人，特別常與下面的形容詞一起使用：

the young	the rich	the sick	the blind	the injured
the old	the poor	the disabled	the deaf	the dead
the elderly	the homeless	the unemployed		

the young 意思是年輕人，**the rich** 意思是有錢人等等：

- Do you think **the rich** should pay higher taxes?
- The government has promised to provide more money to help **the homeless**.

此種用法通常表複數意思。不可用 a young 或 the injured 表達「一個年輕人」或「那個受傷的人」；必須說 **a** young **person**、**the** injured **woman** 等。

注意 the **poor** 不能寫成 the poors，the **young** 不能寫成 the youngs 等。

C

the + 國籍之用法：(-ch 或 -sh 為子字尾的形容詞，例如 the French / the English / the Spanish 等)。

the + 表國籍的形容詞意思是「該國的全體人民」：

- **The French** are famous for their food. (法國全體人民)

注意 the French / the English 等表複數意思，不可以說 a French / an English 表達「一個法國人/英國人」，必須說 **a Frenchman** / **an Englishman** 等。

the 也可以與國籍字尾為 **-ese** 的名詞一起使用(the Chinese / the Sudanese 等)：

- **The Chinese** invented printing.

這些 -ese 結尾的字也可表示單數意思 (a Japanese / a Sudanese / a Vietnamese 等)。

Swiss 的用法也是如此：**the Swiss** 為複數意思，**a Swiss** 表單數意思。

其他國籍的名詞，表複數意思時名詞字尾須加 **-s**。例如：

an Italian → Italians　　**a Mexican → Mexicans**　　**a Thai → Thais**

這類的字，我們通常不以 the+國籍的表達方式，來表示「該國的人民」的意思。(參見Unit 73)

Exercises

74.1 依各句題意，自下面四個方框的名詞中選出語意適當的答案，並加 *the* 以回答各問句。

1. *Animals*		2. *Birds*		3. *Inventions*		4. *Currencies*	
tiger	elephant	eagle	penguin	telephone	wheel	dollar	peso
rabbit	cheetah	swan	owl	telescope	laser	euro	rupee
giraffe	kangaroo	parrot	robin	helicopter	typewriter	ruble	yen

1. a) Which of the animals is the tallest? *the giraffe*
   b) Which animal can run the fastest? _____
   c) Which of these animals is found in Australia? _____

2. a) Which of these birds has a long neck? _____
   b) Which of these birds cannot fly? _____
   c) Which bird flies at night? _____

3. a) Which of these inventions is the oldest? _____
   b) Which one is the most recent? _____
   c) Which one was especially important for astronomy? _____

4. a) What is the currency of India? _____
   b) What is the currency of Canada? _____
   c) And the currency of your country? _____

74.2 依各句題意，在空格中填入 *the* 或 *a*。(有些空格不需填入任何字。)

1. When was __*the*__ telephone invented?
2. Can you play _____ musical instrument?
3. Jill plays _____ violin in an orchestra.
4. There was _____ piano in the corner of the room.
5. Can you play _____ piano?
6. Our society is based on _____ family.
7. Michael comes from _____ large family.
8. _____ computer has changed the way we live.

74.3 依各句題意，自下面形容詞中選出適當者，以 *the* + 形容詞的表達方式完成各句。

injured   poor   rich   sick   unemployed   ~~young~~

1. __*The young*__ have the future in their hands.
2. Ambulances arrived at the scene of the accident and took _____ to the hospital.
3. Life is all right if you have a job, but things are not so easy for _____ .
4. Julia has been a nurse all her life. She has spent her life caring for _____ .
5. In England, there is an old story about a man called Robin Hood. It is said that he took money from _____ and gave the money to _____ .

74.4 如何表達下列各國的國民？

	one person (a/an . . .)	*the people in general*
1. Canada	*a Canadian*	*Canadians*
2. Germany	_____	_____
3. France	_____	_____
4. Russia	_____	_____
5. China	_____	_____
6. Brazil	_____	_____
7. Japan	_____	_____
8. and your country	_____	_____

專有名詞加 the 與不加 the 1

A

人名(例如 Ann、Ann Taylor 等)不加 the；同樣地，地名通常也不加 the。例如：

洲名：	Africa (並非 the Africa), Asia, South America
國家及州名：	France (並非 the France), Japan, Brazil, Texas
島嶼名：	Sicily, Bermuda, Vancouver Island, Cuba
城、鎮名：	Cairo, New York, Bangkok
山嶽名：	Everest, Kilimanjaro, Fuji

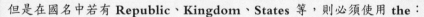

但是在國名中若有 **Republic**、**Kingdom**、**States** 等，則必須使用 **the**：

the Czech **Republic**	**the** United **Kingdom** (the UK)
the Dominican **Republic**	**the** United **States** of America (the USA)

比較下面例句裡國名的用法：

■ We visited **Canada** and **the United States**.

B

使用稱謂語 **Mr.** / **Mrs.** / **Captain** / **Doctor** 等+姓名，不可以加 **the**：
Mr. Johnson / **Doctor** Johnson / **Captain** Johnson / **President** Johnson 等。(並非 the ...)
Uncle Robert / **Saint** Catherine / **Princess** Anne 等。(並非 the ...)

比較下面例句：

■ We called **the doctor**.
We called **Doctor** Johnson. (並非 the Doctor Johnson)

山嶽名 (mount = mountain) 與湖泊名，也不加 **the**：
Mount Everest　**Mount** McKinley　**Lake** Superior　**Lake** Victoria (並非 the ...)

■ They live near **the lake**.
They live near **Lake Superior**. (不加 the)

C

海洋、海、河流、以及運河的名字均須加 **the**：

the Atlantic (Ocean)	**the** Gulf of Mexico	**the** Amazon
the Indian Ocean	**the** Channel (between	**the** Nile
the Caribbean (Sea)	France and Britain)	**the** Panama Canal

沙漠的名字也必須加 **the**
　the Sahara (Desert)　　**the** Gobi Desert

D

人名與地名使用複數形時必須加 **the**：

人名	**the** Mitchell**s** (意思是 Mitchell 一家人), **the** Johnson**s**
國名	**the** Netherland**s**, **the** Philippine**s**, **the** United State**s**
群島名	**the** Bahama**s**, **the** Canarie**s**, **the** Hawaiian Island**s**
山脈名	**the** Rocky Mountain**s** / **the** Rockie**s**, **the** Ande**s**, **the** Alp**s**

■ The highest mountain in **the Andes** is **Mount Aconcagua**.

E

請看下面用法:

　the north (of Mexico) (墨西哥)北部　　　但是　**northern** Mexico (北墨西哥) (不加 the)
　the southeast (of Canada) (加拿大)東南部　但是　**southeastern** Canada (東南加拿大)

比較下面例句中地名的用法：

■ Sweden is in **northern Europe**; Spain is in **the south**.

因此，中東為 **the** Middle East 遠東為 **the** Far East。

north/south等+區域或國家的名字，也不可以加 **the**。

North America	**South Africa**	**southeast Texas**

注意，在地圖上地名通常不加 **the**。

Exercises

75.1 依各句題意，判斷是否該填入 *the*，或僅留空白不需填任何字。

1. Who is ___-___ Doctor Johnson?
2. I was sick, so I went to see _____ doctor.
3. The most powerful person in _____ United States is _____ president.
4. _____ President Kennedy was assassinated in 1963.
5. Do you know _____ Wilsons? They're a very nice couple.
6. Do you know _____ Professor Brown's phone number?

75.2 依各句題意，判斷下面各句是否正確，或是需要加入 *the*。

1. Everest was first climbed in 1953.   _OK_
2. Sapporo is in north of Japan.   _in the north of Japan_
3. Africa is much larger than Europe.   _____
4. Last year I visited Mexico and United States.   _____
5. South of India is warmer than north.   _____
6. Portugal is in western Europe.   _____
7. France and Britain are separated by Channel.   _____
8. Jim has traveled a lot in Middle East.   _____
9. Chicago is on Lake Michigan.   _____
10. Next year we're going skiing in Swiss Alps.   _____
11. UK consists of Great Britain and Northern Ireland.   _____
12. Seychelles are a group of islands in Indian Ocean.   _____
13. The highest mountain in Africa is Kilimanjaro.   _____
14. Hudson River flows into Atlantic Ocean.   _____

75.3 依各句題意，自下面各方框的名詞中選出正確的答案，並視語意需要加 *the* 或不加 *the*，以完成各問句。必要時請參考地圖。

Continents	Countries	Oceans and seas	Mountains	Rivers and canals	
Africa	Canada	~~Atlantic Ocean~~	Alps	Amazon	Suez Canal
Asia	Denmark	Indian Ocean	Andes	Danube	Thames
Australia	Indonesia	Pacific Ocean	Himalayas	Mississippi	Volga
Europe	Sweden	Black Sea	Rockies	Nile	
North America	Thailand	Mediterranean	Urals	Panama Canal	
South America	United States	Red Sea		Rhine	

1. What do you have to cross to travel from Europe to America? _the Atlantic Ocean_
2. Where is Argentina? _____
3. What is the longest river in Africa? _____
4. Of which country is Stockholm the capital? _____
5. Of which country is Washington, D.C., the capital? _____
6. What is the name of the mountain range in the west of North America? _____
7. What is the name of the sea between Africa and Europe? _____
8. What is the smallest continent in the world? _____
9. What is the name of the ocean between North America and Asia? _____
10. What is the name of the ocean between Africa and Australia? _____
11. Which river flows through London? _____
12. Which river flows through Memphis and New Orleans? _____
13. Of which country is Bangkok the capital? _____
14. What joins the Atlantic and Pacific Oceans? _____
15. What is the longest river in South America? _____

專有名詞加 the 與不加 the 2

A

不加 **the** 的專有名詞如下：

大部分的街名、路名、廣場名、公園名等，都不加 **the**：

> Union **Street** (並非 the...)　　Fifth **Avenue**　　Central **Park**
> Wilshire **Boulevard**　　　　　**Broadway**　　　Times **Square**

許多重要建築和機構的名字(例如機場、車站、大學等)通常由兩個字組成，通常不加 **the**：

> **Kennedy Airport**　　　**Cambridge University**

通常第一個字為人名(Kennedy)或地名(Cambridge)，這類專有名詞也通常不加 **the**，例如：

> **Penn Station** (並非 the...)　　**Boston University**　　　**Carnegie Hall**
> **Lincoln Center**　　　　　　　**Buckingham Palace**

比較下面例子：

> **Buckingham Palace** (並非 the...)　但是　**the Royal Palace**
>
> (Royal 是形容詞，而 Buckingham 則為專有名詞。)

B

大部分其他的建築物名要加 **the**。例如：

> 飯店/餐廳　　　**the** Sheraton **Hotel**, **the** Delhi **Restaurant**, **the** Holiday **Inn** (hotel)
> 劇院/電影院　　**the** Shubert **Theater**, **the** Cineplex **Odeon** (movie theater)
> 博物館/藝廊　　**the** Guggenheim **Museum**, **the** National **Gallery**
> 建築物/橋樑　　**the** Empire State **Building**, **the** White **House**, **the** Brooklyn **Bridge**

在使用上述加 **the** 的專有名詞時，有時會省略名詞：

> **the Sheraton** (Hotel)　　**the Palace** (Theater)　　**the Guggenheim** (Museum)

有些專有名詞只由 **the**+名詞組成，例如：

> **the Acropolis**　　**the Kremlin**　　**the Pentagon**

C

含有 **of** 的專有名詞通常會與 **the** 一起使用，例如：

> **the** Bank of England　　　**the** Museum of Modern Art
> **the** Great Wall of China　　**the** Tower of London

注意下列名詞用法：

> **the** University of Michigan　但是　**Michigan State University** (不加 the)

D

許多商店、餐廳、飯店、銀行等是以創辦人的名字命名；這些專有名詞通常以 **–'s** 或 **–s** 結尾。這類名詞通常不加 **the**：

> **Joe's Diner**　　**McDonald's**　　**Macy's** (department store)

教堂的名稱通常以聖徒之名為名：

> **St. John's Church** (並非 the St. John's Church)　　**St. Patrick's Cathedral**

E

許多報紙與組織的名字加了 **the**：

> 報紙　　**the** *Washington Post*, **the** *Financial Times*, **the** *Tribune*
> 組織　　**the** European **Union**, **the** BBC, **the** Red Cross

航空公司等專有名詞通常不加 **the**：

> **Fiat** (並非 the Fiat)　　**Sony**　　　　**Delta Air Lines**
> **Coca-Cola**　　　　　　**Apple Inc.**　　**Cambridge University Press**

Exercises

76.1 依據下面的地圖，回答各題問句。注意：地圖上各專有名詞並不加 *the*，但各句的回答請依實際需要使用 *the*。

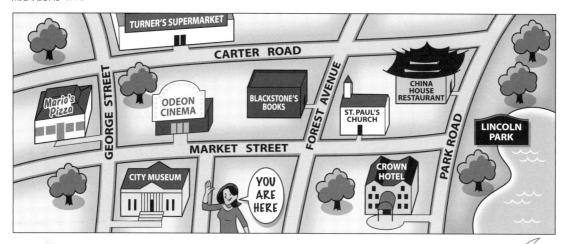

1. Is there a movie theater near here?
2. Is there a supermarket near here?
3. Is there a hotel near here?
4. Is there a church near here?
5. Is there a museum near here?
6. Is there a bookstore near here?
7. Is there a park near here?

8. Is there a restaurant near here?

Yes, *the Odeon on Market Street* .

Yes, _____ on _____ .

Yes, _____ on _____ .

Yes, _____ .

Yes, _____ .

Yes, _____ .

Yes, _____ at the end of

_____ .

There are two. _____

or _____

76.2 依據各句題意，自下列地名或街道名中選出適當者，並判斷是否需要加 *the*，以完成句子。

Acropolis	Broadway	Buckingham Palace	Eiffel Tower
Kremlin	White House	Taj Mahal	~~Times Square~~

1. *Times Square* is in New York.
2. _____ is in Paris.
3. _____ is in Agra, India.
4. _____ is in Washington, D.C.
5. _____ is in Moscow.
6. _____ is in New York.
7. _____ is in Athens.
8. _____ is in London.

76.3 判斷下面各題的名詞用法何者正確。

1. Have you ever been to ~~British Museum~~ / the British Museum? (*the British Museum* 是正確答案)
2. The biggest park in New York is Central Park / the Central Park.
3. My favorite park in London is St. James's Park / the St. James's Park.
4. Ramada Inn / The Ramada Inn is on Main Street / the Main Street.
5. We flew to Mexico City from O'Hare Airport / the O'Hare Airport.
6. Frank is a student at McGill University / the McGill University.
7. If you're looking for a department store, I would recommend Harrison's / the Harrison's.
8. If you're looking for a place to have lunch, I would recommend Ship Inn / the Ship Inn.
9. Statue of Liberty / The Statue of Liberty is at the entrance to New York Harbor / the New York Harbor.
10. You should go to Science Museum / the Science Museum. It's very interesting.
11. John works for IBM / the IBM now. He used to work for General Electric / the General Electric.
12. "Which movie theater are you going to tonight?" "Classic / The Classic."
13. I'd like to go to China and see Great Wall / the Great Wall.
14. "Which newspaper do you want?" "*Washington Post / The Washington Post*."
15. This book is published by Cambridge University Press / the Cambridge University Press.

單數與複數

A

表示成對的物品通常為複數形，例如：

pants (兩隻腳、兩支褲管)　　pajamas　　glasses　　binoculars　　scissors
此外還有 jeans / slacks /　　(上衣與褲子)
shorts / trousers

上列名詞為複數形，所以使用複數動詞：

- My **pants are** too long. (並非 my pants is)

這類名詞也可以與量詞 **a pair of** 一起使用：

- **Those are** nice **jeans**.　或　That**'s a** nice **pair** of jeans. (並非 a nice jeans)
- I need **some** new **glasses**.　或　I need **a new pair of** glasses.

B

有些名詞結尾為 –ics，但通常不是複數之意，所以使用單數動詞，例如：

economics	electronics	gymnastics	mathematics	physics	politics

- **Gymnastics** is my favorite sport. (並非 Gymnastics are)

news 非複數之意(參見 Unit 68B)

- What time **is the news** on television? (並非 are the news)

有些名詞結尾為 **–s**，可以是單數形或複數形。例如：

means	**a means** of transportation	**many means** of transportation
series	**a television series**	**two** television **series**
species	**a species** of bird	**200 species** of birds

C

police 通常與複數動詞一起使用：

- The **police are** investigating the murder, but **haven't** arrested anyone yet.
  (並非 The police is . . . hasn't)

注意：表示「一名員警」要用 **a police officer** / **a policeman** / **a policewoman** (而非 a police)。

D

person 的複數形 (persons) 較少使用，通常用 **people** 表複數之意思：

- He's **a** nice **person**.　但是　They are nice **people**. (並非 nice persons)
- **Many people don't** have enough to eat. (並非 Many people doesn't)

E

一筆錢、一段時間、一段距離等通常視為「一件事」，因此使用單數動詞：

- **Twenty thousand dollars** (= it) **was** stolen in the robbery. (並非 were stolen)
- **Three years** (= it) **is** a long time to be without a job. (並非 Three years are)
- **Six miles is** a long way to walk every day.

Exercises

77.1 依各句題意，自 **A** 小節或 **B** 小節所列的名詞中，選出適當者，並使用 *a* 或 *some* 以完成句子。

1. My eyesight isn't very good. I need ___glasses___ .
2. ___A species___ is a group of animals or plants that have the same characteristics.
3. Soccer players don't wear pants when they play. They wear _____ .
4. The bicycle is _____ of transportation.
5. The bicycle and the car are _____ of transportation.
6. I want to cut this piece of material. I need _____ .
7. A friend of mine is writing _____ of articles for the local newspaper.
8. There are a lot of American TV _____ shown throughout the world.
9. While we were out walking, we saw 25 different _____ of birds.

77.2 依據各題左側所列名詞的屬性，寫出他們所屬的運動、學科名稱或活動。

1. calculate   algebra   equation   m _athematics_ _____
2. government   election   senator   p _____
3. finance   trade   employment   e _____
4. light   heat   gravity   ph _____
5. exercises   somersault   parallel bars   gy _____
6. computer   silicon chip   video games   el _____

77.3 依各句題意，選擇單數形動詞或複數形動詞。

1. Gymnastics is / ~~are~~ my favorite sport. (*is* 是正確答案)
2. The pants you bought for me doesn't / don't fit me.
3. The police want / wants to interview two men about the robbery last week.
4. Physics was / were my best subject at school.
5. Can I borrow your scissors? Mine isn't / aren't sharp enough.
6. Fortunately the news wasn't / weren't as bad as we expected.
7. Three days isn't / aren't long enough for a good vacation.
8. I can't find my binoculars. Do you know where it is / they are?
9. It's a nice place to visit. The people is / are very friendly.
10. Does / Do the police know how the accident happened?
11. I don't like very hot weather. Ninety degrees is / are too hot for me.

77.4 下面各題的句子大部分不正確；因此請依據各句題意，改正各個錯誤的句子。

1. (Three years are) a long time to be without a job.   _Three years is a long time_
2. The news is very depressing these days.   _OK_
3. Susan was wearing a black jeans.   _____
4. I like Matt and Jill. They're very nice persons.   _____
5. I need more than ten dollars. Ten dollars isn't enough. _____
6. I'm going to buy a new pajama.   _____
7. There was a police directing traffic on the street.   _____
8. What are the police going to do?   _____
9. This scissors isn't very sharp.   _____
10. Do you think two days are enough to see all the sights
    of Toronto?   _____
11. Many people has heard about the problem.   _____

名詞+名詞 (a tennis ball / a headache 等)

A

名詞+名詞用來表示一件事/一個人/一個觀念等，例如：

| a **tennis ball** | a **bank manager** | a **car accident** |
| **income tax** | the **water temperature** | |

上述例子中，第一個名詞的功能就如同形容詞，用以說明這是一件什麼樣的事物/人/觀念等。例如：

a **tennis ball** = 打網球時所用的球
a **car accident** = 開車時所發生的意外
income tax = 為所得所繳的稅
the **water temperature** = 水的溫度
a **Boston doctor** = 一位來自 Boston 的醫生
my **life story** = 我一生的故事

所以我們可以說：

| a **television** camera | a **television** program | a **television** studio | a **television** producer |

(上述的名詞片語皆表示與電視有關的事物)

| language **problems** | marriage **problems** | health **problems** | work **problems** |

(上述的名詞片語則表示各種不同的問題)

比較下面兩個名詞片語：
garden vegetables (種在園子裡的菜)
a **vegetable garden** (種菜的園子；菜園)

若名詞片語中的第一個字為 **-ing** 的字，通常表示這是一個用作某用途的東西，例如：
a **frying** pan (= a pan for frying)　a **sleeping** bag　a **swimming** pool　a **dining** room

有時候名詞片語是由兩個以上的名詞所組成：

- I waited at the **hotel reception desk**.
- We watched the **World Swimming Championships** on television.
- Everyone is talking about the **government corruption scandal**.

B

這類由兩個名詞所組成的名詞片語，有時可以寫成一個字，有時則兩個字分開寫。例如：

a **headache**　**toothpaste**　a **weekend**　**pea soup**　a **road sign**

並沒有既定的規則，規定哪些應寫成一個字，哪些該分開寫。不確定時，可以分開寫成兩個字的名詞片語。

C

注意下面的例子意思不同：
a **sugar bowl** (糖碗，可能是空的) and a **bowl of sugar** (一個裝了糖的碗；一碗糖)
a **toolbox** (工具箱，可能是空的) and a **box of tools** (一箱工具)

D

如上所述，「名詞+名詞」中的第一個名詞作用就如同形容詞，其形式通常是單數形，但意思則通常是複數。例如：a **book**store，在書店裡可以買好多書，an **apple** tree 蘋果樹上結了很多蘋果。

同樣地，我們可以使用下列的表達方式：
a three-**hour** trip (歷時 3 小時的旅行)　　two 14-**year**-old girls (並非 years)
a 10-**dollar** bill (並非 dollars)　　a six-**page** letter (並非 pages)
a four-**week** course (並非 weeks)　　a two-**story** house (並非 stories)

比較下面的例句：

- It was a three-**hour** trip.　但是　The trip took three **hours**.

Exercises

78.1 以名詞+名詞的方式，寫出下列各題所描述的事物。

1. A ticket for a concert is ___a concert ticket___ .
2. Problems concerning health are ___health problems___ .
3. A magazine about computers is _____ .
4. Pictures taken on your vacation are your _____ .
5. Chocolate made with milk is _____ .
6. Somebody whose job is to inspect factories is _____ .
7. A horse that runs in races is _____ .
8. A race for horses is _____ .
9. A lawyer in Los Angeles is _____ .
10. The results of your exams are your _____ .
11. The carpet in the dining room is _____ .
12. A scandal involving an oil company is _____ .
13. A building with five stories is _____ .
14. A plan to improve traffic is _____ .
15. A course that lasts five days is _____ .
16. A question that has two parts is _____ .
17. A girl who is seven years old is _____ .

78.2 依各句的描述，自下面名詞中選出兩個適當字，組成名詞片語。

~~accident~~	belt	card	credit	editor	forecast	newspaper
number	~~car~~	room	seat	shop	weather	window

1. This can be caused by bad driving.   ___a car accident___
2. If you're staying at a hotel, you need to remember this.   your _____
3. You should wear this when you're in a car.   a _____
4. You can often use this to pay for things instead of cash.   a _____
5. If you want to know if it's going to rain, you can read or listen to this.   the _____
6. This person is a top journalist.   a _____
7. You might stop to look in this when you're walking along a street.   a _____

78.3 依各句題意，自下面名詞片語中選出適當者，以完成句子。

15 minute(s)	six mile(s)	five day(s)	~~10 page(s)~~
six mile(s)	two hour(s)	five course(s)	500 year(s)
60 minute(s)	20 dollar(s)	two year(s)	~~450 page(s)~~

有些句子需要單數形名詞片語，有些則需要複數形。

1. It's quite a long book. There are ___450 pages___ .
2. A few days ago I received a ___10-page___ letter from Julia.
3. I didn't have any change. I only had a _____ bill.
4. At work in the morning I usually have a _____ break for coffee.
5. There are _____ in an hour.
6. It's only a _____ flight from New York to Montreal.
7. It was a very big meal. There were _____
8. Mary has just started a new job. She's got a _____ contract.
9. The oldest building in the city is the _____ castle.
10. I work _____ a week. Saturday and Sunday are free.
11. We went for a long walk in the country. We walked _____ .
12. We went for a _____ walk in the country.

-'s (your sister's name) 與 of . . . (the name of the book)

A 通常 -'s 用於表示人或動物的所有格(例如 the girl's . . . / the horse's . . . 等)：
- **Tom's** computer isn't working. (並非 the computer of Tom)
- How old are **Chris's** children? (並非 the children of Chris)
- What's (= What is) **your sister's** name?
- What's **Tom's sister's** name?
- Be careful. Don't step on **the cat's** tail.

注意，-'s 後面也可以不接名詞：
- This isn't my book. It's **my sister's**. (= my sister's book)

of . . . 也可以用來表示人的所有格，例如：
- What was the name **of the man who called you**? (the man who called you 這個名詞片語太長，所以不用 -'s 而用of . . . 表所有格)

注意，-'s 也用於下列說法：**a woman's hat** (女人戴的帽子)、**a boy's name** (男孩的名字)、**a bird's egg** (小鳥下的蛋)等。

B 單數形名詞所有格用 -'s：
　　my **sister's** room (= **her** room – one sister)　　**Mr. Carter's** house (= **his** house)

複數形名詞(如sisters/friends等)，則是在字尾 s 後加上 ' (-s')：
　　my **sisters'** room (= **their** room – *two* or *more* sisters)
　　the Carters' house (= **their** house – Mr. and Mrs. Carter)

如果複數形名詞的字尾並不是 s (例如，**men / women / children / people**)，則加 -'s 表所有格：
　　the men's changing room　　a **children's** book (= a book for children)

注意下面用法中，-'s 加在第二個名詞或第三個名詞之後：
　　Jack and Karen's wedding　　**Mr. and Mrs. Carter's** house

C 表示事物、觀念等的所有格通常用of . . . (例如 . . . of the book / . . . of the restaurant 等)：
　　the door **of the garage** (並非 the garage's door)
　　the name **of the book**　　the owner **of the restaurant**

上述名詞也可以用名詞+名詞的方式表達(參見 Unit 78)：
　　the **garage door**　　the **restaurant owner**

of . . . 也用於 the **beginning/end/middle of** . . .、the **top/bottom of** . . .、the **front/back/side of** . . .等用語中：
　　the beginning of the month (並非 the month's beginning)
　　the top of the hill　　**the back of** the car

D -'s 與 of . . . 皆可以用來表達組織或機構的所有格。因此我們說：
　　the government's decision　　或　　the decision **of the government**
　　the company's success　　　　或　　the success **of the company**

地方的所有格也可以用 -'s 表示。因此我們說：
　　the city's streets　　**the world's** population　　**Brazil's** largest city

E 時間的名詞(如 **yesterday/next week** 等) 也可以用 -'s 表所有格：
- Do you still have **yesterday's** newspaper?
- **Next week's** meeting has been canceled.

除上述例子外，我們也可以說 **today's / tomorrow's / tonight's / Monday's** 等。

一段時間的名詞片語也可以用 -'s，其複數型名詞則用 -s' 表所有格：
- I've got **a week's** vacation starting on Monday.
- Sally needs **eight hours'** sleep a night.
- Brenda got to work 15 minutes late but lost **an hour's** pay.

Exercises

79.1 依各句題意，判斷下列各句中劃底線部份的名詞片語應以 **-'s**、**-s'** 或 **. . . of . . .** 表示所有格，並
加以必要的改寫。

1. Who is <u>the owner of this restaurant</u>? *OK*
2. Where are <u>the children of Chris</u>? *Chris's children*
3. Is this <u>the umbrella of your friend</u>? _____
4. Write your name at <u>the top of the page</u>. _____
5. I've never met <u>the daughter of Charles</u>. _____
6. Have you met <u>the son of Mary and Dan</u>? _____
7. We don't know <u>the cause of the problem</u>. _____
8. Do we still have <u>the newspaper of yesterday</u>? _____
9. What's <u>the name of this street</u>? _____
10. What is <u>the cost of a new computer</u>? _____
11. <u>The friends of your children</u> are here. _____
12. <u>The garden of our neighbors</u> is very nice. _____
13. I work on <u>the ground floor of the building</u>. _____
14. <u>The hair of Bill</u> is very long. _____
15. I couldn't go to <u>the party of Catherine</u>. _____
16. What's <u>the name of the woman who lives next door</u>? _____
17. Have you seen <u>the car of the parents of Mike</u>? _____
18. What's <u>the meaning of this expression</u>? _____
19. Do you agree with <u>the economic policy of the government</u>? _____

79.2 以 **-'s** 的表達方式，改寫各題的名詞片語。

1. a hat for a woman *a woman's hat*
2. a name for a boy _____
3. clothes for children _____
4. a school for girls _____
5. a nest for a bird _____
6. a magazine for women _____

79.3 依各句題意，以各題畫底線的語詞為句子的開頭，改寫各句。

1. The meeting <u>tomorrow</u> has been canceled.
   Tomorrow's meeting has been canceled.
2. The storm <u>last week</u> caused a lot of damage.
   Last _____
3. The only movie theater in <u>the town</u> has closed down.
   The _____
4. The weather in <u>Chicago</u> is very changeable.
   _____
5. Tourism is the main industry in <u>the region</u>.
   _____

79.4 依各題的情境，以括號中提供的字，完成句子。

1. I bought groceries at the supermarket last night. They will last us for a week.
   So I bought *a week's groceries* last night. (groceries)
2. Kim got a new car. It cost the same as her salary for a year.
   So Kim's new car cost her _____ . (salary)
3. Jim lost his job. His company gave him extra money equal to his pay for four weeks.
   So Jim got _____ when he lost his job. (pay)
4. Last night I went to bed at midnight and woke up at 5 a.m. After that I couldn't sleep.
   So I only had _____ . (sleep)
5. I haven't been able to rest all day. I haven't rested for even a minute.
   So I haven't had _____ all day. (rest)

myself / yourself / themselves 等

A

請看下面的例子：

Hi, I'm Steve.

Steve

Steve 將自己介紹給其他的客人。
當主詞和受詞為同一人時，用 **myself/yourself/himself** 等(反身代名詞)：

Steve	introduced	**himself**
主詞		受詞

反身代名詞如下：

單數	my**self**	your**self** (一個人)	him**self**/her**self**/it**self**
複數	our**selves**	your**selves** (一個人以上)	them**selves**

- I don't want you to pay for me. **I'll** pay for **myself**. (並非 I'll pay for me)
- Julia had a great vacation. **She** really enjoyed **herself**.
- Do **you** talk to **yourself** sometimes? (一個人)
- If **you** want more to eat, help **yourselves**. (一個人以上)

比較下面的例句：

- It's not our fault. **You** can't blame **us**.
- It's our own fault. **We** should blame **ourselves**.

B

動詞 **concentrate** / **feel** / **relax** / **meet** 後面不使用反身代名詞：

- I **feel** nervous. I can't **relax**.
- You have to try and **concentrate**. (並非 concentrate yourself)
- What time should we **meet**? (並非 meet ourselves, 也非 meet us)

通常 **wash/shave/dress** 後面也不使用反身代名詞：

- He got up, **washed**, **shaved**, and **dressed**. (並非 washed himself、shaved himself 以及 dressed himself)

上述動詞也可以用 get **dressed** (例如 He **got dressed**)來表達。

C

比較 **-selves** 與 **each other** 用法之不同：

- Kate and Joe stood in front of the mirror and looked at **themselves**.
  (在鏡子前面，Kate 看著她自己，Joe 也看著他自己。)
- Kate looked at Joe; Joe looked at Kate. They looked at **each other**.

Themselves

Each other

one another 可以與 **each other** 互換使用，意思相同：

- How long have you and Bill known **each other**? 或 . . . known **one another**?
- Sue and Ann don't like **each other**. 或 . . . don't like **one another**.
- Do you and Sarah live near **each other**? 是 . . . near **one another**?

D

myself/yourself 等反身代名詞也可以用於下面的表達方式。例如：

- "Who repaired your bicycle for you?" "I repaired it **myself**."

I repaired it myself 意思是，是我自己修的，不是別人。此處 *myself* 是用來加強語氣，強調 I。
其他例子如下：

- I'm not going to do your work for you. **You** can do it **yourself**. (= you, not me)
- Let's paint the house **ourselves**. It will be much cheaper.
- The **movie itself** wasn't very good, but I loved the music.
- I don't think Sue will get the job. **Sue herself** doesn't think she'll get it.
  (或 **Sue** doesn't think she'll get it **herself**.)

get dressed / get married 等 Unit 42D *by myself / by yourself* 等 Unit 81D

Exercises

80.1 依各句題意，在下列動詞中選出適當者，並與反身代名詞一起使用，完成各句。

> blame   burn   enjoy   express   hurt   ~~introduce~~   put

1. Steve _introduced himself_ to the other guests at the party.
2. Bill fell down some steps, but fortunately he didn't _____ badly.
3. It isn't Sue's fault. She really shouldn't _____ .
4. Please try and understand how I feel. _____ in my position.
5. The children had a great time at the beach. They really _____ .
6. Be careful! That pan is very hot. Don't _____ .
7. Sometimes I can't say exactly what I mean. I wish I could _____ better.

80.2 依各句題意，填入代名詞的受格 (*me/you/us* 等) 或反身代名詞 (*myself/yourself* 等)。

1. Julia had a great vacation. She enjoyed _herself_ .
2. It's not my fault. You can't blame _____ .
3. What I did was really bad. I'm ashamed of _____ .
4. We've got a problem. I hope you can help _____ .
5. "Can I have another cookie?" "Of course. Help _____ !"
6. I want you to meet Sarah. I'll introduce _____ to her.
7. Don't worry about Tom and me. We can take care of _____ .
8. I gave them a key to our house so that they could let _____ in.
9. I didn't want anybody to see the letters, so I burned _____ .

80.3 依各句題意，自下列動詞中選出適當者，以完成句子。有些動詞必須與反身代名詞 *myself / yourself* 等一起使用。

> concentrate   defend   dry   ~~feel~~   meet   relax

1. I was sick yesterday, but I _feel_ much better today.
2. She climbed out of the swimming pool and _____ with a towel.
3. I tried to study, but I couldn't _____ .
4. If somebody attacks you, you need to be able to _____ .
5. I'm going out with Chris tonight. We're _____ at 7:30.
6. You're always rushing around. Why don't you sit down and _____ ?

80.4 依各句題意，以反身代名詞 *-selves* 或 *each other* 完成各句。

1. How long have you and Bill known _each other_ ?
2. If people work too hard, they can make _____ sick.
3. I need you and you need me. We need _____ .
4. In the U.S., friends often give _____ presents at Christmas.
5. Some people are very selfish. They think only of _____ .
6. Tracy and I don't see _____ very often these days.
7. We couldn't get back into the house. We had locked _____ out.
8. They've had an argument. They're not speaking to _____ at the moment.
9. We'd never met before, so we introduced _____ to _____ .

80.5 依各句題意，以反身代名詞 *myself/yourself/itself* 等完成各個對話。

1. Who repaired the bicycle for you?	Nobody. I _repaired it myself._
2. Who cuts Brian's hair for him?	Nobody. He cuts _____
3. Do you want me to mail that letter for you?	No, I'll _____
4. Who told you that Linda was getting married?	Linda _____
5. Can you call John for me?	Why can't you _____ ?

a friend **of mine**   **my own** house   **by myself**

A

a friend of mine / a friend of Tom's 等

a friend of **mine / yours / his / hers / ours / theirs** 意思是我的/你的/他的/她的/我們的/他們的朋友之一:

- ■ I'm going to a wedding on Saturday. **A friend of mine** is getting married.
  (並非 a friend of me)
- ■ We took a trip with **some friends of ours**. (並非 some friends of us)
- ■ Michael had an argument with **a neighbor of his**.
- ■ It was **a good idea of yours** to go to the movies.

同樣地,a friend **of Tom's / of my sister's** 意思是 Tom 的朋友之一/我妹妹的朋友之一:

- ■ That woman over there is **a friend of my sister's**.
- ■ It was **a good idea of Tom's** to go to the movies.

B

my own ... / your own ... 等

所有格 **my / your / his / her / its / our / their** 用於 **own** 之前:

> **my own** house   **your own** car   **her own** room
> (並非 an own house, an own car, etc.)

my own ... / your own ... 等是表示某樣東西是我自己的/你自己的,不是與他人共有的,也不是借來的:

- ■ I don't want to share a room with anybody. I want **my own room**.
- ■ Vicky and George would like to have **their own house**.
- ■ It's a shame that the apartment doesn't have **its own parking space**.
- ■ It's **my own fault** that I don't have any money. I buy too many things I don't need.
- ■ Why do you want to borrow my car? Why don't you use **your own**? (= your own car)

...own ... 也可以用來表示你親自做某事,而不是別人幫你做的,例如:

- ■ Bill usually cuts **his own hair**. (他的頭髮是自己剪的,沒有去理髮店。)
- ■ I'd like to have a garden so that I could grow **my own vegetables**. (菜是我自己種的,不是到店裡去買的。)

Bill usually cuts **his own hair**.

C

on my own / on your own 等意思是「獨立地」:

- ■ My children are living **on their own**. (住在他們自己的地方,自己養活自己)
- ■ I traveled around Japan **on my own**. (並非參加旅行團)
- ■ Are you raising your children **on your own**? (獨自撫養小孩)

D

by myself / by yourself 等

by myself / by yourself / by themselves 等意思是「獨自」:

- ■ I like living **by myself**.
- ■ "Did you go to Hawaii **by yourself**?"   "No, with a friend."
- ■ Jack was sitting **by himself** in a corner of the café.
- ■ Student drivers are not allowed to drive **by themselves**.

Exercises

81.1 依各句題意，以 **A** 小節中的用法（*a friend of mine* 等），改寫下列各句。

1. I am meeting <u>one of my friends</u> tonight. *I'm meeting a friend of mine tonight.*
2. We met <u>one of your relatives</u>. We met a _____
3. Jason borrowed <u>one of my books</u>. Jason _____
4. Ann invited <u>some of her friends</u> to her place. Ann _____
5. We had dinner with <u>one of our neighbors</u>. _____
6. I took a trip with <u>two of my friends</u>. _____
7. Is that man <u>one of your friends</u>? _____
8. I met <u>one of Amy's friends</u> at the party. _____

81.2 依各句題意，自下列名詞中選出適當者，並以 *my own / your own* 等用法，完成句子。

~~bedroom~~　　**business**　　**opinions**　　**private beach**　　**words**

1. I share a kitchen and bathroom, but I have *my own bedroom* _____ .
2. Gary doesn't think the same as me. He's got _____ .
3. Julia is fed up with working for other people. She wants to start _____ .
4. We stayed at a luxury hotel on the ocean. The hotel had _____ .
5. On the test we had to read a story, and then write it in _____ .

81.3 依各句題意，以 *my own / your own* 等用法，完成句子。

1. Why do you want to borrow my car?
   Why don't you use your own car? _____
2. How can you blame me? It's not my fault.
   It's _____ .
3. She's always using my ideas.
   Why can't she use _____ ?
4. Please don't worry about my problems.
   You've got _____ .
5. I can't make his decisions for him.
   He has to make _____ .

81.4 依各句題意，自下列動詞中選出適當者，並以 *my own / your own* 等用法，完成句子。

bake　　~~cut~~　　**make**　　**write**

1. Bill never goes to the barber. He *cuts his own hair* _____ .
2. Mary doesn't buy many clothes. She usually _____ .
3. We don't often buy bread. We usually _____ .
4. Paul is a singer. He sings songs written by other people, but he also _____
   _____

81.5 依各句題意，以 *on my own / by myself* 等用法，完成句子。

1. Did you go to Hawaii by *yourself* ?
2. I'm glad I live with other people. I wouldn't like to live on _____ .
3. The box was too heavy for me to lift by _____ .
4. "Who was Tom with when you saw him?" "Nobody. He was by _____ ."
5. I think my brother is too young to make that decision on _____ .
6. I don't think she knows many people. When I see her, she is always by _____ .
7. My sister graduated from college and is living on _____ .
8. Do you like working with other people, or do you prefer working by _____ ?
9. We had no help decorating the apartment. We did it completely on _____ .
10. I went out with Sally because she didn't want to go out by _____

there . . . 與 it . . .

there 與 it

> **There's** a new restaurant on Main Street.
> Main Street 上開了一家新的餐廳。

> Yes, I know. I went there last night. **It's** very good.
> 是啊，我知道。我昨天晚上去了，非常好。

第一次提到某個東西時，通常用 **there** 來表達該東西的存在：

- **There's** a new restaurant on Main Street. (並非 A new restaurant is on Main Street)
- I'm sorry I'm late. **There was** a lot of traffic. (並非 It was a lot of traffic)
- Things are more expensive now. **There has been** a big increase in the cost of living.

it 用來指某一特定的事物、地方、事實、情況等(參見 C 小節)：

- We went to the new restaurant. **It's** very good. (**It** = the restaurant)
- I wasn't expecting them to come. **It** was a complete surprise. (**It** = that they came)

比較 **there** 與 **it** 之用法：

- I don't like this town. **There's** nothing to do here. **It's** a boring place.

there 也可以用來表示 to/at/in that place 的意思 (去/在某處)：

- The new restaurant is very good. I went **there** (= to the restaurant) last night.
- When we got to the party, there were already a lot of people **there** (= at the party).

there 可以用於 **there will be**、**there must be**、**there used to be** 等：

- **Will there be** many people at the party?
- "**Is there** a flight to Miami tonight?" "**There might be**. I'll check."
- If people drove more carefully, **there wouldn't be** so many accidents.

there 也可以用在 **there must have been**、**there should have been** 等：

- There was music playing. **There must have been** somebody at home.

比較 **there** 與 **it** 之用法：

- They live on a busy street. **There must be** a lot of noise from the traffic.
  They live on a busy main street. **It must be** very noisy.
- **There used to be** a movie theater on Main Street, but it closed a few years ago.
  That building is now a supermarket. **It used to be** a movie theater.

there 也可以用於 **there is sure/certain/likely/bound** to be 之句型：

- **There is bound** (= sure) **to be** a flight to Miami tonight.

在下面的例句中，可以用 **it** 當作主詞：

- **It**'s dangerous to **walk in the street**. (**It** = to walk in the street)

通常較少使用 To walk in the street is dangerous，而是較常以 **it** 當主詞，代替 to walk in the street。

其他例子如下：

- **It** didn't take us long **to get here**.
- **It**'s too bad **(that) Sandra can't come to the party**.
- Let's go. **It**'s not worth **waiting any longer.**

it 也可以用來指距離、時間和天氣：

- How far is **it** from here to the airport?
- What day is **it** today?
- **It**'s been a long time since I saw you.
- **It** was windy. (但是 **There** was **a cold wind**.)

it's worth / it's no use / there's no point Unit 61A   *there is + -ing / -ed* Unit 95

82.1 填入 *there is/was* 或 *it is/was*，並依各句題意，使用肯定句、否定句 (*isn't/wasn't*) 或疑問句 (*is there . . . ? / is it . . . ?*)

1. I'm sorry I'm late. _There was_ a lot of traffic.
2. What's the new restaurant like? _Is it_ good?
3. " _____ a bookstore near here?" "Yes, _____ one on Hill Street."
4. When we got to the movie theater, _____ a line outside. _____ a very long line, so we decided not to wait.
5. I couldn't see anything. _____ completely dark.
6. _____ trouble at the basketball game last night. They had to call the police.
7. How far _____ from Hong Kong to Taipei?
8. _____ Keith's birthday yesterday. We had a party.
9. _____ too windy to play tennis today. Let's play tomorrow instead.
10. I wanted to visit the museum, but _____ enough time.
11. " _____ time to leave?" "Yes, _____ almost midnight."
12. A few days ago _____ a storm. _____ a lot of damage.
13. _____ a beautiful day yesterday. We went on a picnic.
14. _____ anything on television, so I turned it off.
15. _____ an accident on Main Street, but _____ very serious.

82.2 依各句題意，以 *There . . .* 的句型改寫各句。

1. The roads were busy today.   _There was a lot of traffic._
2. This soup is very salty.   There _____ in the soup.
3. The box was empty.   _____ in the box.
4. The movie was very violent.   _____
5. The shopping mall was very crowded.   _____
                                                  _____
6. I like this town – it's lively.   _____

82.3 依各句題意，以 *there will be / there would be* 等句型，配合下列適當之助動詞，完成句子。

| will | might | ~~would~~ | wouldn't | should | used to | (be) going to |

1. If people drove more carefully, _there would be_ fewer accidents.
2. "Do we have any eggs?" "I'm not sure. _____ some in the fridge."
3. I think everything will be OK. I don't think _____ any problems.
4. Look at the sky. _____ a storm.
5. "Is there a school in this town?" "Not now. _____ one, but it closed."
6. People drive too fast on this road. I think _____ a speed limit.
7. If people weren't aggressive, _____ any wars

82.4 判斷下列各句是否正確。若不正確，則將 *it* 改為 *there* 之句型。

1. They live on a busy street. (It must be) a lot of noise.   _There must be a lot of noise._
2. Last winter it was very cold, and it was a lot of snow.   _____
3. It used to be a church here, but it was torn down.   _____
4. Why was she so unfriendly? It must have been a reason.   _____
5. It's a long way from my house to the nearest store.   _____
6. A: Where can we park the car?
   B: Don't worry. It's sure to be a parking lot somewhere.   _____
7. After the lecture, it will be an opportunity to
   ask questions.   _____
8. I like the place where I live, but it would be nicer
   to live by the ocean.   _____
9. I was told that it would be somebody to meet me
   at the airport, but it wasn't anybody.   _____
10. The situation is still the same. It has been no change.   _____
11. I don't know who'll win, but it's sure to be a good game. _____

some 與 any

A

一般而言，some (包括 somebody/someone/something)用於肯定句，而 any (包括 anybody 等)
則用於否定句

some	any
■ We bought **some** flowers.	■ We did**n't** buy **any** flowers.
■ He's busy. He's got **some** work to do.	■ He's lazy. He **never** does **any** work.
■ There's **somebody** at the door.	■ There is**n't anybody** at the door.
■ I'm hungry. I want **something** to eat.	■ I'm not hungry. I do**n't** want **anything** to eat.

下面例句表示否定的意思，因此使用 **any**：
- ■ She went out **without any** money. (she did**n't** take **any** money with her)
- ■ He **refused** to eat **anything**. (he did**n't** eat **anything**)
- ■ **Hardly anybody** passed the examination. (= almost **nobody** passed)

B

問句中可以用 some 或 any。當我們知道或認為某人或某事物存在時，通常使用 **some**：
- ■ Are you waiting for **somebody**? (I think you are waiting for somebody)

表達提供或要求某事物的問句中，也用 **some**：
- ■ Would you like **something** to eat? (there is something to eat)
- ■ Can I have **some** sugar, please? (there is probably some sugar I can have)

但大部分問句中使用 **any** 因為我們不知道某人或某事物是否存在：
- ■ "Do you have **any** luggage?" "No, I don't."
- ■ I can't find my bag. Has **anybody** seen it?

C

if 的句子中通常用 **any**：
- ■ **If** there are **any** letters for me, can you send them on?
- ■ **If anyone** has any questions, I'll be glad to answer them.
- ■ Let me know **if** you need **anything**.

下面的例句中雖然沒有if這個字，但有 **if** 的意思，因此用 **any**：
- ■ I'm sorry for **any** trouble I've caused. (= if I have caused any trouble)
- ■ **Anyone** who wants to take the exam should tell me by Friday. (= if there is anyone)

D

any 可以用來表示「任何一個都可以」：
- ■ You can take **any** bus. They all go downtown. (你搭哪一班公車都可以)
- ■ "Sing a song." "Which song should I sing?" "**Any** song. I don't care."
  (任何一首歌都可以)
- ■ Come and see me **anytime** you want.
- ■ "Let's go out somewhere." "Where should we go?" "**Anywhere**. It doesn't matter."
- ■ We left the door unlocked. **Anybody** could have come in.

比較 **something** 與 **anything** 之用法：
- ■ A: I'm hungry. I want **something** to eat.
  B: What would you like?
  A: I don't care. **Anything**. (= something, but it doesn't matter what)

E

somebody / someone / anybody / anyone 都是單數形的名詞：
- ■ **Someone** is here to see you.

這些名詞雖是單數形，但是通常使用複數形的代名詞 they/them/their：
- ■ **Someone** has forgotten **their** umbrella. (= his or her umbrella)
- ■ If **anybody** wants to leave early, **they** can. (= he or she can)

83.1 依各句題意，填入 *some* 或 *any*。

1. We didn't buy ___any___ flowers.
2. I'm going out tonight with _____ friends of mine.
3. *A:* Have you seen _____ good movies recently?
   B: No, I haven't been to the movies in ages.
4. I didn't have _____ money, so I had to borrow _____ .
5. Can I have _____ milk in my coffee, please?
6. I was too tired to do _____ work.
7. You can cash these traveler's checks at _____ bank.
8. Can you give me _____ information about places of interest in the area?
9. With the special tourist bus pass, you can travel on _____ bus you like.
10. If there are _____ words you don't understand, use a dictionary.

83.2 依各句題意，填入 *some* 或 *any* + *body / one / thing / where*。

1. I was too surprised to say ___anything___ .
2. There's _____ at the door. Can you go and see who it is?
3. Does _____ mind if I open the window?
4. I wasn't feeling hungry, so I didn't eat _____ .
5. You must be hungry. Would you like _____ to eat?
6. Quick, let's go! There's _____ coming and I don't want _____ to see us.
7. Sarah was upset about _____ and refused to talk to _____ .
8. This machine is very easy to use. _____ can learn to use it very quickly.
9. There was hardly _____ on the beach. It was almost deserted.
10. "Do you live _____ near Jim?" "No, he lives in another part of town."
11. *A:* Where do you want to go on vacation?
    B: Let's go _____ warm and sunny.
12. They stay at home all the time. They never seem to go _____ .
13. I'm going out now. If _____ calls while I'm out, tell them I'll be back at 11:30.
14. Why are you looking under the bed? Did you lose _____ ?
15. _____ who saw the accident should contact the police.
16. "Can I ask you _____ ?" "Sure. What do you want to ask?"
17. Sue is very secretive. She never tells _____ . *(2 words)*

83.3 依各句題意，填入 *any* + 名詞或 *anybody / anyone / anything / anywhere*。

1.	Which bus do I have to catch?	___Any bus.___ They all go downtown.
2.	Which day should I come?	It doesn't matter. _____ .
3.	What do you want to eat?	_____ . I don't care. Whatever you have.
4.	Where should I sit?	It's up to you. You can sit _____ you like.
5.	What kind of job are you looking for?	_____ . It doesn't matter.
6.	What time should I call tomorrow?	_____ . I'll be home all day.
7.	Who should I invite to the party?	I don't care. _____ you like.
8.	Which newspaper should I buy?	_____ . Whatever they have at the store.

no / none / any   nothing / nobody 等

A

no 與 none

no + 名詞；**no** 意思就等於 **not a** 或 **not any**：

- We had to walk home because there was **no bus**. (= there was**n't** a bus)
- Sue will have **no difficulty** finding a job. (= Sue wo**n't** have **any** difficulty . . .)
- There were **no stores** open. (= There were**n't any** stores open.)

no + 名詞可以置於句首：

- **No reason** was given for the change of plan.

none 單獨使用，後面不接名詞：

- "How much money do you have?" "**None**." (= no money)
- All the tickets have been sold. There are **none** left. (= no tickets left)

也可以用 **none of** 來表達：

- This money is all yours. **None of it** is mine.

none of + 複數形名詞(none of **the students**、none of **them** 等)當主詞時，動詞可以是複數形或單數形；複數形動詞較普遍：

- None of the stores **were** (或 **was**) open.

B

nothing   nobody/no one   nowhere

nothing、**nobody/no one**、**nowhere** 等表否定意思的字可以置於句首，也可以單獨使用作為問句的回答：

- **Nobody** (或 **No one**) came to visit me while I was in the hospital.
- "What happened?" "**Nothing**."
- "Where are you going?" "**Nowhere**. I'm staying here."

這些字也常用於動詞之後，特別是在 **be** 與 **have** 之後：

- The house is empty. There**'s no one** living there.
- We **had nothing** to eat.

nothing/nobody 等意思就等於 **not** + **anything/anybody** 等：

- I didn't say anything. (= I said **nothing**.)
- Jane didn't tell **anybody** about her plans. (= Jane told **nobody** . . .)
- They don't have **anywhere** to live. (= They have **nowhere** to live.)

使用 **nothing/nobody** 等表否定意思的字時，不可以使用否定動詞(isn't、didn't 等)：

- I **said** nothing. (並非 I didn't say nothing)
- Nobody **tells** me anything. (並非 Nobody doesn't tell me)

C

any/anything/anybody 等不與 not 一起使用時，可以表示「任何一個/任何東西/任何人都可以」(參見 Unit 83D)。比較 **no-** 與 **any-** 之用法：

- There was **no** bus, so we walked home.
  You can take **any** bus. They all go downtown. (無論哪一班公車都可以。)
- "What do you want to eat?" "**Nothing**. I'm not hungry."
  I'm so hungry I could eat **anything**. (無論哪一種東西都可以。)
- The exam was extremely difficult. **Nobody** passed. (每一個人都沒有通過。)
  The exam was very easy. **Anybody** could have passed. (無論哪一個人都可以通過。)

D

nobody/no one 之代名詞可以用 **they/them/their** (參見 Unit 83E)：

- **Nobody** called, did **they**? (= did he or she)
- **No one** did what I asked **them** to do. (= him or her)
- **Nobody** in the class did **their** homework. (= his or her homework)

some 與 *any* Unit 83   *none of . . .* Unit 86   *any bigger / no better* 等 Unit 103B

Exercises

84.1 依各句題意，填入 *no*、*none* 或 *any*。

1. It was a holiday, so there were __*no*__ stores open.
2. I don't have __*any*__ money. Can you lend me some?
3. We had to walk home because there were _____ taxis.
4. We had to walk home because there weren't _____ taxis.
5. "How many eggs do we have?" " _____ . Should I go and get some?"
6. We took a few pictures, but _____ of them were very good.
7. What a stupid thing to do! _____ intelligent person would do something like that.
8. I'll try to answer _____ questions you ask me.
9. I couldn't answer _____ of the questions they asked me.
10. We canceled the party because _____ of the people we invited were able to come.
11. I tried to call Chris, but there was _____ answer.

84.2 依各問句之意思，以 *none / nobody / no one / nothing / nowhere* 回答問句。

1. What did you do? — *Nothing.*
2. Who were you talking to? _____
3. How much luggage do you have? _____
4. Where are you going? _____
5. How many mistakes did you make? _____
6. How much did you pay? _____

以 *any / anybody / anything / anywhere* 回答以上的問題。

7. (1) __*I didn't do anything.*__
8. (2) I _____
9. (3) _____
10. (4) _____
11. (5) _____
12. (6) _____

84.3 依各句題意，填入 *no* 或 *any + body / one / thing / where*。

1. I don't want __*anything*__ to drink. I'm not thirsty.
2. The bus was completely empty. There was _____ on it.
3. "Where did you go for vacation?" " _____ . I stayed home."
4. I went to the mall, but I didn't buy _____ .
5. A: What did you buy?
   B: _____ . I couldn't find _____ I wanted.
6 The town is still the same as it was years ago. _____ has changed.
7. Have you seen my watch? I can't find it _____ .
8. There was complete silence in the room. _____ said _____ .

84.4 依各句題意，判斷劃線部份的兩個詞何者正確。

1. She didn't tell ~~nobody~~ / anybody about her plans. (*anybody* 是正確答案)
2. The accident looked serious, but fortunately nobody / anybody was injured.
3. I looked out the window, but I couldn't see no one / anyone.
4. My job is very easy. Nobody / Anybody could do it.
5. "What's in that box?" "Nothing / Anything. It's empty."
6. The situation is uncertain. Nothing / Anything could happen.
7. I don't know nothing / anything about economics.

much、many、little、few、a lot、plenty

A　much 與 little 通常和不可數名詞一起使用：

　　much time　　much luck　　little energy　　little money

much 與 few 通常和可數複數名詞一起使用：

　　many friends　　many people　　few cars　　few countries

B　a lot of / lots of / plenty of 可以和不可數名詞，以及可數複數名詞一起使用：

　　a lot of luck　　　lots of time　　　plenty of money
　　a lot of friends　　lots of people　　plenty of ideas

plenty 意思是充足，比足夠還多：

　■ There's no need to hurry. We've got **plenty of time**.

C　much 較少用於肯定句(特別是口語中)。比較下面例句：

　■ We did**n't** spend **much** money.

但是　We spent **a lot of** money. (並非 We spent much money)

　■ Do you see David **much**?

但是　I see David **a lot**. (並非 I see David much)

many、a lot 與 lots of 可以用於各種句子：

　■ **Many** people drive too fast.　或　**A lot of / Lots of** people drive too fast.
　■ Do you know **many** people?　或　Do you know **a lot of / lots of** people?
　■ There aren't **many** tourists here.　或　There aren't **a lot of** tourists here.

注意：我們通常說 **many years / many weeks / many days** (而非 a lot of . . .)：

　■ We've lived here for **many years**. (並非 a lot of years)

D　little 和 few 是表否定的意思，意思等於 not much 和 not many：

　■ Gary is very busy with his job. He has **little time** for other things.
　　(時間不多，比他想的少)
　■ Vicky doesn't like living in Paris. She has **few** friends there.
　　(朋友不多，不如她想要的多)

表示「極少」通常會說 **very little** 與 **very few**：

　■ Gary has **very little** time for other things.
　■ Vicky has **very few** friends in Paris.

E　a little 與 a few 則是表肯定的意思。

a little 意思是「一些」，相當於 some 或 a small amount：

　■ Let's go and get something to drink. We have **a little** time before the train leaves.
　　(一些時間；有足夠的時間喝飲料)
　■ "Do you speak English?" "**A little**." (所以我們與彼此交談。)

a few 意思等於 some、a small number：

　■ I enjoy my life here. I have **a few** friends, and we get together pretty often.
　　(a few friends 意思是朋友不多，但足夠一起玩得愉快)
　■ "When was the last time you saw Claire?" "**A few** days ago." (= some days ago)

比較下面的例子：

　■ He spoke **little** English, so it was difficult to communicate with him.
　■ He spoke **a little** English, so we were able to communicate with him.
　■ She's lucky. She has **few** problems. (= not many problems)
　■ Things are not going so well for her. She has **a few** problems. (= some problems)

注意：我們說 **only a little** 和 **only a few**：

　■ Hurry! We have **only a little** time. (並非 only little time)
　■ The town was very small. There were **only a few** streets. (並非 only few streets)

Exercises

85.1 依各句題意，判斷哪些句子中的 *much* 應改為 *many* 或 *a lot (of)*。若句子正確，則填入 *OK*。

1. We didn't spend much money. — *OK*
2. Sue drinks (much tea). — *a lot of tea*
3. Joe always puts much salt on his food. — _____
4. We'll have to hurry. We don't have much time. — _____
5. It cost much to fix the car. — _____
6. Did it cost much to fix the car? — _____
7. I don't know much people in this town. — _____
8. I use the phone much at work. — _____
9. There wasn't much traffic this morning. — _____
10. You need much money to travel around the world. — _____

85.2 依各句題意，自下列名詞中選出適當者，並與 *plenty of* 一起完成各句。

> hotels   money   room   things to see   ~~time~~   to learn

1. There's no need to hurry. There's _plenty of time._
2. He doesn't have any financial problems. He has _____
3. Come and sit with us. There's _____
4. She knows a lot, but she still has _____
5. It's an interesting town to visit. There _____
6. I'm sure we'll find somewhere to stay. _____

85.3 依各句題意，填入 *much / many / few / little* (限填一字)。

1. He isn't very popular. He has very _few_ friends.
2. Ann is very busy these days. She has _____ free time.
3. Did you take _____ pictures when you were on vacation?
4. I'm not very busy today. I don't have _____ to do.
5. This is a very modern city. There are _____ old buildings.
6. The weather has been very dry recently. We've had very _____ rain.
7. "Do you know Boston?" "No, I haven't been there for _____ years."

85.4 依各句題意，判斷哪些句子中的 *little/few* 應改為 *a little / a few*。若句子正確，則填入 *OK*。

1. She's lucky. She has <u>few problems</u>. — *OK*
2. Things are not going so well for her. She has <u>few problems</u>. — *a few problems*
3. Can you lend me <u>few dollars</u>? — _____
4. There was <u>little traffic</u>, so the trip didn't take very long. — _____
5. I can't give you a decision yet. I need <u>little time</u> to think. — _____
6. It was a surprise that he won the match. <u>Few people</u> expected him to win. — _____
7. I don't know much Spanish – <u>only few words</u>. — _____
8. I wonder how Sam is. I haven't seen him for <u>few months</u>. — _____

85.5 依各句題意，填入 *little / a little / few / a few*。

1. Gary is very busy with his job. He has _little_ time for other things.
2. Listen carefully. I'm going to give you _____ advice.
3. Do you mind if I ask you _____ questions?
4. It's not a very interesting place to visit, so _____ tourists come here.
5. I don't think Jill would be a good teacher. She has _____ patience.
6. "Would you like cream in your coffee?" "Yes, please, _____."
7. This is a very boring place to live. There's _____ to do.
8. "Have you ever been to Paris?" "Yes, I've been there _____ times."

all / all of   most / most of   no / none of 等

all	some	any	most	much/many	little/few	no

上述的字都可以置於名詞之前(例如 some food / few books 等)：

- **All cars** have wheels.
- **Some cars** can go faster than others.
- (在警告標示上) **NO CARS**. (= no cars allowed)
- **Many people** drive too fast.
- I don't go out very often. I stay home **most days**.

通常不可用 all of cars、most of people (參見 B 小節)：

- **Some people** learn languages more easily than others.
  (並非 Some of people)

注意必須用 **most** 而不是 the most：

- **Most tourists** don't visit this part of town. (並非 The most tourists)

all	some	any	most	much/many	little/few	half	none

上述的字都可以與 of 一起使用(some of / most of 等)：

我們用 some of / most of / none of 等 + the / this / that / these / those / my 等，所以可以說 some of the people、some of those people (而非 some of people)：

- **Some of the people** I work with are not very friendly.
- **None of this money** is mine.
- Have you read **any of these books**?
- I was sick yesterday. I spent **most of the day** in bed.

all 和 half 可以直接置於名詞之前，不需要 of，所以可以說：

- **All my friends** live in Los Angeles.   或   All **of** my friends . . .
- **Half this money** is mine.   或   Half **of** this money . . .

比較下面的例句：

- **All flowers** are beautiful. (泛指所有的花)
  All (of) **the flowers in this garden** are beautiful. (某些特定的花，即這個花園裡所有的花)
- **Most problems** have a solution. (泛指大部分的問題)
  We were able to solve **most of the problems we had**. (某些特定的問題，即我們所面臨的問題之中大部分的問題)

也可以用 all of / some of / none of 等 + it / us / you / them：

- "How many of these people do you know?" "**None of them. / A few of them.**"
- Do **any of you** want to come to a party tonight?
- "Do you like this music?" "**Some of it.** Not **all of it.**"

all 和 half 不可以直接置於 it / us / you / them 之前，一定要有 of，如 all of us / all of you / half of it / half of them 等：

- **All of us** were late. (並非 All us)
- I haven't finished the book yet. I've only read **half of it**. (並非 half it)

some/most/none 等可以單獨使用：

- Some cars have four doors and **some** have two.
- A few of the shops were open, but **most** (of them) were closed.
- Half this money is mine, and **half** (of it) is yours. (並非 the half)

Exercises

86.1 依各句題意需要，填入 *of* 或保留空白。

1. All ___–___ cars have wheels.
2. None ___of___ this money is mine.
3. Some _____ movies are very violent.
4. Some _____ the movies I've seen recently have been very violent.
5. Jim has lived in Houston all _____ his life.
6. Many _____ people watch too much TV.
7. Are any _____ those letters for me?
8. Kate has lived in Miami most _____ her life.
9. Jim thinks all _____ museums are boring.
10. Most _____ days I get up before 7:00.

86.2 依各句題意，自下列名詞中選出適當者，並依需要配合 *of* (*some of / most of* 等) 以完成句子。

accidents	large cities	my dinner	my teammates
birds	her friends	my spare time	the population
~~cars~~	her opinions	the buildings	~~these books~~

1. I haven't read many __*of these books*__ .
2. All __*cars*__ have wheels.
3. I spend much _____ gardening.
4. Many _____ are caused by bad driving.
5. It's an old town. Many _____ are over 400 years old.
6. When she got married, she kept it a secret. She didn't tell any _____ .
7. Not many people live in the north of the country. Most _____ live in the south.
8. Not all _____ can fly. For example, the penguin can't fly.
9. Our team played badly and lost the game. None _____ played well.
10. Julia and I have very different ideas. I don't agree with many _____ .
11. New York, like most _____ , has a traffic problem.
12. I had no appetite. I could only eat half _____ .

86.3 依各句題意，並依你自己的想法完成句子。

1. The building was damaged in the explosion. All __*the windows*__ were broken.
2. We had a very lazy vacation. We spent most of _____ on the beach.
3. I went to the movies by myself. None of _____ wanted to come.
4. The test was difficult. I could only answer half _____ .
5. Some of _____ you took at the wedding were very good.
6. *A:* Have you spent all _____ I gave you?
   B: No, there's still some left.

86.4 依各句題意，以 *all of / some of / none of* + *it/them/us* (*all of it / some of them* 等) 的用法完成句子。

1. These books are all Jane's. __*None of them*__ belong to me.
2. "How many of these books have you read?" "_____ . Every one."
3. We all got wet in the rain because _____ had an umbrella.
4. Some of this money is yours, and _____ is mine.
5. I asked some people for directions, but _____ was able to help me.
6. She made up the whole story from beginning to end. _____ was true.
7. Not all the tourists in the group were Spanish. _____ were French.
8. I watched most of the movie, but not _____ .

both / both of   neither / neither of
either / either of

both/neither/either 都用來談論兩件事或物；可以置於名詞前，與名詞一起使用(**both books**、**neither books**等)。例如你正要外出用餐，有兩家餐廳可供選擇，因此你說：

- **Both restaurants** are very good. (並非 The both restaurants)
- **Neither restaurant** is expensive.
- We can go to **either restaurant**. I don't care.
  (我們去兩家中的任何一家都可以。)

both of . . . / neither of . . . / either of . . .

可以用 **both of / neither of / either of** + **the** / **these** / **my** / **Tom's** . . . 等，例如我們可以說 both of **the** restaurants、both of **those** restaurants 等，但不可說 both of restaurants：

- **Both of these** restaurants are very good.
- **Neither of the** restaurants we went to was (或 were) expensive.
- I haven't been to **either of those** restaurants. (兩家餐廳我都沒有去過。)

both 可以直接置於名詞之前，不需要 of，所以我們可以說：

- **Both my parents** are from Michigan.   或   Both **of** my parents . . .

也可以用 **both of / neither of / either of** + **us/you/them**：

- (對著兩個人說話) Can **either of you** speak Spanish?
- I asked two people the way to the station, but **neither of them** knew.

both of + **us/you/them** 的用法中，**of** 不可省略：

- **Both of us** were very tired. (並非 Both us were . . .)

neither of 後可以使用單數動詞或複數動詞：

- Neither of the children **wants** (或 **want**) to go to bed.

both/neither/either 也可以單獨使用：

- I couldn't decide which of the two shirts to buy. I liked **both**.
  (或 I liked **both** of them.)
- "Is your friend British or American?" "**Neither**. She's Australian."
- "Do you want tea or coffee?" "**Either**. It doesn't matter."

請看下面的用法：

both . . . and . . .	■ **Both** Ann **and** Tom were late.
	■ I was **both** tired **and** hungry when I got home.
neither . . . nor . . .	■ **Neither** Liz **nor** Robin came to the party.
	■ She said she would contact me, but she **neither** wrote **nor** called.
either . . . or . . .	■ I'm not sure where he's from. He's **either** Spanish **or** Italian.
	■ **Either** you apologize, **or** I'll never speak to you again.

比較 **either/neither/both** (用於談論兩樣東西)，與 **any/none/all** (用於談論兩樣以上的東西)用法之不同：

■ There are **two** good hotels here. You could stay at **either** of them.	■ There are **many** good hotels here. You could stay at **any** of them.
■ We tried **two** hotels. **Neither** of them had any rooms. **Both** of them were full.	■ We tried **a lot of** hotels. **None** of them had any rooms. **All** of them were full.

Exercises

87.1 依各句題意，填入 **both/neither/either**。

1. "Do you want tea or coffee?" __"Either.__ It really doesn't matter."
2. "What's the date today – the 18th or the 19th?" " _____ . It's the 20th."
3. *A:* Where did you go for vacation – Florida or Puerto Rico?
   B: We went to _____ . A week in Florida and a week in Puerto Rico.
4. "When should I call you, morning or afternoon?" " _____ . I'll be home all day."
5. "Where's Kate? Is she at work or at home?" " _____ . She's out of town."

87.2 依各句題意，填入 **both/neither/either**，並視需要加入 **of**。

1. __Both__ my parents are from California.
2. To get downtown, you can take the city streets or you can take the freeway. You can go _____ way.
3. I tried to call George twice, but _____ times he was out.
4. _____ Tom's parents is American. His father is Polish, and his mother is Italian.
5. I saw an accident this morning. One car drove into the back of another. Fortunately _____ driver was injured, but _____ cars were badly damaged.
6. I have two sisters and a brother. My brother is working, but _____ my sisters are still in school.

87.3 依各句題意，以 **both/neither/either of + us/them** 之用法，完成句子。

1. I asked two people the way to the airport, but __neither of them__ could help me.
2. I was invited to two parties last week, but I couldn't go to _____ .
3. There were two windows in the room. It was very warm, so I opened _____ .
4. Sarah and I play tennis together regularly, but _____ can play very well.
5. I tried two bookstores for the book I wanted, but _____ had it.

87.4 依各句題意，以 **both . . . and . . . / neither . . . nor . . . / either . . . or . . .** 改寫各句。

1. Chris was late. So was Pat. __Both Chris and Pat were late.__
2. He didn't write and he didn't call. __He neither wrote nor called.__
3. Joe is on vacation and so is Sam. _____
4. Joe doesn't have a car. Sam doesn't have one either. _____
5. Brian doesn't watch TV, and he doesn't read newspapers. _____
   _____
6. It was a boring movie. It was long, too.
   The movie _____
7. Is that man's name Richard? Or is it Robert? It's one or the other.
   That man's name _____
8. I don't have time to go on vacation. And I don't have the money.
   I have _____
9. We can leave today, or we can leave tomorrow – whichever you prefer.
   We _____

87.5 依各句題意，填入 **neither / either / none / any**。

1. We tried a lot of hotels, but __none__ of them had any rooms
2. I took two books with me on vacation, but I didn't read _____ of them.
3. I took five books with me on vacation, but I didn't read _____ of them.
4. There are a few stores on the next block, but _____ of them sells newspapers.
5. You can call me at _____ time during the evening. I'm always at home.
6. I can meet you next Monday or Friday. Would _____ of those days be convenient for you?
7. John and I couldn't get into the house because _____ of us had a key.

all、every 與 whole

A

all 與 everybody/everyone

all 通常並不用來表示 everybody/everyone：
- **Everybody** enjoyed the party. (並非 All enjoyed)

可以用 **all of us/you/them**，但不用 everybody of . . . ：
- **All of us** enjoyed the party. (並非 Everybody of us)

B

all 與 everything

有時 **all** 與 **everything** 可以互換使用：
- I'll do **all I can** to help.　或　I'll do **everything I can** to help.

all 可用於 all **I can** / all **you need** 等，但是 all 通常不單獨使用：
- He thinks he knows **everything**. (並非 he knows all)
- Our vacation was a disaster. **Everything** went wrong. (並非 All went wrong)

all 也可以用於 **all about**：
- He knows **all about** computers.

all 還可以用來表示「唯一的東西」(但不可以用 everything)：
- **All** I've eaten today is a sandwich. (我今天唯一吃的東西)

C

every / everybody / everyone / everything 都是單數名詞，所以必須用單數形動詞：
- **Every seat** in the theater **was** taken.
- **Everyone has** arrived. (並非 have arrived)

但是 everybody/everyone 的代名詞通常用 they/them/their：
- **Everybody** said **they** enjoyed **themselves**. (= he or she enjoyed himself or herself)

D

whole 與 all

whole 的意思是整體、全部；whole 通常與單數名詞一起使用：
- Did you read **the whole book**? (整本書，不僅是一部份)
- Lila has lived **her whole life** in Chile.
- I was so hungry, I ate **a whole package** of cookies. (一整包)

可以用 **the/my/her** 等，置於 whole 之前。比較 whole 與 all 之用法：
- **the whole** way / **all the** way　　**her whole** life / **all her** life

whole 通常不與不可數名詞一起使用：
- I've spent **all the money** you gave me. (並非 the whole money)

E

every/all/whole 與表時間的名詞

every 用來表示某事多久發生一次(**every day** / **every Monday** / **every 10 minutes** / **every three week**s等)：
- When we were on vacation, we went to the beach **every day**. (並非 all days)
- The bus service is very good. There's a bus **every 10 minutes**.
- We don't see each other very often – about **every six months**.

all day / the whole day 意思是一整天，從早到晚：
- We spent **all day** / **the whole day** at the beach.
- Dan was very quiet. He didn't say a word **all night** / **the whole night**.

注意我們說 **all day** (而不是 all the day)、**all week**(而不是 all the week)等。

比較 **all the time** 與 **every time** 之用法：
- They never go out. They are at home **all the time**. (= always, continuously)
- **Every time** I see you, you look different. (= each time, on every occasion)

可數名詞與不可數名詞 Unit 67 與 Unit 68　*all / all of* Unit 86　*each* 與 *every* Unit 89　*every one* Unit 89D
all (詞語順序) Unit 107C

Exercises

88.1 依各句題意，填入 *all*、*everything* 或 *everybody/everyone*。

1. It was a good party. __*Everyone*__ enjoyed it.
2. __*All*__ I've eaten today is a sandwich.
3. _____ has their faults. Nobody is perfect.
4. Nothing has changed. _____ is the same as it was.
5. Kate told me _____ about her new job. It sounds very interesting.
6. Can _____ write their name on a piece of paper, please?
7. Why are you always thinking about money? Money isn't _____ .
8. I didn't have much money with me. _____ I had was 10 dollars.
9. When the fire alarm rang, _____ left the building immediately.
10. Sue didn't say where she was going. _____ she said was that she was going away.
11. We have completely different opinions. I disagree with _____ she says.
12. We all did well on the exam. _____ in our class passed.
13. We all did well on the exam. _____ of us passed.
14. Why are you so lazy? Why do you expect me to do _____ for you?

88.2 依各句題意，以 *whole* 改寫各句。

1. I read the book from beginning to end.
   __*I read the whole book.*__
2. Everyone on the team played well.
   The _____
3. Paul opened a box of chocolates. When he finished eating, there were no chocolates left in the box. He ate _____
4. The police came to the house. They were looking for something. They searched everywhere, every room. They _____
5. Everyone in Dave and Jane's family plays tennis. Dave and Jane play, and so do all their children. The _____
6. Ann worked from early in the morning until late at night.
   _____
7. Jack and Lisa spent a week at the beach on vacation. It rained from the beginning of the week to the end. It _____

以 *all* 改寫第 6 句與第 7 句。

8. (6) Ann _____
9. (7) _____

88.3 依各句題意，自下列時間中選出適當者，配合 *every* 完成句子。

five minutes   ~~**10 minutes**~~   **four hours**   **six months**   **four years**

1. The bus service is very good. There's a bus __*every 10 minutes.*__
2. Tom is sick. He has some medicine. He has to take it _____
3. The Olympic Games take place _____
4. We live near a busy airport. A plane flies over our house _____
5. It's a good idea to have a check-up with the dentist _____

88.4 依各句題意，判斷劃線部份的兩個詞何者正確。

1. I spent ~~the whole money~~ / all the money you gave me. (*all the money* 是正確答案)
2. Sue works every day / all days except Sunday.
3. I'm tired. I've been working hard all the day / all day.
4. It was a terrible fire. Whole building / The whole building was destroyed.
5. I've been trying to call her, but every time / all the time I call, the line is busy.
6. I don't like the weather here. It rains every time / all the time.
7. When I was on vacation, all my luggage / my whole luggage was stolen.

each 與 every

A

each 與 every 的意思相近，有時可以互換使用：

- **Each** time (或 **Every** time) I see you, you look different.
- There's a ceiling fan in **each** room (或 **every** room) of the house.

但是 each 和 every 的意思並不盡相同，請看下面的比較：

each 是用來表示一個一個、個別的東西。 ■ Study **each sentence** carefully. (一句一句讀) each = **X** + **X** + **X** + **X**	every 用來表示一群東西中的每一個，意思與 **all** 類似。 ■ **Every sentence** must have a verb. (每一個句子，所有的句子) every = ⬭XXXXXXX⬭
each 通常用於較小的數量： ■ There were four books on the table. **Each book** was a different color. ■ (在遊戲中) At the beginning of the game, **each player** has three cards.	every 通常用於較大的數量： ■ Kate loves reading. She has read **every book** in the library. (= all the books) ■ I would like to visit **every country** in the world. (= all the countries)

each 可以用於說明兩樣東西，但 every 不可以，例如：

- In a baseball game, **each team** has nine players. (並非 every team)

every 用於描述某事發生的頻率，但 each 不可以，例如：

- "How often do you use your computer?" "**Every day.**" (並非 Each day)
- There's a bus **every 10 minutes**. (並非 each 10 minutes)

B

比較下面 each 與 every 之用法：

each 可以置於名詞之前： **each book**　　**each student** each 可以單獨使用： ■ None of the rooms was the same. **Each** (= each room) was different. 也可以用 **each one**： ■ **Each one** was different. 可以用 **each of**(the .../ these ..., them 等)： ■ Read **each of these** sentences carefully. ■ **Each of the** books is a different color. ■ **Each of them** is a different color.	every 可以置於名詞之前： **every book**　　**every student** every 不可以單獨使用，必須用 **every one**： ■ *A:* Have you read all these books? 　*B:* Yes, **every one**. 可以用 **every one of** ...(而非 every of)： ■ I've read **every one of those** books. (並非 every of those books) ■ I've read **every one of them**.

C

each 也可以單獨用於句中或句尾，例如：

- The students were **each** given a book. (每一位學生都獲得一本書)
- These oranges cost 75 cents **each**.

D

everyone 與 every one

everyone 意思是 everybody，只用於指人。
every one 可以用來指事物或人，意思與 **each one** 類似(參見 B 小節)：

- **Everyone** enjoyed the party. (= **Everybody** ...)
- Sarah is invited to lots of parties and she goes to **every one**. (= to **every party**)

Exercises

89.1 依各句題意與各圖片的情境，填入 *each* 或 *every* 以完成句子。

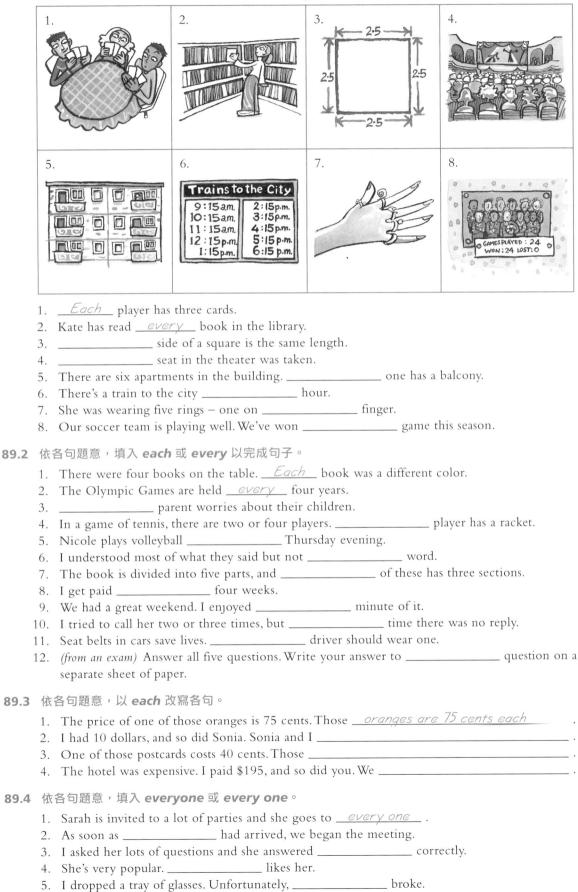

1. __*Each*__ player has three cards.
2. Kate has read __*every*__ book in the library.
3. _____ side of a square is the same length.
4. _____ seat in the theater was taken.
5. There are six apartments in the building. _____ one has a balcony.
6. There's a train to the city _____ hour.
7. She was wearing five rings – one on _____ finger.
8. Our soccer team is playing well. We've won _____ game this season.

89.2 依各句題意，填入 *each* 或 *every* 以完成句子。

1. There were four books on the table. __*Each*__ book was a different color.
2. The Olympic Games are held __*every*__ four years.
3. _____ parent worries about their children.
4. In a game of tennis, there are two or four players. _____ player has a racket.
5. Nicole plays volleyball _____ Thursday evening.
6. I understood most of what they said but not _____ word.
7. The book is divided into five parts, and _____ of these has three sections.
8. I get paid _____ four weeks.
9. We had a great weekend. I enjoyed _____ minute of it.
10. I tried to call her two or three times, but _____ time there was no reply.
11. Seat belts in cars save lives. _____ driver should wear one.
12. *(from an exam)* Answer all five questions. Write your answer to _____ question on a separate sheet of paper.

89.3 依各句題意，以 *each* 改寫各句。

1. The price of one of those oranges is 75 cents. Those __*oranges are 75 cents each*__ .
2. I had 10 dollars, and so did Sonia. Sonia and I _____ .
3. One of those postcards costs 40 cents. Those _____ .
4. The hotel was expensive. I paid $195, and so did you. We _____ .

89.4 依各句題意，填入 *everyone* 或 *every one*。

1. Sarah is invited to a lot of parties and she goes to __*every one*__ .
2. As soon as _____ had arrived, we began the meeting.
3. I asked her lots of questions and she answered _____ correctly.
4. She's very popular. _____ likes her.
5. I dropped a tray of glasses. Unfortunately, _____ broke.

關係子句 1:
有 who / that / which 之關係子句

A

請看下面的例句

The woman who lives next door is a doctor.
　　　　　　　關係子句

子句是句子的一部份。關係子句用來表示說話者所指的人或事物為何，或是什麼樣的人或事物：

- The woman **who lives next door** ... (who lives next door 告訴聽話者是哪一個女人。)
- People **who live in the country** ... (who live in the country 告訴聽話者是哪一種人。)

關係子句中，**who** 用來描述說話者所談論的人(而非事物)：

> the woman – she lives next door – is a doctor
> ↓
> → The woman **who lives next door** is a doctor.
>
> we know a lot of people – they live in the country
> ↓
> → We know a lot of people **who live in the country**.

- An architect is someone **who designs buildings**.
- What was the name of the person **who called you**?
- Anyone **who wants to apply for the job** must do so by Friday.

who 也可以用 **that** 來替代，但是談論人時不可以用 **which**：

- The woman **that lives next door** is a doctor. (並非 the woman **which**)

但是有時候談論人時一定要用 **who** 而非 that，參見 Unit 93。

B

關係子句中，用 **that** 或 **which** 而非 who 來描述事物：

> where is the cheese? – it was in the refrigerator
> ↓
> → Where is the cheese { **that** / **which** } **was in the refrigerator?**

- I don't like stories **that have unhappy endings**. (或 stories **which** have ...)
- Barbara works for a company **that makes furniture**.
  (或 a company **which** makes furniture)
- The machine **that broke down** is working again now.
  (或 The machine **which** broke down)

that 比 **which** 更常使用，但有時候一定要用 **which**，參見 Unit 93。

C

what 意思是 the thing that。比較 **what** 與 **that** 之用法：

- **What** happened was my fault. (= the thing that happened)
- Everything **that happened** was my fault. (並非 Everything what happened)
- The machine **that broke down** is now working again.
  (並非 The machine what broke down)

D

記得，關係子句中要用 **who/that/which**，而不可以用 **he / she / they / it**：

- I've never spoken to the woman **who lives** next door. (並非 the woman she lives)

Exercises

90.1 依各題括號中的提示，自下列的描述中選出適當者，以關係子句 (談論人用 *who*) 解釋括號內提示的字。

he/she	steals from a store ~~designs buildings~~ doesn't believe in God is not brave	he/she	buys something from a store pays rent to live in a room or apartment breaks into a house to steal things expects the worst to happen

1. (an architect) _An architect is someone who designs buildings._
2. (a burglar) A burglar is someone _____
3. (a customer) _____
4. (a shoplifter) _____
5. (a coward) _____
6. (an atheist) _____
7. (a pessimist) _____
8. (a tenant) _____

90.2 依各句題意，以 *who/that/which* 合併句子。

1. A girl was injured in the accident. She is now in the hospital.
   The girl who was injured in the accident is now in the hospital.
2. A waitress served us. She was impolite and impatient.
   The _____
3. A building was destroyed in the fire. It has now been rebuilt.
   The _____
4. Some people were arrested. They have now been released.
   The _____
5. A bus goes to the airport. It runs every half hour.
   The _____

90.3 依各句題意，自下列描述中選出適當者，並以關係子句完成句子。

he invented the telephone	~~it makes furniture~~
she runs away from home	it gives you the meanings of words
they stole my car	it can support life
they were on the wall	it cannot be explained

1. Barbara works for a company _that makes furniture_ .
2. The book is about a girl _____ .
3. What happened to the pictures _____ ?
4. A mystery is something _____
5. The police have caught the men _____
6. A dictionary is a book _____
7. Alexander Bell was the man _____
8. It seems that Earth is the only planet _____

90.4 依各句題意，判斷各句是否正確。若句子不正確，請加以更正。

1. I don't like (stories who have) unhappy endings. _stories that have_
2. What was the name of the person who called you? _OK_
3. Where's the nearest shop who sells newspapers? _____
4. The driver which caused the accident was fined $500. _____
5. Do you know the person that took these photographs? _____
6. We live in a world what is changing all the time. _____
7. Dan said some things about me that were not true. _____
8. What was the name of the horse it won the race? _____

關係子句 2:
有與沒有 who / that / which 之關係子句

A　請再看一次 Unit 90 中的例子：

- The woman **who** lives next door is a doctor.　(或 The woman **that** lives ...)

  The woman ⎯⎯ lives next door.　　　　**who** (= the woman) 為關係子句的主詞

- Where is the cheese **that** was in the refrigerator?　(或 the cheese **which** was ...)

  The cheese ⎯⎯ was in the refrigerator.　　**that** (= the cheese) 也是關係子句的主詞

當 **who/that/which** 為關係子句中的主詞時，不可以省略。因此，我們不可以說
The woman lives next door is a doctor 或 Where is the cheese was in the refrigerator?

B　**who/that/which** 也可以作為關係子句中的受詞，例如：

- The woman **who** I wanted to see was away on vacation.

  I wanted to see the **woman**.　　**who** = the woman 為關係子句的受詞，**I** 是主詞。

- Have you found the keys **that** you lost?

  You lost the **keys**.　　**that** = the keys 為關係子句的受詞，**you** 是主詞。

當 **who/that/which** 為關係子句中的受詞時，可以省略。因此，我們可以說：

- The **woman I wanted to see** was away.　或　The woman **who** I wanted to see ...
- Have you found **the keys you lost**?　或　...the keys **that** you lost?
- **The dress Ann bought** doesn't fit her very well.　或　The dress **that** Ann bought ...
- Is there **anything I can do**?　或　...anything **that** I can do?

注意下列的表達方式：
the keys you lost (並非 the keys you lost them)
the dress Ann bought (並非 the dress Ann bought it)

C　注意介係詞 (**in/at/with** 等) 在關係子句中的位置：

Tom is talking **to** a woman – do you know her?

→ Do you know the woman (who/that) **Tom is talking to**?

I slept **in** a bed last night – it wasn't very comfortable

→ The bed (that/which) **I slept in last night** wasn't very comfortable.

- Are these the books **you were looking for**?　或　...the books **that/which** you were ...
- The woman **he fell in love with** left him after a month.　或　The woman **who/that** he ...
- The man **I was sitting next to on the plane** talked all the time.　或
  The man **who/that** I was sitting next to ...

注意下列的表達方式：
the books you were looking for (並非 the books you were looking for them)

D　下面句子中，關係子句中必須用 **that**，不可以用 **what** (參見 Unit 90C)：

- Everything (**that**) **they said** was true. (並非 Everything what they said)
- I gave her all the money (**that**) **I had**. (並非 all the money what I had)

what 在關係子句中的意思 the thing(s) that：

- Did you hear **what they said**? (= the things that they said)

Exercises

91.1 依各句題意，判斷句子是否正確，並以 *who* 或 *that* 改正句子。

1. (The woman lives next door) is a doctor   _The woman who lives next door_
2. Have you found the keys you lost?   _OK_
3. The people we met last night were very nice.   _____
4. The people work in the office are very nice.   _____
5. The people I work with are very nice.   _____
6. What have you done with the money I gave you?   _____
7. What happened to the money was on the table?   _____
8. What's the worst film you've ever seen?   _____
9. What's the best thing it has ever happened to you?   _____

91.2 依各題所描述的情境，以正確關係子句完成各句。

1. Your friend lost some keys. You want to know if he has found them. You say:
   Have you found the keys _you lost_ ?
2. A friend is wearing a dress. You like it. You tell her:
   I like the dress _____ .
3. A friend is going to see a movie. You want to know the name of the movie. You say:
   What's the name of the movie _____ ?
4. You wanted to visit a museum. It was closed when you got there. You tell a friend:
   The museum _____ was closed when we got there.
5. You invited some people to your party. Some of them couldn't come. You tell someone:
   Some of the people _____ couldn't come.
6. Your friend had to do some work. You want to know if she has finished. You say:
   Have you finished the work _____ ?
7. You rented a car. It broke down after a few miles. You tell a friend:
   The car _____ broke down after a few miles.
8. You stayed at a hotel. Tom had recommended it to you. You tell a friend:
   We stayed at a hotel _____ .

91.3 依各句題意，自下列句子中選出適當者，並以關係子句與介係詞完成句子。

we went to a party last night	you can rely on Brian	we were invited to a wedding
I work with some people	I applied for a job	you told me about a hotel
~~you were looking for some books~~	I saw you with a man	

1. Are these the books _you were looking for_ ?
2. Unfortunately we couldn't go to the wedding _____ .
3. I enjoy my job. I like the people _____ .
4. What's the name of that hotel _____ .
5. The party _____ wasn't very much fun.
6. I didn't get the job _____ .
7. Brian is a good person to know. He's somebody _____ .
8. Who was that man _____ in the restaurant?

91.4 依各句題意需要，填入 *that* 或 *what*；若句中之關係子句正確則保留空白。

1. I gave her all the money _–_ I had. (all the money **that** I had 也是正確答案)
2. Did you hear _what_ they said?
3. They give their children everything _____ they want.
4. Tell me _____ you want, and I'll try to get it for you.
5. Why do you blame me for everything _____ goes wrong?
6. I won't be able to do much, but I'll do _____ I can.
7. I won't be able to do much, but I'll do the best _____ I can.
8. I don't agree with _____ you've just said.
9. I don't trust him. I don't believe anything _____ he says.

關係子句 3: whose / whom / where

A

whose

在關係子句中，**whose** 用來代表 **his/her/their**：

> we saw some people – their car had broken down
>
> → We saw some people **whose car had broken down**.

whose 大多用來描述人：

- A widow is a woman **whose husband is dead**. (**her** husband is dead)
- What's the name of the man **whose car you borrowed**? (you borrowed **his** car)
- I met someone **whose brother I went to school with**.
  (I went to school with **his/her** brother)

比較 **who** 與 **whose** 之用法：

- I met a man **who** knows you. (**he** knows you)
- I met a man **whose sister** knows you. (**his sister** knows you)

B

whom

當關係代名詞在關係子句中作為受詞時，**whom** 與 **who** 可以互換使用 (參見 Unit 91B)：

- The woman **whom I wanted to see** was away on vacation. (I wanted to see **her**)

與介係詞一起使用時，必須用 **whom** (to whom / from whom / with whom等)：

- The people **with whom I work** are very nice. (I work **with them**)

但是在口語中，較少使用 **whom**，通常用 **who**、**that**，或是省略不用 (參見 Unit 91)；因此，我們通常說：

- The woman **I wanted to see** ...　或　The woman **who/that** I wanted to see ...
- The people **I work with** ...　或　The people **who/that** I work with ...

C

where

在關係子句中，**where** 用來描述地方：

> the restaurant – we had dinner there – it was near the airport
>
> → The restaurant **where we had dinner** was near the airport.

- I recently went back to **the town where I grew up**.
  (或 ...the town I grew up in 或 ...the town **that** I grew up in)
- I would like to live in **a place where there is plenty of sunshine**.

D

請看下面的句型：

the day / the year / the time 等 { something happens　或
　　　　　　　　　　　　　　　　　 that something happens

- Do you remember **the day (that) we went to the zoo**?
- **The last time (that) I saw her**, she looked fine.
- I haven't seen them since **the year (that) they got married**.

E

請看下面的句型：

the reason { something happens　或
　　　　　　　　 that/why something happens

- **The reason I'm calling you** is to ask your advice.
  (或 The reason **that** I'm calling / The reason **why** I'm calling)

92.1 以下是你在聚會中所見到的人。

請以 **who** 或 **whose** 作為關係代名詞，以關係子句描述你所遇見的人，轉述給你的朋友。

1. I met somebody _whose mother writes detective stories_ .
2. I met a man _____ .
3. I met a woman _____ .
4. I met somebody _____ .
5. I met a couple _____ .
6. I met somebody _____ .

92.2 依各題所描述的情境，以 **where** 的關係子句完成句子。

1. You grew up in a small town. You went back there recently. You tell someone this.
   I recently went back to the small town _where I grew up_ .
2. You want to buy some postcards. You ask a friend where you can do this.
   Is there someplace near here _____ ?
3. You work in a factory. The factory is going to close down next month. You tell a friend:
   The factory _____ is going to close down next month.
4. Sue is staying at a hotel. You want to know the name of the hotel. You ask a friend:
   Do you know the name of the hotel _____ ?
5. You play baseball in a park on Sundays. You show a friend the park. You say:
   This is the park _____ on Sundays.

92.3 依各句題意，填入 **who / whom / whose / where**。

1. What's the name of the man _whose_ car you borrowed?
2. A cemetery is a place _____ people are buried.
3. A pacifist is a person _____ believes that all wars are wrong.
4. An orphan is a child _____ parents are dead.
5. What was the name of the person to _____ you spoke on the phone?
6. The place _____ we spent our vacation was really beautiful.
7. This school is only for children _____ first language is not English.
8. The woman with _____ he fell in love left him after a month.

92.4 依你自己的意思，參照 D 小節與 E 小節的例句，以完成句子。

1. I'll always remember the day _I first met you_ .
2. I'll never forget the time _____ .
3. The reason _____ was that I didn't know your address.
4. Unfortunately I wasn't at home the evening _____ .
5. The reason _____ is that they don't need one.
6. _____ was the year _____ .

關係子句 4:
補述用法關係子句 (1)

關係子句有兩種；下面的例句中，劃線的部份即為關係子句：

比較下列用法：

<table>
<tr><td>

第一類

- The woman <u>who lives next door</u> is a doctor.
- Barbara works for a company <u>that makes furniture</u>.
- We stayed at the hotel <u>(that) you recommended</u>.

在上述例句中，關係子句是用來指明說話者所談論的是哪個人或哪件事物，或哪一類的人或哪一類事物：

   The woman **who lives next door** 告訴聽話者是哪個女人。
A company **that makes furniture** 告訴聽話者是哪一種公司。
The hotel **(that) you recommended** 告訴聽話者是哪家旅館。

限定用法的關係子句不可以用逗點 (,)：

- People <u>who come from Texas love football</u>.

</td><td>

第二類

- My brother Jim, <u>who lives in Houston</u>, is a doctor.
- Brad told me about his new job, which <u>he's enjoying a lot</u>.
- We stayed at the Grand Hotel, <u>which a friend of ours recommended</u>.

在上述的例句中，聽話者已經知道說話者談論的是那個人、那件事物是「我哥哥Jim」、「Brad 的新工作」、「圓山飯店」。因此，關係子句的功能並不是告訴聽話者是何人、何事物。

在這些例句中的關係子句，是對於所談論的人、或事物，提供更多的訊息。

此類補述用法的關係子句，通常使用逗點 (,)：

- My English teacher, <u>who comes from Texas</u>, loves computers.

</td></tr>
</table>

在這兩類的關係子句中，**who** 皆用來代表人，**which** 皆用來代表事物；然而：

<table>
<tr><td>

第一類

可以用 **that** 代替 **who** 或 **which**：

- Do you know anyone **who/that** speaks French and Italian?
- Barbara works for a company **which/that** makes furniture.

當 **that/who/which** 於關係子句中作為受詞時，可以省略 (參見 Unit 91)：

- We stayed at the hotel (that/which) you recommended.
- This morning I met somebody (who/that) I hadn't seen for ages.

whom 於限定用法中較少使用(參見 Unit 92B)。

</td><td>

第二類

不可以用 **that** 代替 **who** 或 **which**：

- John, **who** (並非 that) speaks French and Italian, works as a tour guide.
- Brad told me about his new job, **which** (並非 that) he's enjoying a lot.

當 **who/which** 於此種用法的關係子句中作為受詞時，仍然不可以省略：

- We stayed at the Grand Hotel, **which** a friend of ours recommended.
- This morning I met Chris, **who** I hadn't seen for ages.

可以使用 **whom** 作為關係子句中的受詞：

- This morning I met Chris, **whom** I hadn't seen for ages.

</td></tr>
</table>

在兩類的關係子句中，都可以使用 **whose** 與 **where**：

<table>
<tr><td>

- We met some people **whose** car had broken down.
- What's the name of the place **where** you spent your vacation?

</td><td>

- Amy, **whose** car had broken down, was in a very bad mood.
- Mrs. Bond is spending a few weeks in Sweden, **where** her daughter lives.

</td></tr>
</table>

Exercises

93.1 以 *who(m)* / *whose* / *which* / *where* 作為關係代名詞，將括號中的句子寫成關係子句 (第二類之補述用法)，以完成句子合併。

1. Ann is very friendly. (She lives next door.)
   Ann, who lives next door, is very friendly.
2. We stayed at the Grand Hotel. (A friend of ours had recommended it.)
   We stayed at the Grand Hotel, which a friend of ours had recommended.
3. We often go to visit our friends in New York. (It is not very far away.)
   _____
4. I went to see the doctor. (He told me to rest for a few days.)
   _____
5. John is one of my closest friends. (I have known him for a very long time.)
   John, _____
6. Sheila is away from home a lot. (Her job involves a lot of travel.)
   _____
7. The new stadium will be opened next month. (It can hold 90,000 people.)
   _____
8. Alaska is the largest state in the United States. (My brother lives there.)
   _____
9. A friend of mine helped me to get a job. (His father is the manager of a company.)
   _____

93.2 依各句題意，以關係子句改寫句子；請判斷各句中的關係子句應為第一類 (限定用法) 或第二類 (補述用法) 的關係子句。

1. There's a woman living next door to me. She's a doctor.
   The woman *who lives next door to me is a doctor.*
2. I have a brother named Jim. He lives in Houston. He's a doctor.
   My brother Jim, *who lives in Houston, is a doctor.*
3. There was a strike at the car factory. It began 10 days ago. It is now over.
   The strike at the car factory _____
4. I was looking for a book this morning. I've found it now.
   I've found _____
5. London was once the largest city in the world, but the population is now decreasing.
   The population of London, _____
6. A job was advertised. A lot of people applied for it. Few of them had the necessary
   qualifications. Few of _____
7. Amanda has a son. She showed me a picture of him. He's a police officer.
   Amanda showed me _____

93.3 依各句題意，判斷關係子句應為第一類 (限定用法) 或第二類 (補述用法)、是否需要加逗點 (,)。若句子正確，則填入**OK**。

1. Brad told me about his new job that he's enjoying a lot.
   Brad told me about his new job, which he's enjoying a lot.
2. My office that is on the second floor is very small.
   _____
3. The office I'm using these days is very small.
   _____
4. Ben's father that used to be a teacher now works for a TV company.
   _____
5. The doctor that examined me couldn't find anything wrong.
   _____
6. The sun that is one of millions of stars in the universe provides us with heat and light.
   _____

關係子句 5:
補述用法關係子句 (2)

A

介係詞 + **whom/which**

在補述用法的關係子句中，**whom**(指人)與**which**(指事物)前都可以使用介係詞。因此，可以說 **to whom** / **with whom** / **about which** / **for which**等：

- Mr. Carter, **to whom** I spoke at the meeting, is very interested in our plan.
- Fortunately we had a map, **without which** we would have gotten lost.

在口語中，關係子句中的介係詞通常會置於動詞的後面；因此，通常使用 **who** (而不是 whom) 來指人：

- This is my friend from Canada, **who** I was telling you **about**.
- Yesterday we visited the City Museum, **which** I'd never been **to** before.

B

all of / **most of** 等 + **whom/which**

請看下面的例子：

Mary has three brothers. All of them are married. *(2 sentences)*

→ Mary has three brothers, **all of whom** are married. *(1 sentence)*

They asked me a lot of questions. I couldn't answer most of them . *(2 sentences)*

→ They asked me a lot of questions, **most of which** I couldn't answer. *(1 sentence)*

類似的用法請看下面各例：

none of / **neither of** / **any of** / **either of**
some of / **many of** / **much of** / **(a) few of**   + **whom** (指人)
both of / **half of** / **each of** / **one of** / **two of** (等)   + **which** (指事或物)

- Tom tried on three jackets, **none of which** fit him.
- Two men, **neither of whom** I had ever seen before, came into the office.
- They have three cars, **two of which** they rarely use.
- Sue has a lot of friends, **many of whom** she went to school with.

也可以用 **the cause of which** / **the name of which** 等：

- The building was destroyed in a fire, **the cause of which** was never established.
- We stayed at a beautiful hotel, **the name of which** I can't remember now.

C

which (並非 **what**)

請看下面的例子：

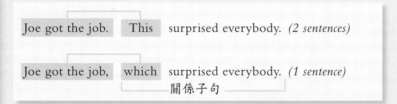

Joe got the job. This surprised everybody. *(2 sentences)*

Joe got the job, which surprised everybody. *(1 sentence)*
關係子句

在上例中，**which** 意思是指 Joe 獲得工作這件事；此種表達方式只可用 **which**，不可用 **what**：

- Sarah couldn't meet us, **which** was a shame. (並非 what was a shame)
- The weather was good, **which** we hadn't expected. (並非 what we hadn't expected)

what 在關係子句中的用法，請見 Unit 90 與 Unit 91D。

94.1 依據各題意，以介係詞 + **whom/which** 之句型改寫各句。

1. Yesterday we visited the City Museum, which I'd never been to before.
Yesterday we visited the City Museum, _to which I'd never been before_ .
2. My brother showed us his new car, which he's very proud of.
My brother showed us his new car, _____ .
3. This is a picture of our friends Chris and Sam, who we went on vacation with.
This is a picture of our friends Chris and Sam, _____ .
4. The wedding, which only members of the family were invited to, took place on Friday.
The wedding, _____ ,
took place on Friday.

94.2 依各句題意，以 **all of / most of** 等 + **whom/which** 改寫各句。

1. All of Mary's brothers are married.
Mary has three brothers, _all of whom are married_ .
2. Most of the information we were given was useless.
We were given a lot of information, _____ .
3. Jane has received neither of the letters I sent her.
I sent Jane two letters, _____ .
4. None of the ten people who applied for the job was suitable.
Ten people applied for the job, _____ .
5. Kate hardly ever uses one of her computers.
Kate has got two computers, _____ .
6. Mike gave half of the $50,000 he won to his parents.
Mike won $50,000, _____ .
7. Both of Julia's sisters are teachers.
Julia has two sisters, _____ .
8. I went to a party – I knew only a few of the people there.
There were a lot of people at the party, _____ .
9. The sides of the road we drove along were lined with trees.
We drove along the road, the _____ .
10. The aim of the company's new business plan is to save money.
The company has a new business plan, _____ .

94.3 請從下列兩個框框中各選出一個句子，並以 **which** 將兩個句子合併為一句。

1. ~~Laura couldn't come to the party.~~
2. Jane doesn't have a phone.
3. Neil has passed his exams.
4. Our flight was delayed.
5. Kate offered to let me stay at her house.
6. The street I live on is very noisy at night.
7. Our car has broken down.

This was very nice of her.
This means we can't take our trip tomorrow.
This makes it difficult to contact her.
This makes it difficult to sleep sometimes.
~~This was a shame.~~
This is good news.
This meant we had to wait three hours at the airport.

1. Laura couldn't come to the party, _which was a shame._ _____
2. Jane _____
3. _____
4. _____
5. _____
6. _____
7. _____

-ing 與 -ed 片語 (the woman **talking to Tom**、 the boy **injured in the accident**)

A

片語是句子的一部分。有些片語以 **-ing** 為首,有些則以 **-ed** 為首。請看下面的例句:

Do you know the woman **talking to Tom**?

└──**-ing** 片語──┘

(你認識正在和Tom談話的那個女人嗎?)

the woman
talking to Tom
正在和 Tom 談
話的那個女人

The boy **injured in the accident** was taken to the hospital.

└──**-ed** 片語──┘

(在車禍中受傷的那個男孩被送到醫院。)

the boy injured
in the accident
在車禍中受傷
的那個男孩

B

-ing 片語用來描述在某一特定時間(現在或過去),某人(或某物)正在做什麼:

- Do you know the woman **talking to Sam**? (the woman **is talking** to Sam)
- Police **investigating the crime** are looking for three men. (police **are investigating** the crime)
- Who were those people **waiting outside**? (they **were waiting**)
- I was awakened by a bell **ringing**. (a bell **was ringing**)

-ing 片語也可以用來描述一般性的狀況,而不只是在某特定時間發生的事件。例如:

- The road **connecting the two towns** is very narrow.
  (the road **connects** the two towns)
- I have a large bedroom **overlooking the garden**.
  (the room **overlooks** the garden)
- Can you think of the name of a flower **beginning with "t"**?
  (the name **begins** with "t")

C

-ed 片語有被動語氣的意涵

- The boy **injured in the accident** was taken to the hospital.
  (he **was injured** in the accident)
- George showed me some pictures **painted by his father**.
  (they **had been painted** by his father)

在上例中,**injured** 與 **painted** 皆為過去分詞。注意,許多動詞的過去分詞為不規則變化,並不以 **-ed** 為字尾(例如 **stolen/made/written** 等):

- The police never found the money **stolen in the robbery**.
- Most of the goods **made in this factory** are exported.

left 用於 **-ed** 片語時,意思是「沒有用完,還在那兒」:

- We've eaten almost all the chocolates. There are only a few **left**.

D

there is / there was 等句型後經常使用 **-ing** 片語與 **-ed** 片語:

- **There were** some children **swimming** in the river.
- **Is there** anybody **waiting**?
- **There was** a big red car **parked** outside the house.

Exercises

95.1 請將括號中的句子以 **-ing** 片語的形式，併入前一句的句中或置於句尾，以合併成一個句子。

1. A bell was ringing. I was awakened by it.
   I was awakened by ___*a bell ringing*___ .
2. A man was sitting next to me on the plane. I didn't talk much to him.
   I didn't talk much to the _____ .
3. A taxi was taking us to the airport. It broke down.
   The _____ broke down.
4. There's a path at the end of this street. The path leads to the river.
   At the end of the street there's a _____ .
5. A factory has just opened in town. It employs 500 people.
   A _____ has just opened in town.
6. The company sent me a brochure. It contained the information I needed.
   The company sent me _____ .

95.2 請依各句題意，以 **-ed** 片語的方式，將兩句話合併為一個句子。

1. A boy was injured in the accident. He was taken to the hospital.
   The boy ___*injured in the accident*___ was taken to the hospital.
2. A gate was damaged in the storm. It has now been repaired.
   The gate _____ has now been repaired.
3. A number of suggestions were made at the meeting. Most of them were not very practical.
   Most of the _____ were not very practical.
4. Some paintings were stolen from the museum. They haven't been found yet.
   The _____ haven't been found yet.
5. A man was arrested by the police. What was his name?
   What was the name of _____ ?

95.3 依各句題意，自下列動詞中選出適當者，並以 **-ing** 或 **-ed** 的形式完成句子。

blow	drive	~~invite~~	live	name	offer	read	~~ring~~	sell	sit

1. I was awakened by a bell ___*ringing*___ .
2. Some of the people ___*invited*___ to the party can't come.
3. Life must be very unpleasant for people _____ near busy airports.
4. A few days after the interview, I received a letter _____ me the job.
5. Somebody _____ Jack phoned while you were out.
6. There was a tree _____ down in the storm last night.
7. The waiting room was empty except for a young man _____ by the
   window _____ a magazine.
8. Look! The man _____ the red car almost hit the person
   _____ newspapers on the street corner.

95.4 依各句題意，將括號中所提供的字以 **there is / there was** 的句型寫成完整的句子。

1. That house is empty. (nobody / live / in it) ___*There's nobody living in it.*___
2. The accident wasn't serious. (nobody / injure) ___*There was nobody injured.*___
3. I can hear footsteps. (somebody / come)
   There _____
4. The train was full. (a lot of people / travel)
   _____
5. We were the only guests at the hotel. (nobody else / stay there)
   _____
6. The piece of paper was blank. (nothing / write / on it)
   _____
7. The school offers English courses in the evening. (a new course / begin / next Monday)
   _____

-ing 與 -ed 為字尾的形容詞
(boring / bored 等)

許多形容詞為 **-ing** 與 **-ed** 為字尾的字，例如 **boring** 與 **bored**。

bored

boring

Jane has been doing the same job for a very long time. Every day she does exactly the same thing again and again. She doesn't enjoy her job any more and would like to do something different.

Jane 做同樣的工作已經很長一段時間了，每天她都重複一遍又一遍做著相同的工作。她再也不喜歡這樣的工作，想要做不同的工作。

Jane's job is **boring.**
Jane 的工作很無聊。
Jane is **bored** (with her job).
Jane 覺得很無聊。

某人覺得 **bored** (無聊)是因為某事 (或某個其他的人) 很 **boring** (令人覺得無聊)；換言之，假如某事很 **boring**，那麼它讓你覺得 **bored**。因此，請看下面的例句：

- Jane is **bored** because her job is **boring**.
- Jane's job is **boring**, so Jane is **bored**. (並非 Jane is boring)

如果說某人很 **boring** (令人覺得無聊)，意思就是這個人讓其他的人覺得 **bored**(無聊)：

- George always talks about the same things. He's really **boring**.

比較 **-ing** 結尾與 **-ed** 結尾之形容詞：

- My job is
  - boring.
  - interesting.
  - tiring.
  - satisfying.
  - depressing. (等)

- I'm **bored** with my job.
- I'm not **interested** in my job any more.
- I get very **tired** doing my job.
- I'm not **satisfied** with my job.
- My job makes me **depressed**. (等)

上述 **-ing** 結尾的形容詞是描述工作。

上述 **-ed** 結尾的形容詞是描述某人 (對某事) 的感覺。

比較下面例子：

interesting
- Julia thinks politics is **interesting**.
- Did you meet anyone **interesting** at the party?

surprising
- It was **surprising** that he passed the exam.

disappointing
- The movie was **disappointing**. We expected it to be much better.

shocking
- The news was **shocking**.

interested
- Julia is **interested** in politics. (並非 interesting in politics)
- Are you **interested** in buying a car? I'm trying to sell mine.

surprised
- Everybody was **surprised** that he passed the exam.

disappointed
- We were **disappointed** with the movie. We expected it to be much better.

shocked
- I was **shocked** when I heard the news.

Exercises

96.1 依各句題意，將括號中的字改為 *-ing* 或 *-ed* 的形容詞。

1. The movie wasn't as good as we had expected. (disappoint-)
   a) The movie was __*disappointing*__ .
   b) We were __*disappointed*__ with the movie.

2. Diana teaches young children. It's a very hard job, but she enjoys it. (exhaust-)
   a) She enjoys her job, but it's often _____ .
   b) At the end of a day's work, she is often _____ .

3. It's been raining all day. I hate this weather. (depress-)
   a) This weather is _____ .
   b) This weather makes me _____ .
   c) It's silly to get _____ because of the weather.

4. Claire is going to Mexico next month. She has never been there before. (excit-)
   a) It will be an _____ experience for her.
   b) Going to new places is always _____ .
   c) She is really _____ about going to Mexico.

96.2 依各句題意，判斷劃線部份的形容詞何者正確。

1. I was ~~disappointing~~ / disappointed with the movie. I had expected it to be better. (*disappointed* 是正確答案)
2. Are you <u>interesting / interested</u> in tennis?
3. The tennis match was very <u>exciting / excited</u>. I had a great time.
4. It's sometimes <u>embarrassing / embarrassed</u> when you have to ask people for money.
5. Do you get <u>embarrassing / embarrassed</u> easily?
6. I never expected to get the job. I was really <u>amazing / amazed</u> when it was offered to me.
7. She has learned really fast. She has made <u>astonishing / astonished</u> progress.
8. I didn't find the situation funny. I was not <u>amusing / amused</u>.
9. It was a really <u>terrifying / terrified</u> experience. Everybody was very <u>shocking / shocked</u>.
10. Why do you always look so <u>boring / bored</u>? Is your life really so <u>boring / bored</u>?
11. He's one of the most <u>boring / bored</u> people I've ever met. He never stops talking and he never says anything <u>interesting / interested</u>.

96.3 依各句題意，自下列形容詞中選出適當者，並判斷應為 *-ing* 或 *-ed* 的形式。

amusing/amused	**annoying/annoyed**	**boring/bored**
confusing/confused	**disgusting/disgusted**	**exciting/excited**
exhausting/exhausted	**interesting/interested**	~~**surprising**~~/**surprised**

1. He works very hard. It's not __*surprising*__ that he's always tired.
2. I don't have anything to do. I'm _____ .
3. The teacher's explanation was _____ . Most of the students didn't understand it.
4. The kitchen hadn't been cleaned in ages. It was really _____ .
5. I seldom go to art galleries. I'm not particularly _____ in art.
6. You don't have to get _____ just because I'm a few minutes late.
7. The lecture was _____ . I fell asleep.
8. I've been working very hard all day and now I'm _____ .
9. I'm starting a new job next week. I'm very _____ about it.
10. Tom is very good at telling funny stories. He can be very _____ .
11. Liz is a very _____ person. She knows a lot, she's traveled a lot, and she's done lots of different things.

形容詞: a **nice new** house、you look **tired**

A

有時候兩個或兩個以上的形容詞，會同時置於名詞前修飾名詞：

- My brother lives in a **nice new** house.
- There was a **beautiful large round wooden** table in the kitchen.

類似 **new / large / round / wooden** 等之形容詞屬於描述「事實」的形容詞；這類形容詞提供有關年齡、大小、顏色等事實的訊息。

另一類形容詞像 **nice/beautiful** 等屬於陳述「意見」的形容詞；這類形容詞描述某人對於某人或某事物的看法。

陳述意見的形容詞通常置於描述事實的形容詞之前：

	意見	事實	
a	**nice**	**long**	summer vacation
an	**interesting**	**young**	man
	delicious	**hot**	vegetable soup
a	**beautiful**	**large round wooden**	table

B

有時兩個或兩個以上描述事實的形容詞會同時置於名詞之前，其排列順序通常如下：(注意這是一般的順序，但並非絕對的順序)

| 1. how big? 大小 | → | 2. how old? 新舊 | → | 3. what color? 顏色 | → | 4. where from? 源由起源 | → | 5. what is it made of? 材質 | → | NOUN 名詞 |

a **tall young** man (1 → 2)   a **large wooden** table (1 → 5)
big blue eyes (1 → 3)   an **old Russian** song (2 → 4)
a **small black plastic** bag (1 → 3 → 5)   an **old white cotton** shirt (2 → 3 → 5)

描述大小與長度的形容詞 (例如 **big / small / tall / short / long** 等) 通常用於描述形狀與寬度的形容詞 (例如 **round / fat / thin / slim / wide** 等) 之前：

a **large round** table   a **tall thin** girl   a **long narrow** street

使用兩個或兩個以上的顏色形容詞時，必須使用連接詞 **and**：

a **black and white** dress   a **red, white, and green** flag

但是顏色形容詞與其他形容詞一起用於名詞前時，通常不使用連接詞 and：

a **long black** dress (並非 a long and black dress)

C

形容詞可以用於 **be / get / become / seem** 等動詞之後：

- **Be careful**!
- I'm **tired** and I'm **getting hungry**.
- As the movie went on, it **became** more and more **boring**.
- Your friend **seems** very **nice**.

形容詞也與 look、feel、sound、taste 或 smell 一起使用，表示某人或某事物看起來、感覺起來、聽起來、嚐起來、或聞起來怎麼樣：

- You **look tired**. / I **feel tired**. / She **sounds tired**.
- The dinner **smells good**.
- This milk **tastes** a little **strange**.

但描述某人如何做某事，則必須使用副詞 (參見 Unit 98 與 Unit 99)：

- Drive **carefully**! (並非 Drive careful)
- Susan plays the piano very **well**. (並非 plays . . . very good)

D

我們可以說 the **first two** days / the **next few** weeks / the **last 10** minutes 等：

- I didn't enjoy the **first two** days of the course. (並非 the two first days)
- They'll be away for the **next few** weeks. (並非 the few next weeks)

副詞 Unit 98 與 Unit 99   比較級 (**cheaper** 等) Unit 102 至 Unit 104   最高級 (**cheapest** 等) Unit 105

Exercises

97.1 將括號中的形容詞，依正確的順序置於名詞之前。

1. a beautiful table (wooden / round)   _a beautiful round wooden table_
2. an unusual ring (gold)   _____
3. an old house (beautiful)   _____
4. black gloves (leather)   _____
5. an Italian film (old)   _____
6. a long face (thin)   _____
7. big clouds (black)   _____
8. a sunny day (lovely)   _____
9. an ugly dress (yellow)   _____
10. a wide avenue (long)   _____
11. a red car (old / little)   _____
12. a new sweater (green / nice)   _____
13. a metal box (black / small)   _____
14. a big cat (fat / black)   _____
15. a little country inn (old / charming)   _____
16. long hair (black / beautiful)   _____
17. an old painting (interesting / French)   _____
18. an enormous umbrella (red / yellow)   _____

97.2 依各句題意，分別自下列左框中選出適當的動詞，自右框中選出適當的形容詞，以完成句子。

feel	look	~~seem~~		awful	fine	interesting
smell	sound	taste		nice	~~upset~~	wet

1. Helen _seemed upset_ this morning. Do you know what was wrong?
2. I can't eat this. I just tried it and it _____ .
3. I was sick yesterday, but I _____ today.
4. What beautiful flowers! They _____ , too.
5. You _____ . Have you been out in the rain?
6. Jim was telling me about his new job. It _____ – much better than his old job.

97.3 依各句題意，判斷應填入形容詞或副詞。

1. This milk tastes _strange_ . (strange / strangely)
2. I always feel _____ when the sun is shining. (happy / happily)
3. The children were playing _____ in the yard. (happy / happily)
4. The man became _____ when the manager of the restaurant asked him to leave. (violent / violently)
5. You look _____ ! Are you all right? (terrible / terribly)
6. There's no point in doing a job if you don't do it _____ . (proper / properly)
7. The soup tastes _____ . (good / well)
8. Hurry up! You're always so _____ . (slow / slowly)

97.4 依各題題意，以 *the first . . . / the next . . . / the last . . .* 改寫各個語詞。

1. the first day and the second day of the course   _the first two days of the course_
2. next week and the week after   _the next two weeks_
3. yesterday and the day before yesterday   _____
4. the first week and the second week of May   _____
5. tomorrow and a few days after that   _____
6. questions 1, 2, and 3 on the exam   _____
7. next year and the year after   _____
8. the last day of our vacation and the two days before that   _____

形容詞與副詞 1
(quick / quickly)

請看下面的例子：

- Our vacation was too short – the time passed very **quickly**.
- Two people were **seriously** injured in the accident.

上面例句中的 **quickly** 與 **seriously** 皆為副詞。許多副詞是由形容詞 + **-ly**所形成：

形容詞：	quick	serious	careful	quiet	heavy	bad
副詞：	quickly	seriously	carefully	quietly	heavily	badly

拼字規則，參見附錄 6。

並非所有 **-ly** 結尾的字都是副詞；例如，下列 **-ly** 結尾的字即為形容詞：

friendly   lively   elderly   lonely   silly   lovely

形容詞或副詞

形容詞 (**quick/careful** 等) 用來描述名詞(某人或某物)；通常置於名詞之前：

- Tom is a **careful driver**.
  (並非 a carefully driver)
- We didn't go out because of the **heavy rain**.

副詞 (**quickly/carefully** 等) 用來描述動詞；副詞用來說明某人如何做某事，或某事是如何發生的：

- Tom **drove carefully** along the narrow road. (並非 drove careful)
- We didn't go out because it was **raining heavily**. (並非 raining heavy)

比較下面的例句：

- She speaks **perfect English**.
  形容詞 + 名詞

- She **speaks** English **perfectly**.
  動詞 + 名詞 + 副詞

形容詞也用於 **look/feel/sound** 等動詞，以及 **be** 動詞之後。
比較下面的例句：

- Please **be quiet**.
- I was disappointed that my exam results **were** so **bad**.
- Why do you always **look** so **serious**?
- I **feel happy**.

- Please **speak quietly**.
- I was unhappy that I **did** so **badly** on the exam. (並非 did so bad)
- Why do you never **take** me **seriously**?
- The children were **playing happily**.

副詞也可以用於形容詞或其他副詞之前，例如：

reasonably cheap	(副詞+形容詞)
terribly sorry	(副詞+形容詞)
incredibly quickly	(副詞+副詞)

- It's a **reasonably cheap** restaurant, and the food is **extremely good**.
- I'm **terribly sorry**. I didn't mean to push you. (並非 terrible sorry)
- Maria learns languages **incredibly quickly**.
- The test was **surprisingly easy**.

副詞也可以用於過去分詞 (例如 **injured/organized/written** 等) 之前：

- Two people were **seriously injured** in the accident. (並非 serious injured)
- The conference was very **badly organized**.

Exercises

98.1 依各句題意，並依所提供的字首字母填入適當的副詞。

1. We didn't go out because it was raining he_avily_ .
2. Our team lost the game because we played very ba_____ .
3. I had little trouble finding a place to live. I found an apartment quite ea_____ .
4. We had to wait for a long time, but we didn't complain. We waited pat_____ .
5. Nobody knew Steve was coming to see us. He arrived unex_____ .
6. Mike stays in shape by playing tennis reg_____ .
7. I don't speak French very well, but I can understand per_____ if people
   speak sl_____ and cl_____ .

98.2 依各句題意，判斷應填入形容詞或副詞。

1. Two people were _seriously_ injured in the accident. (serious / seriously)
2. The driver of the car had _serious_ injuries. (serious / seriously)
3. I think you behaved very _____ . (selfish / selfishly)
4. Kelly is _____ upset about losing her job. (terrible / terribly)
5. There was a _____ change in the weather. (sudden / suddenly)
6. Everybody at the party was _____ dressed. (colorful / colorfully)
7. Linda likes wearing _____ clothes. (colorful / colorfully)
8. Liz fell and hurt herself really _____ . (bad / badly)
9. These pants are already coming apart. They're _____ made. (bad / badly)
10. Don't go up that ladder. It doesn't look _____ . (safe / safely)

98.3 依各句題意，自下面的形容詞/副詞中選出適當者，以完成句子。

careful(ly)	complete(ly)	continuous(ly)	financial(ly)	fluent(ly)
happy / happily	nervous(ly)	perfect(ly)	~~quick(ly)~~	special(ly)

1. Our vacation was too short. The time passed very _quickly_ .
2. Tom doesn't take risks when he's driving. He's always _____ .
3. Sue works _____ . She never seems to stop.
4. Amy and Eric are very _____ married.
5. Nicole's English is very _____ although she makes a lot of mistakes.
6. I cooked this meal _____ for you, so I hope you like it.
7. Everything was very quiet. There was _____ silence.
8. I tried on the shoes and they fit me _____ .
9. Do you usually feel _____ before exams?
10. I'd like to buy a car, but it's _____ impossible for me at this time.

98.4 依各句題意，分別自兩個框框中各選出一個適當的詞，以完成句子。

absolutely	badly	completely
~~reasonably~~	seriously	slightly
unnecessarily	unusually	

changed	~~cheap~~	damaged
enormous	ill	long
planned	quiet	

1. I thought the restaurant would be expensive, but it was _reasonably cheap_ .
2. Steve's mother is _____ in the hospital.
3. What a big house! It's _____ .
4. It wasn't a serious accident. The car was only _____ .
5. The children are normally very lively, but they're _____ today.
6. When I returned home after 20 years, everything had _____ .
7. The movie was _____ . It could have been much shorter.
8. A lot went wrong during our vacation because it was _____ .

形容詞與副詞 2
(well/fast/late, hard/hardly)

A

good/well

good 是形容詞，副詞為 well：

- Your English is **good**.　　並非　You **speak** English **well**.
- Susan is a **good** pianist.　　並非　Susan **plays** the piano **well**.

well (而非 good) 可以用於過去分詞(例如 **dressed/known** 等)之前：

well dressed　　**well known**　　**well educated**　　**well paid**

- Gary's father is a **well known** writer.

然而 **well** 也可以當作形容詞，意思是「身體健康」：

- "How are you today?"　"I'm very **well**, thanks."

B

fast/hard/late

fast、**hard** 與 **late** 是形容詞，也是副詞：

形容詞	副詞
■ Jack is a **very fast runner**.	■ Jack can **run** very **fast**.
■ Kate is a **hard worker**.	■ Kate **works hard**. (並非 works hardly)
■ I was **late**.	■ I **got up late** this morning.

lately 意思是最近 (副詞)：

- Have you seen Tom **lately**?

C

hardly

hardly 意思是很少，幾乎沒有。請看下面的例句：

- Sarah wasn't very friendly at the party. She **hardly** spoke to me.
  (她很少和我說話，幾乎完全沒有)
- We've only met once or twice. We **hardly** know each other.

hard 與 **hardly** 的意思完全不同。比較下面的例句：

- He tried **hard** to find a job, but he had no luck. (他非常努力地去試)
- I'm not surprised he didn't find a job. He **hardly** tried to find one. (他幾乎沒有試)

hardly 常與 **any / anybody / anyone / anything / anywhere** 一起使用：

- *A:* How much money have we got?
  B: **Hardly any**. (很少，幾乎沒有)
- These two cameras are very similar. There's **hardly any** difference between them.
- The results of the test were very bad. **Hardly anybody** in our class passed. (很少學生通過)

注意下列的表達方式：

- She said **hardly anything**.　或　She **hardly** said **anything**.
- We've got **hardly any** money.　或　We've **hardly** got any **money**.

I **can hardly** do something 意思是「我幾乎不可能做某件事」：

- Your writing is terrible. I **can hardly** read it. (你寫的字我幾乎看不懂)
- My leg was hurting me. I **could hardly** walk.

hardly ever 意思是幾乎從來沒有：

- I'm nearly always at home at night. I **hardly ever** go out.

hardly 也可以表示「當然不」的意思。例如:

- It's **hardly surprising** that you're tired. You haven't slept for three days. (當然不令人訝異)
- The situation is serious, but it's **hardly a crisis**. (當然不算是危機)

There's **hardly anything** in the fridge.
我們冰箱裡幾乎沒有任何食物。

Exercises

99.1 依各句題意，填入 *good* 或 *well*。

1. I play tennis but I'm not very ___good___ .
2. Your test results were very _____ .
3. You did _____ on the test.
4. The weather was _____ while we were on vacation.
5. I didn't sleep _____ last night.
6. Jason speaks Spanish very _____ .
7. Jason's Spanish is very _____ .
8. Our new business isn't doing very _____ at the moment.
9. I like your jacket. It looks _____ on you.
10. I've met her a few times, but I don't know her _____ .

99.2 依各句題意，自下列形容詞中選出適當者，與 *well* 一起完成各句。

behaved **dressed** **informed** **known** **maintained** **paid** **written**

1. The children were very good. They were ___well behaved___ .
2. I'm surprised you haven't heard of her. She is quite _____ .
3. Our neighbors' yard is neat and clean. It is very _____ .
4. I enjoyed the book you lent me. It's a great story, and it's very _____ .
5. Tania knows a lot about many things. She is very _____ .
6. Mark always wears nice clothes. He is always _____ .
7. Jane has a lot of responsibility in her job, but she isn't very _____ .

99.3 依各句題意，判斷各題中劃底線的字是否正確，若有錯誤請加以更正。

1. I'm tired because I've been working <u>hard</u>.   ___OK_____
2. I tried <u>hard</u> to remember her name, but I couldn't.   _____
3. This coat is practically unused. I've <u>hardly</u> worn it.   _____
4. Judy is a good tennis player. She hits the ball <u>hardly</u>.   _____
5. Don't walk so <u>fast</u>! I can't keep up with you.   _____
6. I had plenty of time, so I was walking <u>slow</u>.   _____

99.4 依各句題意，自下列動詞中選出適當者，與 *hardly* 一起完成各句。

change **hear** **know** **recognize** **say** **sleep** **speak**

1. Scott and Amy have only met once before. They ___hardly know___ each other.
2. You're speaking very quietly. I can _____ you.
3. I'm very tired this morning. I _____ last night.
4. We were so shocked when we heard the news, we could _____ .
5. Kate was very quiet this evening. She _____ a word.
6. You look the same now as you looked 15 years ago. You've _____ .
7. I met Dave a few days ago. I hadn't seen him for a long time and he looks very different now.
   I _____ him.

99.5 依各句題意，以 *hardly + any / anybody / anything / anywhere / ever* 的用法完成句子。

1. I'll have to go shopping. There's ___hardly anything___ to eat.
2. It was a very warm day. There was _____ wind.
3. "Do you know much about computers?" "No, _____ ."
4. The hotel was almost empty. There was _____ staying there.
5. I listen to the radio a lot, but I _____ watch television.
6. Our new boss is not very popular. _____ likes her.
7. It was very crowded in the room. There was _____ to sit.
8. We used to be good friends, but we _____ see each other now.
9. It was nice driving this morning. There was _____ traffic.
10. I hate this town. There's _____ to do and
    _____ to go.

so 與 such

比較 so 與 such 用法之不同：

so 用於形容詞/副詞之前：
- **so stupid** **so quick**
- **so nice** **so quickly**

- I didn't like the book. The story was **so stupid.**
- I like Liz and Joe. They are **so nice.**

such 用於名詞之前：
- **such a story** **such people**

也可以用 **such** + 形容詞 + 名詞：
- **such** a stupid **story** **such** nice **people**

- I didn't like the book. It was **such** a stupid **story.** (並非 a so stupid story)
- I like Liz and Joe. They are **such nice people.** (並非 so nice people)

注意 such 後接單數名詞時是用 **such a** ...(而非 a such)：
- **such a** big **dog** (並非 a such big dog)

so 與 such 皆用來加強形容詞或副詞的語意：

- It's a beautiful day, isn't it? It's **so warm.** (= really warm)
- It's difficult to understand him because he talks **so quietly.**

可以用 **so ... that ...** 的句型：
- The book was **so good that** I couldn't put it down.
- I was **so tired that** I fell asleep in the armchair.

上述句型中，**that** 可以省略：
- I was **so tired** I fell asleep.

- It was a great holiday. We had **such a good time.** (= a really good time)

可以用 **such ... that ...** 的句型：
- It was **such a good book that** I couldn't put it down.
- It was **such nice weather that** we spent the whole day on the beach.

上述句型中，**that** 可以省略：
- It was **such nice weather** we spent ...

so 與 such 也可以表示「像這樣」的意思：

- Somebody told me the house was built 100 years ago. I didn't realize it was **so old.** (= as old as it is)
- I'm tired because I got up at six. I don't usually get up **so early.**
- I expected the weather to be cooler. I'm surprised it is **so warm.**

- I didn't realize it was **such an old house.**
- You know it's not true. How can you say **such a thing?**

注意 **no such** 的用法：
- You won't find the word 'blid' in the dictionary. There's **no such word.** (= this word does not exist)

so 用於 so long / so far / so much 等用法，而 such 則用於 **such a long time/way**、**such a lot of** 等用法。比較下面的例句：

so long
- I haven't seen her for **so long** I've forgotten what she looks like.

so far
- I didn't know it was **so far.**

so much, so many
- I'm sorry I'm late – there was **so much** traffic.

such a long time
- I haven't seen her for **such a long time.** (並非 so long time)

such a long way
- I didn't know it was **such a long way.**

such a lot (of)
- I'm sorry I'm late – there was **such a lot** of traffic.

Exercises

100.1 依各句題意，填入 *so*、*such* 或 *such a*。

1. It's difficult to understand him because he speaks ___so___ quietly.
2. I like Liz and Joe. They're ___such___ nice people.
3. It was a great vacation. We had ___such a___ good time.
4. I was surprised that he looked _____ good after his recent illness.
5. Everything is _____ expensive these days, isn't it?
6. The weather is beautiful, isn't it? I didn't expect it to be _____ nice day.
7. I have to go. I didn't realize it was _____ late.
8. He always looks good. He wears _____ nice clothes.
9. It was _____ boring movie that I fell asleep while I was watching it.
10. I couldn't believe the news. It was _____ shock.
11. I think she works too hard. She looks _____ tired all the time.
12. The food at the hotel was _____ awful. I've never eaten _____ awful food.
13. They've got _____ much money that they don't know what to do with it.
14. I didn't realize you lived _____ long way from downtown.
15. The party was really great. It was _____ shame you couldn't come.

100.2 請從下面的兩個框框中各選出一個句子，再以 *so . . . (that) . . .* 或 *such . . . (that) . . .* 的句型，將各題中的兩個句子合併為一句。

1. ~~She worked hard.~~	You could hear it from miles away.
2. ~~It was a beautiful day.~~	You would think it was her native language.
3. I was tired.	We spent the whole day indoors.
4. We had a good time on vacation.	~~She made herself sick.~~
5. She speaks English well.	I couldn't keep my eyes open.
6. I've got a lot to do.	I didn't eat anything else for the rest of the day.
7. The music was loud.	~~We decided to go to the beach.~~
8. I had a big breakfast.	I didn't know what to say.
9. It was terrible weather.	I don't know where to begin.
10. I was surprised.	We didn't want to come home.

1. _She worked so hard (that) she made herself sick._
2. _It was such a beautiful day (that) we decided to go to the beach._
3. I was _____
4. _____
5. _____
6. _____
7. _____
8. _____
9. _____
10. _____

100.3 依你自己意思，完成下列各組句子。

1. a) We enjoyed our vacation. It was so ___relaxing_____ .
   b) We enjoyed our vacation. We had such ___a good time_____ .

2. a) I like Catherine. She's so _____ .
   b) I like Catherine. She's such _____ .

3. a) I like New York. It's so _____ .
   b) I like New York. It's such _____ .

4. a) I wouldn't like to be a teacher. It's so _____ .
   b) I wouldn't like to be a teacher. It's such _____ .

5. a) It's great to see you again! I haven't seen you for so ____ .
   b) It's great to see you again! I haven't seen you for such __ .

enough 與 too

A

enough 用於形容詞與副詞之後：

- I can't run very far. I'm not **fit enough**. (並非 enough fit)
- Let's go. We've waited **long enough**.
- Is Joe going to apply for the job? Is he **experienced enough**?

I'm not **fit enough**.

比較 **too . . .** 與 **not . . . enough** 的用法：

- You never stop working. You work **too hard**.
  (超過必要的程度)
- You're lazy. You do**n't** work **hard enough**.
  (不足必要的程度)

B

enough 通常用於名詞之前：

- I can't run very far. I don't have **enough energy**. (並非 energy enough)
- Is Joe going to apply for the job? Does he have **enough experience**?
- We've got **enough money**. We don't need any more.
- Some of us had to sit on the floor because there weren't **enough chairs**.

注意下面的表達方式:

- We didn't have **enough time**. (並非 the time wasn't enough)
- There is **enough money**. (並非 the money is enough)

enough 也可以單獨使用，不必後接名詞：

- We don't need any more money. We've got **enough**.

比較 **too much / too many** 與 **enough**：

- There's **too much** furniture in this room. There's not **enough space**.
- There were **too many people** and not **enough chairs**.

C

我們可以說 **enough/too . . . for** somebody/something：

- We don't have **enough** money **for a vacation**.
- Is Joe experienced **enough for the job**?
- This shirt is **too** big **for me**. I need a smaller size.

但是我們通常用 **enough/too . . . to** do something (而非 for doing)。例如：

- We don't have **enough money to go** on vacation. (並非 for going)
- Is Joe **experienced enough to do** the job?
- They're **too young to get** married. / They're not **old enough to get** married.
- Let's take a taxi. It's **too far to walk** home from here.
- The bridge is just **wide enough** for two cars **to pass** each other.

D

在下面 **too . . . to . . .** 的句型中，動詞後不可以接代名詞：

> The food was very hot. We couldn't eat **it**.
>
> 與　　The food was so hot that we couldn't eat **it**.
>
> 但是　The food was **too** hot **to eat**. (沒有 it)

其他類似的例子如下：

- These boxes are **too heavy to carry**.
  (並非 too heavy to carry them)
- The wallet was **too big to put** in my pocket.
  (並非 too big to put it)
- This chair isn't **strong enough to stand** on.
  (並非 strong enough to stand on it)

Exercises

101.1 依各句題意，自下列形容詞或名詞中選出適當的字與 *enough* 合用，一起完成句子。

big	~~chairs~~	cups	~~fit~~	milk	money
qualified	room	time	warm	well	

1. I can't run very far. I'm not ___*fit enough*___ .
2. Some of us had to sit on the floor because there weren't ___*enough chairs*___ .
3. I'd like to buy a car, but I don't have _____ right now.
4. Do you have _____ in your coffee, or would you like some more?
5. Are you _____ ? Or should I turn up the heat?
6. It's only a small car. There isn't _____ for all of us.
7. Steve didn't feel _____ to go to work this morning.
8. I enjoyed my trip to Paris, but there wasn't _____ to do everything I wanted.
9. Do you think I am _____ to apply for the job?
10. Try this jacket on and see if it's _____ for you.
11. There weren't _____ for everybody to have coffee at the same time.

101.2 依各對話的情境，以括號中所提供的字與 *enough* 或 *too* 合用，一起完成各個對話。

1. Are they going to get married? — (old) No, they're not ___*old enough to*___ ___*get married*___ .
2. I need to talk to you about something. — (busy) Well, I'm afraid I'm _____ to you now.
3. Let's go to the movies. — (late) No, it's _____ to the movies.
4. Why don't we sit outside? — (warm) It's not _____ outside.
5. Would you like to be a politician? — (shy) No, I'm _____ a politician.
6. Would you like to be a teacher? — (patience) No, I don't have _____ a teacher.
7. Did you hear what he was saying? — (far away) No, we were _____ what he was saying.
8. Can he read a newspaper in English? — (English) No, he doesn't know _____ a newspaper.

101.3 依各句題意，以 *too* 或 *enough* 將各題中的兩個句子合併成為一句。

1. We couldn't carry the boxes. They were too heavy.
   ___*The boxes were too heavy to carry.*___
2. I can't drink this coffee. It's too hot.
   This coffee is _____
3. Nobody could move the piano. It was too heavy.
   The piano _____
4. Don't eat these apples. They're not ripe enough.
   These apples _____
5. I can't explain the situation. It is too complicated.
   The situation _____
6. We couldn't climb over the wall. It was too high.
   The wall _____
7. Three people can't sit on this sofa. It isn't big enough.
   This sofa _____
8. You can't see some things without a microscope. They are too small.
   Some _____

比較級 1
(cheaper、more expensive 等)

A

請看下面的例子：

> Should I drive or take the train? 我應該開車，或是搭火車？
>   You should drive. It's **cheaper**. 你應該開車，開車比較便宜。
>   Don't take the train. It's **more expensive**. 不要搭火車，搭火車比較貴。
> 例子中 cheaper 與 more expensive 為形容詞的比較級。

在句子中，比較級後可以用 **than** (參見 Unit 104)：

- It's **cheaper** to go by car **than** by train.
- Going by train is **more expensive than** going by car.

B

比較級的形式有兩種，**-er** 與 **more**：

-er 用於較短的字(單音節字)：
- **cheap** → cheap**er**　　**fast** → fast**er**
- **large** → larg**er**　　**thin** → thin**ner**

雙音節以 -y 結尾的字也可以用 -er (-y → ier)：
- lucky → luck**ier**　　early → earl**ier**
- easy → eas**ier**　　pretty → prett**ier**

有關拼音規則，參見附錄 6。

more 用於較長的字(雙音節或雙音節以上的字)：
- **more serious**　　**more often**
- **more expensive**　　**more comfortable**

more 也用於 -ly 結尾的副詞：
- **more slowly**　　**more seriously**
- **more quietly**　　**more carefully**

比較下面的例子：

- You're **older** than me.
- The test was pretty easy – **easier** than I expected.
- Can you walk a little **faster**?
- I'd like to have a **bigger** car.
- Last night I went to bed **earlier** than usual.

- You're **more patient** than me.
- The test was pretty difficult – **more difficult** than I expected.
- Can you walk a little **more slowly**?
- I'd like to have a **more reliable** car.
- I don't play tennis much these days. I used to play **more often**.

有一些雙音節形容詞可以用 -er 或 more 形成比較級：

> **clever**　　**narrow**　　**quiet**　　**shallow**　　**simple**

- It's too noisy here. Can we go somewhere **quieter** / **more quiet**?

C

下列形容詞與副詞之比較為不規則形式：

good/well → **better**
- The yard looks **better** since you cleaned it up.
- I know him **well** – probably **better** than anybody else knows him.

bad/badly → **worse**:
- "How is your headache? Better?" "No, it's **worse**."
- He did very badly on the test – **worse** than expected.

far → **farther** (或 **further**):
- "It's a long walk from here to the park – **farther** than I thought. (或 **further** than)

further (而非 farther) 也可以表示「更多」或「額外的」之意思：
- Let me know if you hear any **further** news. (= any more news)

Exercises

102.1 依各句題意，填入適當的比較級形容詞 (**older** / **more important** 等)。

1. It's too noisy here. Can we go somewhere __quieter__ ?
2. This coffee is very weak. I like it a little _____ .
3. The hotel was surprisingly big. I expected it to be _____ .
4. The hotel was surprisingly cheap. I expected it to be _____ .
5. The weather is too cold here. I'd like to live somewhere _____ .
6. My job is kind of boring sometimes. I'd like to do something _____ .
7. It's too bad you live so far away. I wish you lived _____ .
8. I was surprised how easy it was to use the computer. I thought it would be
   _____ .
9. Your work isn't very good. I'm sure you can do _____ .
10. Don't worry. The situation isn't so bad. It could be _____ .
11. I was surprised we got here so quickly. I expected the trip to take _____ .
12. You're talking very loudly. Can you speak a little _____ ?
13. You hardly ever call me. Why don't you call me _____ ?
14. You're standing too close to the camera. Can you move a little _____ away?
15. You were a little depressed yesterday, but you look _____ today.

102.2 依各句題意，自下列形容詞中選出適當者，並以比較級形式填入句中；必要時需填入 **than**。

big	crowded	~~early~~	easily	high	important
interested	peaceful	~~reliable~~	serious	simple	thin

1. I was feeling tired last night, so I went to bed __earlier than__ usual.
2. I'd like to have a __more reliable__ car. Mine keeps breaking down.
3. Unfortunately, her illness was _____ we thought at first.
4. You look _____ . Have you lost weight?
5. I want a _____ apartment. We don't have enough space here.
6. He doesn't study very hard. He's _____ in having a good time.
7. Health and happiness are _____ money.
8. The instructions were very complicated. They could have been _____ .
9. There were a lot of people on the bus. It was _____ usual.
10. I like living in the country. It's _____ living in a city.
11. You'll find your way around the city _____ if you have a good map.
12. In some parts of the country, prices are _____ in others.

102.3 依各句題意，以比較級 (**-er** 或 **more** . . .) 完成各句。

1. Yesterday the temperature was 6 degrees. Today it is only 3 degrees.
   It's __colder today than it was yesterday__ _____ .
2. The trip takes four hours by car and five hours by train.
   It takes _____ .
3. Dave and I went for a run. I ran five miles. Dave stopped after three.
   I ran _____ .
4. Chris and Joe both did badly on the test. Chris got a C, but Joe only got a C–.
   Joe did _____ .
5. I expected my friends to arrive at about 4:00. In fact they arrived at 2:30.
   My friends _____ .
6. You can go by bus or by train. The buses run every 30 minutes. The trains run every hour.
   The buses _____ .
7. We were very busy at work today. We're not usually so busy.
   We _____ .

比較級 2 (much better / any better / better and better / the sooner the better)

A

下列副詞可以置於比較級形容詞之前：

| **much**　　**a lot**　　**far** (= a lot)　　**a bit**　　**a little**　　**slightly** (= a little) |

■ Let's drive. It's **much cheaper**. (或 **a lot cheaper**)
■ "How do you feel?"　"**Much better**, thanks."
■ Don't go by train. It's **a lot more expensive**. (或 **much more expensive**)
■ Could you speak **a bit more slowly**? (或 **a little more slowly**)
■ This bag is **slightly heavier** than the other one.
■ Her illness was **far more serious** than we thought at first.
(或 **much more serious** / **a lot more serious**)

B

any 或 **no** 可以用於比較級形容詞之前(**any longer** / **no bigger** 等)：
■ I've waited long enough. I'm not waiting **any longer**. (= not even a little longer)
■ We expected their house to be very big, but it's **no bigger** than ours.　或
　. . . it is**n't any bigger** than ours. (= not even a little bigger)
■ How do you feel now? Do you feel **any better**?
■ This hotel is better than the other one, and it's **no more expensive**.

C

better and better / **more and more** 等

比較級 + **and** + 比較級 (**better and better** 等) 用來表示某事正持續在改變：
■ Your English is improving. It's getting **better and better**.
■ The city is growing fast. It's getting **bigger and bigger**.
■ Cathy got **more and more bored** in her job. In the end, she quit.
■ These days **more and more** people are learning English.

D

the sooner the better

the + 比較級(**sooner/bigger/more** 等) + **the better** 表示「越…越好」：
■ "What time should we leave?"　"**The sooner the better**." (越快越好)
■ *A:* What sort of box do you want? A big one?
　B: Yes, **the bigger the better**. (越大越好)
■ When you're traveling, **the less luggage** you have **the better**.

the + 比較級 + **the** + 比較級也可以用來表示某一件事取決於另一件事：
■ **The warmer** the weather, **the better** I feel. (假如氣候溫暖些，我就覺得好些。)
■ **The sooner** we leave, **the earlier** we will arrive.
■ **The younger** you are, **the easier** it is to learn.
■ **The more expensive** the hotel, **the better** the service.
■ **The more electricity** you use, **the higher** your bill will be.
■ **The more** I thought about the plan, **the less** I liked it.

E

older 與 **elder** 用法之不同：

old 之比較級為 **older**：
■ David looks **older** than he really is.

談論家庭成員時可以用 **elder** 或(**older**)；我們可以說 (**my/your** 等) **elder sister** / **brother** / **daughter** / **son**：
■ **My elder sister** is a TV producer. (或 My **older** sister . . .)

「我的姐姐」以 my **elder sister** 來表達，但是我們不能說 somebody is elder：
■ My sister is **older** than me. (並非 elder than me)

any / no Unit 84　比較級 **1**、**3** Unit 102 與 Unit 104　*eldest* Unit 105D　*even* + 比較級 Unit 109C

103.1 依各句題意，用括號內所提供的字，以 *much / a bit* 等 + 比較級形容詞的用法完成句子；必要時請使用 *than*。

1. Her illness was __*much more serious than*__ we thought at first. (much / serious)
2. This bag is too small. I need something _____ . (much / big)
3. I'm afraid the problem is _____ it seems. (much / complicated)
4. It was very hot yesterday. Today it's _____ . (a little / cool)
5. I enjoyed our visit to the museum. It was _____ I expected. (far / interesting)
6. You're driving too fast. Can you drive _____ ? (a little / slowly)
7. It's _____ to learn a foreign language in a country where it is spoken. (a lot / easy)
8. I thought she was younger than me, but in fact she's _____ . (slightly / old)

103.2 依各句題意，以 *any/no* + 比較級形容詞的用法完成句子；必要時請使用 *than*。

1. I've waited long enough. I'm not waiting __*any longer*__ .
2. I'm sorry I'm a little late, but I couldn't get here _____ .
3. This store isn't expensive. The prices are _____ anywhere else.
4. I need to stop for a rest. I can't walk _____ .
5. The traffic isn't particularly bad today. It's _____ usual.

103.3 依各句題意，用括號內所提供的字，以 C 小節中的句型完成句子。

1. Cathy got __*more and more bored*__ in her job. In the end she quit. (bored)
2. That hole in your sweater is getting _____ . (big)
3. My bags seemed to get _____ as I carried them. (heavy)
4. As I waited for my interview, I became _____ . (nervous)
5. As the day went on, the weather got _____ . (bad)
6. Health care is becoming _____ . (expensive)
7. Since Anna went to Canada, her English has gotten _____ . (good)
8. As the conversation went on, Paul became _____ . (talkative)

103.4 依各句題意，用括號內所提供的字，以 D 小節中的句型完成句子。

1. I like warm weather.
   The warmer the weather, __*the better I feel*__ . (feel)
2. I didn't really like him when we first met.
   But the more I got to know him, _____ . (like)
3. If you're in business, you want to make a profit.
   The more goods you sell, _____ . (profit)
4. It's hard to concentrate when you're tired.
   The more tired you are, _____ . (hard)
5. Kate had to wait a very long time.
   The longer she waited, _____ . (impatient / become)

103.5 依各句題意，判斷 *older* 與 *elder* 何者正確，或兩者皆正確。

1. My older / elder ✓ ✓ sister is a TV producer. (*older* 與 *elder* 皆為正確答案)
2. I'm surprised Diane is only 25. I thought she was older / elder.
3. Jane's younger sister is still in school. Her older / elder sister is a nurse.
4. Martin is older / elder than his brother.

比較級 3 (as . . . as / than)

請看下面的例子：

Sarah   Eric   David

Sarah, Eric 與 David 都非常富有。Sarah 有二千萬，Eric 有一千五百萬，David 有一千萬，所以我們說：

Eric is rich. Eric 很富有。
He is **richer than** David. 他比 David 富有。
But he is**n't as rich as** Sarah. 但是他不如 Sarah 富有 。
(= Sarah is **richer than** he is) (Sarah 比他富有)

not as . . . (**as**) 用法的其他例子如下：
- Richard is**n't as old as** he looks. (他看起來比實際年齡老)
- The shopping mall was**n't as crowded as** usual. (通常比較擁擠)
- Jenny did**n't** do **as well** on the test **as** she had hoped.
  (她本來希望可以做得更好)
- The weather is better today. It's **not as cold**. (昨天比較冷)
- I don't know **as many** people **as** you do. (你認識的人比較多)
- *A:* How much did it cost? Fifty dollars?
  B: No, **not as much as** that. (少於五十塊錢)

也可以用 **not so . . .** (**as**)：
- It's not warm, but it is**n't so** cold **as** yesterday. (= it is**n't as** cold **as . . .**)

less . . . (**than**) 的意思與 **not as . . .** (**as**) 類似：
- I spent **less money than** you. (我花的錢沒有你花的多)
- The shopping mall was **less crowded than** usual. (沒有平常那麼擁擠)
- Ted talks **less than** his brother. (他說話說得不像他哥哥那麼多)

as . . . as 用於肯定句與問句中(不可以用 **so . . . as**)：
- I'm sorry I'm late. I got here **as fast as** I could.
- There's plenty of food. You can have **as much as** you want.
- Let's walk. It's **just as quick as** taking the bus.
- Can you send me the money **as soon as possible**, please?

其他類似用法還有 **twice as . . . as**、**three times as . . . as** 等：
- Gas is **twice as expensive as** it was a few years ago.
- Their house is about **three times as big as** ours.

我們說 **the same as** (而不是 the same like)：
- Ann's salary is **the same as** mine.   或   Ann gets **the same** salary **as** me.
- David is **the same** age **as** James.
- "What would you like to drink?"   "I'll have **the same as** you."

than me / than I am 等
我們通常說：
- You're taller **than I am**.   或   You're taller **than me**.
  (通常不說 You're taller than I)
- He's not as clever **as she is**.   或   He's not as clever **as her**.
- They have more money **than we do**.   或   They have more money **than us**.
- I can't run as fast as **he can**.   或   I can't run as fast **as him**.

Exercises

104.1 依各句題意，以 *as . . . as* 的句型完成句子。

1. I'm pretty tall, but you are taller. I'm not __as tall as you__ .
2. My salary is high, but yours is higher.
   My salary isn't _____ .
3. You know a little about cars, but I know more.
   You don't _____ .
4. It's still cold, but it was colder yesterday.
   It isn't _____ .
5. I still feel tired, but I felt a lot more tired yesterday.
   I don't _____ .
6. Our neighbors have lived here quite a while, but we've lived here longer.
   Our neighbors haven't _____ .
7. I was a little nervous before the interview, but usually I'm a lot more nervous.
   I wasn't _____ .

104.2 改寫下面各句，使之與原句意思相同。

1. Jack is younger than he looks. Jack isn't __as old as he looks__ .
2. I didn't spend as much money as you. You __spent more money than me__ .
3. The station was closer than I thought. The station wasn't _____ .
4. The meal didn't cost as much as I expected. The meal cost _____ .
5. I go out less than I used to. I don't _____ .
6. Karen's hair isn't as long as it used to be. Karen used to _____ .
7. I know them better than you do. You don't _____ .
8. There are fewer people at this meeting than at the last one.
   There aren't _____ .

104.3 依各句題意，自下列形容詞中選出適當者，以 *as . . . as* 之句型完成各句。

bad	**comfortable**	~~**fast**~~	**long**	**often**
quietly	**well qualified**	**well**	**soon**	

1. I'm sorry I'm late. I got here __as fast as__ I could.
2. It was a difficult question. I answered it _____ I could.
3. "How long can I stay with you?" "You can stay _____ you like."
4. I need the information quickly, so let me know _____ possible.
5. I like to stay in shape, so I go swimming _____ I can.
6. I didn't want to wake anybody, so I came in _____ I could.

以 *just as . . . as* 的句型完成以下各句。

7. I'm going to sleep on the floor. It's _____ the bed.
8. Why did he get the job rather than me? I'm _____ him.
9. At first I thought he was nice, but really he's _____ everybody else.

104.4 依各句題意，以 *the same as* 的句型完成句子。

1. David and James are both 22 years old. David __is the same age as James__ .
2. You and I both have dark brown hair. Your hair _____ .
3. I arrived at 10:25 and so did you. I _____ .
4. My birthday is April 5. Tom's birthday is April 5, too. My _____ .

104.5 依各句題意，以 *than . . .* 或 *as . . .* 完成句子。

1. I can't reach as high as you. You are taller __than me__ .
2. He doesn't know much. I know more _____ .
3. I don't work especially hard. Most people work as hard _____ .
4. We were very surprised. Nobody was more surprised _____ .
5. She's not a very good player. I'm a better player _____ .
6. They've been very lucky. I wish we were as lucky _____ .

最高級
(the longest / the most enjoyable 等)

A　請看下面的例句：

> What is the **longest river** in the world?
> What was **the most enjoyable** vacation you've ever taken?
>
> 上面例句中的 **longest** 與 **most enjoyable** 為形容詞的最高級。

B　最高級的兩種形式為 **-est** 或 **most . . .**。一般而言，**-est** 用於較短的字，**most . . .** 用於較長的字。
用 **-est** 或 **most . . .** 之規則與比較級的規則相同，參見 Unit 102。

long → long**est**	**hot** → hot**test**	**easy** → easi**est**	**hard** → hard**est**
但是 **most** famous	**most** boring	**most** difficult	**most** expensive

下列形容詞之最高級為不規則變化：

> good → **best**　　　bad → **worst**　　　far → **farthest/furthest**

有關拼字規則，參見附錄 6。

C　在最高級形容詞之前通常會加 **the** (**the** longest / **the** most famous 等)：

- Yesterday was **the hottest** day of the year.
- The film was really boring. It was **the most boring** film I've ever seen.
- She is a really nice person – one of **the nicest** people I know.
- Why does he always come to see me at **the worst** possible time?

> 比較最高級與比較級之用法：
> - This hotel is **the cheapest** in town. (最高級)
>   This hotel is **cheaper** than all the others in town. (比較級)
> - He's **the most patient** person I've ever met.
>   He's much **more patient** than I am.

D　**oldest** 與 **eldest**

old 之最高級為 **oldest**：

- That church is **the oldest** building in the town. (並非 the eldest)

談論家庭的成員時，可以用 **eldest**(或 **oldest**)：

- **My eldest son** is 13 years old. (或 My **oldest** son)
- Are you **the eldest** in your family? (或 the **oldest**)

E　在最高級的句子中，表地點的詞必須用 **in** (例如 towns、buildings 等)：

- What's the longest river **in the world**? (並非 of the world)
- We had a nice room. It was one of the best **in the hotel**. (並非 of the hotel)

表示組織或一群人的詞也用 **in** (a class / a company 等)：

- Who is the youngest student **in the class**? (並非 of the class)

表一段時間的詞則通常用 **of**：

- What was the happiest day **of your life**?
- Yesterday was the hottest day **of the year**.

F　最高級經常與現在完成式(I **have done**)一起使用(參見 Unit 7B)：

- What's **the most important** decision you**'ve** ever **had** to make?
- That was **the best** vacation I**'ve taken** for a long time.

比較級 (*cheaper / more expensive* 等) Unit 102 至 Unit 104　*elder* Unit 103E

Exercises

105.1 依各句題意，以最高級 + 介係詞的句型完成句子。

1. It's a very good room. It _is the best room in_ the hotel.
2. It's a very cheap restaurant. It's _____ town.
3. It was a very happy day. It was _____ my life.
4. She's a very intelligent student. She _____ the class.
5. It's a very valuable painting. It _____ the gallery.
6. Spring is a very busy time for me. It _____ the year.

以 **one of** + 最高級 + 介係詞 (**of** 或 **in**) 的句型完成下面的句子。

7. It's a very good room. It _is one of the best rooms in_ the hotel.
8. He's a very rich man. He's one _____ the world.
9. It's a very old house. It _____ the city.
10. It's a very good college. It _____ the state.
11. It was a very bad experience. It _____ my life.
12. He's a very dangerous criminal. He _____ the country.

105.2 依各句題意，以最高級 (**-est** 或 **most** . . .) 或比較級 (**-er** 或 **more** . . .) 完成各句。

1. We stayed at _the cheapest_ hotel in town. (cheap)
2. Our hotel was _cheaper_ than all the others in town. (cheap)
3. The United States is very large, but Canada is _____ . (large)
4. What's _____ country in the world? (small)
5. I wasn't feeling well yesterday, but I feel a little _____ today. (good)
6. It was an awful day. It was _____ day of my life. (bad)
7. What is _____ sport in your country? (popular)
8. Everest is _____ mountain in the world. It is _____ than any other mountain. (high)
9. We had a great vacation. It was one of _____ vacations we've ever taken. (enjoyable)
10. I prefer this chair to the other one. It's _____ . (comfortable)
11. What's _____ way to get to the station? (quick)
12. Sue and Kevin have three daughters. _____ is 14 years old. (old)

105.3 在下列情境下，你會怎麼說？用括號內所提供的字，以最高級 + **ever** 之句型完成句子。

1. You've just been to the movies. The movie was extremely boring. You tell your friend:
   (boring / movie / see) That's _the most boring movie I've ever seen_ .
2. Your friend has just told you a joke, which you think is very funny. You say:
   (funny / joke / hear) That's _____ .
3. You're drinking coffee with a friend. It's really good coffee. You say:
   (good / coffee / taste) This _____ .
4. You are talking to a friend about Mary. Mary is very generous. You tell your friend about her: (generous / person / meet) She _____ .
5. You have just run 10 miles. You've never run farther than this. You say to your friend:
   (far / run) That _____ .
6. You decided to quit your job. Now you think this was a bad mistake. You say to your friend: (bad / mistake / make) It _____ .
7. Your friend meets a lot of people, some of them famous. You ask your friend:
   (famous / person / meet?) Who _____ ?

語詞順序 1:
動詞+受詞; 地點與時間

A 動詞+受詞

受詞通常直接置於動詞之後，中間通常不插入其他字：

	動詞	受詞	
I	**like**	**my job**	very much. (並非 I like very much my job)
Did you	**see**	**your friends**	yesterday?
Ann often	**plays**	**tennis**.	

請看下面的例句。注意，例句中受詞皆直接置於動詞之後：

■ Do you **eat meat** every day? (並非 Do you eat every day meat?)

■ Everybody **enjoyed the party** very much. (並非 enjoyed very much the party)

■ Our guide **spoke English** fluently. (並非 spoke fluently English)

■ I lost all my money, and I also **lost my passport**. (並非 I lost also my passport)

■ At the end of the block, you'll **see a supermarket** on your left.
(並非 see on your left a supermarket)

B 地點與時間

通常地點(where?)置於動詞之後：

go home　　**live in a city**　　**walk to work** 等

若動詞後有受詞，則地點置於動詞+受詞之後：

take somebody home　　**meet a friend on the street**

時間 (when? / how often? / how long?) 通常置於地點之後：

	地點 +	時間
Tom walks	**to work**	**every morning**. (並非 every morning to work)
Sam has been	**in Canada**	**since April**.
We arrived	**at the airport**	**early**.

請看下面的例子。注意，例句中時間皆置於地點之後：

■ I'm going **to Paris on Monday**. (並非 I'm going on Monday to Paris)

■ They have lived **in the same house for a long time**.

■ Don't be late. Make sure you're **here by 8:00**.

■ Sarah gave me a ride **home after the party**.

■ You really shouldn't go **to bed so late**.

但是時間也常可置於句首：

■ **On Monday** I'm going to Paris.
■ **Every morning** Tom walks to work.

部分表時間的字(例如 **always/never/often**)通常緊跟著動詞置於句子中。參見 Unit 107。

問句中的語詞順序 Unit 47 與 Unit 48　形容詞的順序 Unit 97　語詞順序 2 Unit 107

Exercises

106.1 判斷各題中語詞的順序是否正確，並將錯誤的句子更正。

1. Everybody enjoyed the party very much.   *OK*
2. Tom walks ⟨every morning to work.⟩   *Tom walks to work every morning.*
3. Jim doesn't like very much basketball. _____
4. I drink three or four cups of coffee every morning. _____
5. I ate quickly my breakfast and went out. _____
6. Are you going to invite to the party a lot of people? _____
7. I called Tom immediately after hearing the news. _____
8. Did you go late to bed last night? _____
9. Did you learn a lot of things at school today? _____
10. I met on my way home a friend of mine. _____

106.2 將括號中所提供的語詞，以正確的順序寫出正確的句子。

1. (the party / very much / everybody enjoyed) *Everybody enjoyed the party very much.*
2. (we won / easily / the game) _____
3. (quietly / the door / I closed) _____
4. (Diane / quite well / speaks / Chinese) _____
5. (Tim / all the time / TV / watches) _____
6. (again / please don't ask / that question)
   _____
7. (golf / every weekend / does Ken play?)
   _____
8. (some money / I borrowed / from a friend of mine)
   _____

106.3 將括號中所提供的語詞，以正確的順序寫出正確的句子。

1. (for a long time / have lived / in the same house)
   They *have lived in the same house for a long time* .
2. (to the supermarket / every Friday / go)
   I _____ .
3. (home / did you come / so late)
   Why _____ ?
4. (her children / takes / every day / to school)
   Sarah _____ .
5. (been / recently / to the movies)
   I haven't _____ .
6. (at the top of the page / your name / write)
   Please _____ .
7. (her name / after a few minutes / remembered)
   I _____ .
8. (around the town / all morning / walked)
   We _____ .
9. (on Saturday night / didn't see you / at the party)
   I _____ .
10. (some interesting books / found / in the library)
    We _____ .
11. (her umbrella / last night / in a restaurant / left)
    Jackie _____ .
12. (across from the park / a new hotel / are building)
    They _____

語詞順序 2:
副詞與動詞

A 有些副詞(例如 **always/also/probably** 等)通常緊跟著動詞，置於句子中：
- Helen **always drives** to work.
- We were feeling very tired, and we **were also** hungry.
- The concert **will probably be** canceled.

B 請看下面各項副詞於句中位置之規則(這些只是一般的規定，因此會有例外。)

(1) 若動詞為一個字(例如 **drives/fell/cooked** 等)，副詞通常置於動詞之前：

	副詞	動詞	
Helen	**always**	**drives**	to work.
I	**almost**	**fell**	as I was going down the stairs.

- I cleaned the house and **also cooked** dinner. (並非 cooked also)
- Lucy **hardly ever watches** television and **rarely reads** newspapers.
- "Should I give you my address?" "No, I **already have** it."

注意，這些副詞(例如 **always/often/also**)置於 **have to** 之前：
- Joe never calls me. I **always have to** call him. (並非 I have always to call)

(2) 但副詞必須置於 **am / is / are / was / were** 之後：
- We were feeling very tired, and we **were also** hungry.
- Why are you always late? You**'re never** on time.
- The traffic **isn't usually** as bad as it was this morning.

(3) 當動詞包含兩個或兩個以上的字時(例如 **can remember / doesn't eat /**
   will be canceled 等)，副詞必須置於第一個動詞 (如 **can/doesn't/will** 等)之後：

	動詞 1	副詞	動詞 2	
I	**can**	**never**	**remember**	her name.
Claire	**doesn't**	**often**	**eat**	meat.
	Are you	**definitely**	**going**	to the party tomorrow?
The concert	**will**	**probably**	**be**	canceled.

- You **have always been** very kind to me.
- Jack can't cook. He **can't even boil** an egg.
- **Do** you **still work** for the same company?
- The house **was only built** a year ago, and it**'s already falling** down.

注意，**probably** 必須置於否定詞(**isn't/won't** 等)之前，所以我們說：
- I **probably won't** see you. 或 I will **probably not** see you. (並非 I won't probably)

C **all** 與 **both** 出現的位置也與上述副詞一樣：
- We **all felt** sick after we ate. (並非 we felt all sick)
- My parents **are both** teachers. (並非 my parents both are teachers)
- Sarah and Jane **have both applied** for the job.
- We **are all going** out tonight.

D 有時候 **is/will/did** 等可用於下面的句型，以避免句子重複(參見 Unit 49)；注意副詞於此句
型下之位置：
- He always says he won't be late, but he **always is**. (= he **is always** late)
- I've never done it, and I **never will**. (= I **will never** do it)

在此類避免重複的短句中，副詞 **always/never** 等通常置於動詞之前。

Exercises

107.1 判斷下列各題中劃線部分的字順序是否正確，並將錯誤之處更正。

1. Helen drives <u>always</u> to work.   *Helen always drives to work.*
2. I cleaned the house and <u>also</u> cooked dinner.   *OK*
3. I take <u>usually</u> a shower in the morning   _____
4. We <u>soon</u> found the solution to the problem.   _____
5. Steve gets <u>hardly ever</u> angry.   _____
6. I did some shopping, and I went <u>also</u> to the bank.   _____
7. Jane has <u>always</u> to hurry in the morning.   _____
8. We <u>all</u> were tired, so we <u>all</u> fell asleep.   _____
9. She <u>always</u> says she'll call me, but she <u>never</u> does.   _____

107.2 將括號內的副詞填入各句中的正確位置。

1. Claire doesn't eat meat. (often) *Claire doesn't often eat meat.*
2. a) We were on vacation in Spain. (all) _____
   b) We were staying at the same hotel. (all) _____
   c) We enjoyed ourselves. (all) _____
3. Catherine is very generous. (always) _____
4. I don't have to work on Saturdays. (usually) _____
5. Do you watch TV in the evenings? (always) _____
6. Josh is studying Spanish, and he is studying Japanese. (also)
   Josh is studying Spanish, and he _____
7. a) The new hotel is very expensive. (probably) _____
   b) It costs a lot to stay there. (probably) _____
8. a) I can help you. (probably) _____
   b) I can't help you. (probably) _____

107.3 將括號內所提供的語詞，以正確的順序填入各句中，完成句子。

1. I *can never remember* her name. (remember / never / can)
2. I _____ sugar in my coffee. (take / usually)
3. I _____ hungry when I get home from work. (am / usually)
4. *A:* Where's Joe?
   B: He _____ home early. (gone / has / probably)
5. Mark and Diane _____ in Texas. (both / were / born)
6. Liz is a good pianist. She _____ very well.
   (sing / also / can)
7. Our cat _____ under the bed. (often / sleeps)
8. They live on the same street as me, but I _____ to them.
   (never / have / spoken)
9. We _____ a long time for the bus.
   (have / always / to wait)
10. My eyesight isn't very good. I _____ with glasses.
    (read / can / only)
11. I _____ early tomorrow. (probably / leaving / will / be)
12. I'm afraid I _____ able to come to the party.
    (probably / be / won't)
13. It's hard to contact Sue. Her cell phone _____ on when I call
    her. (is / hardly ever)
14. We _____ in the same place. We haven't moved.
    (still / are / living)
15. If we hadn't taken the same train, we _____ each other.
    (never / met / would / have)
16. *A:* Are you tired?
    B: Yes, I _____ at this time of day. (am / always)

still、yet, 與 already
anymore / any longer / no longer

A

still

still 表示某個情況或動作仍持續中，該情況或動作並未改變或停止：

- It's 10:00 and Joe is **still** in bed.
- When I went to bed, Chris was **still** working.
- Do you **still** want to go to the party, or have you changed your mind?

still 通常緊跟著動詞出現於句中。參見 Unit 107。

B

anymore / any longer / no longer

not ... anymore 或 **not ... any longer** 用來表示某情況已經改變。**Anymore** 與 **any longer** 置於句尾：

- Lucy doesn**'t** work here **anymore** (或 **any longer**). She left last month.
  (並非 Lucy doesn't still work here.)
- We used to be good friends, but we are**n't anymore** (或 **any longer**).

也可以用 **no longer** 來表示某情況已經改變；但 **no longer** 通常需置於句中：

- Lucy **no longer** works here.

注意，**no more** 通常不用於上述用法：

- We are **no longer** friends. (並非 We are no more friends.)

比較 **still** 與 **not ... anymore** 之用法：

- Sally **still** works here, but Ann doesn**'t** work here **anymore**.

C

yet

yet 意思等於 until now，主要用於否定句(**He isn't** here **yet**)與問句(**Is he** here **yet**?)中，表示說話者期待某事發生。

yet 通常置於句尾：

- It's 10:00 and Joe **isn't** here **yet**.
- **Have** you **met** your new neighbors **yet**?
- "Where are you going for vacation?" "We **don't** know **yet**."

yet 經常與現在完成式(**Have** you **met** ... **yet**?)一起使用。參見 Unit 8D。

比較 **yet** 與 **still** 之用法：

- Mike lost his job six months ago and **is still** unemployed.
  Mike lost his job six months ago and **hasn't found** another job **yet**.
- **Is** it **still** raining?
  Has it **stopped** raining **yet**?

still 也可以用於否定句中(置於否定詞之前)：

- She said she would be here an hour ago, and she **still** has**n't** come.

She **still** has**n't** come 與 She hasn't come **yet** 的意思類似，但 **still ... not** 表示更強烈的驚訝或不耐煩。比較下面的例子：

- I wrote to him last week. He has**n't** replied **yet**. (但是我預期他很快會回覆。)
- I wrote to him months ago and he **still** has**n't** replied. (他早就該回覆了。)

D

already

already 用來表示某事比預期的早發生，通常置於句中(參見 Unit 107)或句尾：

- "What time is Sue leaving?" "She has **already** left." (比聽話者預期的早)
- Should I tell Joe what happened, or does he **already** know?
- I've just had lunch, and I'm **already** hungry.

Exercises

108.1 比較下面 Paul 在幾年前所説的話與他目前説的話。有些事和過去一樣，有些事已經改變了。以 *still* 和 *not...anymore* 描述 Paul 的情況。

Paul a few years ago

I travel a lot.
I work in a store.
I write poems.
I want to be a teacher.
I'm interested in politics.
I'm single.
I go fishing a lot.

Paul now

I travel a lot.
I work in a hospital.
I gave up writing poems.
I want to be a teacher.
I'm not interested in politics.
I'm single.
I haven't been fishing in years.

1. (travel) *He still travels a lot.*
2. (store) *He doesn't work in a store anymore.*
3. (poems) He _____
4. (teacher) _____

5. (politics) _____
   _____
6. (single) _____
7. (fishing) _____
8. (beard) _____

以 *no longer* 寫出三句描寫 Paul 的情況的句子。

9. *He no longer works in a store.*
10. _____
11. _____
12. _____

108.2 依各句題意，自下列動詞中選出一個適當的字，並配合 *not ... yet* 之句型，將各題改寫為意思相近的句子。

decide   find   finish   leave   ~~stop~~   take off   wake up

1. It's still raining. *It hasn't stopped raining yet* .
2. Gary is still here. He _____ .
3. They're still repairing the road. They _____ .
4. The children are still asleep. _____ .
5. Is Ann still looking for a place to live? _____ ?
6. I'm still wondering what to do. _____ .
7. The plane is still waiting on the runway. _____ .

108.3 依各句題意，在各題的劃線部分填入 *still*、*yet*、*already* 或 *anymore*，以改寫該部分的語句。

1. Mike lost his job a year ago, and <u>he is unemployed</u>. *he is still unemployed*
2. Should I tell Joe what happened, or <u>does he know</u>? *does he already know*
3. I'm hungry. <u>Is dinner ready</u>? *Is dinner ready yet*
4. I was hungry earlier, but <u>I'm not hungry</u>. *I'm not hungry anymore*
5. Can we wait a few minutes? I <u>don't want to go out</u> _____
6. Jenny used to work at the airport, but <u>she doesn't work there</u>. _____
7. I used to live in Tokyo. <u>I have a lot of friends there</u>. _____
8. "Let me introduce you to Jim." "You don't have to. <u>We've met</u>." _____
9. <u>Do you live in the same place</u>, or have you moved? _____
10. Would you like to eat with us, or <u>have you eaten</u>? _____
11. "Where's John?" "<u>He's not here</u>. He'll be here soon." _____
12. Tim said he'd be here at 8:30. It's 9:00 now, and <u>he isn't here</u>. _____
13. Do you want to join the club, or <u>are you a member</u>? _____
14. It happened a long time ago, but <u>I can remember it very clearly</u>. _____
15. I've put on weight. <u>These pants don't fit me</u>. _____
16. "<u>Have you finished with the paper</u>?" "No, <u>I'm reading it</u>." _____

A

請看下面的例子：

Tina 喜歡看電視。

She has a TV set in every room of the house – **even** the bathroom. (她的房子裡每個房間都有電視機─甚至浴室都有。)

even 表示某事不尋常或令人訝異。在上例中，**even** 表示浴室裡有電視機並不尋常。

其他例子如下：

- These pictures are really awful. **Even I** could take better pictures than these. (我當然不是個好的攝影師。)
- He always wears a coat – **even in hot weather**.
- Nobody would help her – **not even her best friend**.

或   **Not even** her best friend would help her.

B

even 通常緊跟著動詞，置於句中(參見 Unit 107)：

- Sue has traveled all over the world. She has **even** been to the Antarctic. (到南極並不尋常，因此她必定去過很多地方。)
- They are very rich. They **even** have their own private jet.

請看下面 **not even** 的例句：

- I can't cook. I can**'t even** boil an egg. (煮蛋是一件非常容易的事)
- They weren't very friendly to us. They did**n't even** say hello.
- Jenny is in great shape. She's just run five miles, and she's **not even** out of breath.

C

我們可以用 **even** + 比較級(例如 **cheaper / more expensive** 等)

- I got up very early, but Jack got up **even earlier**.
- I knew I didn't have much money, but I have **even less** than I thought.
- We were surprised to get a letter from her. We were **even more surprised** when she came to see us a few days later.

D

even though / even when / even if

even though / even when / even if + 主詞+動詞：

- **Even though she can't** drive, she bought a car.

    主詞+動詞
- He never shouts, **even when he's** angry.
- I'll probably see you tomorrow. But **even if I don't see** you tomorrow, I'm sure we'll see each other before the weekend.

even + **though / when / if** 可用以連接句子。注意：在下面的例句中，**even** 不可單獨使用：

- **Even though she can't** drive, she bought a car. (並非 Even she can't drive)
- I can't reach the shelf **even if I stand** on a chair. (並非 even I stand)

比較 **even if** 與 **if**：

- We're going to the beach tomorrow. It doesn't matter what the weather is like. We're going **even if** it's raining.
- We want to go to the beach tomorrow, but we won't go **if** it's raining.

Exercises

109.1 Julie、Sarah 和 Amanda 一起去渡假，下面是有關她們的描述。根據這些描述，配合 *even* 或 *not even* 完成各個句子。

Julie	Sarah	Amanda
is usually happy	doesn't really like art	is almost always late
is usually on time	is usually miserable	is a good photographer
likes getting up early	usually hates hotels	loves staying at hotels
is very interested in art	doesn't have a camera	isn't good at getting up early

1. They stayed at a hotel. Everybody liked it, _even Sarah_ .
2. They arranged to meet. They all arrived on time, _____ .
3. They went to an art gallery. Nobody enjoyed it, _____ .
4. Yesterday they had to get up early. They all managed to do this, _____ .
5. They were together yesterday. They were all in a good mood, _____ .
6. None of them took any pictures, _____ .

109.2 依各句題意，以 *even* 和括號中所提供的語詞完成句子。

1. Sue has been all over the world. (the Antarctic) _She has even been to the Antarctic._
2. We painted the whole room. (the floor) We _____
3. Rachel has met lots of famous people. (the president)
   She _____
4. You could hear the noise from a long way away. (from two blocks away)
   You _____

以 *not even* 和括號中所提供的語詞完成以下的句子。

5. They didn't say anything to us. (hello) _They didn't even say hello._
6. I can't remember anything about her. (her name)
   I _____
7. There isn't anything to do in this town. (a movie theater)
   _____
8. He didn't tell anybody where he was going. (his wife)
   _____
9. I don't know anyone on my street. (the people next door)
   _____

109.3 依各句題意，以 *even* + 比較級形容詞完成各句。

1. It was very hot yesterday, but today it's _even hotter_ .
2. The church is 200 years old, but the house next to it is _____ .
3. That's a very good idea, but I've got an _____ one.
4. The first question was very difficult to answer. The second one was _____ .
5. I did very badly on the test, but most of my friends did _____ .
6. Neither of us was hungry. I ate very little, and my friend ate _____ .

109.4 依各句題意，填入 *if*、*even*、*even if* 或 *even though*。

1. _Even though_ she can't drive, she bought a car.
2. The bus leaves in five minutes, but we can still catch it _____ we run.
3. The bus leaves in two minutes. We won't catch it now _____ we run.
4. His Spanish isn't very good – _____ after three years in Mexico.
5. His Spanish isn't very good _____ he's lived in Mexico for three years.
6. _____ with the heat on, it was very cold in the house.
7. I couldn't sleep _____ I was very tired.
8. I won't forgive them for what they did _____ they apologize.
9. _____ I hadn't eaten anything for 24 hours, I wasn't hungry.

although / though / even though / in spite of / despite

請看下面的例子：

去年 Paul 和 Joanne 在海邊度假。雖然雨下得很多，但是他們玩得很開心。

我們可以說：

Although it rained a lot, they had a good time.

(= It rained a lot, *but* they . . .)

或

In spite of
Despite } the rain, they had a good time.

---

although 後需有主詞+動詞：

- **Although it rained** a lot, we enjoyed our vacation.
- I didn't get the job **although I was** well qualified.

比較 **although** 與 **because** 之意思：

- We went out **although** it was raining.
- We didn't go out **because** it was raining.

---

in spite of 或 **despite** 後必須用名詞、代名詞(**this/that/what** 等)，或 **-ing**：

- **In spite of the rain**, we enjoyed our vacation.
- I didn't get the job **in spite of being** well qualified.
- She wasn't feeling well, but **in spite of this** she went to work.
- **In spite of what** I said yesterday, I still love you.

despite 的意思以及用法與 **in spite of** 相同；注意 **despite** 後沒有 **of**：

- She felt sick, but **in spite of this** she went to work. (並非 despite of this)

我們可以用 **in spite of the fact** (**that**) 與 **despite the fact** (**that**)：

- I didn't get the job { **in spite of the fact** (**that**) / **despite the fact** (**that**) } I was extremely qualified.

比較 **in spite of** 與 **because of**：

- We went out . **in spite of the rain** (或 . . . **despite the rain**.)
- We didn't go out **because of the rain**.

比較 **although** 與 **in spite of** / **despite**：

- **Although the traffic was** bad, / **In spite of the traffic**, } we arrived on time. (並非 In spite of the traffic was bad)
- I couldn't sleep { **although I was** very tired. / **despite being** very tired. } (並非 despite I was tired)

有時候可以用 **though** 取代 **although**：

- I didn't get the job **though** I had all the necessary qualifications.

口語中，**though** 常置於句尾：

- The house isn't very nice. I like the garden, **though**. (= but I like the garden)
- I see them every day. I've never spoken to them, **though**.
  (= but I've never spoken to them)

even though 表示 **although** 的加強語氣（注意：此種用法不可單獨使用 **even**）：

- **Even though** I was really tired, I couldn't sleep. (並非 Even I was really tired . . .)

Exercises

110.1 依各句題意，自下列句子中選出適當者，以 *although* 子句完成句子。

I didn't speak the language	~~he has a very important job~~
I had never seen her before	we don't like them very much
it was quite cold	the heat was on
I'd met her twice before	we've known each other a long time

1. _Although he has a very important job_ , he isn't particularly well paid.
2. _____ , I recognized her from a photograph.
3. She wasn't wearing a coat _____ .
4. We thought we'd better invite them to the party _____ .
5. _____ , I managed to make myself understood.
6. _____ , the room wasn't warm.
7. I didn't recognize her _____ .
8. We're not very good friends _____ .

110.2 依各句題意，填入 *although* / *in spite of* / *because* / *because of*。

1. _Although_ it rained a lot, we enjoyed our vacation.
2. a) _____ all our careful plans, a lot of things went wrong.
   b) _____ we had planned everything carefully, a lot of things went wrong.
3. a) I went home early _____ I wasn't feeling well.
   b) I went to work the next day _____ I was still feeling sick.
4. a) She only accepted the job _____ the salary, which was very high.
   b) She accepted the job _____ the salary, which was rather low.
5. a) I managed to get to sleep _____ there was a lot of noise.
   b) I couldn't get to sleep _____ the noise.

依你自己的意思完成下面各句。

6. a) He passed the exam although _____ .
   b) He passed the exam because _____ .
7. a) I didn't eat anything although _____ .
   b) I didn't eat anything in spite of _____ .

110.3 用括號中字將下列各題中的兩個句子合併為一句。

1. I couldn't sleep. I was very tired. (despite)
   I couldn't sleep despite being very tired.
2. They have very little money. They are happy. (in spite of)
   In spite _____
3. My foot was injured. I managed to walk to the nearest town. (although)
   _____
4. I enjoyed the movie. The story was silly. (in spite of)
   _____
5. We live on the same street. We hardly ever see each other. (despite)
   _____
6. I got very wet in the rain. I was only out for five minutes. (even though)
   _____

110.4 依各句題意，用括號中的字造出以 *though* 為結尾的句子。

1. The house isn't very nice. (like / yard) _I like the yard, though._
2. It's warm today. (very windy) _____
3. We didn't like the food. (ate) _____
4. Liz is very nice. (don't like / husband) I _____

in case

請看下面的例子：

你的車應該要有備胎，因為可能發生輪胎破了的情形。

Your car should have a spare tire **in case** you have a flat tire.
你的車應該有備胎，萬一輪胎破了(才能換胎)。

In case you have a flat tire 意思是輪胎可能會破。

其他例子如下：

- I'll leave my cell phone on **in case Jane calls**. (因為她可能會打來。)
- I'll draw a map for you **in case you can't find our house**. (因為你可能會找不到。)
- I'll remind them about the meeting **in case they've forgotten**. (因為他們可能會忘記)

just in case 用來表達可能性更小：

- I don't think it will rain, but I'll take an umbrella **just in case**. (= **just in case** it rains)

in case 後不可以使用 **will**，而必須使用現在式來表示未來意思 (參見 Unit 24)：

- I'll leave my phone on **in case** Jane **calls**. (並非 in case Jane will call)

in case 的意思與 **if** 不同。**in case** 是說明某人為何做或不做某事，意思是某人現在做某事是因為有可能另一件事稍後會發生。

比較 **in case** 與 **if** 的用法：

in case	if
■ We'll buy some more food **in case** Tom comes. (Tom 可能會來。不論他來不來，我們現在就多買些食物；假如(if)他來了，那麼我們就已經準備好食物了。)	■ We'll buy some more food **if** Tom comes. (Tom 可能會來。假如他來了，我們就多買些食物；假如他不來，我們就不用多買食物了。)
■ I'll give you my phone number **in case** you need to contact me.	■ You can call me at the hotel **if** you need to contact me.
■ You should register your bike **in case** it is stolen.	■ You should inform the police **if** your bike is stolen.

in case 後使用過去式，是說明某人為何做某事：

- I left my phone on **in case Jane called**.
  (因為當時 Jane 有可能打電話來)
- I drew a map for Sarah **in case** she **couldn't** find the house.
- We rang the doorbell again **in case** they **hadn't** heard it the first time.

in case of . . . 與 **in case** 的意思並不相同；**in case of . . .** = if there is . . . (特別是用於公告或招牌等)：

- **In case of fire**, please leave the building as quickly as possible. (假如發生火災)
- **In case of emergency**, call this number. (假如發生意外)

Exercises

111.1 Barbara 將要到鄉村去郊遊，你認為她應該攜帶以下的物品：

~~some chocolate~~　**a map**　**a raincoat**　**her camera**　**some water**

你認為她應該帶這些東西是因為下面各項原因：

> it's possible she'll get lost
> perhaps she'll be thirsty
> she might want to take some pictures

> ~~she might get hungry~~
> maybe it will rain

請以 *in case* 造句，説明為什麼你認為 Barbara 應該帶這些東西。

1. *Take some chocolate with you in case you get hungry.*
2. Take _____
3. _____
4. _____
5. _____

111.2 依各題的情境，以 *in case* 完成你將回應的話。

1. It's possible that Mary will need to contact you, so you give her your phone number.
   You say: Here's my phone number *in case you need to contact me* .
2. A friend of yours is going away for a long time. Maybe you won't see her again before she goes, so you decide to say good-bye now.
   You say: I'll say good-bye now _____ .
3. You are shopping in a supermarket with a friend. You think you have everything you need, but perhaps you've forgotten something. Your friend has the list. You ask her to check it.
   You say: Can you _____ ?
4. You are giving a friend some advice about using a computer. You think he should back up (= *copy*) his files because the computer might crash (and he would lose all his data).
   You say: You should back up _____ .

111.3 依各句題意，以 *in case* 完成句子。

1. There was a possibility that Jane would call. So I left my phone switched on.
   I left *my phone switched on in case Jane called* .
2. Mike thought that he might forget the name of the book. So he wrote it down.
   He wrote down _____ .
3. I thought my parents might be worried about me. So I called them.
   I called _____
4. I sent an e-mail to Liz, but I didn't get an answer. So I sent another e-mail because I thought that maybe she hadn't received the first one.
   I sent _____ .
5. I met some people when I was on vacation in France. They said they might come to New York one day. I live in New York, so I gave them my address.
   I gave _____ .

111.4 依各句題意，填入 *in case* 或 *if*。

1. I'll draw a map for you *in case* you can't find our house.
2. You should tell the police *if* you have any information about the crime.
3. I hope you'll come to Chicago sometime. _____ you come, you can stay with us.
4. This letter is for Susan. Can you give it to her _____ you see her?
5. Write your name and address on your bag _____ you lose it.
6. Go to the Lost and Found office _____ you lose your bag.
7. The burglar alarm will ring _____ somebody tries to break into the house.
8. You should lock your bike to something _____ somebody tries to steal it.
9. I was advised to get insurance _____ I needed medical treatment while I was abroad.

unless   as long as   provided / providing

A

unless

請看下面的例子：

The club is for members only.
這個俱樂部只有會員可以進入。

You can't go in **unless you are a member**.

上句話意思是除非你是會員，否則你不能進入。
You can't go in *except if* you are a member.
或
You can go in *only if* you are a member.
只有會員才能進去那裡打球。

unless = except if

其它 **unless** 例句如下：

- I'll see you tomorrow **unless I have to work late**. (除非我必須工作到很晚)
- There are no buses to the beach. **Unless you have a car**, it's difficult to get there.
  (除非你有車)
- "Should I tell Liz what happened?" "**Not unless she asks you.**"
  (除非她問你)
- Sally hates to complain. She wouldn't complain about something **unless it was really bad**. (除非事情真的很糟)
- We can take a taxi to the restaurant – **unless you'd prefer to walk**.
  (除非你比較喜歡走路)

除了 **unless**，也可以用 **if . . . not** 來表達同樣的意思：

- **Unless we leave now**, we'll be late. 或 **If we don't leave now**, we'll . . .

B

As long as 等

as long as 或 **so long as**
provided (that) 或 **providing** (that)

這些表達方式意思都是 if (假如) 或 on condition that (在某情況下)

例如：

- You can borrow my car { **as long as** / **so long as** } you promise not to drive too fast.
  (你可以用我的車，但你必須小心開車－這是唯一的條件。)

- Traveling by car is convenient { **provided** (that) / **providing** (that) } you have somewhere to park.
  (假如你有地方可以停車的話。)

- { **Providing** (that) / **Provided** (that) } the room is clean, I don't care which hotel we stay at.
  (假如房間乾淨，我不在乎住哪家旅館)

C

unless / **as long as** / **so long as** / **provided** / **providing** 後不可以使用 **will**；表未來時必須使用現在式表未來的意思(參見 Unit 24A)：

- I'm not going out **unless** it **stops** raining. (並非 unless it will stop)
- **Providing** the weather is good, we're going on a picnic.
  (並非 providing the weather will be good)

Exercises

112.1 依各句題意，以 *unless* 將各句改寫成為意思相似的句子。

1. You need to try a little harder, or you won't pass the exam.
   You won't pass the exam unless you try a little harder.
2. Listen carefully, or you won't know what to do.
   You won't know what to do _____
3. She has to apologize to me, or I'll never speak to her again.
   _____
4. You have to speak very slowly, or he won't be able to understand you.
   _____
5. Business has got to improve soon, or the company will have to close.
   _____

112.2 依各句題意，以 *unless* 將各句改寫成為意思相似的句子。將各題的兩個句子合併成一句或改寫成為意思相近的句子。

1. The club isn't open to everyone. You are allowed in only if you're a member.
   You aren't allowed in the club unless you're a member.
2. I don't want to go to the party alone. I'm going only if you go, too.
   I'm not going _____
3. Don't worry about the dog. It will attack you only if you move suddenly.
   The dog _____
4. Ben isn't very talkative. He'll speak to you only if you ask him something.
   Ben _____
5. The doctor will see you only if it's an emergency.
   The doctor _____

112.3 依各句題意，選出正確的字或片語。

1. You can borrow my car ~~unless~~ / as long as you promise not to drive too fast.
   (*as long as* 是正確答案)
2. I'm playing tennis tomorrow unless / providing it rains.
3. I'm playing tennis tomorrow unless / providing it doesn't rain.
4. I don't mind if you come home late unless / as long as you come in quietly.
5. I'm going now unless / provided you want me to stay.
6. I don't watch TV unless / as long as I've got nothing else to do.
7. Children are allowed to use the swimming pool unless / provided they are with an adult.
8. Unless / Provided they are with an adult, children are not allowed to use the swimming pool.
9. We can sit here in the corner unless / as long as you'd rather sit over there by the window.
10. *A:* Our vacation cost a lot of money.
    B: Did it? Well, that doesn't matter unless / as long as you had a good time.

112.4 依你自己的意思完成下面各句。

1. We'll be late unless *we take a taxi* _____ .
2. I like hot weather as long as _____ .
3. It takes Kate about 20 minutes to drive to work provided _____ .
4. I don't mind walking home as long as _____ .
5. I like to walk to work in the morning unless _____ .
6. We can meet tomorrow unless _____ .
7. You can borrow the money providing _____ .
8. You won't achieve anything unless _____ .

as (= at the same time) 與 as (= because)

as = at the same time as

as 用以表達當兩件事在同時間發生：

- We all waved good-bye to Liz **as** she drove away.
  (we **waved** 與 she **drove** away 兩件事發生於同時。)
- I watched her **as** she opened the letter.
- **As** I walked along the street, I looked in the store windows.
- Can you turn off the light **as** you go out, please?

Bye!

Liz

Something happened **as you were doing** something else

意思是，某事發生在某人正在做另一件事的時候
(正當做另一件事的期間)：

- Jill slipped **as she was getting off** the bus.
- We met Paul **as we were leaving** the hotel.

關於過去進行式的用法(例如 **was getting / were going** 等)，
參見 Unit 6。

just as (= exactly at that moment)意思是「就在那個時候」：

- **Just as** I sat down, the phone rang.
- I had to leave **just as** the conversation was getting interesting.

as 也可以表達兩件事於一段長時間裡一起改變：

- **As** the day went on, the weather got worse.
- I began to enjoy the job more **as** I got used to it.

> the day went on
> the weather got worse

As the day went on, the weather got worse.

比較 **as** 與 **when** 之用法：

as 用於當兩件事同時發生的情形； ■ **As we walked home**, we talked about what we would have for dinner. (= at the same time)	如果是一件事較另一件事晚發生的情況則用 **when** (而非 as)： ■ **When we got home**, we started cooking dinner. (並非 As we got home)

as = because

as 有時候意思為「因為」：

- **As it was a national holiday** last Thursday, all the banks were closed.
  (因為是國定假日)
- The thief was difficult to identify **as he was wearing a mask** during the robbery.

since 也可以這樣用以表示「因為」：

- **Since it was a national holiday** last Thursday, all the banks were closed.
- The thief was difficult to identify **since he was wearing a mask** during the robbery.

比較 **as** 與 **when** 之用法：

■ I couldn't contact David **as he was on a business trip**, and he doesn't have a cell phone. (因為他們在旅途中)	■ David's passport was stolen **when he was on a business trip**. (在他出差的時候)
■ **As they lived near us**, we used to see them pretty often. (因為他們住得離我們很近)	■ **When they lived near us**, we used to see them pretty often. (在他們他們住得離我們很近的時候)

as . . . as Unit 104 *like* 與 *as* Unit 114 *as if* Unit 115

Exercises

113.1 自下面兩個框框中各選出一個句子，並且以 *as* 將兩句話合併成為一句話。

1. ~~we all waved goodbye to Liz~~	we were driving along the road
2. we all smiled	I was taking a hot dish out of the oven
3. I burned myself	~~she drove away~~
4. the crowd cheered	we posed for the photograph
5. a dog ran out in front of the car	the two teams ran onto the field

1. _We all waved goodbye to Liz as she drove away._
2. _____
3. _____
4. _____
5. _____

113.2 依各句題意，判斷 *as* 在該句的意思是 *because* 還是 *at the same time as*。

	because	at the same time as
1. **As** they live near me, I see them fairly often.	✔	
2. Jill slipped **as** she was getting off the bus.		✔
3. **As** I was tired, I went to bed early.		
4. Unfortunately, **as** I was parking the car, I hit the car behind me.		
5. **As** we climbed the hill, we got more and more tired.		
6. We decided to go out to eat **as** we had no food at home.		
7. **As** we don't use the car very often, we've decided to sell it.		

將各句中 *as* 解釋作「因為」的句子，並以 *since* 改寫。

8. _Since they live near me, I see them pretty often._
9. _____
10. _____
11. _____

113.3 依各句題意，判斷各句中的 *as* 是否需要改為 *when*。

1. Maria got married (as she was 22.)   _when she was 22_
2. As the day went on, the weather got worse.   _OK_
3. He dropped the glass as he was taking it out of the cabinet.   _____
4. My camera was stolen as I was asleep on the beach.   _____
5. As I finished high school, I went into the army.   _____
6. The train slowed down as it approached the station.   _____
7. I used to live near the ocean as I was a child.   _____

113.4 依你自己的意思完成下面各句。

1. I saw you as _____
2. It started to rain just as _____
3. As I didn't have enough money for a taxi, _____
4. Just as I took the photograph, _____

like 與 as

like 意思是「像」、「和...一樣」時,不可以用 **as** 來代替:

- What a beautiful house! It's **like a palace**. (並非 as a palace)
- "What does Sandra do?"　"She's a teacher, **like me**." (並非 as me)
- Be careful! The floor has been polished. It's **like walking on ice**. (並非 as walking)
- It's raining again. I hate weather **like this**. (並非 as this)

在上述例句中 **like** 為介係詞,所以後面接名詞(like **a palace**)、代名詞(like **me** / like **this**)、或 **-ing** (like walk**ing**)。

上述的用法也可以使用 . . . **like** (somebody / something) do**ing** something 之句型:

- "What's that noise?"　"It sounds **like a baby** cry**ing**."

有時候 **like** = for example,意思是「舉例」,例如:

- Some sports, **like** race-car driving, can be dangerous.

這種用法也可以用 **such as**:

- Some sports, **such as** race-car driving, can be dangerous.

as (= in the same way 或 in the same condition as 相同地),通常用於主詞+動詞之前:

- I didn't move anything. I left everything **as it was**.
- You should have done it **as I showed you**. (= the way I showed you)

在非正式的用法中,上述例句中也可以用 **like** 代替 **as**:

- I left everything **like it was**.

比較 **as** 與 **like** 用法的不同:

- You should have done it **as I showed you**. (或 **like I showed you**)
- You should have done it **like this**. (並非 as this)

注意下面 **as usual** / **as always** 的用法:

- You're late **as usual**.
- **As always**, Nick was the first to complain.

有時 **as** (+主詞+動詞)有別的意思。例如,在 **do** 之後:

- You can do **as you like**. (= do what you like)
- They did **as they promised**. (= They did what they promised)

除上述例句外,我們也說 **as you know** / **as I said** / **as she expected** / **as I thought** 等:

- **As you know**, it's Emma's birthday next week. (= you know this already)
- Ann failed her driving test, **as she expected**. (= she expected this before)

上述用法中通常不用 **like** 代替 **as**,但 **like I said** 則可以用 **like**:

- **As I said** yesterday, I'm sure we can solve the problem.　或　**Like I said** yesterday . . .

as 也可以用作介係詞,但意思與 **like** 不同。比較下面的例子:

- Brenda Casey is the manager of a company. **As the manager,** she has to make many important decisions. Brenda Casey 是一家公司的經理。身為經理,她必須作很多重要的決定。 (**as** the manager 意思是作為經理)	- Mary Stone is the assistant manager. **Like the manager** (Brenda Casey), she also has to make important decisions. Mary Stone 是協理。和經理(Brenda Casey)一樣,她也必須作很多重要的決定。 (**like** the manager 意思是和經理一樣)

as 作為介係詞的用法,意思是在某個職位、以某種形式等:

- A few years ago I worked **as a taxi driver**. (並非 like a taxi driver)
- We don't have a car, so we use the garage **as a workshop**.
- Many words, for example "work" and "rain," can be used **as verbs or nouns**.
- New York is all right **as a place to visit**, but I wouldn't like to live there.
- The news of the tragedy came **as a great shock**.

as . . . as Unit 104　*as* (= at the same time as / because) Unit 113　*as if* Unit 115

Exercises

114.1 依各句題意判斷各句中的 *as* 是否需要改為 *like*。

1. It's raining again. I hate (weather as this.)   *weather like this*
2. Ann failed her driving test, as she expected.   *OK*
3. Do you think Carol looks as her mother?   _____
4. Tim gets on my nerves. I can't stand people as him.   _____
5. Why didn't you do it as I told you to do it?   _____
6. Brian is a student, as most of his friends.   _____
7. You never listen. Talking to you is as talking to the wall.   _____
8. As I said yesterday, I'm thinking of changing my job.   _____
9. Tom's idea seemed to be a good one, so we did as he suggested.   _____
10. I'll call you tomorrow as usual, OK?   _____
11. Suddenly there was a terrible noise. It was as a bomb exploding.   _____
12. She's a very good swimmer. She swims as a fish.   _____

114.2 依各句題意，以 *like* 或 *as* 配合自下列名詞中所選出之適當者，完成各句。

| a beginner | blocks of ice | ~~a palace~~ | a birthday present |
| a child | a church | winter | a tour guide |

1. This house is beautiful. It's _like a palace_____ .
2. My feet are really cold. They're _____ .
3. I've been playing tennis for years, but I still play _____ .
4. Margaret once had a part-time job _____ .
5. I wonder what that building with the tower is. It looks _____ .
6. My brother gave me this watch _____ a long time ago.
7. It's very cold for the middle of summer. It's _____ .
8. He's 22 years old, but he sometimes behaves _____ .

114.3 依各句題意，填入 *like* 或 *as*；有時兩者皆可。

1. We heard a noise __like__ a baby crying.
2. Your English is very fluent. I wish I could speak _____ you.
3. Don't take my advice if you don't want to. You can do _____ you like.
4. You waste too much time doing things _____ sitting in cafés all day.
5. I wish I had a car _____ yours.
6. You don't need to change your clothes. You can go out _____ you are.
7. My neighbor's house is full of lots of interesting things. It's _____ a museum
8. We saw Kevin last night. He was very cheerful, _____ always.
9. Sally has been working _____ a waitress for the last two months.
10. While we were on vacation, we spent most of our time doing active things _____ sailing, water skiing, and swimming.
11. You're different from the other people I know. I don't know anyone _____ you.
12. We don't need all the bedrooms in the house, so we use one of them _____ a study.
13. The news that Sue and Gary were getting married came _____ a complete surprise to me.
14. _____ her father, Catherine has a very good voice.
15. At the moment I've got a temporary job in a bookstore. It's OK _____ a temporary job, but I wouldn't like to do it permanently.
16. _____ you can imagine, we were very tired after such a long trip.
17. This tea is awful. It tastes _____ water.
18. I think I preferred this room _____ it was, before we decorated it.

like / as if / as though

A

like 可以表達某人或某事看起來、聽起來、感覺上(**looks/sounds/feels**等)如何：

■ That house **looks like** it's going to fall down.
■ Helen **sounded like** she had a cold, didn't she?
■ I've just come back from vacation, but I feel very tired. I don't **feel like** I just had a vacation.

as if 與 **as though** 也可以用於上述用法：

■ That house looks **as if** it's going to fall down.
■ I don't feel **as though** I just had a vacation.

在口語中較常使用 **like**。

比較下面的例句：

■ You look **tired**. (**look** + 形容詞)
■ You look $\left\{ \begin{array}{l} \textbf{like} \\ \textbf{as if} \end{array} \right\}$ **you didn't sleep** last night.

(**look like / as if** + 主詞 + 動詞)

B

我們可以說 **It looks like** . . . / **It sounds like** . . .

■ Sandra is very late, isn't she? **It looks like** she isn't coming.
■ We took an umbrella because **it looked like** it was going to rain.
■ Do you hear that music next door? **It sounds like** they are having a party.

此用法也可以使用 **as if** 與 **as though**：

■ It looks **as if** she isn't coming.
■ It looks **as though** she isn't coming.

It sounds like they're having a party next door.
聽起來隔壁正有聚會。

C

like / **as if** / **as though** 也可以和其他動詞一起使用，表示某人如何做某事：

■ He **ran like** he was running for his life.
■ After the interruption, the speaker **went on talking as if** nothing had happened.
■ When I told them my plan, they **looked at me as though** I was crazy.

D

有時候雖然談論的是目前的事，但 **as if** 之後使用過去式動詞。例如：

■ I don't like Tim. He talks **as if** he **knew** everything.

在上例中，動詞雖然為過去式，但意思是現在式；使用過去式動詞(as if he **knew**)是因為這件事並不是真的，也就是說，Tim 並不知道每一件事。此處過去式的用法表假設語氣，與 **if** 與 **wish** 後之動詞用法相同(參見 Unit 37)。

其他例子如下：

■ She's always asking me to do things for her – **as if I didn't** have enough to do already.
(我真的有很多事要做)
■ Gary's only 40. Why do you talk about him **as if he was** an old man?
(他不是老人)

上述用法，以過去式用來表示某件事不是真的時，則 **was** 可以與 **were** 互換使用：

■ Why do you talk about him **as if he were** (或 **was**) an old man?
■ They treat me **as if I were** (或 **was**) their own son. (我不是他們的兒子)

If I was / were Unit 37C   *look / sound* 等+形容詞 Unit 97C   *like* 與 *as* Unit 114

115.1 依各題的情境，以 *look/sound/feel + like ...* 的句型與括號內的字，完成句子。

1. You meet Bill. He has a black eye and some bandages on his face. (be / a fight)
   You say to him:
   You look like you've been in a fight.

2. Christine comes into the room. She looks absolutely terrified. (see / a ghost)
   You say to her: What's the matter? You _____

3. Joe is on vacation. He's talking to you on the phone and sounds very happy. (enjoy / yourself)
   You say to him: You _____

4. You have just run a mile. You are absolutely exhausted. (run / a marathon)
   You say to a friend: I _____

115.2 依各句題意，自下列句子中選出適當者，以 *It looks like ... / It sounds like ...* 的句型完成句子。

you should see a doctor	there's been an accident	they are having an argument
it's going to rain	~~she isn't coming~~	we'll have to walk

1. Sandra said she would be here an hour ago.
   You say: _It looks like she isn't coming._

2. The sky is full of black clouds.
   You say: It _____

3. You hear two people shouting at each other next door.
   You say: _____

4. You see an ambulance, some police officers, and two damaged cars at the side of the road.
   You say: _____

5. You and a friend have just missed the last bus home.
   You say: _____

6. Dave isn't feeling well. He tells you all about it.
   You say: _____

115.3 依各句題意，自下列句子中選出適當者，並配合 *as if* 完成句子。

she / enjoy / it	I / go / be sick	not / eat / for a week
~~he / need / a good rest~~	she / hurt / her leg	he / mean / what he / say
I / not / exist	she / not / want / come	

1. Mark looks very tired. He looks _as if he needs a good rest_ .
2. I don't think Paul was joking. He looked _____
3. What's the matter with Liz? She's walking _____
4. Peter was extremely hungry and ate his dinner very quickly.
   He ate _____ .
5. Carol had a bored expression on her face during the concert.
   She didn't look _____
6. I've just eaten too many chocolates. Now I don't feel well.
   I feel _____
7. I called Liz and invited her to the party, but she wasn't very enthusiastic about it.
   She sounded _____ .
8. I went into the office, but nobody spoke to me or looked at me.
   Everybody ignored me _____

115.4 依各句題意，參照 D 小節之例句，以 *as if* 完成各句。

1. Brian is a terrible driver. He drives _as if he were_ the only driver on the road.
2. I'm 20 years old, so please don't talk to me _____ I _____ a child.
3. Steve has never met Maria, but he talks about her _____ his best friend.
4. It was a long time ago that we first met, but I remember it _____ yesterday.

for、during 與 while

for 與 during

for + 一段時間表示某件事持續、進行了多久：

for **two hours**　　for **a week**　　for **ages**

- We watched television **for two hours** last night.
- Diane is going away **for a week** in September.
- Where have you been? I've been waiting **for ages**.
- Are you going away **for the weekend**?

during + 名詞表示某事何時發生(而非發生了多久)：

during **the movie**　　during **our vacation**　　during **the night**

- I fell asleep **during the movie**.
- We met some really nice people **during our vacation**.
- The ground is wet. It must have rained **during the night**.

表時間的名詞(例如 **the morning** / **the afternoon** / **the summer**)，通常與 **in** 或 **during** 一起使用：

- It must have rained **in the night**. (或 **during the night**)
- I'll call you sometime **during the afternoon**. (或 **in the afternoon**)

during 不可以用來表示某件事進行了有多久：

- It rained **for** three days without stopping. (並非 during three days)

比較 **during** 與 **for**：

- I fell asleep **during the movie**. I was asleep **for half an hour**.

during 與 while

比較下面的用法：

during + 名詞：	**while** +主詞+動詞：
■ I fell asleep **during the movie** .　名詞	■ I fell asleep **while I was watching TV**.　主詞+動詞
■ We met a lot of interesting people **during our vacation**.	■ We met a lot of interesting people **while we were on vacation**.
■ Robert suddenly began to feel sick **during the exam**.	■ Robert suddenly began to feel sick **while he was taking the exam**.

while 其他的例句如下：

- We saw Claire **while we were waiting** for the bus.
- **While you were** out, there was a phone call for you.
- Chris read a book **while I watched** TV.

若表示未來的意思，則 **while** 後必須使用現在式動詞：

- I'll be in Toronto next week. I hope to see Tom **while I'm** there.
  (並非 while I will be there)
- What are you going to do **while** you **are** waiting? (並非 while you will be waiting)

參見 Unit 24。

for 與 *since* Unit 12A　*while* + *-ing* Unit 66B

116.1 依各句題意，填入 *for* 或 *during*。

1. It rained __*for*__ three days without stopping.
2. I fell asleep __*during*__ the movie.
3. I went to the theater last night. I met Sue _____ the intermission.
4. Matt hasn't lived in the United States all his life. He lived in Brazil _____ four years.
5. Production at the factory was seriously affected _____ the strike.
6. I felt really sick last week. I could hardly eat anything _____ three days.
7. I waited for you _____ half an hour and decided that you weren't coming.
8. Sarah was very angry with me. She didn't speak to me _____ a week.
9. We usually go out on weekends, but we don't often go out _____ the week.
10. Jack started a new job a few weeks ago. Before that he was out of work _____ six months.
11. I need a change. I think I'll go away _____ a few days.
12. The president gave a long speech. She spoke _____ two hours.
13. We were hungry when we arrived. We hadn't had anything to eat _____ the trip.
14. We were hungry when we arrived. We hadn't had anything to eat _____ eight hours.

116.2 依各句題意，填入 *during* 或 *while*。

1. We met a lot of interesting people __*while*__ we were on vacation.
2. We met a lot of interesting people __*during*__ our vacation.
3. I met Mike _____ I was shopping.
4. _____ I was on vacation, I didn't read any newspapers or watch TV.
5. _____ our stay in Paris, we visited a lot of museums and galleries.
6. The phone rang three times _____ we were having dinner.
7. The phone rang three times _____ the night.
8. I had been away for many years. _____ that time, many things had changed.
9. What did they say about me _____ I was out of the room?
10. I went out for dinner last night. Unfortunately, I began to feel sick _____ the meal and had to go home.
11. Please don't interrupt me _____ I'm speaking.
12. There were many interruptions _____ the president's speech.
13. Can you set the table _____ I get dinner ready?
14. We were hungry when we arrived. We hadn't had anything to eat _____ we were traveling.

116.3 依你自己的意思，完成各句。

1. I fell asleep while __*I was watching television.*__
2. I fell asleep during __*the movie.*__
3. I hurt my arm while _____
4. Can you wait here while _____
5. Most of the students looked bored during _____
6. I was asked a lot of questions during _____
7. Don't open the car door while _____
8. The lights suddenly went out while _____
9. It started to rain during _____
10. It started to rain while _____

by 與 until　by the time . . .

A

by + 時間意思是在(某時間)之前：

- I sent the letter to them today, so they should receive it **by Monday**.
  (在星期一那天或星期一之前)

- We'd better hurry. We have to be home **by 5:00**.
  (在五點鐘或五點鐘之前)

- Where's Sue? She should be here **by now**.
  (現在或之前，所以她早就應該到了。)

This milk should be sold **by August 14**.
這罐牛奶必須在8月14日前賣出
(亦即其保存期限為8月14日)

B

until (或 till)表示某個情況持續了有多久：

- "Shall we go now?"　"No, let's wait **until** (或 till) it stops raining."

- I couldn't get up this morning. { I stayed in bed **until** half past ten.
  I didn't get up **until** half past ten.

比較 until 與 by：

某事持續進行到未來的某個時間：	某事將於未來的某個時間以前發生：
■ Fred **will be away until** Monday. (他將於星期一回來)	■ Fred **will be back by** Monday. (他將會在星期一之前回來)
■ **I'll be working until** 11:30. (我將會在 11:30 停止工作)	■ **I'll have finished my work by** 11:30. (我將會在 11:30 以前結束工作)

C

by the time something happens 之句型用法，請看下面的例句：

- It's too late to go to the bank now. **By the time we get there**, it will be closed.
  (在我們抵達以前銀行將已經關門)

- (在明信片上) Our vacation ends tomorrow. So **by the time you receive this postcard**, I'll be back home.
  (在你收到這封明信片以前，我將已經回到家了)

- Hurry up! **By the time we get to the theater**, the play will already have started.

by the time something happened 之句型用法則可用於表過去式：

- Karen's car broke down on the way to the party last night. **By the time she arrived**, most of the other guests had left.
  (他花了很多的時間才到達那個聚會，而在他到達之前大部分的客人都回家了。)

- I had a lot of work to do last night. I was very tired **by the time I finished**.
  (我花了很久的時間才把工作做完，工作期間我越來越累。)

- We went to the theater last night. It took us a long time to find a place to park.
  By the time we got to the theater, the play had already started.

類似用法還有 **by then** 或 **by that time**：

- Karen finally arrived at the party at midnight, but **by then** (或 **by that time**), most of the guests had left.

Exercises

117.1 依各句題意，以 **by** 改寫各句。

1. We have to be home no later than 5:00.
   We have to be home by 5:00.

2. I have to be at the airport no later than 8:30.
   I have to be at the airport _____

3. Let me know no later than Saturday whether you can come to the party.
   Let me know _____

4. Please make sure that you're here no later than 2:00.
   Please make sure that _____

5. If we leave now, we should arrive no later than lunchtime.
   If we leave now, _____

117.2 依各句題意，填入 **by** 或 **until**。

1. Fred is out of town. He'll be away _until_ Monday.
2. Sorry, but I have to go. I have to be home _____ 5:00.
3. I've been offered a job. I haven't decided yet whether to accept it or not.
   I have to decide _____ Friday.
4. I think I'll wait _____ Thursday before making a decision.
5. It's too late to go shopping. The stores are open only _____ 5:30 today.
   They'll be closed _____ now.
6. I'd better pay the phone bill. It has to be paid _____ tomorrow.
7. Don't pay the bill today. Wait _____ tomorrow.
8. *A:* Have you finished redecorating your house?
   B: Not yet. We hope to finish _____ the end of the week.
9. *A:* I'm going out now. I'll be back at about 10:30. Will you still be here?
   B: I don't think so. I'll probably have left _____ then.
10. I'm moving into my new apartment next week. I'm staying with a friend
    _____ then.
11. I've got a lot of work to do. _____ the time I finish, it will be time to go to bed.
12. If you want to take the exam, you have to register _____ April 3.

117.3 依你自己的意思，用 **by** 或 **until** 完成句子。

1. Fred is out of town at the moment. He'll be away _until Monday_____ .
2. Fred is out of town at the moment. He'll be back _by Monday_____ .
3. I'm going out. I won't be very long. Wait here _____ .
4. I'm going out to buy a few things. It's 4:30 now. I won't be long. I'll be back _____ .
5. If you want to apply for the job, your application must be received _____ .
6. Last night I watched TV _____ .

117.4 依各題的情境，用 **By the time ...** 完成句子。

1. I was invited to a party, but I got there much later than I intended.
   By the time I got to the party , most of the other guests had left.
2. I wanted to catch a train, but it took me longer than expected to get to the station.
   _____ , my train had already left.
3. I intended to go shopping after finishing work. But I finished much later than expected.
   _____ , it was too late to go shopping.
4. I saw two men who looked as if they were trying to steal a car. I called the police, but it was some time before they arrived.
   _____ , the two men had disappeared.
5. We climbed a mountain, and it took us a very long time to get to the top. There wasn't much time to enjoy the view.
   _____ , we had to come down again.

at / on / in (表時間)

A

比較 at、on 與 in：
- They arrived **at 5:00**.
- They arrived **on Friday**.
- They arrived **in October**. / They arrived **in 1968**.

請看下面的用法：

at 用於一天裡的某個時間：
at 5:00　　**at 11:45**　　**at midnight**　　**at lunchtime**　　**at sunset** 等

on 用於日期：
on Friday / **on Fridays**　　　**on May 16, 1999**　　**on Christmas Day**　　　**on my birthday**
此外也用於 **on the weekend**、**on weekends**

in 用於較長的時間(例如月/年/季節)：
in October　　　　**in 1988**　　　**in the 18th century**　　**in the past**
in (the) winter　　**in the 1990s**　　**in the Middle Ages**　　**in the future**

B

at 也用於表示下面的時間：

at night | I don't like going out **at night**.
at Christmas | Do you give each other presents **at Christmas**?
at this time / **at the moment** | Mr. Brown is busy **at this time** / **at the moment**.
at the same time | Liz and I arrived **at the same time**.

C

請看下面的用法：

in the morning(s)　　　　但是　　**on Friday morning(s)**
in the afternoon(s)　　　　　　　**on Sunday afternoon(s)**
in the evening(s)　　　　　　　　**on Monday evening(s)**, 等

- I'll see you **in the morning**.
- Do you work **in the evenings**?
- I'll see you **on Friday morning**.
- Do you work **on Saturday evenings**?

D

last / **next** / **this** / **every** 的時間詞之前不可以用 **at/on/in**：
- I'll see you **next Friday**. (並非 on next Friday)
- They got married **last March**.

在口說中日期前(**Sunday**、**Monday** 等)的 **on** 通常可以省略：
- I'll see you **on Friday**.　或　I'll see you **Friday**.
- She works **on Saturday** mornings.　或　She works **Saturday** mornings.
- They got married **on March 12**.　或　They got married **March 12**.

E

in a few minutes / **in six months** 等用法是表示未來的時間：
- The train will be leaving **in a few minutes**. (現在起的幾分鐘後)
- Andy has left town. He'll be back **in a week**. (現在起一個星期後)
- She'll be here **in a moment**. (現在起不久之後)

也可以用 **in** six months' **time**、**in** a week's **time** 等：
- They're getting married **in six months' time**.　或　. . . **in six months**.

in . . . 也可以表示完成某件事需要多少時間：
- I learned to drive **in four weeks**. (學開車花了我四個星期。)

on / in time, at / in the end Unit 119　　*in / at / on* (表位置) Unit 120 至 Unit 122　　*in / at / on* (其他用法) Unit 124

英式英文 附錄 7

118.1 依各句題意，自下列時間中選出適當者，並搭配正確的介係詞 *at*、*on* 或 *in*，以完成句子。

the evening	about 20 minutes	~~1492~~	the same time
the moment	July 21, 1969	the 1920s	night
Saturdays	the Middle Ages	11 seconds	

1. Columbus made his first voyage from Europe to America _in 1492_____ .
2. If the sky is clear, you can see the stars _____ .
3. After working hard during the day, I like to relax _____ .
4. Neil Armstrong was the first man to walk on the moon _____ .
5. It's difficult to listen if everyone is speaking _____ .
6. Jazz became popular in the United States _____ .
7. I'm just going out to the store. I'll be back _____ .
8. *(on the phone)* "Can I speak to Dan?" "I'm sorry, but he's not here _____ ."
9. Many of Europe's great cathedrals were built _____ .
10. Bob is a very fast runner. He can run 100 meters _____ .
11. Liz works from Monday to Friday. Sometimes she also works _____ .

118.2 依各句題意，填入適當的介係詞 *at*、*on* 或 *in*。

1. Mozart was born in Salzburg _in__ 1756.
2. "Have you seen Kate recently?" "Yes, I saw her _____ Tuesday."
3. The price of electricity is going up _____ October.
4. _____ weekends, we often go for long walks in the country.
5. I've been invited to a wedding _____ February 14.
6. Henry is 63. He'll be retiring from his job _____ two years.
7. I'm busy right now, but I'll be with you _____ a moment.
8. Jenny's brother is an engineer, but he doesn't have a job _____ the moment.
9. There are usually a lot of parties _____ New Year's Eve.
10. I don't like driving _____ night.
11. My car is being repaired. It will be ready _____ two hours.
12. The telephone and the doorbell rang _____ the same time.
13. Mary and David always go out for dinner _____ their wedding anniversary.
14. It was a short book and easy to read. I read it _____ a day.
15. _____ Saturday night I went to bed _____ midnight.
16. We traveled overnight to Paris and arrived _____ 5:00 _____ the morning.
17. The course begins _____ January 7 and ends sometime _____ April.
18. I might not be at home _____ Tuesday morning, but I'll be there _____ the afternoon.

118.3 下列何者正確，(a)、(b) 或兩者皆可？

1. a) I'll see you on Friday. | b) I'll see you Friday. | _both_
2. a) I'll see you on next Friday. | b) I'll see you next Friday. | _b_
3. a) Paul got married in April. | b) Paul got married April. | _____
4. a) They never go out on Sunday evenings. | b) They never go out Sunday evenings. | _____
5. a) We usually take a short vacation on Christmas. | b) We usually take a short vacation at Christmas. | _____
6. a) What are you doing the weekend? | b) What are you doing on the weekend? | _____
7. a) Will you be here on Tuesday? | b) Will you be here Tuesday? | _____
8. a) We were sick at the same time. | b) We were sick in the same time. | _____
9. a) Sue got married at May 18, 2002. | b) Sue got married on May 18, 2002. | _____
10. a) He finished school last June. | b) He finished school in last June. | _____

on time 與 in time
at the end 與 in the end

on time 與 in time

on time 意思是「準時」。something happens **on time** 意思是某事依計畫準時在某時間發生：
- The 11:45 train left **on time**. (火車準時 11:45 開)
- "I'll meet you at 7:30." "OK, but please be **on time**." (不要遲到，在 7:30 準時到)
- The conference was well organized. Everything began and ended **on time**.

on time 的反義詞為 **late**：
- Be **on time**. Don't be **late**.

in time (for something / to do something) 意思是「及時」、「來得及」(做某事)：
- Will you be home **in time for dinner**? (來得及吃晚餐)
- I've sent Jill a birthday present. I hope it arrives **in time** (for her birthday).
  (在她生日當天或生日之前)
- I'm in a hurry. I want to be home **in time to see** the game on television.
  (來得及看球賽)

in time 的反義詞為 **too late**：
- I got home **too late** to see the game on television.

just in time 意思是幾乎太遲了：
- We got to the station **just in time** for our train.
- A child ran into the street in front of the car – I managed to stop **just in time**.

at the end 與 in the end

At the end of (something) 意思是在某事結束的時候。例如：

at the end of the month   at the end of January   at the end of the game
at the end of the movie   at the end of the course   at the end of the concert

- I'm going away **at the end of January** / **at the end of the month**.
- **At the end of the concert**, there was great applause.
- The players shook hands **at the end of the game**.

不可以用 in the end of something，所以不可以說 in the end of January 或 in the end of the concert。

at the end of 的反義詞為 **at the beginning of**：
- I'm going away **at the beginning of January**. (並非 in the beginning)

in the end 意思是「最後」、「終於」。
in the end 表示某狀況最後的結果是什麼：
- We had a lot of problems with our car. We sold it **in the end**. (最後我們把車賣了)
- He got angrier and angrier. **In the end** he just walked out of the room.
- Alan couldn't decide where to go on vacation. He didn't go anywhere **in the end**.
  (並非 at the end)

in the end 的反義詞為 **at first**：
- **At first** we didn't get along very well, but **in the end** we became good friends.

Exercises

119.1 依各句題意，填入 *on time* 或 *in time*。

1. The bus was late this morning, but it's usually _____on time_____ .
2. The movie was supposed to start at 8:30, but it didn't begin _____ .
3. I like to get up _____ to have a big breakfast before going to work.
4. We want to start the meeting _____ , so please don't be late.
5. I just washed this shirt. I want to wear it tonight, so I hope it will dry _____ .
6. The train service isn't very good. The trains are seldom _____ .
7. I nearly missed my flight this morning. I got to the airport just _____ .
8. I almost forgot that it was Joe's birthday. Fortunately I remembered _____ .
9. Why aren't you ever _____ ? You always keep everybody waiting.

119.2 依各題的情況，以括號內的字詞搭配 *just in time* 完成各句。

1. A child ran into the street in front of your car. You saw the child at the last moment. (manage / stop) ____*I managed to stop just in time.*____
2. You were walking home. Just after you got home, it started to rain very heavily.
   (get / home) I _____
3. Tim was going to sit on the chair you had just painted. You said, "Don't sit on that chair!" so he didn't. (stop / him) I _____
4. You and a friend went to the movies. You were late, and you thought you would miss the beginning of the film. But the film began just as you sat down in the theater.
   (get / theater / beginning of the film)
   We _____

119.3 依各句題意，自下列名詞選出適當者，以 *at the end of* 的片語完成各句。

    the course   ~~the game~~   **the interview**   **the month**   **the race**

1. The players shook hands ____*at the end of the game*____ .
2. I usually get paid _____ .
3. The students had a party _____ .
4. Two of the runners collapsed _____ .
5. To my surprise, I was offered the job _____ .

119.4 依各句題意，以括號內的字搭配 *In the end ...*，以完成各句。

1. We had a lot of problems with our car.
   (sell) ____*In the end we sold it.*____
2. Judy got more and more fed up with her job.
   (resign) _____
3. I tried to learn German, but I found it too difficult.
   (give up) _____
4. We couldn't decide whether to go to the party or not.
   (not / go) _____

119.5 填入適當的介係詞 *at* 或 *in*。

1. I'm going away ____*at*____ the end of the month.
2. It took me a long time to find a job. _____ the end I got a job in a hotel.
3. Are you going away _____ the beginning of August or _____ the end?
4. I couldn't decide what to buy Laura for her birthday. I didn't buy her anything _____ the end.
5. We waited ages for a taxi. We gave up _____ the end and walked home.
6. I'll be moving to a new address _____ the end of September.
7. We had a few problems at first, but _____ the end everything was OK.
8. I'm going away _____ the end of this week.
9. *A:* I didn't know what to do.
   B: Yes, you were in a difficult position. What did you do _____ the end?

in / at / on (表位置) 1

A

in

in a room
在房間裡
in a building
在建築物裡
in a box
在箱子裡

in a garden
在花園裡
in a town/city
在鎮上/在城裡
in a country
在國家裡

in a pool
在池子裡
in an ocean
在海洋裡
in a river
在河裡

- There's somebody **in the room** / **in the building** / **in the garden**.
- What do you have **in your hand** / **in your mouth**?
- When we were **in Taiwan**, we spent a few days **in Hualien**.
- I have a friend who lives **in a small village in the mountains**.
- There were some people swimming **in the pool** / **in the ocean** / **in the river**.

B

at

at the bus stop
在公車站

at the door
在門前

at the intersection
在十字路口

at the front desk
在櫃台

- Do you know that man standing **at the bus stop** / **at the door** / **at the window**?
- Turn left **at the traffic light** / **at the church** / **at the intersection**.
- We have to get off the bus **at the next stop**.
- When you leave the hotel, please leave your key **at the front desk**.

C

on

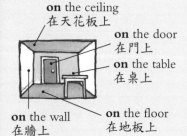

on the ceiling
在天花板上
on the door
在門上
on the table
在桌上
on the wall
在牆上
on the floor
在地板上

on her nose
在她的鼻子上

on a page
在(某一)頁上

on an island
在島上

- I sat **on the floor** / **on the ground** / **on the grass** / **on the beach** / **on a chair**.
- There's a dirty mark **on the wall** / **on the ceiling** / **on your nose** / **on your shirt**.
- Have you seen the notice **on the bulletin board** / **on the door**?
- You'll find the listings of TV programs **on page 7** (of the newspaper).
- The hotel is **on a small island** in the middle of the lake.

D

比較 **in** 與 **at**：
- There were a lot of people **in the store**. It was very crowded.
  Go along this road, then turn left **at the store**.
- I'll meet you **in the hotel lobby**.
  I'll meet you **at the entrance to the hotel**.

比較 **in** 與 **on**：
- There is some water **in the bottle**.
  There is a label **on the bottle**.

比較 **at** 與 **on**：
- There is somebody **at the door**. Should I go and see who it is?
  There is a sign **on the door**. It says "Do not disturb."

in the bottle
在瓶子裡

on the bottle
在瓶子上

Exercises

120.1 依據下面的圖片，以圖片中提供的名詞或名詞片語搭配適當的介係詞 *in*、*at* 或 *on*，回答下面各項問題。

1. (bottle)	2. (arm)	3. (traffic light)	4. (door)
5. (wall)	6. (Paris)	7. (front desk)	8. (beach)

1. Where's the label? _____On the bottle._____
2. Where's the butterfly? _____
3. Where is the car waiting? _____
4. a) Where's the sign? _____
   b) Where's the key? _____
5. Where are the shelves? _____
6. Where's the Eiffel Tower? _____
7. a) Where's the man standing? _____
   b) Where's the telephone? _____
8. Where are the children playing? _____

120.2 依各句題意，自下列名詞片語選出適當者，搭配適當的介係詞 *in*、*at* 或 *on* 完成各句。

the window	your coffee	the mountains	that tree
my guitar	~~the river~~	the island	the next gas station

1. Look at those people swimming __in the river__ .
2. One of the strings _____ is broken.
3. There's something wrong with the car. We'd better stop _____ .
4. Would you like sugar _____ ?
5. The leaves _____ are a beautiful color.
6. Last year we had a wonderful ski trip _____ .
7. There's nobody living _____ . It's uninhabited.
8. He spends most of the day sitting _____ and looking outside.

120.3 填入適當的介係詞 *in*、*at* 或 *on*。

1. There was a long line of people __at__ the bus stop.
2. Nicole was wearing a silver ring _____ her little finger.
3. There was an accident _____ the intersection this morning.
4. I wasn't sure whether I had come to the right office. There was no name _____ the door.
5. There are some beautiful trees _____ the park.
6. You'll find the sports results _____ the back page of the newspaper.
7. I wouldn't like an office job. I couldn't spend the whole day sitting _____ a desk.
8. My brother lives _____ a small town _____ eastern Tennessee.
9. The man the police are looking for has a scar _____ his right cheek.
10. The headquarters of the company are _____ Tokyo.
11. I like that picture hanging _____ the wall _____ the kitchen.
12. If you come here by bus, get off _____ the stop after the traffic light.

in / at / on (表位置) 2

A

請看下面的用法。somebody/something is 意思是某人/某物在：

in a row
在一排裡面

in a line / **in a row**	**in bed**
in the sky / **in the world**	**in the country** / **in the countryside**
in an office / **in a department**	**in a photograph** / **in a picture**
in a book / **in a (news)paper** / **in a magazine** / **in a letter**	

- When I go to the movies, I like to sit **in the front row**.
- I just started working **in the sales department**.
- Who is the woman **in that photo**?
- Have you seen this picture **in today's paper**?

表達在車子、房子、戲院、一群人等的前面/後面，要用
in the front / **in the back** of：

- I was sitting **in the back** (of the car) when we crashed.
- Let's sit **in the front** (of the movie theater).
- John was standing **in the back** of the crowd.

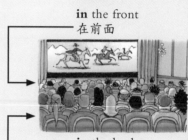

in the front
在前面

in the back
在後面

B

on the left / **on the right**	**on the left-hand side** / **right-hand side**	
on the ground floor / **on the first floor** / **on the second floor**, etc.		
on a map / **on a menu** / **on a list**		
on a farm / **on a ranch**		

- In Britain they drive **on the left**. (或 . . . **on the left-hand side**.)
- Our apartment is **on the second floor** of the building.
- Here's a shopping list. Don't buy anything that's not **on the list**.
- Have you ever worked **on a farm**? It's a lot like working **on a ranch**.

我們說 a place is **on a river** / **on a street** / **on a road** / **on the coast** 意思
是某個地方在河面上/在街上/在道路上/在岸邊：

- Washington, D.C., is **on the East Coast** of the United States,
  on the Potomac River.
- I live **on Main Street**. My brother lives **on Elm**. (= on Elm Street)

on the way 意思是在(去某處)路上：

- We stopped at a small town **on the way** to Atlanta.

表達在一張紙、一個信封、一張相片(the letter / piece of paper / photo)等
的正面或背面，要用 **on the front** / **on the back**：

- I wrote the date **on the back** of the photo.

C

at the top (of) / **at the bottom** (of) / **at the end** (of)

- Write your name **at the top of the page**.
- Jane's house is **at the other end of the street**.

at the top (of the page)
在(一張紙)的頂端

at the bottom (of the page)
在(一張紙)的底部

D

在房間的角落為 **in the corner** of a room：

- The television is **in the corner** of the room.

在街角為 **at the corner** 或 **on the corner** of a street：

- There is a mailbox **at/on the corner** of the street.

in the corner   **at/on** the corne

121.1 依據下面的圖片，以適當的介係詞 *in*、*at* 或 *on*，回答下面各項問題。

1. Sue (sales department)	2. (second floor)	3. (corner)	4. (corner)	5. (top / stairs)
6. (back / car)	7. (front) Liz	8. (left)	9. Gary (back row)	10. Kate (farm)

1. Where does Sue work? __*In the sales department.*__
2. Sue lives in this building. Where's her apartment exactly? _____
3. Where is the woman standing? _____
4. Where is the man standing? _____
5. Where's the cat? _____
6. Where's the dog? _____
7. Liz is in this group of people. Where is she? _____
8. Where's the post office? _____
9. Gary is at the movies. Where is he sitting? _____
10. Where does Kate work? _____

121.2 依各句題意，自下列名詞片語選出適當者，搭配適當的介係詞 *in*、*at* 或 *on* 完成各句。

the West Coast	the world	the back of the class	~~the sky~~
the front row	the right	the back of this card	the way to work

1. It was a lovely day. There wasn't a cloud __*in the sky*__ .
2. In most countries people drive _____ .
3. What is the tallest building _____ ?
4. I usually buy a newspaper _____ in the morning.
5. San Francisco is _____ of the United States.
6. We went to the theater last night. We had seats _____ .
7. I couldn't hear the teacher. She spoke quietly and I was sitting _____ .
8. I don't have your address. Could you write it _____ ?

121.3 填入適當的介係詞 *in*、*at* 或 *on*。

1. Write your name __*at*__ the top of the page.
2. Is your sister _____ this photo? I don't recognize her.
3. I didn't feel very well when I woke up, so I stayed _____ bed.
4. We normally use the front entrance to the building, but there's another one _____ the back.
5. Is there anything interesting _____ the paper today?
6. There was a list of names, but my name wasn't _____ the list.
7. _____ the end of the block, there is a small store. You'll see it _____ the corner.
8. I love to look up at the stars _____ the sky at night.
9. When I'm a passenger in a car, I prefer to sit _____ the front.
10. It's a very small town. You probably won't find it _____ your map.
11. Joe works _____ the furniture department of a large store.
12. Paris is _____ the Seine River.
13. I don't like cities. I'd rather live _____ the country.
14. My office is _____ the top floor. It's _____ the left as you come out of the elevator.

in / at / on (表位置) 3

A at home / in the hospital 等

somebody is **at home** / **at work**意思是某人在家/在工作：
- I'll be **at work** until 5:30, but I'll be **at home** all evening.

也可以用 **be/stay home** (注意：不用介係詞 at)：
- You can stop by anytime. I'll **be home** all evening.

somebody is **in the hospital** / **in prison** / **in jail**意思某人在住院、在坐牢：
- Ann's mother is **in the hospital**.

我們可以說 **at** 或 **in school/college**。表示某人在哪裡時用 **at school/college**：
- Kim is not living at home. She's away **at college**.

而表示某人正在做什麼則用 **in school/college**：
- Amy works at a bank and her brother is **in medical school**. (他正就讀醫科)

B at a party / at a concert 等

用 **at** 表達某人出席、參加某個活動(**at a party**，**at a conference** 等)：
- Were there many people **at the party** / **at the meeting** / **at the wedding**?
- I saw Steve **at a tennis match** / **at a concert** on Saturday.

C in 與 at 用於建築物之用法

在建築物裡可以用 **in** 或 **at**，但意思稍有不同。例如 you can eat **in a café** 或 **at a restaurant** 皆表示你在餐廳用餐(You can buy something **in a supermarket** 或 **at a supermarket**意思都是在超市買東西)。**At** 通常用於描述事件是於某一地點發生 (例如 a concert、a movie、a party、a meeting)：
- We went to a concert **at Lincoln Center**.
- The meeting took place **at the company's headquarters** in New York.

我們說 **at the station** / **at the airport**：
- Don't meet me **at the station**. I can get a taxi.

at somebody's house 意思是「在某人家」：
- I was **at Sue's house** last night. 或 I was **at Sue's** last night.

此外，我們說 **at the doctor's**, **at the hairdresser's** 等。

in 通常用於指某建築物本身。比較下面例句：
- We had dinner **at the hotel**. 但是
  All the rooms **in the hotel** have air conditioning. (並非 at the hotel)
- I was **at Sue's** (house) last night. 但是
  It's always cold **in Sue's house**. The heating doesn't work very well. (並非 at Sue's house)

D in 與 at 用於城鎮的用法

in 通常與 cities (城市)、towns (城鎮)、與鄉村(village)一起使用：
- Sam's parents live **in St. Louis**. (並非 at St. Louis)
- The Louvre is a famous art museum **in Paris**. (並非 at Paris)

但如果將某個地方視為旅遊或行程中的一個地點或一個站，則 **at** 或 **in** 都可以用：
- Does this train stop **at** (或 **in**) **Denver**? (= at the Denver station)
- We stopped **at** (或 **in**) a small **town** on the way to Denver.

E on a bus / in a car 等

我們通常說 **on a bus** / **on a train** / **on a plane** / **on a ship**，但是**in a car** / **in a taxi**：
- **The bus** was very full. There were too many people **on it**.
- Mary arrived **in a taxi**.

我們說 **on a bike** (= bicycle) / **on a motorcycle** / **on a horse**：
- Jane passed me **on her bike**.

at school / *in prison* 等 Unit 72   *in* / *at* / *on* (表位置) Unit 120 與 Unit 121   *to* / *at* / *in* / *into* Unit 123
by car / *by bike* 等 Unit 125B

Exercises

122.1 依據下面的圖片，以適當的介係詞 *in*、*at* 或 *on*，完成各句。

1. (the airport)	2. Dave (a train)	3. CONFERENCE (a conference) Karen	4. Martin (the hospital)
5. Judy (the hairdresser's)	6. Gary (his bike)	7. (New York)	8. THE FORD THEATER (the Ford Theater)

1. You can rent a car ___at the airport___ .
2. Dave is _____ .
3. Karen is _____ .
4. Martin is _____ .
5. Judy is _____ .
6. I saw Gary _____ .
7. We spent a few days _____ .
8. We went to a show _____ .

122.2 依各句題意，自下列名詞片語選出適當者，搭配適當的介係詞 *in*、*at* 或 *on* 完成各句。

> the plane   the hospital   a taxi   ~~the station~~   the party
> the gym   school   prison   the airport

1. My train arrives at 11:30. Can you meet me ___at the station___ ?
2. We walked to the restaurant, but we went home _____ .
3. Did you have a good time _____ ? I heard it was a lot of fun.
4. I enjoyed the flight, but the food _____ wasn't very good.
5. *A:* What does your sister do? Does she have a job?
   B: No, she's only 16. She's still _____ .
6. I play basketball _____ on Friday evenings.
7. A friend of mine was injured in an accident a few days ago. She's still _____ .
8. Our flight was delayed. We had to wait _____ for four hours.
9. Some people are _____ for crimes that they did not commit.

122.3 填入適當的介係詞 *in*、*at* 或 *on*。

1. We went to a concert ___at___ Lincoln Center.
2. It was a very slow train. It stopped _____ every station.
3. My parents live _____ a suburb of Chicago.
4. I haven't seen Kate for some time. I last saw her _____ David's wedding.
5. We stayed _____ a very nice hotel when we were _____ Amsterdam.
6. There were 50 rooms _____ the hotel.
7. I don't know where my umbrella is. Maybe I left it _____ the bus.
8. I wasn't home when you called. I was _____ my sister's house.
9. There must be somebody _____ the house. The lights are on.
10. The exhibition _____ the Museum of Modern Art closed on Saturday.
11. Should we go _____ your car or mine?
12. What are you doing _____ home? I expected you to be _____ work.
13. "Did you like the movie?" "Yes, but it was too hot _____ the theater."
14. Paul lives _____ Boston. He's a student _____ Boston University.

to / at / in / into

A

我們說 go/come/travel (等) to 某一地點或事件。例如：

go to China	**go to** bed	**come to** my house
go back to Italy	**go to** the bank	**be taken to** the hospital
return to Boston	**go to** a concert	**be sent to** prison
welcome (somebody) **to** (a place)		**drive to** the airport

■ When are your friends **going back to** Italy? (並非 going back in Italy)
■ Three people were injured in the accident and **taken to** the hospital.
■ **Welcome to** our country! (並非 Welcome in)

相同地，我們說 a **trip to** / a **visit to** / on **my way to** ... 等：

■ Did you enjoy **your trip to** Paris / **your visit to** the zoo?

比較 **to** (表移動)與 **in/at** (表定點位置)的用法：

■ They are **going to** France.　但是　They **live in** France.
■ Can you **come to** the party?　但是　I'll see **you at** the party.

B

been to

been to (地點)意思是「曾經到過…」：

■ I've **been to Italy** four times, but I've never **been to Rome**.
■ Amanda has never **been to a hockey game** in her life.

C

get 與 **arrive**

我們說「**get to** + 地點」意思是「到達某地」：

■ What time did they **get to London** / **get to work** / **get to the party** / **get to the hotel**?

但我們說 **arrive in** ... 或 **arrive at** ... (而非 arrive to)。
arrive in + 國家或城市/城鎮：

■ They **arrived in Rio de Janeiro** / **in Brazil** a week ago.

arrive at 用於其他的地方(例如建築物)，或事件：

■ When did they **arrive at the hotel** / **at the airport** / **at the party**?

D

home

go home / **come home** / **get home** / **arrive home** / **on the way home** 等用語前面不需要介係詞。

不可以用 to home：

■ I'm tired. Let's **go home** now. (並非 go to home)
■ I met Linda **on my way home**. (並非 my way to home)

E

into

go into/ **get into** 等用法的意思是 enter (a room / a building / a car 等)：

■ I opened the door, **went into** the room, and sat down.
■ A bird **flew into** the kitchen through the window.

上述片語(特別是 **go/get/put**)中的 **into** 也可以用 **in** 替換：

■ She **got in** the car and drove away. (或 She **got into** the car ...)
■ I read the letter and **put it** back **in the envelope**.

into 的反義為 **out of**：

■ She **got out of** the car and **went into** a shop.

注意：我們通常說 **get on/off** a bus / a train / a plane (通常不是 get into/out of)：

■ She **got on the** bus and I never saw her again.

Exercises

123.1 依各句題意，填入 *to / at / in / into*；若題意不需要介係詞，則保留空白。

1. Three people were taken __to__ the hospital after the accident.
2. I met Kate on my way __–__ home. *(no preposition)*
3. We left our luggage _____ the hotel and went to find something to eat.
4. Should we take a taxi _____ the station, or should we walk?
5. I have to go _____ the bank today to change some money.
6. The Mississippi River flows _____ the Gulf of Mexico.
7. "Do you have your camera?" "No, I left it _____ home."
8. Have you ever been _____ China?
9. I had lost my key, but I managed to climb _____ the house through a window.
10. We got stuck in a traffic jam on our way _____ the airport.
11. We had lunch _____ the airport while we were waiting for our plane.
12. Welcome _____ the hotel. We hope you enjoy your stay here.
13. I got a flat tire, so I turned _____ a parking lot to change it.
14. Did you enjoy your visit _____ the zoo?
15. I'm tired. As soon as I get _____ home, I'm going _____ bed.
16. Marcel is French. He has just returned _____ France after two years _____ Brazil.
17. Carl was born _____ Chicago, but his family moved _____ New York when he was three. He still lives _____ New York.

123.2 你去過下面的地方嗎？去過幾次呢？自下面的地點選出三個，以 *been to* 造句。

Australia   Hong Kong   Mexico   Paris   Thailand   Tokyo   Washington, D.C.

1. (範例答案) *I've never been to Australia. / I've been to Thailand once.*
2. _____
3. _____
4. _____

123.3 依各句題意，填入 *to / at / in / into*；若題意不需要介係詞，則保留空白。

1. What time does this bus get __to__ Vancouver?
2. What time does this bus arrive _____ Vancouver?
3. What time did you get _____ home last night?
4. What time do you usually arrive _____ work in the morning?
5. When we got _____ the theater, there was a long line outside.
6. I arrived _____ home feeling very tired.

123.4 依各句題意，以 *got + into / out of / on / off* 完成答句。

1. You were walking home. A friend passed you in her car. She saw you, stopped, and offered you a ride. She opened the door. What did you do? *I got into the car.*
2. You were waiting for the bus. At last your bus came. The doors opened. What did you do then? I _____
3. You drove home in your car. You stopped outside your house and parked the car. What did you do then? _____
4. You were traveling by train to Chicago. When the train got to Chicago, what did you do? _____
5. You needed a taxi. After a few minutes a taxi stopped for you. You opened the door. What did you do then? _____
6. You were traveling by air. At the end of your flight, your plane landed at the airport and stopped. The doors were opened. You took your bag and stood up. What did you do then? _____

補充練習 34 **(315–316 頁)**

247

UNIT 124

in / at / on (其他用法)

A

請看下面使用 **in** 之片語：

in the rain / **in the sun** (= sunshine) / **in the shade** / **in the dark** / **in bad weather** 等，
意思是在雨中/在太陽下/在影子下/在黑暗中/在壞天氣(的情況)下等：

■ We sat **in the shade**. It was too hot to sit **in the sun**.
■ Don't go out **in the rain**. Wait until it stops.

(write) **in ink** / **in pen** / **in pencil** 意思是以鋼筆/以原子筆/以鉛筆書寫：

■ When you take the exam, you're not allowed to write **in pencil**.

(write) **in words** / **in numbers** / **in capital letters** 等，意思是以文字、以數字、以大寫字
母等書寫：

■ Please write your name **in capital letters**.
■ Write the story **in your own words**. (= don't copy somebody else)

(be/fall) **in love** (**with** somebody) ，意思是(與某人)談戀愛：

■ Have you ever been **in love with** anybody?

in (my) **opinion** 意思是依我之意見：

■ **In my opinion**, the movie wasn't very good.

B

at the age of ... 等

at the age of 16 / **at 120 miles an hour** / **at 100 degrees** 等意思是在
16 歲(的年紀)/以時速 120 英里的速度/在 100 度等：

■ Tracy left school **at 16**.　或　... **at the age of 16**.
■ The train was traveling **at 120 miles an hour**.
■ Water boils **at 100 degrees Celsius**.

We are now flying **at a speed of** 500 miles per hour **at an altitude of** 30,000 feet.
我們現在正以時速 500 英里的速度，在 30000 英呎的高空飛行。

C

on vacation / **on a tour** 等

(be/go) **on vacation** / **on business** / **on a trip** / **on a tour** / **on a cruise** 等，意思是去度
假、去出差、去旅遊等：

■ I'm going **on vacation** next week.
■ Emma's away **on business** at this time.
■ One day I'd like to go **on a world tour**.

也可以說「go to 某地點 **for vacation**」：

■ Steve has gone to France **for vacation**.

D

其他使用 **on** 的片語如下：

on television / **on the radio** 意思是「在電視上/在廣播中」：

■ I didn't watch the news **on television**, but I heard it **on the radio**.

on the phone/telephone 意思是「在電話上」：

■ I've never met her, but I've spoken to her **on the phone** a few times.

(be/go) **on strike** 意思是「罷工」：

■ There are no trains today. The railroad workers are **on strike**.

(be/go) **on a diet** 意思是「節食」：

■ I've put on a lot of weight. I'll have to go **on a diet**.

(be) **on fire** 意思是「失火了」：

■ Look! That car is **on fire**.

on the whole 意思是「整體而言」、「一般來說」：

■ Sometimes I have problems at work, but **on the whole** I enjoy my job.

on purpose 意思是「故意地」：

■ I'm sorry. I didn't mean to annoy you. I didn't do it **on purpose**.

Exercises

124.1 依各句題意，自下列名詞中選出適當的字，搭配介係詞 *in* 以完成句子。

capital letters	cold weather	love	my opinion
pencil	~~the rain~~	the shade	

1. Don't go out ___in the rain___ . Wait until it stops.
2. Matt likes to keep warm, so he doesn't go out much _____ .
3. If you write _____ and make a mistake, you can erase it and correct it.
4. They fell _____ almost immediately and were married a few weeks later.
5. Please write your address clearly, preferably _____ .
6. It's too hot in the sun. I'm going to sit _____ .
7. Ann thought the restaurant was OK, but _____ it wasn't very good.

124.2 依各句題意，自下列名詞中選出適當的字，搭配介係詞 *on* 以完成句子。

business	~~fire~~	purpose	television	vacation
a diet	the phone	strike	a tour	the whole

1. Look! That car is ___on fire___ ! Somebody call the fire department.
2. Workers at the factory have gone _____ for better pay and conditions.
3. Soon after we arrived, we were taken _____ of the city.
4. I feel lazy tonight. Is there anything worth watching _____ ?
5. I'm sorry. It was an accident. I didn't do it _____ .
6. Richard has put on a lot of weight recently. I think he should go _____ .
7. Jane's job involves a lot of traveling. She is out of town a lot _____ .
8. *A:* I'm going _____ next week.
   B: Where are you going? Somewhere nice?
9. *A:* Is Sarah here?
   B: Yes, but she's _____ at the moment. She won't be long.
10. *A:* How did your exams go?
    B: Well, there were some difficult questions, but _____ they were OK.

124.3 依各句題意，填入適當的介係詞 *on*、*in*、*at* 或 *for*。

1. Water boils ___at___ 100 degrees Celsius.
2. When I was 14, I went _____ a trip to Mexico organized by my school.
3. There was panic when people realized that the building was _____ fire.
4. Julia's grandmother died recently _____ the age of 79.
5. Can you turn the light on, please? I don't want to sit _____ the dark.
6. We didn't go _____ vacation last year. We stayed at home.
7. I'm going to Miami _____ a short vacation next month.
8. I won't be here next week. I'll be _____ vacation.
9. Technology has developed _____ great speed.
10. Allan got married _____ 17, which is really young to get married.
11. I heard an interesting program _____ the radio this morning.
12. _____ my opinion, violent films should not be shown _____ television.
13. I wouldn't want to go _____ a cruise. I think I'd get bored.
14. I can't eat a lot. I'm supposed to be _____ a diet.
15. I wouldn't want his job. He spends most of his time talking _____ the phone.
16. The earth travels around the sun _____ a speed of 67,000 miles an hour.
17. "Did you enjoy your vacation?" "Not every minute, but _____ the whole, yes."
18. When you write a check, you have to write the amount _____ words and figures.

A

by 用於許多用語中，表示如何做某事。例如：

send something **by mail**　　　　　contact somebody **by phone** / **by e-mail** / **by fax**
意思是以郵寄的方式寄出某物　　意思是以電話/電子郵件/傳真聯絡某人
do something **by hand**　　　　　pay **by check** / **by credit card**
意思是以手工做某事　　　　　　意思是以支票、信用卡付款

- Can I pay **by credit card**?
- You can contact me **by phone**, **by fax**, or **by e-mail**.

但是付現必須用 **pay cash** 或 **pay in cash** (而非 by cash)。

此外，表示某事因為疏忽/意外/偶然而發生也用 **by**，如 **by mistake** / **by accident** / **by chance**：

- We hadn't arranged to meet. We met **by chance**.

但是表示故意做某事則用 **on**，如 do something **on purpose**：

- I didn't do it **on purpose**. It was an accident.

在上述 **by** + 名詞的用法中，名詞前不可以加 a 或 the。例如，我們說 by chance / by check
等，而不是 by the chance / by a check)。

B

by 也用於表達某人以何種方式到達某處：

by car / **by train** / **by plane** / **by boat** / **by ship** / **by bus** / **by bike** 等
by road / **by rail** / **by air** / **by sea** / **by subway**

- Joanne usually goes to work **by bus**.
- Do you prefer to travel **by plane** or **by train**?

但是表示步行則用 **on foot**：

- Did you come here **by car** or **on foot**?

在上述 **by** + 名詞的用法中，名詞前面不可以加 a/the/my 等，所以不可以說 **by my car** /
the train / **a taxi** 等。比較下列用法：

by car　　但是　**in my** car (並非 by my car)
by train　但是　**on the** train (並非 by the train)

in 用於轎車和計程車：

- They didn't come **in their car**. They came **in a taxi**.

on 用於腳踏車與大眾交通工具(例如，公車、火車等)：

- We came **on the 6:45 train**.

C

被動句也用於表達某事是由某人所做或由某事所造成的情況：

- Have you ever been bitten **by a dog**?
- The program was watched **by millions of people**.

比較被動句中 **by** 與 **with** 的用法：

- The door must have been opened **with a key**. (並非 by a key)
  (有人用鑰匙開了門)
- The door must have been opened **by somebody** with a key.

by 用於表達「由某人所寫、所創作」，例如 a play **by Shakespeare** / a painting **by Rembrandt** / a
novel **by Tolstoy** 等：

- Have you read anything **by** Ernest Hemingway?

D

by 也用作 next to / beside 表示在…旁邊之意：

- Come and sit **by me**. (= beside me)
- "Where's the light switch?" "**By the door**."

light switch

E

by 也用於下面的用語：

- Claire's salary has just gone up **from** $3,000 a month **to**
  $3,300. So it has increased **by $300** / **by 10 percent**.
- Carl and Mike ran a 100-meter race. Carl won
  by about three meters.

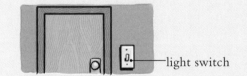

New Salary ——— $3,300/month
(新的薪資)　↑　(每月 3,300 元)
salary increased **by $300**
(薪資增加了 300 元)
Old Salary ——— $3,000/month
(舊的薪資)　　(每月 3,000 元)

Exercises

UNIT **125**

125.1 依各句題意，自下列名詞中選出適當的字，搭配介係詞 *by* 以完成句子。

~~chance~~   credit card   hand   mistake   satellite

1. We hadn't arranged to meet. We met __by chance__ .
2. I didn't mean to take your umbrella. I took it _____ .
3. Don't put the sweater in the washing machine. It has to be washed _____ .
4. I don't need cash. I can pay the bill _____ .
5. The two cities were connected _____ for a television program.

125.2 依各句題意，填入適當的介係詞 *by*、*in* 或 *on*。

1. Joanne usually goes to work __by__ bus.
2. I saw Jane this morning. She was _____ the bus.
3. How did you get here? Did you come _____ train?
4. I decided not to go _____ car. I went _____ my bike instead.
5. I didn't feel like walking home, so I came home _____ a taxi.
6. Sorry we're late. We missed the bus, so we had to come _____ foot.
7. How long does it take to cross the Atlantic _____ ship?

125.3 依下面範例所示，寫出三個句子描述某本書、某首歌、某幅畫、某部電影等為某人所作。

1. _War and Peace is a book by Tolstoy._
2. _Romeo and Juliet is a play by Shakespeare._
3. _____
4. _____
5. _____

125.4 依各句題意，填入適當的介係詞 *by*、*in*、*on* 或 *with*。

1. Have you ever been bitten __by__ a dog?
2. The plane was badly damaged _____ lightning.
3. We managed to put the fire out _____ a fire extinguisher.
4. Who is that man standing _____ the window?
5. These photos were taken _____ a friend of mine.
6. I don't mind going _____ car, but I don't want to go _____ your car.
7. There was a small table _____ the bed _____ a lamp and a clock _____ it.

125.5 請找出下面各句中的錯誤，並加以更正。

1. Did you come here (by Kate's car) or yours?   _in Kate's car_
2. I don't like traveling on bus.   _____
3. These photographs were taken by a very good camera.   _____
4. I know this music is from Beethoven, but I can't remember what it's called.   _____
5. I couldn't pay by cash – I didn't have any money on me.   _____
6. We lost the game only because of a mistake of one of our players.   _____

125.6 依各句題意，以 *by* 完成各句。

1. Claire's salary was $2,000 a month. Now it is $2,200.
   Her salary _has increased by $200 a month._
2. My daily newspaper used to cost a dollar. Starting today, it will cost $1.25.
   The price has gone up _____
3. There was an election. Helen won. She got 25 votes and Norman got 23.
   Helen won _____
4. I went to Kate's house to see her, but she had gone out five minutes before I arrived.
   I missed _____

補充練習 34 (315–316 頁)251

名詞 + 介係詞
(reason for、cause of 等)

A 名詞 + for...

a **check FOR** (a sum of money) 意思是「(一筆⋯的)支票」:
- They sent me **a check for** $200.

a **demand** / a **need FOR** ... 意思是「⋯之需求」:
- The company closed down because there wasn't enough **demand for** its product.
- There's no excuse for behavior like that. There's no **need for** it.

a **reason FOR** ... 意思是「⋯的理由」:
- The train was late, but nobody knew the **reason for** the delay. (並非 reason of)

B 名詞 + of...

an **advantage** / a **disadvantage OF** ... 意思是「⋯的優/缺點」:
- The **advantage of living alone** is that you can do what you like.

但是在 **there is** an advantage **to** (或 **in**) doing something 的句型中則用 **to** 或 **in** 而不用 of:
- **There are** many advantages **to** living alone. (或 ... **in** living alone)

a **cause OF** ... 意思是「⋯之原因」:
- The **cause of** the explosion is unknown.

a **photo** / a **picture** / a **map** / a **plan** / a **drawing**, etc. 意思是「⋯之相片/圖片/地圖/計畫/圖畫等」:
- Rachel showed me some **photos of** her family.
- I had a **map of** the town, so I was able to find my way around.

C 名詞 + in...

an **increase** / a **decrease** / a **rise** / a **drop IN** (價錢、銷售量等):
- There has been an **increase in** the number of traffic accidents recently.
- Last year was a bad one for the company. There was a big **drop in** sales.

D 名詞 + to ... /toward ...

damage TO ... 意思是「⋯之損害」:
- The accident was my fault, so I had to pay for the **damage to** the other car.

an **invitation TO** ... (a party / a wedding, etc.) 意思是(聚會、婚禮等)之邀請:
- Did you get an **invitation to** the party?

a **solution TO** (a problem) / a **key TO** (a door) / an **answer TO** (a question) /
a **reply TO** (a letter) / a **reaction TO** ... 意思是問題的解決之道/門的鑰匙/問題的答案/信件的
回覆/對⋯的反應:
- I hope we find a **solution to** the problem. (並非 a solution of the problem)
- I was surprised at her **reaction to** my suggestion.

an **attitude TOWARD** ... 意思是對於⋯之態度:
- His **attitude toward** his job is very negative.

E 名詞 + with ... / between ...

a **relationship** / a **connection** / contact **WITH** ... 意思是與⋯之關係/關聯/接觸:
- Do you have a good **relationship with** your parents?
- The police want to question a man in **connection with** the robbery.

但是 a **relationship** / a **connection** / contact / a **difference BETWEEN** two things
or people 則是指兩件事或兩者之間的關係/關聯/接觸/差別:
- The police believe that there is no **connection between** the two crimes.
- There are some **differences between** British and American English.

Exercises

126.1 依照範例所示，以適當的介係詞片語改寫句子，使改寫後的句子與原句意思一樣。

1. What caused the explosion?
   What was the cause _of the explosion_ ?
2. We're trying to solve the problem.
   We're trying to find a solution _____ .
3. Sue gets along well with her brother.
   Sue has a good relationship _____ .
4. The cost of living has gone up a lot.
   There has been a big increase _____ .
5. I don't know how to answer your question.
   I can't think of an answer _____ .
6. I don't think that a new road is necessary.
   I don't think there is any need _____ .
7. I think that working at home has many advantages.
   I think that there are many advantages _____ .
8. The number of people without jobs fell last month.
   Last month there was a drop _____ .
9. Nobody wants to buy shoes like these any more.
   There is no demand _____ .
10. In what way is your job different from mine?
    What is the difference _____ ?

126.2 依各句題意，自下列名詞中選出適當者，配合正確的介係詞填入句子。

cause	connection	contact	damage	invitation
key	~~map~~	pictures	reason	reply

1. On the wall there were some pictures and a _map of_ the world.
2. Thank you for the _____ your party next week.
3. Since she left home two years ago, Sofia has had little _____ her family.
4. I can't open this door. Do you have a _____ the other door?
5. The _____ the fire at the hotel last night is still unknown.
6. I e-mailed Jim last week, but I still haven't received a _____ my message.
7. The two companies are completely independent. There is no _____ them.
8. Jane showed me some old _____ the city the way it looked 100 years ago.
9. Carol has decided to quit her job. I don't know her _____ doing this.
10. It wasn't a bad accident. The _____ the car wasn't serious.

126.3 依各句題意，填入正確的介係詞。

1. There are some differences _between_ British and American English.
2. Money isn't the solution _____ every problem.
3. There has been an increase _____ the amount of traffic using this road.
4. When I opened the envelope, I was delighted to find a check _____ $500.
5. The advantage _____ having a car is that you don't have to rely on public transportation.
6. There are many advantages _____ being able to speak a foreign language.
7. Everything can be explained. There's a reason _____ everything.
8. When Paul left home, his attitude _____ his parents seemed to change.
9. Ben and I used to be good friends, but I don't have much contact _____ him now.
10. There has been a sharp rise _____ property values in the past few years.
11. What was Ann's reaction _____ the news?
12. If I give you the camera, can you take a picture _____ me?
13. The company has rejected the workers' demands _____ an increase _____ pay.
14. What was the answer _____ question 3 on the test?
15. The fact that Jane was offered a job has no connection _____ the fact that she is a friend of the managing director.

形容詞 + 介係詞 1

A

It was **nice of** you to . . .

注意在此句型中形容詞nice / kind / good / generous / polite / stupid / silly 等之後的介係詞為 **OF** + somebody (+ to do something)，意思是某人做某事是很仁慈(或大方等)的：
- Thank you. It was very **kind of** you to help me.
- It is **stupid of** me to go out without a coat in such cold weather.

但是在 nice / kind / good / generous / polite / rude / friendly / cruel 等形容詞 + **TO** + somebody 的句型中，介係詞則為 to，例如：
- They have always been very **nice to** me. (並非 with me)
- Why were you so **unfriendly to** Lucy?

B

形容詞 + **about / with / at**

furious / angry / mad / upset ABOUT something
- Max is really **angry about** what his brother said.

mad	**AT**	
upset	**WITH**	somebody **FOR** doing something
furious / angry	**AT / WITH**	

- My parents are **mad at** me **for** disobeying them.
- Are you **upset with** me **for** being late?
- Pat's **furious with** me **for** telling her secret. (或 **furious at** me)

excited / worried / upset / nervous / happy, etc. **ABOUT** 某個情況：
- Are you **excited about** going away next week?
- Lisa is **upset about** not being invited to the party.

delighted / pleased / satisfied / happy / disappointed WITH 你所收到的東西或是某事的結果：
- I was very **pleased with** the present you gave me.
- Were you **happy with** your exam results?

C

形容詞 + **at / by / with**

surprised / shocked / amazed / astonished AT / BY something
- Everybody was **surprised AT** (或 **BY**) the news.
- I hope you weren't **shocked BY** (或 **AT**) what I said.

impressed WITH / BY somebody/something
- I'm very **impressed with** (或 **by**) her English. It's very good.

fed up / bored WITH something
- I don't enjoy my job any more. I'm **fed up with** it. / I'm **bored with** it.

D

sorry about / for

sorry ABOUT 某個情況或發生的某件事：
- I'm **sorry about** the mess. I'll clean it up later.
- We're all **sorry about** Julie losing her job.

sorry FOR / ABOUT 你所做的事：
- Alex is very **sorry for** what he said. (或 **sorry about** what he said)
- I'm **sorry for** shouting at you yesterday. (或 **sorry about** shouting)

也可以用 I'm sorry I (did something) 的句型：
- I'm **sorry I shouted** at you yesterday.

feel / be sorry FOR 處在不好的情況下的某個人：
- I **feel sorry for** Matt. He's had a lot of bad luck. (並非 I feel sorry about Matt)

介係詞 + -ing Unit 58　形容詞 + to Unit 63　*sorry to . . . / sorry for . . .* Unit 64C　形容詞 + 介係詞 2 Unit 128

127.1 依各題的對話內容，以括號中的字，配合 *nice of* ... , *kind of* ... 的句型以完成句子。

1. I went out in the cold without a coat.
2. Sue offered to drive me to the airport.
3. I needed money and Tom gave me some.

4. They didn't invite us to their party.

5. Can I help you with your luggage?
6. Kevin didn't thank me for the present.

7. They've had an argument and now they refuse to speak to each other.

(silly) _That was silly of you._

(nice) That was _____ her.

(generous) That _____

(not very nice) That _____

(very kind) _____ you.

(not very polite) _____

(a little childish) _____

127.2 依各句題意，自下列形容詞中選出適當者，配合正確的介係詞以完成各句。

astonished   bored   ~~excited~~   impressed   kind   nervous   sorry   upset

1. Are you _excited about_ going away next week?
2. Thank you for all your help. You've been very _____ me.
3. I wouldn't want to be in her position. I feel _____ her.
4. I'm really _____ taking my driver's test. I hope I don't fail.
5. Why do you always get so _____ things that don't matter?
6. I wasn't very _____ the service at the restaurant. We had to wait ages before our food arrived.
7. Ben isn't very happy at college. He says he's _____ the classes he's taking.
8. I had never seen so many people before. I was _____ the crowds.

127.3 依各句題意，填入正確的介係詞。

1. I was delighted _with_ the present you gave me.
2. It was very nice _____ you to do my shopping for me. Thank you very much.
3. Why are you always so rude _____ your parents? Can't you be nice _____ them?
4. It was careless _____ you to leave the door unlocked when you went out.
5. They didn't reply to our letter, which wasn't very polite _____ them.
6. We always have the same food every day. I'm fed up _____ it.
7. I can't understand people who are cruel _____ animals.
8. We enjoyed our vacation, but we were a little disappointed _____ the hotel.
9. I was surprised _____ the way he behaved. It was completely out of character.
10. I've been trying to learn Spanish, but I'm not very satisfied _____ my progress.
11. Linda doesn't look very well. I'm worried _____ her.
12. Are you angry _____ what happened?
13. I'm sorry _____ what I did. I hope you're not mad _____ me.
14. The people next door are furious _____ us _____ making so much noise last night.
15. Jill starts her new job next week. She's quite excited _____ it.
16. I'm sorry _____ the smell of paint in this room. I'm redecorating it.
17. I was shocked _____ what I saw. I'd never seen anything like it before.
18. The man we interviewed for the job was intelligent, but we weren't very impressed _____ his appearance.
19. Are you still upset _____ what I said to you yesterday?
20. He said he was sorry _____ the situation, but there was nothing he could do.
21. I felt sorry _____ the children when we went on vacation. It rained every day and they had to spend most of the time indoors.

形容詞 + 介係詞 2

A 形容詞 + of (1)

afraid / frightened / terrified / scared OF . . .
- ■ "Are you **afraid of** spiders?" "Yes, I'm **terrified of** them."

fond / proud / ashamed / jealous / envious OF . . .
- ■ Why are you always so **jealous of** other people?

suspicious / critical / tolerant OF . . .
- ■ He didn't trust me. He was **suspicious of** my intentions.

B 形容詞 + of (2)

aware / conscious OF . . .
- ■ "Did you know he was married?" "No, I wasn't **aware of** that."

capable / incapable OF . . .
- ■ I'm sure you are **capable of** passing the exam.

full / short OF . . .
- ■ The letter I wrote was **full of** mistakes. (並非 full with)
- ■ I'm a little **short of** money. Can you lend me some?

typical OF . . .
- ■ He's late again. It's **typical of** him to keep everybody waiting.

tired / sick OF . . .
- ■ Come on, let's go! I'm **tired of** waiting. (= I've had enough of waiting)

certain / sure OF 或 **ABOUT** . . .
- ■ I think she's arriving tonight, but I'm not **sure of** that.   或   . . . sure **about** that.

C 形容詞 + at / to / from / in / on / with / for

good / bad / excellent / better / hopeless 等 **AT** . . .
- ■ I'm not very **good at** repairing things. (並非 good in repairing things)

married / engaged TO . . .
- ■ Linda is **married to** an American. (並非 married with)

但是 Linda is married **with three children**. (= she is married and has three children)

similar TO . . .
- ■ Your writing is **similar to** mine.

different FROM 或 **different THAN** . . .
- ■ The film was **different from** what I'd expected. (或 **different than** what I'd expected.)

interested IN . . .
- ■ Are you **interested in** art?

dependent ON . . . (但是 **independent OF** . . .)
- ■ I don't want to be **dependent on** anybody.

crowded WITH (people, etc.)
- ■ The streets were **crowded with** tourists. (但是 **full of** tourists)

famous FOR . . .
- ■ The Italian city of Florence is **famous for** its art treasures.

responsible FOR . . .
- ■ Who was **responsible for** all that noise last night?

介係詞 + -ing Unit 58   *afraid of / to* . . . Unit 64A   形容詞+介係詞 1 Unit 127   英式英文 附錄 7

Exercises

128.1 以適當的介係詞片語改寫句子,使改寫後的句子與原句的意思一樣。

1. There were lots of tourists in the streets.   The streets were crowded _with tourists_ .
2. There was a lot of furniture in the room.   The room was full _____ .
3. Who made this mess?   Who is responsible _____ ?
4. We don't have enough time.   We're a little short _____ .
5. I'm not a very good tennis player.   I'm not very good _____ .
6. Catherine's husband is Russian.   Catherine is married _____ .
7. I don't trust Robert.   I'm suspicious _____ .
8. My problem is not the same as yours.   My problem is different _____ .

128.2 依各句題意,自下列形容詞中選出適當者,並配合正確的介係詞以完成各句。

afraid   different   interested   proud   responsible   similar   ~~sure~~

1. I think she's arriving tonight, but I'm not _sure of_ that.
2. Your camera is _____ mine, but it isn't exactly the same.
3. Don't worry. I'll take care of you. There's nothing to be _____ .
4. I never watch the news on television. I'm not _____ the news.
5. The editor is the person who is _____ what appears in a newspaper.
6. Sarah loves gardening. She's very _____ her garden and loves showing it to visitors.
7. I was surprised when I met Lisa for the first time. She was _____ what I expected.

128.3 依各句題意,填入正確的介係詞。

1. The letter I wrote was full _of_ mistakes.
2. My hometown is not an especially interesting place. It's not famous _____ anything.
3. Kate is very fond _____ her younger brother.
4. I don't like climbing ladders. I'm scared _____ heights.
5. You look bored. You don't seem interested _____ what I'm saying.
6. Did you know that Liz is engaged _____ a friend of mine?
7. I'm not ashamed _____ what I did. In fact I'm quite proud _____ it.
8. Mark has no money of his own. He's totally dependent _____ his parents.
9. These days everybody is aware _____ the dangers of smoking.
10. The station platform was crowded _____ people waiting for the train.
11. Sue is much more successful than I am. Sometimes I feel a little jealous _____ her.
12. I'm tired _____ doing the same thing every day. I need a change.
13. Do you know anyone who might be interested _____ buying an old car?
14. We've got plenty to eat. The fridge is full ____ food.
15. She is a very honest person. I don't think she is capable _____ telling a lie.
16. Helen works hard and she's extremely good _____ her job.
17. I'm not surprised he changed his mind at the last minute. That's typical _____ him.
18. The woman Sam is married _____ runs a software business.
19. We're short _____ staff in our office at the moment. We need more people to do the work.

128.4 你對下列各題括號中所描述的事情是否在行呢?請依照你自己的情況從下列形容詞片語中選出適當者, 回答下面的問題。

good   pretty good   not very good   hopeless

1. (repairing things) _I'm not very good at repairing things._
2. (telling jokes) _____
3. (mathematics) _____
4. (remembering names) _____

A　動詞 + to

talk / speak TO somebody (也可以用 **with**，但較少使用)
- ■ Who was that man you were **talking to**?

listen TO . . .
- ■ We spent the evening **listening to** music. (並非 listening music)

apologize TO somebody (for . . .)
- ■ They **apologized to me** for what happened. (並非 They apologized me)

explain something **TO** somebody
- ■ Can you **explain** this word **to me**? (並非 explain me this word)

explain / describe (**to** somebody) what/how/why . . .
- ■ I **explained to them** why I was worried. (並非 I explained them)
- ■ Let me **describe to you** what I saw. (並非 Let me describe you)

B　下列動詞不可與 to 一起使用：

call / phone / telephone somebody
- ■ Did you **call your father** yesterday? (並非 call to your father)

answer somebody/something
- ■ He refused to **answer my question**. (並非 answer to my question)

ask somebody
- ■ Can I **ask you** a question? (並非 ask to you)

thank somebody (for something)
- ■ He **thanked me** for helping him. (並非 He thanked to me)

C　動詞 + at

look / stare / glance AT . . . , **have a look / take a look AT** . . .
- ■ Why are you **looking at** me like that?

laugh AT . . .
- ■ I look stupid with this haircut. Everybody will **laugh at** me.

aim / point (something) **AT** . . . , **shoot / fire** (a gun) **AT** . . .
- ■ Don't **point** that knife **at** me. It's dangerous.
- ■ We saw someone with a gun **shooting at** birds, but he didn't hit any.

D　有些動詞可以與 at 或 to 一起使用，但意思不同。例如：

shout AT somebody (當某人生氣時)
- ■ He got very angry and started **shouting at** me.

shout TO somebody (為了讓對方聽得見)
- ■ He **shouted to** me from the other side of the street.

throw something **AT** somebody/something (為了打中對方)
- ■ Somebody **threw** an egg **at** the politician.

throw something **TO** somebody (為了讓對方接住)
- ■ Lisa shouted "Catch!" and **threw** the keys **to** me from the window.

動詞+介係詞2–4 Unit 130 至 Unit 132　*ask for* Unit 130C　*apologize for / thank somebody for* Unit 132B
其他動詞 + *to* Unit 133D　英式英文 附錄 7

Exercises

129.1 以 ***Can you explain . . . ?*** 的句型，依下列各句括號內的字寫出問句，請求他人為你解釋你不了解的事。

1. (I don't understand this word.)
   Can you explain this word to me?

2. (I don't understand what you mean.)
   Can you explain to me what you mean?

3. (I don't understand this question.)
   Can you explain _____

4. (I don't understand the problem.)
   Can _____

5. (I don't understand how this machine works.)
   _____

6. (I don't understand what I have to do.)
   _____

129.2 依各句題意，判斷是否需要填入介係詞 ***to***；若不需任何介係詞則保留空白。

1. I know who she is, but I've never spoken __to__ her.
2. Why didn't you answer __–__ my letter?
3. I like to listen _____ the radio while I'm having breakfast.
4. We'd better call _____ the restaurant to reserve a table.
5. "Did Mike apologize _____ you?" "Yes, he said he was very sorry."
6. I explained _____ everybody the reasons for my decision.
7. I thanked _____ everybody for all the help they had given me.
8. Ask me what you like, and I'll try and answer _____ your questions.
9. Mike described _____ me exactly what happened.
10. Karen won't be able to help you, so there's no point in asking _____ her.

129.3 依各句題意，自下列動詞中選出適當者，以正確的動詞形式並配合正確的介係詞以完成句子。

~~explain~~   glance   ~~laugh~~   listen   point   speak   throw   throw

1. I look stupid with this haircut. Everybody will _laugh at_ me.
2. I don't understand this. Can you _explain_ it _to_ me?
3. Sue and Kevin had an argument and now they're not _____ each other.
4. Be careful with those scissors! Don't _____ them _____ me!
5. I _____ my watch to see what time it was.
6. Please _____ me! I've got something important to tell you.
7. Don't _____ stones _____ the birds! It's cruel.
8. If you don't want that sandwich, _____ it   the birds They'll eat it.

129.4 依各句題意，填入介係詞 ***to*** 或 ***at***。

1. Lisa shouted, "Catch!" and threw the keys __to__ me from the window.
2. Look _____ these flowers. Aren't they pretty?
3. Please don't shout _____ me! Try to calm down.
4. I saw Sue as I was riding along the road. I shouted _____ her, but she didn't hear me.
5. Don't listen _____ what he says. He doesn't know what he's talking about.
6. What's so funny? What are you laughing _____ ?
7. Do you think I could have a look _____ your magazine, please?
8. I'm a little lonely. I need somebody to talk _____ .
9. She was so angry she threw a book _____ the wall.
10. The woman sitting opposite me on the train kept staring _____ me.
11. Can I speak _____ you a moment? There's something I want to ask you.

動詞 + 介係詞 2　　about / for / of / after

A　動詞 + about

talk / read / know ABOUT . . . , **tell** somebody **ABOUT** . . .
- We **talked about** a lot of things at the meeting.

我們說 **have a discussion ABOUT** something，但是 **discuss** something 後則不需有介係詞：
- We **had a discussion about** what we should do.
- We **discussed** a lot of things at the meeting. (並非 discussed about)

do something **ABOUT** something 意思是做某事以便改善某一個不好的情況：
- If you're worried about the problem, you should **do** something **about** it.

B　care about、care for 與 take care of

care ABOUT somebody/something 意思是認為某人/某事是重要的：
- He's very selfish. He doesn't **care about** other people.

care what/where/how . . . 等之用法中，不需介係詞 about
- You can do what you like. I don't **care what** you do.

care FOR somebody/something
意思是喜歡某事(通常用於問句與否定句)：
- Would you **care for** a cup of coffee? (= Would you like . . . ?)
- I don't **care for** very hot weather. (= I don't like . . .)

意思是確定某人安好無恙：
- Alan is 85 and lives alone. He needs somebody to **care for** him.

take care OF . . . 意思是照顧；確定某人/某事處於安全、良好的狀況，為某事負責：
- John gave up his job to **take care of** his elderly parents.
- I'll **take care of** all the travel arrangements – you don't need to do anything.

C　動詞 + for

ask (somebody) **FOR** . . .
- I wrote to the company **asking** them **for** more information about the job.

但是 I **asked** him **the way** to . . . , She **asked** me **my name**. (不需介係詞)

apply (**TO** 人、公司等) **FOR** 工作等：
- I think you'd be good at this job. Why don't you **apply for** it?

wait FOR . . .
- Don't **wait for** me. I'll join you later.
- I'm not going out yet. I'm **waiting for** the rain to stop.

search (人、地點、包包等) **FOR** . . .
- I've **searched** the house **for** my keys, but I still can't find them.

leave (a place) **FOR** another place 意思是離開某地前往他處：
- I haven't seen her since she **left** (home) **for** the office this morning. (並非 left to the office)

D　look for 與 look after

look FOR . . . 意思是「尋找」：
- I've lost my keys. Can you help me **look for** them?

look AFTER . . . 意思是「照顧」：
- Alan is 85 and lives alone. He needs somebody to **look after** him. (並非 look for)
- You can borrow this book if you promise to **look after** it.

動詞 + *about* / *of* (*think* / *hear* 等) Unit 131　其他動詞 + *for* Unit 132B

Exercises

130.1 依各句題意，填入正確的介係詞；若不需任何介係詞，則保留空白。

1. I'm not going out yet. I'm waiting _for_ the rain to stop.
2. I couldn't find the street I was looking for, so I stopped someone to ask _____ directions.
3. I've applied _____ a job at the factory. I don't know if I'll get it.
4. I've applied _____ three colleges. I hope one of them accepts me.
5. I've searched everywhere _____ John, but I haven't been able to find him.
6. I don't want to talk _____ what happened last night. Let's forget it.
7. I don't want to discuss _____ what happened last night. Let's forget it.
8. We had an interesting discussion _____ the problem, but we didn't reach a decision.
9. We discussed _____ the problem, but we didn't reach a decision.
10. I don't want to go out yet. I'm waiting _____ the mail to arrive.
11. Ken and Sonia are touring Italy. They're in Rome right now, but tomorrow they leave _____ Venice.
12. The roof of the house is in very bad condition. I think we ought to do something _____ it.
13. We waited _____ Steve for half an hour, but he never came.
14. Tomorrow morning I have to catch a plane. I'm leaving my house _____ the airport at 7:30.

130.2 依各句題意，自下列動詞中選出適當者，以正確的動詞形式並配合正確的介係詞完成各句。

apply   ask   do   leave   look   ~~search~~   talk   wait

1. Police are _searching for_ the man who escaped from prison.
2. We're still _____ a reply to our letter. We haven't heard anything yet.
3. I think Ben likes his job, but he doesn't _____ it much.
4. When I'd finished my meal, I _____ the waiter _____ the check.
5. Cathy is unemployed. She has _____ several jobs, but she hasn't had any luck.
6. If something is wrong, why don't you _____ something _____ it?
7. Linda's car is very old, but it's in excellent condition. She _____ it very well.
8. Diane is from Boston, but now she lives in Paris. She _____ Boston _____ Paris when she was 19.

130.3 依各句題意，在動詞 *care* 後填入適當的介係詞；若不需任何介係詞，則保留空白。

1. He's very selfish. He doesn't care _about_ other people.
2. Are you hungry? Would you care _____ something to eat?
3. She doesn't care _____ the exam. She doesn't care whether she passes or fails.
4. Please let me borrow your camera. I promise I'll take good care _____ it.
5. "Do you like this coat?"   "Not really. I don't care _____ the color."
6. Don't worry about the shopping. I'll take care _____ that.
7. I want to have a nice vacation. I don't care _____ the cost.
8. I want to have a nice vacation. I don't care _____ how much it costs.

130.4 依各句題意，填入 *look for* 或 *look after*；注意： *look* 需使用適當的動詞形式(*looks / looked / looking*)。

1. I _looked for_ my keys, but I couldn't find them anywhere.
2. Kate is _____ a job. I hope she finds one soon.
3. Who _____ you when you were sick?
4. I'm _____ Elizabeth. Have you seen her?
5. The parking lot was full, so we had to _____ somewhere else to park.
6. A babysitter is somebody who _____ other people's children.

A

dream ABOUT . . . (在睡覺時)
- I **dreamed about** you last night.

dream OF/ABOUT being something / doing something 意思是「想像」:
- Do you **dream of/about** being rich and famous?

(I) **wouldn't dream OF** doing something 意思是我絕對不會做某事:
- "Don't tell anyone what I said." "No, I **wouldn't dream of** it." (= I would never do it)

B

hear ABOUT . . . 意思是「聽說、被告知」:
- Did you **hear about** what happened at the club on Saturday night?

hear OF . . . 意思是知道某人/某事的存在:
- "Who is Tom Hart?" "I have no idea. I've never **heard of** him." (並非 heard from him)

hear FROM . . . 意思是接獲某人的信、電話或訊息:
- "Have you **heard from** Jane recently?" "Yes, she called a few days ago."

C

比較 **think ABOUT** 和 **think OF** . . . 的用法
think ABOUT something 意思是考慮某事,集中心思在某事上面:
- I've **thought about** what you said, and I've decided to take your advice.
- "Will you lend me the money?" "I'll **think about** it."

think OF something 意思是想到或想起某事:
- He told me his name, but I can't **think of** it now. (並非 think about it)
- That's a good idea. Why didn't I **think of** that? (並非 think about that)

think of 也可以用來詢問或表達意見:
- "What did you **think of** the film?" "I didn't **think** much **of** it." (我不是很喜歡那部電影)

有時候 **of** 或 **about** 意思差別不大,兩者均可以用:
- When I'm alone, I often **think of** (或 **about**) you.

think of / **think about** doing something 皆可用於描述未來可能的行動:
- My sister is **thinking of** (或 **about**) going to Canada. (她正在考慮)

D

remind somebody **ABOUT** . . . 意思是提醒某人不要忘記:
- I'm glad you **reminded** me **about** the meeting. I had completely forgotten about it.

remind somebody **OF** . . . 意思是使某人想起:
- This house **reminds** me **of** the one I lived in when I was a child.
- Look at this picture of Richard. Who does he **remind** you **of**?

E

complain (**TO** somebody) **ABOUT** . . . 意思是表達對某事不滿意:
- We **complained to** the manager of the restaurant **about** the food.

complain OF a pain, an illness 等,意思是表達有某種病痛:
- We called the doctor because George was **complaining of** a pain in his stomach.

F

warn somebody **ABOUT** 意思是警告某人某件事或某個人是危險的、不正常等:
- I knew he was a strange person. I had been **warned about** him. (並非 warned of him)
- Vicky **warned** me **about** the traffic. She said it would be bad.

warn somebody **ABOUT/OF** a danger 意思是向某人預警某件不好的事將有可能會發生:
- Scientists have **warned** us **about**/**of** the effects of global warming.

Exercises

131.1 依各句題意，填入正確的介係詞(*about*、*of* 或 *from*)。

1. Did you hear __*about*__ what happened at the party on Saturday?
2. "I had a strange dream last night." "Did you? What did you dream _____?"
3. Our neighbors complained _____ us _____ the noise we made last night.
4. Kevin was complaining _____ pains in his chest, so he went to the doctor.
5. I love this music. It reminds me _____ a warm day in spring.
6. He loves his job. He thinks _____ his job all the time, he dreams _____ it, he talks _____ it, and I'm sick of hearing _____ it.
7. I tried to remember the name of the book, but I couldn't think _____ it.
8. Jackie warned me _____ the water. She said it wasn't safe to drink.
9. We warned our children _____ the dangers of playing in the street.

131.2 依各句題意，自下列動詞中選出適當者，以正確的動詞的形式並配合正確的介係詞以完成各句。

complain	dream	hear	remind	remind	~~think~~	think	warn

1. That's a good idea. Why didn't I __*think of*__ that?
2. Bill is never satisfied. He is always _____ something.
3. I can't make a decision yet. I need time to _____ your proposal.
4. Before you go into the house, I should _____ you _____ the dog. He is very aggressive sometimes, so be careful.
5. She's not a well-known singer. Not many people have _____ her.
6. A: You wouldn't leave without telling me, would you?
   B: Of course not. I wouldn't _____ it.
7. I would have forgotten my appointment if Jane hadn't _____ me _____ it.
8. Do you see that man over there? Does he _____ you _____ anybody you know?

131.3 依各句題意，填入動詞 *hear* 或 *heard* 以及適當的介係詞。

1. I've never __*heard of*__ Tom Hart. Who is he?
2. "Did you _____ the accident last night?" "Yes, Vicky told me."
3. Jill used to call quite often, but I haven't _____ her for a long time now.
4. A: Have you _____ a writer called William Hudson?
   B: No, I don't think so. What sort of writer is he?
5. Thank you for your letter. It was good to _____ you again.
6. "Do you want to _____ our vacation?" "Not now. Tell me later."
7. I live in a small town in Texas. You've probably never _____ it.

131.4 依各句題意，填入 *think about* 或 *think of*，有些句子 *think about* 與 *think of* 皆適用；注意：需使用適當的動詞形式(*think/thinking/thought*)。

1. You look serious. What are you __*thinking about*__?
2. I like to have time to make decisions. I like to _____ things carefully.
3. I don't know what to get Sarah for her birthday. Can you _____ anything?
4. A: I've finished reading the book you lent me.
   B: You have? What did you _____ it? Did you like it?
5. We're _____ going out for dinner tonight. Would you like to come?
6. I don't really want to go out with Tom tonight. I'll have to _____ an excuse.
7. When I was offered the job, I didn't accept immediately. I went away and _____ it for a while. In the end I decided to take the job.
8. I don't _____ much _____ this coffee. It's like water.
9. Carol is very homesick. She's always _____ her family back home.

A　動詞 + of

accuse / suspect 某人 **OF** ...，意思是控訴/懷疑某人…：
- Sue **accused** me **of** being selfish.
- Some students were **suspected of** cheating on the exam.

approve / disapprove OF ...，意思是許可/核准某事：
- His parents don't **approve of** what he does, but they can't stop him.

die OF (或 **FROM**) 某種疾病等，意思是死於某種疾病：
- "What did he **die of**?" "A heart attack."

consist OF ...
- We had an enormous meal. It **consisted of** seven courses.

B　動詞 + for

pay (somebody) **FOR** ... 意思是為某人所買的東西付錢：
- I didn't have enough money to **pay for** the meal. (並非 pay the meal)

但是 **pay** a bill / a fine / tax / rent / a sum of money 等用法中，不需介係詞：
- I didn't have enough money to **pay the rent**.

thank / forgive somebody **FOR** ... 意思是因某事感謝/原諒某人：
- I'll never **forgive** them **for** what they did.

apologize (to somebody) **FOR** ... 意思是因某事向某人道歉：
- When I realized I was wrong, I **apologized** (to them) **for** my mistake.

blame somebody/something **FOR** ...，somebody is **to blame FOR** ... 意思是因某事怪罪某人：
- Everybody **blamed** me **for** the accident.
- Everybody said that I was **to blame for** the accident.

blame (a problem, etc.) **ON** ... 意思是將某事怪罪某人：
- Everybody **blamed** the accident **on** me.

C　動詞 + from

suffer FROM an illness, etc. ，意思是為疾病等所苦：
- The number of people **suffering from** heart disease has increased.

protect somebody/something **FROM** (或 **AGAINST**) ...，意思是保護某人免於或遠離某事：
- Sun block **protects** the skin **from** the sun. (或 ... **against** the sun.)

D　動詞 + on

depend / rely ON ... 意思是「依靠」、「取決於」：
- "What time will you be home?" "I don't know. It **depends on** the traffic."
- You can **rely on** Jill. She always keeps her promises.

depend (on) + when/where/how 等疑問詞，此種用法中，可以省略 on：
- "Are you going to buy it?" "It **depends how** much it is." (或 It depends **on** how much)

live ON 金錢/食物
- Michael's salary is very low. It isn't enough to **live on**.

congratulate / compliment somebody **ON** ...，意思是因某事恭喜/讚美某人：
- I **congratulated** her **on** being admitted to law school.

Exercises

132.1 依各句題意，以適當的介係詞片語完成第二個句子，使之與第一個句子意思相同。

1. Sue said I was selfish.
   Sue accused me ___of being selfish___.
2. The misunderstanding was my fault, so I apologized.
   I apologized _____.
3. Jane won the tournament, so I congratulated her.
   I congratulated Jane _____.
4. He has enemies, but he has a bodyguard to protect him.
   He has a bodyguard to protect him _____.
5. There are nine players on a baseball team.
   A baseball team consists _____.
6. Sandra eats only bread and eggs.
   She lives _____.

132.2 下列句子的動詞皆為 **blame**；請依題意以 **for** 或 **on** 完成第二個句子。

1. Liz said that what happened was Joe's fault.
   Liz blamed Joe ___for what happened___.
2. You always say everything is my fault.
   You always blame me _____.
3. Do you think the economic crisis is the fault of the government?
   Do you blame the government _____?
4. I think the increase in violent crime is the fault of television.
   I blame the increase in violent crime _____.

以 **blame for** 改寫第 3 句與第 4 句。

5. (3.) Do you think the government _____?
6. (4.) I think that _____.

132.3 依各句題意，自下列動詞中選出適當者，以正確的動詞形式並配合正確的介係詞以完成句子。

> **accuse   apologize   ~~approve~~   congratulate   depend   live   pay**

1. His parents don't ___approve of___ what he does, but they can't stop him.
2. When you went to the theater with Paul, who _____ the tickets?
3. It's a terrible feeling when you are _____ something you didn't do.
4. A: Are you going to the beach tomorrow?
   B: I hope so. It _____ the weather.
5. Things are very cheap there. You can _____ very little money.
6. When I saw David, I _____ him _____ passing his driving test.
7. You were very rude to Liz. Don't you think you should _____ her?

132.4 依各句題意，填入正確的介係詞；若不需介係詞，則保留空白。

1. Some students were suspected ___of___ cheating on the exam.
2. Sally is often sick. She suffers _____ very bad headaches.
3. You know that you can rely _____ me if you ever need any help.
4. It is terrible that some people are dying _____ hunger while others eat too much.
5. Are you going to apologize _____ what you did?
6. The accident was my fault, so I had to pay _____ the repairs.
7. I didn't have enough money to pay _____ the bill.
8. I complimented her _____ her English. She spoke very fluently, and her pronunciation was excellent.
9. She doesn't have a job. She depends _____ her parents for money.
10. I don't know whether I'll go out tonight. It depends _____ how I feel.
11. They wore warm clothes to protect themselves _____ the cold.
12. Cake consists mainly _____ sugar, flour, and butter.

動詞 + 介係詞 5　　in / into / with / to / on

A　動詞 + **in**

believe IN . . .
- Do you **believe in** God? (你相信上帝存在嗎?)
- I **believe in** saying what I think. (我相信說出我的想法是對的。)

但是 **believe** something 意思是「相信某事是真的」,而 **believe** somebody 意思則是「相信某人是說實話」:
- The story can't be true. I don't **believe it**. (並非 believe in it)

specialize IN . . .
- Helen is a lawyer. She **specializes in** corporate law.

succeed IN . . .
- I hope you **succeed in** finding the job you want.

B　動詞 + **into**

break INTO . . .
- Our house was **broken into** a few days ago, but nothing was stolen.

crash / drive / bump / run INTO . . .
- He lost control of the car and **crashed into** a wall.

divide / cut / split something **INTO** two or more parts,意思是將某物分成兩個或多個部分:
- The book is **divided into** three parts.

translate a book, etc., **FROM** one language **INTO** another,意思是將書等從一種語言翻譯成另一種語言:
- Ernest Hemingway's books have been **translated into** many languages.

C　動詞 + **with**

collide WITH . . .
- There was an accident this morning. A bus **collided with** a car.

fill something **WITH** . . . (**full of** . . . 的用法,參見 Unit 128B)
- Take this pot and **fill** it **with** water.

provide / supply somebody **WITH** . . .
- The school **provides** all its students **with** books.

D　動詞 + **to**

happen TO . . .
- What **happened to** that gold watch you used to have? (= where is it now?)

invite somebody **TO** a party / a wedding 等
- They only **invited** a few people **to** their wedding.

prefer one thing/person **TO** another
- I **prefer** tea **to** coffee.

E　動詞 + **on**

concentrate ON . . .
- Don't look out the window. **Concentrate on** your work.

insist ON . . .
- I wanted to go alone, but some friends of mine **insisted on** coming with me.

spend (money) **ON** . . .
- How much do you **spend on** food each week?

Exercises

133.1 完成下列各題中的第二個句子，使之與第一個句子的意思相同。

1. There was a collision between a bus and a car.
   A bus collided _with a car_____.
2. I don't mind big cities, but I prefer small towns.
   I prefer _____.
3. I got all the information I needed from Jane.
   Jane provided me _____.
4. This morning I bought a pair of shoes, which cost $70.
   This morning I spent _____.

133.2 依各句題意，自下列動詞中選出適當者，以正確的動詞形式並配合正確的介係詞完成句子。

believe   concentrate   divide   drive   fill   happen   ~~insist~~   invite   succeed

1. I wanted to go alone, but Sue _insisted on__ coming with me.
2. I haven't seen Mike for ages. I wonder what has _____ him.
3. We've been _____ the party, but unfortunately we can't go.
4. It's a very large house. It's _____ four apartments.
5. I don't _____ ghosts. I think people only imagine that they see them.
6. Steve gave me an empty bucket and told me to _____ it _____ water.
7. I was driving along when the car in front of me stopped suddenly. Unfortunately I couldn't stop in time and _____ the back of it.
8. Don't try and do two things together. _____ one thing at a time.
9. It wasn't easy, but in the end we _____ finding a solution to the problem.

133.3 依各句題意，填入正確的介係詞；若不需要介係詞，則保留空白。

1. The school provides all its students _with__ books.
2. A strange thing happened _____ me a few days ago.
3. Mark decided to give up sports so that he could concentrate _____ his studies.
4. I don't believe _____ working very hard. It's not worth it.
5. My present job isn't wonderful, but I prefer it _____ what I did before.
6. I hope you succeed _____ getting what you want.
7. As I was coming out of the room, I collided _____ somebody who was coming in.
8. There was an awful noise as the car crashed _____ a tree.
9. Patrick is a photographer. He specializes _____ sports photography.
10. Do you spend much money _____ clothes?
11. The country is divided _____ six regions.
12. I prefer traveling by train _____ driving. It's much more pleasant.
13. I was amazed when Joe walked into the room. I couldn't believe _____ it.
14. Somebody broke _____ my car and stole the radio.
15. I was very cold, but Tom insisted _____ keeping the window open.
16. Some words are difficult to translate _____ one language _____ another.
17. What happened _____ the money I lent you? What did you spend it _____ ?
18. The teacher decided to split the class _____ four groups.
19. I filled the tank, but unfortunately I filled it _____ the wrong kind of gas.

133.4 依你自己的意思，使用適當的介係詞以完成各句。

1. I wanted to go out alone, but my friend insisted _on coming with me_____.
2. I spend a lot of money _____.
3. I saw the accident. The car crashed _____.
4. Chris prefers basketball _____.
5. Shakespeare's plays have been translated _____.

片語動詞 1　概論

A

有些動詞經常與下面的字一起使用：

in	on	up	away	around	about	over		by
out	off	down	back	through	along	forward	

所以 **look out / get on / take off / run away** 等皆為片語動詞。

on/off/out 經常與表移動之動詞一起使用。例如：

get on	■	The bus was full. We couldn't **get on**.
drive off	■	A woman got into the car and **drove off**.
come back	■	Sally is leaving tomorrow and **coming back** on Saturday.
turn around	■	When I touched him on the shoulder, he **turned around**.

片語動詞中的第二個字(**on/off/out** 等)，常賦予前面的動詞特殊的意思。例如：

break down	■	Sorry I'm late. The car **broke down**. (引擎壞了)
take off	■	It was my first flight. I was nervous as the plane **took off**. (飛入空中)
run out	■	We don't have any more milk. We **ran out**. (用/喝完了)
get along	■	My brother and I **get along** well. (對待彼此很友善/相處得很好)
get by	■	My French isn't very good, but it's enough to **get by**. (應付得來。)

其它片語動詞的用法參見 Unit 135 至 Unit 142。

B

有時候片語動詞後會加介係詞。例如：

片語動詞	介係詞		
run away	**from**	■	Why did you **run away from** me?
keep up	**with**	■	You're walking too fast. I can't **keep up with** you.
look up	**at**	■	We **looked up at** the plane as it flew above us.
look forward	**to**	■	Are you **looking forward to** the weekend?
get along	**with**	■	Do you **get along with** your boss?

C

有時候片語動詞可以有受詞，其受詞通常可以置於兩種位置。

我們可以說：

I **turned on** the light.　或　I **turned** the light **on**.
　　　　受詞　　　　　　　　　　　　　　受詞

如果受詞為代名詞 (**it/them/me/him** 等)，則只可以置於片語動詞中，即動詞與第二個字之間：

I **turned** it **on**. (並非 I turned on it)

其他例子如下：

■ Could you { **fill out** this form? / **fill** this form **out**? }

但是　They gave me a form and told me to **fill it out**. (並非 fill out it)

■ Don't { **throw away** this postcard. / **throw** this postcard **away**. }

但是　I want to keep this postcard, so don't **throw it away**. (並非 throw away it)

■ I'm going to { **take off** my shoes. / **take** my shoes **off**. }

但是　These shoes are uncomfortable. I'm going to **take them off**. (並非 take off them)

■ Don't { **wake up** the baby. / **wake** the baby **up**. }

但是　The baby is asleep. Don't **wake her up**. (並非 wake up her)

134.1 依各句題意，自 A 表與 B 表中各選出一個適當的字，以完成句子。動詞需使用正確的形式；A 表與 B 表中的字可重複使用。

A | **fly   get   go   look   sit   run** | B | **away   by   down   on   out   around   up**

1. The bus was full. We couldn't __*get on*__ .
2. I've been standing for the last two hours. I'm going to _____ for a bit.
3. A cat tried to catch the bird, but the bird _____ just in time.
4. We were trapped in the building. We couldn't _____ .
5. "Did you get fish at the store?" "I couldn't. They had _____ ."
6. "Do you speak German?" "Not very well, but I can _____ ."
7. The cost of living is higher now. Prices have _____ a lot.
8. I thought there was somebody behind me, but when I _____ , there was nobody there.

134.2 依各句題意，自 A 表與 B 表中各選出一個適當的字，以完成句子。A 表與 B 表中的字可重複使用。

A | **along   away   back   forward   in   up** | B | **at   through   to   with**

1. You're walking too fast. I can't keep __*up with*__ you.
2. My vacation is nearly over. Next week I'll be _____ work.
3. We went _____ the top floor of the building to admire the view.
4. Are you looking _____ the party next week?
5. There was a bank robbery last week. The robbers got _____ $50,000.
6. I love to look _____ the stars in the sky at night.
7. I was sitting in the kitchen when suddenly a bird flew _____ the open window.
8. "Why did Sally quit her job?" "She didn't get _____ her co-workers."

134.3 依各句題意，自下列片語動詞中選出適當者，以適當的形式與受詞 (*it* / *them* / *me*) 完成句子。

~~**fill out**~~   **get out   give back   turn on   take off   wake up**

1. They gave me a form and told me to __*fill it out*__ .
2. I'm going to bed now. Can you _____ at 6:30?
3. I've got something in my eye and I can't _____ .
4. I don't like it when people borrow things and don't _____ .
5. I want to use the heater. How do I _____ ?
6. My shoes are dirty. I'd better _____ before going into the house.

134.4 依你自己的意思，用名詞 (*this newspaper* 等) 或代名詞 (*it* / *them* 等)，並配合括號中的字 (*away* / *up* 等) 一起完成句子。

1. Don't throw __*away this newspaper*__ . I want to read it. (away)
2. "Do you want this postcard?" "No, you can throw __*it away*__ ." (away)
3. I borrowed these books from the library. I have to take _____ tomorrow. (back)
4. We can turn _____ . Nobody is watching it. (off)
5. *A*: How did the vase get broken?
   B: Unfortunately, I knocked _____ while I was cleaning. (over)
6. Shh! My mother is asleep. I don't want to wake_____ . (up)
7. It's pretty cold. You should put _____ if you're going out. (on)
8. It was only a small fire. I was able to put _____ easily. (out)
9. I took _____ because they were uncomfortable and my feet were hurting. (off)
10. It's a little dark in this room. Should I turn _____ ? (on)

片語動詞 2　in / out

比較 **in** 與 **out** 的意思不同如下：

in 意思是進入房間、建築物、汽車等：

- How did the thieves **get in**?
- Here's a key, so you can **let yourself in**.
- Sally walked up to the edge of the pool and **dived in**. (進入水裡)
- I've got a new apartment. I'm **moving in** on Friday.
- As soon as I got to the airport, I **checked in**.

相同地，我們可以用 **go in**、**come in**、**walk in**、**break in** 等。

比較 **in** 與 **into**：

- I'm moving **in** next week.
- I'm moving **into my new apartment** on Friday.

out 意思是走出房間/建築物/汽車等：

- He just stood up and **walked out**.
- I had no key, so I was **locked out**.
- She swam up and down the pool, and then **climbed out**.
- Tim opened the window and **looked out**.
- (在飯店裡) What time do we have to **check out**?

類似的用法有 **go out**、**get out**、**move out**、**let** somebody **out** 等。

比較 **out** 與 **out of**：

- He walked **out**.
- He walked **out of the room**.

其他與 **in** 一起使用的動詞如下：

drop in 意思是短暫地拜訪某人：

- I **dropped in** to see Chris on my way home.

join in 意思是加入已經在進行中的活動：

- We're playing a game. Why don't you **join in**?

plug in an electrical machine 意思是將電器用品插上插頭：

- The fridge isn't working because you haven't **plugged** it **in**.

hand in / **turn in** homework, a report, a resignation 意思是繳交書寫文件給老師、老闆等：

- Your report is due this week. Please **hand** it **in** by Friday at 3 p.m.

fit in 意思是感覺自己成為某團體、或為某團體所接納：

- Some children have trouble **fitting in** at a new school.

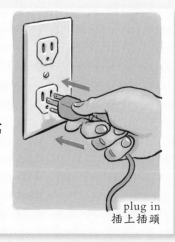

plug in
插上插頭

其他與 **out** 一起使用的動詞如下：

eat out 意思是在餐廳而非在家中用餐：

- There wasn't anything to eat at home, so we decided to **eat out**.

drop out of college / school / a course / a race 意思是在完成一門課/一項比賽等之前停止修課/比賽：

- Gary went to college but **dropped out** after a year.

get out of something that you arranged to do 意思是避免做已經安排好的事：

- I promised I'd go to the wedding. I don't want to go, but I can't **get out** of it now.

cut something **out** 意思是(自報紙等)剪下：

- There was a beautiful picture in the magazine, so I **cut** it **out** and kept it.

leave something **out** 意思是「省略」、「不包括」：

- In the sentence "She said that she was sick," you can **leave out** the word "that."

fill out a form, a questionnaire 意思是填寫表格問卷等：

- I have to **fill out** this application by the end of the week.

Exercises

135.1 依據各題題意，填入正確形式的適當動詞以完成各句。

1. Here's a key so that you can __*let*__ yourself in.
2. Liz doesn't like cooking, so she _____ out a lot.
3. Eva isn't living in this apartment anymore. She _____ out a few weeks ago.
4. If you're in our part of town, you should _____ in and see us.
5. When I _____ in at the airport, I was told my flight was delayed.
6. There were some advertisements in the paper that I wanted to keep, so I _____ them out.
7. I wanted to iron some clothes, but there was nowhere to _____ the iron in.
8. Everyone else at the party was dressed up. In my jeans, I didn't _____ in.
9. Throw this away. I don't have time to _____ out useless questionnaires.
10. Sue is going to _____ in her essay a week early in order to be free next weekend.
11. Soup isn't very tasty if you _____ out the salt.
12. Paul started taking a Spanish class, but he _____ out after a few weeks.

135.2 依據各題題意，填入 *in*、*into*、*out* 或 *out of* 以完成各句。

1. I've got a new apartment. I'm moving __*in*__ on Friday.
2. We checked _____ the hotel as soon as we arrived.
3. As soon as we arrived at the hotel, we checked _____ .
4. The car stopped and the driver got _____ .
5. Thieves broke _____ the house while we were away.
6. Why did Sarah drop _____ college? Did she fail her exams?

135.3 依據各題題意，以適當的動詞與 *in* 或 *out (of)* 完成各句。

1. Sally walked to the edge of the pool, __*dived in*__ , and swam to the other end.
2. Not all the runners finished the race. Three of them _____ .
3. I went to see Joe and Sue in their new house. They _____ last week.
4. I've told you everything you need to know. I don't think I've _____ anything.
5. Some people in the crowd started singing. Then a few more people _____ , and soon everybody was singing.
6. We go to restaurants a lot. We like _____ .
7. Sam is still new at the job, but his co-workers already like him. Everyone agrees that he _____ well.
8. I _____ to see Laura a few days ago. She was fine.
9. *A:* Can we meet tomorrow morning at 10:00?
   B: Probably. I'm supposed to go to another meeting, but I think I can _____ it.

135.4 依據各題對話內容，用括號內的字，以正確的動詞形式完成各句。

1. *A:* The fridge isn't working.
   B: That's because you haven't __*plugged it in*__ . (plug)
2. *A:* What do I have to do with these forms?
   B: _____ and send them to this address. (fill)
3. *A:* Your book report is better than mine, but you got a lower grade.
   B: That's because I _____ late. (hand)
4. *A:* Don't you usually put nuts in these cookies?
   B: This time I _____ because Jill is allergic to them. (leave)
5. *A:* Have you been to that new club on Bridge Street?
   B: We wanted to go there a few nights ago, but the doorman wouldn't _____ because we weren't members. (let)

片語動詞 3　out

out = 停止燃燒、停止發光發亮

go out ■ Suddenly all the lights in the building **went out**.

put out a fire / a cigarette / a light ■ We managed to **put** the fire **out**.

turn out a light ■ I **turned** the lights **out** before leaving.

blow out a candle ■ We don't need the candle. You can **blow** it **out**.

B

work out 可以用來表達以下各種不同的意思：

work out 意思是「做運動」：
■ Rachel **works out** at the gym three times a week.

work out 意思是「發展」、「進展」：
■ Good luck for the future. I hope everything **works out** well for you.
■ A: Why did James leave the company?
　B: Things didn't **work out**. (= things didn't work out well)

work out a problem / difficulties 等意思是「解決」：
■ The family has been having some problems, but I'm sure they'll **work** things **out**.

work out a plan / an agreement / a contract, etc 意思是產生、達成計畫、同意、約定等：
■ The two sides in the conflict are trying to **work out** a peace plan.

C

其他與 **out** 一起使用的動詞如下：

carry out an order / an experiment / a survey / an investigation / a plan 等，意思是執行一項命令/實驗/調查/計畫等：
■ Soldiers are expected to **carry out** orders.
■ An investigation into the accident will be **carried out** as soon as possible.

figure out something/somebody 意思是「瞭解」：
■ Can you help me **figure out** why my answer to this math problem is wrong?
■ Why did Erica do that? I can't **figure** her **out**.

find out that/what/when . . . , etc., **find out about** something 意思是「獲得資訊」：
■ The police never **found out** who committed the murder.
■ I just **found out** that it's Helen's birthday today.
■ I went online to **find out about** hotels in the town.

hand/**give** things **out** 意思是分給每一個人：
■ At the end of the lecture, the speaker **handed out** information sheets to the audience.

point something **out** (**to** somebody) 意思是引起(某人)對某事的注意：
■ As we drove through the city, our guide **pointed out** all the sights.
■ I didn't realize I'd made a mistake until somebody **pointed** it **out to** me.

run out (**of** something) 意思是「用完」、「用盡」：
■ We **ran out of** gas on the freeway. (汽油用完了)

turn out to be . . . / **turn out** good/nice, etc. / **turn out** that . . .
■ Nobody believed Paul at first, but he **turned out** to be right.
(最後很清楚地他是對的)
■ The weather wasn't so good in the morning, but it **turned out** nice later.
■ I thought they knew each other, but it **turned out** that they'd never met.

try out a machine, a system, a new idea, etc. 意思是測試機器/系統/新的主意等是否可用/可行：
■ The company is **trying out** a new computer system at the moment.

Exercises

136.1 依各題的片語動詞，自名詞中選出適當者，填入語意適當的名詞。

a candle	a campfire	~~a light~~	a problem	a mistake	a new product	an order

1. turn out _a light_ _____
2. point out _____
3. blow out _____
4. carry out _____
5. put out _____
6. try out _____
7. work out _____

136.2 依據各句題意，以適當的動詞與 *out* 完成各句。

1. The company is ___trying out___ a new computer system at the moment.
2. Steve is in shape. He plays a lot of sports and _____ regularly.
3. The road will be closed for two days next week while repairs are _____ .
4. We didn't manage to discuss everything at the meeting. We _____ of time.
5. My father helped me _____ a plan to save money.
6. I called the station to _____ what time the train arrived.
7. The new drug will be _____ on a small group of patients.
8. I thought the two books were the same until a friend of mine _____ the difference.
9. They got married a few years ago, but it didn't _____ , and they separated.
10 There was a power outage and all the lights _____ .
11. We thought she was American at first, but she _____ to be Swedish.
12. I haven't been able to _____ how the water is getting into the house.
13. I haven't applied for the job yet. I want to _____ more about the company first.
14. It took the fire department two hours to _____ the fire.

136.3 依據下面的圖片，以適當的動詞與 *out* 完成圖中各句。

1. 8:01 p.m.   8:02 p.m.
The lights have _gone out_ .

2. The man with a beard is _____ _____ leaflets.

3. *earlier*   *now*
The weather has _____ .

4. Sally   Kim
Sally and Kim are _____ _____ at the gym.

5. Joe
Joe has _____ of water.

6. Lisa
Lisa is trying to _____ how to _____ .

136.4 依各題對話內容，以適當的動詞與 *out* 完成各對話。

1. *A:* Do we still need the candle?
   B: No, you can _blow it out_ .
2. *A:* This recipe looks interesting.
   B: Yes, let's _____
3. *A:* Jason is strange. I'm not sure I like him.
   B: I agree. I can't _____
4. *A:* You realize that tomorrow's a holiday, don't you?
   B: No, I completely forgot. Thanks for _____ to me.

片語動詞 4　on / off (1)

A　on 與 off 用於燈、機器等

我們說 the light **is on** / **put** the light **on** / **leave** the light **on**，以及
　　　turn the light **on/off**　或　**shut** the light **off** 等：
- Should I **leave** the lights **on** or **turn** them **off**?
- "**Is** the heat **on**?"　"No, I **shut** it **off**."
- Who **left** the computer **on**?

相同地，我們也可以用 **put on** some music / a CD / a DVD 等：
- "What's this CD like?"　"It's great. Should I **put** it **on**?"

B　on 與 off 用於事件等

go on 意思是「發生」：
- What's all that noise? What's **going on**? (發生了什麼事)

call something **off** 意思是「取消」：
- The open air concert had to be **called off** because of the weather.

put something **off**, **put off** doing something 意思是「延期」：
- The wedding has been **put off** until January.
- We can't **put off** making a decision. We have to decide now.

C　on 與 off 用於衣物等

put on clothes, glasses, makeup, a seat belt 等，意思是「穿上」/「戴上」：
- My hands were cold, so I **put** my gloves **on**.

此外，**put on** weight 意思即為體重增加、變胖：
- I've **put on** five pounds in the last month.

try on clothes 意思是試穿衣服(看看是否合適)：
- I **tried on** a jacket in the store, but it didn't fit me very well.

have something **on** 意思是穿著、戴著(衣服、珠寶、香水等)：
- I like the perfume you **had on** yesterday.

take off clothes, glasses 等，意思是「脫下」：
- It was warm, so I **took off** my jacket.

D　off 意思是離開某人或某地：

be off (to 某一地點) 意思是出發到某地：
- Tomorrow I'**m off** to Paris / I'**m off** to the store.
  (我將去巴黎/我要去逛街)

walk off / **run off** / **drive off** / **ride off** / **go off** (與 **walk away** / **run away** 等意思類似)
- Diane got on her bike and **rode off**.
- Mark left home at the age of 18 and **went off** to Canada.

take off 意思是(飛機)起飛：
- After a long delay the plane finally **took off**.

see somebody **off** 意思是至機場/車站送行：
- Helen was going away. We went to the station with her to **see her off**.

Exercises

137.1 依據各句題意，以 **put on** 與自下列名詞中選出者完成各句。

~~a CD~~   the heat   the light   a DVD   the radio

1. I wanted to listen to some music, so I _put a CD on_____ .
2. It was getting cold, so I _____ .
3. I wanted to hear the news, so I _____ .
4. It was getting dark, so I _____ .
5. I wanted to watch a movie, so I _____ .

137.2 依據各句題意，以適當的動詞配合 **on** 或 **off** 完成各句。

1. It was warm, so I __took off___ my jacket.
2. What are all these people doing? What's _____ ?
3. The weather was too bad for the plane to _____ , so the flight was delayed.
4. I didn't want to be disturbed, so I _____ my cell phone.
5. Rachel got into her car and _____ at high speed.
6. Tim has _____ weight since I last saw him. He used to be quite thin.
7. The clothes Bill _____ weren't warm enough so he borrowed my jacket.
8. Don't _____ until tomorrow what you can do today.
9. There was going to be a strike by bus drivers, but now they have been offered more money and the strike has been _____ .
10. Are you cold? Should I get you a sweater to _____ ?
11. When I go away, I prefer to be alone at the station or airport. I don't like it when people come to _____ me _____ .

137.3 依據下面的圖片，以適當的片語動詞完成圖中各句。

1. Her hands were cold, so she _put her gloves on___ .

2. The plane _____ at 10:55.

3. Maria _____ , but it was too big for her.

4. The game _____ because of the weather.

5. Mark's parents went to the airport to _____ .

6. He took his sunglasses out of his pocket and _____ .

A

動詞 + **on** 意思是繼續走路/開車/遊玩等：

drive on / walk on / play on 意思是繼續走路/開車/遊玩等：
- Should we stop at this gas station or should we **drive on** to the next one?

go on 意思是「繼續」：
- The party **went on** until 4 o'clock in the morning.

go on doing something 意思是繼續做某事：
- We can't **go on** spending money like this. We'll have nothing left soon.

繼續做某事也可以用 **go on with** something
- Don't let me disturb you. Please **go on with** what you were doing.

keep on doing something 意思是持續、反覆做某事：
- He **keeps on** criticizing me. I'm really tired of it!

drag on 意思是拖延太久：
- Let's make a decision now. I don't want this problem to **drag on**.

B

其他與 **on** 一起使用的動詞如下：

hold on / hang on 意思是「等待」、「等候」：
- (在電話中) **Hold on** a minute. I'll see if Max is home.

move on 意思是開始一項新的活動、開始談論一個新的主題：
- (在演說中) That's enough about the political situation. Let's **move on** to the economy.

take on a job / extra work / a responsibility 意思是接受一項工作/額外工作/一項責任等，並且盡力完成：
- When Sally was sick, a friend **took on** her work at the office.

C

動詞 + **off**

doze off / drop off / nod off 意思是「睡著」：
- The lecture wasn't very interesting. In fact, I **dozed off** in the middle of it.

drop somebody/something **off** 意思是將某人或某物用車載至某處後離開：
- Sue **drops** her children **off** at school before she goes to work every morning.

go off 意思是「爆炸」：
- A bomb **went off** in a hotel downtown, but fortunately nobody was hurt.

an alarm can **goes off** 意思是警鈴作響：
- Did you hear the alarm **go off**?

lay someone **off** 意思是裁員，亦即因工作員額不足所以停止聘用某人：
- My brother was **laid off** two months ago and still hasn't found another job.

rip somebody **off** 意思是欺騙某人(非正式用法)：
- Did you really pay $2,000 for that painting? I think you were **ripped off**.
  (你付太多錢了)

show off 意思是誇示；試圖藉由自己的能力、知識等，令人印象深刻：
- Look at that boy on the bike riding with no hands. He's just **showing off**.

tell somebody **off** 意思是生氣地對某人說話因為他們做錯事：
- Claire's mother **told** her **off** for wearing dirty shoes in the house.

138.1 以適當的動詞配合 *on* 或 *off* 改寫各題畫線部分，使第二個句子與第一個句子意思相同。

1. Did you hear the bomb <u>explode</u>?
   Did you hear the bomb ___*go off*___ ?
2. The meeting <u>continued</u> longer than I expected.
   The meeting _____ longer than I expected.
3. We didn't stop to rest. We <u>continued walking</u>.
   We didn't stop to rest. We _____ .
4. I <u>fell asleep</u> while I was watching TV.
   I _____ while I was watching TV.
5. Gary doesn't want to retire. He wants to <u>continue working</u>.
   Gary doesn't want to retire. He wants to _____ working.
6. The fire alarm <u>rang</u> in the middle of the night.
   The fire alarm _____ in the middle of the night.
7. Martin <u>calls me continuously</u>. It's very annoying.
   Martin _____ . It's very annoying.

138.2 依據各句題意，以適當的動詞配合 *on* 或 *off* 完成各句。

1. We can't ___*go on*___ spending money like this. We'll have nothing left soon.
2. I was standing by the car when suddenly the alarm _____ .
3. I _____ my clothes at the laundry and then I went shopping.
4. *A:* Michael seems very busy at the office these days.
   B: Yes, he has _____ too much extra work, I think.
5. Bill paid too much for the car he bought. I think he was _____ .
6. As time _____ , I feel less and less upset about what happened.
7. I was very tired at work today. I nearly _____ at my desk a couple of times.
8. Ben was _____ by his boss for being late for work repeatedly.
9. If business doesn't improve, my company may have to _____ some employees.
10. There was a very loud noise. It sounded like a bomb _____ .
11. I _____ making the same mistake. It's very frustrating.
12. Please _____ with what you were saying. I'm sorry I interrupted you.
13. Peter is always trying to impress people. He's always _____ .
14. "Are you ready to go yet?" "Almost. Can you _____ just a while longer?"

138.3 依據各句題意，自下列動詞中選出適當者，以正確的動詞形式配合 *on* 或 *off* 完成各句。有些句子需要填入兩個以上的字。

> drag   go   go   ~~hold~~   lay   move   rip   tell

1. *A: (on the phone)* May I speak to Mrs. Jones?
   B: ___*Hold on*___ a second. I'll get her for you.
2. *A:* Are you still working on that project? I can't believe it isn't finished.
   B: I know. I'm fed up with it. It's really _____ .
3. *A:* We took a taxi to the airport. It cost forty dollars.
   B: Forty dollars! Normally it costs about twenty dollars. You _____ .
4. *A:* Why were you late for work this morning?
   B: I overslept. My alarm clock didn't _____ .
5. *A:* Have we discussed this point enough?
   B: I think so. Let's _____ to the next point on our agenda.
6. *A:* There won't be any more interruptions. I've turned off my phone.
   B: Good. Let's _____ what we were doing.
7. *A:* Some children at the next table in the restaurant were behaving very badly.
   B: Why didn't their parents _____ ?
8. *A:* Why did Paul quit his job?
   B: He didn't quit. He was _____ .

片語動詞 6 up / down

A

比較 up 與 down 之意思不同：

put something **up** (在牆上等)
- I **put** some pictures **up** on the wall.

pick something **up**
- There was a letter on the floor. I **picked** it **up** and looked at it.

stand up
- Alan **stood up** and walked out.

turn something **up**
- I can't hear the TV. Can you **turn** it **up** a little?

take something **down** (從牆上等)
- I didn't like the picture, so I **took** it **down**.

put something **down**
- I stopped writing and **put down** my pen.

sit down / bend down / lie down
- I **bent down** to tie my shoes.

turn something **down**
- The oven is too hot. **Turn** it **down** to 325 degrees.

B

tear down、**cut down** 等

tear down a building / **cut down** a tree / **blow** something **down**
- Some old houses were **torn down** to make room for the new shopping mall.
- *A:* Why did you **cut down** the tree in your yard?
  B: I didn't. It was **blown down** in the storm last week.

burn down 意思是被火摧毀：
- They were able to put out the fire before the house **burned down**.

C

down 的意思是「變少」、「吃少」：

slow down 意思是「慢下來」：
- You're driving too fast. **Slow down**.

calm somebody **down** 意思是冷靜下來，使某人冷靜：
- **Calm down**. There's no point in getting mad.

cut down (**on** something) 意思是吃得較少、喝得較少，或較不常做某事：
- I'm trying to **cut down on** coffee. I drink too much of it.

D

其他與 **down** 一起使用的動詞如下

break down 意思是機器、汽車停止運轉：
- The car **broke down** and I had to call for help.

discussions、talks 等 **break down** 意思是討論、談話失敗：
- Talks between the two groups **broke down** without a solution being reached. (談話失敗)

close down 意思是「停止營業」：
- There used to be a shop on this street; it **closed down** a few years ago.

let somebody **down** 意思是因為你沒有做到某人希望你做的，所以你令他們失望了：
- You can always rely on Pete. He'll never **let** you **down**.

turn somebody/something **down** 意思是拒絕一項申請、提供等：
- I applied for several jobs, but I was **turned down** for all of them.
- Rachel was offered the job, but she decided to **turn** it **down**.

write something **down** 意思是因為你稍後可能需要這項訊息，所以把它寫在紙上：
- I can't remember Tim's address. I **wrote** it **down**, but I can't find it.

Exercises

139.1 依據各句題意，自下列動詞中選出適當者，以正確的動詞形式配合 *up* 或 *down* 完成各句。

calm	let	put	~~take~~	turn	turn

1. I don't like this picture on the wall. I'm going to __take it down__ .
2. The music is too loud. Can you _____ ?
3. David was very angry. I tried to _____ .
4. I've bought some new curtains. Can you help me _____ ?
5. I promised I would help Anna. I don't want to _____ .
6. I was offered the job, but I decided I didn't want it. So I _____ .

139.2 依據下面的圖片，以適當的動詞配合 *up* 或 *down* 完成各句。有些句子需要填入兩個以上的字。

1. There used to be a tree in front of the house, but we __cut it down__ .
2. There used to be some shelves on the wall, but I _____ .
3. The ceiling was so low, he couldn't _____ straight.
4. She couldn't hear the radio very well, so she _____ .
5. While they were waiting for the bus, they _____ on the ground.
6. A lot of trees _____ in the storm last week.
7. Sarah gave me her phone number. I _____ on a piece of paper.
8. Liz dropped her keys, so she _____ and _____ .

139.3 依據各題題意，以適當的動詞配合 *up* 或 *down* 完成各句。

1. I stopped writing and __put down__ my pen.
2. I was really upset. It took me a long time to _____ .
3. The train _____ as it approached the station.
4. Sarah applied for medical school, but she _____ .
5. Our car is very reliable. It has never _____ .
6. I need to spend less money. I'm going to _____ on things I don't really need.
7. I didn't play very well. I felt that I had _____ the other players on the team.
8. The shop _____ because it was losing money.
9. This is a very ugly building. Many people would like it to _____ .
10. I don't understand why you _____ the chance to work abroad for a year. It would have been a great experience.
11. Unfortunately, the house _____ before the fire department got there, but no one was hurt.
12. The strike is going to continue. Talks between the two sides have _____ without agreement.

A

go up / come up / walk up (to ...) 意思是「接近」：
- A man **came up to** me in the street and asked me for money.

catch up (with somebody) 意思是比前面的人移動更快，以便趕上他們：
- I'm not ready to go yet. You go on and I'll **catch up with** you.

keep up (with somebody) 意思是繼續保持相同的速度或程度：
- You're walking too fast. I can't **keep up** (**with** you).
- You're doing well. **Keep** it **up**!

B

set up an organization, a company, a business, a system, a Web site, etc. 意思是「成立」、「設立」：
- The government has **set up** a committee to investigate the problem.

take up a hobby, a sport, an activity, etc. 意思是開始做某事：
- Laura **took up** photography a few years ago. She takes really good pictures.

C

grow up 意思是「長大成人」：
- Sara was born in Mexico but **grew up** in the United States.

bring up a child 意思是將小孩扶養長大：
- Her parents died when she was a child, so she was **brought up** by her grandparents.

D

back up

back someone up 意思是支持某人：
- Will you **back** me **up** if I tell the police what happened? (= say I'm telling the truth)

back up computer files 意思是製作備份：
- You've spent a long time on that document; you'd better **back up** your files.

back up a car 意思是「倒車」：
- I couldn't turn around in the narrow street. I had to **back** the car **up** for a block.

back up 也可以指(交通)停止前進：
- Cars are **backed up** for a mile at the entrance to the stadium.

E

end up somewhere、end up doing something 等
- There was a fight in the street and three men **ended up** in the hospital.
  (這就是這些人的下場)
- I couldn't find a hotel and **ended up** sleeping on a bench at the station.
  (這就是我的下場)

give up 意思是「放棄嘗試」，give something up 意思是放棄做某事：
- Don't **give up**. Keep trying!
- Ted failed his driving test at age 80, so he had to **give up** driving. (停止開車)

make up something / be made up of something
- Children under 16 **make up** half the population of the city.
  (半數的人口為 16 歲以下的兒童)
- Air is **made up** mainly **of** nitrogen and oxygen. (空氣是由…所組成)

take up space or time 意思是佔用空間或時間：
- Most of the space in the room was **taken up** by a large table.

turn up / show up 意思是「抵達」、「出現」：
- We arranged to meet Dave last night, but he didn't **turn up**.

use something up 意思是用盡某物，所以一點也不剩：
- I'm going to make some soup. I want to **use up** the vegetables I have.

Exercises

140.1 依據下面圖片，以 A 小節中的動詞與其他兩個字，完成圖中各句。

1. Can you tell me . . .?

A man __came up to__ me in the street and asked me the way to the station.

2. Sue

Sue _____ the front door of the house and rang the doorbell.

3. Tom   Tom

Tom was a long way behind the other runners, but he managed to _____ them.

4. Tanya   Paul

Tanya was running too fast for Paul. He couldn't _____ her.

140.2 依據各題題意，自下列動詞選出適當者，以正確的動詞形式與 *up* 完成各句。

> **back**   ~~**end**~~   **end**   **give**   **give**   **grow**   **make**   **take**   **take**   **turn**   **use**

1. I couldn't find a hotel and __ended up__ sleeping on a bench at the station.
2. I'm feeling very tired now. I've _____ all my energy.
3. I hadn't _____ my files and my computer crashed. I lost everything I was working on.
4. People often ask children what they want to be when they _____ .
5. We invited Tim to the party, but he didn't _____ .
6. Two years ago Mark _____ his studies to be a professional basketball player.
7. *A:* Do you play any sports?
   B: Not right now, but I'm thinking of _____ tennis.
8. You don't have enough determination. You _____ too easily.
9. Karen traveled a lot for a few years and _____ in Canada, where she still lives.
10. I do a lot of gardening. It _____ most of my free time.
11. There are two universities in the city, and students _____ 20 percent of the population.

140.3 依據各題題意，自下列動詞選出適當者，以正確的動詞形式與 *up* 完成各句。有些句子需要填入兩個以上的字。

> **back**   **back**   **bring**   ~~**catch**~~   ~~**give**~~   **go**   **keep**   **keep**   **make**   **set**

1. Sue was on the volleyball team, but she got injured and had to __give it up__ .
2. I'm not ready yet. You go on and I'll __catch up with__ you.
3. Helen has her own Web site. A friend of hers helped her to _____ .
4. Steven is having problems at school. He can't _____ the rest of the class.
5. Although I _____ in the country, I have always preferred cities.
6. Our team started the game well, but we couldn't _____ , and in the end we lost.
7. Traffic has been _____ on this road for an hour. Is there another way to go?
8. I saw Mike at the party, so I _____ him and said hello.
9. When I was on my trip, I joined a tour group. The group _____ two Americans, three Germans, five Italians, and myself.
10. "I agree with your solution and will give you my support." "Thanks for _____ ."

A

bring up a topic 等意思是在談話中提及某話題等：
- I don't want to hear any more about this issue. Please don't **bring** it **up** again.

come up 意思是在談話中提及、談起：
- Some interesting issues **came up** in our discussion yesterday.

come up with an idea, a suggestion 等意思是產生、想出一個主意、建議等：
- Sarah is very creative. She's always **coming up with** new ideas.

make something **up** 意思是編造不真的事：
- What Kevin told you about himself wasn't true. He **made** it all **up**.

B

cheer up 意思是「快樂些」，**cheer** somebody **up** 意思是使某人覺得快樂些：
- You look so sad! **Cheer up!**
- Helen is depressed these days. What can we do to **cheer her up**?

save up for something / to do something 意思是存錢以便買某事物：
- Dan is **saving up** for a trip around the world.

clear up 意思是天氣放晴：
- It was raining when I got up, but it **cleared up** during the morning.

C

blow up 意思是「爆炸」，**blow** something **up** 意思是用炸彈將某物摧毀：
- The engine caught fire and **blew up**.
- The bridge was **blown up** during the war.

tear something **up** 意思是將某物撕成碎片：
- I didn't read the letter. I just **tore** it **up** and threw it away.

beat somebody **up** 意思是連續揍某人使其因此受傷嚴重：
- A friend of mine was attacked and **beaten up** a few days ago. He was badly hurt and had to go to the hospital.

D

break up / **split up** (with somebody) 意思是「分居」、「分開」：
- I'm surprised to hear that Sue and Paul have **split up**. They seemed very happy together the last time I saw them.

clean something **up** 意思是將某物清理乾淨：
- Look at this mess! Who is going to **clean** it **up**?

fix up a building, a room, a car 等意思是修理建築物、房間、汽車等：
- I love how you've **fixed up** this room. It looks so much nicer.

look something **up** in a dictionary/encyclopedia, etc.
- If you don't know the meaning of a word, you can **look** it **up** in a dictionary.

put up with something 意思是容忍某事：
- We live on a busy road, so we have to **put up with** a lot of noise from the traffic.

hold up a person, a plan 等意思是「拖延」、「延遲」：
- Don't wait for me. I don't want to **hold** you **up**.
- Plans to build a new factory have been **held up** because of the company's financial problems.

mix up people/things, **get** people/things **mixed up** 意思是無法分辨是何者：
- The two brothers look very similar. Many people **mix** them **up**.
  (或 . . . **get** them **mixed up**)

Exercises

141.1 依據各句題意，判斷各題的片語動詞與右邊的名詞是否相合。

1. I'm going to tear up	A a new camera	1. ___F___
2. Jane came up with	B a lot of bad weather	2. _____
3. Paul is always making up	C the two medicines	3. _____
4. Be careful not to mix up	D an interesting suggestion	4. _____
5. I don't think you should bring up	E excuses	5. _____
6. I'm saving up for	F ~~the letter~~	6. _____
7. We had to put up with	G that subject	7. _____

141.2 依據下面的圖片，以片語動詞完成各句。每題都需填入 2 或 3 個字。

this morning / *now*

The weather was horrible this morning, but it's ___cleared up___ now.

Linda
Sorry I'm late.

Linda was late because she was _____ by the traffic.

They bought an old house and _____ _____ . It's really nice now.

Pete
Come out to dinner with us!

Pete was really depressed. We took him out for dinner to _____ .

141.3 依據各題題意，以適當的動詞 **up** 完成各句。有些句子需填入 2 個以上的字。

1. I love how you've ___fixed up___ this room. It looks so much nicer.
2. The ship _____ and sank. The cause of the explosion was never discovered.
3. Two men have been arrested after a man was _____ outside a restaurant last night. The injured man was taken to the hospital.
4. "Is Robert still going out with Tina?" "No, they've _____ ."
5. An interesting question _____ in class today.
6. The weather is terrible this morning, isn't it? I hope it _____ later.
7. I wanted to call Chris, but I dialed Laura's number by mistake. I got their phone numbers _____ .

141.4 依據各題題意，以適當的動詞 **up** 完成各句。有些句子需填入 2 個以上的字。

1. Don't wait for me. I don't want to ___hold you up___ .
2. I don't know what this word means. I'll have to _____ .
3. There's nothing we can do about the problem. We'll just have to _____ it.
4. "Was that story true?" "No, I _____ ."
5. I think we should follow Tom's suggestion. Nobody has _____ a better plan.
6. I hate this photo of me. I'm going to _____ .
7. I'm trying to spend less money these days. I'm _____ a trip to Australia.
8. After the party, my place was a mess. Some friends helped me _____ .

片語動詞 9　away / back

比較 away 與 back 之意思不同如下：

away 意思是「離開家」：
- We're **going away** on a trip today.

away 意思是離開某地、某人等：
- The woman got into her car and **drove away**.
- I tried to take a picture of the bird, but it **flew away**.
- I dropped the ticket and it **blew away** in the wind.
- The police searched the house and **took away** a computer.

同樣地，我們可以說：
walk away、**run away**、**look away** 等。

back 意思是「回家」：
- We'll **be back** in three weeks.

back 意思是回到某地、歸還某人等：
- *A:* I'm going out now.
  B: What time will you **be back**?
- After eating at a restaurant, we **walked back** to our hotel.
- I've still got Jane's keys. I forgot to **give** them **back** to her.
- When you're finished with that book, can you **put** it **back** on the shelf?

同樣地，我們可以說：
go back、**come back**、**get back**、**take** something **back** 等。

其他與 away 一起使用的動詞如下：

get away 意思是逃離、困難地離開：
- We tried to catch the thief, but he managed to **get away**.

get away with something 意思是做了不對的事但沒有被發現：
- I parked in a no-parking zone, but I **got away with** it.

keep away (from …) 意思是不要靠近：
- **Keep away from** the edge of the pool. You might fall in.

give something **away** 意思是因為不再需要某物，所以將它給了別人：
- "Did you sell your old computer?" "No, I **gave** it **away**."

put something **away** 意思是將某物放回它原來的地方，通常不在視線範圍內：
- When the children had finished playing with their toys, they **put** them **away**.

throw something **away** 意思是丟棄為垃圾：
- I kept the letter, but I **threw away** the envelope.

其他與 back 一起使用的動詞：

wave back / **smile back** / **shout back** / **write back** / **hit** somebody **back**
- I waved to her and she **waved back**.

call/phone (somebody) **back** 意思是回電、回覆電話：
- I can't talk to you now. I'll **call** you **back** in 10 minutes.

get back to somebody 意思是以電話等方式回覆某人：
- I sent him an e-mail, but he never **got back to** me.

look back (**on** something) 意思是回想過去發生的事：
- My first job was at a travel agency. I didn't like it very much at the time but, **looking back on** it, I learned a lot, and it was a very useful experience.

pay back money, **pay** somebody **back**
- If you borrow money, you have to **pay** it **back**.
- Thanks for lending me the money. I'll **pay** you **back** next week.

Exercises

142.1 依據各句題意，填入正確形式的適當動詞以完成各句。

1. The woman got into her car and __*drove*__ away.
2. Here's the money you need. _____ me back when you can.
3. Don't _____ that box away. It could be useful.
4. Jane doesn't do anything at work. I don't know how she _____ away with it.
5. I'm going out now. I'll _____ back at about 10:30.
6. You should think more about the future; don't _____ back all the time.
7. Gary is very generous. He won some money in the lottery and _____ it all away.
8. I'll _____ back to you as soon as I have the information you need.

142.2 依據各句題意，以適當的動詞與 *away* 或 *back* 完成各句。

1. I was away all day yesterday. I __*got back*__ very late.
2. I haven't seen our neighbors for a while. I think they must _____ .
3. "I'm going out now." "OK. What time will you _____ ?"
4. A man was trying to break into a car. When he saw me, he _____ .
5. I smiled at him, but he didn't _____ .
6. If you cheat on the exam, you might _____ with it. But you might get caught.
7. Be careful! That's an electric fence. _____ from it.

142.3 依據下面圖片，填入適當的片語動詞以完成各句。

1. She waved to him, and he __*waved back*__ .

2. It was windy. I dropped a $20 bill and it _____ .

3. Sue

Sue opened the letter, read it, and _____ in the envelope.

4. He tried to talk to her, but she just _____ .

5. Ellie   Ben

Ellie threw the ball to Ben, and he _____ .

6. His shoes were worn out, so he _____ .

142.4 依據各句題意，以括號中的動詞與 *away* 或 *back* 完成各句。

1. *A:* Do you still have my keys?
   B: No. Don't you remember? I __*gave them back*__ to you yesterday. (give)
2. *A:* Do you want this magazine?
   B: No, I'm finished with it. You can _____ . (throw)
3. *A:* How are your new jeans? Do they fit you OK?
   B: No, I'm going to _____ to the shop. (take)
4. *A:* Here's the money you asked me to lend you.
   B: Thanks. I'll _____ as soon as I can. (pay)
5. *A:* What happened to all the books you used to have?
   B: I didn't want them any more, so I _____ . (give)
6. *A:* Did you call Sarah?
   B: She wasn't there. I left a message asking her to _____ . (call)

規則動詞與不規則動詞

1.1 規則動詞

規則動詞之過去簡單式與過去分詞皆為 **-ed** 結尾。請看以下例子：

動詞原型 過去簡單式 過去分詞	clean	finish	use	paint	stop	carry
	cleaned	finished	used	painted	stopped	carried

拼字規則參見附錄 6。

過去簡單式 (I **cleaned** / they **finished** / she **carried** 等) 之用法，參見 Unit 5。

過去分詞用於形成完成式以及被動式。

完成式 (**have/has/had** cleaned)，請看下面例子：

- I **have cleaned** the windows. (現在完成式，參見 Units 7–9)
- They were still working. They **hadn't finished**. (過去完成式，參見 Unit 14)

被動式 (**is** clean**ed** / **was** cleaned 等)，請看下面例子：

- He **was carried** out of the room. (過去簡單被動式)
- This gate has just **been painted**. (現在完成被動式) 參見 Units 40–42。

1.2 不規則動詞

過去簡單式或過去分詞不以 **-ed** 結尾的動詞 (例如：**I saw** / **I have seen**)，稱為不規則動詞。

有些不規則動詞的過去簡單式以及過去分詞，其形式與動詞原型相同。例如，**hit**：

- Don't **hit** me. (動詞原型)
- Somebody **hit** me as I came into the room. (過去簡單式)
- I've never **hit** anybody in my life. (過去分詞 – 現在完成式)
- George was **hit** on the head by a stone. (過去分詞 – 被動式)

另外有些不規則動詞的過去簡單式與過去分詞形式相同 (但與動詞原型不同)。
例如，**tell** → **told**：

- Can you **tell** me what to do? (動詞原型)
- She **told** me to come back the next day. (過去簡單式)
- Have you **told** anybody about your new job? (過去分詞 – 現在完成式)
- I was **told** to come back the next day. (過去分詞 – 被動式)

其他不規則動詞的動詞原型、過去簡單式以及過去分詞形式皆不相同。例如，**wake** → **woke/ woken**：

- I'll **wake** you up. (動詞原型)
- I **woke** up in the middle of the night. (過去簡單式)
- The baby has **woken** up. (過去分詞 – 現在完成式)
- I was **woken** up by a loud noise. (過去分詞 – 被動式)

1.3 不規則動詞表

動詞原型	過去簡單式	過去分詞	動詞原型	過去簡單式	過去分詞
be	was/were	been	**blow**	blew	blown
beat	beat	beaten	**break**	broke	broken
become	became	become	**bring**	brought	brought
begin	began	begun	**broadcast**	broadcast	broadcast
bend	bent	bent	**build**	built	built
bet	bet	bet	**burst**	burst	burst
bite	bit	bitten	**buy**	bought	bought

動詞原型	過去簡單式	過去分詞
catch	caught	caught
choose	chose	chosen
come	came	come
cost	cost	cost
creep	crept	crept
cut	cut	cut
deal	dealt	dealt
dig	dug	dug
do	did	done
draw	drew	drawn
drink	drank	drunk
drive	drove	driven
eat	ate	eaten
fall	fell	fallen
feed	fed	fed
feel	felt	felt
fight	fought	fought
find	found	found
fit	fit	fit
flee	fled	fled
fly	flew	flown
forbid	forbade	forbidden
forget	forgot	forgotten
forgive	forgave	forgiven
freeze	froze	frozen
get	got	gotten
give	gave	given
go	went	gone
grow	grew	grown
hang	hung	hung
have	had	had
hear	heard	heard
hide	hid	hidden
hit	hit	hit
hold	held	held
hurt	hurt	hurt
keep	kept	kept
kneel	knelt	knelt
know	knew	known
lay	laid	laid
lead	led	led
leave	left	left
lend	lent	lent
let	let	let
lie	lay	lain
light	lit/lighted	lit/lighted
lose	lost	lost
make	made	made
mean	meant	meant
meet	met	met
pay	paid	paid
put	put	put

動詞原型	過去簡單式	過去分詞
quit	quit	quit
read	read [red]★	read [red]★
ride	rode	ridden
ring	rang	rung
rise	rose	risen
run	ran	run
say	said	said
see	saw	seen
seek	sought	sought
sell	sold	sold
send	sent	sent
set	set	set
sew	sewed	sewn/sewed
shake	shook	shaken
shine	shone/shined	shone/shined
shoot	shot	shot
show	showed	shown/showed
shrink	shrank	shrunk
shut	shut	shut
sing	sang	sung
sink	sank	sunk
sit	sat	sat
sleep	slept	slept
slide	slid	slid
speak	spoke	spoken
spend	spent	spent
spit	spit/spat	spit/spat
split	split	split
spread	spread	spread
spring	sprang	sprung
stand	stood	stood
steal	stole	stolen
stick	stuck	stuck
sting	stung	stung
stink	stank	stunk
strike	struck	struck
swear	swore	sworn
sweep	swept	swept
swim	swam	swum
swing	swung	swung
take	took	taken
teach	taught	taught
tear	tore	torn
tell	told	told
think	thought	thought
throw	threw	thrown
understand	understood	understood
wake	woke	woken
wear	wore	worn
weep	wept	wept
win	won	won
write	wrote	written

★ 讀音

現在式與過去式

	簡單式	進行式
現在式	**I do** 現在簡單式 (→ Unit 2 至 Unit 4) ■ Ann often **plays** tennis. ■ I **work** in a bank, but **I don't enjoy** it much. ■ **Do** you **like** parties? ■ It **doesn't rain** so much in summer.	**I am doing** 現在進行式 (→ Unit 1 與 Unit 3 至 Unit 4) ■ "Where's Ann?" "She**'s playing** tennis." ■ Please don't disturb me now. **I'm working**. ■ Hello. **Are** you **enjoying** the party? ■ It isn't **raining** right now.
現在 完成式	**I have done** 現在完成簡單式 (→ Unit 7 至 Unit 9 與 Unit 11 至 Unit 13) ■ Ann **has played** tennis many times. ■ Where's Tom? **Have** you **seen** him this morning? ■ How long **have** you and Chris **known** each other? ■ *A:* Is it still raining? 　*B:* No, it **has stopped**. ■ I'm hungry. I **haven't eaten** anything since breakfast.	**I have been doing** 現在完成進行式 (→ Unit 10 至 Unit 13) ■ Ann is tired. She **has been playing** tennis. ■ You're out of breath. **Have** you **been running**? ■ How long **have** you **been studying** English? ■ It's still raining. It **has been raining** all day. ■ I **haven't been feeling** well recently. Maybe I should go to the doctor.
過去式	**I did** 過去簡單式 (→ Unit 5 至 Unit 6 與 Unit 8 至 Unit 9) ■ Ann **played** tennis yesterday afternoon. ■ **I lost** my key a few days ago. ■ There was a movie on TV last night, but we **didn't watch** it. ■ What **did** you **do** when you finished work yesterday?	**I was doing** 過去進行式 (→ Unit 6) ■ I saw Ann at the park yesterday. She **was playing** tennis. ■ I dropped my key when I **was trying** to open the door. ■ The television was on, but we **weren't watching** it. ■ What **were** you **doing at** this time yesterday?
過去 完成式	**I had done** 過去完成式 (→ Unit 14) ■ It wasn't her first game of tennis. She **had played** many times before. ■ They couldn't get into the house because they **had lost** the key. ■ The house was dirty because I **hadn't cleaned** it for weeks.	**I had been doing** 過去完成進行式 (→ Unit 15) ■ Ann was tired last night because she **had been playing** tennis in the afternoon. ■ George decided to go to the doctor because he **hadn't been feeling** well.

被動式之用法，參見 Unit 40 至 Unit 42。

3.1 表示未來之句型如下：

■ I'm **leaving tomorrow**.	現在進行式	(Unit 18A)
■ My train **leaves** at 9:30.	現在簡單式	(Unit 18B)
■ I'm **going to leave** tomorrow.	**(be) going to**	(Unit 19 與 Unit 22)
■ I'll **leave** tomorrow.	**will**	(Unit 20 至 Unit 22)
■ I'll **be leaving** tomorrow.	未來進行式	(Unit 23)
■ I'll **have left** by this time tomorrow.	未來完成式	(Unit 23)
■ I hope to see you before I **leave** tomorrow.	現在簡單式	(Unit 24)

3.2 未來的動作

現在進行式 (I'm **doing**) 表示已經安排好未來將做的事，例如：

- ■ I'm **leaving** tomorrow. I've got my plane ticket. (已經計畫且安排好)
- ■ "When **are** they **getting** married?" "On July 24."

現在簡單式 (I **leave** / it **leaves** 等) 表示未來的行程、計畫等，例如：

- ■ My train **leaves** at 11:30. (依據時刻表)
- ■ What time **does** the movie **start**?

(be) going to . . . 表示某人已經決定將做某件事，例如：

- ■ I've decided not to stay here any longer. I'm **going to leave** tomorrow. 或
  I'm **leaving** tomorrow.
- ■ "Your shoes are dirty." "Yes, I know. I'm **going to clean** them."

will (**'ll**) 表示在說話的當時，我們決定或同意將做某事，例如：

- ■ *A:* I don't want you to stay here any longer.
  B: OK. I'll **leave** tomorrow. (B 在說話的此刻決定他將明天離開。)
- ■ That bag looks heavy. I'll **help** you with it.
- ■ I **won't tell** anybody what happened. I promise. (**won't = will not**)

3.3 未來將發生的事情以及狀況

will 通常用於談論未來會發生的事情 (something **will happen**) 或是狀況 (something **will be**)，例如：

- ■ I don't think John is happy at work. I think he'll **leave** soon.
- ■ This time next year I'll **be** in Japan. Where **will** you **be**?

(be) going to 表示目前的狀況顯示未來即將發生某事，例如：

- ■ Look at those black clouds. It's **going to rain**. (你現在就可以看到烏雲。)

3.4 未來進行式與未來完成式

will be (**do**)**ing** = will be in the middle of (doing something)，表示正在做某件事當中：

- ■ This time next week I'll **be** on vacation. I'll **be lying** on a beach or **swimming** in the ocean.

will be –ing 也用於表示未來的動作 (參見 Unit 23C)，例如：

- ■ What time **will** you **be leaving** tomorrow?

will have (**done**) 表示在未來某個時間之前，將會完成某事，例如：

- ■ I won't be here this time tomorrow. I'll **have** already **left**.

3.5 *when* / *if* / *while* / *before* 等之後必須使用現在式(而非 **will**，未來式)，(參見 Unit 24)，例如：

- ■ I hope to see you **before** I **leave** tomorrow. (並非 before I will leave)
- ■ **When** you **are** in New York again, come and see us. (並非 When you will be)
- ■ **If** we **don't hurry**, we'll be late.

情態助動詞 (can / could / will / would 等)

本附錄為情態助動詞用法摘要，詳細用法請見 Unit 25 至 Unit 35。

4.1 比較 *can/could* 等表動作之用法：

can	■ I **can go** out tonight. (沒有事情可以阻止我) ■ I **can't go** out tonight.
could	■ I **could go** out tonight, but I don't feel like it. ■ I **couldn't go** out last night. (= I wasn't able)
can 或 may	■ **Can** **May** I **go** out tonight? (你能否允許我)
will/won't	■ I think I**'ll go** out tonight. ■ I promise I **won't go** out.
would	■ I **would go** out tonight, but I have too much to do. ■ I promised I **wouldn't go** out.
should/shall	■ **Should** we **go** out tonight? (或 **Shall** we . . .) (= do you think it is a good idea?)
should 或 ought to	■ I { **should** / **ought to** } **go** out tonight. (這將是件好事)

比較 **could have . . .** / **would have . . .** 等之用法：

could	■ I **could have gone** out last night, but I decided to stay at home.
would	■ I **would have gone** out last night, but I had too much to do.
should	■ I **should have gone** out last night. I'm sorry I didn't.

4.2 *will/would/may* 等用於表示某事是否可能、不可能、確定等。比較下列用法：

will	■ "What time **will** she **be** here?" "She**'ll be** here soon."
would	■ She **would be** here now, but she's been delayed.
should 或 ought to	■ She { **should** / **ought to** } **be** here soon. (我期待她很快會在/抵達這裡)
may 或 might 或 could	■ She { **may** / **might** / **could** } **be** here now. I'm not sure. (她可能會在這裡)
must	■ She **must be** here. I saw her come in. ■ She **must not be** here. I've looked everywhere for her.
can't	■ She **can't be** here. I know for sure she is away on vacation.

比較 **would have . . .** / **should have . . .** 等之用法：

will	■ She **will have arrived** by now. (此刻之前)
would	■ She **would have arrived** earlier, but she was delayed.
should	■ I wonder where she is. She **should have arrived** by now.
may 或 might 或 could	■ She { **may** / **might** / **could** } **have arrived**. I'm not sure. (她可能已經到達)
must	■ She **must have arrived** by now. (我確定，沒有其他的可能性)
couldn't	■ She **couldn't have arrived** yet. It's much too early. (可能)

縮寫形式 (I'm / you've / didn't 等)

5.1　在口語表達時，通常使用 **I'm** / **you've** / **didn't** 等(縮寫形式)，而非 **I am** / **you have** / **did not** 等。非正式的書面英文中也可以使用縮寫(例如，寫給朋友的信或留言)，但正式書面英文中不得使用縮寫(例如，學校作業或商業報告等)。

使用縮寫時，縮寫符號 *' (apostrophe)* 用以表示被縮寫的字母，例如：

I'm = I a̲m̲　　you've = you ha̲v̲e̲　　didn't = did no̲t̲

5.2　**be** 動詞與助動詞縮寫形式表

'm = am	I'm						
's = is *or* has		he's	she's	it's			
're = are					you're	we're	they're
've = have	I've				you've	we've	they've
'll = will	I'll	he'll	she'll		you'll	we'll	they'll
'd = would *or* had	I'd	he'd	she'd		you'd	we'd	they'd

's 可以是 **is** 或 **has**，例如：
- She's sick. (= She **is** sick.)
- She's gone away. (= She **has** gone)

但是 let's 表示 **let us**，例如：
- Let's go now. (= Let **us** go)

'd 可以是 **would** 或 **had**，例如：
- I'd see a doctor if I were you. (= I **would** see)
- I'd never seen her before. (= I **had** never seen)

疑問詞 (例如 **who/what** 等) 以及 **that/there/here** 之後，也常使用這些縮寫形式(尤其是 **'s**)，例如：

who's　what's　where's　how's　that's　there's　here's　who'll　there'll　who'd
- Who's that woman over there? (= who **is**)
- What's happened? (= what **has**)
- Do you think there'll be many people at the party? (= there **will**)

名詞之後也可以使用縮寫形式(尤其是 **'s**)，例如：
- Catherine's going out tonight. (= Catherine **is**)
- My best friend's just gotten married. (= My best friend **has**)

縮寫形式 **'m** / **'s** / **'re** / **'ve** / **'ll** / **'d** 不得用於句尾(因為句尾的動詞通常為訊息的重點)，例如：
- "Are you tired?" "Yes, I **am**." (並非 Yes, I'm.)
- Do you know where she **is**? (並非 Do you know where she's?)

5.3　否定縮寫形式

isn't (= is not)	**don't** (= do not)	**haven't** (= have not)
aren't (= are not)	**doesn't** (= does not)	**hasn't** (= has not)
wasn't (= was not)	**didn't** (= did not)	**hadn't** (= had not)
weren't (= were not)		
can't (= cannot)	**couldn't** (= could not)	
won't (= will not)	**wouldn't** (= would not)	
	shouldn't (= should not)	

is 和 **are** 的否定縮寫形式有兩種：

he **isn't** / she **isn't** / it **isn't**　　　或　he's **not** / she's **not** / it's **not**
you **aren't** / we **aren't** / they **aren't**　或　you're **not** / we're **not** / they're **not**

拼字

6.1 名詞、動詞以及形容詞後可以加以下的字尾：

noun + **-s/-es** (複數形)	books	ideas	matches
verb + **-s/-es** (after **he**/**she**/**it**)	works	enjoys	washes
verb + **-ing**	work**ing**	enjoy**ing**	wash**ing**
verb + **-ed**	work**ed**	enjoy**ed**	wash**ed**
adjective + **-er** (比較級)	cheap**er**	quick**er**	bright**er**
adjective + **-est** (最高級)	cheap**est**	quick**est**	bright**est**
adjective + **-ly** (副詞)	cheap**ly**	quick**ly**	bright**ly**

加上這些字尾時，有時會造成拼字的改變，其規則條列如下：

6.2 名詞及動詞 + -s/-es

以 **-s**、**-ss**、**-sh**、**-ch** 或 **-x** 結尾的字是加上 **-es**，例如：

bu**s**/bus**es**　　　　mi**ss**/miss**es**　　　　wa**sh**/wash**es**

mat**ch**/match**es**　　sear**ch**/search**es**　　bo**x**/box**es**

注意下面以 **-o** 結尾的字的拼法：

potat**o**/potato**es**　　tomat**o**/tomato**es**

d**o**/do**es**　　　　　g**o**/go**es**

6.3 以 **-y** 結尾的字 (例如 **baby**、**carry**、**easy** 等)

若某字是以子音* + **-y** 結尾 (例如 **-by**、**-ry**、**-sy**、**-vy** 等)，

把 **y** 改成 **ie** 再加 **-s**，例如：

bab**y**/bab**ies**　　　story/stor**ies**　　　countr**y**/countr**ies**　　　secretar**y**/secretar**ies**
hurr**y**/hurr**ies**　　　stud**y**/stud**ies**　　appl**y**/appl**ies**　　　tr**y**/tr**ies**

把 **y** 改成 **i** 再加 **-ed**，例如：

hurr**y**/hurr**ied**　　　stud**y**/stud**ied**　　appl**y**/appl**ied**　　　tr**y**/tr**ied**

把 **y** 改成 **i** 再加 **-er** 以及 **-est**，例如：

eas**y**/eas**ier**/eas**iest**　　heav**y**/heav**ier**/heav**iest**　　luck**y**/luck**ier**/luck**iest**

把 **y** 改成 **i** 再加 **-ly**，例如：

eas**y**/eas**ily**　　　　　　heav**y**/heav**ily**　　　　temporar**y**/temporar**ily**

加 **-ing** 時，**y** 不改變，例如：

hurr**ying**　　study**ing**　　apply**ing**　　try**ing**

以母音 + **y** 結尾 (例如 **-ay**、**-ey**、**-oy**、**-uy**) 的字，**y** 不做改變，例如：

pl**ay**/pl**ays**/pl**ayed**　　monk**ey**/monk**eys**　　enj**oy**/enj**oys**/enj**oyed**　　b**uy**/b**uys**

d**ay**/d**aily** 是例外。

注意：**pay**/**paid**　　　**lay**/**laid**　　　**say**/**said**

6.4 以 **-ie** 結尾的動詞 (例如 **die**、**lie**、**tie**)

若動詞以 **-ie** 結尾，將 **ie** 改成 **y** 後加 **-ing**：

d**ie**/d**ying**　　　l**ie**/l**ying**　　　t**ie**/t**ying**

* **a e i o u** 為母音字母

而其他字母 (如 **b c d f g** 等) 為子音字母。

6.5 以 -e 結尾的字 (例如 hope、dance、wide 等)

動詞

若動詞以 **-e** 結尾，把 **e** 去掉再加 **-ing**，例如：

hop**e**/hop**ing**   smile/smil**ing**   danc**e**/danc**ing**   confus**e**/confus**ing**

但 **be**/**being** 為例外

以 **-ee** 結尾之動詞也除外，例如：   s**ee**/s**eeing**   agr**ee**/agr**eeing**

若動詞以 **-e** 結尾，則加上 **-d** 使之成為(規則動詞之)過去式，例如：

hop**e**/hop**ed**   smile/smil**ed**   danc**e**/danc**ed**   confus**e**/confus**ed**

形容詞和副詞

若形容詞以 **-e** 結尾，加上 **-r** 以及 **-st** 使之成為比較級和最高級，例如：

wid**e**/wid**er**/wid**est**   lat**e**/lat**er**/lat**est**   larg**e**/larg**er**/larg**est**

若形容詞以 **-e** 結尾，保留 **e** 再加上 **-ly** 成為副詞，例如：

polit**e**/polit**ely**   extrem**e**/extrem**ely**   absolut**e**/absolut**ely**

若形容詞以 **-le** 結尾(例如 simp**le**、terrib**le** 等)，去掉 **e** 並加 **y**，形成以 **-ly** 結尾之副詞，如 **-ply**、**-bly** 等，例如：

simp**le**/simp**ly**   terrib**le**/terri**bly**   reasona**ble**/reasona**bly**

6.6 重複子音字母 (stop/stopping/stopped、wet/wetter/wettest 等)

有些字以母音 + 子音為結尾，例如：

st**op**   pl**an**   r**ub**   b**ig**   w**et**   th**in**   pref**er**   regr**et**

此類的字必須重複字尾的子音字母之後再加上 **-ing**/**-ed**/**-er**/**-est**。亦即 **p → pp**，**n → nn** 等，例如：

sto**p**	p → **pp**	sto**pp**ing	sto**pp**ed
pla**n**	n → **nn**	pla**nn**ing	pla**nn**ed
ru**b**	b → **bb**	ru**bb**ing	ru**bb**ed
bi**g**	g → **gg**	bi**gg**er	bi**gg**est
we**t**	t → **tt**	we**tt**er	we**tt**est
thi**n**	n → **nn**	thi**nn**er	thi**nn**est

此類的字若多於一個音節(例如 **prefer**、**begin** 等)，只有當重音落在最後一個音節時，才重複子音字母，例如：

preFER / prefe**rr**ing / prefe**rr**ed   perMIT / permi**tt**ing / permi**tt**ed

reGRET / regre**tt**ing / regre**tt**ed   beGIN / begi**nn**ing

若最後一個音節並非重音節，則不重複子音字母，例如：

VISit / visi**t**ing / visi**t**ed   deVELop / develo**p**ing / develo**p**ed

HAPpen / happe**n**ing / happe**n**ed   reMEMber / remembe**r**ing / remembe**r**ed

英式英文拼法參見附錄 7。

注意下面各情形：

兩個不同子音結尾的字(例如**-rt**、**-lp**、**-ng** 等)，不需重複最後一個子音字母，例如：

sta**rt** / sta**rt**ing / sta**rt**ed   he**lp** / he**lp**ing / he**lp**ed   lo**ng** / lo**ng**er / lo**ng**est

若字尾的子音前為兩個母音字母(例如 **-oil**、**-eed** 等)，也不需重複最後一個子音字母，例如：

b**oil** / b**oil**ing / b**oil**ed   n**eed** / n**eed**ing / n**eed**ed   expl**ain** / expl**ain**ing / expl**ain**ed

ch**eap** / ch**eap**er / ch**eap**est   l**oud** / l**oud**er / l**oud**est   qu**iet** / qu**iet**er / qu**iet**est

以 **y** 或 **w** 結尾的字，不需重複該子音字母(因為在字尾的 **y** 或 **w** 不是子音)，例如：

sta**y** / sta**y**ing / sta**y**ed   gro**w** / gro**w**ing   ne**w** / ne**w**er / ne**w**est

英式英文

美式英文與英式英文在文法規則上有部分不同。

Unit	美式英文	英式英文
8A–C	過去簡單式與現在完成式皆可以表示剛剛或最近發生的事，例如： ■ I **lost** my keys. **Did** you **see** them? 或 I**'ve lost** my keys. **Have** you **seen** them? ■ Sally isn't here. { She **went** out. / She**'s gone** out. 過去簡單式與現在完成式皆可以和 **just**、**already** 以及 **yet** 一起使用，例如： ■ I'm not hungry. { I **just had** lunch. / I**'ve just had** lunch. ■ *A:* What time is Mark leaving? *B:* { He **already left**. / He **has already left**. ■ **Did** you **finish** your work **yet**? 或 **Have** you **finished** your work **yet**?	通常只有現在完成式用於表示剛剛或最近發生的事，例如： ■ I**'ve lost** my keys. **Have** you **seen** them? ■ Sally isn't here. She**'s gone** out. 通常只有現在完成式可以和 **just**、**already** 以及 **yet** 一起使用，例如： ■ I'm not hungry. I**'ve just had** lunch. ■ *A:* What time is Mark leaving? *B:* He **has already left**. ■ **Have** you **finished** your work **yet**?
27	美式英文用 **must not** 表示說話者確定某事不是真的，例如： ■ Their car isn't outside their house. They **must not** be at home. ■ She walked past me without speaking. She **must not** have seen me.	英式英文則通常以 **can't** 表示確定某事不是真的，例如： ■ Their car isn't outside their house. They **can't** be at home. ■ She walked past me without speaking. She **can't** have seen me.
32	在 **demand**、**insist** 等之後，通常使用假設語氣，例如： ■ I **insisted** he **have** dinner with us.	英式英文則較常使用 **should**，或過去簡單式和現在簡單式，例如： ■ I **insisted** that he **should have** dinner with us. 或 I **insisted** that he **had** dinner with us.
49B	美式英語通常用 **You have?** / **She isn't?** 等，例如： ■ *A:* Liz isn't feeling very well today. *B:* **She isn't?** What's wrong with her?	英式英語通常用 **Have you?** / **Isn't she?** 等，例如： ■ *A:* Liz isn't feeling very well today. *B:* **Isn't she?** What's wrong with her?
70C, 122A	美式英文用 to/in **the hospital** 表達「送到醫院」，例如： ■ Two people were taken to **the hospital** after the accident.	英式英文則通常用 to/in **hospital** (沒有 the)，例如： ■ Two people were taken to **hospital** after the accident.
118A	美式英文用 **on the weekend** / **on weekends** 表示「在週末」，例如： ■ Will you be here **on the weekend**?	英式英文則用 **at the weekend** / **at weekends**，例如： ■ Will you be here **at the weekend**?
121A	美式英文用 **in** the front / **in** the back (a group 等)，例如： ■ Let's sit **in** the front (of the movie theater).	英式英文則用 **at** the front / **at** the back group 等)，例如： ■ Let's sit **at** the front (of the cinema).

Unit	美式英文	英式英文
128	美式英文用 **different from** 或 **different than** 表示「與…不同」，例如： ■ It was **different from/than** what I'd expected.	英式英文則用 **different from** 或 **different to**，例如： ■ It was **different from/to** what I'd expected.
134A	美式英語通常用 **around**，例如： ■ He turned **around**.	英式英語通常 **round** 與 **around** 皆可使用，例如： ■ He turned **round**. 或 He turned **around**.
134A–B	美式英文用 **get along** (with 某人) 表示「與某人相處」，例如： ■ Do you **get along with** your boss?	英式英文則用 **get on** 或 **get along** (with 某人)，例如： ■ Do you **get on with** your boss? 或 …**get along with** your boss?
134C, 135C	美式英文用 **fill out** (a form 等)，例如： ■ Could you **fill out** this form?	英式英文則用 **fill in** 或 **fill out** (a form 等)，例如： ■ Could you **fill in** this form? 或 …**fill out** this form?
139B	美式英文用 **tear down** (a building) 表示「拆除(建築物)」，例如： ■ Some old houses were **torn down** to make room for a new shopping mall.	英式英文則用 **knock down** (a building)，例如： ■ Some old houses were **knocked down** to make room for a new shopping mall.
141D	美式英文用 **fix up** (a house 等) 表示「修繕(房子等)」，例如： ■ That old house looks great now that it has been **fixed up**.	英式英文則用 **do up** (a house 等)，例如： ■ That old house looks great now that it has been **done up**.

附錄	美式英文	英式英文
1.3	下列動詞在美式英文中為規則動詞： **burn** → burned **dream** → dreamed **lean** → leaned **learn** → learned **smell** → smelled **spell** → spelled **spill** → spilled **spoil** → spoiled **get** 的過去分詞是 **gotten**，例如： ■ Your English has **gotten** much better. (= has become much better) 但是 **have got** (而不是 gotten)意思與 **have** 相同，例如： ■ I've got two brothers. (= I have two brothers.)	下列動詞在英式英文中可以是規則動詞或不規則動詞： **burn** → burned 或 burnt **dream** → dreamed 或 dreamt **lean** → leaned 或 leant **learn** → learned 或 learnt **smell** → smelled 或 smelt **spell** → spelled 或 spelt **spill** → spilled 或 spilt **spoil** → spoiled 或 spoilt **get** 的過去分詞是 **got**，例如： ■ Your English has **got** much better. 與美式英文相同，**have got** 意思與 have 相同，例如： ■ I've got two brothers.
6.6	美式英文拼法： travel → traveling, traveled cancel → canceling, canceled	英式英文拼法： travel → travelling, travelled cancel → cancelling, cancelled

補充練習

補充練習分為下列各部分：

現在式與過去式　　　　　　　　　　　　　Unit 1 至 Unit 6, 附錄 2

1　依各句題意，填入正確的動詞時式：現在簡單式 (*I do*)、現在進行式 (*I am doing*)、過去簡單式 (*I did*) 或過去進行式 (*I was doing*)。

1. We can go out now. It _isn't raining_ (not / rain) anymore.
2. Catherine _was waiting_ (wait) for me when I _arrived_ (arrive).
3. I _____ (get) hungry. Let's go and have something to eat.
4. What _____ (you / do) in your spare time? Do you have any hobbies?
5. The weather was horrible when we _____ (arrive). It was cold and it _____ (rain) hard.
6. Louise usually _____ (call) me on Fridays, but she _____ (not / call) last Friday.
7. *A:* The last time I saw you, you _____ (think) of moving to a new apartment.
   B: That's right, but in the end I _____ (decide) to stay where I was.
8. Why _____ (you / look) at me like that? What's the matter?
9. It's usually dry here at this time of the year. It _____ (not / rain) much.
10. The phone _____ (ring) three times while we _____ (have) dinner last night.
11. Linda was busy when we _____ (go) to see her yesterday. She _____ (study) for an exam. We _____ (not / want) to bother her, so we _____ (not / stay) very long.
12. When I _____ (tell) Tom the news, he _____ (not / believe) me at first. He _____ (think) that I _____ (joke).

2 依各句題意，選出正確的動詞時式。

1. Everything is going well. We ~~didn't have~~ / haven't had any problems so far. (*haven't had* is correct)
2. Lisa didn't go / hasn't gone to work yesterday. She wasn't feeling well.
3. Look! That man over there wears / is wearing the same sweater as you.
4. I went / have been to New Zealand last year.
5. I didn't hear / haven't heard from Ann in the last few days. I wonder why.
6. I wonder why Jim is / is being so nice to me today. He isn't usually like that.
7. Jane had a book open in front of her, but she didn't read / wasn't reading it.
8. I wasn't very busy. I didn't have / wasn't having much to do.
9. It begins / It's beginning to get dark. Should I turn on the light?
10. After finishing high school, Tim got / has got a job in a factory.
11. When Sue heard the news, she wasn't / hasn't been very pleased.
12. This is a nice restaurant, isn't it? Is this the first time you are / you've been here?
13. I need a new job. I'm doing / I've been doing the same job for too long.
14. "Anna has gone out." "She has? What time did she go / has she gone?"
15. "You look tired." "Yes, I've played / I've been playing basketball."
16. Where are you coming / do you come from? Are you Australian?
17. I'd like to see Tina again. It's been a long time since I saw her / that I didn't see her.
18. Robert and Maria have been married since 20 years / for 20 years.

依各句題意，填入適當的動詞以完成各個對話。

1. *A:* I'm looking for Paul. *Have you seen* him?
   B: Yes, he was here a minute ago.
2. *A:* Why *did you go* to bed so early last night?
   B: Because I was very tired.
3. *A:* Where _____ ?
   B: To the post office. I want to mail these letters. I'll be back in a few minutes.
4. *A:* _____ television every night?
   B: No, only if there's something special on.
5. *A:* Your house is very beautiful. How long _____ here?
   B: Almost 10 years.
6. *A:* How was your vacation? _____ a nice time?
   B: Yes, thanks. It was great.
7. *A:* _____ Julie recently?
   B: Yes, we had lunch together a few days ago.
8. *A:* Can you describe the woman you saw? What _____ ?
   B: A red sweater and black jeans.
9. *A:* I'm sorry to keep you waiting. _____ long?
   B: No, only about 10 minutes.
10. *A:* How long _____ you to get to work in the morning?
    B: Usually about 45 minutes. It depends on the traffic.
11. *A:* _____ a horse before?
    B: No, this is the first time.
12. *A:* _____ to Australia?
    B: No, never, but I went to New Zealand a few years ago.

4 依你自己的意思完成各個對話。

1. *A:* What's the new restaurant like? Is it good?
   B: I have no idea. ___*I've never been*___ there.
2. *A:* How well do you know Bill?
   B: Very well. We _____ since we were children.
3. *A:* Did you enjoy your vacation?
   B: Yes, it was fantastic. It's the best vacation _____ .
4. *A:* Is David still here?
   B: No, I'm afraid he isn't. _____ about 10 minutes ago.
5. *A:* I like your suit. I haven't seen it before.
   B: It's new. It's the first time _____ .
6. *A:* How did you cut your knee?
   B: I slipped and fell while _____ tennis.
7. *A:* Do you ever go swimming?
   B: Not these days. I haven't _____ a long time.
8. *A:* How often do you go to the movies?
   B: Hardly ever. It's been almost a year _____ to the movies.
9. *A:* I've bought some new shoes. Do you like them?
   B: Yes, they're very nice. Where _____ them?

現在式與過去式   Unit 1 至 Unit 15 與 Unit 107, 附錄 2

5 依下列圖片與各句題意，填入正確的動詞時式：過去簡單式 (*I did*)、過去進行式 (*I was doing*)、過去完成式 (*I had done*) 或過去完成進行式 (*I had been doing*)。

1.

Yesterday afternoon Sarah ___*went*___ (go) to the station to meet Paul. When she
_____ (get) there, Paul _____ (already / wait)
for her. His train _____ (arrive) early.

2.

When I got home, Bill _____ (lie) on the sofa. The television was on,
but he _____ (not / watch) it. He _____ (fall)
asleep and _____ (snore) loudly. I _____ (turn)
the television off and just then he _____ (wake) up.

3.

Last night I _____ (just / go) to bed and _____ (read)
a book when suddenly I _____ (hear) a noise. I _____
(get) up to see what it was, but I _____ (not / see) anything, so I
_____ (go) back to bed.

4.

Lisa had to go to Tokyo last week, but she almost _____ (miss) the plane. She
_____ (stand) in line at the check-in counter when she suddenly
_____ (realize) that she _____ (leave) her passport
at home. Fortunately she lives near the airport, so she _____ (have) time to
take a taxi home to get it. She _____ (get) back to the airport just in time
for her flight.

5.

I _____ (meet) Peter and Lucy yesterday as I _____
(walk) through the park. They _____ (be) to the Sports Center where they
_____ (play) tennis. They _____ (go) to a café and
_____ (invite) me to join them, but I _____ (arrange)
to meet another friend and _____ (not / have) time.

依各句題意，以括號中的字配合正確的動詞時式完成句子：現在完成式 (*I have done*)、現在完成進行式
(*I have been doing*)、過去完成式 (*I had done*) 或過去完成進行式 (*I had been doing*)。

1. Amanda is sitting on the ground. She's out of breath.
   (she / run) *She has been running.*

2. Where's my bag? I left it under this chair.
   (somebody / take / it) _____

3. We were all surprised when Jenny and Andy got married last year.
   (they / only / know / each other / a few weeks)
   _____

4. It's still raining. I wish it would stop.
   (it / rain / all day) _____

5. Suddenly I woke up. I was confused and didn't know where I was.
   (I / dream) _____

6. I wasn't hungry at lunchtime, so I didn't have anything to eat.
   (I / have / a big breakfast) _____
7. Every year Robert and Tina spend a few days at the same hotel in Hawaii.
   (they / go / there for years) _____
8. I've got a headache.
   (I / have / it / since I got up) _____
9. Next week Gary is going to run in a marathon.
   (he / train / very hard for it) _____

7 依各句題意，填入正確的動詞時式。

Julia and Kevin are old friends. They meet by chance at the train station.

Julia: Hello, Kevin. (1) _____ (I / not / see)
you in ages. How are you?

Kevin: I'm fine. How about you?
(2) _____ (you / look) good.

Julia: Thanks. So, (3) _____ (you / go) somewhere or
(4) _____ (you / meet) somebody?

Kevin: (5) _____ (I / go) to New York for a business meeting.

Julia: Oh. (6) _____ (you / travel / a lot) on business?

Kevin: Fairly often, yes. And you? Where (7) _____ (you / go)?

Julia: Nowhere. (8) _____ (I / meet) a friend. Unfortunately,
her train (9) _____ (be) delayed – (10) _____
(I / wait) here for nearly an hour.

Kevin: How are your children?

Julia: They're all fine, thanks. The youngest (11) _____ (just / start)
school.

Kevin: How (12) _____ (she / do)?
(13) _____ (she / like) it?

Julia: Yes, (14) _____ (she / think) it's great.

Kevin: (15) _____ (you / work) these days? The last time I
(16) _____ (speak) to you, (17) _____
(you / work) in a travel agency.

Julia: That's right. Unfortunately, the company (18) _____ (go) out
of business a couple of months after (19) _____ (I / start)
work there, so (20) _____ (I / lose) my job.

Kevin: And (21) _____ (you / not / have) a job since then?

Julia: Not a permanent job. (22) _____ (I / have) a few temporary
jobs. By the way, (23) _____ (you / see) Joe recently?

Kevin: Joe? He's in Canada.

Julia: Really? How long (24) _____ (he / be) in Canada?

Kevin: About a year now. (25) _____ (I / see) him a few days before
(26) _____ (he / leave). (27) _____ (he / be)
unemployed for months, so (28) _____ (he / decide) to try his
luck somewhere else. (29) _____ (he / really / look forward)
to going.

Julia: So, what (30) _____ (he / do) there?

Kevin: I have no idea. (31) _____ (I / not / hear) from him since
(32) _____ (he / leave). Anyway, I have to go – my train is
here. It was really nice to see you again.

Julia: You, too. Bye. Have a good trip.

Kevin: Thanks. Bye.

8 依各句題意，填入最適當的動詞時式。

1. Who _____ (invent) the bicycle?
2. "Do you still have that class on Wednesdays?" "No, _____ (it / end)."
3. I was the last to leave the office last night. Everybody else _____ (go) home when I _____ (leave).
4. What _____ (you / do) last weekend? _____ (you / go) away?
5. I like your car. How long _____ (you / have) it?
6. It's a shame the trip was canceled. I _____ (look) forward to it.
7. Jane is an experienced teacher. _____ (she / teach) for 15 years.
8. _____ (I / buy) a new jacket last week, but _____ (I / not / wear) it yet.
9. A few days ago _____ (I / see) a man at a party whose face _____ (be) very familiar. At first I couldn't think where _____ (I / see) him before. Then suddenly _____ (I / remember) who _____ (he / be).
10. _____ (you / hear) of Agatha Christie? _____ (she / be) a writer who _____ (die) in 1976. _____ (she / write) more than 70 detective novels. _____ (you / read) any of them?
11. *A:* What _____ (this word / mean)?
    B: I have no idea. _____ (I / never / see) it before. Look it up in the dictionary.
12. *A:* _____ (you / get) to the theater in time for the play last night?
    B: No, we were late. By the time we got there, _____ (it / already / begin).
13. I went to Sarah's room and _____ (knock) on the door, but there _____ (be) no answer. Either _____ (she / go) out or _____ (she / not / want) to see anyone.
14. Patrick asked me how to use the photocopier. _____ (he / never / use) it before, so _____ (he / not / know) what to do.
15. Liz _____ (go) for a swim after work yesterday. _____ (she / need) some exercise because _____ (she / sit) in an office all day in front of a computer.

過去進行式與 *used to*　　　　　　　　　　Unit 6 與 Unit 17

依各句題意，用括號中的字，以過去進行式 (*was/were -ing*) 或 *used to . . .* 完成各句。

1. I haven't been to the movies in ages now. We _used to go_ a lot. (go)
2. Ann didn't see me wave to her. She _was looking_ in the other direction. (look)
3. I _____ a lot, but I don't use my car very much these days. (drive)
4. I asked the taxi driver to slow down. She _____ too fast. (drive)
5. Rosemary and Jonathan met for the first time when they _____ at the same bank. (work)
6. When I was a child, I _____ a lot of bad dreams. (have)
7. I wonder what Joe is doing these days. He _____ in Spain when I last heard from him. (live)
8. "Where were you yesterday afternoon?" "I _____ volleyball." (play)
9. "Do you play any sports?" "Not these days, but I _____ volleyball." (play)
10. George looked very nice at the party. He _____ a very stylish suit. (wear)

10 依下列各題的情境，用括號中的字，以現在進行式 (*I am doing*)、*going to* 或 *will* (*I'll*)，完成各個對話。

1. You have made all your vacation plans. Your destination is Japan.
   Friend: Have you decided where you're going on vacation yet?
   You: ___*I am going to Japan.*___ (I / go)

2. You have made an appointment with the dentist for Friday morning.
   Friend: Do you want to get together on Friday morning?
   You: I can't on Friday. _____ (I / go)

3. You and some friends are planning a vacation in Mexico. You have decided to rent a car, but you haven't arranged this yet.
   Friend: How do you plan to travel around Mexico? By bus?
   You: No, _____ (we / rent)

4. Your friend has two young children. She wants to go out tomorrow night. You offer to take care of the children.
   Friend: I want to go out tomorrow night, but I don't have a babysitter.
   You: That's no problem. _____ (I / take care of)

5. You have already arranged to have lunch with Sue tomorrow.
   Friend: Are you free at lunchtime tomorrow?
   You: No, _____ (have lunch)

6. You are in a restaurant. You and your friend are looking at the menu. Maybe your friend has decided what to have. You ask her/him.
   You: What _____ ? (you / have)
   Friend: I don't know. I can't make up my mind.

7. You and a friend are reading. It's getting dark, and your friend is having trouble reading. You decide to turn on the light.
   Friend: It's getting dark, isn't it? It's difficult to read.
   You: Yes. _____ (I / turn on)

8. You and a friend are reading. It's getting dark and you decide to turn on the light. You stand up and walk toward the light switch.
   Friend: What are you doing?
   You: _____ (I / turn on)

11 依以下 Jenny 與 Helen 對話的內容，填入最適當的動詞時式：現在式(簡單式或進行式)、*will* (*I'll*) 或 *shall/should*。

Conversation 1 *(in the morning)*

Jenny: (1) ___*Are you doing*___ (you / do) anything tomorrow night, Helen?

Helen: No, why?

Jenny: Well, do you feel like going to the movies? *Strangers on a Plane* is playing. I want to see it, but I don't want to go alone.

Helen: OK, (2) _____ (I / go) with you. What time
(3) _____ (we / meet)?

Jenny: Well, the movie (4) _____ (start) at 8:45, so
(5) _____ (I / meet) you at about 8:30 outside the theater, OK?

Helen: Fine. (6) _____ (I / see) Tina later on tonight.
(7) _____ (I / ask) her if she wants to come, too?

Jenny: Yes, why don't you? (8) _____ (I / see) you tomorrow then. Bye.

Conversation 2 *(later the same day)*

Helen: Jenny and I (9) _____ (go) to the movies tomorrow
night to see *Strangers on a Plane*. Why don't you come with us?

Tina: I'd love to come. What time (10) _____ (the movie / start)?

Helen: 8:45.

Tina: (11) _____ (you / meet) outside the theater?

Helen: Yes, at 8:30. Is that OK for you?

Tina: Yes, (12) _____ (I / be) there at 8:30.

2 依下列各個對話的內容，填入最適當的動詞時式；有時可能會有一個以上適當的時式。

1. *A has decided to learn a language.*
   A: I've decided to try and learn a foreign language.
   B: You have? Which language (1) __*are you going to learn*__ (you / learn)?
   A: Spanish.
   B: (2) _____ (you / take) a class?
   A: Yes, (3) _____ (it / start) next week.
   B: That's great. I'm sure (4) _____ (you / enjoy) it.
   A: I hope so. But I think (5) _____ (it / be) a lot of work.

2. *A wants to know about B's vacation plans.*
   A: I hear (1) _____ (you / go) on vacation soon.
   B: That's right. (2) _____ (we / go) to Brazil.
   A: I hope (3) _____ (you / have) a nice time.
   B: Thanks. (4) _____ (I / send) you a postcard and
   (5) _____ (I / get) in touch with you when
   (6) _____ (I / get) back.

3. *A invites B to a party.*
   A: (1) _____ (I / have) a party next Saturday. Can you come?
   B: On Saturday? I'm not sure. Some friends of mine (2) _____ (come) to
   stay with me next week, but I think (3) _____ (they / leave) by
   Saturday. But if (4) _____ (they / be) still here,
   (5) _____ (I / not / be) able to come to the party.
   A: OK. Well, tell me as soon as (6) _____ (you / know).
   B: All right. (7) _____ (I / call) you during the week.

4. *A and B are two secret agents arranging a meeting. They are talking on the phone.*
   A: Well, what time (1) _____ (we / meet)?
   B: Come to the café by the station at 4:00.
   (2) _____ (I / wait) for you
   when (3) _____ (you / arrive).
   (4) _____ (I / sit) by the window
   and (5) _____ (I / wear) a bright green sweater.
   A: OK. (6) _____ (Agent 307 / come), too?
   B: No, she can't come.
   A: Oh. (7) _____ (I / bring) the documents?
   B: Yes. (8) _____ (I / explain) everything when
   (9) _____ (I / see) you. And don't be late.
   A: OK. (10) _____ (I / try) to be on time.

13 依各句題意，自下列時式中選出正確者，以填入正確的動詞時式完成句子。

現在進行式 (**I am doing**)   will (**'ll**) / **won't**
現在簡單式 (**I do**)   **will be doing**
going to (**I'm going to do**)   **should / shall**

1. I'm a little hungry. I think _____ (I / have) something to eat.
2. Why are you putting on your coat? _____ (you / go) somewhere?
3. What time _____ (I / call) you tonight? About 7:30?
4. Look! That plane is flying toward the airport. _____ (it / land).
5. We have to do something soon before _____ (it / be) too late.
6. I'm sorry you've decided to leave the company. _____ (I / miss) you
   when _____ (you / go).
7. _____ (I / give) you my address? If _____
   (I / give) you my address, _____ (you / send) me a postcard?
8. Are you still watching that TV program? What time _____ (it / end)?
9. _____ (I / go) to Chicago next weekend for a wedding.
   My sister _____ (get) married.
10. I'm not ready yet. _____ (I / tell) you when _____
    (I / be) ready. I promise _____ (I / not / be) very long.
11. *A:* Where are you going?
    B: To the hairdresser. _____ (I / have) my hair cut.
12. She was very rude to me. I refuse to speak to her again until _____ (she /
    apologize).
13. I wonder where _____ (we / live) 10 years from now?
14. What do you plan to do when _____ (you / finish) college?

過去式、現在式與未來式   Unit 1 至 Unit 24

依你自己的意思完成各個對話。

14
1. *A:* How did the accident happen?
   B: I _was going_ too fast and couldn't stop in time.
2. *A:* Is that a new camera?
   B: No, I _____ it a long time.
3. *A:* Is that a new computer?
   B: Yes, I _____ it a few weeks ago.
4. *A:* I can't talk to you right now. You can see I'm very busy.
   B: OK. I _____ back in about half an hour.
5. *A:* This is a nice restaurant. Do you come here often?
   B: No, it's the first time I _____ here.
6. *A:* Do you play any sports?
   B: No, I _____ tennis, but I gave it up.
7. *A:* I'm sorry I'm late.
   B: That's OK. I _____ long.
8. *A:* When you went to Russia last year, was it your first visit?
   B: No, I _____ there twice before.
9. *A:* Do you have any plans for the weekend?
   B: Yes, I _____ to a party on Saturday night.
10. *A:* Do you know what Steve's doing these days?
    B: No, I _____ him in ages.
11. *A:* Will you still be here by the time I get back?
    B: No, I _____ by then.

5 Robert 正在美國旅遊，他寄送電子郵件給在 Winnipeg (加拿大) 的友人。依各句題意，填入最適當的動詞時式。

North American travels

To: Chris

Subject: North American travels

Hi

(1) _I've just arrived_ (I / just / arrive) in Minneapolis. (2) _____ (I / travel) for more than a month now, and (3) _____ (I / begin) to think about coming home. Everything (4) _____ (I / see) so far (5) _____ (be) really interesting, and (6) _____ (I / meet) some really kind people.

(7) _____ (I / leave) Kansas City a week ago. (8) _____ (I / stay) there with Emily, the aunt of a friend from college. She was really helpful and hospitable and although (9) _____ (I / plan) to stay only a couple of days, (10) _____ (I / end up) staying more than a week.

(11) _____ (I / enjoy) the trip from Kansas City to here. (12) _____ (I / take) the Greyhound bus and (13) _____ (meet) some really interesting people – everybody was really friendly.

So now I'm here, and (14) _____ (I / stay) here for a few days before (15) _____ (I / continue) up to Canada. I'm not sure exactly when (16) _____ (I / get) to Winnipeg – it depends what happens while (17) _____ (I / be) here. But (18) _____ (I / let) you know as soon as (19) _____ (I / know) myself.

(20) _____ (I / stay) with a family here – they're friends of some people I know at home. Tomorrow (21) _____ (we / visit) some people they know who (22) _____ (build) a house on a lake. It isn't finished yet, but (23) _____ (it / be) interesting to see what it's like.

Anyway, that's all for now. (24) _____ (I / be) in touch again soon.

Robert

情態助動詞 (*can/must/would* 等)　　Unit 25 至 Unit 34, 附錄 4

依各句題意，自選項中選出正確的時式；有時可能會有一個以上適當的時式。

1. "What time will you be home tonight?" "I'm not sure. I __*A or B*__ late."
   A may be　　**B** might be　　**C** can be　　(both *A* and *B* are correct)
2. I can't find the theater tickets. They _____ out of my pocket.
   A must have fallen　　**B** should have fallen　　C had to fall
3. Somebody ran in front of the car as I was driving. Fortunately, I _____ just in time.
   A could stop　　**B** could have stopped　　**C** managed to stop
4. We've got plenty of time. We _____ yet.
   A must not leave　　**B** couldn't leave　　**C** don't have to leave
5. I _____ out but I didn't feel like it, so I stayed at home.
   A could go　　**B** could have gone　　**C** must have gone

6. I'm sorry I _____ to your party last week.
   A couldn't come   **B** couldn't have come   **C** wasn't able to come
7. "What do you think of my theory?" "I'm not sure. You _____ right."
   A could be   **B** must be   **C** might be
8. I couldn't wait for you any longer. I _____ , and so I went.
   A must go   **B** must have gone   **C** had to go
9. "Do you know where Liz is?" "No. I suppose she _____ shopping."
   A should have gone   **B** may have gone   **C** could have gone
10. At first they didn't believe me when I told them what had happened, but in the end
    I _____ them that I was telling the truth.
    A was able to convince   **B** managed to convince   **C** could convince
11. I promised I'd call Gary tonight. I _____ .
    A can't forget   **B** must not forget   **C** don't have to forget
12. Why did you leave without me? You _____ for me.
    A must have waited   **B** had to wait   **C** should have waited
13. Lisa called and suggested _____ lunch together.
    A we have   **B** having   **C** to have
14. You look nice in that jacket, but you hardly ever wear it. _____ it more often.
    A You'd better wear   **B** You should wear   **C** You ought to wear
15. Should I buy a car? What's your advice? What _____ ?
    A will you do   **B** would you do   **C** should you do

17 以括號內的字，依各句題意，完成句子。

1. Don't call them now. (they might / have / lunch)
   *They might be having lunch.*

2. I ate too much. Now I feel sick. (I shouldn't / eat / so much)
   *I shouldn't have eaten so much.*

3. I wonder why Tom didn't call me. (he must / forget)
   _____

4. Why did you go home so late? (you shouldn't / leave / so late)
   _____

5. You signed the contract. (it can't / change / now)
   _____

6. Why weren't you here earlier? (you could / get / here earlier)
   _____

7. "What's Linda doing?" "I'm not sure." (she may / watch / television)
   _____

8. Laura was standing outside the movie theater. (she must / wait / for somebody)
   _____

9. He was in prison at the time that the crime was committed. (he couldn't / do / it)
   _____

10. Why didn't you ask me to help you? (I would / help / you)
    _____

11. I'm surprised you weren't told that the road was dangerous. (you should / warn / about it)
    _____

12. Gary was in a strange mood yesterday. (he might not / feel / very well)
    _____

8 依各題對話內容，以 *can / could / might / must / should / would* + 括號中的動詞，填入適當的動詞時式完成句子。有些句子需要使用 *must have . . . / should have . . .* 等動詞時式；並視需要使用否定形式 (*can't/couldn't* 等)。

1. *A:* I'm hungry.
   B: But you just had lunch. You __*can't be*__ hungry already. (be)
2. *A:* I haven't seen our neighbors in ages.
   B: Neither have I. They __*must have gone*__ away. (go)
3. *A:* What's the weather like? Is it raining?
   B: Not right now, but it _____ later. (rain)
4. *A:* Where's Julia?
   B: I'm not sure. She _____ to the bank. (go)
5. *A:* I didn't see you at Michael's party last week.
   B: No, I had to work that night, so I _____ (go)
6. *A:* I saw you at Michael's party last week.
   B: No, you _____ me. I didn't go to Michael's party. (see)
7. *A:* What time will we get to Sue's house?
   B: Well, it's about a two-hour drive, so if we leave at 3:00, we _____ there by 5:00. (get)
8. *A:* When was the last time you saw Bill?
   B: Years ago. I _____ him if I saw him now. (recognize)
9. *A:* Did you hear the explosion?
   B: What explosion?
   A: There was a loud explosion about an hour ago. You _____ it. (hear)
10. *A:* We weren't sure which way to go. In the end we turned right.
    B: You went the wrong way. You _____ left. (turn)

If (條件句)   Unit 24 與 Unit 36 至 Unit 38

依各句題意，填入正確的動詞形式。

1. If you __*found*__ a wallet in the street, what would you do with it? (find)
2. I have to hurry. My friend will be upset if I __*'m not*__ on time. (not / be)
3. I didn't realize that Gary was in the hospital. If I __*had known*__ he was in the hospital, I would have gone to visit him. (know)
4. If the phone _____ , can you answer it? (ring)
5. I can't decide what to do. What would you do if you _____ in my position? (be)
6. *A:* What should we do tomorrow?
   B: Well, if it _____ a nice day, we can go to the beach. (be)
7. *A:* Let's go to the beach.
   B: No, it's too cold. If it _____ warmer, I wouldn't mind going. (be)
8. *A:* Did you go to the beach yesterday?
   B: No, it was too cold. If it _____ warmer, we might have gone. (be)
9. If you _____ enough money to go anywhere in the world, where would you go? (have)
10. I'm glad we had a map. I'm sure we would have gotten lost if we _____ one. (not / have)
11. The accident was your fault. If you _____ more carefully, it wouldn't have happened. (drive)
12. *A:* Why do you read newspapers?
    B: Well, if I _____ newspapers, I wouldn't know what was happening in the world. (not / read)

20 依各句提示完成句子。

1. Liz is tired all the time. She shouldn't go to bed so late.
   If _Liz didn't go to bed so late, she wouldn't be tired all the time._

2. It's getting late. I don't think Sarah will come to see us now.
   I'd be surprised if Sarah _____

3. I'm sorry I disturbed you. I didn't know you were busy.
   If I'd known you were busy, I _____

4. I don't want them to be upset, so I've decided not to tell them what happened.
   They'd _____ if _____

5. The dog attacked you, but only because you frightened it.
   If _____

6. Unfortunately, I didn't have an umbrella, so I got very wet in the rain.
   I _____

7. Martin failed his driver's test last week. He was very nervous and that's why he failed.
   If he _____

21 依你自己的意思完成下面各句。

1. I'd go out tonight if _____ .
2. I'd have gone out last night if _____ .
3. If you hadn't reminded me, _____ .
4. We wouldn't have been late if _____ .
5. If I'd been able to get tickets, _____ .
6. Who would you call if _____ ?
7. Cities would be nicer places if _____ .
8. If there were no television, _____ .

被動語氣 Unit 40 至 Unit 43

22 依各句題意，填入最適當的被動語氣動詞。

1. There's somebody behind us. I think we _are being followed_ (follow).
2. A mystery is something that _can't be explained_ (can't / explain).
3. We didn't play baseball yesterday. The game _____ (cancel).
4. The television _____ (repair). It's working again now.
5. In the middle of town there is a church, which _____ (restore) at this time. The work is almost finished.
6. The tower is the oldest part of the church. It _____ (believe) to be more than 100 years old.
7. If I didn't do my job right, I _____ (would / fire).
8. *A:* I left a newspaper on the desk last night and it isn't there now.
   B: It _____ (might / throw) away.
9. I learned to swim when I was very young. I _____ (teach) by my mother.
10. After _____ (arrest), I was taken to the police station.
11. "_____ (you / ever / arrest)?" "No, never."
12. *(TV news report)* Two people _____ (report) to _____ (injure) in an explosion at a factory in Miami early this morning.

3 依各句題意，填入主動或被動語氣動詞。

1. This house is very old. It ___was built___ (build) over 100 years ago.
2. My grandfather was a builder. He ___built___ (build) this house many years ago.
3. "Is your car still for sale?" "No, I _____ (sell) it."
4. *A:* Is the house at the end of the street still for sale?
   B: No, it _____ (sell).
5. Sometimes mistakes _____ (make). It's inevitable.
6. I wouldn't leave your car unlocked. It _____ (might / steal).
7. My bag has disappeared. It _____ (must / steal).
8. I can't find my hat. Somebody _____ (must / take) it by mistake.
9. It's a serious problem. I don't know how it _____ _____ (can / solve).
10. We didn't leave early enough. We _____ (should / leave) earlier.
11. Nearly every time I travel by plane, my flight _____ (delay).
12. A new bridge _____ (build) across the river. Work started last year
    and the bridge _____ (expect) to open next year.

4 下列為四則新聞報導。依各篇新聞內容，填入最適當的動詞形式。

1.

Fire at City Hall

City Hall (1) ___was damaged___ (damage) in a fire last night. The fire, which (2) _____ _____ (discover) at about 9:00 p.m., spread very quickly. Nobody (3) _____ (injure), but two people had to (4) _____ _____ (rescue) from an upstairs room. A large number of documents (5) _____ _____ (believe / destroy). It (6) _____ _____ (not / know) how the fire started.

2.

Convenience Store Robbery

A convenience store clerk (1) _____ _____ (force) to hand over $500 after (2) _____ (threaten) by a man with a gun. The man escaped in a car, which (3) _____ (steal) earlier in the day. The car (4) _____ _____ (later / find) in a parking lot, where it (5) _____ (abandon) by the thief. A man (6) _____ _____ (arrest) in connection with the robbery and (7) _____ _____ (still / question) by the police.

3.

Road Delays

Repair work started yesterday on Route 22. The road (1) _____ (resurface), and there will be long delays. Drivers (2) _____ (ask) to use an alternate route if possible. The work (3) _____ (expect) to last two weeks. Next Sunday the road (4) _____ (close), and traffic (5) _____ (reroute).

4.

Accident

A woman (1) _____ (take) to the hospital after her car collided with a truck on the freeway yesterday. She (2) _____ _____ (allow) to go home later that day after treatment. The road (3) _____ _____ (block) for an hour after the accident, and traffic had to (4) _____ _____ (reroute). A police investigator said afterward: "The woman was lucky. She could (5) _____ _____ (kill)."

25 依各題的情境，以間接敘述完成各個句子。

1.

> Can I speak to Paul, please?

> I'll try again later.

> Paul's gone out. I don't know when he'll be back.
> Do you want to leave a message?

You

A woman called at lunchtime yesterday and asked __*if she could speak to Paul*__ . I told
_____ and _____
_____ . I asked _____
_____ , but she said _____ later. But she never did.

2.

> We have no record of a reservation in your name.

> We're sorry, but the hotel is full.

> Do you have any rooms available?

RECEPTION

I went to New York recently, but my trip didn't begin well. I had reserved a hotel room, but when I got
to the hotel, they told _____ no _____ . When I
asked _____ ,
they said _____ , but _____ .
There was nothing I could do. I just had to look for somewhere else to stay.

3.

> Why are you visiting the country?

> How long do you intend to stay?

> Where will you be staying during your visit?

> We're on vacation.

After getting off the plane, we had to stand in line for an hour to get through immigration. Finally
it was our turn. The immigration official asked us _____
_____ , and we told _____ .
Then he wanted to know _____ and
_____ .
He seemed satisfied with our answers, checked our passports, and wished us a pleasant stay.

4.

> I'll call you from the airport when I arrive.

> Don't come to the airport. I'll take the bus.

Sue

A: What time is Sue arriving this afternoon?

B: About three. She said _____
_____ .

A: Aren't you going to meet her?

B: No, she said _____ . She said
_____ .

5.

A few days ago a man called from a marketing company and started asking me questions.

He wanted to know _____ and asked _____ .

I don't like people calling and asking questions like that, so I told _____

_____ and I put the phone down.

6. *now*

Louise   Sarah

Paul

Louise and Sarah are in a restaurant waiting for Paul.

Louise: I wonder where Paul is. He said _____ .

Sarah: Maybe he got lost.

Louise: I don't think so. He said _____ .

And I told _____ .

7.

Jane   Joe

Joe: Is there anything to eat?

Jane: You just said _____ .

Joe: Well, I am now. I'd love a banana.

Jane: A banana? But you said _____ .

You told _____ .

-ing 與不定詞   Unit 51 至 Unit 64

依各句題意，填入正確的動詞形式。

1. How old were you when you learned __to drive__ ? (drive)
2. I don't mind __walking__ home, but I'd rather __take__ a taxi. (walk / take)
3. I can't make a decision. I keep _____ my mind. (change)
4. He had made his decision and refused _____ his mind. (change)
5. Why did you change your decision? What made you _____ your mind? (change)
6. It was a really good vacation. I really enjoyed _____ by the ocean again. (be)
7. Did I really tell you I was unhappy? I don't remember _____ that. (say)
8. "Remember _____ Tom tomorrow." "OK, I won't forget." (call)
9. The water here is not very good. I'd avoid _____ it if I were you. (drink)
10. I pretended _____ interested in the conversation, but it was really very boring. (be)
11. I got up and looked out the window _____ what the weather was like. (see)
12. I have a friend who claims _____ able to speak five languages. (be)
13. I like _____ carefully about things before _____ a decision. (think / make)

14. I had an apartment downtown but I didn't like _____ there, so I decided _____ . (live / move)

15. Steve used _____ a hockey player. He had to stop _____ because of an injury. (be / play)

16. After _____ by the police, the man admitted _____ the car but denied _____ 100 miles an hour. (stop / steal / drive)

17. *A:* How do you make this machine _____ ? (work)
    B: I'm not sure. Try _____ that button and see what happens. (press)

27 以括號中的字，依各句題意造句。

1. I can't find the tickets. (I / seem / lose / them)
   I seem to have lost them.

2. I don't have far to go. (it / not / worth / take / a taxi)
   It's not worth taking a taxi.

3. The game was getting boring. (we / stop / watch / after a while)
   _____

4. Tim isn't very reliable. (he / tend / forget / things)
   _____

5. I've got a lot of luggage. (you / mind / help / me?)
   _____

6. There's nobody at home. (everybody / seem / go out)
   _____

7. We don't like our apartment. (we / think / move)
   _____

8. The vase was very valuable. (I / afraid / touch / it)
   _____

9. Bill never carries money with him. (he / afraid / robbed)
   _____

10. I wouldn't go to see that movie. (it / not / worth / see)
    _____

11. I'm very tired after that long walk. (I / not / used / walk / so far)
    _____

12. Sue is on vacation. I received a postcard from her yesterday. (she / seem / enjoy / herself)
    _____

13. Dave had lots of vacation pictures. (he / insist / show / them to me)
    _____

14. I don't want to do the shopping. (I'd rather / somebody else / do / it)
    _____

28 完成下列各題中的第二句話，使之與第一句話意思相似。

1. I was surprised I passed the exam.
   I didn't expect _to pass the exam_____ .

2. Did you manage to solve the problem?
   Did you succeed _in solving the problem_____ ?

3. I don't read newspapers anymore.
   I've given up _____ .

4. I'd prefer not to go out tonight.
   I'd rather _____ .

5. He can't walk very well.
   He has trouble _____ .

6. Should I call you tonight?
   Do you want _____ ?

7. Nobody saw me come in.
   I came in without _____ .

8. They said I was a liar.
   I was accused _____ .
9. It will be good to see them again.
   I'm looking forward _____ .
10. What do you think I should do?
   What do you advise me _____ ?
11. It's too bad I couldn't go out with you.
   I'd like _____ .
12. I'm sorry that I didn't take your advice.
   I regret _____ .

---

a/an 與 the   Unit 67 至 Unit 76

9 依各句題意，填入 **a/an** 或 **the**。若不須冠詞則空白。

1. I don't usually like staying at __—__ hotels, but last summer we spent a few days at __a__ very nice hotel at __the__ beach.
2. _____ tennis is my favorite sport. I play once or twice _____ week if I can, but I'm not _____ very good player.
3. I won't be home for _____ dinner this evening. I'm meeting some friends after _____ work, and we're going to _____ movies.
4. _____ unemployment is increasing, and it's very difficult for _____ people to find _____ work.
5. There was _____ accident as I was going _____ home last night. Two people were taken to _____ hospital. I think _____ most accidents are caused by _____ people driving too fast.
6. Carol is _____ economist. She used to work in _____ investment department of _____ Lloyds Bank. Now she works for _____ American bank in _____ United States.
7. *A:* What's _____ name of _____ hotel where you're staying?
   B: _____ Royal. It's on _____ West Street in _____ suburbs. It's near _____ airport.
8. I have two brothers. _____ older one is training to be _____ pilot with _____ Western Airlines. _____ younger one is still in _____ high school. When he finishes _____ school, he wants to go to _____ college to study _____ engineering.

代名詞與限定詞   Unit 80 至 Unit 89

依各句題意，自選項中選出正確者；可能會有一個或兩個適當的選項。

1. I don't remember __A__ about the accident. (*A* 是正確答案)
   A anything   **B** something   **C** nothing
2. Chris and I have known _____ for quite a long time.
   A us   **B** each other   **C** ourselves
3. "How often do the buses run?" "_____ 20 minutes."
   A All   **B** Each   **C** Every
4. I shouted for help, but _____ came.
   A nobody   **B** no one   **C** anybody
5. Last night we went out with some friends of _____ .
   A us   **B** our   **C** ours
6. It didn't take us a long time to get here. _____ traffic.
   A It wasn't much   **B** There wasn't much   **C** It wasn't a lot
7. Can I have _____ milk in my coffee, please?
   A a little   **B** any   **C** some
8. Sometimes I find it difficult to _____ .
   A concentrate   **B** concentrate me   **C** concentrate myself
9. There's _____ on at the movies that I want to see, so there's no point in going.
   A something   **B** anything   **C** nothing

10. I drink _____ water every day.

    A much   **B** a lot of   **C** lots of

11. _____ in the mall are open on Sunday.

    A Most of stores   **B** Most of the stores   **C** The most of the stores

12. There were about 20 people in the photo. I didn't recognize _____ of them.

    A any   **B** none   **C** either

13. I've been waiting _____ for Sarah to call.

    A all morning   **B** the whole morning   **C** all the morning

14. I can't afford to buy anything in this store. _____ so expensive.

    A All is   **B** Everything is   **C** All are

形容詞與副詞   Unit 96 至 Unit 105

31 依各句題意判斷下列各句是否正確。若有錯誤請更正；句子若正確無誤，請填入 *OK*。

1. The building was (total destroyed) in the fire.   *totally destroyed*
2. I didn't like the book. It was such a stupid story.   *OK*
3. The city is very polluted. It's the more polluted place I've ever been to. _____
4. I was disappointing that I didn't get the job. I was well qualified and the interview went well. _____
5. Could you walk a little more slowly? _____
6. Joe works hardly, but he doesn't get paid very much. _____
7. The company's offices are in a modern large building. _____
8. Dan is a very fast runner. I wish I could run as fast as him. _____
9. I missed the three last days of the course because I was sick. _____
10. You don't look happy. What's the matter? _____
11. The weather has been unusual cold for this time of year. _____
12. The water in the pool was too dirty to swim in it. _____
13. I got impatient because we had to wait so long time. _____
14. Is this box big enough, or do you need a bigger one? _____
15. This morning I got up more early than usual. _____

連接詞   Unit 24, Unit 36 與 Unit 109 至 Unit 115

32 依各句題意，選擇正確的連接詞。

1. I'll try to be on time, but don't worry if / ~~when~~ I'm late. (*if* 是正確答案)
2. Don't throw that bag away. If / When you don't want it, I'll take it.
3. Please go to the reception desk if / when you arrive at the hotel.
4. We've arranged to play tennis tomorrow, but we won't play if / when it's raining.
5. Jennifer is in her final year at school. She still doesn't know what she's going to do if / when she graduates.
6. What would you do if / when you lost your keys?
7. I hope I'll be able to come to the party, but I'll let you know if / unless I can't.
8. I don't want to be disturbed, so don't call me if / unless it's something important.
9. Please sign the contract if / unless you're happy with the conditions.
10. I like traveling by ship as long as / unless the sea is not rough.
11. You might not remember the name of the hotel, so write it down if / in case you forget it.
12. It's not cold now, but take your coat with you if / in case it gets cold later.

13. Take your coat with you, and then you can put it on <u>if / in case</u> it gets cold later.
14. They always have the television on, <u>even if / if</u> nobody is watching it.
15. <u>Even / Although</u> we played very well, we lost the game.
16. <u>Despite / Although</u> we've known each other a long time, we're not especially close friends.
17. "When did you graduate from high school?" "<u>As / When</u> I was 18."
18. I think Ann will be very pleased <u>as / when</u> she hears the news.

介係詞 (表時間) Unit 13 與 Unit 116 至 Unit 119

3 依各句題意，自下列介係詞中選出適當者填入，以完成各句。

at   on   in   during   for   since   by   until

1. Jack is out of town. He'll be back <u>in</u> a week.
2. We're having a party _____ Saturday. Can you come?
3. I've got an interview next week. It's _____ 9:30 _____ Tuesday morning.
4. Sue isn't usually here _____ weekends. She goes away.
5. The train service is very good. The trains are nearly always _____ time.
6. It was a confusing situation. Many things were happening _____ the same time.
7. I couldn't decide whether or not to buy the sweater. _____ the end I decided not to.
8. The road is busy all the time, even _____ night.
9. I met a lot of nice people _____ my stay in New York.
10. I saw Helen _____ Friday, but I haven't seen her _____ then.
11. Brian has been doing the same job _____ five years.
12. Lisa's birthday is _____ the end of March. I'm not sure exactly which day it is.
13. We have some friends staying with us _____ the moment. They're staying _____ Friday.
14. If you're interested in applying for the job, your application must be received _____ Friday.
15. I'm just going out. I won't be long — I'll be back _____ 10 minutes.

介係詞 (表位置與其他用法) Unit 120 至 Unit 125

依各句題意，填入適當的介係詞。

1. I'd love to be able to visit every country _____ the world.
2. Jessica White is my favorite author. Have you read anything _____ her?
3. "Is there a bank near here?" "Yes, there's one _____ the end of this block."
4. Tim is out of town at the moment. He's _____ vacation.
5. We live _____ the country, a long way from the nearest town.
6. I've got a stain _____ my jacket. I'll have to have it cleaned.
7. We went _____ a party _____ Linda's house on Saturday.
8. Boston is _____ the East Coast of the United States.
9. Look at the leaves _____ that tree. They're a beautiful color.
10. "Have you ever been _____ Tokyo?" "No, I've never been _____ Japan."
11. Mozart died _____ Vienna in 1791 _____ the age of 35.
12. "Are you _____ this photograph?" "Yes, that's me, _____ the left."
13. We went _____ the theater last night. We had seats _____ the front row.
14. "Where's the light switch?" "It's _____ the wall _____ the door."
15. It was late when we arrived _____ the hotel.
16. I couldn't decide what to eat. There was nothing _____ the menu that I liked.
17. We live _____ a high rise. Our apartment is _____ the fifteenth floor.
18. *A:* What did you think of the movie?
    B: Some parts were a little stupid, but _____ the whole I enjoyed it.
19. "When you paid the hotel bill, did you pay cash?" "No, I paid _____ credit card."
20. "How did you get here? _____ the bus?" "No, _____ car."
21. *A:* I wonder what's _____ TV tonight. Do you have a newspaper?
    B: Yes, the TV listings are _____ the back page.

22. Helen works for a telecommunications company. She works _____ the customer service department.
23. Anna spent two years working _____ Chicago before returning _____ Italy.
24. "Did you enjoy your trip _____ the beach?" "Yes, it was great."
25. Next summer we're going _____ a trip to Canada.

名詞/形容詞 + 介係詞 Unit 126 至 Unit 128

35 依各句題意，填入適當的介係詞。

1. The plan has been changed, but nobody seems to know the reason _____ this.
2. Don't ask me to decide. I'm not very good _____ making decisions.
3. Some people say that Sue is unfriendly, but she's always very nice _____ me.
4. What do you think is the best solution _____ the problem?
5. There has been a big increase _____ the price of land recently.
6. He lives a rather lonely life. He doesn't have much contact _____ other people.
7. Paul is a wonderful photographer. He likes taking pictures _____ people.
8. Michael got married _____ a woman he met when he was in college.
9. He's very brave. He's not afraid _____ anything.
10. I'm surprised _____ the amount of traffic today. I didn't think it would be so heavy.
11. Thank you for lending me the guidebook. It was full _____ useful information.
12. Please come in and sit down. I'm sorry _____ the mess.

動詞 + 介係詞 Unit 129 至 Unit 133

36 依各句題意，填入適當的介係詞。若不須介係詞則空白。

1. She works very hard. You can't accuse her _____ being lazy.
2. Who's going to look _____ your children while you're at work?
3. The problem is becoming serious. We have to discuss _____ it.
4. The problem is becoming serious. We have to do something _____ it.
5. I prefer this chair _____ the other one. It's more comfortable.
6. I have to call _____ the office to tell them I won't be at work today.
7. The river divides the city _____ two parts.
8. "What do you think _____ your new boss?" "She's all right, I guess."
9. Can somebody please explain _____ me what I have to do?
10. I said hello to her, but she didn't answer _____ me.
11. "Do you like staying at hotels?" "It depends _____ the hotel."
12. "Have you ever been to Borla?" "No, I've never heard _____ it. What is it?"
13. You remind me _____ somebody I knew a long time ago. You look just like her.
14. This is wonderful news! I can't believe _____ it.
15. George is not an idealist – he believes _____ being practical.
16. What's so funny? What are you laughing _____ ?
17. What have you done with all the money you had? What did you spend it _____ ?
18. If Kevin asks _____ you _____ money, don't give him any.
19. I apologized _____ Sarah _____ keeping her waiting so long.
20. Lisa was very helpful. I thanked _____ her _____ everything she'd done.

7 依各題情境，自 B 框中選出能配合 A 框的句子，以完成各個對話。

A

1. I'd like to apply for a license.
2. I'm too warm with my coat on.
3. This jacket looks nice.
4. My phone number is 555-9320.
5. I don't think my car will fit in that space.
6. I'm glad we have a plan.
7. How did you find the mistake?
8. I'm not sure whether to accept their offer or not.
9. I don't know how to put this toy together.
10. It's a subject he doesn't like to talk about.
11. I don't know what this word means.

B

a. I can back up and give you more room.
b. Let me try. I'm sure I can figure it out.
c. Kate pointed it out.
d. Sure, just fill out this form.
e. Yes, why don't you try it on?
f. OK, I won't bring it up.
g. Just a minute. I'll write it down.
h. Why don't you take it off then?
i. You can look it up.
j. I think you should turn it down.
k. Yes, now let's work out the details.

1. _d_   2. _____   3. _____   4. _____   5. _____   6. _____
7. _____   8. _____   9. _____   10. _____   11. _____

8 依各句題意，自選項中選出正確者。

1. Nobody believed Paul at first but he __B__ to be right. (*B 是正確答案*)
   A came out   **B** turned out   **C** worked out   **D** carried out
2. Here's some good news. It will _____ .
   A turn you up   **B** put you up   **C** blow you up   **D** cheer you up
3. I was annoyed with the way the children were behaving, so I _____ .
   A told them up   **B** told them off   **C** told them out   **D** told them over
4. The club committee is _____ of the president, the secretary, and seven other members.
   A set up   **B** made up   **C** set out   **D** made out
5. When you are finished with those board games, please _____ ?
   A put them away   **B** put them out   **C** turn them off   **D** turn them away
6. We moved the table to another room. It _____ too much space here.
   A took in   **B** took up   **C** took off   **D** took over
7. Barbara started taking classes in college, but she _____ after six months.
   A went out   **B** fell out   **C** turned out   **D** dropped out
8. You can't predict everything. Often things don't _____ the way you expect.
   A make out   **B** break out   **C** work out   **D** get out
9. Why are all these people here? What's _____ ?
   A going off   **B** getting off   **C** going on   **D** getting on
10. It's a very busy airport. There are planes _____ or landing every few minutes.
    A going up   **B** taking off   **C** getting up   **D** driving off
11. The traffic was moving slowly because a bus had _____ and was blocking the road.
    A broken down   **B** fallen down   **C** fallen over   **D** broken up
12. Pat feels different from other kids at her school. She doesn't think she _____ .
    A hands in   **B** turns in   **C** drops in   **D** fits in

依各句題意，每題填入兩個字以完成句子。

1. Keep _away from_ the edge of the pool. You might fall in.
2. I didn't notice that the two pictures were different until Liz pointed it _____ me.
3. I asked Dan if he had any suggestions about what we should do, but he didn't come _____ anything.
4. I'm glad Sarah is coming to the party. I'm really looking _____ seeing her again.
5. Things are changing all the time. It's difficult to keep _____ all these changes.
6. I don't want to run _____ food for the party. Are you sure we have enough?
7. Don't let me interrupt you. Go _____ your work.

8. I'd love to go to your party, but I promised to go see my grandparents this weekend, and I can't get _____ it. They'd be disappointed if I didn't go.

9. I've had enough of being treated like this. I'm not going to put _____ it anymore.

10. I didn't enjoy the trip very much at the time, but when I look _____ it now, I realize it was a good experience and I'm glad I went on it.

11. The wedding was supposed to be a secret, so how did you find _____ it? Did Jenny tell you?

12. There is a very nice atmosphere in the office where I work. Everybody gets _____ everybody else.

40 依各句題意，使用與括號中的動詞意思相同的片語動詞，完成各句。

1. The football game had to be _called off_ because of the weather. (canceled)

2. The story Kate told wasn't true. She _made it up_ . (invented it)

3. A bomb _____ near the station, but no one was injured. (exploded)

4. George finally _____ nearly an hour late. (arrived)

5. Here's an application form. Can you _____ and sign it, please? (complete it)

6. A number of buildings are going to be _____ to make way for the new road. (demolished)

7. Since my father became ill, my older brother has _____ more responsibilities in the family. (accepted)

8. Be positive! You must never _____ ! (stop trying)

9. I was very tired and _____ in front of the television. (fell asleep)

10. After eight years together, they've decided to _____ . (separate)

11. The noise is terrible. I can't _____ any longer. (tolerate it)

12. We don't have a lot of money, but we have enough to _____ . (manage)

13. I'm sorry I'm late. The meeting _____ longer than I expected. (continued)

14. We need to make a decision today. We can't _____ any longer. (delay it)

41 依各句題意，每題填入一個字以完成句子。

1. You're driving too fast. Please _slow_ down.

2. It was only a small fire, and I managed to _____ it out with a bucket of water.

3. The house is empty at the present time, but the new tenants are _____ in next week.

4. I've _____ on weight. My clothes don't fit any more.

5. Their house is really nice now. They've _____ it up really well.

6. I was talking to the woman sitting next to me on the plane, and it _____ out that she works for the same company as my brother.

7. "Do you know what happened?" "Not yet, but I'm going to _____ out."

8. There's no need to get angry. _____ down!

9. Come and see us more often. You can _____ in any time you like.

10. Sarah has just called to say that she'll be late. She's been _____ up.

11. You've written my name wrong. It's Martin, not Marin — you _____ out the T.

12. My mom wants me to take her downtown and _____ her off at city hall this morning.

13. We had a really interesting discussion, but Jane didn't _____ in. She just listened.

14. Jonathan is in good shape. He _____ out at the gym every day.

15. Jenny said she would help me move, but she never came. I can't believe that she _____ me down.

16. We are still discussing the contract. There are a few things we need to _____ out.

17. My alarm clock _____ off in the middle of the night and _____ me up.

學習指引

學習指引能夠幫助您決定應該研讀哪些單元。以下的測驗與目錄(第 iii–vi 頁)中各單元內容的編排方式相同(現在式與過去式，冠詞與名詞等)。

下面測驗中的每一個句子皆有二至五個選項 (A、B、C 等)，請自選項中選出最適當者以完成各句；部分句子可以複選。

如果您不知道或不確定某題的選項何者正確，那麼您可能需要研讀該題右側所列的單元；您可以在該單元找到正確的句子 (若所列的單元超過一個，您會在第一個單元中找到正確的句子)。

學習指引中各題的答案參見第 362 頁。

如果您不確定選項何者正確，請研讀這些單元

現在式與過去式

1.1 At first I didn't like my job, but _____ to enjoy it now.
    A I'm beginning   **B** I begin | **1, 3**

1.2 I don't understand this sentence. What _____ ?
    A does mean this word   **B** does this word mean   **C** means this word | **2, 4, 7**

1.3 Robert _____ away two or three times a year.
    A is going usually   **B** is usually going   **C** usually goes   **D** goes usually | **2, 3, 107**

1.4 How _____ now? Better than before?
    A you are feeling   **B** do you feel   **C** are you feeling | **4**

1.5 It was a boring weekend. _____ anything.
    A I didn't   **B** I don't do   **C** I didn't do | **5**

1.6 Matt _____ while we were having dinner.
    A called   **B** was calling   **C** has called | **6, 9**

現在完成式與過去式

2.1 Everything is going well. We _____ any problems so far.
    A didn't have   **B** don't have   **C** haven't had | **7**

2.2 Sarah has lost her passport again. It's the second time this _____ .
    A has happened   **B** happens   **C** happened   **D** is happening | **7**

2.3 "Are you hungry?" "No, _____ lunch."
    A I just had   **B** I just have   **C** I've just had | **8**

2.4 It _____ raining for a while, but now it's raining again.
    A stopped   **B** has stopped   **C** was stopped | **8**

2.5 My mother _____ in Taichung.
    A grew up   **B** has grown up   **C** had grown up | **8, 14**

2.6 _____ a lot of candy when you were a child?
    A Have you eaten   **B** Had you eaten   **C** Did you eat | **9**

2.7 John _____ in New York for 10 years. Now he lives in Los Angeles
    A lived   **B** has lived   **C** has been living | **9, 12**

2.8 You're out of breath. _____ ?
    A Are you running?   **B** Have you run?   **C** Have you been running? | **10**

2.9 Where's the book I gave you? What _____ with it?
    A have you done   **B** have you been doing   **C** are you doing | **11**

2.10 *A:* _____ each other for a long time?
    B: Yes, since we were in high school.
    A Do you know   **B** Have you known   **C** Have you been knowing | **12, 11**

2.11 Kelly has been working here _____ .

| 13
A for six months   **B** since six months   **C** six months ago

2.12 It's been two years _____ Joe.

| 13
A that I don't see   **B** that I haven't seen   **C** since I didn't see
D since I saw

2.13 The man sitting next to me on the plane was very nervous. He _____ before.

| 14
A hasn't flown   **B** didn't fly   **C** hadn't flown   **D** wasn't flying

2.14 Stephanie was sitting in an armchair resting. She was tired because _____ very hard.

| 15
A she was working   **B** she's been working   **C** she'd been working

2.15 _____ a car when they were living in Miami?

| 16, 9
A Do they have   **B** Were they having   **C** Have they had
D Did they have

2.16 I _____ tennis a lot, but I don't play very often now.

| 17
A was playing   **B** was used to play   **C** used to play

未來式

3.1 I'm tired. _____ to bed now. Good night.

| 18
A I go   **B** I'm going

3.2 _____ tomorrow, so we can go out somewhere.

| 18, 20
A I'm not working   **B** I don't work   **C** I won't work

3.3 That bag looks heavy. _____ you with it.

| 20
A I'm helping   **B** I help   **C** I'll help

3.4 I think the weather _____ be nice this afternoon.

| 22, 21
A will   **B** shall   **C** is going to

3.5 "Ann is in the hospital." "Yes, I know. _____ her tonight."

| 22, 19
A I visit   **B** I'm going to visit   **C** I'll visit

3.6 We're late. The movie _____ by the time we get to the theater.

| 23
A will already start   **B** will be already started   **C** will already have started

3.7 Don't worry _____ late tonight.

| 24
A if I'm   **B** when I'm   **C** when I'll be   **D** if I'll be

情態助動詞

4.1 The fire spread through the building very quickly, but fortunately everybody _____ .

| 25
A was able to escape   **B** managed to escape   **C** could escape

4.2 I'm so tired I _____ for a week.

| 26
A can sleep   **B** could sleep   **C** could have slept

4.3 The story _____ be true, but I don't think it is.

| 26, 28
A might   **B** can   **C** could   **D** may

4.4 Why did you stay at a hotel when you were in Paris? You _____ with Julia.

| 26
A can stay   **B** could stay   **C** could have stayed

4.5 "I've lost one of my gloves." "You _____ it somewhere."

| 27
A must drop   **B** must have dropped   **C** must be dropping
D must have been dropping

4.6 *A:* I was surprised that Sarah wasn't at the meeting yesterday.
B: She _____ about it.
A might not know **B** may not know
C might not have known **D** may not have known

28

4.7 What was the problem? Why _____ leave early?
A had you to **B** did you have to **C** must you **D** you had to

30

4.8 You missed a great party last night. You _____ . Why didn't you?
A must have come **B** should have come **C** ought to come
D had to come

31

4.9 Lisa _____ some new clothes.
A suggested that Mary buy **B** suggested that Mary buys
C suggested Mary to buy

32

4.10 You're always at home. You _____ out more often.
A should go **B** had better go **C** had better to go

33

4.11 It's late. It's time _____ home.
A we go **B** we must go **C** we should go **D** we went

33

4.12 _____ a little longer, but I really have to go now.
A I'd stay **B** I'll stay **C** I can stay **D** I'd have stayed

34

if 與 wish

5.1 I'm not tired enough to go to bed. If I _____ to bed now,
I wouldn't sleep.
A go **B** went **C** had gone **D** would go

36

5.2 If I were rich, _____ a yacht.
A I'll have **B** I can have **C** I'd have **D** I had

37

5.3 I wish I _____ have to work tomorrow, but unfortunately I do.
A don't **B** didn't **C** wouldn't **D** won't

37, 39

5.4 The view was wonderful. If _____ a camera with me, I would
have taken some photos.
A I had **B** I would have **C** I would have had **D** I'd had

38

5.5 The weather is horrible. I wish it _____ raining.
A would stop **B** stopped **C** stops **D** will stop

39

被動語氣

6.1 We _____ by a loud noise during the night.
A woke up **B** are woken up **C** were woken up **D** were waking up

40

6.2 A new supermarket is going to _____ next year.
A build **B** be built **C** be building **D** building

41

6.3 There's somebody walking behind us. I think _____ .
A we are following **B** we are being following
C we are followed **D** we are being followed

41

6.4 "Where _____ ?" "In Los Angeles."
A were you born **B** are you born **C** have you been born
D did you born

42

6.5 There was a fight at the game, but nobody _____ .
A was hurt **B** got hurt **C** hurt

42

6.6 Jane _____ to call me last night, but she didn't. **43**
   A supposed   **B** is supposed   **C** was supposed

6.7 Where _____ ? Which hairdresser did you go to? **44**
   A did you cut your hair   **B** have you cut your hair
   C did you have cut your hair   **D** did you have your hair cut

間接敘述

7.1 Paul left the room suddenly. He said he _____ to go. **46, 45**
   A had   **B** has   **C** have

7.2 Hi, Joe. I didn't expect to see you today. Sonia said you _____ in the hospital. **46, 45**
   A are   **B** were   **C** was   **D** should be

7.3 Ann _____ and left. **46**
   A said goodbye to me   **B** said me goodbye   **C** told me goodbye

問句與助動詞

8.1 "What time _____ ?"   "At 8:30." **47**
   A begins the film   **B** does begin the film   **C** does the film begin

8.2 "Do you know where _____ ?"   "No, he didn't say." **48**
   A Tom has gone   **B** has Tom gone   **C** has gone Tom

8.3 The police officer stopped us and asked us where _____ . **48**
   A were we going   **B** are we going   **C** we are going   **D** we were going

8.4 "Do you think it will rain?"   "_____" **49**
   A I hope not.   **B** I don't hope.   **C** I don't hope so.

8.5 "You don't know where Lauren is, _____ ?"   "Sorry, I have no idea." **50**
   A don't you   **B** do you   **C** is she   **D** are you

-ing 與不定詞

9.1 Suddenly everybody stopped _____ . There was silence. **51**
   A talking   **B** talk   **C** to talk   **D** that they talked

9.2 I have to go now. I promised _____ late. **52, 34**
   A not being   **B** not to be   **C** to not be   **D** I wouldn't be

9.3 Do you want _____ with you, or do you want to go alone? **53**
   A me coming   **B** me to come   **C** that I come   **D** that I will come

9.4 I know I locked the door. I clearly remember _____ it. **54**
   A locking   **B** to lock   **C** to have locked

9.5 She tried to be serious, but she couldn't help _____ . **55**
   A laughing   **B** to laugh   **C** that she laughed   **D** laugh

9.6 Paul lives in Vancouver now. He likes _____ there. **56**
   A living   **B** to live

9.7 It's not my favorite job, but I like _____ the kitchen as often as possible. **56**
   A cleaning   **B** clean   **C** to clean   **D** that I clean

9.8 I'm tired. I'd rather _____ out tonight, if you don't mind. **57**
   A not going   **B** not to go   **C** don't go   **D** not go

9.9 "Should I stay here?"   "I'd rather _____ with us." **57**
   A you come   **B** you to come   **C** you came   **D** you would come

9.10 Are you looking forward _____ on vacation?　　**58, 60**
　　A going　　**B** to go　　**C** to going　　**D** that you go

9.11 When Lisa went to Japan, she had to get used _____ on the left.　　**59**
　　A driving　　**B** to driving　　**C** to drive

9.12 I'm thinking _____ a house. Do you think that's a good idea?　　**60, 64**
　　A to buy　　**B** of to buy　　**C** of buying

9.13 I had no _____ a place to live. In fact it was surprisingly easy.　　**61**
　　A difficulty to find　　**B** difficulty finding
　　C trouble to find　　**D** trouble finding

9.14 A friend of mine called _____ me to a party.　　**62**
　　A for invite　　**B** to invite　　**C** for inviting　　**D** for to invite

9.15 Jim doesn't speak very clearly. _____　　**63**
　　A It is hard to understand him.　　**B** He is hard to understand.
　　C He is hard to understand him.

9.16 The sidewalk was icy, so we walked very carefully. We were afraid _____ .　　**64**
　　A of falling　　**B** from falling　　**C** to fall　　**D** to falling

9.17 I didn't hear you _____ in. You must have been very quiet.　　**65**
　　A come　　**B** to come　　**C** came

9.18 _____ a hotel, we looked for somewhere to have dinner.　　**66**
　　A Finding　　**B** After finding　　**C** Having found　　**D** We found

冠詞與名詞

10.1 It wasn't your fault. It was _____ .　　**67**
　　A accident　　**B** an accident　　**C** some accident

10.2 Where are you going to put all your _____ ?　　**68**
　　A furniture　　**B** furnitures

10.3 "Where are you going?" "I'm going to buy _____ ."　　**68**
　　A a bread　　**B** some bread　　**C** a loaf of bread

10.4 Sandra is _____ . She works at a large hospital.　　**69, 70**
　　A nurse　　**B** a nurse　　**C** the nurse

10.5 Helen works six days _____ week.　　**70**
　　A in　　**B** for　　**C** a　　**D** the

10.6 There are millions of stars in _____ .　　**71**
　　A space　　**B** a space　　**C** the space

10.7 Every day _____ starts at 9:00 and ends at 3:00.　　**72**
　　A school　　**B** a school　　**C** the school

10.8 _____ a problem in most big cities.　　**73**
　　A Crime is　　**B** The crime is　　**C** The crimes are

10.9 When _____ invented?　　**74**
　　A was telephone　　**B** were telephones
　　C were the telephones　　**D** was the telephone

10.10 Have you been to _____ ?　　**75**
　　A Canada or United States　　**B** the Canada or the United States
　　C Canada or the United States　　**D** the Canada or United States

10.11 On our first day in Moscow, we visited _____ .　　**76**
　　A Kremlin　　**B** a Kremlin　　**C** the Kremlin

10.12 What time _____ on television?

    A is the news   **B** are the news   **C** is news   **D** is the new

          77, 68

10.13 It took us quite a long time to get here. It was _____ trip.

    A three hour   **B** a three-hours   **C** a three-hour

          78

10.14 This isn't my book. It's _____ .

    A my sister   **B** my sister's   **C** from my sister

    D of my sister   **E** of my sister's

          79

代名詞與限定詞

11.1 What time should we _____ tomorrow?

    A meet   **B** meet us   **C** meet ourselves

          80

11.2 I'm going to a wedding on Saturday. _____ is getting married.

    A A friend of me   **B** A friend of mine   **C** One my friends

          81

11.3 They live on a busy street. _____ a lot of noise from the traffic.

    A It must be   **B** It must have   **C** There must have   **D** There must be

          82

11.4 He's lazy. He never does _____ work.

    A some   **B** any   **C** no

          83

11.5 *A:* What would you like to eat?

    B: I don't care. _____ – whatever you have.

    A Something   **B** Anything   **C** Nothing

          83

11.6 We couldn't buy anything because _____ of the stores were open.

    A all   **B** no one   **C** none   **D** nothing

          84

11.7 We went shopping and spent _____ money.

    A a lot of   **B** much   **C** lots of   **D** many

          85

11.8 _____ don't visit this part of the town.

    A The most tourists   **B** Most of tourists   **C** Most tourists

          86

11.9 I asked two people the way to the station, but _____ of them could help me.

    A none   **B** either   **C** both   **D** neither

          87

11.10 _____ enjoyed the party. It was great.

    A Everybody   **B** All   **C** All of us   **D** Everybody of us

          88

11.11 The bus service is excellent. There's a bus _____ 10 minutes.

    A each   **B** every   **C** all

          88, 89

關係子句

12.1 I don't like stories _____ have unhappy endings.

    A that   **B** they   **C** which   **D** who

          90

12.2 I didn't believe them at first, but in fact everything _____ was true.

    A they said   **B** that they said   **C** what they said

          91

12.3 What's the name of the man _____ ?

    A you borrowed his car   **B** which car you borrowed

    C whose car you borrowed   **D** his car you borrowed

          92

12.4 Brad told me about his new job, _____ very much.

    A that he's enjoying   **B** which he's enjoying   **C** he's enjoying

    D he's enjoying it

          93

12.5 Sarah couldn't meet us, _____ was a shame.

A that   **B** it   **C** what   **D** which

94

12.6 George showed me some pictures _____ by his father.

A painting   **B** painted   **C** that were painted   **D** they were painted

95, 90

形容詞與副詞

13.1 Jane doesn't enjoy her job anymore. She's _____ because every day she does exactly the same thing.

A boring   **B** bored

96

13.2 Lisa was carrying a _____ bag.

A black small plastic   **B** small and black plastic
C small black plastic   **D** plastic small black

97

13.3 Maria's English is excellent. She speaks _____ .

A perfectly English   **B** English perfectly
C perfect English   **D** English perfect

98

13.4 He _____ to find a job, but he had no luck.

A tried hard   **B** tried hardly   **C** hardly tried

99

13.5 I haven't seen her for _____ , I've forgotten what she looks like.

A so long   **B** so long time   **C** a such long time   **D** such a long time

100

13.6 We haven't got _____ on vacation at the moment.

A money enough to go   **B** enough money to go
C money enough for going   **D** enough money for going

101

13.7 The test was fairly easy – _____ I expected.

A more easy that   **B** more easy than   **C** easier than   **D** easier as

102

13.8 The more electricity you use, _____ .

A your bill will be higher   **B** will be higher your bill
C the higher your bill will be   **D** higher your bill will be

103

13.9 Patrick is a fast runner. I can't run as fast as _____ .

A he   **B** him   **C** he can

104

13.10 The film was really boring. It was _____ I've ever seen.

A most boring film   **B** the more boring film
C the film more boring   **D** the most boring film

105

13.11 Ben likes walking. _____

A Every morning he walks to work.   **B** He walks to work every morning.
C He walks every morning to work.   **D** He every morning walks to work.

106

13.12 Joe never calls me. _____

A Always I have to call him.   **B** I always have to call him.
C I have always to call him.   **D** I have to call always him.

107

13.13 Lucy _____ . She left last month.

A still doesn't work here   **B** doesn't still work here
C no more works here   **D** doesn't work here anymore

108

13.14 _____ she can't drive, she has bought a car.

A Even   **B** Even when   **C** Even if   **D** Even though

109, 110

連接詞與介係詞

14.1 I couldn't sleep _____ very tired.
    A although I was   **B** despite I was   **C** despite of being
    D in spite of being

14.2 You should register your bike _____ stolen.
    A in case it will be   **B** if it will be   **C** in case it is   **D** if it is

14.3 The club is for members only. You _____ you're a member.
    A can't go in if   **B** can go in only if   **C** can't go in unless
    D can go in unless

14.4 _____ the day went on, the weather got worse.
    A When   **B** As   **C** While   **D** Since

14.5 "What's that noise?" "It sounds _____ a baby crying."
    A as   **B** like   **C** as if   **D** as though

14.6 They are very kind to me. They treat me _____ their own son.
    A like I'm   **B** as if I'm   **C** as if I was   **D** as if I were

14.7 I'll be in Toronto next week. I hope to see Tom _____ there.
    A while I'll be   **B** while I'm   **C** during my visit   **D** during I'm

14.8 Fred is away at the moment. I don't know exactly when he's coming back, but I'm sure he'll be back _____ Monday.
    A by   **B** until

介係詞

15.1 Goodbye! I'll see you _____ .
    A at Friday morning   **B** on Friday morning
    C in Friday morning   **D** Friday morning

15.2 I'm going away _____ the end of January.
    A at   **B** on   **C** in

15.3 When we were in France, we spent a few days _____ Paris.
    A at   **B** to   **C** in

15.4 Our apartment is _____ the second floor of the building.
    A at   **B** on   **C** in   **D** to

15.5 I saw Steve _____ a concert on Saturday.
    A at   **B** on   **C** in   **D** to

15.6 When did they _____ the hotel?
    A arrive to   **B** arrive at   **C** arrive in   **D** get to   **E** get in

15.7 I'm going _____ vacation next week. I'll be away for two weeks.
    A at   **B** on   **C** in   **D** for

15.8 We came _____ 6:45 train, which arrived at 8:30.
    A in the   **B** on the   **C** by the   **D** by

15.9 *A:* Have you read anything _____ Ernest Hemingway?
    B: No, what sort of books did he write?
    A of   **B** from   **C** by

15.10 The accident was my fault, so I had to pay for the damage _____ the other car.
    A of   **B** for   **C** to   **D** on   **E** at

15.11 I like them very much. They have always been very nice _____ me.　**127**
    A of　　**B** for　　**C** to　　**D** with

15.12 I'm not very good _____ fixing things.　**128**
    A at　　**B** for　　**C** in　　**D** about

15.13 I don't understand this sentence. Can you _____ ?　**129**
    A explain to me this word　　　**B** explain me this word
    C explain this word to me

15.14 If you're worried about the problem, you should do something _____　**130**
    it.
    A for　　**B** about　　**C** against　　**D** with

15.15 "Who is Tom Hart?" "I have no idea. I've never heard _____ him."　**131**
    A about　　**B** from　　**C** after　　**D** of

15.16 *A:* What time will you be home?　**132**
    B: I don't know. It depends _____ the traffic.
    A of　　**B** for　　**C** from　　**D** on

15.17 I prefer tea _____ coffee.　**133, 57**
    A to　　**B** than　　**C** against　　**D** over

片語動詞

16.1 These shoes are uncomfortable. I'm going to _____ .　**134**
    A take off　　**B** take them off　　**C** take off them

16.2 We're playing a game. Why don't you _____ ?　**135**
    A join in　　**B** come in　　**C** get in　　**D** break in

16.3 Nobody believed Paul at first, but he _____ to be right.　**136**
    A worked out　　**B** came out　　**C** found out　　**D** turned out

16.4 We can't _____ making a decision. We have to decide now.　**137**
    A put away　　**B** put over　　**C** put off　　**D** put out

16.5 The party _____ until 4:00 in the morning.　**138**
    A went by　　**B** went to　　**C** went on　　**D** went off

16.6 You can always rely on Pete. He'll never _____ .　**139**
    A put you up　　**B** let you down　　**C** take you over　　**D** see you off

16.7 Children under 16 _____ half the population of the city.　**140**
    A make up　　**B** put up　　**C** take up　　**D** bring up

16.8 I'm surprised to hear that Sue and Paul have _____ . They seemed very　**141**
    happy together the last time I saw them.
    A broken up　　**B** ended up　　**C** finished up　　**D** split up

16.9 I parked in a no-parking zone, but I _____ it.　**142**
    A came up with　　**B** got away with　　**C** made off with　　**D** got along with

解答 (Exercises)

部份練習題是請您依自己的意思完成句子，因此解答中提供之例句僅作為參考。

UNIT 1

1.1
2. 'm looking (am looking)
3. 's getting (is getting)
4. 're staying (are staying)
5. is losing
6. 's starting (is starting)
7. 're making (are making)
   'm trying (am trying)
8. 's happening (is happening)

1.2
3. 'm not listening (am not listening)
4. 's having (is having)
5. 'm not eating (am not eating)
6. 's studying (is studying)
7. aren't speaking / 're not speaking
   (are not speaking)
8. 'm getting (am getting)
9. isn't working / 's not working
   (is not working)

1.3
1. What's he studying
   Is he enjoying
   he's learning
2. is your new job going
   it's getting
   he isn't enjoying / he's not enjoying
   he's beginning

1.4
2. is changing
3. 's getting (is getting)
4. is rising
5. is beginning

UNIT 2

2.1
2. drink
3. opens
4. causes
5. live
6. take
7. connects

2.2
2. do the banks close
3. don't watch (do not watch)
4. does Hiroshi come
5. do you do
6. takes . . . does it take
7. does this word mean
8. doesn't exercise (does not exercise)

2.3
3. rises
4. make
5. don't eat

6. doesn't believe
7. translates
8. don't tell
9. flows

2.4
2. Does . . . play tennis?
3. Which newspaper do you read?
4. What does your brother do?
5. How often do you go to the movies?
6. Where do your grandparents live?

2.5
2. I promise
3. I insist
4. I apologize
5. I recommend

UNIT 3

3.1
3. is trying
4. are they talking
5. OK
6. It's getting (It is getting)
7. OK
8. I'm coming (I am coming)
9. is it going
10. He always gets
11. OK

3.2
3. 's waiting (is waiting)
4. Are you listening
5. Do you listen
6. flows
7. 's flowing (is flowing)
8. grow . . . aren't growing / 're not
   growing (are not growing)
9. 's improving (is improving)
10. 's staying (is staying) . . . stays
11. 'm starting (am starting)
12. 'm learning (am learning) . . .
    's teaching (is teaching)
13. finish . . . 'm working
    (am working)
14. live . . . do your parents live
15. 's looking (is looking) . . . 's staying
    (is staying)
16. does your brother do . . . isn't
    working / 's not working
    (is not working)
17. enjoy . . . 'm not enjoying
    (am not enjoying)

3.3
2. 's always breaking down.
3. 'm always making the same
   mistake. / . . . that mistake.

4. You're always forgetting your
   glasses.

UNIT 4

4.1
2. Do you believe
3. OK
4. It tastes
5. I think

4.2
2. What are you doing? I'm thinking.
3. Who does this umbrella belong to?
4. Dinner smells good.
5. Is anybody sitting there?
6. These gloves don't fit me.

4.3
2. 'm using
3. need
4. does he want
5. is he looking
6. believes
7. don't remember 或 can't
   remember
8. 'm thinking
9. think . . . don't use
10. consists

4.4
2. is being
3. 's
4. are you being
5. Is he

UNIT 5

5.1
2. had
3. walked to work
4. took her (about) half an hour
5. She started work
6. She didn't have / She didn't eat
   (She did not have/eat)
7. She finished work
8. She was . . . she got
9. She cooked
10. She didn't go
11. She went to bed
12. She slept

5.2
2. taught
3. sold
4. fell . . . hurt
5. threw . . . caught
6. spent . . . bought . . . cost

5.3

2. did you travel / did you go
3. did it take (you) / were you there
4. did you stay
5. How was the weather?
6. Did you go to / Did you see / Did you visit

5.4

3. didn't disturb
4. left
5. didn't sleep
6. flew
7. didn't cost
8. didn't have
9. were

UNIT 6

6.1

參考答案:
3. I was working.
4. I was in bed asleep. / I was sleeping.
5. I was getting ready to go out.
6. I was watching TV at home.

6.2

參考答案:
2. was taking a shower
3. were driving to work
4. was reading the paper
5. was watching it

6.3

1. didn't see . . . was looking
2. met . . . were going . . . was going . . . talked . . . were waiting 或 waited
3. was riding . . . stepped . . . was going . . . managed . . . didn't hit

6.4

2. were you doing
3. Did you go
4. were you driving . . . happened
5. took . . . wasn't looking
6. didn't know
7. saw . . . was trying
8. was walking . . . heard . . . was following . . . started
9. wanted
10. dropped . . . was doing . . . didn't break

UNIT 7

7.1

2. . . . you ever been to Mexico?
3. Have you ever run [in] a marathon?
4. Have you ever spoken to a famous person?
5. . . . the most beautiful place you've ever visited? (. . . you have ever visited?)

7.2

2. haven't seen (have not seen)
3. I haven't eaten (I have not eaten . . .)
4. I haven't played (I have not played)
5. I've had / I have had
6. I've never read (I have never)
7. I've never been / I haven't been
8. 's been (has been)
9. I've never tried / I have never tried
10. it's happened / it has happened
11. I've never seen / I have never seen

7.3

2. haven't read one / haven't read a newspaper
3. it hasn't made a profit
4. she hasn't worked hard this semester
5. it hasn't snowed [a lot] this winter
6. haven't won many/any games this season

7.4

2. you played tennis before?
   time I've played tennis.
3. Have you ridden a horse before? / Have you been on a horse before?
   No, this is the first time I've ridden a horse. / . . . I've been on a horse.
4. Have you been in Los Angeles before?
   No, this is the first time I've been in Los Angeles.

UNIT 8

8.1

2. has changed
3. forgot
4. went
5. had
6. 've lost / have lost

8.2

3. 兩者皆為正確答案
4. a
5. h
6. 兩者皆為正確答案
7. 兩者皆為正確答案
8. 兩者皆為正確答案
9. b
10. a

8.3

2. he just went out 或 he's just gone out
3. I didn't finish yet. 或 I haven't finished yet.
4. I already did it. 或 I've already done it.

5. Did you find a place to live yet?
   或 Have you found a place to live yet?
6. I didn't decide yet. 或 I haven't decided yet.
7. she just came back 或 she's just come back
8. already invited me 或 has already invited me

UNIT 9

9.1

3. OK
4. I bought
5. Where were you
6. graduated
7. OK
8. OK
9. OK
10. was this book

9.2

2. has been cold recently.
3. was cold last week.
4. didn't read a newspaper yesterday.
5. haven't read a newspaper today.
6. has made a lot of money this year.
7. She didn't make so much last year.
8. Have you taken a vacation recently?

9.3

2. got . . . was . . . went
3. Did you eat . . .   We've been
4. weren't (were not)
5. worked
6. 's lived (has lived)
7. Did you go . . . was . . . was
8. died . . . never met
9. 've never met (have never met)
10. haven't seen
11. have you lived / have you been living . . . did you live . . . did you live

9.4

參考答案:
2. I haven't bought anything today.
3. I didn't watch TV yesterday.
4. I went out with some friends last night.
5. I haven't been to the movies recently. / I haven't gone to . . .
6. I've read a lot of books recently.

UNIT 10

10.1

2. 's been watching television (has been watching)
3. 've been playing tennis (have been playing)
4. 's been running (has been running) / has been jogging

10.2

2. Have you been waiting long?
3. What have you been doing?
4. How long have you been working there?
5. How long have you been selling computers?

10.3

2. 've been waiting (have been waiting)
3. 've been studying Spanish (have been studying Spanish)
4. She's been working there (She has been working there)
5. They've been going there (They have been going there)

10.4

2. I've been looking (I have been looking)
3. are you looking
4. She's been teaching (She has been teaching)
5. I've been thinking (I have been thinking)
6. she's working (she is working)
7. she's been working (she has been working)

UNIT 11

11.1

2. She's been traveling for three months. / She has been traveling . . .
   She's visited six countries so far. / She has visited . . .
3. He's won the national championships four times. / He has won . . .
   He's been playing tennis since he was 10. / He has been playing . . .
4. They've made five movies since they finished college. / They have made . . .
   They've been making movies since they finished college. / They have been making . . .

11.2

2. Have you been waiting long?
3. Have you caught any fish?
4. How many people have you invited?
5. How long have you been teaching?
6. How many books have you written? How long have you been writing books?
7. How long have you been saving? How much money have you saved?

11.3

2. Somebody's broken / Somebody has broken

3. Have you been working
4. Have you ever worked
5. 's gone / has gone
6. He's appeared / He has appeared
7. I haven't been waiting
8. it's stopped / it has stopped
9. I've lost / I have lost . . . Have you seen
10. I've been reading / I have been reading . . . I haven't finished
11. I've read / I have read

UNIT 12

12.1

3. have been married
4. *OK*
5. It's been raining / It has been raining
6. have you been living
7. has been working
8. *OK*
9. I haven't drunk
10. have you had

12.2

2. How long have you been teaching English? / How long have you taught . . .
3. How long have you known Carol?
4. How long has your brother been in Costa Rica?
5. How long have you had that car?
6. How long has Scott been working at the airport? / How long has Scott worked . . .
7. How long have you been taking guitar lessons?
8. Have you always lived in Chicago?

12.3

3. 's been / has been
4. 've been waiting / have been waiting
5. 've known / have known
6. haven't played
7. 's been watching / has been watching
8. haven't watched
9. 've had / have had
10. hasn't been
11. 've been feeling / have been feeling 或 've felt / have felt
12. 's lived / has lived 或 's been living / has been living
13. haven't been
14. 've always wanted / have always wanted

UNIT 13

13.1

2. since
3. for

4. for
5. since
6. for / in
7. since
8. since
9. for

13.2

2. How long has Kate been studying Japanese?
   When did Kate start studying Japanese?
3. How long have you known Jeff? When did you first meet Jeff? / When did you and Jeff first meet?
4. How long have Rebecca and David been married?
   When did Rebecca and David get married?

13.3

3. been sick since
4. been sick for
5. married a year ago
6. had a headache since
7. to France three weeks ago.
8. been working in a hotel for six months. / I've worked in a hotel for six months.

13.4

2. No, I haven't seen Laura/her for/in about a month.
3. No, I haven't been to the movies for/in a long time.
4. No, I haven't eaten out in ages. / No, I haven't been to a restaurant in ages.
6. been about a month since I (last) saw Laura/her.
7. it's been a long time since I (last) went to the movies.
8. No, it's been ages since I (last) ate out. 或 . . . since I went to a restaurant.

UNIT 14

14.1

2. It had changed a lot.
3. She'd made plans to do something else. (She had made plans . . .)
4. The movie had already begun.
5. I hadn't seen him in five years.
6. She'd just had breakfast. (She had just had . . .)

14.2

2. 'd never seen her before. (had never seen . . .)
3. 'd never played (tennis) before. (had never played . . .)
4. 'd never been there before. (had never been . . .)

14.3

1. called the police
2. there was . . . had gone
3. He'd just . . . come back from (He had just come back from)
   He looked
4. got a phone call . . . was
   'd sent her (had sent her)
   'd never answered them (had never answered them)

14.4

2. went
3. had gone
4. broke
5. saw . . . had broken . . . stopped

UNIT 15

15.1

2. They'd been playing soccer. (They had been playing . . .)
3. I'd been looking forward to it. (I had been looking forward . . .)
4. She'd been dreaming. (She had been dreaming.)
5. He'd been watching a DVD. (He had been watching . . .)

15.2

2. 'd been waiting . . . [suddenly] realized that I was in . . . 或
   . . . that I had come to . . .
3. closed down, . . . had been working . . .
4. had been playing for about 10 minutes . . . a man in the audience started shouting.
5. 参考答案：
   'd been driving along the road for about 10 minutes . . . the car behind me started honking its horn.

15.3

3. was walking
4. 'd been running (had been running)
5. were eating
6. 'd been eating (had been eating)
7. was looking
8. was waiting . . . 'd been waiting (had been waiting)
9. 'd had (had had)
10. 'd been traveling (had been traveling)

UNIT 16

16.1

3. I don't have a ladder. / I haven't got a ladder.
4. didn't have enough time.
5. He didn't have a map.
6. She doesn't have any money.
7. I don't have enough energy.
8. They didn't have a camera.

16.2

2. Do you have / Have you got
3. Did you have
4. Do you have / Have you got
5. Do you have / Have you got
6. did you have
7. Did you have

16.3

参考答案：
2. I don't have a bike (now).
   I had a bike (10 years ago).
3. I have a cell phone / I've got a cell phone (now).
   I didn't have a cell phone (10 years ago).
4. I don't have a dog (now).
   I didn't have a dog (10 years ago).
5. I have a guitar / I've got a guitar (now).
   I had a guitar (10 years ago).
6. I don't have long hair (now).
   I didn't have long hair (10 years ago).
7. I have a driver's license / I've got a driver's license (now).
   I didn't have a driver's license (10 years ago).

16.4

2. have a talk
3. had a party
4. have a look
5. 's having a nice time (is having . . .)
6. had a dream
7. Did you have trouble
8. had a baby
9. were having dinner
10. Did you have a good flight?

UNIT 17

17.1

2. used to have/ride
3. used to live
4. used to eat/like/love
5. used to be
6. used to take [me]
7. used to be
8. did you use to go

17.2

3.–6.
He used to go to bed early.
He didn't use to go out every night.
He used to run three miles every morning.
He didn't use to spend much money. / . . . a lot of money.

17.3

2.–10.
used to have lots of friends, . . . she doesn't see many people these days.

used to be very lazy, . . . she works very hard these days.
didn't use to like cheese, . . . she eats lots of cheese now.
used to be a hotel desk clerk, . . . she works in a bookstore now.
used to play the piano, . . . she hasn't played the piano for years.
never used to read newspapers, . . . she reads a newspaper every day now.
didn't use to drink tea, . . . she likes it now.
used to have a dog, . . . it died two years ago.
used to go to a lot of parties, . . . she hasn't been to a party for ages.

UNIT 18

18.1

2. How long are you staying?
3. When are you leaving?
4. Are you going alone?
5. Are you traveling by car?
6. Where are you staying?

18.2

2. 'm working late. / 'm working till 9:00.
3. I'm going to the theater.
4. I'm meeting Julia.

18.3

参考答案：
2. 'm working tomorrow morning.
3. I'm not doing anything tomorrow night.
4. I'm playing football next Sunday.
5. I'm going to a party this evening.

18.4

3. 're having / are having
4. opens
5. 'm not going / am not going . . . 'm staying / am staying
6. Are you doing
7. 're going / are going . . . starts
8. 'm leaving / am leaving
9. 're meeting / are meeting
10. does this train get
11. 'm going / am going . . . Are you coming
12. does it end
13. 'm not using / am not using
14. 's coming / is coming . . . 's flying / is flying . . . arrives

UNIT 19

19.1

2. What are you going to wear?
3. Where are you going to put it?
4. Who are you going to invite?

19.2

2. I'm going to take it back.
3. I'm not going to take it.
4. I'm going to call her tonight.
5. I'm going to complain.

19.3

2. 's going to be late. (is going to be late.)
3. boat is going to sink.
4. 're going to run out of gas. (are going to . . .)

19.4

2. was going to buy
3. were going to play
4. was going to call
5. was going to quit
6. were going to have

UNIT 20

20.1

2. I'll turn / I'll put
3. I'll go
4. I'll do
5. I'll show / I'll teach
6. I'll have
7. I'll send
8. I'll give / I'll bring
9. I'll stay / I'll wait

20.2

2. I'll go to bed.
3. I'll walk.
4. I'll play tennis (today).
5. I don't think I'll go swimming.

20.3

3. I'll meet
4. I'll lend
5. I'm having
6. I won't forget
7. does your plane leave
8. won't tell
9. Are you doing
10. Will you come

20.4

2. shall I give/buy/get
3. I'll do / I will do
4. shall we go?
5. I won't tell
6. I'll try

UNIT 21

21.1

2. I'm going
3. will get
4. is coming
5. we are going
6. It won't hurt

21.2

2. 'll look / will look
3. 'll like / will like
4. 'll get / will get
5. will live
6. 'll see / will see
7. 'll come / will come
8. will take

21.3

2. won't
3. 'll / will
4. won't
5. 'll / will
6. 'll / will
7. won't
8. 'll / will

21.4

參考答案：

2. I'll be in bed.
3. I'll be at work.
4. I'll probably be at home.
5. I don't know where I'll be this time next year.

21.5

2. think it will rain?
3. think it will end?
4. do you think it will cost?
5. you think they'll get married? / . . . they will get married?
6. do you think you'll be back? / . . . you will be back?
7. do you think will happen?

UNIT 22

22.1

2. I'll lend
3. I'll get
4. I'm going to wash
5. are you going to paint
6. I'm going to buy
7. I'll show
8. I'll do
9. it's going to fall
10. He's going to take . . . he's going to start

22.2

2. I'm going to take . . . I'll join
3. you'll find
4. I'm not going to apply
5. You'll wake
6. I'll take . . . we'll leave . . . Ann is going to take

UNIT 23

23.1

2. b 為正確答案
3. a 與 c 皆為正確答案
4. b 與 d 皆為正確答案

5. c 與 d 皆為正確答案
6. c 為正確答案

23.2

2. We'll have finished
3. we'll be playing
4. I'll be working
5. the meeting will have ended
6. he'll have spent
7. you'll still be doing
8. she'll have traveled
9. I'll be staying
10. Will you be seeing

UNIT 24

24.1

2. goes
3. 'll tell / will tell . . . come
4. see . . . won't recognize / will not recognize
5. Will you miss . . . 'm/am
6. 's/is
7. 'll wait / will wait . . . 're/are
8. 'll be / will be . . . gets
9. is
10. calls . . . 'm/am

24.2

2. I'll give you my address . . . I find somewhere to live. 或 . . . I've found somewhere to live.
3. I'll come straight home . . . I do the shopping. 或 . . . I've done the shopping.
4. Let's go home . . . it gets dark.
5. I won't speak to her . . . she apologizes. 或 . . . she has apologized.

24.3

2. you go / you leave
3. you decide 或 you've decided / you have decided
4. you're in Hong Kong / you are in Hong Kong
5. finish the new road / 've finished the new road / have finished the new road 或 build the new road / 've built the new road / have built the new road

24.4

2. If
3. When
4. if
5. If
6. when
7. if
8. if

UNIT 25

25.1

3. can
4. be able to

332 解答 (EXERCISES)

5. been able to
6. can
7. be able to

25.2
参考答案：
2. I used to be able to run fast.
3. I'd like to be able to play the piano.
4. I've never been able to get up early.

25.3
2. could run
3. can wait
4. couldn't eat
5. can't hear
6. couldn't sleep

25.4
2. was able to finish it
3. were able to find it
4. was able to get away

25.5
4. couldn't
5. managed to
6. could
7. managed to
8. could
9. managed to
10. couldn't

UNIT 26

26.1
2. could have fish.
3. could call (her) now.
4. You could give her a book.
5. We could go on Friday.

26.2
3. I could scream.
4. *OK – could have 也可以作為正確答案*
5. I could stay here all day
6. it could be in the car (may/might 也可以作為正確答案)
7. *OK*
8. *OK – could borrow 也可以作為正確答案*
9. it could change later (may/might 也可以作為正確答案)

26.3
2. could have come/gone
3. could apply
4. could have been
5. could have taken
6. could come

26.4
3. couldn't wear
4. couldn't have found
5. couldn't get
6. couldn't have been
7. couldn't have come/gone

UNIT 27

27.1
2. must
3. must not

4. must
5. must not
6. must

27.2
3. be
4. have been
5. go
6. be going
7. have taken / have stolen / have moved
8. have been
9. be following

27.3
3. It must have been very expensive.
4. I must have left it in the restaurant last night.
5. The exam must not have been very difficult.
6. She must have listened to our conversation.
7. She must not have understood what I said.
8. I must have forgotten to turn it off.
9. The neighbors must have been having a party.

27.4
3. can't
4. must not
5. can't
6. must not

UNIT 28

28.1
2. She might/may be busy.
3. She might/may be working.
4. She might/may want to be alone.
5. She might/may have been sick yesterday.
6. She might/may have gone home early.
7. She might/may have had to go home early.
8. She might/may have been working yesterday.
9. She might/may not want to see me.
10. She might/may not be working today.
11. She might/may not have been feeling well yesterday.

28.2
2. be
3. have been
4. be waiting
5. have

28.3
2. a) She might be watching TV in her room.
   b) She might have gone out.
3. a) It might be in the car.
   b) You might have left it in the

restaurant last night.
4. a) He might not have heard the doorbell.
   b) He might have been in the shower.
在這些句子中，**may** 可以取代 **might**。

28.4
3. might not have received it
4. couldn't have been an accident
5. couldn't have tried
6. might not have been Chinese

UNIT 29

29.1
2. I might/may buy a Toyota.
3. I might/may go to the movies.
4. He might/may come on Saturday.
5. I might/may hang it in the dining room.
6. She might/may go to college.

29.2
2. might wake up
3. might bite
4. might need
5. might slip
6. might break
在這些句子中，**may** 可以取代 **might**。

29.3
2. might be able to meet/see
3. might have to work
4. might have to go/leave
在這些句子中，**may** 可以取代 **might**。

29.4
2. might not go out tonight.
3. might not like the present you bought him. 或 . . . bought for him.
4. Sue might not be able to get together with us tonight.
在這些句子中，**may** 可以取代 **might**。

29.5
2. might as well go to the concert.
3. might as well paint the bathroom.
4. We might as well watch the movie.
在這些句子中，**may** 可以取代 **might**。

UNIT 30

30.1
2. had to
3. have to
4. have to
5. has to
6. had to
7. had to
8. have to

30.2

2. do you have to go
3. Did you have to wait
4. do you have to be
5. Does he have to travel

30.3

3. have to make
4. had to ask
5. doesn't have to shave
6. didn't have to go
7. has to make
8. don't have to do

30.4

3. might have to
4. will have to
5. might have to
6. won't have to

30.5

3. don't have to
4. must not
5. don't have to
6. must not
7. doesn't have to
8. must not
9. don't have to

UNIT 31

31.1

2. should look for another job.
3. shouldn't go to bed so late.
4. should take a photo.
5. shouldn't use her car so much.
6. should put some pictures on the walls.

31.2

2. I don't think you should go out tonight.
3. you should apply for the job.
4. I don't think the government should raise taxes.

31.3

3. should come
4. should do
5. should have done
6. should have won
7. should be
8. should have arrived

31.4

3. should have reserved a table.
4. The store should be open by now. 或 The store should have opened by now.
5. shouldn't be driving so fast. / 50 miles an hour. 或 should be driving 30 miles an hour.
6. should have written it down
7. I shouldn't have been driving right behind another car.
8. I should have looked where I was going. 或 I should have been looking . . .

UNIT 32

32.1

3. I stay a little longer.
4. she visit the museum after lunch.
5. I see a specialist.
6. I not lift anything heavy.
7. we pay the rent by Friday.
8. I go away for a few days.
9. I not give my children snacks before mealtime.
10. we have dinner early.

32.2

3. spend / take
4. apologize
5. be
6. wait
7. be
8. wear
9. have / be given
10. remember / not forget
11. drink / have

32.3

2. walk to work in the morning.
3. that he eat more fruit and vegetables.
4. suggested that he take vitamins.

UNIT 33

33.1

2. You'd better put a bandage on it. (You had better put . . .)
3. 'd better make a reservation. (We had better make a reservation . . .)
4. You'd better not go to work (You had better not go . . .)
5. I'd better pay the phone bill (soon). (I had better pay . . .)
6. I'd better not go out (yet). (I had better not go out . . .)
7. We'd better take/get a taxi. (We had better take . . .)

33.2

3. 'd better (had better)
4. should
5. should
6. 'd better (had better)
7. should
8. should

33.3

1. b) 'd (had)
   c) close/shut
2. a) did
   b) was done
   c) thought

33.4

2. took / had a vacation
3. It's time the train left.
4. It's time I/we had a party.
5. It's time some changes were made.
6. It's time he tried something else.

UNIT 34

34.1

参考答案：

2. I wouldn't like to be a teacher.
3. I'd love to learn to fly a plane. (I would love to learn . . .)
4. It would be nice to have a big garden.
5. I'd like to go to Mexico. (I would like to go . . .)

34.2

2. 'd enjoy (would enjoy)
3. would have enjoyed
4. would . . . do
5. would have stopped
6. would have been
7. 'd be (would be)
8. would have passed
9. would have

34.3

2. e
3. b
4. f
5. a
6. d

34.4

2. he'd call. (. . . he would call)
3. promised you wouldn't tell her.
4. promised they'd wait (for us).

34.5

2. wouldn't tell
3. wouldn't speak / talk
4. wouldn't let

34.6

2. would shake
3. would . . . help
4. would share
5. would . . . forget

UNIT 35

35.1

2. Can/Could I leave a message (for her)? 或 Can/Could you give her a message?
3. Can/Could you tell me how to get to the post office? 或 . . . the way to the post office? 或 . . . where the post office is?
4. Can/Could I try on these pants? 或 Can/Could I try these [pants] on?
5. Can/Could you give me a ride home? 或 Can/Could I [please] have a ride home?

35.2

3. Do you think you could check this letter (for me)? / . . . check my letter?
4. Do you mind if I leave work early?

5. Do you think you could turn the music down? / . . . turn it down?
6. Is it OK if I come and see the apartment today?
7. Do you think I could have a look at your newspaper?

35.3

2. Can/Could/Would you show me? 或 Do you think you could show me? 或 . . . do it for me?
3. Would you like to sit down? 或 Would you like a seat? 或 Can I offer you a seat?
4. Can/Could/Would you slow down? 或 Do you think you could . . . ?
5. Can/Could/May I/we have the check, please? 或 Do you think I/we could have . . . ? 或 Can I get . . .
6. Would you like to borrow it?

UNIT 36

36.1

3. 'd take (would take)
4. closed down
5. wouldn't get
6. pressed
7. refused
8. 'd be (would be)
9. didn't come
10. borrowed
11. walked
12. would understand

36.2

2. would you do if you lost your passport?
3. What would you do if there was/were a fire in the building?
4. What would you do if you were in an elevator and it stopped between floors?

36.3

2. took his driving test, he'd fail (it). / . . . he would fail (it).
3. we stayed at a hotel, it would cost too much.
4. she applied for the job, she wouldn't get it.
5. we told them the truth, they wouldn't believe us.
6. If we invited Bill, we'd have to invite his friends, too. (. . . we would have to . . .)

36.4

参考答案：
2. somebody broke into my house.
3. I'd have a much nicer day than usual.
4. you were invited?

5. you'd save a lot of time.
6. I didn't go out with you this evening?

UNIT 37

37.1

3. 'd help (would help)
4. lived
5. 'd live (would live)
6. would taste
7. were/was
8. wouldn't wait . . . 'd go (would go)
9. didn't go
10. weren't . . . wouldn't be

37.2

2. buy it . . . it weren't/wasn't so expensive. (I would buy it) 或 . . . if it were/was cheaper.
3. 'd go out to eat more often if we could afford it. (We would go out . . .)
4. I didn't have to work late, I could meet you tomorrow. 或 . . . I'd meet (I would meet . . .) 或 . . . I'd be able to meet . . .
5. could have lunch on the patio if it weren't raining / wasn't raining.
6. I wanted his advice, I'd ask for it (I would ask for it.)

37.3

2. I had a cell phone.
3. I wish Amanda was/were here.
4. I wish it weren't/wasn't so cold.
5. I wish I didn't live in a big city.
6. I wish I could go to the party.
7. I wish I didn't have to work tomorrow.
8. I wish I knew something about cars.
9. I wish I was feeling / were feeling better.

37.4

参考答案：
2. I wish I had a big garden.
3. I wish I could tell jokes. 或 . . . I wish I was/were able to . . .
4. I wish I was/were taller.

UNIT 38

38.1

2. he'd missed (he had missed) . . . , he would have been.
3. I would have forgotten . . . you hadn't reminded
4. I'd had (I had had) . . . I would have sent
5. we would have enjoyed . . . the weather had been
6. It would have been . . . I had walked
7. I was / I were
8. I'd been (I had been)

38.2

2. hadn't been icy, the accident wouldn't have happened.
3. had known [that Matt had to get up early], I would have woken him up.
4. If Jim hadn't lent me the money, I wouldn't have been able to buy the car. 或 . . . I couldn't have bought the car.
5. If Michelle hadn't been wearing a seat belt, she would have been injured [in the crash].
6. If you had had (some) breakfast, you wouldn't be hungry now.
7. If I had had (some) money, I would have taken a taxi.

38.3

2. 'd applied (I wish I had applied) for the job.
3. I wish I'd learned to play a musical instrument [when I was younger]. (I wish I had learned . . .)
4. I wish I hadn't painted it red. 或 . . . the door red.
5. I wish I'd brought my camera. (I wish I had brought . . .)
6. I wish they'd called first [to say they were coming]. (I wish they had called) 或 I wish I'd known they were coming. (I wish I had known)

UNIT 39

39.1

2. hope
3. wish
4. wished
5. hope
6. wish . . . hope

39.2

2. Jane/she would come. 或 . . . would hurry up.
3. would give me a job.
4. I wish the/that baby would stop crying.
5. wouldn't drive so fast.
6. I wish you wouldn't leave the door open [all the time].
7. wouldn't drop litter in the street.

39.3

2. OK
3. I wish I had more free time.
4. I wish our house was/were a little bigger.
5. OK
6. OK
7. I wish everything wasn't/weren't so expensive.

39.4

3. I knew
4. I'd taken (I had taken)
5. I could come
6. I wasn't / I weren't
7. they'd hurry (they would hurry)
8. we didn't have
9. we could have stayed 或 we had been able to stay
10. it wasn't/weren't
11. he'd decide (he would decide)
12. we hadn't gone

UNIT 40

40.1

2. is made
3. was damaged
4. were invited
5. are shown
6. are held
7. was written . . . was translated
8. were passed
9. is surrounded

40.2

2. When was television invented?
3. How are mountains formed?
4. When was Neptune discovered?
5. What is silver used for?

40.3

3. covers
4. is covered
5. are locked
6. was mailed . . . arrived
7. sank . . . was rescued
8. died . . . were brought up
9. grew up
10. was stolen
11. disappeared
12. did Sue quit
13. was Bill fired
14. is owned
15. called . . . was injured . . . wasn't needed
16. were these picture taken . . . Did you take

40.4

2. flights were canceled because of fog.
3. This road isn't used much.
4. was accused of stealing money.
5. are languages learned?
6. We were warned not to go out alone.

UNIT 41

41.1

2. can't be broken
3. it can be eaten
4. it can't be used
5. it can't be seen
6. it can be carried

41.2

3. be made
4. be spent
5. have been repaired
6. be carried
7. be woken up
8. have been arrested
9. have been caused

41.3

2. is being used right now.
3. our conversation was being recorded.
4. the game had been canceled.
5. A new highway is being built around the city.
6. A new hospital has been built near the airport.

41.4

3. was stolen! 或 It has been stolen! (It's been)
4. took it! 或 Somebody has taken it!
5. furniture had been moved.
6. hasn't been seen since then.
7. haven't seen her for ages.
8. the computers were being used.
9. 's being redecorated.
10. 's working again. (is working . . .) . . . It's been repaired. (It has been repaired)
11. Have you ever been mugged?

UNIT 42

42.1

2. was asked some difficult questions at the interview.
3. was given a present by her colleagues when she retired.
4. told about the meeting.
5. be paid for your work?
6. should have been offered the job.
7. been shown what to do?

42.2

2. being invited
3. being given
4. being hit
5. being treated
6. being paid

42.3

2.–6.
Beethoven was born in 1770.
John Lennon was born in 1940.
Galileo was born in 1564.
Mahatma Gandhi was born in 1869.
Martin Luther King Jr. was born in 1929.
Elvis Presley was born in 1935.
Leonardo da Vinci was born in 1452.
William Shakespeare was born in 1564.
was born in . . .

42.4

2. got stung
3. get used
4. got stolen
5. get paid
6. got stopped
7. get damaged
8. get asked

UNIT 43

43.1

3. are reported to be homeless after the floods.
4. is alleged to have robbed the store of $3,000.
5. is reported to have been badly damaged by the fire.
6. a) is said to be losing a lot of money
   b) is believed to have lost a lot of money last year.
   c) is expected to lose money this year

43.2

2. is supposed to know a lot of famous people. (He's supposed . . .)
3. He is supposed to be very rich.
4. He is supposed to have 12 children
5. He is supposed to have been an actor when he was younger.

43.3

2. You're supposed to be my friend.
3. I'm supposed to be on a diet. (I am supposed . . .)
4. It was supposed to be a joke.
5. Or maybe it's supposed to be a flower. (it is supposed . . .)
6. You're supposed to be working. (You are supposed . . .)

43.4

2. 're supposed to start (We are supposed . . .)
3. was supposed to call
4. aren't / 're not supposed to block (are not supposed . . .)
5. was supposed to arrive

UNIT 44

44.1

1. b
2. a
3. a
4. b

44.2

2. have my jacket cleaned.
3. To have my watch repaired.
4. To have my eyes tested.

44.3

2. had it cut.
3. had it painted.
4. He had it built.
5. I had them delivered.

44.4

2. have another key made.
3. had your hair cut
4. Do you have a newspaper delivered
5. 're having a garage built
6. have your eyes checked
8. get it cleaned
9. get your ears pierced
10. got it repaired 或 've gotten it repaired
12. had her purse stolen
13. had his nose broken

UNIT 45

45.1

2. his father wasn't very well.
3. said [that] Amanda and Paul were getting married next month.
4. He said [that] his sister had had a baby.
5. He said [that] he didn't know what Eric was doing.
6. He said [that] he'd seen Nicole at a party in June and she'd seemed fine / he had . . . she had seemed fine 或 He said [that] he saw Nicole . . . and she seemed . . .
7. He said [that] he hadn't seen Diane recently.
8. He said [that] he wasn't enjoying his job very much.
9. He said [that] I could come and stay at his place if I was ever in Chicago.
10. He said [that] his car had been stolen a few days ago. 或 . . . his car was stolen a few days ago.
11. He said [that] he wanted to take a trip, but [he] couldn't afford it.
12. He said [that] he'd tell Amy he'd seen me. / . . . he would tell . . . he had seen 或 . . . he saw me.

45.2

参考答案:

2. wasn't coming / . . . was going somewhere else / . . . was staying at home
3. she didn't like him
4. you didn't know anybody / you didn't know many people
5. she wouldn't be here / she would be away / she was going away
6. you were staying at home / you weren't going out
7. you couldn't speak (any) French / were fluent in French
8. you went to the movies last week / you had gone to the movies last week

UNIT 46

46.1

2. you said you didn't like fish.
3. But you said you couldn't drive.
4. But you said she had a very well-paid job.
5. But you said you didn't have any brothers or sisters.
6. But you said you'd never been to Peru. (you had never been)
7. But you said you were working tomorrow night.
8. But you said she was a friend of yours.

46.2

2. Tell
3. Say
4. said
5. told
6. said
7. tell . . . said
8. tell . . . say
9. told
10. said

46.3

2. her to slow down
3. her not to worry
4. asked Tom to give me a hand 或 . . . to help me
5. asked me to open my bag
6. told him to mind his own business
7. asked her to marry him
8. told her not to wait [for me] if I was late

UNIT 47

47.1

2. Were you born there?
3. Are you married?
4. How long have you been married?
5. Do you have (any) children? 或 Have you got (any) children?
6. How old are they?
7. What do you do?
8. What does your wife do?

47.2

3. paid the bill?
4. happened?
5. What did she/Diane say?
6. Who does it/this book belong to?
7. Who lives in that house? / Who lives there?
8. What did you fall over?
9. What fell on the floor?
10. What does it/this word mean?
11. Who did you borrow it/the money from?
12. What are you worried about?

47.3

2. How is cheese made?
3. When was the computer invented?
4. Why isn't Sue working today?
5. What time are your friends coming?
6. Why was the concert canceled?
7. Where was your mother born?
8. Why didn't you come to the party?
9. How did the accident happen?
10. Why doesn't this machine work?

47.4

2. Don't you like him?
3. Isn't it good?
4. Don't you have any?

UNIT 48

48.1

2. where the post office is?
3. what time it is.
4. what this word means.
5. if/whether the plane has left?
6. if/whether Sue is going out tonight.
7. where Carol lives?
8. where I parked the car.
9. if/whether there is a bank near here?
10. what you want.
11. why Kelly didn't come to the party.
12. how much it costs to park here?
13. who that woman is.
14. if/whether Ann got my letter?
15. how far it is to the airport?

48.2

1. Amy is?
2. when she'll be back. (. . . she will be back)
3. if/whether she went out alone?

48.3

2. where I'd been. (. . . where I had been)
3. asked me how long I'd been back. (. . . how long I had been back)
4. He asked me what I was doing now.
5. He asked me why I'd come back. (. . . why I had come back) 或 . . . why I came back.
6. He asked me where I was living.
7. He asked me if/whether I was glad to be back.
8. He asked me if/whether I had plans to stay for a while.
9. He asked me if/whether I could lend him some money.

UNIT 49

49.1

2. doesn't
3. was

4. will
5. am . . . isn't 或 'm not . . . is
6. should
7. won't
8. do
9. could
10. would . . . could . . . can't

49.2

3. You do? I don't.
4. You didn't? I did.
5. You haven't? I have.
6. You did? I didn't.

49.3

参考答案：
3. So did I. 或 You did? What did you watch?
4. Neither will I. 或 You won't? Where will you be?
5. So do I. 或 You do? What kind of books do you like?
6. So would I. 或 You would? Where would you like to live?
7. Neither can I. 或 You can't? Why not?

49.4

2. I guess so.
3. I don't think so.
4. I hope so.
5. I'm afraid not.
6. I'm afraid so.
7. I hope not.
8. I think so.
9. I suppose so.

UNIT 50

50.1

3. haven't you
4. were you
5. does she
6. isn't he
7. has he
8. can't you
9. will he
10. aren't there
11. shall we
12. is it
13. aren't I
14. would you
15. will you
16. should I
17. had he

50.2

2. 's (very) expensive, isn't it?
3. was great, wasn't it?
4. 've had your hair cut, haven't you? 或 You had your hair cut, didn't you?
5. has a good voice, doesn't she? 或 She's got / She has got . . . doesn't / . . . doesn't she?

6. doesn't look very good, does it?
7. isn't very safe, is it?

50.3

2. don't have paper bags, do you?
3. don't know where Ann is, do you? 或 . . . you haven't seen Ann, have you?
4. you haven't got a bicycle pump, have you? 或 . . . you don't have a bicycle pump, do you?
5. you haven't seen my keys, have you? 或 you didn't see my keys, did you?
6. you couldn't take me to the station, could you? 或 . . . you couldn't give me a lift to the station, could you?

UNIT 51

51.1

2. making
3. listening
4. applying
5. reading
6. paying
7. using
8. forgetting
9. writing
10. being
11. trying
12. losing

51.2

2. driving too fast.
3. going swimming 或 going for a swim
4. breaking the DVD player
5. waiting a few minutes

51.3

2. traveling during rush hour
3. leaving . . . tomorrow
4. turning the radio down
5. not interrupting me all the time

51.4

参考答案：
2. standing
3. having a picnic
4. laughing
5. breaking down

UNIT 52

52.1

2. to help him
3. to carry her bags (for her)
4. to meet at 8:00
5. to tell him her name / to give him her name
6. not to tell anyone

52.2

2. to go
3. to get

4. waiting
5. to eat
6. how to use
7. barking
8. to call
9. having
10. to say / say
11. missing
12. to find

52.3

2. to be worried about something.
3. seem to know a lot of people.
4. My English seems to be getting better.
5. That car appears to have broken down.
6. David tends to forget things.
7. They claim to have solved the problem.

52.4

2. how to use
3. what to do
4. how to ride
5. what to say / what to do
6. whether to go

UNIT 53

53.1

2. me to lend you some
3. like me to shut it
4. you like me to show you (how)
5. you want me to repeat it
6. you want me to wait

53.2

2. to stay with them
3. him use her phone
4. her to be careful
5. her to give him a hand

53.3

2. it to rain.
3. him do what he wants.
4. him look older.
5. you to know the truth.
6. me to call my sister.
7. me to apply for the job.
8. advised me not to say anything to the police.
9. not to believe everything he says.
10. you to get around more easily.

53.4

2. to go
3. to do
4. cry
5. to study
6. eating
7. read
8. to make
9. think

UNIT 54

54.1
2. driving
3. to go
4. to go
5. raining
6. to win
7. asking
8. asking
9. to answer
10. breaking
11. to pay
12. losing 或 to lose
13. to tell
14. crying 或 to cry
15. to get
16. meeting . . . to see

54.2
2. He can remember crying on his first day of school.
3. He can't remember wanting to be a doctor.
4. He can remember going to Miami when he was eight.
5. He can't remember falling into a river.
6. He can't remember being bitten by a dog.

54.3
1. b) lending
   c) to call
   d) to say
   e) leaving/putting
2. a) saying
   b) to say
3. a) to become
   b) working
   c) reading

UNIT 55

55.1
2. turning it the other way.
3. tried taking an aspirin?
4. try calling his office?

55.2
2. It needs painting. / needs to be painted.
3. It needs cutting. / needs to be cut.
4. They need tightening. / need to be tightened.
5. It needs emptying. / to be emptied.

55.3
1. b) knocking
   c) to put
   d) asking
   e) to reach
   f) to concentrate
2. a) to go
   b) looking / to be looked
   c) washing / to be washed

d) cutting / to be cut
e) to iron . . . ironing / to be ironed
3. a) overhearing
   b) get 或 to get
   c) smiling
   d) make 或 to make

UNIT 56

56.1
参考答案：
2. I don't mind playing cards.
3. I don't like being alone. 或
   . . . to be alone.
4. I enjoy going to museums.
5. I love cooking. 或 I love to cook.

56.2
2. likes teaching biology.
3. He likes taking photographs. 或
   He likes to take photographs.
4. I didn't like working there.
5. She likes studying medicine.
6. He doesn't like being famous.
7. She doesn't like taking risks.
   或 She doesn't like to take risks.
8. I like to know things ahead of time.

56.3
2. to sit
3. waiting
4. going 或 to go
5. to get
6. being
7. to come / to go
8. living
9. to talk
10. to hear / hearing / to be told

56.4
2. I would like / I'd like to have seen the program.
3. I would hate / I'd hate to have lost my watch.
4. I would love / I'd love to have met your parents.
5. I wouldn't like to have been alone.
6. I would prefer / I'd prefer to have traveled by train. 或 I would have preferred to travel . . .

UNIT 57

57.1
参考答案：
2. tennis to soccer.
3. prefer calling people . . . sending e-mails.
4. I prefer going to the movies to watching videos at home.
5. call people rather than send e-mails.
6. I prefer to go to the movies rather than watch videos at home.

57.2
3. I'd rather listen to some music.
4. I'd prefer to eat at home.

5. I'd rather wait a few minutes.
6. I'd rather go for a swim.
7. I'd prefer to think about it for a while.
8. I'd rather stand.
9. I'd prefer to go alone.
11. rather than play tennis.
12. than go to a restaurant.
13. rather than decide now.
14. than watch TV.

57.3
2. I told her
3. would you rather I did it
4. would you rather I called her

57.4
2. stayed/remained/waited
3. stay
4. didn't
5. were
6. didn't

UNIT 58

58.1
2. applying for the job
3. remembering names
4. passing the exam
5. being late
6. eating at home, we went to a restaurant
7. having to wait in line 或 waiting in line
8. playing well

58.2
2. by standing on a chair
3. by turning a key
4. by borrowing too much money
5. by driving too fast
6. by putting some pictures on the walls

58.3
2. paying
3. going
4. using
5. going
6. being/traveling/sitting
7. asking/telling/consulting
8. doing/having
9. turning/going
10. taking

58.4
2. looking forward to seeing her/Diane.
3. looking forward to going to the dentist (tomorrow).
4. She's looking forward to graduating (next summer).
5. I'm looking forward to playing tennis (tomorrow).

UNIT 59

59.1
1. When Juan first went to Canada,

he **wasn't used to having** dinner so early, but after a while he **got used to** it. Now he finds it normal. He is **used to eating / is used to having dinner** at 6:00.

2. She **wasn't used to working** nights and it took her a few months to **get used to** it. Now, after a year, she's pretty happy. She **is used to working** nights.

59.2

2. 'm used to sleeping on the floor.
3. 'm used to working long hours.
4. I'm not used to going to bed so late.

59.3

2. get used to living in a much smaller house.
3. got used to her. / . . . to the/their new teacher.
4. 参考答案:
   They'll have to get used to the weather. / . . . to the food. / . . . to speaking a foreign language.

59.4

3. drink
4. eating
5. having
6. have
7. go
8. be
9. being

UNIT 60

60.1

2. doing
3. coming/going
4. doing/trying
5. buying/getting
6. hearing
7. going
8. having/using
9. being
10. watching
11. inviting/asking

60.2

2. in solving
3. of living
4. of causing
5. (from) walking
6. for interrupting
7. of spending
8. from escaping
9. on carrying
10. to seeing

60.3

2. on driving Ann to the station / . . . on taking Ann . . .
3. on getting married

4. Sue for coming to see her
5. (to me) for not calling earlier
6. me of being selfish

UNIT 61

61.1

2. There's no point in working if you don't need money.
3. There's no point in trying to study if you feel tired.
4. There's no point in hurrying if you've got plenty of time.

61.2

2. asking Dave
3. in going out
4. calling her
5. complaining (about what happened)
6. taking
7. keeping

61.3

2. remembering people's names
3. getting a job
4. getting a ticket for the game
5. understanding him

61.4

2. reading
3. packing / getting ready
4. watching
5. going/climbing/walking
6. applying
7. getting / being

61.5

2. went swimming
3. go skiing
4. goes riding
5. 's gone shopping / went shopping

UNIT 62

62.1

2. to get some money.
3. 'm saving money to go to Canada.
4. I went into the hospital to have an operation.
5. I'm wearing two sweaters to keep warm.
6. I called the police to report that my car had been stolen.

62.2

2. to read
3. to walk
4. to drink
5. to put / to carry
6. to discuss / to talk about
7. to buy / to get
8. to talk / to speak
9. to wear / to put on
10. to celebrate
11. to help

62.3

2. for
3. to
4. to
5. for
6. to
7. for
8. for . . . to

62.4

2. warm clothes so that I wouldn't be cold.
3. left Dave my phone number so that he could contact me. / . . . would be able to contact me.
4. We whispered so that . . . else would hear our conversation. / . . . so that nobody could hear . . . / would be able to hear . . .
5. arrive early so that we can start the meeting on time. / . . . so that we'll be able to start . . .
6. Jennifer locked the door so that she wouldn't be disturbed.
7. I slowed down so that the car behind me could pass. / . . . would pass.

UNIT 63

63.1

2. easy to use.
3. was very difficult to open.
4. are impossible to translate.
5. car is expensive to maintain.
6. chair isn't safe to stand on.

63.2

2. easy mistake to make.
3. nice place to live. 或 . . . a nice place to live in.
4. good game to watch.

63.3

2. 's careless of you to make the same mistake again and again.
3. It was nice of them to invite me (to stay with them). / It was nice of Dan and Jenny to . . .
4. It's inconsiderate of them to make so much noise (at night). / It's inconsiderate of the neighbors to . . .

63.4

2. am glad to hear 或 was glad to hear
3. were surprised to see
4. 'm/am sorry to hear 或 was sorry to hear

63.5

2. Paul was the last (person) to arrive.
3. Jenny was the only student to pass (the exam). / . . . the only one to pass (the exam).

4. I was the second customer/person to complain.
5. Neil Armstrong was the first person/man to walk on the moon.

63.6
2. 're/are bound to be
3. 's/is sure to forget
4. 's/is not likely to rain 或 isn't likely to rain
5. 's/is likely to be

UNIT 64

64.1
3. I'm afraid of losing it.
4. I was afraid to tell her.
5. We were afraid of missing our train.
6. We were afraid to look.
7. I was afraid of dropping it.
8. a) I was afraid to eat it.
   b) I was afraid of getting sick.

64.2
2. in starting
3. to read
4. in getting
5. to know
6. in looking

64.3
2. sorry to hear
3. sorry for saying / sorry about saying
4. sorry to bother
5. sorry for losing / sorry about losing

64.4
1. b) to leave
   c) from leaving
2. a) to solve
   b) in solving
3. a) of/about going
   b) to go
   c) to go
   d) to going
4. a) to buy
   b) to buy
   c) on buying
   d) of buying

UNIT 65

65.1
2. arrive
3. take it / do it
4. it ring
5. him play / him playing
6. you lock it / you do it
7. her fall

65.2
2. playing tennis.
3. Claire eating.
4. Bill playing his guitar.
5. smell the dinner burning.

6. We saw Linda jogging/running.

65.3
3. tell
4. crying
5. riding
6. say
7. run . . . climb
8. explode
9. crawling
10. slam
11. sleeping

UNIT 66

66.1
2. in an armchair reading a book.
3. opened the door carefully trying not to make any noise.
4. Sarah went out saying she would be back in an hour.
5. Linda was in London for two years working as a teacher.
6. Mary walked around the town looking at the sights and taking pictures.

66.2
2. fell asleep watching television.
3. slipped and fell getting off a bus.
4. got very wet walking home in the rain.
5. Laura had an accident driving to work yesterday.
6. Two kids got lost hiking in the woods.

66.3
2. Having bought our tickets, we went into the theater.
3. Having had dinner, they continued their trip.
4. Having done the shopping, I stopped for a cup of coffee.

66.4
2. Thinking they might be hungry, I offered them something to eat.
3. Being a vegetarian, Sally doesn't eat meat of any kind.
4. Not knowing his e-mail address, I wasn't able to contact him.
5. Having traveled a lot, Sarah knows a lot about other countries.
6. Not being able to speak the local language, I had trouble communicating.
7. Having spent nearly all our money, we couldn't afford to stay at a hotel.

UNIT 67

67.1
3. We went to **a** very nice restaurant . . .

4. *OK*
5. I use **a** toothbrush . . .
6. . . . if there's **a** bank near here?
7. . . . for **an** insurance company
8. *OK*
9. *OK*
10. . . . we stayed in **a** big hotel.
11. . . . I hope we come to **a** gas station soon.
12. . . . I have **a** problem.
13. . . . It's **a** very interesting idea.
14. John has **an** interview for **a** job tomorrow.
15. . . . It's **a** good game.
16. *OK*
17. Jane was wearing **a** beautiful necklace.

67.2
3. a key
4. a coat
5. sugar
6. a cookie
7. electricity
8. an interview
9. blood
10. a question
11. a minute
12. a decision

67.3
2. days
3. meat
4. a line
5. letters
6. friends
7. people
8. air
9. patience
10. an umbrella
11. languages
12. space

UNIT 68

68.1
2. a) a paper
   b) paper
3. a) a light
   b) Light
4. a) time
   b) a wonderful time
5. a nice room
6. advice
7. nice weather
8. bad luck
9. job
10. trip
11. total chaos
12. some

13. doesn't
14. Your hair is . . . it
15. The damage

68.2
2. information
3. chairs
4. furniture
5. hair
6. progress
7. job
8. work
9. permission
10. advice
11. experience
12. experiences

68.3
2. some information about places to see in the city.
3. some advice about which courses to take? / . . . courses I can take?
4. is the news on (TV)?
5. 's a beautiful view, isn't it?
6. horrible/awful weather!

UNIT 69

69.1
3. It's a vegetable.
4. It's a game. / It's a board game.
5. They're musical instruments.
6. It's a (tall/high) building.
7. They're planets.
8. It's a flower.
9. They're rivers.
10. They're birds.
12. He was a writer / a poet / a playwright / a dramatist.
13. He was a scientist / a physicist.
14. They were U.S. presidents / American presidents / presidents of the U.S.
15. She was an actress / a movie actress / a movie star.
16. They were singers.
17. They were painters / artists.

69.2
2. 's a waiter.
3. 's a travel agent.
4. He's a surgeon.
5. He's a chef.
6. She's a journalist.
7. He's a plumber.
8. She's an interpreter.

69.3
4. a
5. an
6. – (Do you collect stamps?)
7. a
8. Some
9. – (Do you enjoy going to concerts?)
10. – (I've got sore feet.)

11. a
12. some
13. a . . . a
14. – (Those are nice shoes.)
15. some
16. a . . . some
17. a . . . – (Her parents were teachers, too.)
18. a . . . – (He's always telling lies.)

UNIT 70

70.1
1. . . . and **a** magazine. **The** newspaper is in my briefcase, but I can't remember where I put **the** magazine.
2. I saw **an** accident this morning. **A** car crashed into **a** tree. **The** driver of **the** car wasn't hurt, but **the** car was badly damaged.
3. . . . **a** blue one and **a** gray one. **The** blue one belongs to my neighbors; I don't know who **the** owner of **the** gray one is.
4. My friends live in **an** old house in **a** small town. There is **a** beautiful garden behind **the** house. I would like to have **a** garden like that.

70.2
1. b) the
   c) the
2. a) a
   b) a
   c) the
3. a) a
   b) the
   c) the
4. a) an . . . The
   b) the
   c) the
5. a) the
   b) a
   c) a

70.3
2. **the** dentist
3. **the** door
4. **a** mistake
5. **the** bus station
6. **a** problem
7. **the** post office
8. **the** floor
9. **the** book
10. **a** job at **a** bank
11. **a** small apartment near **the** hospital
12. **a** supermarket on **the** corner

70.4
参考答案：
3. About once a month.
4. Once or twice a year.
5. About 55 miles an hour.

6. About seven hours a night.
7. Two or three times a week.
8. About two hours a day.

UNIT 71

71.1
2. *A:* a; *B:* the
3. *A:* the; *B:* the
4. *A:* the; *B:* a
5. *A:* –; *B:* the
6. *A:* the; *B:* –
7. *A:* a; *B:* the
8. *A:* –; *B:* –
9. *A:* –; *B:* the
10. *A:* the; *B:* a

71.2
2. the . . . the
3. –
4. The
5. the
6. –
7. the . . . the . . . – . . .
8. the

71.3
2. in a small town in the country
3. The moon goes around the earth every 27 days.
4. the same thing
5. a very hot day . . . the hottest day of the year
6. usually have lunch . . . eat a good breakfast
7. live in a foreign country . . . learn the language
8. on the wrong platform
9. The next train . . . from Platform 3

71.4
2. the ocean
3. question 8
4. the movies
5. breakfast
6. the gate
7. Gate 21

UNIT 72

72.1
2. to school
3. at home
4. to work
5. in high school
6. in bed
7. to prison

72.2
1. c) school
   d) school
   e) . . . school . . . The school
   f) school
   g) the school
2. a) college
   b) college
   c) the college

3. a) church
    b) church
    c) the church
4. a) class
    b) the class
    c) class
    d) the class
5. a) prison
    b) the prison
    c) prison
6. a) bed
    b) home
    c) work
    d) bed
    e) work
    f) work

UNIT 73

73.1
参考答案：
2.–5.
I like cats.
I don't like zoos.
I don't mind fast food restaurants.
I'm not interested in football.

73.2
3. spiders
4. meat
5. the questions
6. the people
7. History
8. lies
9. the hotels
10. The water
11. the grass
12. patience

73.3
3. Apples
4. the apples
5. Women . . . men
6. tea
7. The vegetables
8. Life
9. skiing
10. the people
11. people . . . aggression
12. All the books
13. the beds
14. war
15. The First World War
16. the Pyramids
17. the history . . . modern art
18. the marriage
19. Most people . . . marriage . . .
    family life . . . society

UNIT 74

74.1
1. b) the cheetah
    c) the kangaroo (and the rabbit)
2. a) the swan
    b) the penguin
    c) the owl

3. a) the wheel
    b) the laser
    c) the telescope
4. a) the rupee
    b) the (Canadian) dollar
    c) the . . .

74.2
2. a
3. the
4. a
5. the
6. the
7. a
8. The

74.3
2. the injured
3. the unemployed
4. the sick
5. the rich . . . the poor

74.4
2. a German   Germans
3. a Frenchman/Frenchwoman
    the French
4. a Russian   Russians
5. a Chinese   the Chinese
6. a Brazilian   Brazilians
7. a Japanese man/woman
    Japanese
8. . . .

UNIT 75

75.1
2. the
3. the . . . the
4. – (President Kennedy was
    assassinated in 1963.)
5. the
6. – (Do you know Professor Brown's
    phone number?)

75.2
3. OK
4. the United States
5. The south of India . . . the north
6. OK
7. the Channel
8. the Middle East
9. OK
10. the Swiss Alps
11. The UK
12. The Seychelles . . . the Indian
    Ocean
13. OK
14. The Hudson River . . . the Atlantic
    Ocean

75.3
2. (in) South America
3. the Nile
4. Sweden
5. the United States
6. the Rockies
7. the Mediterranean
8. Australia

9. the Pacific
10. the Indian Ocean
11. the Thames
12. the Mississippi
13. Thailand
14. the Panama Canal
15. the Amazon

UNIT 76

76.1
2. Turner's on Carter Road
3. the Crown (Hotel) on Park Road
4. St. Paul's on Market Street
5. the City Museum on George Street
6. Blackstone's on Forest Avenue
7. Lincoln Park at the end of Market
    Street
8. The China House on Park
    Road 或 Mario's Pizza on
    George Street

76.2
2. The Eiffel Tower
3. the Taj Mahal
4. The White House
5. The Kremlin
6. Broadway
7. The Acropolis
8. Buckingham Palace

76.3
2. Central Park
3. St. James's Park
4. The Ramada Inn . . . Main Street
5. O'Hare Airport
6. McGill University
7. Harrison's
8. the Ship Inn
9. The Statue of Liberty . . . New
    York Harbor
10. the Science Museum
11. IBM . . . General Electric
12. The Classic
13. the Great Wall
14. The Washington Post
15. Cambridge University Press

UNIT 77

77.1
3. shorts
4. a means
5. means
6. some scissors 或 a pair of scissors
7. a series
8. series
9. species

77.2
2. politics
3. economics
4. physics
5. gymnastics
6. electronics

77.3
2. don't

3. want
4. was
5. aren't
6. wasn't
7. isn't
8. they
9. are
10. Do
11. is

77.4
3. . . . wearing black jeans.
4. very nice people.
5. OK
6. . . . buy some new pajamas. 或
   . . . buy a new pair of pajamas.
7. There was a police officer / a
   policeman / a policewoman . . .
8. OK
9. These scissors aren't . . .
10. . . . two days is . . .
11. Many people have . . .

UNIT 78

78.1
3. a computer magazine
4. (your) vacation pictures
5. milk chocolate
6. a factory inspector
7. a race horse
8. a horse race
9. a Los Angeles lawyer
10. (your) exam results
11. the dining room carpet
12. an oil company scandal
13. a five-story building
14. a traffic plan
15. a five-day course
16. a two-part question
17. a seven-year-old girl

78.2
2. room number
3. seat belt
4. credit card
5. weather forecast
6. newspaper editor
7. shop window

78.3
3. 20-dollar
4. 15-minute
5. 60 minutes
6. two-hour
7. five courses
8. two-year
9. 500-year-old
10. five days
11. six miles
12. six-mile

UNIT 79

79.1
3. your friend's umbrella
4. OK
5. Charles's daughter
6. Mary and Dan's son
7. OK
8. yesterday's newspaper
9. OK
10. OK
11. Your children's friends
12. Our neighbors' garden
13. OK
14. Bill's hair
15. Catherine's party
16. OK
17. Mike's parents' car
18. OK
19. OK (the government's economic
    policy 也可以作為正確答案)

79.2
2. a boy's name
3. children's clothes
4. a girls' school
5. a bird's nest
6. a women's magazine

79.3
2. week's storm caused a lot of damage.
3. town's only movie theater has closed
   down.
4. Chicago's weather is very
   changeable.
5. The region's main industry is
   tourism.

79.4
2. a year's salary
3. four weeks' pay
4. five hours' sleep
5. a minute's rest

UNIT 80

80.1
2. hurt himself
3. blame herself
4. Put yourself
5. enjoyed themselves
6. burn yourself
7. express myself

80.2
2. me
3. myself
4. us
5. yourself
6. you
7. ourselves
8. themselves
9. them

80.3
2. dried herself
3. concentrate
4. defend yourself
5. meeting
6. relax

80.4
2. themselves
3. each other
4. each other
5. themselves
6. each other
7. ourselves
8. each other
9. ourselves . . . each other

80.5
2. it himself.
3. mail/do it myself.
4. told me herself. / herself told me. /
   did herself.
5. call him yourself? / . . . do it
   yourself?

UNIT 81

81.1
2. relative of yours.
3. borrowed a book of mine.
4. invited some friends of hers to her
   place.
5. We had dinner with a neighbor of
   ours.
6. I took a trip with two friends of
   mine.
7. Is that man a friend of yours?
8. I met a friend of Amy's at the party.

81.2
2. his own opinions
3. her own business
4. its own (private) beach
5. our own words

81.3
2. your own fault
3. her own ideas
4. your own problems
5. his own decisions

81.4
2. makes her own clothes
3. bake/make our own bread
4. writes his own songs

81.5
2. my own
3. myself
4. himself
5. his own
6. herself
7. her own
8. yourself
9. our own
10. herself

UNIT 82

82.1
3. Is there . . . there's / there is
4. there was . . . It was
5. It was
6. There was
7. is it
8. It was
9. It's / It is
10. there wasn't
11. Is it . . . it's / it is
12. there was . . . There was
13. It was
14. There wasn't
15. There was . . . it wasn't

82.2
2. is a lot of salt
3. There was nothing
4. There was a lot of violence in the film. / There was a lot of fighting . . .
5. There were a lot of people in the stores / the mall.
6. There is a lot to do in this town. / There is a lot happening in this town.

82.3
2. There might be
3. there will be / there'll be 或 there are going to be
4. There's going to be / There is going to be
5. There used to be
6. there should be
7. there wouldn't be

82.4
2. and there was a lot of snow
3. There used to be a church here
4. There must have been a reason.
5. *OK*
6. There's sure to be a parking lot somewhere.
7. there will be an opportunity
8. *OK*
9. there would be somebody . . . but there wasn't anybody.
10. There has been no change.
11. *OK*

UNIT 83

83.1
2. some
3. any
4. any . . . some
5. some
6. any
7. any
8. some
9. any
0. any

83.2
2. somebody/someone
3. anybody/anyone
4. anything
5. something
6. somebody/someone . . . anybody/anyone
7. something . . . anybody/anyone
8. Anybody/Anyone
9. anybody/anyone
10. anywhere
11. somewhere
12. anywhere
13. anybody/anyone
14. something
15. Anybody/Anyone
16. something
17. anybody/anyone . . . anything

83.3
2. Any day
3. Anything
4. anywhere
5. Any job 或 Anything
6. Any time
7. Anybody/Anyone
8. Any newspaper 或 Any one

UNIT 84

84.1
3. no
4. any
5. None
6. none
7. No
8. any
9. any
10. none
11. no

84.2
2. Nobody/No one.
3. None.
4. Nowhere.
5. None.
6. Nothing.
8. I wasn't talking to anybody/anyone.
9. I don't have any luggage.
10. I'm not going anywhere.
11. I didn't make any mistakes.
12. I didn't pay anything.

84.3
2. nobody/no one
3. Nowhere
4. anything
5. Nothing. I couldn't find anything . . .
6. Nothing
7. anywhere
8. Nobody/No one said anything.

84.4
2. nobody
3. anyone
4. Anybody
5. Nothing
6. Anything
7. anything

UNIT 85

85.1
3. a lot of salt
4. *OK*
5. It cost a lot
6. *OK*
7. many people 或 a lot of people
8. I use the phone a lot
9. *OK*
10. a lot of money

85.2
2. plenty of money.
3. plenty of room.
4. plenty to learn.
5. are plenty of things to see.
6. There are plenty of hotels.

85.3
2. little
3. many
4. much
5. few
6. little
7. many

85.4
3. a few dollars
4. *OK*
5. a little time
6. *OK*
7. only a few words
8. a few months

85.5
2. a little
3. a few
4. few
5. little
6. a little
7. little
8. a few

UNIT 86

86.1
3. –
4. of
5. –
6. –
7. of
8. of
9. –
10. –

86.2

3. of my spare time
4. accidents
5. of the buildings
6. of her friends
7. of the population
8. birds
9. of my teammates
10. of her opinions
11. large cities
12. (of) my dinner

86.3

参考答案：

2. the time / the day
3. my friends
4. (of) the questions
5. the photos / the photographs / the pictures
6. (of) the money

86.4

2. All of them
3. none of us
4. some of it
5. none of them
6. None of it
7. Some of them
8. all of it

UNIT 87

87.1

2. Neither
3. both
4. Either
5. Neither

87.2

2. either
3. both
4. Neither of
5. neither ... both / both the / both of the
6. both / both of

87.3

2. either of them
3. both of them
4. neither of us
5. neither of them

87.4

3. Both Joe and Sam are on vacation.
4. Neither Joe nor Sam has a car.
5. Brian neither watches TV nor reads newspapers.
6. The movie was both boring and long.
7. That man's name is either Richard or Robert.
8. I've got neither the time nor the money to go on vacation.
9. We can leave either today or tomorrow.

87.5

2. either
3. any
4. none
5. any
6. either
7. neither

UNIT 88

88.1

3. Everybody/Everyone
4. Everything
5. all/everything
6. everybody/everyone
7. everything
8. All
9. everybody/everyone
10. All
11. everything/all
12. Everybody/Everyone
13. All
14. everything

88.2

2. whole team played well.
3. the whole box (of chocolates).
4. searched the whole house.
5. whole family plays tennis.
6. Ann/She worked the whole day.
7. It rained the whole week.
8. worked all day.
9. It rained all week.

88.3

2. every four hours
3. every four years
4. every five minutes
5. every six months

88.4

2. every day
3. all day
4. The whole building
5. every time
6. all the time
7. all my luggage

UNIT 89

89.1

3. Each
4. Every
5. Each
6. every
7. each
8. every

89.2

3. Every
4. Each
5. every
6. every
7. each
8. every
9. every

10. each
11. Every
12. each

89.3

2. had 10 dollars each. / ... and I each had 10 dollars.
3. postcards cost 40 cents each. / ... postcards are 40 cents each.
4. paid $195 each. / ... each paid $195.

89.4

2. everyone
3. every one
4. Everyone
5. every one

UNIT 90

90.1

2. who breaks into a house to steal things.
3. A customer is someone who buys something from a store.
4. A shoplifter is someone who steals from a store.
5. A coward is someone who is not brave.
6. An atheist is someone who doesn't believe in God.
7. A pessimist is someone who expects the worst to happen.
8. A tenant is someone who pays rent to live in a room or apartment.

90.2

2. waitress who/that served us was impolite and impatient.
3. building that/which was destroyed in the fire has now been rebuilt.
4. people who/that were arrested have now been released.
5. bus that/which goes to the airport runs every half hour.

90.3

2. who/that runs away from home
3. that/which were on the wall
4. that/which cannot be explained
5. who/that stole my car
6. that/which gives you the meaning of words
7. who/that invented the telephone
8. that/which can support life

90.4

3. that/which sells
4. who/that caused
5. *OK* (who took 也可以作為正確答案)
6. that/which is changing
7. *OK* (which were 也可以作為正確答案)
8. that/which won

UNIT 91

91.1

3. *OK* (the people who/that we met 也可以作為正確答案)

4. The people who/that work in the office
5. *OK* (the people who/that I work with 也可以作為正確答案)
6. *OK* (the money that/which I gave you 也可以作為正確答案)
7. the money that/which was on the table
8. *OK* (the worst film that/which you've ever seen 也可以作為正確答案)
9. the best thing that/which has ever happened to you

91.2

2. you're wearing 或 that/which you're wearing
3. you're going to see 或 that/which you're going to see
4. I/we wanted to visit 或 that/which I/we wanted to visit
5. I/we invited to the party 或 who/whom/that we invited . . .
6. you had to do 或 that/which you had to do
7. I/we rented 或 that/which I/we rented
8. Tom had recommended (to us) 或 that/which Tom had recommended . . .

91.3

2. we were invited to 或 that/which we were invited to
3. I work with 或 who/that I work with
4. you told me about 或 that/which you told me about
5. we went to last night 或 that/which we went to . . .
6. I applied for 或 that/which I applied for
7. you can rely on 或 who/that you can rely on
8. I saw you with 或 who/that I saw you with

91.4

3. – (that 也可以作為正確答案)
4. what
5. that
6. what
7. – (that 也可以作為正確答案)
8. what
9. – (that 也可以作為正確答案)

UNIT 92

92.1

2. whose wife is an English teacher
3. who owns a restaurant
4. whose ambition is to climb Everest
5. who have just gotten married / just got married
6. whose parents used to work in a circus

92.2

2. where I can buy some postcards
3. where I work
4. where Sue is staying
5. where I/we play baseball

92.3

2. where
3. who
4. whose
5. whom
6. where
7. whose
8. whom

92.4

參考答案：
2. I'll never forget the time we got stuck in an elevator.
3. The reason I didn't write to you was that I didn't know your address.
4. Unfortunately I wasn't at home the evening you called.
5. The reason they don't have a car is that they don't need one.
6. 1996 was the year Amanda got married.

UNIT 93

93.1

3. We often go to visit our friends in New York, which is not very far away.
4. I went to see the doctor, who told me to rest for a few days.
5. John, who/whom I've known for a very long time, is one of my closest friends.
6. Sheila, whose job involves a lot of travel, is away from home a lot.
7. The new stadium, which can hold 90,000 people, will be opened next month.
8. Alaska, where my brother lives, is the largest state in the United States.
9. A friend of mine, whose father is the manager of a company, helped me to get a job.

93.2

3. which began 10 days ago, is now over.
4. the book I was looking for this morning. 或 . . . the book that/which I was looking for.
5. which was once the largest city in the world, is now decreasing.
6. the people who/that applied for the job had the necessary qualifications.
7. a picture of her son, who is a police officer.

93.3

2. My office, which is on the second floor, is very small.
3. *OK* (The office that/which I'm using . . . 也可以作為正確答案)

4. Ben's father, who used to be a teacher, now works for a TV company.
5. *OK* (The doctor who examined me . . . 也可以作為正確答案)
6. The sun, which is one of millions of stars in the universe, provides us with heat and light.

UNIT 94

94.1

2. of which he's very proud
3. with whom we went on vacation
4. to which only members of the family were invited

94.2

2. most of which was useless
3. neither of which she has received
4. none of whom was suitable
5. one of which she hardly ever uses
6. half of which he gave to his parents
7. both of whom are teachers
8. only a few of whom I knew
9. (the) sides of which were lined with trees
10. the aim of which is to save money

94.3

2. doesn't have a phone, which makes it difficult to contact her.
3. Neil has passed his exams, which is good news.
4. Our flight was delayed, which meant we had to wait three hours at the airport.
5. Kate offered to let me stay at her house, which was very nice of her.
6. The street I live on is very noisy at night, which makes it difficult to sleep sometimes.
7. Our car has broken down, which means we can't take our trip tomorrow.

UNIT 95

95.1

2. the man sitting next to me on the plane
3. The taxi taking us to the airport
4. a path leading to the river
5. A factory employing 500 people
6. a brochure containing the information I needed

95.2

2. damaged in the storm
3. suggestions made at the meeting
4. paintings stolen from the museum
5. the man arrested by the police

95.3

3. living
4. offering

5. named
6. blown
7. sitting . . . reading
8. driving . . . selling

95.4

3. is somebody coming.
4. There were a lot of people traveling.
5. There was nobody else staying there.
6. There was nothing written on it.
7. There's a new course beginning next Monday.

UNIT 96

96.1

2. a) exhausting
   b) exhausted
3. a) depressing
   b) depressed
   c) depressed
4. a) exciting
   b) exciting
   c) excited

96.2

2. interested
3. exciting
4. embarrassing
5. embarrassed
6. amazed
7. astonishing
8. amused
9. terrifying . . . shocked
10. bored . . . boring
11. boring . . . interesting

96.3

2. bored
3. confusing
4. disgusting
5. interested
6. annoyed
7. boring
8. exhausted
9. excited
10. amusing
11. interesting

UNIT 97

97.1

2. an unusual gold ring
3. a beautiful old house
4. black leather gloves
5. an old Italian film
6. a long thin face
7. big black clouds
8. a lovely sunny day
9. an ugly yellow dress
10. a long wide avenue
11. a little old red car
12. a nice new green sweater
13. a small black metal box
14. a big fat black cat
15. a charming little old country inn
16. beautiful long black hair

17. an interesting old French painting
18. an enormous red and yellow umbrella

97.2

2. tastes/tasted awful
3. feel fine
4. smell nice
5. look wet
6. sounds/sounded interesting

97.3

2. happy
3. happily
4. violent
5. terrible
6. properly
7. good
8. slow

97.4

3. the last two days
4. the first two weeks of May
5. the next few days
6. the first three questions (in the exam)
7. the next two years
8. the last three days of our vacation

UNIT 98

98.1

2. badly
3. easily
4. patiently
5. unexpectedly
6. regularly
7. perfectly . . . slowly . . . clearly

98.2

3. selfishly
4. terribly
5. sudden
6. colorfully
7. colorful
8. badly
9. badly
10. safe

98.3

2. careful
3. continuously
4. happily
5. fluent
6. specially
7. complete
8. perfectly
9. nervous
10. financially 或 completely

98.4

2. seriously ill
3. absolutely enormous
4. slightly damaged
5. unusually quiet
6. completely changed
7. unnecessarily long
8. badly planned

UNIT 99

99.1

2. good
3. well
4. good
5. well
6. well
7. good
8. well
9. good
10. well

99.2

2. well known
3. well maintained
4. well written
5. well informed
6. well dressed
7. well paid

99.3

2. *OK*
3. *OK*
4. hard
5. *OK*
6. slowly

99.4

2. hardly hear
3. hardly slept
4. hardly speak
5. hardly said
6. hardly changed
7. hardly recognized

99.5

2. hardly any
3. hardly anything
4. hardly anybody/anyone
5. hardly ever
6. Hardly anybody/anyone
7. hardly anywhere
8. hardly 或 hardly ever
9. hardly any
10. hardly anything . . . hardly anywhere

UNIT 100

100.1

4. so
5. so
6. such a
7. so
8. such
9. such a
10. such a
11. so
12. so . . . such
13. so
14. such a
15. such a

100.2

3. I was so tired (that) I couldn't keep my eyes open.
4. We had such a good time on our vacation (that) we didn't want to come home.

5. She speaks English so well (that) you would think it was her native language. 或 She speaks such good English (that) . . .

6. I've got such a lot to do (that) I don't know where to begin. 或 I've got so much to do (that) . . .

7. The music was so loud (that) you could hear it from miles away.

8. I had such a big breakfast (that) I didn't eat anything else for the rest of the day.

9. It was such terrible weather (that) we spent the whole day indoors.

10. I was so surprised (that) I didn't know what to say.

100.3
参考答案：

2. a) friendly.
   b) a nice person.
3. a) lively.
   b) an exciting place.
4. a) exhausting.
   b) a difficult job.
5. a) long.
   b) a long time.

UNIT 101

101.1
3. enough money
4. enough milk
5. warm enough
6. enough room
7. well enough
8. enough time
9. qualified enough
10. big enough
11. enough cups

101.2
2. too busy to talk
3. too late to go
4. warm enough to sit
5. too shy to be
6. enough patience to be
7. too far away to hear
8. enough English to read

101.3
2. too hot to drink.
3. was too heavy to move.
4. aren't / are not ripe enough to eat.
5. is too complicated (for me) to explain.
6. was too high (for us) to climb over.
7. isn't / is not big enough for three people (to sit on).
8. things are too small to see without a microscope.

UNIT 102

102.1
2. stronger
3. smaller
4. more expensive
5. warmer/hotter
6. more interesting / more exciting
7. nearer/closer
8. more difficult / more complicated
9. better
10. worse
11. longer
12. more quietly
13. more often
14. farther/further
15. happier

102.2
3. more serious than
4. thinner
5. bigger
6. more interested
7. more important than
8. simpler / more simple
9. more crowded than
10. more peaceful than
11. more easily
12. higher than

102.3
2. longer by train than by car.
3. further/farther than Dave.
4. worse than Chris (on the test).
5. arrived earlier than I expected.
6. run more often than the trains. 或 The buses run more frequently than . . .
7. were busier than usual (at work today). 或 We were busier at work today than usual.

UNIT 103

103.1
2. much bigger
3. much more complicated than
4. a little cooler
5. far more interesting than
6. a little more slowly
7. a lot easier
8. slightly older

103.2
2. any sooner / any earlier
3. no higher than / no more expensive than
4. any farther/further
5. no worse than

103.3
2. bigger and bigger
3. heavier and heavier
4. more and more nervous

5. worse and worse
6. more and more expensive
7. better and better
8. more and more talkative

103.4
2. the more I liked him 或 the more I got to like him
3. the more profit you (will) make 或 the higher your profit (will be) 或 the more your profit (will be)
4. the harder it is to concentrate
5. the more impatient she became

103.5
2. older
3. older 或 elder
4. older

UNIT 104

104.1
2. as high as yours.
3. know as much about cars as me. 或 . . . as I do.
4. as cold as it was yesterday.
5. feel as tired as I did yesterday. 或 . . . as I felt yesterday.
6. lived here as long as us. 或 . . . as we have.
7. as nervous (before the interview) as I usually am. 或 . . . as usual.

104.2
3. as far as I thought.
4. less than I expected.
5. go out as much as I used to. 或 . . . as often as I used to.
6. have longer hair.
7. know them as well as me. 或 . . . as I do.
8. as many people at this meeting as at the last one.

104.3
2. as well as
3. as long as
4. as soon as
5. as often as
6. as quietly as
7. just as comfortable as
8. just as well-qualified as
9. just as bad as

104.4
2. is the same color as mine.
3. arrived at the same time as you did.
4. birthday is the same day as Tom's. 或 birthday is the same as Tom's.

104.5
2. than him / than he does
3. as me / as I do
4. than us / than we were

5. than her / than she is
6. as them / as they have been

UNIT 105

105.1

2. the cheapest restaurant in the town.
3. the happiest day of my life.
4. 's the most intelligent student in the class.
5. 's the most valuable painting in the gallery.
6. 's the busiest time of the year.
8. of the richest men in the world.
9. 's one of the oldest houses in the city.
10. 's one of the best colleges in the state.
11. was one of the worst experiences of my life.
12. 's one of the most dangerous criminals in the country.

105.2

3. larger
4. the smallest
5. better
6. the worst
7. the most popular
8. ... the highest mountain in the world ... It is higher than ...
9. the most enjoyable
10. more comfortable
11. the quickest
12. The oldest 或 The eldest

105.3

2. the funniest joke I've ever heard.
3. is the best coffee I've ever tasted.
4. 's the most generous person I've ever met.
5. 's the furthest/farthest I've ever run.
6. 's the worst mistake I've ever made. 或 was the worst ...
7. 's the most famous person you've ever met?

UNIT 106

106.1

3. Jim doesn't like basketball very much.
4. OK
5. I ate my breakfast quickly and ...
6. ... a lot of people to the party?
7. OK
8. Did you go to bed late last night?
9. OK
10. I met a friend of mine on my way home.

106.2

2. We won the game easily.
3. I closed the door quietly.
4. Diane speaks Chinese quite well.
5. Tim watches TV all the time.
6. Please don't ask that question again.

7. Does Ken play golf every weekend?
8. I borrowed some money from a friend of mine.

106.3

2. go to the supermarket every Friday.
3. did you come home so late?
4. takes her children to school every day.
5. been to the movies recently.
6. write your name at the top of the page.
7. remembered her name after a few minutes.
8. walked around the town all morning.
9. didn't see you at the party on Saturday night.
10. found some interesting books in the library.
11. left her umbrella in a restaurant last night.
12. are building a new hotel across from the park.

UNIT 107

107.1

3. I usually take ...
4. OK
5. Steve hardly ever gets angry.
6. ... and I also went to the bank.
7. Jane always has to hurry ...
8. We were all ... OK
9. OK

107.2

2. a) We were all on vacation in Spain.
   b) We were all staying at the same hotel.
   c) We all enjoyed ourselves.
3. Catherine is always very generous.
4. I don't usually have to work on Saturdays.
5. Do you always watch TV in the evenings?
6. ... is also studying Japanese.
7. a) The new hotel is probably very expensive.
   b) It probably costs a lot to stay there.
8. a) I can probably help you.
   b) I probably can't help you.

107.3

2. usually take
3. am usually
4. has probably gone
5. were both born
6. can also sing
7. often sleeps
8. have never spoken
9. always have to wait
10. can only read
11. will probably be leaving
12. probably won't be

13. is hardly ever
14. are still living
15. would never have met
16. always am

UNIT 108

108.1

3. He doesn't write poems anymore.
4. He still wants to be a teacher.
5. He isn't / He's not interested in politics anymore.
6. He's still single.
7. He doesn't go fishing anymore.
8. He doesn't have a beard anymore.
10.–12.
   He no longer writes poems.
   He is / He's no longer interested in politics.
   He no longer goes fishing.
   He no longer has a beard.

108.2

2. hasn't left yet.
3. haven't finished (repairing the road) yet.
4. They haven't woken up yet.
5. Has she found a place to live yet?
6. I haven't decided (what to do) yet.
7. It hasn't taken off yet.

108.3

5. I don't want to go out yet.
6. she doesn't work there anymore
7. I still have a lot of friends there. 或 I've still got ...
8. We've already met.
9. Do you still live in the same place
10. have you already eaten
11. He's not here yet.
12. he still isn't here (he isn't here yet 也可以作為正確答案)
13. are you already a member
14. I can still remember it very clearly
15. These pants don't fit me anymore.
16. "Have you finished with the paper yet?" "No, I'm still reading it." 或 Are you finished with ...?

UNIT 109

109.1

2. even Amanda
3. not even Julie
4. even Amanda
5. even Sarah
6. not even Amanda

109.2

2. even painted the floor.
3. 's even met the president. 或 even met ...
4. could even hear it from two blocks away. 或 You could even hear the noise from ...
6. I can't even remember her name.
7. There isn't even a movie theater.

8. He didn't even tell his wife (where he was going).
9. I don't even know the people next door.

109.3
2. even older
3. even better
4. even more difficult
5. even worse
6. even less

109.4
2. if
3. even if
4. even
5. even though
6. Even
7. even though
8. even if
9. Even though

UNIT 110

110.1
2. Although I had never seen her before
3. although it was quite cold
4. although we don't like them very much
5. Although I didn't speak the language
6. Although the heat was on
7. although I'd met her twice before
8. although we've known each other a long time

110.2
2. a) In spite of (或 Despite)
   b) Although
3. a) because
   b) although
4. a) because of
   b) in spite of (或 despite)
5. a) although
   b) because of
参考答案：
6. a) he hadn't studied very hard
   b) he had studied very hard
7. a) I was hungry
   b) being hungry / my hunger / the fact (that) I was hungry

110.3
2. In spite of having very little money, they are happy. 或 In spite of the fact (that) they have very little money . . .
3. Although my foot was injured, I managed to walk to the nearest town. 或 I managed to walk to the nearest town although my . . .
4. I enjoyed the movie in spite of the silly story. / . . . in spite of the story being silly. / . . . in spite of the fact (that) the story was silly. 或 In spite of . . . , I enjoyed the movie.

5. Despite living on the same street, we hardly ever see each other. 或 Despite the fact (that) we live on . . . 或 We hardly ever see each other despite . . .
6. Even though I was only out for five minutes, I got very wet in the rain. 或 I got very wet in the rain even though I was . . .

110.4
2. It's very windy though.
3. We ate it though.
4. I don't like her husband though.

UNIT 111

111.1
2.–5.
a map with you in case you get lost. Take a raincoat with you in case it rains.
Take a camera with you in case you want to take some pictures/photos. Take some water with you in case you're thirsty. 或 . . . you get thirsty.

111.2
2. in case I don't see you again (before you go).
3. check the list in case we forgot something? 或 . . . forgot anything?
4. your files in case the computer crashes.

111.3
2. the name (of the book) in case he forgot it.
3. my parents in case they were worried (about me).
4. (Liz) another e-mail in case she hadn't received the first one.
5. them my address in case they came to New York (one day).

111.4
3. If
4. if
5. in case
6. if
7. if
8. in case
9. in case

UNIT 112

112.1
2. unless you listen carefully.
3. I'll never speak to her again unless she apologizes to me. 或 Unless she apologises to me, I'll . . .
4. He won't be able to understand you unless you speak very slowly. 或 Unless you speak very slowly, he . . .

5. The company will have to close unless business improves soon. 或 Unless business improves soon, the company . . .

112.2
2. (to the party) unless you go too.
3. won't attack you unless you move suddenly.
4. won't speak to you unless you ask him something.
5. won't see you unless it's an emergency.

112.3
2. unless
3. providing
4. as long as
5. unless
6. unless
7. provided
8. Unless
9. unless
10. as long as

112.4
参考答案：
2. it's not too hot
3. there isn't too much traffic
4. it isn't raining
5. I'm in a hurry
6. you have something else to do
7. you pay it back next week
8. you take risks

UNIT 113

113.1
2. We all smiled as we posed for the photograph.
3. I burned myself as I was taking a hot dish out of the oven.
4. The crowd cheered as the two teams ran onto the field.
5. A dog ran out in front of the car as we were driving along the road.

113.2
3. because
4. at the same time as
5. at the same time as
6. because
7. because
参考答案：
9. Since I was tired, I went to bed early.
10. We decided to go out to eat since we had no food at home.
11. Since we don't use the car very often, we've decided to sell it.

113.3
3. OK
4. when I was asleep
5. When I finished high school
6. OK
7. when I was a child

113.4
参考答案：
1. you were getting into your car.
2. we started playing tennis.
3. I had to walk home.
4. somebody walked in front of the camera.

UNIT 114

114.1
3. like her mother
4. people like him
5. *OK*
6. like most of his friends
7. like talking to the wall
8. *OK*
9. *OK*
10. *OK*
11. like a bomb exploding
12. like a fish

114.2
2. like blocks of ice
3. like a beginner
4. as a tour guide
5. like a church
6. as a birthday present
7. like winter
8. like a child

114.3
2. like
3. as
4. like
5. like
6. as (like 也可以作為正確答案)
7. like
8. as
9. as
10. like
11. like
12. as
13. as
14. Like
15. as
16. As
17. like
18. as (like 也可以作為正確答案)

UNIT 115

115.1
2. look like you've seen a ghost.
3. sound like you're enjoying yourself.
4. feel like I've (just) run a marathon.

115.2
2. looks like it's going to rain.
3. It sounds like they're having an argument.
4. It looks like there's been an accident.
5. It looks like we'll have to walk.

6. It sounds like you should see a doctor.

115.3
2. as if he meant what he said
3. as if she hurt her leg
4. as if he hadn't eaten for a week
5. as if she was enjoying it
6. as if I'm going to be sick
7. as if she didn't want to come
8. as if I didn't exist

115.4
2. as if [I] was/were
3. as if she was/were
4. as if it was/were

UNIT 116

116.1
3. during
4. for
5. during
6. for
7. for
8. for
9. during
10. for
11. for
12. for
13. during
14. for

116.2
3. while
4. While
5. During
6. while
7. during
8. During
9. while
10. during
11. while
12. during
13. while
14. while

116.3
参考答案：
3. I was doing the housework.
4. I make a quick phone call?
5. the lesson.
6. the interview.
7. the car is moving.
8. we were having dinner.
9. the game.
10. we were walking home.

UNIT 117

117.1
2. by 8:30.
3. by Saturday whether you can come to the party.

4. you're here by 2:00.
5. we should arrive by lunchtime.

117.2
2. by
3. by
4. until
5. until 5:30 . . . by now
6. by
7. until
8. by
9. by
10. until
11. By
12. by

117.3
参考答案：
3. until I come back
4. by 5:00
5. by next Friday
6. until midnight

117.4
2. By the time I got to the station / By the time I'd gotten to the station
3. By the time I finished (my work) / By the time I'd finished (my work)
4. By the time the police arrived
5. By the time we got to the top / By the time we'd gotten to the top

UNIT 118

118.1
2. at night
3. in the evening
4. on July 21, 1969
5. at the same time
6. in the 1920s
7. in about 20 minutes
8. at the moment
9. in the Middle Ages
10. in 11 seconds
11. (on) Saturdays

118.2
2. on
3. in
4. On
5. on
6. in
7. in
8. at
9. on
10. at
11. in
12. at
13. on
14. in
15. On . . . at
16. at . . . in
17. on . . . in
18. on . . . in

118.3

3. a
4. 兩者皆為正確答案
5. b
6. b
7. 兩者皆為正確答案
8. a
9. b
10. a

UNIT 119

119.1

2. on time
3. in time
4. on time
5. in time
6. on time
7. in time
8. in time
9. on time

119.2

2. got home just in time.
3. stopped him just in time.
4. got to the theater just in time for the beginning of the film.

119.3

2. at the end of the month
3. at the end of the course
4. at the end of the race
5. at the end of the interview

119.4

2. In the end she resigned (from her job).
3. In the end I gave up (trying to learn German).
4. In the end we decided not to go (to the party). 或 In the end we didn't go (to the party).

119.5

2. In
3. at . . . at
4. in
5. in
6. at
7. in
8. at
9. in

UNIT 120

120.1

2. On his arm. 或 On the man's arm.
3. At the traffic light.
4. a) On the door.
   b) In the door.
5. On the wall.
6. In Paris.
7. a) At the front desk.
   b) On the desk.
8. On/At the beach.

120.2

2. on my guitar

3. at the next gas station
4. in your coffee
5. on that tree
6. in the mountains
7. on the island
8. at the window

120.3

2. on
3. at
4. on
5. in
6. on
7. at
8. in . . . in
9. on
10. in
11. on . . . in
12. at

UNIT 121

121.1

2. On the second floor.
3. At/On the corner.
4. In the corner.
5. At the top of the stairs.
6. In the back of the car.
7. In the front.
8. On the left.
9. In the back row.
10. On a farm.

121.2

2. on the right
3. in the world
4. on the way to work
5. on the West Coast
6. in the front row
7. in/at the back of the class
8. on the back of this card

121.3

2. in
3. in
4. in/at
5. in
6. on
7. At . . . on
8. in
9. in
10. on
11. in
12. on
13. in
14. on . . . on ,

UNIT 122

122.1

2. on a train
3. at a conference
4. in the hospital
5. at the hairdresser's
6. on his bike
7. in New York
8. at the Ford Theater

122.2

2. in a taxi
3. at the party
4. on the plane
5. at school
6. at the gym
7. in the hospital
8. in/at the airport
9. in prison

122.3

2. at
3. in
4. at
5. at/in . . . in
6. in
7. on
8. at
9. in
10. at
11. in
12. at . . . at
13. in
14. in . . . at

UNIT 123

123.1

3. at
4. to
5. to
6. into
7. at 或 —
8. to
9. into
10. to
11. at
12. to
13. into
14. to
15. — . . . to
16. to . . . in
17. in . . . to . . . in

123.2

參考答案：

2.–4.
   I've been to Hong Kong once.
   I've never been to Tokyo.
   I've been to Paris a few times.

123.3

2. in
3. –
4. at
5. to
6. –

123.4

2. got on the bus.
3. I got out of the car.
4. I got off the train.
5. I got into the taxi. 或 I got in the taxi.
6. I got off the plane.

UNIT 124

124.1
2. in cold weather
3. in pencil
4. in love
5. in capital letters
6. in the shade
7. in my opinion

124.2
2. on strike
3. on a tour
4. on television
5. on purpose
6. on a diet
7. on business
8. on vacation
9. on the phone
10. on the whole

124.3
2. on
3. on
4. at
5. in
6. on
7. for
8. on
9. at
10. at
11. on
12. In . . . on
13. on
14. on
15. on
16. at
17. on
18. in

UNIT 125

125.1
2. by mistake
3. by hand
4. by credit card
5. by satellite

125.2
2. on
3. by
4. by . . . on
5. in
6. on
7. by

125.3
参考答案：
3.–5.
   Ulysses is a novel by James Joyce.
   "Yesterday" is a song by Paul
   McCartney.
   Guernica is a painting by Pablo Picasso.

125.4
2. by
3. with
4. by

5. by
6. by . . . in
7. by . . . with . . . on

125.5
2. traveling by bus 或 traveling on
   the bus 或 traveling on buses
3. taken with a very good camera
4. this music is by Beethoven
5. pay cash 或 pay in cash
6. a mistake by one of our players

125.6
2. by 25 cents.
3. by two votes.
4. her/Kate by five minutes.

UNIT 126

126.1
2. to the problem
3. with her brother
4. in the cost of living
5. to your question
6. for a new road
7. in/to working at home
8. in the number of people without
   jobs
9. for shoes like these any more
10. between your job and mine

126.2
2. invitation to
3. contact with
4. key to
5. cause of
6. reply to
7. connection between
8. pictures of
9. reason for
10. damage to

126.3
2. to
3. in
4. for
5. of
6. in 或 to
7. for
8. to 或 toward
9. with
10. in
11. to
12. of
13. for . . . in
14. to
15. with

UNIT 127

127.1
2. nice of
3. was generous of him.
4. wasn't very nice of them.
5. That's very kind of
6. That wasn't very polite of him.
7. That's a little childish of them.

127.2
2. kind to
3. sorry for
4. nervous about
5. upset about
6. impressed by / with
7. bored with 或 bored by
8. astonished at/by

127.3
2. of
3. to . . . to
4. of
5. of
6. with
7. to
8. with
9. at/by
10. with
11. about
12. about
13. for/about . . . at
14. at/with . . . for
15. about
16. about
17. at/by
18. by/with
19. about
20. about
21. for

UNIT 128

128.1
2. of furniture
3. for this mess
4. of time
5. at tennis
6. to a Russian (man)
7. of him / of Robert
8. from yours / than yours

128.2
2. similar to
3. afraid of
4. interested in
5. responsible for
6. proud of
7. different from/than

128.3
2. for
3. of
4. of
5. in
6. to
7. of . . . of
8. on
9. of
10. with
11. of
12. of
13. in
14. of
15. of
16. at

17. of
18. to
19. of

128.4
参考答案：
2. I'm hopeless at telling jokes.
3. I'm not very good at mathematics.
4. I'm pretty good at remembering names.

UNIT 129

129.1
3. this question to me? / Can you explain it to me?
4. you explain the problem to me? / Can you explain it to me?
5. Can you explain to me how this machine works?
6. Can you explain to me what I have to do?

129.2
3. to
4. –
5. to
6. to
7. –
8. to
9. to
10. –

129.3
3. speaking to
4. point . . . at
5. glanced at
6. listen to
7. throw . . . at
8. throw . . . to

129.4
2. at
3. at
4. to
5. to
6. at
7. at
8. to
9. at
10. at
11. to

UNIT 130

130.1
2. for
3. for
4. to
5. for
6. about
7. –
8. about
9. –
10. for
11. for
12. about

13. for
14. for

130.2
2. waiting for
3. talk about
4. asked . . . for
5. applied for
6. do . . . about
7. looks after 或 has looked after
8. left . . . for

130.3
2. for
3. about
4. of
5. for
6. of
7. about
8. –

130.4
2. looking for
3. looked after
4. looking for
5. look for
6. looks after

UNIT 131

131.1
2. about
3. to . . . about
4. of
5. of
6. about . . . about . . . about . . . about
7. of
8. about
9. about/of

131.2
2. complaining about
3. think about
4. warn . . . about
5. heard of
6. dream of
7. reminded . . . about
8. remind . . . of

131.3
2. hear about
3. heard from
4. heard of
5. hear from
6. hear about
7. heard of

131.4
2. think about
3. think of
4. think of
5. thinking of/about
6. think of
7. thought about
8. think . . . of
9. thinking about/of

UNIT 132

132.1
2. for the misunderstanding
3. on winning the tournament
4. from/against his enemies
5. of nine players
6. on bread and eggs

132.2
2. for everything
3. for the economic crisis
4. on television
5. is to blame for the economic crisis
6. television is to blame for the increase in violent crime

132.3
2. paid for
3. accused of
4. depends on
5. live on
6. congratulated . . . on
7. apologize to

132.4
2. from
3. on
4. of/from
5. for
6. for
7. –
8. on
9. on
10. – 或 on
11. from/against
12. of

UNIT 133

133.1
2. small towns to big cities.
3. with all the information I needed.
4. $70 on a pair of shoes.

133.2
2. happened to
3. invited to
4. divided into
5. believe in
6. fill . . . with
7. drove into
8. Concentrate on
9. succeeded in

133.3
2. to
3. on
4. in
5. to
6. in
7. with
8. into
9. in
10. on
11. into
12. to
13. –

14. into
15. on
16. from . . . into
17. to . . . on
18. into
19. with

133.4
参考答案：
2. on CDs
3. into a wall
4. to volleyball
5. into many languages

UNIT 134

134.1
2. sit down
3. flew away
4. get out
5. run out
6. get by
7. gone up
8. looked around

134.2
2. back at
3. up to
4. forward to
5. away with
6. up at
7. in through
8. along with

134.3
2. wake me up
3. get it out
4. give them back
5. turn it on
6. take them off

134.4
3. them back
4. the television off 或 off the television
5. it over
6. her up
7. 参考答案：
   your coat on 或 on your coat
8. it out
9. my shoes off 或 off my shoes
10. the light(s) on 或 on the light(s)

UNIT 135

135.1
2. eats
3. moved
4. drop
5. checked
6. cut
7. plug
8. fit
9. fill
10. hand/turn
11. leave
12. dropped

135.2
2. into
3. in
4. out
5. into
6. out of

135.3
2. dropped out
3. moved in
4. left out
5. joined in
6. eating out 或 to eat out
7. fits in
8. dropped in
9. get out of

135.4
2. Fill them out
3. handed it in
4. left them out
5. let us in

UNIT 136

136.1
2. a mistake
3. a candle
4. an order
5. a campfire
6. a new product
7. a problem

136.2
2. works out
3. carried out
4. ran out
5. work out
6. find out
7. tried out
8. pointed out
9. work out
10. went out
11. turned out
12. figure out
13. find out
14. put out

136.3
2. giving/handing out
3. turned out nice/fine/sunny
4. working out
5. run out
6. figure out . . . use the camera / her new camera

136.4
2. try it out
3. figure him out
4. pointing it out

UNIT 137

137.1
2. put the heat on
3. put the radio on
4. put the light on
5. put a DVD on

137.2
2. going on
3. take off
4. turned off
5. drove off / went off
6. put on
7. had on
8. put off
9. called off
10. put on
11. see . . . off

137.3
2. took off
3. tried on a/the hat 或 tried a/the hat on
4. was called off
5. see him off
6. put them on

UNIT 138

138.1
2. went on
3. went on walking
4. dozed off / dropped off / nodded off
5. go on
6. went off
7. keeps on calling me

138.2
2. went off
3. dropped off
4. taken on
5. ripped off
6. goes on
7. dozed off / dropped off / nodded off
8. told off
9. lay off
10. going off
11. keep on
12. go on
13. showing off
14. hold on/hang on

138.3
2. dragging on
3. were ripped off
4. go off
5. move on / go on
6. go on with
7. tell them off
8. laid off

UNIT 139

139.1
2. turn it down
3. calm him down
4. put them up
5. let her down
6. turned it down

139.2
2. took them down
3. stand up
4. turned it up

5. put their bags down
6. were blown/knocked down
7. wrote it down
8. bent down . . . picked them up

139.3
2. calm down
3. slowed down
4. was turned down
5. broken down
6. cut down
7. let down
8. (has) closed down
9. be torn down
10. turned down
11. burned down
12. broken down

UNIT 140

140.1
2. went up to / walked up to
3. catch up with
4. keep up with

140.2
2. used up
3. backed up
4. grow up
5. turn up
6. gave up
7. taking up
8. give up
9. ended up
10. takes up
11. make up

140.3
3. set it up
4. keep up with
5. was brought up / grew up
6. keep it up
7. backed up
8. went up to
9. was made up of
10. backing me up

UNIT 141

141.1
2. D
3. E
4. C
5. G
6. A
7. B

141.2
2. held up
3. fixed it up
4. cheer him up

141.3
2. blew up
3. beaten up
4. broken up / split up
5. came up
6. clears up
7. mixed up

141.4
2. look it up
3. put up with
4. made it up

5. come up with
6. tear it up
7. saving up for
8. clean it up

UNIT 142

142.1
2. Pay
3. throw
4. gets
5. be
6. look
7. gave
8. get

142.2
2. be away / have gone away
3. be back
4. ran away
5. smile back
6. get away
7. Keep away

142.3
2. blew away
3. put it back
4. walked away
5. threw it back (to her)
6. threw them away

142.4
2. throw it away
3. take them back
4. pay you back / pay it back
5. gave them away
6. call back / call me back

解答（補充練習）

(請見 296 頁)

1

3. 'm getting / am getting
4. do you do
5. arrived . . . was raining
6. calls . . . didn't call
7. were thinking . . . decided
8. are you looking
9. doesn't rain
10. rang . . . were having
11. went . . . was studying . . . didn't want . . . didn't stay
12. told . . . didn't believe . . . thought . . . was joking

2

2. didn't go
3. is wearing
4. went
5. haven't heard
6. is being
7. wasn't reading
8. didn't have
9. It's beginning
10. got
11. wasn't
12. you've been
13. I've been doing
14. did she go
15. I've been playing
16. do you come
17. since I saw her
18. for 20 years

3

3. are you going
4. Do you watch
5. have you lived / have you been living / have you been
6. Did you have
7. Have you seen
8. was she wearing
9. Have you been waiting / Have you been here
10. does it take
11. Have you ridden
12. Have you (ever) been

4

2. 've known each other / have known each other 或 've been friends / have been friends
3. I've ever had / I've ever been on / I've had in ages (等)
4. He left / He went home / He went out
5. I've worn it
6. I was playing
7. been swimming for 或 gone swimming for

5

8. since I've been / since I (last) went
9. did you buy / did you get

1. got . . . was already waiting . . . had arrived
2. was lying . . . wasn't watching . . . 'd fallen / had fallen . . . was snoring . . . turned . . . woke
3. 'd just gone / had just gone . . . was reading . . . heard . . . got . . . didn't see . . . went
4. missed . . . was standing . . . realized . . . 'd left / had left . . . had . . . got
5. met . . . was walking . . . 'd been / had been . . . 'd been playing / had been playing . . . were going . . . invited . . . 'd arranged / had arranged . . . didn't have

6

2. Sombody's taken it. / Somebody has taken it.
3. They'd only known / They had only known each other (for) a few weeks.
4. It's been raining / It has been raining all day. 或 It's rained / It has rained all day.
5. I'd been dreaming. / I had been dreaming.
6. I'd had / I had had a big breakfast.
7. They've been going / They have been going there for years.
8. I've had it / I have had it since I got up.
9. He's been training / He has been training very hard for it.

7

1. I haven't seen
2. You look 或 You're looking
3. are you going
4. are you meeting
5. I'm going
6. Do you travel a lot
7. are you going
8. I'm meeting
9. has been 或 was
10. I've been waiting
11. has just started 或 just started
12. is she doing
13. Does she like
14. she thinks
15. Are you working 或 Do you work
16. spoke
17. you were working
18. went

19. I started / I had started
20. I lost
21. you haven't had
22. I've had
23. have you seen
24. has he been
25. I saw
26. he left
27. He'd been
28. he decided / he'd decided
29. He was really looking forward
30. is he doing
31. I haven't heard
32. he left

8

1. invented
2. it's ended / it has ended / it ended
3. had gone . . . left
4. did you do . . . Did you go
5. have you had
6. was looking
7. She's been teaching / She has been teaching
8. I bought . . . I haven't worn
9. I saw . . . was . . . I'd seen / I had seen . . . I remembered . . . he was
10. Have you heard . . . She was . . . died . . . She wrote . . . Have you read
11. does this word mean . . . I've never seen
12. Did you get . . . it had already begun
13. knocked . . . was . . . she'd gone / had gone . . . she didn't want
14. He'd never used / He had never used . . . he didn't know
15. went . . . She needed . . . she'd been sitting / she had been sitting

9

3. used to drive
4. was driving
5. were working
6. used to have
7. was living
8. was playing
9. used to play
10. was wearing

10

2. I'm going to the dentist.
3. No, we're going to rent a car.
4. I'll take care of the children.
5. I'm having lunch with Sue.
6. What are you going to have?
7. I'll turn on the light.
8. I'm going to turn on the light.

11

2. I'll go
3. should/shall we meet
4. starts
5. I'll meet
6. I'm seeing
7. Should/Shall I ask
8. I'll see
9. are going
10. does the movie start
11. Are you meeting
12. I'll be

12

1. (2) Are you going to take
   (3) it starts
   (4) you'll enjoy
   (5) it will / it's going to be
2. (1) you're going
   (2) We're going
   (3) you have
   (4) I'll send
   (5) I'll get
   (6) I get
3. (1) I'm having / I'm going to have
   (2) are coming
   (3) they'll have left
   (4) they're
   (5) I won't be / I will not be
   (6) you know
   (7) I'll call
4. (1) should/shall we meet
   (2) I'll be waiting
   (3) you arrive
   (4) I'll be sitting
   (5) I'll be wearing
   (6) Is Agent 307 coming / Is Agent 307 going to come / Will Agent 307 be coming
   (7) Should/Shall I bring
   (8) I'll explain
   (9) I see
   (10) I'll try

13

1. I'll have
2. Are you going
3. should/shall I call
4. It's going to land
5. it's / it is
6. I'll miss / I'm going to miss . . . you go (或 you've gone)
7. Should/Shall I give . . . I give . . . will you send
8. does it end
9. I'm going . . . is getting
10. I'll tell . . . I'm . . . I won't be
11. I'm going to have / I'm having
12. she apologizes
13. we'll be living
14. you finish

14

2. 've had
3. I bought 或 I got
4. 'll come
5. 've been 或 've eaten
6. used to play
7. haven't been waiting 或 haven't been here
8. 'd been
9. 'm going
10. haven't seen 或 haven't heard from
11. 'll have gone 或 'll have left

15

2. I've been traveling
3. I'm beginning
4. I've seen
5. has been
6. I've met
7. I left
8. I stayed 或 I was staying
9. I'd planned 或 I was planning
10. I ended up
11. I enjoyed
12. I took
13. met
14. I'm staying 或 I'm going to stay 或 I'll be staying 或 I'll stay
15. I continue
16. I'll get
17. I'm
18. I'll let
19. I know
20. I'm staying
21. we're going to visit 或 we're visiting
22. are building 或 have been building
23. it will be
24. I'll be

16

2. A
3. C
4. C
5. B
6. A 或 C
7. A 或 C
8. C
9. B 或 C
10. A 或 B
11. A 或 B
12. C
13. A 或 B
14. B 或 C
15. B

17

3. He must have forgotten.
4. You shouldn't have left so late.
5. It can't be changed now.
6. You could have gotten here earlier.
7. She may be watching television.
8. She must have been waiting for somebody.
9. He couldn't have done it.
10. I would have helped you.
11. You should have been warned about it.
12. He might not have been feeling very well. 或 He might not have felt . . .

18

3. could rain / might rain
4. might have gone / could have gone
5. couldn't go
6. couldn't have seen / can't have seen
7. should get
8. wouldn't recognize / might not recognize
9. must have heard
10. should have turned

19

4. rings
5. were
6. 's / is
7. was/were
8. had been
9. had
10. hadn't had
11. 'd driven / had driven 或 'd been driving / had been driving
12. didn't read

20

2. came (to see us now).
3. wouldn't have disturbed you.
4. be upset . . . I told them what happened.
5. you hadn't frightened the dog, it wouldn't have attacked you.
6. wouldn't have gotten (so) wet if I'd had an umbrella. 或 . . . if I had had an umbrella.
7. hadn't been (so) nervous, he wouldn't have failed (his driver's test).

21

參考答案：
1. I wasn't feeling so tired
2. I hadn't had so much to do
3. I would have forgotten Jane's birthday
4. you hadn't taken so long to get ready
5. I would have gone to the concert
6. you were in trouble
7. there was less traffic
8. people would go out more

22

3. was canceled

4. has been repaired
5. is being restored
6. 's believed / is believed
7. 'd be fired / would be fired
8. might have been thrown
9. was taught
10. being arrested / having been arrested
11. Have you ever been arrested
12. are reported . . . have been injured 或 be injured

23

3. sold 或 've sold / have sold
4. 's been sold / has been sold
5. are made
6. might be stolen
7. must have been stolen
8. must have taken
9. can be solved
10. should have left
11. is delayed
12. is being built . . . is expected

24

Fire at City Hall
2. was discovered
3. was injured
4. be rescued
5. are believed to have been destroyed
6. is not known

Convenience Store Robbery
1. was forced
2. being threatened
3. had been stolen
4. was later found
5. had been abandoned
6. has been arrested / was arrested
7. is still being questioned

Road Delays
1. is being resurfaced
2. are asked / are being asked / have been asked
3. is expected
4. will be closed
5. will be rerouted

Accident
1. was taken
2. was allowed
3. was blocked
4. be rerouted
5. have been killed

25

1. I told **her** (**that**) **Paul had gone out** and **I didn't know when he'd be back**. I asked (**her**) **if/whether she wanted to leave a message**, but she said (**that**) **she'd try again** later.
2. I had reserved a hotel room, but when I got to the hotel, they told **me** (**that**) **they had** no **record of a reservation in my name**. When I asked (**them**) **if/whether they had**

any rooms available anyway, they said (**that**) **they were sorry**, but **the hotel was full**.
3. The immigration official asked us **why we were visiting the country**, and we told **him** (**that**) **we were on vacation**. Then he wanted to know **how long we intended to stay** and **where we would be staying during our visit**.
4. She said (**that**) **she'd call us from the airport when she arrived**. 或 She said (**that**) **she'll call us from the airport when she arrives**. No, she said **not to come to the airport**. She said (**that**) **she'd take the bus**. 或 She said (**that**) **she'll take the bus**.
5. He wanted to know **what my job was** and asked (**me**) **how much I made**. 或 He wanted to know **what my job is** and asked (**me**) **how much I made**. . . . so I told **him to mind his own business** and I put the phone down.
6. He said (**that**) **he'd be at the restaurant at 7:30**. He said (**that**) **he knew where the restaurant was**. And I told **him to call me if there was any problem**.
7. You just said (**that**) **you weren't hungry**. But you said (**that**) **you didn't like bananas**. You told **me not to buy any**.

26

3. changing
4. to change
5. change
6. being
7. saying
8. to call
9. drinking
10. to be
11. to see
12. to be
13. to think . . . making
14. living . . . to move
15. to be . . . playing
16. being stopped . . . to stealing . . . driving
17. work . . . pressing

27

3. We stopped watching after a while.
4. He tends to forget things.
5. Would you mind helping me? / Do you mind helping me?
6. Everybody seems to have gone out.

7. We're thinking of moving.
8. I was afraid to touch it.
9. He's / He is afraid of being robbed.
10. It's not worth seeing.
11. I'm not used to walking so far.
12. She seems to be enjoying herself.
13. He insisted on showing them to me.
14. I'd rather somebody else did it.

28

3. reading newspapers.
4. not go out tonight / . . . stay at home tonight.
5. walking
6. me to call you tonight?
7. anybody seeing me / . . . without being seen.
8. of being a liar/ . . . of lying.
9. to seeing them again.
10. to do?
11. to have gone out with you.
12. not taking your advice / . . . that I didn't take your advice.

29

2. Tennis . . . twice a week . . . a very good player
3. for dinner . . . after work . . . to the movies
4. Unemployment . . . for people . . . find work
5. an accident . . . going home . . . taken to the hospital. I think most accidents . . . by people driving
6. an economist . . . in the investment department of Lloyds Bank . . . for an American bank . . . in the United States
7. the name of the hotel . . . The Royal . . . on West Street in the suburbs . . . near the airport.
8. The older one . . . a pilot with Western Airlines . . . The younger one . . . in high school. . . . he finishes school . . . go to college . . . study engineering.

30

2. B
3. C
4. A 或 B
5. C
6. B
7. A 或 C
8. A
9. C
10. B 或 C
11. B
12. A
13. A 或 B
14. B

31

3. It's the most polluted place . . .
4. I was disappointed that . . .
5. *OK*
6. Joe works hard, but . . .
7. . . . in a large modern building.
8. *OK* (as fast as he can 也可以作為正確答案)
9. I missed the last three days . . .
10. *OK*
11. The weather has been unusually cold . . .
12. The water in the pool was too dirty to swim in.
13. . . . to wait such a long time. (so long 也可以作為正確答案)
14. *OK*
15. . . . I got up earlier than usual.

32

2. If
3. when
4. if
5. when
6. if
7. if
8. unless
9. if
10. as long as
11. in case
12. in case
13. if
14. even if
15. Although
16. Although
17. When
18. when

33

2. on
3. at . . . on
4. on
5. on
6. at
7. In
8. at
9. during
10. on . . . since
11. for
12. at
13. at . . . until
14. by
15. in

34

1. in
2. by
3. at
4. on
5. in
6. on
7. to . . . at
8. on

9. on
10. to . . . to
11. in . . . at
12. in . . . on
13. to . . . in
14. on . . . by
15. at
16. on
17. in . . . on
18. on
19. by
20. On . . . by
21. on . . . on
22. in
23. in . . . to
24. to
25. on

35

1. for
2. at
3. to
4. to
5. in
6. with
7. of
8. to
9. of
10. at/by
11. of
12. about

36

1. of
2. after
3. − (不需介係詞)
4. about
5. to
6. − (不需介係詞)
7. into
8. of
9. to
10. − (不需介係詞)
11. on
12. of
13. of
14. − (不需介係詞)
15. in
16. at (about 也可以作為正確答案)
17. on
18. − (不需介係詞) . . . for
19. to . . . for
20. − (不需介係詞) . . . for

37

2. h
3. e
4. g
5. a
6. k
7. c
8. j
9. b
10. f
11. i

38

2. D
3. B
4. B
5. A
6. B
7. D
8. C
9. C
10. B
11. A
12. D

39

2. out to
3. up with
4. forward to
5. up with
6. out of
7. on with
8. out of
9. up with
10. back on
11. out about
12. along with

40

3. went off
4. turned up / showed up
5. fill it out / fill it in
6. torn down / knocked down
7. taken on
8. give up
9. dozed off / dropped off / nodded off
10. split up / break up
11. put up with it
12. get by
13. went on
14. put it off

41

2. put
3. moving
4. put
5. fixed
6. turned / turns
7. find
8. Calm
9. drop
10. held
11. left 或 've left / have left
12. drop
13. join
14. works
15. let
16. work
17. went . . . woke

解答 (學習指引)

(請見 319 頁)

現在式與過去式

1.1　A
1.2　B
1.3　C
1.4　B, C
1.5　C
1.6　A

現在完成式與過去式

2.1　C
2.2　A
2.3　A, C
2.4　A
2.5　A
2.6　C
2.7　A
2.8　C
2.9　A
2.10　B
2.11　A
2.12　D
2.13　C
2.14　C
2.15　D
2.16　C

未來式

3.1　B
3.2　A
3.3　C
3.4　A, C
3.5　B
3.6　C
3.7　A

情態助動詞

4.1　A, B
4.2　B
4.3　A, C, D
4.4　C
4.5　B
4.6　C, D
4.7　B
4.8　B
4.9　A
4.10　A
4.11　B
4.12　A

If 與 Wish

5.1　B
5.2　C
5.3　B
5.4　D
5.5　A

被動語氣

6.1　C
6.2　B
6.3　D
6.4　A
6.5　A, B
6.6　C
6.7　D

間接敘述

7.1　A
7.2　B
7.3　A

問句與助動詞

8.1　C
8.2　A
8.3　D
8.4　A
8.5　A

-ing 與不定詞

9.1　A
9.2　B, D
9.3　B
9.4　A
9.5　A
9.6　A
9.7　C
9.8　D
9.9　C
9.10　C
9.11　B
9.12　C
9.13　B, D
9.14　B
9.15　A, B
9.16　A
9.17　A
9.18　B, C

冠詞與名詞

10.1　B
10.2　A
10.3　B, C
10.4　B
10.5　C
10.6　A
10.7　A
10.8　A
10.9　D
10.10　C
10.11　C
10.12　A
10.13　C
10.14　D

代名詞與限定詞

11.1　A
11.2　B
11.3　D
11.4　B
11.5　B
11.6　C
11.7　A, C
11.8　C
11.9　D
11.10　A, C
11.11　B

關係子句

12.1　A, C
12.2　A, B
12.3　C
12.4　B
12.5　D
12.6　B, C

形容詞與副詞

13.1　B
13.2　C
13.3　B
13.4　A
13.5　A, D
13.6　B
13.7　C
13.8　C
13.9　B, C
13.10　D
13.11　A, B
13.12　B
13.13　D
13.14　D

連接詞與介係詞

14.1　A, D
14.2　C
14.3　B
14.4　B
14.5　B
14.6　C, D
14.7　B, C
14.8　A

介係詞

15.1　B, D
15.2　A
15.3　C
15.4　B
15.5　A
15.6　B, D
15.7　B
15.8　B
15.9　C
15.10　C
15.11　C
15.12　A
15.13　C
15.14　B
15.15　D
15.16　D
15.17　A

片語動詞

16.1　B
16.2　A
16.3　D
16.4　C
16.5　C
16.6　B
16.7　A
16.8　A, D
16.9　B

英文索引

索引中所列的號碼並非頁數，而是相對應的單元（Unit）。

中文索引

索引中所列的號碼並非頁數，而是相對應的單元（Unit）。